THE RAILWAY DETECTIVE OMNIBUS

By Edward Marston

THE RAILWAY DETECTIVE SERIES

The Railway Detective
The Excursion Train
The Railway Viaduct
The Iron Horse
Murder on the Brighton Express
The Silver Locomotive Mystery
Railway to the Grave
Blood on the Line

The Railway Detective Omnibus:
The Railway Detective, The Excursion Train, The Railway Viaduct

THE RESTORATION SERIES

The King's Evil
The Amorous Nightingale
The Repentant Rake
The Frost Fair
The Parliament House
The Painted Lady

THE CAPTAIN RAWSON SERIES

Soldier of Fortune
Drums of War
Fire and Sword
Under Siege
A Very Murdering Battle

THE HOME FRONT DETECTIVE SERIES

A Bespoke Murder

a&b

THE RAILWAY DETECTIVE OMNIBUS

EDWARD MARSTON

This omnibus first published in Great Britain in 2011 by
Allison & Busby Limited
13 Charlotte Mews
London W1T 4EJ
www.allisonandbusby.com

A CIP catalogue record for this book is available from the British Library.

10 9 8 7 6 5 4 3 2 1

ISBN 978-0-7490-0964-9

Typeset in 10.25/14.5 pt Sabon by
Allison & Busby Ltd.

The paper used for this Allison & Busby publication has been produced from trees that have been legally sourced from well-managed and credibly certified forests.

Printed and bound by
CPI Group (UK) Ltd, Croydon, CR0 4Y

In loving memory of my father,
who spent his working life as an engine driver,
and who instructed me in the mystery
of steam locomotion.

THE RAILWAY DETECTIVE

The landed proprietor often refused admission to the trespasser and his theodolite. At Addington the surveyors were met and defied in such force, that after the brief fight they were secured, carried before a magistrate and fined . . . The engineers were in truth driven to adopt whatever methods might occur to them. While people were at church; while the villager took his rustic meal; with dark lanthorns during the dark hours; by force, by fraud, by any and every mode they could devise, they carried the object which they felt to be necessary but knew to be wrong.

JOHN FRANCIS
A History of the English Railroads (1851)

CHAPTER ONE

London, 1851

Euston Station was one of the architectural marvels of the day. Even the most regular passengers on the London and North Western Railway could still be impressed by the massive portico with its four Doric columns built of adamantine Bramley Fall sandstone, flanked by two pairs of pavilions, and standing on the north side of a large open space. The addition of two hotels, one either side of the portico, introduced a functional element that did not lessen the stunning impact of the facade. Those who passed through the imposing entrance found themselves in the Great Hall, a combined concourse and waiting room. It was a magnificent chamber in the Roman-Ionic style with a high, deeply coffered ceiling that made newcomers gape in astonishment.

Caleb Andrews did not even notice it, nor did he spare a glance for the majestic curved double flight of steps at the northern end of the hall that led to a gallery and vestibule. Only one thing in the station interested him, and that was the locomotive he and his fireman were about to drive to Birmingham. Andrews was a short, wiry character in his early fifties with a fringe beard that was peppered with grey. There was a jauntiness about him that belied his age and that concealed his deep sense of dedication to his work. Caleb Andrews was a man who thrived on responsibility.

'It's a fine day, Frank,' he observed. 'We should have a clear run.'

'God willing,' said Pike.

'God doesn't come into it, man. *We* are the people in charge. If we do our jobs properly, everything will go well. The important thing is to get there on time. Do that and we'll earn ourselves another pat on the back.'

'That would be nice, Caleb.'

'It would indeed.'

'Extra money would be even nicer.'

Andrews gave a hollow laugh. 'From *this* company?'

Frank Pike nodded resignedly. Now in his thirties, the big, shambling man from the West Country knew that they would only get their stipulated wage. Fireman Pike had a round, flat, moon face that was marked by routine exposure to the elements and, as a rule, darkened by a somnolent expression. His large hands were badly scarred by his trade. He had the deepest respect for his companion and was delighted to work alongside him. Technically, a conductor was in charge of a train, but not when Caleb Andrews was there. The driver always asserted his authority and his colleagues knew better than to arouse his combative streak.

The two men were on the footplate, checking that everything was in readiness. Pike had got up a good head of steam and his fire shovel was at hand to add more fuel from the tender when necessary. The engine was throbbing with suppressed power. Andrews studied his instruments with a mixture of pride and affection. A locomotive was much more than an inanimate piece of machinery to him. She was a trusted friend, a living creature with moods, likes and dislikes, a complex lump of metal with her own idiosyncrasies, a sublime being, blessed with awesome might, who had to be treated correctly in order to get the best out of her.

'Mr Allan knows how to design an engine,' he said, appreciatively.

'She's one of the best,' agreed Pike.

'Mind you, there's still room for improvement. They ought to let me spend a week or two at Crewe. I could point out a number of things that would make her run better yet use less oil.'

'You always were a man of opinions, Caleb.'

'They're not opinions – they're plain common sense. The people who can give the best advice about how to build a locomotive are the men who drive her.'

'I got no complaints.'

'That's because you're too easily satisfied, Frank.'

'I do what I'm paid to do, that's all.'

There was an air of fatalism about Pike. Though Andrews was very fond of him, he had long ago accepted that his fireman lacked any real urgency or ambition. Frank Pike was a reliable workhorse, a quiet, efficient, unassuming, conscientious man who never questioned what he was doing or looked beyond it to something better. Andrews, by contrast, had enough aspiration for the two of them. He was bubbling with energy. While most men of his years were anticipating retirement, all that he could think about was promotion.

Like his fireman, Andrews wore a uniform of light-coloured corduroy and a cap. Pulling a watch from his pocket to consult it, he clicked his tongue in irritation.

'What's keeping them?' he said.

'There's minutes to go yet, Caleb.'

'I like to leave on time.'

'We will,' said Pike, turning round to look back down the train. 'I think they're loading the last box now.'

Andrews put his watch away and gazed back down the platform. It was a short train, comprising an empty first class carriage, a bright red mail coach, a luggage van and a guard's van. The locomotive and tender bore the distinctive livery of the northern division of the company. The engine was painted green, with main frames a paler shade of the same hue. Smoke box and chimney were black. The dome was green, as was the base of the safety valve, though the casing of the latter was polished brass. Hand-rails were covered polished brass and splashers were brass-headed. Wheels were black. The front cylinder caps were made of iron, polished to a sheen. Before she set out, she was positively gleaming.

'Come on, come on,' said Andrews, tapping his foot.

Pike gave a tolerant smile. 'You're too impatient.'

'I want to be on my way, Frank.'

'So do I,' admitted the other. 'I always feel a bit nervous when we've so much money aboard. It must worry you as well.'

'Not in the least.'

'But we must be carrying a small fortune.'

'I don't care if we've got the Crown Jewels tucked away in the luggage van,' boasted Andrews, sticking out his chest. 'Makes no difference at all to me. Besides, we have plenty of guards on board to watch over the mail and the money. No,' he went on, 'the only thing that unsettles me is time-keeping. I've a reputation to maintain.' He heard a shrill blast on a whistle. 'At last!' he said with relief. 'Stand by, Frank.'

'I'm ready.'

'Then let's take her to Birmingham.'

With a venomous hiss of steam and a loud clanking of wheels, the engine moved slowly forward as she pulled her carriages on the first stage of their fateful journey.

By the time they hit open country, they had built up a steady speed. Caleb Andrews was at the controls and Frank Pike shovelled more coal into the firebox at regular intervals. The train surged on, rattling noisily and leaving clouds of dark smoke in its wake. Its iron wheels clicked rhythmically on the track. Having driven over the route many times, the two men were familiar with every bridge, viaduct, tunnel, change of gradient and curve in the line. They were also known to many of the people who manned the various stations, and they collected endless waves and greetings as they steamed past. Andrews acknowledged them all with a cheerful grin. Pike lifted his shovel in response.

It was a glorious April afternoon and the men enjoyed the warm sunshine. After the harsh winter they had endured, it was a pleasant change. Their work took them out in all weathers and they had little protection against wind, rain, snow, sleet, or insidious fog. Driver and fireman had often arrived at their destination, soaked to the skin or chafed by an icy blast. Even the heat from the firebox could not keep out all of the cold. Today, however, it was different. It was a perfect day. Lush green fields surrounded them and trees were in first leaf. The train was running smoothly over the flanged rails.

Forty miles passed uneventfully. It was only when they had raced through Leighton Buzzard Junction that they had their first hint of trouble. One of the railway policemen, who acted as signalman, stood beside the line and waved his red flag to stop the train. Andrews reacted immediately. Without shutting off steam, he put the engine into reverse so that her speed was gradually reduced. Only when she had slowed right down was the tender hand-brake applied along with the brake in the guard's van. Since she had been moving fast, it had taken almost half a mile to bring her to a halt.

Driver Andrews opened the cylinder cocks with the regulator open, so that steam continued to flow without working on the pistons. The water level in the boiler was maintained. Andrews leant out to look at the bulky figure of another railway policeman, who was striding towards them in the official uniform of dark, high-necked frock coat, pale trousers and stovepipe hat. He too had been signalling with his red flag for the train to stop. Andrews was annoyed by the delay.

'You'd better have good cause to hold us up,' he warned.

'We do,' said the policeman.

'Well?'

'There's a problem with the Linslade Tunnel.'

'What sort of problem?'

'You're not going through it, Mr Andrews.'

Tossing his flag to the ground, the policeman suddenly pulled a pistol from his belt and pointed it at the driver. Following his example, a group of armed men emerged swiftly from behind the bushes on either side of the line and made for the mail coach and the guard's van. The latter was easy to enter, but the locked doors of the mail coach had to be smashed open with sledgehammers before they could rush in and overpower the mail guards in their scarlet uniforms. While that was happening, someone was uncoupling the mail coach from the first class carriage in front of it.

As he watched the burst of activity, Caleb Andrews was outraged.

'What's going on?' he demanded.

'The train is being robbed,' replied the policeman, still

holding the weapon on him. 'All you have to do is to obey orders. Stand back.'

'Why?'

'Do as I tell you.'

'No.'

'Stand back!' ordered another voice, 'or I'll shoot you.'

Andrews looked up to see a well-dressed man at the top of a shallow embankment, aiming a rifle at him. There was an air of certainty about him that suggested he was more than ready to carry out his threat. Pike tugged anxiously at his friend's elbow.

'Do as they say, Caleb,' he advised.

Andrews was truculent. 'Nobody tells me what to do on my engine,' he said, as he was pulled back a little. 'I won't let this happen.'

'They have guns.'

'They'll need more than that to frighten me, Frank.'

'Will we?' asked the bogus policeman.

Having hauled himself up onto the footplate, he levelled the pistol at the driver's temple. Pike let out a cry of protest but Andrews was unmoved. He stared at the interloper with defiance.

'Take her on, Mr Andrews,' said the other, crisply.

'What do you mean?'

'Drive the train, man.'

'Not without the mail coach, the luggage van and the guard's van.'

'You won't be needing those.'

'I've got my responsibilities,' argued the driver.

'Your only responsibility is to stay alive,' said the policeman, letting him feel the barrel of the weapon against his skull. 'Now – are you going to obey orders?'

Andrews put his hands on his hips. 'Make me,' he challenged.

For a moment, the other man hesitated, not quite knowing what to do in the face of unexpected resistance. Then he moved quickly. Grabbing the pistol by the barrel, he used the butt to club the driver to the floor, opening up a gash on the side of his head that sent blood oozing down his cheek. When the fireman tried to intervene, the gun was pointed at him and he was forced to step back. Badly dazed, Andrews was groaning at their feet.

'Don't hit Caleb again,' pleaded Pike.

'Then do as I tell you. Start her up.'

'Let me see to that wound of his first.'

'No,' snapped the other, turning the pistol towards Andrews. 'Drive the engine or your friend is a dead man.'

Pike obeyed at once. More concerned about the driver's safety than his own, he released the brake as fast as he could. Andrews, meanwhile, had recovered enough to realise what had happened to him. With a surge of rage, he threw his arms around the ankle of the man who was trying to take over his beloved locomotive. His recklessness was short-lived. It not only earned him two more vicious blows to the head, he was dragged to the edge of the footplate and tossed to the ground.

Horrified at the treatment of his friend, Pike could do nothing to help him. With a loaded pistol at his back, he set the train in motion and prayed that Caleb Andrews had not been too badly injured in the fall. The locomotive, tender and first class carriage trundled forward, leaving the mail coach, luggage van and guard's van behind. Had he been able to glance over his shoulder, Frank Pike would have seen a disconsolate group of guards, surprised by the speed of the ambush, relieved of their weapons and forced to dismount from the train and remove their shoes.

When the engine had gone a hundred yards and started to pick up speed, the man who had pretended to be a railway policeman gave Pike a farewell slap on the back before jumping off the footplate. He made a soft landing on a grassy verge and rolled over. The fireman soon saw why he had been abandoned. Ahead of him in the middle distance was the opening of the Linslade Tunnel, but there was no way that he could reach it. A whole section of track had been levered off its sleepers and cast aside. Those behind the ambush were bent on destruction.

Seized by panic, Pike did what he could to avert disaster, but it was in vain. Though he put the engine into reverse and tried to apply the brake, all that he did was to produce a firework display of sparks as the wheels skidded crazily along the rails. Seconds before he ran out of track, Pike had the presence of mind to leap from the footplate. Hitting the ground hard, he rolled over then watched in alarm as the locomotive veered over sharply, like a giant animal shot for sport.

The noise was deafening. Ploughing after the engine, the tender and the first class carriage ended up as a tangled mass of iron, seen through a fog of billowing smoke and angry steam. Frank Pike had to hold back tears. When he jumped to the ground, he had twisted his ankle but he ignored the pain. Pulling himself up, he turned his back on the hideous sight and limped back along the line to the fallen driver, hoping that Caleb Andrews was still alive.

CHAPTER TWO

As soon as he entered the room, Robert Colbeck knew that a serious crime must have been committed. The air was thick with pungent smoke, and Superintendent Edward Tallis only reached for his cigar case when he was under severe pressure. Seated behind his desk, the older man was scanning a sheet of paper as if trying to memorise important details. Colbeck waited patiently for the invitation to sit down. Tall, slim and well-favoured, he was impeccably dressed in a dark brown frock coat, with rounded edges and a high neck, well-cut fawn trousers and an Ascot cravat. Catching the light that streamed in through the window, his black leather shoes were shining brightly. In the prosaic world of law enforcement, Inspector Robert Colbeck stood out as the unrivalled dandy of Scotland Yard.

Tallis tossed him a cursory glance then waved a podgy hand.

'Take a seat,' he barked. 'We have much to discuss.'

'So I understood from the urgency of your summons,' said Colbeck, lowering himself onto a chair. 'I came as soon as I could, sir.'

'And not before time. We have a robbery on our hands.'

'What kind of robbery, Superintendent?'

'The worst kind,' said Tallis, putting the sheet of paper aside. 'A mail train was ambushed on its way to Birmingham. It was carrying a large consignment of gold sovereigns for delivery to a bank in the city. The thieves got away with every penny.'

'Was anyone hurt in the process?' asked Colbeck with concern.

'Only the driver, it seems. He was foolish enough to offer resistance and suffered for his bravery. The fellow is in a sorry state.'

'Poor man!'

'Save your sympathy for me, Inspector,' said Tallis, ruefully. 'All hell broke loose when word of the crime reached London. I've been hounded by the commissioners, harried by the railway company, hunted by the Post Office and badgered by the Royal Mint.'

Colbeck smiled. 'I thought I caught a whiff of cigar smoke.'

'Anybody would think that *I* was the culprit.'

'Only a bold man would ever accuse you of breaking the law, sir.'

Tallis bristled. 'Are you being facetious, Inspector?'

'Of course not.'

'I'll brook no disrespect.'

'I appreciate that, sir.'

Tallis glared at him. The Superintendent was a stout, red-faced, robust man in his fifties with a military background that had deprived him of his sense of humour and given him, in return, a habit of command, a conviction that he always made the right decisions and a small scar on his right cheek. Tallis had a shock of grey hair and a neat moustache that he was inclined to caress in quieter moments. A lifelong bachelor, he had no family commitments to deflect him from his work in the Detective Department of the Metropolitan Police Force.

'This is no time for drollery,' he warned.

'I was merely making an observation, Superintendent.'

'Keep such observations to yourself in future.'

Colbeck bit back a reply. There was an unresolved tension between the two men that came to the surface whenever they were alone together, and the Inspector had learnt to rein in his urge to provoke Tallis. The Superintendent had a violent temper when roused. Colbeck had been at the mercy of it once too often. He probed for information.

'What exactly happened, sir?' he asked, politely.

'That is what I'm endeavouring to tell you.'

'I'm all ears.'

Clasping his hands together, the Superintendent recited the salient details of the case, stressing the importance of prompt action by Scotland Yard. Colbeck listened carefully to the account. Several questions raised themselves and he put the obvious one to Tallis.

'How did they know that the train was carrying so much money?'

'That's for you to find out, Inspector.'

'They must have had help from an insider.'

'Track him down.'

'We will, sir,' promised Colbeck. 'What interests me is that the locomotive was forced off the tracks and badly damaged.'

'It will be out of service for weeks, I'm told.'

'Why on earth did they do such a thing? I mean, the gang had got what they wanted from the train. There was no need to derail the engine like that. What was the intention?'

'Ask them when you catch up with them.'

'The other thing that worries me,' said Colbeck, reflectively, 'is the ease with which the security arrangements were breached. The money was loaded in boxes that were locked inside Chubb safes. I read an article about those safes when they were installed. They were reckoned to be impregnable.'

'Two keys are needed to open them.'

'As well as a combination number, Superintendent.'

'Only one key was carried on the train,' noted Tallis. 'The other was in the possession of the bank to whom the money was being sent.'

'Yet, according to you,' Colbeck pointed out, 'the safes were opened and emptied within a matter of minutes. That could only be done with a duplicate key and foreknowledge of the combination number. There's collusion at work here.'

Tallis heaved a sigh. 'This robbery was extremely well planned, Inspector. I deplore what was done, but I have to admire the skill of the operation. We've never had to deal with anything on this scale before. That's why we must solve this crime quickly and bring the malefactors to justice,' he went on, banging a fist on the desk in exasperation. 'If they are seen to get away with such a daring exploit, there'll be others who will surely try to copy them.'

'I doubt that, Inspector. Most criminals, fortunately, have no gift for organisation and that's the essence of this robbery. Several men were involved and their timing must have been excellent.'

'Yes,' conceded Tallis, grudgingly. 'They knew what they wanted and took it – including the mail bags. The Post Office is hopping mad about that.'

'It's the people whose correspondence has gone astray who should be really alarmed,' said Colbeck, thinking it through. 'Those mail bags were not taken out of spite. Some envelopes will contain money or valuable items that can be sold for gain, and – by the law of averages – there'll be letters of a highly sensitive nature that may give the villains opportunities for blackmail.'

'That never occurred to me.'

'I'll wager that it occurred to them.'

'The scheming devils!' said Tallis, extracting a cigar case from his pocket. 'Robbery, blackmail, wanton destruction of railway property – these men must be rounded up, Inspector.'

Colbeck rose purposefully to his feet. 'The investigation will begin immediately, Superintendent,' he said, firmly. 'What resources do I have at my disposal?'

'Whatever you ask for – within reason.'

'I presume that the railway company will be offering a reward?'

Tallis nodded. 'Fifty guineas for anyone who can provide information that will lead to an arrest,' he said, selecting a cigar from the case. 'This is a poor advertisement for them. It's the first time their mail train has been robbed.'

'I take it that I'm to work with Victor Leeming on this case?'

'Sergeant Leeming is on his way here, even as we speak.'

'Good,' said Colbeck. 'When he arrives, we'll take a cab to Euston Station and catch the next available train to the scene of the crime. I want to see exactly where and how it all happened.'

'You'll need this, Inspector.' Tallis picked up the sheet of paper. 'It has all the relevant names on it – except those of the criminals, alas.'

Colbeck took it from him. 'Thank you, Superintendent.' His eye ran down the list. 'The driver is the crucial person – this Caleb Andrews. I hope to speak to him in due course.'

Tallis lit his cigar. 'You may need to have a clairvoyant with you.'

'Why?'

'Mr Andrews is still in a coma, and not expected to survive.'

The table in the stationmaster's office at Leighton Buzzard was not the most comfortable bed, but the patient was quite unaware of that. Lying on the bare wood, with a blanket draped over him, Caleb Andrews seemed to have shrunk. His head was heavily bandaged, his face pallid, his breathing laboured. One arm was in a sling, one leg in a splint. He looked as if he were hanging on to life by the merest thread.

Keeping vigil beside the makeshift bed, Frank Pike was torn between fear and guilt, terrified that his friend might die and filled with remorse at his inability to protect the driver from attack. There was another dimension to his anguish. With a pistol held over him, he had been forced to drive the locomotive off the track, something that was anathema to any railwayman. It was no consolation to him that Caleb Andrews had not been able to witness the awful moment when their engine plunged into the grass verge and shed its load of coal and water. Pike winced as he recalled it. His employers were bound to blame him.

He reached out a hand to touch the patient's shoulder.

'I'm sorry, Caleb,' he said. 'I had no choice.'

The older man's eyelids flickered for a second and a soft murmur escaped his lips. Pike needed no interpreter. Caleb Andrews was reproaching him. The driver had been in the same situation as him and he had shown that there was, in fact, a choice. It was between refusal and compliance. While one man had the courage to refuse, the other had opted for compliance. It made Pike feel as if he had betrayed a dear friend and colleague. He drew back his hand involuntarily, no longer entitled to touch Andrews.

Covered in blood, the body had been carried all the way back to the station so that a doctor could be sought. The fractured leg and the broken collarbone were not the real cause for concern. It was the head injuries that made the doctor pessimistic. All that he could do was to clean and bind the wounds. Given their severity, he could offer no hope of recovery. Whatever happened, Pike realised, he would come in for censure. If the driver lived, he would be sure to admonish his fireman for cowardice. If he died, there would be many others who would point an accusatory finger at Frank Pike. Among them was Caleb Andrews's daughter, a young woman whom Pike would not hurt for the world. As an image of her face came into his mind, he let out a gasp of pain.

'Forgive me, Madeleine!' he begged. 'It was not my fault.'

'What about the railway policemen who should have patrolled that line?' asked Victor Leeming. 'Why were they not on duty?'

'Because they were bound and gagged,' explained Colbeck, brushing a speck of dust from his sleeve. 'Apparently, they were found behind some bushes in their underwear. The robbers had borrowed their uniforms.'

'What about their shoes?'

'Those, too, were missing.'

'Along with the shoes from all the people on board the train,' said Leeming. 'Are we looking for criminals with a passion for footwear?'

'No, Victor. We're searching for people who know that the simplest way to slow someone down is to make him walk in stockinged feet. By the time one of the guards reached the station to raise the alarm, the robbers were miles away.'

'With all that money and several pairs of shoes.'

'Don't forget the mail bags. They were a secondary target.'

'Were they?'

Sergeant Victor Leeming was puzzled. His brow wrinkled in concentration. He was a stocky man in his thirties, slightly older than Colbeck but with none of the Inspector's social graces or charm. Leeming's face had a benign ugliness that was not helped by his broken nose and his slight squint. Though he was not the most intelligent of detectives, he was always the first choice of Robert Colbeck, who valued his tenacity, his single-mindedness and his capacity for hard work. Leeming was a loyal colleague.

The two men were sitting in a first class carriage of a train that rumbled its way through Buckinghamshire. When it passed Leighton Buzzard Junction, it slowed by prior arrangement so that it could drop the detectives near the scene of the crime. Colbeck peered through the window as the wrecked locomotive came into sight.

'They've repaired the line,' he said, pointing to the track that curved ahead of them, 'but I suspect it will take a lot longer to mend the engine and the carriage. They'll need a crane to lift them.'

'There's no shortage of railway policemen,' said Leeming, studying the knot of people beside the line. 'I can count a dozen or more.'

'All with their shoes on.'

'What sort of reception can we expect, Inspector?'

'A hostile one. They resent our interference.'

'But we're here to solve the crime.'

'They probably feel that it's their job to do that.'

Colbeck waited until the train shuddered to a halt then opened the door of the carriage. Taking care not to snag the tails of his coat, he jumped down nimbly onto the track. Leeming descended more slowly. Having deposited two of its passengers, the train chugged slowly off towards the Linslade Tunnel.

The newcomers took stock of the situation. Several people were gathered around the stricken engine and carriage. Others were standing in forlorn groups. Colbeck sought out the man whose name has been given to him as the person in charge. Inspector Rory McTurk of the railway police was a huge individual with a black beard and shaggy eyebrows. When he was introduced to them, McTurk was patently unimpressed by Colbeck's tailored elegance and by Leeming's unsightly features. He put a note of disapproval into his gruff voice.

'So you've come at last, have you?' he said.

'Yes,' replied Colbeck, weighing him up. 'I trust that we can count on your full cooperation, Mr McTurk.'

'*Inspector* McTurk,' corrected the other.

'I beg your pardon.'

'We'll give you all the help you need – and some guidance.'

'Do you think that we'll need guidance, Inspector?'

'Yes,' said McTurk, brusquely. 'Railway lore is a complicated thing. You'll need someone to take you through it. As for the robbery,' he continued with an air of complacency, 'I've already made preliminary enquiries among those who were on board the train, and I'm in a position to tell you exactly what happened.'

'I'd prefer to hear it from the lips of the witnesses,' insisted Colbeck. 'That way we eliminate any narrative flourishes you might feel impelled to introduce.'

McTurk was indignant. 'I'll tell you the plain facts. Nothing else.'

'After we've spoken to those who actually travelled on the train, if you don't mind. Second-hand evidence is always suspect, as you know.' Colbeck looked around. 'Where are they?'

'The mail guards are there,' said McTurk, sourly, indicating the men who wore scarlet uniforms. 'The two railway policemen who were aboard are at the station along with Fireman Pike and the guard.'

'What about the driver, Caleb Andrews?'

'He's at Leighton Buzzard as well, Inspector. They took him to the station and sent for a doctor. Driver Andrews was badly hurt.'

'How badly?'

McTurk was blunt. 'This may turn into a murder investigation.'

'Does he have a family?'

'Only a daughter, according to his fireman. We've sent word to her. She'll have heard the worst by now.'

'I hope that tact and consideration were shown,' said Colbeck, glad that McTurk himself had not imparted the distressing news. Discretion did not appear to be one of the Scotsman's virtues. 'Victor?'

'Yes, Inspector?' said Leeming, stepping forward.

'Take full statements from the mail guards.'

'Yes, sir.'

'We'll speak to the others later.'

Leeming went off to interview the men who were sitting on the grass without any shoes and feeling very sorry for themselves. Colbeck was left to survey the scene. After looking up and down the line, he climbed the embankment and walked slowly along the ridge. McTurk felt obliged to follow him, scrambling up the incline and cursing when he lost his footing. The detective eventually paused beside some divots that had been gouged out of the turf. He knelt down to examine them.

'They brought the money this way,' he decided.

'What makes you think that?'

'The sovereigns were in bags that were packed into wooden boxes, Inspector. They were very heavy. It would have taken two men to carry each box and that meant that they had to dig their feet in as they climbed the embankment.' He glanced down at the line. 'What happened to the mail coach, the luggage van and the guard's van?'

'They were towed back to Leighton Buzzard and put in a siding.'

'They should have been left here,' said Colbeck, sharply, 'where the robbery actually took place. It would have made it easier for me to reconstruct events.'

'Railways run on timetables, Inspector Colbeck,' the Scotsman told him. 'As long as that rolling stock remained on the line, no down trains could get beyond this point.' He curled a derisive lip. 'Do you know what a down train is?'

'Of course, Inspector McTurk. I travel by rail frequently.' He looked back in the direction of Leighton Buzzard. 'We'll need to examine them. They may yield valuable clues.'

'We've already searched the mail coach and the luggage van.'

'That's what troubles me,' said Colbeck, meeting his gaze. 'If you and your men have trampled all over them, evidence may unwittingly have been destroyed. Please ensure that nobody else has access to that rolling stock until we've had the chance to inspect it.' McTurk glowered at him. 'It's not a request,' warned Colbeck. 'It's an order.'

McTurk turned away and waved an arm at the cluster of railway policemen gathered below. One of them scampered up the embankment to be given a curt order by his superior. The man then went back down the incline and trotted in the direction of the station. Having asserted his authority,

Colbeck gave his companion a disarming smile.

'Thank you, Inspector,' he said, suavely. 'Your willing cooperation makes my job so much easier.'

McTurk remained silent but his eyes smouldered. He was much more accustomed to giving orders rather than receiving them. Colbeck swung on his heel and followed the marks in the grass. McTurk went after him. After picking their way through the undergrowth, they came to a narrow track that twisted its way off through a stand of trees. Colbeck noticed the fresh manure.

'This is where they left their horses,' he said, 'and the boxes must have been loaded onto a carriage. They chose their spot with care. It's hidden by the trees and only a short distance from the railway.'

'Wait till I get my hands on the rogues!'

'They'll face due process in a court of law, Inspector.'

'I want a word with them first,' growled McTurk, grinding his teeth. 'They stripped two of my men and trussed them up like turkeys.'

'With respect,' said Colbeck, reprovingly, 'there are more serious issues here than the humiliation of two railway policeman. We are dealing with an armed robbery during which the driver of the train was so badly injured that he may not survive.'

'I'd not forgotten that – and I want revenge.'

'Don't take it personally, Inspector McTurk. That will only cloud your judgement. Our job is to apprehend those responsible for this crime, and, if possible, to reclaim the stolen money and mail bags. Revenge has no place in that scheme of things.'

'It does for me,' affirmed McTurk. 'Look what they did,' he added, jabbing a finger at the wreckage below. 'They destroyed railway property. That's the worst crime of all to me.'

'Caleb Andrews is railway property,' Colbeck reminded him. 'His life is in the balance. When they're hauled off to Crewe, the locomotive and the carriage can be repaired, but I don't think that your engineering works runs to spare parts for injured drivers.' He raised his eyes to a sky that was slowly darkening. 'I need to make best use of the light I still have,' he announced. 'Excuse me, Inspector. I want to take a look at the rolling stock that was foolishly moved from the scene of the crime.'

'We only followed instructions,' complained McTurk.

'Do you always do as you're told?'

'Yes, Inspector.'

'Then here's another instruction for you,' said Colbeck, pointedly. 'Keep out of my way. The last thing I want at this moment is some over-obedient railway policeman getting under my feet. Is that understood?'

'You need my help.'

'Then I'll call upon it, as and when necessary.'

'You won't get far without me,' cautioned McTurk.

'I fancy that I will,' said Colbeck, easing him gently aside. 'You cast a long shadow, Inspector. And I want all the light that I can get.'

On the walk back to the station, Sergeant Leeming gave his superior an edited version of the statements he had taken from the mail guards. Not wishing to be left out, Inspector McTurk trailed in their wake. Colbeck was sceptical about what he heard.

'Something is missing, Victor,' he concluded.

'Is it?'

'Every man tells the same tale, using almost identical language. That means they've had time to rehearse their story in order to cover their blushes.'

'What blushes?'

'They were at fault. They were on duty in a locked carriage, yet they were caught napping by the ambush. How? Their assailants were quick but they still had to smash their way into the mail coach.'

'It was all over in a matter of seconds,' said Leeming. 'At least, that's what they told me.'

'Did they tell you why nobody fired a shot in anger?'

'No, Inspector.'

'Then that's what we need to establish,' said Colbeck. 'The train was stopped over a mile from the station but a gunshot would have been heard from here. It's the reason that the robbers took care not to fire themselves. They didn't wish to give themselves away.'

'I never thought of that.'

'They did – and the mail guards should have done so as well. The very least they should have managed was a warning shot. Help would have come from the station.'

'Now that you mention it,' recalled Leeming, scratching his chin, 'they did seem a little embarrassed when I questioned them. I put it down to the fact that they had no shoes on.'

'They're hiding something, Victor.'

'Do you think they might be in league with the robbers?'

'No,' said Colbeck. 'If that had been the case, they'd have fled when the crime was committed. My guess is that they helped the robbers in another way – by being lax in their duties.'

Light was starting to fade noticeably so the Inspector lengthened his stride. Leeming increased his own speed, but Inspector McTurk was panting audibly as he tried to keep pace with them. When they reached Leighton Buzzard Station, they saw that there was a sizeable crowd on the platform. Colbeck ignored them and led the way to the rolling stock that was standing in a siding. The railway policeman who had been dispatched by McTurk was standing officiously beside the guard's van.

Handing his top hat to Leeming, Colbeck first clambered up into the luggage van to examine the huge safe in which the money had been locked. Designed and built at the factory of one of England's most reputable locksmiths, John Chubb, the safe was made of inch thick steel plate. It was three feet high, wide and deep, with a door formed by the hinged lid that swung back on a guard-chain. On the front wall of the safe were keyholes to twin locks, whose interior mechanism was almost six inches deep.

Colbeck admired the quality of construction. The positioning of the locks, and the need for a combination number, confronted any burglar with almost insurmountable problems. Cracksmen whom he had arrested in the past had always admitted how difficult it was to open a Chubb safe. Yet, in this case, the doors of the safe were gaping. Colbeck made a quick search of the van but found nothing that could be construed as a clue. He left the van, dropped to the ground, and moved across to inspect the broken handles on the doors of the mail coach. One blow from a sledgehammer was all that had been required. Opening a door, Colbeck hauled himself up into the coach.

'You're wasting your time,' called McTurk.

'Am I?' he replied.

'I searched it thoroughly myself.'

'I'm sure that I'll see your footprints, Inspector.'

'You'll find nothing, I can tell you that.'

Colbeck beamed at him. 'Thank you for your encouragement,' he said. 'It's heartening to know we have your sage counsel to call upon.'

McTurk replied with a snort but Colbeck did not even hear it. He had already stepped into the coach to begin his search.

Instead of being divided into separate compartments, the carriage consisted of one long space that had been adapted to enable mail to be sorted in transit. A table ran the length of one wall, and above that was a series of wooden pigeonholes into which letters and parcels could be slotted. There were no signs of a struggle.

Robert Colbeck was meticulous. Beginning at one end of the coach, he made his way slowly forward and combed every inch. The search was painstaking and it produced no evidence at first, but he pressed on nevertheless, bending low to peer into every corner. It was when he was almost finished that he saw something that appeared to have fallen down behind the table. It was a small white object, resting against the side of the coach. Colbeck had to get on his knees and stretch an arm to its fullest extent to retrieve the object. When he saw what it was, he gave a smile of satisfaction and went across to the door.

Inspector McTurk and Sergeant Leeming waited beside the track.

'I told you there was nothing to see,' said McTurk, triumphantly.

'But there was,' Colbeck told him. 'You missed something.'

'What?'

'This, Inspector.' He held up the card that he had found. 'Now we know why the mail guards were taken unawares, Victor,' he went on. 'They were too busy playing cards to do their job properly.'

'No wonder they kept their mouths shut,' said Leeming.

'My guess is that the policemen were in there with them. Instead of staying at their post in the luggage van, they preferred to pass the time with a game of cards.' Colbeck leapt down to stand beside McTurk. 'I fear that some of your men are unable to follow your excellent example, Inspector,' he declared. 'Unlike you, they do not know how to obey instructions.'

CHAPTER THREE

It took some while to persuade Frank Pike to abandon his bedside vigil. Consumed with grief, he seemed to feel that it was his bounden duty to remain beside the injured driver, as if his physical presence in the stationmaster's office were the only hope of ensuring recovery. Having instructed his sergeant to take statements from the other people involved, Robert Colbeck turned his attention to Pike, and, with a mixture of patience, sympathy and cool reason, eventually coaxed him into another room, where they could talk alone.

'What about Caleb?' asked Pike, nervously.

'Mr Hayton, the stationmaster, will sit with him,' explained Colbeck, putting his hat on the table. 'If there's any change in his condition, we'll be called immediately.'

'I should have done more to help him, sir.'

'Let me be the judge of that, Mr Pike.'

'When that man hit Caleb, I just went numb. I couldn't move.'

'It's been a very distressing experience for you,' said Colbeck, taking the chair behind the table. 'I daresay that you're still suffering from the shock of it all. Why don't you sit down and rest?'

'I feel that I should be in there with Caleb.'

'Think of the man who attacked him. Do you want him caught?'

'Yes, Inspector,' said Pike with sudden urgency. 'I do.'

'Then you'll have to help us. Every detail you can provide may be of value.' He indicated the bench and the fireman slowly lowered himself on to it. 'That's better,' he said, producing a pencil and pad from his inside pocket. 'Now, in your own time, tell me what happened from the moment that the train was flagged down.'

Pike licked his lips with apprehension. He clearly did not wish to recount a story in which he felt his own conduct had been grievously at fault, but he accepted that it had to be done. On the other side of the wall, Caleb Andrews was fighting for his life. Even if it meant some personal discomfort for Pike, he knew that he had to be honest. It was the only way that he could help in the search for the men who had robbed the train and forced him to drive the locomotive off the track.

'When was your suspicion first aroused?' asked Colbeck.

'Not until the signalman threw his flag aside and drew a pistol.'

'Can you describe the fellow?'

'Oh, yes,' said Pike with feeling. 'He was as close as you are, Inspector. I looked him right in the face. He was a big man, around my own height, and with ginger whiskers. But it was his eyes I remember most clearly, sir. They was cold as death.'

Notwithstanding the fact that he was still badly shaken, Frank Pike gave a full and lucid account of the robbery, albeit punctuated with apologies for the way that he felt he had let the driver down. Noting down everything in his pad, Colbeck prodded him gently with questions until he elicited all the details. The fireman's deep respect and affection for Caleb

Andrews was obvious. Colbeck was touched. He tried to offer a modicum of reassurance.

'From what you tell me,' he said, 'Mr Andrews was a plucky man.'

'Caleb would stand up to anybody.'

'Even when he was threatened with a loaded pistol.'

'Yes,' said Pike with a note of pride. 'He was fearless.'

'That courage will stand him in good stead now. He has a strong will to live and it should help him through. When his condition is more stable, I'll arrange for him to be taken home. Meanwhile, I'll make sure that's he's moved to a proper bed.'

'Thank you, Inspector.'

'I believe that he has a daughter.'

'That's true,' replied the other. 'Madeleine worships her father. This will be a terrible blow to her. It is to us all, of course, but Madeleine is the person who'll suffer most. Caleb is everything to her.'

'What about you, Mr Pike?'

'Me, sir?'

'Do you have someone who can help you through this ordeal?'

'I've a wife and child, Inspector. Heaven knows what Rose will say when she hears what happened today. She worries enough about me, as it is,' he said with a sheepish smile. 'My wife thinks that working on the railway is dangerous.'

'You may find it difficult to convince her otherwise, Mr Pike.'

The fireman sat upright. 'I like my job, sir,' he attested. 'It's the only thing I ever wanted to do. The robbery won't change that.'

'I admire your devotion to duty.' Colbeck glanced down at his notes. 'Let me just read through your statement, if I may, in case there's anything you wish to change or add.'

'There won't be, Inspector.'

'You never know. Please bear with me.'

Referring to his notes, Colbeck repeated the story that he had been told. Pike was astounded by the accuracy with which his words had been recorded and, in hearing them again, his memory was jogged.

'There *was* one more thing,' he said.

'Go on.'

'It may not be important but it struck me as odd at the time.'

'Odd?'

'Yes, Inspector. The man who climbed up onto the footplate called Caleb by his name. He *knew* who was driving that train.'

'I wonder how,' said Colbeck, making another entry in his notebook. He flipped it shut. 'Thank you, Mr Pike. That information is very pertinent. I'm glad that I double-checked your story.'

There was a tap on the door and it opened to admit Hayton, the stationmaster, a stooping man in his forties. His sad expression made Pike leap to his feet in alarm. He grabbed the newcomer by the shoulder.

'Has something happened to Caleb?' he demanded.

'Calm down, Mr Pike,' soothed Colbeck, rising from his chair.

'I want to know the truth.'

'Leave go of me and you shall,' said the stationmaster, detaching the fireman's hand. 'There's no need to be so anxious, Mr Pike. The news is good. I came to tell you that the patient has rallied slightly. Mr Andrews even took a sip of water.'

* * *

Sergeant Victor Leeming had not been idle. He was working in a little room that was used for storage. Having first taken a statement from the guard on the ambushed train, he interviewed the two railway policemen whose task was to protect the money in the safes. Initially, they denied having left the luggage van and insisted that they had not been playing cards in the mail coach. When Leeming told them that the guard had given evidence to the contrary, they blustered, prevaricated, then, under close questioning, they caved in. One of the railway policemen, a surly individual with a walrus moustache, even tried to justify their actions.

'Sitting in a luggage van is very boring,' he said.

'You were not there to be entertained,' observed Leeming.

'We often slip into the mail van on such occasions. Nothing ever happens when we carry money. The train has never been under threat before. Ask yourself this, Sergeant. Who would even think of trying to rob us? It's impossible to open those two safes.'

'Not if you have the keys and the combination. What would have made it more difficult for them, of course,' said Leeming, 'is that they'd met stout resistance from two railway policemen hired to guard that money.'

'We didn't believe that it could ever happen, Sergeant.'

'That's no excuse.'

'It was *their* fault,' said the man, searching desperately for a way to redeem himself. 'We were led astray. The mail guards pleaded with us to join them in their coach. They should carry the blame.'

'If you wanted to play cards,' said Leeming, reasonably, 'you could have done that in the luggage van with your colleague.'

'It's not the same with only two players.'

'Tell that to Inspector McTurk.'

The two policemen quailed. They had already given accounts of the robbery to their superior, carefully omitting any mention of their visit to the mail coach. Thanks to the detective, they would now have to confess that they had lied to McTurk. It was a daunting prospect. In the event, it was Leeming who first informed the Scotsman that he had been misled. When he left the storeroom, he found McTurk lurking outside and told him what had transpired.

'Hell and damnation!' exclaimed McTurk. 'They'll swing for this.'

'They pulled the wool over your eyes, Inspector.'

'I'll make them regret that they did that.'

'You owe a debt to Inspector Colbeck,' said Leeming, enjoying the other's discomfort. 'Had he not searched the mail van, this dereliction of duty may not have come to light. It explains why those employed to look after the mail and the money were caught off guard.'

'I'll see them crucified,' vowed McTurk.

'You need to review your safety procedures.'

'Don't presume to tell me my job, Sergeant.'

'Your men were blatantly at fault.'

'Then they'll be punished accordingly,' said McTurk, nettled by the criticism. 'We have high standards to maintain. But I'll thank you not to pass comments on our police force. Might I remind you that we've been in existence a lot longer than the Detective Department at Scotland Yard?'

'Perhaps that's why complacency has set in.'

'We are not complacent, Sergeant Leeming!'

'Patently, some of your men are.'

'Isolated examples,' argued the Scotsman, barely able to contain his fury. 'And whatever their shortcomings, at least they *look* like policemen. I can't say that about you and Inspector Colbeck.'

'We belong to the Plain Clothes Detail.'

McTurk sniffed. 'There's nothing plain about your colleague's attire. He struts around like a peacock.'

'The Inspector puts a high premium on smartness.'

'Then he'd be more at home in fashionable society.'

'I agree with you there,' said Colbeck, coming into the room in time to hear McTurk's comment. 'Fashionable society is often the place where serious crimes are hatched. Were we to wear police uniform, we would disclose our identity at once and that would be fatal. Being able to move invisibly in society gives us an enormous advantage. It's one of the principles on which we operate.'

'It's not one that appeals to me,' said McTurk, tapping his chest. 'I'm proud to wear a uniform. It shows who I am and what I stand for.'

'But it also warns any criminals that you represent danger.'

'And what do *you* represent, Inspector Colbeck?'

'The veiled sarcasm in your voice suggests that you've already supplied your own answer to that question,' said Colbeck, tolerantly, 'so I'll not confuse you by giving you my reply. I simply came to thank you for your help and to tell you that we'll be leaving for London soon.' He could not resist a smile. 'On what, I believe, you call an up train.'

'What about the others?'

'They're free to leave, Inspector – with the exception of the patient, that is. The stationmaster has very kindly offered a bed in his house to Mr Andrews, who seems to have made a slight improvement.'

'That's cheering news,' said Leeming.

'Yes,' added McTurk. 'The station can get back to normal.'

'Normality will not be completely restored,' said Colbeck, 'until this crime has been solved and the villains are securely behind bars. Sergeant Leeming and I have done all that we can here. We move on to the next stage of the investigation.'

'May one ask where that might be?'

'Of course, Inspector. We're going to pay a visit to the Post Office.' He hovered in the doorway. 'Now, please excuse me while I speak to Fireman Pike. He insists on staying with the driver even though there's nothing that he can do.' He waved to McTurk. 'Goodbye.'

'And good riddance!' muttered the other as Colbeck went out. He turned on Leeming. 'A Detective-Inspector, is he? And how did he get that title?'

'Strictly on merit,' said the other.

'The merit of knowing the right people?'

'Not at all. He achieved his promotion by dint of hard work and exceptional talent. Inspector Colbeck is highly educated.'

'I knew that there was something wrong with him.'

'Don't you believe in education, Inspector McTurk?'

'Only in small doses,' retorted the other. 'Otherwise, it can get in your way. Book-learning is useless in this job. All that a good policeman really needs is a sharp eye and a good nose.'

'Is that what you have?' asked Leeming.

'Naturally.'

'Then they let you down, Inspector. Your sharp eye didn't help you to spot that playing card in the mail coach, and your good nose failed to pick up the smell of deception when you questioned the two policemen who travelled on the train.'

'That's immaterial.'

'Not to me. I put my trust in Inspector Colbeck's education.'

'You'd never get me working for that fop,' sneered McTurk.

'I can see that you don't know him very well,' said Leeming

with a short laugh. 'He's no fop, I can assure you of that. But you're quite safe from him. He'd never even consider employing you.'

'Why not?'

'Because you are what you are, Inspector McTurk. Criminals can see you coming a mile away. Let's be frank about it, shall we? Even if you were stark naked, everyone would know that you were a policeman.'

Herbert Shipperley was a short, thin, harassed man in his fifties with a bald head that was dotted with freckles and a face that was a mass of wrinkles. His responsibilities at the Post Office included supervision of the mail coaches that were run on various lines. News of the train robbery had struck him with the force of a blow and he was quick to see all the implications. Shipperley knew that he would be in the line of fire. Even though it was quite late, he was still in his office when the detectives called on him and introduced themselves. He backed away as if they had come to arrest him.

'We just wish to ask you a few questions,' explained Colbeck.

'I've been bombarded with questions ever since people caught wind of the robbery,' moaned Shipperley. 'It's only a matter of time before I have newspaper reporters banging on my door. They'll blame me as well, whereas it's the railway company that's really at fault.'

'We're not here to apportion blame, Mr Shipperley. We merely wish to establish certain facts. Sergeant Leeming and I have just returned from the scene of the crime.'

'What did you learn?'

'Enough to see that we have a difficult case on our hands.'

'But you will recover everything, won't you?' bleated

Shipperley. 'I need to be able to reassure the Royal Mint and the bank – not to mention my own superiors. The loss of that mail is a tragedy,' he cried. 'It threatens the integrity of our service. Imagine how people will feel when they discover that their correspondence has gone astray. Help me, Inspector Colbeck,' he implored. 'Give me your word. You do expect to catch the robbers, don't you?'

'We hope so.'

'I need more than hope to revive me.'

'It's all that I can offer at the moment.'

'You might try a glass of whisky,' advised Leeming. 'It will calm your nerves. We're not miracle-workers, I fear. We'll do our best but we can give you no firm promises.'

Shipperley sagged visibly. 'Oh, I see.'

'We're dealing with a premeditated crime,' said Colbeck. 'It was conceived and planned with great care, and couldn't possibly have been committed in the way that it was without the direct assistance of insiders.'

'You're surely not accusing *me*?' gasped the other, clutching at his throat. 'I've worked for the Post Office all my life, Inspector. My reputation is spotless.'

'I'm sure that it is, Mr Shipperley, and I can say now that you're not under any suspicion.' He signalled to Leeming, who took out his notepad and pencil. 'We simply want a few details from you, please.'

'About what?'

'The procedure for carrying money on the mail train.'

'We go to great lengths to maintain secrecy.'

'Word obviously got out on this occasion,' said Colbeck. 'We need to know how. Perhaps you can tell me how often you liaise with the Royal Mint or with the Bank of England to carry money on their behalf on the mail train. We'd also like to hear how many of your employees know the exact dates of each transfer.'

'Very few, Inspector.'

'Let's start with the frequency of such deliveries, shall we?'

Herbert Shipperley took a deep breath and launched into what turned out to be a prolonged lecture on how the mail trains operated, giving far more detail than was actually required. Colbeck did not interrupt him. In talking about his work, the man gradually relaxed and some of his facial corrugations began to disappear. The longer he went on, the more enthusiastic he got, as if initiating some new recruits into the mysteries of the Post Office. It was only when he had finished that his eyes regained their hunted look and the anxious furrows returned.

'As you see, gentlemen,' he said, stroking his pate with a sweaty palm, 'our system is virtually foolproof.'

'Until today,' commented Leeming.

'The Post Office was not in error.'

'That remains to be seen.'

'The information must have been leaked by the Royal Mint.'

'Let's consider the names that you've given us, Mr Shipperley,' said Colbeck, thoughtfully. 'Apart from yourself, only three other people here had foreknowledge of the transfer of money by means of mail train.'

'Yes, Inspector, and I can vouch for all of them.'

'But even they – if I understood you right – wouldn't necessarily be able to say what was being carried on any particular day.'

'That's correct,' said Shipperley. 'It's an extra safeguard. Only I would know for certain if the consignment were coming from the Royal Mint or the Bank of England. Coin, bank notes and gold bullion are sent to assorted destinations around the country. Some gold is periodically exported to France from one of the Channel ports.'

'Of the three names you gave us,' said Leeming, glancing at his notebook, 'which employee would you trust least – Mr Dyer, Mr Ings or Mr Finlayson?'

'I have equal faith in all of them,' said the other, loyally.

'Then let me put the question a different way,' suggested Colbeck, taking over. 'Which of the three has the lowest wage?'

'I don't see that that has any relevance, Inspector.'

'It could do.'

'Then the answer is William Ings. He's the most junior of the three in terms of position. However,' Shipperley went on, 'there's not a blemish on his character. Mr Ings has always been strongly committed to the Post Office. He's been with us longer than either Mr Dyer or Mr Finlayson.'

'We'll need to speak to all three of them.'

'Is that necessary, Inspector?'

'I think so,' said Colbeck. 'What time will they arrive for work tomorrow morning?' The other man looked uncomfortable. Colbeck took a step closer. 'Is there a problem, Mr Shipperley?'

'Yes,' he confessed. 'Mr Dyer and Mr Finlayson will definitely be here but I can't guarantee that Mr Ings will turn up.'

'Oh? Why is that, pray?'

'He's been sick all week and unable to work.'

Leeming put a tick against one of the names in his notebook.

When she heard the knock on the front door, Maud Ings rushed to open it, first drawing back the heavy bolts. Her expectation changed instantly to disappointment when she saw, by the light of her lamp, that the caller was a complete stranger. Inspector Robert Colbeck touched the brim of his hat politely then explained who he was. Mrs Ings was alarmed to hear of his occupation.

'Has something happened to William?' she asked.

'Not that I know of, Mrs Ings.'

'That's a relief!'

'My understanding was that your husband was at home.'

She shifted her feet uneasily. 'I'm afraid not, sir.'

'His employer told me that he was ill.'

'Why?' she said in surprise. 'Has he not been to work?'

'I wonder if I might come in,' said Colbeck, quietly.

The house was at the end of a terrace not far from Euston Station. It was small and neat with a presentable exterior. Once inside, however, Colbeck saw signs of sustained neglect. Wallpaper was starting to peel on some walls and the paint work was in a poor condition. There was a distinct smell of damp. The room into which he was conducted had no more than a few sticks of furniture in it and a threadbare carpet. There was an air of neglect about Maud Ings as well. She was a slim, shapeless woman in her late thirties with a haggard face and unkempt hair. He could see from the red-rimmed eyes that she had been crying. A moist handkerchief protruded from the sleeve of her dress.

Embarrassed by her appearance, she took off her apron then adjusted her hair with a hand. She gave him an apologetic smile.

'Excuse me, Inspector,' she said. 'I was not expecting company.'

'But you were expecting someone, Mrs Ings. I could tell that by the alacrity with which you opened the door. Did you think that I might be your husband?'

'Yes.'

'Does he not have a key to his own front door?'

'Of course.'

'Then why did you bolt it against him?'

She shook her head. 'I don't know.'

'Perhaps you should sit down,' he suggested, seeing her distress. 'I'm sorry that I called at such an inopportune hour but I had no choice. It's imperative that I speak to Mr Ings.'

'Why?' she asked, sitting down.

'It's a matter that relates to his work at the Post Office.'

'Is he in trouble, Inspector?'

'I'm not sure.'

'What has he done?'

'Well,' he replied, taking the chair opposite her, 'Mr Ings failed to report for work this week. He sent word to say that he was sick.'

'But there's nothing wrong with him.'

'So why did he lie to his employers?'

Maud Ings bit her lip. 'William has never let them down before,' she said with vestigial affection for her husband. 'He works long hours at the Post Office. They don't appreciate what he does.' She gave a shrug. 'It may be that he *is* unwell. That's the only thing that would keep him away. The truth is that I haven't seen him this week.'

'And why is that, Mrs Ings?'

'My husband is . . . staying elsewhere.'

'Do you have an address for him?'

'No,' she said, bitterly, 'and I don't really want it.'

Colbeck took a swift inventory of the room then looked at her more closely. Maud Ings was evidently a woman who was at the end of her tether. Apparently abandoned by her husband, she was still hoping that he might come back to her even though he had caused her obvious suffering. The remains of her youthful prettiness were all but obscured now. Colbeck treated her with great sympathy.

'I regret that I have to ask you about your private life,' he said, 'but it's germane to my investigation. Mrs Ings, it's not difficult to see that you and your husband were short of money.'

'I did my best,' she said, defensively. 'I always managed on what he gave me, however little it was.'

'Yet Mr Ings earned a reasonable wage at the Post Office.'

'Earned it and threw it away, Inspector.'

'Was he a drinking man?'

'No,' she replied, as another flicker of affection showed, 'William was no drunkard. I can clear him of that charge. He was a good man at heart – kind and considerate.' Her voice darkened. 'At least, he was for a time. That was before he caught the disease.'

'What disease?'

'Gambling. It ruined our marriage, Inspector.'

'I take it that he was not a successful gambler.'

'Only now and then,' she said, wistfully. 'That was the trouble, sir. William had a run of luck at the start and he thought that it would last. He bought me a new coat with his winnings and some lovely furniture.' She shook her head sadly. 'Then his luck changed. We had to sell the furniture last month.'

'Yet he still went on gambling?'

'Yes, Inspector.'

'Do you know where he went to play cards?'

'I do now,' she said, vengefully. 'I got it out of him in the end. I mean, I had a right to know. I'm his wife, Inspector. Sometimes, he'd be away all night at this place. I had a right to be told where it was.'

'And where was it, Mrs Ings?'

'Devil's Acre.'

'I see.'

Colbeck knew the area only too well. It was a favoured haunt of the criminal fraternity and notorious for its brothels and gambling dens. If her husband were a regular visitor to the Devil's Acre, then Maud Ings had been right to describe his addiction as a disease. No decent or sensible man would even dare to venture into such a hazardous district. Colbeck was seeing an aspect of William Ings that had been carefully hidden from his employer. Herbert Shipperley might believe that Ings had an unblemished character but the man consorted regularly with criminals around a card table.

Colbeck was certain that he had picked up a scent at last.

'Is that where your husband is now?' he asked. 'Playing cards?'

'Probably.'

'Can you be a little more precise, Mrs Ings?'

'No,' she replied. 'He wouldn't tell me exactly where he went in case I tried to follow him there. And I would have, Inspector,' she went on with an edge of desperation. 'William left us with no money.'

'He left you with a roof over your head.'

'That's true, Inspector. I've still got a home for myself and the children. It's one consolation. And he did promise that he'd send me something when the money came through.'

'From his wages, you mean?'

'Well, I don't think it would be from his winnings at a card table,' she said, 'because he always seemed to lose.' She peered at Colbeck. 'Why are you so interested in my husband? I still don't understand why you came here looking for him.'

'Earlier today,' he explained, 'there was a train robbery.'

'He'd never get involved in anything like that,' she protested.

'Not directly, perhaps, but the mail train that was ambushed was carrying a consignment of money. Mr Ings was one of the few men who knew that the money would be in transit today.'

'That doesn't mean he betrayed the secret.'

'No,' he conceded, 'and it may well be that your husband is completely innocent. What I need to do is to establish that innocence as soon as is possible so that we can eliminate him from our inquiries. Now,' he said, softly, 'I realise that this is a difficult time for you but I must press you on the matter of his whereabouts.'

'I told you, Inspector. I don't know where he is.'

'You must have some idea, Mrs Ings.'

'None at all.'

'When did he leave?'

'Last weekend.'

'Did he offer you no explanation?'

'William simply packed a bag and walked out of the house.'

'He must have had somewhere to go to,' insisted Colbeck, watching her carefully. 'Somewhere – or someone.'

Her cheeks reddened. 'I don't know what you mean, Inspector.'

'I think that you do.'

'William is not that sort of man.'

'Your husband is a trusted employee at the Post Office,' he told her, calmly, 'a man with access to important information. On the eve of a serious crime that may be linked to his place of work, Mr Ings not only pleads illness and stays away, he leaves his wife and children to fend for themselves while he goes elsewhere.' He fixed her with a piercing stare. 'I think that we have rather more than a curious coincidence here, Mrs Ings. Don't you?'

Maud Ings was in a quandary. Wanting to protect her husband, she was deeply hurt by his treatment of her. Refusing to accept that he could be involved in a crime, she came to see that the evidence was pointing against him. She wrestled with her conscience for a long time but Colbeck did not rush her, recognising that her situation was already exerting almost unbearable pressure upon the woman. She was the discarded wife of a man who might turn out to be involved in a major crime. It took time for her to adjust to the full horror of her predicament.

Eventually, she capitulated and gabbled the information.

'I don't know the woman's name,' she said with rancour, 'but I think that she lives in the Devil's Acre.'

CHAPTER FOUR

Superintendent Edward Tallis was just finishing another cigar when there was a knock on the door of his office. It was late, but he rarely left his desk before ten o'clock at night, believing that long hours and continual vigilance were required to police a city as large and volatile as London. He cleared his throat noisily.

'Come in,' he called, stubbing out his cigar in an ashtray.

Robert Colbeck entered. 'Good evening, sir,' he said.

'I was wondering when you'd deign to put in an appearance.'

'Sergeant Leeming and I have been very busy.'

'To what effect?'

'I believe that we've made slight headway, Superintendent.'

'Is that all?'

'There's still a lot of intelligence to gather,' said Colbeck, 'but I wanted to keep you abreast of developments. Is this a convenient time?'

'No,' said Tallis, grumpily, 'it most definitely is not. My head is pounding, my bad tooth is aching and I'm extremely tired. This is a highly inconvenient time, Inspector, but I'll endure it with good grace. Take a seat and tell me what you have to report.'

Colbeck chose a leather armchair and settled back into it. Relying solely on his memory, he gave a concise account of the progress of the investigation and drew a periodic grunt of approval from the other man. He took it as a good sign that Tallis did not even try to interrupt him. Colbeck just wished that the cigar smoke were not quite so acrid, mingling, as it did, with the stink from the gas lighting to produce a foul compound.

'Where is Sergeant Leeming now?' asked Tallis.

'Questioning senior figures at the railway company,' said Colbeck. 'I left him to do that while I called at the home of William Ings.'

'But the cupboard was bare.'

'The man himself may not have been there, Superintendent, but I feel that I gathered some valuable clues. I strongly advise that we keep the house under surveillance in case Mr Ings should chance to return.'

'Why should he do that?'

'To give his wife money and to see his children.'

'The complications of marriage!' sighed Tallis, sitting back in his chair. 'The more I see of holy matrimony, the more grateful I am that I never got embroiled in it myself. I daresay that you feel the same.'

'Not exactly, sir.'

'Then why have you remained single?'

'It was not a conscious decision,' explained Colbeck, unwilling to go into any detail about his private life. 'I suppose the truth is that I have yet to meet the lady with whom I feel impelled to share my life, but I have every hope of doing so one day.'

'Even if it might impede your career as a detective?'

'Unlike you, sir, I don't see marriage as an impediment.'

'Anything that prevents a man from devoting himself to his work is a handicap,' announced Tallis. 'That's why I limit my social life so strictly. We have an enormous amount to do, Inspector. London is a veritable sewer of crime. Our job is to sluice it regularly.'

'I have a feeling that this case will take us much further afield than the capital, Superintendent,' said Colbeck. 'The robbery occurred in a rural location in Buckinghamshire and that county is hardly a hive of criminal activity. On the other hand, the crucial information about the mail train was doubtless supplied by someone in London.'

'William Ings?'

'I reserve judgement until we get conclusive proof.'

'It sounds to me as if we already have it.'

'The evidence is only circumstantial,' Colbeck pointed out. 'Do I have your permission to arrange for the house to be watched?'

'No, Inspector.'

'Why not, sir?'

'Only a fool would dare to go back there again.'

'Only a fool would run up gambling debts.'

'I can't spare the men.'

'You said that I could have unlimited resources.'

'Within reason,' Tallis reminded him, 'and I don't happen to think that keeping this house under observation is a reasonable use of police time. Ings has obviously gone to ground somewhere else. I doubt if his wife will ever see the rogue again.'

Colbeck was far too used to having his suggestions blocked by his superior to be irritated. It was something he had learnt to accept. Edward Tallis seemed to take pleasure from frustrating any initiatives that the other man put forward. It was one of the reasons why the antipathy between them had deepened over the years.

'It's your decision, sir,' said Colbeck with exaggerated civility.

'Abide by it.'

'What else can I do?'

'Invent some hare-brained scheme of your own to subvert me,' said Tallis with vehemence, 'and I'll not stand for that. It's happened before, as I know to my cost.'

'I only took what I felt were the appropriate steps.'

'You resorted to untried, unauthorised methods. And, yes,' he admitted, raising a hand, 'they did achieve a measure of success, I grant you. But they also left me to face a reprimand from the Commissioners. Never again, Inspector – do you hear me?'

'Loud and clear, sir.'

'Good. You must follow procedure to the letter.'

'Yes, Superintendent.'

'So what's your next step?'

'To meet up with Victor Leeming and hear what he found out at the railway company. He acquitted himself well when he talked to the people who were on board the train. He asked all the right questions.'

'I'll want to know what he gleaned from the railway company.'

'Of course, sir.'

'What are your plans for tomorrow?'

'I intend to catch the earliest possible train to Birmingham.'

'Why?' demanded Tallis.

'Because I need to speak to the manager of the bank to which that money was being sent. He has a key to open that safe. I'd like to know how it came into the possession of the robbers.'

'So you suspect treachery at that end as well?'

'I'm certain of it, Superintendent,' said Colbeck. 'I believe that we're looking at a much wider conspiracy than might at first appear. There was inside help at the Post Office, the bank and, possibly, at the Mint. The robbers might also have had a confederate inside the London and North Western Railway Company,' he argued. 'I don't believe that William Ings is the only man implicated.'

Tallis grimaced. 'In other words,' he said, tartly, 'this case will take a long time to solve.'

'I'm afraid so.'

'Then I'll have to endure even more harassment from all sides.'

'Your back is broad, sir.'

'That's the trouble,' complained Tallis. 'It presents a big target for anybody with a whip in his hand. If we fail to make swift progress in this investigation, I'll be flayed alive. I've already had to fight off the so-called gentlemen of the press. Tomorrow's headlines will not make pleasant reading, Inspector. My bad tooth is throbbing at the prospect.'

'There's a way to solve that problem, Superintendent.'

'Is there?'

'Yes,' said Colbeck, cheerfully. 'Don't buy a newspaper.'

Caleb Andrews had never known such fierce and unremitting pain. He felt as if his skull were about to split apart. The only escape from the agony was to lapse back into unconsciousness. Every so often, however, he recovered enough, if only fleetingly, to remember something of what had happened and he felt the savage blows being administered by the butt of the pistol again and again. When that torment eased slightly with the passage of time, he became more acutely aware of the pain in his body and limbs. He ached all over and one of his legs seemed to be on fire. What frightened him was that he was unable to move it.

As his mind slowly cleared, he hovered for an age between sleep and waking, conscious of the presence of others, but unable to open his eyes to see whom they might be. There was movement at his bedside and he heard whispers, but, before he could identify the voices, he always drifted off again. It was infuriating. He was desperate to reach out, to make contact, to beg for help, to share his suffering with others. Yet somehow he could not break through the invisible barrier between his private anguish and the public world. And then, just as he despaired of ever waking up again, he had a momentary surge of energy, strong enough for him to be able to separate his eyelids at last.

Faces swam in front of him then one of them swooped in close. He felt a kiss on his cheek and his hand was squeezed very gently. A soft female voice caressed his ear.

'Hello, Father,' said Madeleine Andrews. 'I'm here with you.'

Victor Leeming was weary. After conducting a long and taxing series of interviews at the offices of the London and North Western Railway Company, he was grateful that his duties were almost over for the day. All that he had to do was to repair to Colbeck's house in order to compare notes with the Inspector. He hoped that the latter had had a more productive evening than he had managed.

As a cab took him to the house in John Islip Street, he listened to the clacking of the horse's hooves on the hard surface and mused on the seductive simplicity of a cab driver's life. Ferrying passengers to and fro across London was an interesting, practical and undemanding way of life, free from the dangers of police work or from the tedium that often accompanied it. One could even count on generous tips, something that was unheard of among those who toiled at Scotland Yard. By the time he reached his destination, Leeming had come to envy the virtues of a less onerous occupation.

Once inside the house, however, he dismissed such thoughts from his mind. Robert Colbeck had a warm welcome and a bottle of Scotch whisky waiting for him. The two men sat down in a study that was lined with books on all manner of subjects. Neat piles of newspapers and magazines stood on a beautiful mahogany cabinet. Framed silhouettes occupied most of the mantelpiece. Above them, on the wall, in a large, rectangular gilt frame, was a portrait of a handsome middle-aged woman.

'How did you fare?' asked Colbeck, sipping his drink.

'Not very well, Inspector.'

'Did the railway company close ranks on you?'

'That's what it amounted to,' said Leeming, taking a first, much-needed taste of whisky. 'They denied that any of their employees could have leaked information to the robbers and boasted about their record of carrying money safely by rail. I spoke to four different people, and each one told me the same thing. We must search elsewhere.'

'We'll certainly do that, Victor, but I still think that we should take a closer look at the way the company operates its mail trains. We've already exposed the shortcomings of railway policemen.'

'They were rather upset when I told them about that.'

'Understandably.'

'Though not as irate as Inspector McTurk,' recalled Leeming with a broad grin. 'He was in a frenzy. McTurk was such a bad advertisement for Scotland.' He raised his glass. 'Unlike this excellent malt whisky.'

'Yes,' said Colbeck with amusement. 'The good Inspector was not the most prepossessing individual, was he? But I'm sorry that you found the railway company itself in an uncooperative mood. I had a much more profitable time at the home of William Ings.'

'What sort of man is he?'

'An absent one.'

Colbeck told him in detail about the visit to Maud Ings and how his request for the house to be watched had been summarily turned down. Leeming rolled his eyes.

'If only Superintendent Tallis was on *our* side for once.'

'Now, now, Victor,' said Colbeck with mock reproof. 'Do I hear a murmur of insubordination?'

'He's supposed to put handcuffs on the villains, not on us.'

'He does hamper us now and then, I agree, but we must contrive to work around him. One of the things I want you to do in the morning is to find out who patrols the beat that includes the house. Ask the officers in question to keep an eye out for Mr Ings.'

'Yes, Inspector. What else am I to do tomorrow?'

'Report to Superintendent Tallis first thing,' said Colbeck. 'He wishes to know exactly what you found out at the offices of the London and North Western Railway Company.'

'Precious little.'

'That's rather perplexing, I must say. People with nothing to hide are usually more open and helpful.'

'They were neither.'

'Then we must find out why. When you've delivered your report, I want you to go to the Royal Mint to see if there was any breach of security there. I fancy there are more names to unearth than that of William Ings.'

'What if he doesn't make the mistake of returning to his house?'

'We'll have to go looking for him.'

'In the Devil's Acre?' asked Leeming with disbelief. 'You'd be searching for a needle in a haystack. Besides, we couldn't venture in there without a dozen or more uniformed constables at our back.'

'Oh,' said Colbeck, casually, 'that won't be necessary.'

He finished his drink and put his glass on the mahogany desk. He looked at ease in the elegant surroundings. Leeming was making a rare visit to the house and he felt privileged to be there. Colbeck was a private man who invited few colleagues to his home. It was so much larger and more comfortable than the one in which Leeming and his family lived. He gazed at the well-stocked shelves.

'Have you read all these books, Inspector?' he asked.

'Most of them,' replied the other. 'And the ones I haven't read, I've probably referred to. A good library is an asset for a detective. If you're interested, I have a few books here on the development of the steam locomotive.'

'No, thank you. I barely have time to read a newspaper.'

'That's a pity.'

'There's no such thing as leisure when you have a family.'

'I'll take your word for it, Victor.'

Leeming admired the mahogany cabinet beside him. 'My wife would covet some of this lovely furniture,' he said, stroking the wood.

'It's not for sale, I fear,' warned Colbeck with a fond smile. 'I inherited it with the house. My father was a cabinetmaker. Most of the things in here are examples of his handiwork.'

'He must have been a fine craftsman.'

'He was, Victor, but he never wanted his son to follow in his footsteps. My father had boundless faith in the powers of education. That's why I was packed off to school at such an early age.'

The clock on the desk began to strike and Leeming realised how late it was. It was time to go home. He downed the last of the whisky in one gulp then rose to his feet.

'What will *you* be doing tomorrow, sir?' he asked.

'Going to Birmingham. I need to speak to the bank manager.'

'Better you than me. I hate long train journeys. They unsettle my stomach. To be honest, I don't like travelling by rail at all.'

'Really? I love it. Believe it or not, there was a time in my youth when I toyed with the notion of being an engine driver.'

'The life of a cab driver has more attraction for me.'

'You prefer the horse to the steam locomotive?'

'I do, Inspector.'

'Then you're behind the times, Victor,' said Colbeck. 'The railways are here to stay. In any race between them, a steam train will always beat a horse and carriage.'

'That's not what happened today, sir.'

'What do you mean?'

'The mail train came a poor second,' argued Leeming. 'It was put out of action completely while the robbers escaped overland by horse. I think that there's a message in that.'

Colbeck pondered. 'Thank you, Victor,' he said at length. 'I do believe that you're right. There was indeed a message.'

The fight was over almost as soon as it had begun. After exchanging loud threats and colourful expletives, the two men leapt to their feet and squared up to each other. But before either of them could land a telling blow, they were grabbed by the scruff of their necks, marched to the door and thrown out into the alleyway with such force that they tumbled into accumulated filth on the ground. Rubbing his hands together, the giant Irishman who had ejected them sauntered back to the crowded bar.

'I see that you haven't lost your touch,' said a voice in the gloom.

'Who are you?' growled Brendan Mulryne, turning to the man.

'I was waiting for you to remember.'

Mulryne blinked. 'Haven't I heard that voice before somewhere?'

'You should have. It gave you a roasting often enough.'

'Holy Mary!' exclaimed the other, moving him closer to one of the oil lamps so that he could see the stranger more clearly. 'It's never Mr Colbeck, is it?'

'The very same.'

Mulryne stared at him in the amazement. The Black Dog was one of the largest and most insalubrious public houses in Devil's Acre and the last place where the Irishman would have expected to find someone as refined as Robert Colbeck. The detective had taken trouble to blend in. Forsaking his usual attire, he looked like a costermonger down on his luck. His clothes were torn and shabby, his cap pulled down over his forehead. Colbeck had even grimed his face by way of disguise and adopted a slouch. He had been standing next to Mulryne for minutes and evaded recognition. The Irishman was baffled.

'What, in God's sacred name, are you doing here?' he said.

'Looking for you, Brendan.'

'I've done nothing illegal. Well,' he added with a chuckle, 'nothing that I'd own up to in a court of law. The Devil's Acre is a world apart. We have our own rules here.'

'I've just seen one of them being enforced.'

Colbeck bought his friend a pint of beer, then the two of them adjourned to a table in the corner. It was some time since the detective had seen Mulryne but the man had not changed. Standing well over six feet tall, he had the physique of a wrestler and massive hands. His gnarled face looked as if it had been inexpertly carved out of rock, but it was shining with a mixture of pleasure and surprise now. During his years in the Metropolitan Police, Mulryne had been the ideal person to break up a tavern brawl or to arrest a violent offender. The problem was that he had been too eager in the exercise of his duties and was eventually dismissed from the service. The Irishman never forgot that it was Robert Colbeck who had spoken up on his behalf and tried to save his job for him.

A pall of tobacco smoke combined with the dim lighting to make it difficult for them to see each other properly. The place was full and the hubbub loud. They had to raise their voices to be heard.

'How is life treating you, Brendan?' asked Colbeck.

'Very well, sir.'

'You don't have to show any deference to me now.'

'No,' said Mulryne with a grin that revealed several missing teeth. 'I suppose not. Especially when you're dressed like that. But, yes, I'm happy here at The Black Dog. I keep the customers in order and help behind the bar now and then.'

'What do you get in return?'

'Bed, board and all the beer I can drink. Then, of course, there's the privileges.'

'Privileges?'

'We've new barmaids coming here all the time,' said Mulryne with a twinkle in his eye. 'I help them to settle in.'

'Would you be interested in doing some work for me?'

Mulryne was hesitant. 'That depends.'

'I'd pay you well,' said Colbeck.

'It's not a question of money. The Devil's Acre is my home now. I've lots of friends here. If you're wanting help to put any of them in jail, then you've come to the wrong shop.'

'The man I'm after is no friend of yours, Brendan.'

'How do you know?'

'Because he doesn't really belong in this seventh circle of hell,' said Colbeck. 'He's an outsider, who's taken refuge here. A gambler who drifted in here to play cards and to lose his money.'

'We've lots of idiots like that,' said Mulryne. 'They always lose. There's not an honest game of cards in the whole of the Devil's Acre.'

'He still hasn't realised that.'

'Why do you want him?'

'It's in connection with a serious crime that was committed earlier today – a train robbery.'

'Train robbery!' echoed the other with disgust. 'Jesus, what will they think of next? There was never anything like that in my time. The only people I ever arrested were beggars, footpads, cracksmen, flimps, doxies, screevers and murderers – all good, decent, straightforward villains. But now they're robbing trains, are they? That's shameful!'

'It was a mail train,' said Colbeck. 'A substantial amount of money was also being carried. They got away with everything.'

'How does this gambler fit into it?'

'That's what I need to ask him, Brendan – with your help.'

'Ah, no. My days as a bobby are over.'

'I accept that. What I'm asking you is a personal favour.'

'Is it that important, Mr Colbeck?'

'It is,' said the other. 'I'd not be here otherwise. It's been a long day and walking through the Devil's Acre in the dark is not how I'd choose to spend my nights. No offence, Brendan,' he added, glancing around at some of the sinister faces nearby, 'but the company in The Black Dog is a little too primitive for my taste.'

Mulryne laughed. 'That's why I like it here,' he said. 'The place is alive. The sweepings of London come in through that door, looking for a drink, a woman and a fight in that order. I keep very busy.'

'Could you not spare some time to assist me?'

'I'm not sure that I can, Mr Colbeck. I've no idea what this man looks like and not a clue where to start looking.'

'I can help you on both counts,' said the detective. 'When I finally persuaded his wife that I needed to track him down, she gave me a good description of William Ings. He's living with a woman somewhere. But the place to start is among the moneylenders.'

'Why – did he borrow from them?'

'He must have Brendan. He lost so much at the card table that he had to sell or pawn most of the furniture in his house. The only way he could have carried on gambling was to borrow money – probably at an exorbitant rate of interest.'

'There are no philanthropists in the Devil's Acre.'

Colbeck leant in closer. 'I need to locate this man.'

'So I see. But tell me this – does that black-hearted devil, Superintendent Tallis, know that you're here?'

'Of course not.'

'What about Sergeant Leeming?'

'There's no need for Victor to be told,' said Colbeck. 'That way, he can't get into trouble with Mr Tallis. This is my project, Brendan. You'll only be answerable to me.'

'And there's money in it?'

'If you can root out William Ings.'

Mulryne pondered. Before he could reach a decision, however, he saw a drunk trying to molest one of the prostitutes who lounged against the bar. When she pushed the man away, he slapped her hard across the face and produced a squeal of outrage. Mulryne was out of his seat in a flash. He stunned the troublemaker with a solid punch on the side of his head before catching him as he fell. The man was lifted bodily and hurled out of the door into the alleyway, where he lay in a pool of his own vomit. The Irishman returned to his table.

'I'm sorry about the interruption,' he said, sitting down.

'You have a living to earn, Brendan.'

'I do, Mr Colbeck. Mind you, I can always do with extra money. Since I became forty, my charm is no longer enough for some of the girls. They expect me to buy them things as well – as a mark of my affection, you understand.'

'I don't care how you spend what I give you.'

'That's just as well,' said Mulryne. 'Before I agree, promise me there'll be no questions about any friends of mine here who might accidentally have strayed from the straight and narrow.' His eyes glinted. 'I'm not an informer, Mr Colbeck.'

'The only man I'm interested in is William Ings. Will you help me?'

'As long as my name never reaches Mr Tallis.'

'It won't,' said Colbeck, 'I can assure you of that.'

'Then I'm your man.'

'Thank you, Brendan. I appreciate it. Though I'm afraid it won't be easy to find Ings in this rabbit warren.'

Mulryne was confident. 'If he's here – I'll find the bastard!'

Polly Roach was much older than she looked. By dyeing her hair and using cosmetics artfully, she lost over a decade, but her body was more difficult to disguise. She had therefore placed the oil lamp where the spill of its light did not give too much away. As she lay naked in his flabby arms, she made sure that the bed sheet covered her sagging breasts, her spindly legs and the mottled skin on her protruding belly. She nestled against his shoulder.

'When are you going to take me away from here?' she asked.

'All in good time.'

'You said that we'd have a home together.'

'We will, Polly. One day.'

'And when will that be?'

'When it's safe for me to leave here,' he said, unwilling to commit himself to a date. 'Until then, I'll stay with you.'

'But you told me that I didn't belong in the Devil's Acre.'

'You don't, Poll.'

'You promised that we'd live together properly.'

'That's what we are doing,' he said, fondling a breast and kissing her on the lips. 'I left a wife and children for you, remember.'

'I know, Bill.'

'I changed my whole life just to be with you.'

'I simply want you to get me out of the Devil's Acre.'

'Be patient.'

William Ings was a plump man in his forties with large, round eyes that made him look as if he was in a state of constant surprise, and a tiny mouth that was out of proportion with the rest of his facial features. It was lust rather than love that had drawn him to Polly Roach. She offered him the kind of sexual excitement that was unimaginable with his prudish and conventional wife and, once she had a hold on him, she slowly tightened her grasp. During the first few days when he moved in with her, he was in a state of euphoria, enjoying a freedom he had never known before and luxuriating in sheer decadence. It was worlds away from the humdrum routine of the Post Office.

The shortcomings of his situation then became more apparent. Instead of having his own house, he was now sharing two small rooms in a fetid tenement whose thin walls concealed no sounds from the rest of the building. Ings soon learnt that his immediate neighbours, an elderly man and his wife, had ear-splitting arguments several times a day and he had been shocked when he heard the prostitute in the room above them being beaten into silence by one of her more brutal customers. In the room below, a couple had made love to the accompaniment of such vile language that it made his ears burn. In the past, paying an occasional brief visit to Polly Roach had been exhilarating. Living with her in a place of menace was beginning to have distinct drawbacks.

'What are you thinking, Bill?' she asked, gently rubbing his chest.

He sat up. 'I've decided to go out again.'

'*Now*? It must be almost midnight.'

'There are places that never close.'

'You don't want to play cards again, surely?'

'Yes, Poll,' he said, easing her away from him. 'I feel lucky.'

'You always say that,' she complained, jabbing him with a finger, 'yet you always manage to lose somehow.'

'I won this week, didn't I?' he said, peevishly.

'That's what you told me, anyway.'

'Don't you believe me?'

'I'm not sure that I do.'

Anger stirred. 'Where else would I have got so much money from?' he said. 'You should be grateful, Polly. It enabled me to leave my job and move in here with you. Isn't that what you wanted?'

'Yes, Bill. Of course.'

'Then why are you pestering me like this?'

'I just wanted to know where the money came from,' she said, putting a conciliatory hand on his arm. 'Please don't go out again. I know that you feel lucky, but I'd hate you to throw away what you've already earned at the card table. That would be terrible.'

'I only play to win more,' he insisted, getting up and reaching for his clothes. 'This is my chance, don't you see? I can play for higher stakes.'

'Not tonight.'

'I must. I have this feeling inside me.'

Her voice hardened. 'How much have you given to *her*?' she asked, coldly. 'I don't want you wasting any of our money on your wife.'

'That's a matter between me and Maud.'

'No, it isn't, Bill.'

'I have responsibilities.'

'*I'm* your only responsibility now,' she said, climbing out of bed to confront him in the half-dark. 'Have you forgotten what you promised? You swore that I was the only person who mattered in your life.'

'You are, Poll.'

'Then prove it.'

'Leave me be,' he said, fumbling for his trousers.

'Prove it.'

'I've already done that.'

'Not to my satisfaction.'

'What more do you want of me?' he demanded, rounding on her. 'Because of you, I walked out on my wife and children, I gave up my job and I started a whole new life. I tried my best to make you happy.'

'Then take me away from here.'

'I will – in due course.'

'Why the delay?' she challenged. 'What are you hiding from?'

'Nothing.'

'Then why this talk about it not being safe to leave here?'

He pulled on his trousers. 'We'll talk about this in the morning,' he said, evasively. 'I have other things on my mind now.'

She glared at him. 'Are you lying to me, Bill?'

'No!'

'There's something you're not telling me.'

'You've been told everything you need to know, Poll.'

'I'm your woman. There should be no secrets between us.'

'There *are* none,' he said, irritably. 'Now stand out of my way and let me get dressed. I have to go out.'

Polly Roach had played the submissive lover for too long now. She decided that it was time to assert herself. When she got involved with William Ings, she had seen him as her passport out of the squalor and degradation that she had endured for so many years. He represented a last chance for her to escape from the Devil's Acre and its attendant miseries. The thought that he might be deceiving her in some way made her simmer with fury. As he tried to do up the buttons on his shirt, she took him by the shoulders.

'Stay here with me,' she ordered.

'No, Polly. I'm going out.'

'I won't let you. Your place is beside me.'

'Don't you *want* me to make more money, you silly woman?'

'Not that way, Bill. It's too dangerous.'

'Take your hands off me,' he warned.

'Only if you promise to stay here tonight.'

'Don't make me lose my temper.'

'I have a temper as well,' she snarled, digging her nails into his flesh. 'I fight for what's mine. I'm not going to let you sit at a card table and lose money that could be spent on me. I've been in this jungle far too long, Bill. I want to live somewhere *respectable*.'

'Get off me!' he yelled.

'No!'

'Get off!'

Stung by the pain and annoyed by her resistance, he pushed her away and lashed out wildly with a fist, catching her on the chin and sending her sprawling on to the floor. Her head hit the bare wood with a dull thud and she lost consciousness. Ings felt a pang of guilt as he realised what he had done but it soon passed. When he looked down at her, he was repelled by her sudden ugliness. Her mouth was wide open, her snaggly teeth were revealed and he could see the deep wrinkles around her scrawny neck for the first time. Her powdered cheeks were hollow. Ings turned away.

He had never hit a woman before and expected to be horrified at his own behaviour. Yet he felt no remorse. If anything, he felt strangely empowered. He finished dressing as quickly as he could. Polly Roach could do nothing to stop him when he retrieved his belongings from a corner and stuffed them into a leather bag. After taking a farewell look around the tawdry bedroom, he stepped over her body as if it were not there and went out with a swagger.

CHAPTER FIVE

Madeleine Andrews had refused the kind offer of accommodation in the neighbouring house, preferring instead to spend the night beside her father's bed. With a blanket around her shoulders and a velvet cushion beneath her, she sat on an upright wooden chair that was not designed to encourage slumber. Every time she fell asleep, she was awake again within minutes, fearful that she might fall off the chair or miss any sign of recovery by the patient. In fact, Caleb Andrews did not stir throughout the night, lying motionless on his back in the single bed, lost to the world and looking in a pitiful condition. It was only his mild but persistent snore that convinced Madeleine that he was still alive.

She loved her father dearly. In the five years since her mother's death, she had been running their home, taking on full responsibility and treating her father with the kind of affectionate cajolery that was needed. Madeleine was an attractive, alert, self-possessed young woman in her early twenties with an oval face framed by wavy auburn hair and set off by dimpled cheeks. She was calm and strong-willed. Instead of showing panic when told of the attack on her father, she had simply abandoned what she was doing and made her way to Leighton Buzzard as soon as she could.

By the time that she arrived, her father had been moved to the spare bedroom in the stationmaster's house and a penitent Frank Pike was seated beside him. It took her over an hour to convince the fireman that he needed to go home to his wife in order to reassure her that he had not been injured during the robbery. Still troubled in his mind, Pike had finally departed, given some hope by the brief moment when his friend and workmate seemed to rally. He accepted that it was Madeleine's place to keep watch over her father. Both she and the fireman prayed earnestly that she was not sitting beside a deathbed.

It was well after dawn when Caleb Andrews started to wake from his long sleep. Eyes still shut, he rocked from side to side as if trying to shake himself free of something, and a stream of unintelligible words began to tumble from his mouth. Madeleine bent solicitously over him.

'Can you hear me?' she asked.

He puckered his face as he fought to concentrate. When he tried to move the arm that was in a sling, he let out a cry of pain then became silent again. Madeleine thought he had fallen asleep and made no effort to rouse him. She simply sat there and gazed at him by the light that was slanting in through a gap in the curtains. The room was small and featureless, but the bed was a marked improvement on the table in the stationmaster's office. Greater comfort had allowed the patient to rest properly and regain some strength. When his daughter least expected it, Caleb Andrews forced his eyes open and squinted at the ceiling.

'Where am I?' he whispered.

'You're somewhere safe, Father,' she replied.

He recognised her voice. 'Maddy? Is that you?'

He turned his head towards her and let out another yelp of pain.

'Keep still, Father.'

'What's wrong with me?'

'You were badly injured,' she explained, putting a delicate hand on his chest. 'The train was robbed and you were attacked.'

'Where's Frank? Why isn't my fireman here?'

'I sent him home.'

Andrews was bewildered. 'Home? Why?' His eyes darted wildly. 'Where are we, Maddy?'

'In the stationmaster's house at Leighton Buzzard.'

'What am I doing here? I should be at work.'

'You need rest,' she told him, putting her face close to his. 'You took some blows to the head and you fractured a leg when you fell from the footplate. Your arm is in a sling because you have a broken collarbone. Be very careful how you move.'

His face was puce with rage. 'Who *did* this to me?'

'There's no need to worry about that now.'

'Tell me. I want to know.'

'Calm down. You must not get excited.'

'Frank Pike shouldn't have deserted his post. He'll be reported.'

'Forget him, Father,' she advised. 'All we have to think about is how to get you better. It's a miracle that you're alive and able to talk again. I thought I might have lost you.'

She brushed his lips with a tender kiss. Though his face was contorted with pain, he managed a faint smile of thanks and reached up with his free hand to touch her arm. Still hazy, torn between fatigue and anger, puzzled and comforted by his daughter's presence, he struggled to piece together what had happened to him but his memory was hopelessly clouded. All that he could remember was who he was and what he did for a living. When he heard a train steaming through the nearby station, a sense of duty swelled up in him.

'I must get out of here,' he decided, attempting to move.

'No, Father,' she said, using both hands to restrain him gently.

'Frank and I have to take the mail train to Birmingham.'

'It was robbed yesterday. You were assaulted.'

'Help me up, Maddy. We have to get there on time.'

'There *is* no mail train,' she said, trying to break the news to him as softly as she could. 'The men who robbed you removed a section of the track. When you were knocked unconscious, Frank Pike was forced to drive the engine off the rails. He told me that it's lying on its side until they can get a crane to it.'

Andrews was appalled. 'My engine came off the track?' Madeleine nodded sadly. 'Oh, no! That's a terrible thing to hear. She was such a lovely piece of engineering. Mr Allan designed her and I looked after her as if she was my own daughter – as if she was *you*, Maddy.' His eyes moistened. 'I don't care what happened to me. It's her that I worry about. I loved her like a father. She was *mine*.'

Caleb Andrews sobbed as if he had just lost the dearest thing in his life. All that Madeleine could do was to use her handkerchief to wipe away the tears that rolled down his cheeks.

The train that had sped through Leighton Buzzard Station continued on its journey to Birmingham, passing the spot where the robbery had occurred and allowing its passengers a fleeting view of the scene of the crime before taking them on into the Linslade Tunnel. Among those in one of the first class compartments was Inspector Robert Colbeck, who took a keen interest in the sight of the wrecked locomotive that still lay beside the line. He spared a thought for its unfortunate driver.

Though it had given him a very late night, he felt that his visit to the Devil's Acre had been worthwhile and he had been struck once again by the fact that one of the most hideous rookeries in London was cheek by jowl with the uplifting beauty of Westminster Abbey. Rising early the next day, he had travelled by cab to Euston Station where he bought two different newspapers to compare their treatment of the story.

Edward Tallis had been right in his prediction. For anyone involved in law enforcement, reports of the robbery did not make happy reading. The stunning novelty of the crime and the sheer size of the amount stolen – over £3,000 in gold sovereigns – encouraged the newspapers to inject a note of hysteria into their accounts, stressing the ease with which the robbery had been carried out and the apparent inability of either the mail guards or the railway policemen to offer anything but token resistance. The Detective Department at Scotland Yard, they told their readers, had never mounted an investigation of this kind before and were therefore operating in the dark.

Robert Colbeck was mentioned as being in charge of the case and he was surprised to read a quotation from Superintendent Tallis, who referred to him as 'an experienced, reliable and gifted detective'. When he remembered some of the less flattering things that his superior had called him in private, he gave a wry smile. One point made by both newspapers was incontrovertible. No crime of this nature had ever before confronted a Detective Department that, formed only nine years earlier, was still very much in its infancy. They were in uncharted waters.

While the newspapers used this fact as a stick with which to beat the men at Scotland Yard, the Inspector in charge of the investigation saw it as a welcome challenge. He was thrilled by the notion of pitting himself against a man who had organised a crime of such magnitude and audacity. Most of the offenders he had arrested were poor, downtrodden, uneducated men who had turned to crime because there was no honest way for them to make a living. London had its share of seasoned villains, desperate characters who would stop at nothing to achieve their ends, but the majority who trooped through the courts were pathetic figures for whom Colbeck felt a sneaking sympathy.

This time, however, it was different. They were up against a man of clear intelligence, a natural leader who could train and control a gang of almost a dozen accomplices. Instead of fearing him, as the reporters were inclined to do, Colbeck saw him as a worthy adversary, someone who would test his skills of detection and who would stretch the resources of Scotland Yard in a way that had never occurred before. Solving the crime would be an adventure for the mind. However long it might take, Colbeck looked forward to meeting the man behind the train robbery.

Meanwhile, he decided to catch up on some lost sleep. The train was moving along at a comfortable speed, but there were stops to make and it would be hours before it reached Birmingham. He settled back in his upholstered seat and closed his eyes. It was a noisy journey. The chugging of the locomotive combined with the rattling of the carriages and the clicking of the wheels on the rails to produce a cacophony that tried to defy slumber. There was also a lurching motion to contend with as the train powered its way along the standard gauge track.

Because it offered more stability, Colbeck preferred the wider gauge of the Great Western Railway and the greater space in its carriages but he had no choice in the matter on this occasion. The company whose mail train had been robbed was the one taking him to Birmingham, and he was interested to see how it treated its passengers. His compartment was almost full and sleep would offer him a refuge from conversation with any of his companions. Two of them, both elderly men, were scandalised by what they had read in their newspapers.

'A train robbery!' protested one of them. 'It's unthinkable.'

'I agree,' said the other. 'If this kind of thing is allowed to go on, we'll all be in danger. Any passenger train would run the risk of being ambushed and we would be forced to hand over everything we are carrying of value.'

'What a ghastly prospect!'

'It might come to that.'

'Not if this gang is caught, convicted and sent to prison.'

'What chance is there of that?' said the other, sceptically.

'Detectives have already begun an investigation.'

'I find it hard to put much faith in them, sir.'

'Why?'

'Because they have almost no clues to help them. According to *The Times*, these devils came out of nowhere, stole what they wanted, then vanished into thin air. The detectives are chasing phantoms.'

'Yet they claim that this Inspector Colbeck is a gifted policeman.'

'It will need more than a gifted policeman to solve this crime.'

'I agree with you there, my friend.'

'My guess is that this Inspector will not even know where to start.'

On that vote of confidence in his ability, Colbeck fell asleep.

* * *

The Devil's Acre was almost as menacing by day as by night. Danger lurked everywhere in its narrow streets, its twisting lanes and its dark alleyways. There was a pervading stink that never seemed to go away and an unrelenting clamour. Bawling adults and screaming children joined in a mass choir whose repertory consisted solely of a sustained and discordant din that assaulted the eardrums. Scavenging dogs and fighting tomcats added their own descant. Smoke-blackened tenements were built around small shadowed courtyards, thick with assorted refuse and animal excrement. In every sense, it was a most unhealthy place to live.

Brendan Mulryne, however, loved the district. Indeed, he was sad that parts of it had recently been pulled down during the building of Victoria Street, thereby limiting its size and increasing the population of the area that was left, as those who had been evicted moved into houses that were already crowded with occupants. What the Irishman enjoyed about the Devil's Acre was its raucous life and its sense of freedom. It was a private place, set apart from the rest of London, a swirling underworld that offered sanctuary to criminals of every kind in its brothels, its tenements, its opium dens, its gambling haunts and its seedy public houses.

Mulryne felt at home. People he had once hounded as a policeman were now his neighbours and he tolerated their misdemeanours with ease. It was only when a defenceless woman was being beaten, or when a child was in distress, that he felt obliged to intervene. Otherwise, he let the mayhem continue unabated. It was his natural milieu. Unlike strangers who came into the Acre, he could walk its streets without fear of assault or of attracting any of the pickpockets who cruised up and down in search of targets. Mulryne's size and strength bought him respect from almost everyone.

Isadore Vout was the exception to the rule. When the Irishman found him that morning, the moneylender was at his lodging, enjoying a breakfast of stale bread and dripping that he first dipped into a mug of black, brackish tea. Rich by comparison with most people in the area, Vout led a miserly existence, wearing tattered clothes and eating poor food. He was a short, skinny weasel of a man in his fifties, with long grey hair that reached his shoulders and a mean face that was forever set in an expression of distaste. He was not pleased when the landlady showed in his visitor. His voice betrayed no hint of respect.

'Wor d'yer want, Mulryne?' he said through a mouthful of food.

'First of all,' replied the other, standing over him, 'I'd like a little politeness from that arsehole you call a mouth. Unless, that is, you'd like me to pour the rest of that tea over your head.'

'Yer got no right to threaten me.'

'I'm giving you friendly advice.' Pulling up a stool, Mulryne sat beside him at the table and saw what he was eating. 'Bread and dripping, is it?' he noted with disgust. 'And you, able to dine off the finest plate and eat like a lord.'

'It's been a bad month, ain't it?'

'You never have a bad month, you leech. There's always plenty of blood for you to suck out of people who can't afford to lose it. That's why I'm here, Isadore. I want to talk about debts.'

Vout was surprised. 'Yer want to borrow money?'

'I wouldn't borrow a penny from a creeping Shylock like you.'

'Yer'd get a good rate of interest, Mulryne.' He nudged his visitor. 'Friends of mine have special terms, see?'

'I'm no friend of yours, you old skinflint. Special terms?'

repeated Mulryne with derision. 'I don't give a fiddler's fart for your special terms.'

'Then why are yer botherin' me?'

'Because I need information from you. There's a man who probably turned to you for a loan – God help him! I want to know where he is.'

'I can't tell yer,' said Vout, guzzling his tea.

'You haven't heard his name yet.'

'Meks no diff'rence, Mulryne. I never discusses business matters. Them's confeedential.' He jerked his thumb over his shoulder. 'Shut the door when yer leaves – and don't come back.'

'I'm going nowhere until I get an answer,' warned Mulryne.

'Sling yer 'ook, you big, Irish numbskull. Yer wasting yer time.'

'Now you're insulting my nation as well as trying my patience.'

'I wants to finish my grub, that's all.'

'Then let a big, Irish numbskull offer you some assistance,' said Mulryne, grabbing the remainder of the food to stuff into his mouth. 'Like more tea to wash it down, would you?'

Holding the moneylender's hair, he pulled his head back and poured the remaining tea all over his face until Vout was squealing in pain and spluttering with indignation. Mulryne felt that more persuasion was still needed. He got up, pushed the other man to the floor, took him by the heels and lifted him up so that he could shake him vigorously. A waterfall of coins came pouring out of his pockets. Isadore Vout shrieked in alarm and tried to gather up his scattered money. Without any effort, Mulryne held him a foot higher so that he could not reach the floor.

'Put me down, yer madman!' wailed Vout.

'Only when you tell me what I want to know.'

'I'll 'ave yer locked away fer this!'

'Shut up and listen,' Mulryne ordered, 'or I'll bounce your head on the floor until all your hair falls out.'

By way of demonstration, he lowered his captive hard until Vout's head met the carpet with such a bang that it sent up a cloud of dust. The moneylender yelled in agony.

'Stop it!' he pleaded. 'Yer'll crack my skull open.'

'Will you do as you're told, then?'

'No, Mulryne. I never talks about my clients.' His head hit the floor once again. 'No, no!' he cried. 'Yer'll kill me if you do that again.'

'Then I'd be doing the Devil's Acre a favour,' said Mulryne, hoisting him high once more. 'We can do without vultures like you. Now then, you snivelling rogue, what's it to be? Shall I ask my question or would you rather I beat your brains out on the floor?'

It was no idle threat. Seeing that he had no alternative, Vout agreed to help and he was promptly dropped in a heap on the carpet. He immediately began to collect up all the coins he had lost. Mulryne brought a large foot down to imprison one of his hands.

'Yer'll break my fingers!' howled Vout.

'Then leave your money until you've dealt with me.'

Removing his foot, the Irishman took him by the lapels of his coat and lifted him back into his chair. He put his face intimidatingly close. Vout cowered before him.

'Who's this man yer knows?' he asked in a quavering voice.

'His name is William Ings.'

'Never 'eard of 'im.'

'Don't lie to me, Isadore.'

'It's the truth. I never met anyone called that.'

'There's an easy way to prove that, isn't there?' said Mulryne, looking around the dingy room. 'I can check your account book.'

'No!'

'You keep the names of all your victims in there, don't you? If I find that William Ings is among them, I'll know that you're lying to me. Now, where do you keep that book?'

'It's private. Yer can't touch it.'

'I can do anything I like, Isadore,' said Mulryne, walking across to a chest of drawers. 'Who's to stop me?'

As if to prove his point, he pulled out the top drawer and emptied its contents all over the floor. Vout leapt up from his seat and rushed across to grab his arm.

'No, no,' he shouted. 'Leave my things alone.'

'Then tell me about William Ings.'

The moneylender backed away. 'Maybe I *can* help yer,' he said.

'Ah, I've jogged your memory, have I?'

'It was the name that confused me, see? I did business with a Bill Ings, but I can't say for certain that 'e's the same man. Wor does this William Ings look like?'

'I've never seen him myself,' admitted Mulryne, 'but I'm told he's a fat man in his forties who can't resist a game of cards. Since he lost so much, he'd turn to someone like you to borrow. Did he?'

'Yes,' confessed Vout.

'How much does he owe you?'

'Nothing.'

'*Nothing*?'

'He paid off his debt,' said the other. 'In full. Ings told me that 'e 'ad a big win at cards and wanted to settle up. Shame, really. I likes clients of 'is type. They're easy to squeeze.'

'Where can I find him?'

'Who knows?'

'You do, Isadore,' insisted Mulryne. 'You'd never lend a farthing unless you had an address so that you could chase the borrower for repayment. Find your account book. Tell me where this man lives.'

'I can't, Mulryne. I took 'im on trust, see? Someone I knew was ready to vouch for 'im and that was good enough for me.' He gave a sly grin. 'Polly has done a favour or two for me in the past. If 'e's with 'er, Bill Ings is a lucky man, I can tell yer. I knew I could always get to my client through Polly.'

'Polly who? Does she live in the Devil's Acre?'

'Born and bred 'ere. Apprenticed to the trade at thirteen. 'Er name is Polly Roach,' he said, grateful to be getting rid of Mulryne at last. 'Ask for 'er in Hangman's Lane. You may well find Mr Ings there.'

Robert Colbeck woke up as the train was approaching Birmingham and he was able to look through the window at the mass of brick factories and tall chimneys that comprised the outskirts. It was a depressing sight, but, having been there before, he knew that the drab industrial town also boasted some fine architecture and some spacious parks. What made it famous, however, were its manufacturing skills and Colbeck read the names of engineers, toolmakers, potters, metalworkers, builders and arms manufacturers emblazoned across the rear walls of their respective premises. Through the open window, he could smell the breweries.

Arriving at the terminus, he climbed into a cab and issued directions to the driver. During the short ride from Curzon Street to the bank, he was reminded that Joseph Hansom, inventor and architect, had not only built the arresting Town Hall with its Classical colonnade, he had also registered the Patent Safety Cab, creating a model for horse-drawn transport that had been copied down the years. Birmingham was therefore an appropriate place in which to travel in such a vehicle.

Spurling's Bank, one of the biggest in the Midlands, was in the main street between a hotel and an office building of daunting solidity. When he heard that a detective had come to see him, the manager, Ernest Kitson, invited Colbeck into his office at once and plied him with refreshments. A tall, round-faced, fleshy man in his fifties, Kitson was wearing a black frock coat and trousers with a light green waistcoat. He could not have been more willing to help.

'The stolen money must be recovered, Inspector,' he said.

'That's why I'm here, sir. Before we can find it, however, I must first know how it went astray in the first place. Inside help was utilised.'

'Not from Spurling's Bank, of that you can rest assured.'

'Have you questioned the relevant staff?'

'It was the first thing I did when I heard of the robbery,' said Kitson, straightening his cravat. 'Apart from myself, only two other people here have access to the key that would open the safe containing the money. I spoke to them both at length and am satisfied that neither would even consider betraying a trust. Do not take my word for it. You may talk to them yourself, if you wish.'

'That will not be necessary,' decided Colbeck, impressed by his manner and bearing. 'I simply need to examine the key in question.'

'It is locked in the safe, Inspector.'

'Before you take it out, perhaps you could explain to me why the mail train was carrying such a large amount of money in gold coin.'

'Of course,' replied Kitson. 'We abide by the spirit of the Bank Charter Act of 1844. Does that mean anything to you, Inspector?'

'No, Mr Kitson.'

'Then let me enlighten you. Currency crises are the bane of banking and we have suffered them on a recurring basis. When he was Prime Minister, the late Mr Peel sought to end the cycle by imposing certain restrictions. Strict limits were placed on the issue of notes by individual banks and the fiduciary note issue of the Bank of England was set at £14,000,000. Any notes issued above this sum were to be covered by coin or gold bullion.'

'That sounds like a sensible precaution.'

'It is one that Spurling's Bank took to heart,' explained Kitson. 'We stick to that same principle and ensure that notes in all our banks are balanced by a supply of gold coin or bullion. A bank note, after all, is only a piece of paper that bears promise of payment. In the event of a sudden demand for real money, we are in a position to cope. Other banks have collapsed in such situations because they over-extended themselves with loans and had inadequate reserves.'

'How much of the money stolen was destined for this branch?'

'Over a half of it. The rest was to be shared between some of our smaller branches. None of us,' he emphasized, 'can afford to lose that money.' Taking a key from his waistcoat pocket, he crossed to the safe in the corner. 'Let me show you what you came to see.'

'What about the combination number of the safe on the train?'

'That, too, is kept in here.'

'Have you not memorised it, Mr Kitson?'

'I'm a banker, Inspector,' he said. 'I keep a record of everything.'

He opened the safe and took out a metal box that had a separate lock on it. After using a second key to open it, he handed the box to Colbeck. Inside was a slip of paper and a large key on a ring. Colbeck took them out and studied them carefully. Kitson watched in surprise when the detective produced a magnifying glass from his inside pocket to scrutinise the key more carefully. He even held it to his nose and sniffed it.

'May I ask what you are doing?' said Kitson, intrigued.

'Looking for traces of wax, sir. That's the way that duplicates are made. A mould is taken so that it can be used to produce an identical key. Not all locksmiths are as law-abiding as they should be, alas.'

'And this key?'

'It has not been tampered with,' said Colbeck.

'That is what I told you.'

'I needed to check for myself.'

'The only other set of keys is at the Royal Mint.'

'My colleague, Sergeant Leeming, will be visiting the Mint this very day, but I doubt if he will find a lapse in security there. Their procedures are usually faultless. That leaves only a third option.'

'And what is that, Inspector?'

'A visit to the factory where the safe was made,' said Colbeck, handing the key back to him. 'Please excuse me, Mr Kitson. I have to catch a train to Wolverhampton.'

Victor Leeming's day had had an abrasive start to it. When he reported to Tallis, he had found the Superintendent at his most irascible as he read the accounts of the train robbery in the morning newspapers. Seeing himself mocked, and misquoted, Tallis had taken out his anger on the Sergeant and left him feeling as if he had just been mauled by a Bengal tiger. Leeming was glad to escape to the Royal Mint where he could lick his wounds. His guide was a far less truculent companion.

'As you see, Sergeant Leeming,' he said, 'security has absolute priority here. Nobody has sole access to the keys to that safe. There are always two of us present, so it would be impossible for anybody to take a wax impression of the key.'

'I accept that, Mr Omber.'

'There has been a mint here on Tower Hill since Roman times. Methods of guarding the supply of coin thus have a long and honourable history. Having learnt from our predecessors, we feel that we have turned the Royal Mint into an impregnable stronghold.'

'There is no question of that,' conceded Leeming.

He was fascinated by all he had seen, particularly by the thick steel doors that seemed to be fitted everywhere. Once locked, they were almost airtight, and would not buckle before a barrel of gunpowder. Charles Omber took a justifiable pride in their security arrangements. He was a short, stout, middle-aged man whose paunch erupted out of his body and tested the buttons on his trousers to their limit. Having been subjected to Tallis's bellow, Leeming was grateful for Omber's quiet, friendly, helpful voice.

'What else can I show you, Sergeant?' he asked.

'While I'm here, I'd be interested to see the whole process.'

'It will be a pleasure to show you.'

'Thank you.'

Omber waddled off and Leeming fell in beside him. After passing the weighing room, where the amounts of bullion were carefully recorded, they went through some steel doors into the hot metallic atmosphere of the refining shop. Leeming brought up a hand to shield his eyes from the startling brilliance of the furnaces where molten gold was simmering in crucibles like over-heated soup. With long-handled dipping cups, refiners stood in their shirtsleeves before the furnaces to scoop out the liquid gold and pour it into zinc vats of water.

Even those who were used to the heat and the noise had to use their bare forearms to wipe the sweat from their faces. Leeming was loosening his collar with a finger within seconds.

Charles Omber took him on to the corroding shop, where they were met with billowing steam from the porcelain vats in which the golden granules sizzled in hot nitric acid. It was like walking into a golden fog. When his eyes grew accustomed to the haze, Leeming watched the muscular men in their leather aprons and noticed that they all wore hats to protect them from the fumes. Interested to see every stage of the process, he was nevertheless relieved when they moved out of the room, enabling him to breathe more easily.

In the casting shop, with its arched furnace bricked into a wall, he saw the gold being melted again before being poured with utmost care into the moulds of the ingots. Standing at his shoulder, Omber explained what was happening then took his visitor on into the rolling room, the largest and most deafening part of the establishment. The massive steam-driven mill, powered by iron wheels on each side, thundered ceaselessly on, enabling the brick-like ingots to be pressed into long strips from which coins could be punched.

It was when they moved into the coining shop that Leeming suddenly realised something. He had to shout above the metallic chatter of the machines.

'I think I know why the robbers stole coin from that train,' he yelled. 'What is the melting point of gold?'

'That depends on its source and composition,' replied Omber, 'but it is usually between 1,200 and 1,420 degrees centigrade. Why do you ask, Sergeant Leeming?'

'They would need a furnace to handle gold bullion so the robbers let the Royal Mint do their work for them and waited until a shipment of coin was being made. They chose carefully,' he said, watching the blank discs being cut out of the metal. 'Had the train been carrying an issue of notes from the Bank of England, they would have ignored them because they might be traced by their serial numbers. Gold sovereigns are more easily disposed of, Mr Omber.'

'That is certainly true.'

'Then how did they know that you were only sending gold coin yesterday?' wondered Leeming. 'I have an uncomfortable feeling that someone found a way to get past all these steel doors of yours.'

The journey to Wolverhampton obliged Colbeck to travel second class on the Birmingham, Lancaster and Carlisle Railway. It took him through the heart of the Black Country and he looked out with dismay at the forges, mills, foundries, nail factories, coal mines and ironstone pits that stretched for miles beneath the curling dark smoke that spewed from a thousand brick chimneys. Cutting through the smoke, filling the sky with a fierce glare, were lurid flames from countless burning heaps of rubbish. Those who laboured for long hours in heavy industry were unacquainted with the light of day and vulnerable to hideous accidents or cruel diseases. Above the thunder of his train, Colbeck could hear the pounding of hammers and the booming explosion of a blast furnace.

Wolverhampton was a large, dirty, sprawling industrial town that was celebrated for the manufacture of locks, brass, tin, japanned wares, tools and nails. The immaculate detective looked rather incongruous in its workaday atmosphere. Given directions by the stationmaster, he elected to walk to his destination so that he could take a closer look at the people and place. By the time that he arrived at the Chubb Factory, he felt that he had the measure of Wolverhampton.

Silas Harcutt, the manager at the factory, could not understand why someone had come all the way from London to question him. He was a slim individual of middle height with the look of a man who had worked his way up to his position with a slowness that had left a residual resentment. Harcutt was abrupt.

'Your visit is pointless, Inspector,' he declared.

'Not at all,' said Colbeck. 'I've always been curious to see the inside of the Chubb factory. I once had the privilege of a visit to the Bramah Works and it was a revelation.'

'Bramah locks are nothing compared to ours.'

'Your competitors would disagree. At the forthcoming Great Exhibition, they are to display a lock that is impossible to pick.'

'We, too, will have our best lock on show,' boasted Harcutt, 'and we will challenge anyone to open it. I can tell you now that nobody will.'

'You obviously have faith in your product.'

'The Chubb name is a guarantee of quality.'

'Nobody disputes that, Mr Harcutt,' said Colbeck, ignoring the man's brusque manner. 'For professional reasons, I try to keep abreast of developments in the locksmith's trade and I'm always interested to read about your progress. The railway safe that you devised was a marvel of its kind. Even so,' he went on, 'I fear that it was not able to prevent a consignment of money from being stolen.'

'The locks were not picked,' insisted the manager, huffily. 'The safe is specifically designed so that a burglar has nothing to work upon but the keyholes with their protective internal barrels and the steel curtain at their mouths. Do not dare to blame us, Inspector. We were not at fault.'

'I hope that turns out to be the case, sir.'

'It *is* the case, Inspector. Let me show you why.'

Opening the door of his office, he led Colbeck down a corridor to a room that housed dozens of safes and locks. Harcutt walked across to a replica of the safe that the detective had seen on board the train.

'You see?' said the manager, patting the safe. 'Far too heavy to lift without the aid of a crane and resistant to any amount of gunpowder. It is solid and commodious, able to carry a quarter of a ton of gold, coin, or a mixture of both.'

'The robbers showed due respect for the Chubb name,' said Colbeck. 'Instead of trying to pick the locks, they opened them with the keys and the combination number. I am certain that they got neither from Spurling's Bank and security at the Royal Mint is very tight.'

Harcutt was offended. 'Are you suggesting that the keys came from *here*?' he said, drawing himself up to his full height. 'I regard that as an insult, Inspector.'

'It was not meant to be. If I may examine the keys to this safe, I can tell you at once whether there has been subterfuge in your factory.'

'That is inconceivable.'

'I must press you on this point,' said Colbeck, meaningfully.

Lips pursed, Harcutt turned away and strode back to his office with the detective at his heels. He had to use two keys and a combination number to open the wall safe, making sure that he kept his back to his visitor so that Colbeck could see nothing of the operation. Extracting a metal box, the manager unlocked it with a third key and handed it over.

Colbeck took out the keys. Unable to detect anything suspicious with the naked eye, he brought his magnifying glass out again. He saw exactly what he had expected to find.

'Minute traces of wax,' he noted, offering the glass to the other man. 'Would you care to confirm that, Mr Harcutt?'

The manager took the magnifying glass and peered through it with disbelief. Both keys had discernible specks of wax still attached to them.

'Who else was authorised to open your safe?' asked Colbeck.

'Only two people. Mr Dunworth, my deputy, is one of them.'

'And the other?'

'Daniel Slender.'

'I need to speak to both of them at once, Mr Harcutt.'

'Of course,' said the manager, grudgingly. 'Mr Dunworth is in the next office. But you'll have to wait until you get back to London before you question Mr Slender.'

'Oh?'

'He left some weeks ago to take up a new post there.' He saw the suspicion in Colbeck's eyes. 'You are quite wrong, Inspector,' he continued, shaking his head. 'Daniel Slender could not possibly be the culprit. He has been with us for decades. For the last few years, he has been looking after his sick mother in Willenhall. When she died, he felt that it was time to move out of the Midlands.' He thrust the magnifying glass at Colbeck. 'I have complete trust in Daniel Slender.'

The frock coat fitted perfectly. He preened himself in front of the mirror for minutes. Daniel Slender had finally fulfilled his ambition to wear clothing that had been tailored for him in Bond Street. Tall and well-proportioned, he looked as if he belonged in such fine apparel. When he had changed back into his other suit, he took a wad of five pounds notes from his wallet and began to peel them off. Years of self-denial were behind him now. He had enough money to change his appearance, his place in society and his whole life. He was content.

CHAPTER SIX

It was early evening before Robert Colbeck finally got back to his office in Scotland Yard. Victor Leeming was waiting to tell him about his visit to the Royal Mint and to voice his suspicion that someone there might have warned the train robbers when gold coin was actually being dispatched to Birmingham. He took a positive delight in describing the processes by which gold bullion was transformed into coinage.

'I have never seen such a large amount of money,' he said.

'No, Victor,' remarked Colbeck. 'The irony is that the men who sweat and strain to make the money probably get little of it in their wages. It is a cruel paradox. Workers who are surrounded by gold every day remain relatively poor. It must be a vexing occupation.'

'A dangerous one as well, sir. Had I stayed in the refining shop any longer, the heat from those furnaces would have given me blisters. As it is, I can still smell those terrible fumes.'

'I had my own share of fumes in the Midlands.'

'Was the visit a useful one?' asked Leeming.

'Extremely useful. While you were learning about the mysteries of the Royal Mint, I was being taught sensible banking practices and given an insight into the art of the locksmith.'

Colbeck related the events of his day and explained why he had enjoyed travelling by rail so much. Leeming was not convinced that train rides of well over a hundred miles each way were anything but purgatory. He was happy to have missed the ordeal.

'We now know where the keys were obtained,' he said.

'And the combination number, Victor. That, too, was essential.'

'This man, Daniel Slender, must be responsible.'

'Not according to the manager,' said Colbeck, remembering the protestations of Silas Harcutt. 'He claims that the fellow is innocent even though he is the only possible suspect. He set great store by the fact that Slender was a dutiful son who looked after an ailing mother.'

'That certainly shows kindness on his part.'

'It might well have led to frustration. Caring for a sick parent meant that he had no real life of his own. When he was not at the Chubb factory, he was fetching and carrying for his mother. I find it significant that, the moment she died, Daniel Slender sold the house.'

'If he was moving to another post, he would have to do that.'

'I doubt very much if that post exists, Victor.'

'Do you know what it was?'

'Yes,' said Colbeck. 'I even have the address of the factory to which he is supposed to have gone. But I'll wager that we won't find anyone of his name employed there.'

'So why did he come to London?'

Colbeck raised an eyebrow. 'I can see that you've never visited the Black Country. On the journey to Wolverhampton, I saw what the poet meant when he talked about 'dark, satanic mills'.'

'Poet?'

'William Blake.'

'The name means nothing to me, sir,' admitted Leeming, scratching a pimple on his chin. 'I never had much interest in poetry and such things. I know a few nursery rhymes to sing to the children but that's all.'

'It's a start, Victor,' said Colbeck without irony, 'it's a start. Suffice it to say that – with all its faults – London is a much more attractive place to live than Willenhall. Also, of course, Daniel Slender had to get well away from the town where he committed the crime.' He nodded in the direction of the next office. 'What sort of a mood is Mr Tallis in today?'

'A vicious one.'

'I told him not to read the newspapers.'

'They obviously touched him on a raw spot. When I saw the Superintendent this morning, he was breathing fire.'

'I need to report to him myself,' said Colbeck, moving to the door. 'Hopefully, I can dampen down the flames a little. At least we now have the name of the man who made it possible for the robbers to open that safe with such ease.'

'That means we have two suspects.'

'Daniel Slender and William Ings.'

'I did as you told me, Inspector,' said Leeming. 'I asked the men on that beat to keep watch on Mr Ings's house, though I still think that he's unlikely to go back there. It would be too risky.'

'Then we'll have to smoke him out of the Devil's Acre.'

'How on earth could you do that?'

Colbeck suppressed a smile. 'I'll think of a way,' he said.

Work had kept Brendan Mulryne too busy throughout most of the day to continue his search. That evening, however, he took a break from The Black Dog and strode along to Hangman's Lane. The name was apposite. Most of the people he saw loitering there looked if they had just been cut down from the gallows. The man who told him where Polly Roach lived was a typical denizen of the area. Eyes staring, cheeks hollow and face drawn, he spoke in a hoarse whisper as if a noose were tightening around his neck.

Entering the tenement, Mulryne went up the stairs and along a narrow passageway. It was difficult to read the numbers in the gloom so he banged on every door he passed. At the fourth attempt, he came face to face with the woman he was after.

'Polly Roach?' he inquired.

'Who's asking?'

'My name is Brendan Mulryne. I wanted a word with you, darling.'

'You've come to the wrong place,' she said, curtly. 'I don't entertain guests any more.'

'It's not entertainment I want, Polly – it's information.' He looked past her into the room. 'Do you have company, by any chance?'

'No, Mr Mulryne.'

'Would you mind if I came in to look?'

'Yes,' she cautioned, lifting her skirt to remove the knife from the sheath strapped to her thigh. 'I mind very much.'

Mulryne grinned benignly. 'In that case, we'll talk here.'

'Who sent you?'

'Isadore Vout.'

'That mangy cur! If you're a friend of his, away with you!'

'Oh, I'm no friend of Isadore's,' promised Mulryne, 'especially since I lifted him up by the feet and made him dance a jig on his head. He'd probably describe me as his worst enemy.'

'So why have you come to me?'

'I'm looking for someone called William Ings – Billy Ings to you.'

'He's not here,' she snapped.

'So you do know him?'

'I did. I thought I knew him well.'

'So where is he now?'

Polly was bitter. 'You tell me, Mr Mulryne.'

'Is he not coming to see you?'

'Not any more.'

There was enough light from the oil lamp just inside the door for him to see her face clearly. Polly Roach looked hurt and jaded. The thick powder failed to conceal the dark bruise on her chin. Mulryne sensed that she had been crying.

'Did you and Mr Ings fall out, by any chance?' he asked.

'That's my business.'

'It happens to be mine as well.'

'Why – what's Bill to you?'

'A week's wages. That's what I get when I find him.'

'His wife!' she cried, brandishing the knife. 'That bitch sent you after him, didn't she?'

'No, Polly,' replied Mulryne, holding up both hands in a gesture of surrender. 'I swear it. Sure, I've never met the lady and that's the honest truth. Now, why don't you put that knife away before someone gets hurt?' She lowered the weapon to her side. 'That's better. If you were hospitable, you'd invite me in.'

She held her ground. 'Say what you have to say here.'

'A friend of mine is anxious to meet this Billy Ings,' he explained, 'and he's paying me to find him. I'm not a man who turns away the chance of an honest penny and, in any case, I owe this man a favour.'

'What's his name?'

'There's no need for you to know that, darling.'

'Then why is he after Billy?'

'There was a train robbery yesterday and it looks as if Mr Ings may have been involved. His job at the Post Office meant that he had valuable information to sell.'

'So *that's* where he got the money from,' she said. 'He told me that he won it at the card table.'

'Isadore Vout heard the same tale from him.'

'He lied to me!'

'Then you have no reason to protect him.'

Polly Roach became suspicious. She eyed him with disgust. 'Are you a policeman?' she said.

Mulryne laughed. 'Do I *look* like a policeman, my sweetheart?'

'No, you don't.'

'I work at The Black Dog, making sure that our customers don't get out of hand. Policeman, eh? What policeman would dare to live in the Devil's Acre?' He summoned up his most endearing smile. 'Come on now, Polly. Why not lend me a little assistance here?'

'How can I?' she said with a shrug. 'I've no idea where he is.'

'But you could guess where he's likely to be.'

'Sitting at a card table, throwing his money away.'

'And where did he usually go to find a game?'

'Two or three different places.'

'I'll need their names,' he said. 'There's no chance that he'll have sneaked back to his wife then?'

'No, Mr Mulryne. He said that it wouldn't be safe to leave the Acre and I can see why now. He's here somewhere,' she decided, grimly. 'Billy liked his pleasures. That's how we met each other. If he's not gambling, then he's probably lying between the legs of some doxy while he tells her what his troubles are.'

The long day had done nothing to curb Superintendent Tallis's temper or to weaken his conviction that the newspapers were trying to make a scapegoat of him. Even though he brought news of progress, Colbeck still found himself on the receiving end of a torrent of vituperation. He left his superior's office with his ears ringing. Victor Leeming was in the corridor.

'How did you get on, Inspector?' he asked.

'Superintendent Tallis and I have had quieter conversations,' said Colbeck with a weary smile. 'He seemed to believe that he was back on the parade ground and had to bark orders at me.'

'That problem will not arise with your visitor.'

'Visitor?'

'Yes, sir. I just showed her into your office. The young lady was desperate to see you and would speak to nobody else.'

'Did she give a name?'

'Madeleine Andrews, sir. Her father was the driver of the train.'

'Then I'll see her at once.'

Colbeck opened the door of his office and went in. Madeleine Andrews leapt up from the chair on which she had perched. She was wearing a pretty, burgundy-coloured dress with a full skirt, and a poke bonnet whose pink ribbons were tied under her chin. She had a shawl over her arm. Introductions were made then Colbeck indicated the chair.

'Do sit down again, Miss Andrews,' he said, courteously.

'Thank you, Inspector.'

Colbeck sat opposite her. 'How is your father?'

'He's still in great pain,' she said, 'but he felt well enough to be brought home this afternoon. My father hates to impose on anyone else. He did not wish to spend another night at the stationmaster's house in Leighton Buzzard. It will be more comfortable for both of us at home.'

'You went to Leighton Buzzard, then?'

'I sat beside his bed all night, Inspector.'

'Indeed?' He was amazed. 'You look remarkably well for someone who must have had very little sleep.'

She acknowledged the compliment with a smile and her dimples came into prominence. Given her concern for her father, only something of importance could have made her leave him to come to Scotland Yard. Colbeck wondered what it was and why it made her seem so uneasy and tentative. But he did not press her. He waited until she was ready to confide in him.

'Inspector Colbeck,' she began at length, 'I have a confession to make on behalf of my father. He told me something earlier that I felt duty bound to report to you.'

'And what is that, Miss Andrews?'

'My father loves his work. There's not a more dedicated or respected driver in the whole company. However . . .' She lowered her head as if trying to gather strength. He saw her bite her lip. 'However,' she went on, looking at him again, 'he is inclined to be boastful when he has had a drink or two.'

'There's no harm in that,' said Colbeck. 'Most people become a little more expansive when alcohol is consumed.'

'Father was very careless.'

'Oh?'

'At the end of the working day,' she said, squirming slightly with embarrassment, 'he sometimes enjoys a pint of beer with his fireman, Frank Pike, at a public house near Euston. It's a place that is frequented by railwaymen.'

'In my opinion, they're fully entitled to a drink for what

they do. I travelled to the Midlands by train today, Miss Andrews, and am deeply grateful for the engine drivers who got me there and back. I'd have been happy to buy any of them a glass of beer.'

'Not if it made them talkative.'

'Talkative?'

'Let me frank with you,' she said, blurting it out. 'My father blames himself for the robbery yesterday. He thinks that he may have been drinking with his friends one evening and let slip the information that money was being carried on the mail trains.' She held out her hands in supplication. 'It was an accident, Inspector,' she said, defensively. 'He would never willingly betray the company. You may ask Frank Pike. My father stood up to the robbers.'

'I know, Miss Andrews,' said Colbeck, 'and I admire him for it. I also admire you for coming here like this.'

'I felt that you should know the truth.'

'Most people in your situation would have concealed it.'

'Father made me promise that I would tell you the terrible thing that he did,' she said, bravely. 'He feels so ashamed. Even though it will mean his dismissal from the company, he insisted.' She sat forward on her chair. 'Will you have to arrest him, Inspector?'

'Of course not.'

'But he gave away confidential information.'

'Not deliberately,' said Colbeck. 'It popped out when he was in his cups. I doubt very much if that was how the robbers first learnt how money was being carried. They had only to keep watch at the station for a length of time and they would have seen boxes being loaded under armed guard on to the mail train. Such precautions would not be taken for a cargo of fruit or vegetables.'

Her face brightened. 'Then he is *not* to blame for the robbery?'

'No, Miss Andrews. What the villains needed to know was what a particular train was carrying and the exact time it was leaving Euston. That information was obtained elsewhere – along with the means to open the safe that was in the luggage van.'

Madeleine caught her breath. 'I'm so relieved, Inspector!'

'Tell your father that he's escaped arrest on this occasion.'

'It will be a huge load off his mind – and off mine.'

'I'm delighted that I've been able to give you some reassurance.'

Relaxed and happy, Madeleine Andrews looked like a completely different woman. A smile lit up her eyes and her dimples were expressive. She had come to Scotland Yard in trepidation and had feared the worst. Madeleine had not expected to meet such a considerate and well-spoken detective as Robert Colbeck. He did not fit her image of a policeman at all and she was profoundly grateful.

For his part, Colbeck warmed to her. It had taken courage to admit that her father had been at fault, especially when she feared dire consequences from the revelation. There was a quiet integrity about Madeleine Andrews that appealed to him and he was by no means immune to her physical charms. Now that she was no longer so tense, he could appreciate them to the full. Pleased that she had come, he was glad to be able to put her mind at rest.

'Thank you, Inspector,' she said, getting to her feet. 'I must get back home to tell Father. He felt so dreadfully guilty about this.'

Colbeck rose at well. 'I think that some censure is in order,' he pointed out. 'Mr Andrews did speak out of turn about the mail train, that much is clear. On reflection, he will come to see how foolish that was and be more careful in future.'

'Oh, he will, he will.'

'I leave it to you to issue a stern warning.'

'Father needs to be kept in line at times. He can be wayward.'

'What he requires now,' suggested Colbeck, 'is a long rest. Far from dismissing him, the London and North Western Railway Company should be applauding him for trying to protect their train.' He smiled at her. 'When would it be possible for me to call on your father?'

'At home, you mean?'

'I hardly expect Mr Andrews to come hopping around here.'

'No, no,' she said with a laugh.

'Mr Pike has given me his version of events, of course, but I would like to hear what your father has to say. Is there any chance that I might question him tomorrow?'

'Yes, Inspector – if he continues to improve.'

'I'll delay my arrival until late morning.'

'We will expect you,' said Madeleine, glad that she would be seeing him again. Their eyes locked for a moment. Both of them felt a mild *frisson*. It was she who eventually turned away. 'I've taken up too much of your time, Inspector. I look forward to seeing you tomorrow.'

'One moment,' he said, putting a hand on her arm to stop her. 'I may be a detective, but I find it much easier to visit a house when I know exactly where it is.' He took out his notebook. 'Could I trouble you for an address, Miss Andrews?'

She gave another laugh. 'Yes – how silly of me!'

He wrote down the address that she dictated then closed the notebook. When he looked up, she met his gaze once more and there was a blend of interest and regret in her eyes. Colbeck was intrigued.

'I hope that you catch these men soon, Inspector,' she said.

'We will make every effort to do so.'

'What they did to my father was unforgivable.'

'They will be justly punished, Miss Andrews.'

'He was heartbroken when he heard what happened to his locomotive. Father dotes on it. Why did they force it off the track? It seems so unnecessary.'

'It was. Unnecessary and gratuitous.'

'Do you have any idea who the train robbers might be?'

'We have identified two of their accomplices,' he told her, 'and we are searching for both men. One of them – a former employee of the Post Office – should be in custody before too long.'

William Ings was astounded by his good fortune. He never thought that he would meet any woman whose company he preferred to a game of cards but that is what had happened in the case of Kate Piercey. He had shared a night of madness with her and spent most of the next day in her arms. Kate was younger, livelier and more sensual than Polly Roach. Her breath was far sweeter, her body firmer. More to the point, she was not as calculating as the woman he had discarded on the previous night. Ings had bumped into her in the street as he fled from the clutches of Polly Roach. He knew that the collision was no accident – she had deliberately stepped out of the shadows into his path – but that did not matter. He felt that the encounter was fateful.

There was something about Kate that excited him from the start, an amalgam of boldness and vulnerability that he found irresistible. She was half-woman and half-child, mature yet nubile, experienced yet seemingly innocent. William Ings was a realist. He knew that he was not the first man to enjoy her favours and he had no qualms about paying for them, but he was soon overcome by the desire to be the last of her clients, to covet her, to protect her, to rescue her from the hazards of her profession and shape her into something better. Impossible as the dream might appear, he wanted to be both father and lover to Kate Piercey.

As he watched her dress that evening by the light of the lamp, he was enchanted. Polly Roach might have brought him to the Devil's Acre but she had been displaced from his mind completely.

'Where shall we go, Billy?' she asked.

'Wherever you wish,' he replied.

'We can eat well but cheaply at Flanagan's.'

'Then we'll go elsewhere. That place is not good enough for you.'

She giggled. 'You say the nicest things.'

'You deserve the best, Kate. Let me take you somewhere special.'

'You're so kind to me.'

'No, my love,' he said, slipping his arms around her, 'it's you who are kind to me.' He kissed her once more. 'I adore you.'

'But you've known me less than twenty-four hours, Billy.'

'That's long enough. Now, where can we dine together?'

'There's a new place in Victoria Street,' she told him, 'but they say that it's very expensive.'

He thrust his hand deep into his leather bag and brought out a fistful of bank notes. Ings held them proudly beneath her nose, as if offering them in tribute.

'Do you think that this would buy us a good meal?'

'Billy!' she cried with delight. 'Where did you get all that money?'

'I've been saving it up until I met you,' he said.

Madeleine Andrews was touched when Colbeck insisted on escorting her to the front door of the building. Light was beginning to fade and there was a gentle breeze. She turned to look up at him.

'Thank you, Inspector. You are very kind.'

'It must have taken an effort for you to come here.'

'It did,' she said. 'The worst of it was that I felt like a criminal.'

'You've done nothing wrong, Miss Andrews.'

'I shared my father's guilt.'

'All that he was guilty of was thoughtless indiscretion,' he said, 'and I'm sure that nobody could ever accuse you of that.' Her gaze was quizzical. 'What's the matter?'

'Oh, I'm sorry. I did not mean to stare like that.'

'You seem to be puzzled by something.'

'I suppose that I am.'

'Let me see if I can guess what it is, Miss Andrews,' he said with a warm smile. 'The question in your eyes is the one that I've asked myself from time to time. What is a man like me doing in this job?'

'You are so different to any policemen that I have ever met.'

'In what way?'

'They are much more like the man who showed me to your office.'

'That was Sergeant Leeming,' he explained. 'I'm afraid that Victor is not blessed with the most handsome face in London, though his wife loves him dearly nevertheless.'

'It was his manner, Inspector.'

'Polite but rough-edged. I know what you mean. Victor spent years, pounding his beat in uniform. It leaves its mark on a man. My time in uniform was considerably shorter. However,' he went on, looking up Whitehall, 'you did not come here to be bored by my life story. Let me help you find a cab.'

'I had planned to walk some of the way, Inspector.'

'I'd advise against it, Miss Andrews. It is not always safe for an attractive woman to stroll unaccompanied at this time of day.'

'I am well able to look after myself.'

'It will be dark before long.'

'I am not afraid of the dark.'

'Why take any risks?'

Seeing a cab approach in the distance, he raised a hand.

'There is no risk involved,' she said with a show of spirit. 'Please do not stop the cab on my account. If I wished to take it, I am quite capable of hailing it myself.'

He lowered his hand. 'I beg your pardon.'

'You must not worry about me. I am much stronger than I may appear. After all, I did come here on foot.'

He was taken aback. 'You *walked* from Camden Town?'

'It was good exercise,' she replied. 'Goodbye, Inspector Colbeck.'

'Goodbye, Miss Andrews. It was a pleasure to meet you.'

'Thank you.'

'I will see you again tomorrow,' he said, relishing the thought. 'I hope that you'll forgive me if I arrive by Hansom cab.'

She gave him a faint smile before walking off up Whitehall. Colbeck stood for a moment to watch her then he went back into the building. As soon as the detective had disappeared, a figure stepped out from the doorway in which he had been hiding. He was a dark-eyed young man of medium height in an ill-fitting brown suit. Pulling his cap down, he set off in pursuit of Madeleine Andrews.

By the time he got back to The Black Dog, the fight had already started. Several people were involved and they had reached the stage of hurling chairs at each other or defending themselves with a broken bottle. Brendan Mulryne did not hesitate. Hurling himself into the middle of the fray, he banged heads together, kicked one man in the groin and felled a second with an uppercut. But even he could not stop the brawl. When it spilt out into the street, he was carried along with it, flailing away with both fists and inflicting indiscriminate punishment.

Mulryne did not go unscathed. He took some heavy blows himself and the brick that was thrown at him opened a gash above his eye. Blood streamed down his face. It only served to enrage him and to make him more determined to flatten every man within reach. Roaring with anger, he punched, kicked, grappled, gouged and even sank his teeth into a forearm that was wrapped unwisely across his face. Well over a dozen people had been involved in the fracas but, apart from the Irishman, only three were left standing.

As he bore down on them, they took to their heels and Mulryne went after the trio, resolved to teach them to stay away from The Black Dog in future. One of them tripped and fell headlong. Mulryne was on him at once, heaving him to his feet and slamming him against a wall until he heard bones crack. The next moment, a length of iron pipe struck the back of Mulryne's head and sent him to his knees. The two friends of the man who had fallen had come back to rescue him. Hurt by the blow, the Irishman had the presence of mind to roll over quickly so that he dodged a second murderous swipe.

He was on his feet in an instant, grabbing the pipe and wresting it from the man holding it. Mulryne used it to club him to the ground. When the second man started to belabour him, he tossed the pipe away, lifted his assailant up and hurled him through a window. Yells of protest came from the occupants of the house. Dazed by the blow to his head and exhausted by the fight, Mulryne swayed unsteadily on his feet, both hands to his wounds to stem the bleeding. He did not even hear the sound of the police whistles.

Robert Colbeck sat in his office and reviewed the evidence with Victor Leeming. While no arrests had yet been made, they felt that they had a clear picture of how the robbery had taken place, and what help had been given to the gang responsible by employees in the Post Office and the lock industry. The Sergeant still believed that someone from the Royal Mint was implicated as well. Colbeck told him about the interview with Madeleine Andrews and how he had been able to still her fears.

'The young lady was well-dressed for a railwayman's daughter.'

'Did you think that she'd be wearing rags and walking barefoot?'

'She looked so neat and tidy, sir.'

'Engine drivers are the best-paid men on the railway,' said Colbeck, 'and quite rightly. They have to be able to read, write and understand the mechanism of the locomotive. That's why so many of them begin as fitters before becoming firemen. Caleb Andrews earns enough to bring up his daughter properly.'

'I could tell from her voice that she'd had schooling.'

'I think that she's an intelligent woman.'

'And a very fetching one,' said Leeming with a grin.

'She thought that you were a typical policeman, Victor.'

'Is that good or bad, sir?'

Colbeck was tactful. 'You'll have to ask the young lady herself.' There was a tap on the door. 'Come in!' he said.

The door opened and a policeman entered in uniform.

'I was asked to give this to you, Inspector Colbeck,' he said, handing over the envelope that he was carrying.

'I'm told that it's quite urgent. I'm to wait for a reply.'

'Very well.' Colbeck opened the envelope and read the note inside. He scrunched up the paper in his hand. 'There's no reply,' he said. 'I'll come with you myself.'

'Right, sir.'

'Bad news, Inspector?' wondered Leeming.

'No, Victor,' said Colbeck, smoothly. 'A slight problem has arisen, that's all. It will not take me long to sort it out. Excuse me.'

The only time that Brendan Mulryne had seen the inside of a police cell was when he had thrown the people he had arrested into one. It was different being on the other side of the law. When the door had slammed shut upon him, he was locked in a small, bare, cheerless room that was no more than a brick rectangle. The tiny window, high in the back wall, was simply a ventilation slit with thick iron bars in it. The place reeked of stale vomit and urine.

The bed was a hard wooden bench with no mattress or blankets. Sitting on the edge of it, Mulryne wished that his head would stop aching. His wounds had been tended, and the blood wiped from his face, but it was obvious that he had been in a fight. His craggy face was covered with cuts and abrasions, his knuckles were raw. His black eye and split lip would both take time to heal. It had been a savage brawl yet he was not sorry to have been in it. His only regret was that he had been arrested as a result. It meant that he would lose money and leave The Black Dog unguarded for some time.

When a key scraped in the lock, he hoped that someone was bringing him a cup of tea to revive him. But it was not the custody sergeant who stepped into the cell. Instead, Inspector Robert Colbeck came in and looked down at the offender with more disappointment than sympathy. His voice was uncharacteristically harsh.

'Why ever did you get yourself locked up in here, Brendan?'

'It was a mistake,' argued Mulryne.

'Police records do not lie,' said Colbeck. 'According to the book, you have been charged with taking part in an affray, causing criminal damage, inflicting grievous bodily harm and – shocking for someone who used to wear a police uniform – resisting arrest.'

'Do you think that I *wanted* to be shut away here?'

'Why make things worse for yourself?'

'Because I was goaded,' said Mulryne. 'Two of the bobbies that tried to put cuffs on me recognised who I was and had a laugh at my expense. They thought it was great fun to arrest an old colleague of theirs. I'll not stand for mockery, Mr Colbeck.'

'Look at the state of you, man. Your shirt is stained with blood.'

Mulryne grinned. 'Don't worry. Most of it is not mine.'

'I do worry,' said Colbeck, sharply. 'I asked for help and you promised to give it. How can you do that when you're stuck in here?'

'The man to blame is the one who started the fight.'

'You should have kept out of it.'

'Sure, isn't keeping the peace what I'm paid to do?' asked

Mulryne, earnestly. 'I'm a sort of policeman at The Black Dog, excepting that I don't wear a uniform. All I did was to try to calm things down.'

'With your fists.'

'They were not in the mood to listen to a sermon.'

Colbeck heaved a sigh. 'No, I suppose not.'

'Is there anything you can do for me?' said Mulryne, hopefully. 'Ask at The Black Dog. They'll tell that I didn't start the affray. I just got caught up in it. As for criminal damage, the person at fault is the one who dived head first through that window. On my word of honour, I did my best to stop him.'

'I know you too well, Brendan. I've seen you fight.'

'Well, at least get them to drop the charge of grievous bodily harm. Jesus! You should feel the lump on the back of my head. It's the size of an egg, so it is. I was the *victim* of grievous bodily harm.' He got up from the bed. 'Please, Mr Colbeck. I'm a wronged man.'

'Are you?'

'I'm such a peaceable fellow by nature.'

'Tell that to the policeman whose teeth you knocked out.'

'I did apologise to him afterwards.'

'What use is that?' demanded Colbeck. 'And what use are you to me while you're cooling your heels in here?'

'None at all, I admit. That's why you must get me out.'

'So that you can create more havoc?'

'No, Mr Colbeck,' said Mulryne, 'so that I can find out where Billy Ings is hiding. He's within my grasp, I know it. I did as you told me. I spoke to Isadore Vout, the bloodsucker who loaned him money when he lost at the card table.'

'Did he know where Ings could be found?'

'With a doxy named Polly Roach who lives in Hangman's Lane.'

'And?'

'I paid her a call. When I asked her about Billy Ings, she spat out his name like it was a dog turd. They had a disagreement, you see, and he walked out on her. I fancy that he knocked her about before he went. He told Polly that he'd won a lot of money playing cards but she knows better now. It made her livid.'

'I'm the one who is livid,' asserted Colbeck. 'You let me down.'

'I could never walk away from a fight.' He took his visitor by the arms. 'Help me, please. If you don't get me released, it will be too late.'

'What do you mean?'

'Polly Roach has gone looking for Ings as well,' said Mulryne, 'and it's not to give him her best wishes. There's only one thing on her mind.'

'Is there?'

'Revenge.'

The Devil's Acre was a comparatively small district but it was teeming with inhabitants, packed into its houses and tenements until their walls were about to burst. Tracking someone down in its labyrinthine interior was not a simple task, even for someone like Polly Roach who had lived there since birth. It had such a shifting population. She first tried the various gambling dens where William Ings was known but he had not been seen at any of them that day. Polly reasoned that he must have found himself a bed for the night and that meant he paid someone to share it with him.

There was no shortage of prostitutes in the Acre. Clients could pick anyone from young girls to old women. Polly Roach knew from personal experience the sordid acts that they were called upon to perform. It was what set William Ings apart from all the other men who had paid for her services. He had made no demands on her. He came in search of a friend rather than a nameless whore who would simply satisfy his urges and send him on his way. Ings wanted a confidante, a source of sympathy, someone who would listen patiently to his bitter complaints about his private life and offer him succour.

Polly Roach felt that she had done just that. Over a period of several months, she had soothed his wounded pride. She had lost count of the number of times he talked about his unhappy marriage, his problems at work and his disputes with his neighbours. Until he met her, his life had had no joy or purpose. Polly had given him direction. Seeing how she could benefit herself, she had flattered him, advised him, supported him, even pretended that she loved him. If he had come into some money, she had earned her share of it and was determined to get it. William Ings was going to pay for all the time she had devoted to him.

Hours of searching for him eventually paid off. After questioning almost anybody she encountered, Polly met an old acquaintance who recognised the description of William Ings and said that he had seen him in the company of Kate Piercey. He was even able to give her an address. Incensed that she had been replaced by a younger woman, Polly fingered the knife under her skirt and went off to confront the man who had cast her aside so unfairly.

When she reached the tenement, she hastened up the stairs to the attic room and saw the light under the door. It was no time for social niceties. She kicked the timber hard.

'Come out of there, Billy!' she shouted.

To her surprise, the door swung back on its hinges to reveal the hazy outline of a small, dirty, cluttered room with bare rafters. What hit her nostrils was a smell of damp mixed with the aroma of cheap perfume, a kind that she herself had used in the past. There was an oil lamp in the corner but it had been turned down so that it gave only the faintest glow. Polly turned up the flame in order to see more clearly. A hideous sight was suddenly conjured out of the dark. When she realised that she was not alone in the room, she let out a cry of horror. On a bed in the corner, lying side by side as if they were asleep, were William Ings and Kate Piercey. Their throats had been cut.

Polly began to retch and her first instinct was to run from the scene. Self-interest then slowly got the better of fear. Though Ings was dead, she might still get what she wanted. She breathed in deeply as she tried to compose herself. Averting her gaze from the bed, she used the lamp to illumine the corners of the room as she looked for Ings's leather bag so that she could take the money that she felt was hers. But she was too late. His belongings were scattered all over the floor and the bag was empty. In desperation, she grabbed his jacket and felt in the inside pocket but his wallet was no longer there. Not a penny of his money was left. Whoever had murdered them, had known exactly where to look. She gazed ruefully at William Ings. Her hopes of escape had bled to death. Polly Roach was condemned to stay in the Devil's Acre forever.

CHAPTER SEVEN

When word of the crime reached him, Inspector Robert Colbeck took an immediate interest. Murder was not a rare phenomenon in the Devil's Acre, and ordinarily, he would have been content to let someone else lead the investigation. But the fact that one of the victims was a middle-aged man alerted him and he persuaded Superintendent Tallis to let him look into the case. After collecting Victor Leeming, he left Scotland Yard and took a cab to the scene of the crime.

Policemen were already on duty, guarding the room where the victims lay and questioning other occupants of the building. There was no sign of Polly Roach. Additional lamps had been brought in so that the attic room was ablaze with light. When the detectives entered, the grisly scene was all too visible. In spite of the number of times he had seen murder victims, Leeming was inclined to be squeamish but Colbeck had no qualms about examining the dead bodies at close range. Both were partly clothed, their garments spattered with blood. The sheets and pillows were also speckled.

After inspecting the corpses for some time, Colbeck stood up.

'At least, they did not suffer too much,' he observed.

'How do you know that?' asked Leeming.

'Both of them have wounds on the back of their heads, Victor. I think that they were knocked unconscious before their throats were cut. One neat incision was all that it took. The killer knew his trade.'

'So I see, Inspector.' He looked at the face of the dead man and quailed slightly. 'Do you think it's William Ings?'

'Yes,' said Colbeck, sifting through the items on the floor. 'He matches the description that Mrs Ings gave me and nobody who lives in the Acre dresses quite as smartly as he did. This man is an outsider.' Picking up a jacket, he searched the pockets and found a small brown envelope. 'This confirms it,' he said.

'What is it?'

'An empty pay packet from the Post Office. His very last wages.'

'Does he have a wallet on him?'

'That appears to have been taken,' said Colbeck, putting the jacket aside. 'It must have contained money. Judging by the way that it was emptied all over the floor, so did that bag.'

Leeming was annoyed. 'We've lost one of our suspects to a thief.'

'This was not the work of a thief, Victor.'

'It must have been. They were obviously killed for the money.'

'Not at all,' contradicted the other. 'The young lady died because she had the misfortune to be with Mr Ings at the time. *He* was the target. In my opinion, the murder was directly connected to the train robbery. He was silenced because he knew too much. Since Ings no longer had any need of it, his paymaster took the opportunity to repossess the hefty bribe that must have been paid to him.'

'These men are more dangerous than I thought,' said Leeming.

'They'll go to any lengths to cover their tracks.'

'Does that mean the other accomplice is at risk?'

'Yes, Victor,' said Colbeck. 'Unless we can find him first.'

'And how do we do that?'

'To be honest, I'm not sure.' He glanced at the policeman by the door. 'Who discovered the body?'

'A woman named Polly Roach, sir,' replied the man.

'I'll need to speak to her,' said Colbeck, recalling that Mulryne had mentioned her name. 'I've reason to believe that she knew at least one of the victims. Where is she?'

'Being held at the station, Inspector. I must warn you that she's very jittery. Walking in on this has upset her badly.'

'I daresay that it has. A lot of people are going to be upset when they learn what happened here tonight. The person I feel sorry for is the man's wife,' said Colbeck with a sigh. 'I'm not looking forward to breaking the news to Mrs Ings.'

Maud Ings was about to retire to bed when she heard the click of her letterbox. Taking the lamp, she went to the front door to investigate and saw a small package lying on the doormat. Puzzled as to what it might contain, she picked it up and read the bold capitals that ran across the front of it – from your husband. She was even more mystified. She put her lamp on the hall table so that she could use both hands to open the package. As she peeled back the brown paper, she found, to her utter astonishment, that it was covering a sizeable wad of five pound notes. The arrival of such unexpected bounty was too much for her. Overcome with emotion, she burst into tears.

'I want results, Inspector,' shouted Tallis, rising angrily to his feet. 'I want progress, not this incessant litany of excuses.'

'We could not foresee that William Ings would be murdered.'

'Perhaps not, but you could have prevented the crime by reaching him before anyone else did.'

'That's what I attempted to do, sir,' said Colbeck.

'Yes,' snarled Tallis, 'by employing that Irish maniac, Mulryne. Whatever possessed you to do that? The fellow is a confounded menace. When he was in the police force, his notion of making an arrest was to beat the offender to a pulp.'

'Brendan was simply too zealous in the execution of his duties.'

'Zealous! He was uncontrollable. I'm told that it took four officers to subdue him this evening. Was that another example of his zeal?' asked Tallis with heavy sarcasm. 'Why ever did you turn to him?'

'Because he knows the Devil's Acre from the inside.'

'He'll know a prison cell from the inside before I'm done with him.'

'There were extenuating circumstances about the brawl,' said Colbeck, 'and, when the time is ripe, I'd like to speak up on Mulryne's behalf. The reason that I engaged him is that he's a good bloodhound. He did, after all, find the woman with whom William Ings had been living. Her name was Polly Roach. She was the person who raised the alarm tonight.'

'What did she have to say for herself?'

'She was very bitter when I questioned her earlier. Mr Ings had promised to take her away from the Acre to start a new life with him. Polly Roach offered him something that he could not find at home.'

'I was in the army, Inspector,' said Tallis, darkly. 'You don't need to tell me why married men visit whores. Our doctor was the busiest man in the regiment, trying to cure them of their folly.' He sat down again behind his desk. 'Now, tell me in detail what this Polly Roach said.'

Standing in front of him, Robert Colbeck gave him a terse account of his interview with the woman who had found the dead bodies and who had provided confirmation that one of the victims was William Ings. Wreathed in cigar smoke, Tallis listened in stony silence. His eye occasionally drifted to the newspapers that lay on his desk. When Colbeck finished, the Superintendent fired questions at him.

'Do you believe this woman?'

'Yes, sir.'

'Did you find any witnesses?'

'None, sir.'

'How many people live in that tenement?'

'Dozens.'

'Yet not one of them saw or heard a stranger entering or leaving the premises? Is the place a home for the blind and deaf?'

'People in the Devil's Acre do not like assisting the police.'

'So why did you rely on someone like Mulryne?'

'Brendan is the exception to the rule.'

'He's a liability,' said Tallis, acidly. 'Whatever you do, make sure that the newspapers don't get hold of the fact that you sought his help. I'll have enough trouble keeping those reporters at bay when they ask me about the murder.'

'Would you rather I spoke to them, sir?'

'No, it's my duty.'

'Of course.'

'Yours is to find these villains before they commit any more crimes. What's your plan of campaign?'

'Courtesy must come before anything else, Superintendent.'

'In what way?'

'Mrs Ings has a right to be informed of the death of her husband,' said Colbeck. 'It was far too late to call on her tonight. It would only have given her additional distress if she'd been hauled out of bed to be told that her husband had been murdered.'

'While lying between foul sheets beside some pox-ridden whore.'

'I'll try to put it a little more diplomatically than that, sir.'

'And then what?'

'It seems that the driver of the train has recovered somewhat, sir, so I intend to visit him to see if he can give us any useful information.' Colbeck remembered that he would be seeing Madeleine Andrews again. 'I think that it's very important for me to question the man.'

Tallis narrowed his eyes to peer at him through the cigar smoke.

'We are dealing with armed robbery and brutal murder, Inspector,' he reminded him. 'What the devil are you *smiling* about?'

Caleb Andrews was well enough to sit up in bed and sip tea from the cup that his daughter had brought him. Still in pain, he moved his limbs very gingerly. His pugnacity, however, had been restored in full. Now that his mind had cleared, he had vivid memories of the moment when his train was ambushed, and he was anxious to confront the man who had knocked him down with a pistol butt. Madeleine came into the room to see how he was and, as they talked, she tidied the place up.

'Why are you wearing your best dress?' he wondered.

'I always like to look smart, Father.'

'But you usually save that one for church. Is it Sunday?'

'You know that it isn't,' she said, repositioning the two china dogs on the mantelpiece. 'Are you sure that you're well enough to speak to Inspector Colbeck?'

'Yes, I think so.'

'I can always send word to Scotland Yard to ask him to postpone the visit. Would you like me to do that?'

'No, Maddy. I want to see him today. Apart from anything, I want to know if he's caught anybody yet. Those men deserve to be strung up for what they did to my locomotive.'

'Frank Pike still has nightmares about that.'

'I don't hold it against him.'

'His wife told me that he's racked with guilt.'

'Frank always was a sensitive lad,' said Andrews, fondly. 'None of us likes to go off the road like that. It's the thing a driver hates most.'

'You forget about your fireman,' she said, adjusting his pillows to make him more comfortable. 'All you have to worry about is getting better. Have you finished your tea?'

'Yes, Maddy.'

'Then I'll take the cup downstairs with me.'

'What time is Her Majesty due to arrive?'

Madeleine was baffled. 'Her Majesty?'

'That's what all of this in aid of, isn't it?'

'All what?'

'Your best dress, tidying up my room, clearing my cup away, putting on something of a show. At the very least, I expect a visit from Queen Victoria.'

'Stop teasing me, Father.'

'Then tell me why you're making such an effort,' he said with a lopsided grin. 'You even changed the bandaging on my wounds so that I looked a little better. Why did you do that? Are you going to put me on display at the Great Exhibition?'

Seated in her armchair, Maud Ings received the news without flinching. It was almost as if she had expected it. Colbeck spoke as gently as he could be but he did not disguise any of the salient details from her. It was only when he told her the name of the other murder victim that she winced visibly.

'And how old was this Kate Piercey?' she asked.

'Somewhat younger than your husband.'

'Is that why he ran off with her?'

'Does that matter, Mrs Ings?'

'What was she like?'

'I did not exactly see her at her best,' he said.

Colbeck saw no point in telling her that the woman to whom William Ings had first gone was Polly Roach. The widow had enough to contend with as it was. To explain that he had abandoned one prostitute and immediately shared a bed with another would only be adding further to her misery. Bitter and bereaved, Maud Ings nevertheless had some sympathy for the man who had betrayed her. Colbeck did not wish to poison any last, lingering, pleasant memories of their marriage.

'I'm sorry to be the bearer of such sad tidings,' he said.

'It was kind of you to come, Inspector.'

'This has been a shock for you, Mrs Ings. Would you like me to ask one of the neighbours to come in and sit with you?'

'No, no. I prefer to be alone. Besides,' she said, 'our neighbours were never fond of William. I don't think many tears will be shed for him in this street.'

'As long as you are not left alone to brood.'

'I have the children. They are my life now.'

'Family is so important at a time like this, Mrs Ings. Well,' he said, relieved that there had been no outpouring of grief,

'I'll intrude no longer. You'll be informed when the body is ready to be released.'

'Wait!' she said, getting up. 'Before you go, Inspector, I need your advice. I can see that I've been living on false hope.'

'False hope?'

'Yes. Last night, before I went to bed, a package was put through my letterbox. Inside it was almost two hundred pounds.'

'Really?' Colbeck was curious. 'Was there any note enclosed?'

'No,' she said, 'but there was something written on the paper. I still have it, if you'd like to see it.'

'I would, Mrs Ings.' He waited as she lifted the cushion of her chair to take out the brown paper in which the money had been wrapped. When she handed it to him, he read the words on the front. 'At what time did this arrive?' he asked.

'It must have been close to eleven o'clock,' she replied. 'I thought at first that William had brought it. But, by the time I had unbolted the door and opened it, there was nobody to be seen in the street. Having the money gave me the best night's sleep I've had since he left.' Her face went blank. 'I was misled. From what you've told me, it obviously could not have been delivered by my husband.'

'I fear not. By that time, his body had already been discovered.'

'Then who could have brought the money?'

'The person who stole it from Mr Ings.'

She was bewildered. 'I do not understand, Inspector.'

'I'm not certain that I do,' he said, 'but I can see no other explanation. That money was paid to your husband in return for vital information about the mail train. Somebody was clearly aware of his domestic situation. When your husband was killed, this person somehow felt that his widow was entitled to the money.'

'So it is not really mine at all.'

'Why not?'

'It is money that was made from crime. I'll have to surrender it.'

'That's the last thing you should do,' advised Colbeck. 'It was money that your husband earned from a source that has yet to be identified. It was not part of the haul from the train robbery so there is no onus on you to return it. In view of the situation,' he went on, 'I believe that you are fully entitled to hold on to that money. Nobody need know how it came into your hands.'

'Then I am not breaking the law?'

'No, Mrs Ings. You are simply inheriting something that belonged to your husband. Look upon it as a welcome gift. It may not bring Mr Ings back to you, but it may help to console you in your grief.'

'I'll not deny that we *need* the money,' she said, looking balefully around the bare room. 'But I find it hard to accept that the man who murdered my husband and stole money from him should bring it to me.'

'It is an unusual situation, I grant you.'

'Why did he do it, Inspector?'

'It may have been an act of atonement.'

'Atonement?'

'Even the most evil men sometimes have a spark of goodness.'

Maud Ings fell silent as she thought about the life she had shared with her husband. It was a painful exercise. She remembered how they had met, married and set off together with such high expectations. Few of them had been fulfilled. Yet, soured as her memories were by his recent treatment of her, she could still think of the dead man with a distant kindness.

'You are right,' she said, coming out of her reverie. 'Evil men sometimes do good deeds. The problem is,' she added with tears at last threatening to come, 'that good men – and William was the soul of goodness when I first knew him – sometimes do evil.'

With his arm in a sling, it was impossible for Caleb Andrews to hold the newspaper properly so he had to rely on his daughter to fold it over in such a way that he could grasp it with one hand to read it. It had gone to press too early to carry news of the murder in the Devil's Acre but there was an article about the train robbery and it was critical both of the railway policemen on duty that day, and of the Detective Department of the Metropolitan Police. Andrews saw his own name mentioned.

'Have you read this, Maddy?' he asked, petulantly. 'It says that Driver Andrews is still unable to remember what happened during the ambush. I can recall *exactly* what happened.'

'I know, Father,' said Madeleine.

'So why do they make me sound like an invalid?'

'Because you *are* an invalid.'

'My body may be injured but there's nothing wrong with my mind. This article says that I'm still in a complete daze.'

'That was my doing.'

'What do you mean?'

'Some reporters came knocking on our door this morning,' she explained. 'They wanted to interview you about the robbery. I told them that you were in no fit state to speak to anyone and that your mind was still very hazy. I was trying to protect you, Father.'

'By telling everyone in London that I cannot think straight.'

'I had to get rid of the reporters somehow. I was not going to have them pestering you when you need rest.'

'Yet you let this Inspector Colbeck pester me,' he argued.

'He is trying to solve the crime,' she said. 'Inspector Colbeck wants to catch the men who ambushed the train and did this to you. He knows that you were badly injured and will be very considerate.'

Andrews tossed the newspaper aside. 'If he reads this first, he'll think that he's coming to speak to a distracted fool who's unable to tell what day of the week it is.'

'The Inspector will not think that at all, Father.'

Gathering up the newspaper, Madeleine put it on the table beside the bed. The sound of an approaching horse took her to the window and she looked down to see a cab pulling up outside the house. After a quick glance around the room, she adjusted her dress and went quickly out. Caleb Andrews gave a tired smile.

'Ah!' he said. 'I think that Queen Victoria has arrived at last.'

Two minutes later, Robert Colbeck was being shown into the bedroom to be introduced to the wounded railwayman.

'Can I offer you any refreshment, Inspector?' said Madeleine.

'No, thank you, Miss Andrews.'

'In that case, I'll leave you alone with Father.'

'There's no need to do that,' said Colbeck, enjoying her company too much to lose it. 'I'm quite happy for you to stay while we talk and, in any case, there's something that you need to know.'

Madeleine was cheered. 'You've arrested someone?'

'Not exactly,' he replied, 'but we have caught up with one of the accomplices who was involved. His name was William Ings.'

'Let me get my hands on the devil,' said Andrews.

'That's not possible, I fear. Mr Ings was killed last night.'

'Killed?' echoed Madeleine, shocked at the news.

'Yes, Miss Andrews,' said Colbeck. 'It means that we are no longer merely investigating a train robbery. This is now a murder case as well.'

'Do you have any clue who the killer might be?'

'Someone employed to make sure that Mr Ings's tongue would tell no tales. Once we discovered that he was implicated, we were very close to apprehending him. The assassin got to him first.'

'I wish that I had!' said Andrews, truculently. 'If he helped that gang to ambush my train, I'd have throttled him.'

'Father!' reproached his daughter.

'I would have, I swear it.'

'You are hardly in a position to throttle anyone, Mr Andrews,' noted Colbeck with a sympathetic smile. 'Mr Ings, alas, was not alone when he was attacked. The young lady with him also had her throat cut.'

'How horrible!' exclaimed Madeleine.

'It shows you the sort of men we are up against.'

'The worst kind,' said Andrews. 'They destroyed my locomotive. They made Frank Pike drive it off the track.' He indicated the chair beside the bed and Colbeck sat down. 'Do you know anything about the railway, Inspector?'

'I travel by train regularly, Mr Andrews.'

'But do you know anything about the locomotive that pulls it?'

'A little,' replied Colbeck. 'I'm familiar with the engines designed by Mr Bury; four-wheeled, bar-framed locomotives with haystack fireboxes, and tight coupling between locomotive and tender to give more stability.'

Andrews was impressed. 'You obviously know far more than most passengers,' he said. 'They have no clue how a steam locomotive works. Like many others, I began driving Bury locomotives, but they had too little power. We had to use two, three, sometimes four locomotives to pull a heavy train. If there were steep gradients to go up, we might need as many as six to give us enough traction power.'

'The mail train that you were taking to Birmingham was pulled by a Crampton locomotive – at least, that's what it looked like to me.'

'It was very similar to a Crampton, I agree, but it was designed by Mr Allan at the Crewe Works. He's the foreman there and assistant to Mr Trevithick. Allan locomotives have double frames that extend the whole length of the engine with the cylinders located between the inside and outside frames.'

'Inspector Colbeck does not want a lecture,' warned Madeleine.

'I'm always ready to learn from an expert,' said Colbeck.

'There you are, Maddy,' said Andrews, happily. 'The Inspector is really interested in the railways.' He turned to Colbeck. 'When we used inside cylinders, we were always having crank-axle breakages. Mr Allan was one of the men who began to develop horizontal outside cylinders. He may not be as famous as Mr Bury or Mr Crampton but I'd drive any locomotive that Alexander Allan built.'

'Why is that?' prompted Colbeck.

Caleb Andrews was in his element. He got so carried away describing the technicalities of locomotive construction that he forgot all about the nagging pain in his broken leg and the dull ache in one shoulder. Colbeck's interest was genuine but that was not the only reason he had asked for instruction. He wanted the driver to relax, to feel at ease with him, to trust him. Watching from the other side of the room, Madeleine was struck by the way that the detective gently guided her father around to the subject of the train robbery and coaxed far more detail out of him about the event than she had managed to do. During the interview, Colbeck jotted down a few things in his notebook.

'Would you recognise the man who attacked you?' asked Colbeck.

'I'll never forget that face of his,' replied Andrews.

'Mr Pike gave us a good description.'

'If my daughter were not present, Inspector, then I'd give you a good description of him – in one word.'

'We do not wish to hear it, Father,' scolded Madeleine.

'That's what he was, Maddy.'

'Forgive him, Inspector.'

'There's nothing to forgive, Miss Andrews,' said Colbeck, getting up and putting his notebook away. 'In view of what happened, your father has been remarkably restrained. He's also added some new details for me and that was very useful. One last question,' he said, looking at the driver once more. 'Is the London and North Western Railway a good company to work for, Mr Andrews?'

'The best, Inspector.'

'Are you saying that out of loyalty?'

'No, Inspector Colbeck – I speak from experience. I hope to see out my time working for the London and North Western. And my link with the company will not end there.'

'Oh?'

'I have every hope that my son-in-law will be a driver one day.'

Madeleine blushed instantly. 'Father!' she cried.

'Gideon would make a good husband.'

'This is not the place to bring up the subject.'

'The two of you were made for each other.'

'That is not true at all,' she asserted, 'and you know it.'

'Gideon loves you.'

'Perhaps I ought to withdraw,' volunteered Colbeck, seeing Madeleine's patent discomfort. 'Thank you for talking to me, Mr Andrews. Meeting you has been an education.'

'Let me know when you catch up with those villains.'

'I will, I promise you.' He moved to the door. 'Goodbye, Miss Andrews. I can see myself out.'

'Wait,' she said. 'Let me come to the front door with you.'

'But you clearly have something to discuss with your father.'

'High time that she discussed it with Gideon Little,' said Andrews.

Madeleine shot him a look of reproof and followed Colbeck down the stairs. Before she could apologise to him, the detective retrieved his silk hat from the table and opened the front door.

'Goodbye, Miss Andrews,' he said, masking his disappointment behind a smile. 'Allow me congratulate you on your forthcoming engagement.'

It was Victor Leeming's turn to face the wrath of Superintendent Tallis once more. A night's sleep had not improved the older man's temper. He was pacing up and down his room like a caged animal. When Leeming came in, Tallis rounded on him accusingly.

'Where have you been, man?' he demanded.

'Making inquiries, sir.'

'That is exactly what those jackals from the press have been doing. They almost drove me insane by making their damned inquiries. I had a dozen of them in here this morning,' he complained, 'wanting to know why we had made no progress with our investigation into the robbery, and why Inspector Colbeck was also in charge of this latest murder case.'

'The two crimes are connected, Superintendent.'

'They could not understand how.'

'Why not let the Inspector deal with the newspapers in future?'

'I'd never countenance that,' affirmed Tallis. 'My seniority obliges me to take on that particular duty and I have never been one to shun the cares of office. Besides, I want you and the Inspector out there, solving the crime, not getting distracted by a bevy of reporters.'

'What did you tell them?' asked Leeming.

'Enough to give them a story but no more. The information we feed to the press has to be carefully controlled. Give too much away and we alert the very people we are trying to apprehend.'

'I agree with you there, sir.'

'The main thing was,' said Tallis, 'to ensure that they did not get wind of Mulryne's role in this whole sorry affair. It was reckless of Inspector Colbeck to use that Irish blockhead in the way that he did.' He confronted the Sergeant. 'I presume that you condoned his decision.'

'Not entirely,' admitted Leeming, uneasily.

Tallis blenched. 'You mean that he did not even have the grace to tell you what he was proposing? That is unpardonable.'

'The Inspector did raise the matter,' said the other, lying to protect his colleague, 'and I could see the advantage of using Brendan Mulryne.'

'What advantage?'

'He knew where to look for William Ings.'

'So did the killer.'

'That's why we're making efforts to track down the other suspect, sir. Inspector Colbeck gave me an address that was passed on to him at the Chubb factory in Wolverhampton. It was a locksmith's where a man called Daniel Slender was supposed to have worked.' He put a hand in his pocket. 'I have just returned from the factory.'

'But this Daniel Slender was not employed there?'

'No, sir.'

'I daresay that they never heard of him.'

'That's not true,' said Leeming, taking out a letter to pass to him. 'When they advertised a post, Daniel Slender was among those who applied for it, as you will see from that letter.' Tallis began to read the missive. 'His qualifications are good and he could have expected a strong recommendation from the Chubb factory. Mr Slender was invited to come for an interview.'

'But?'

'He never turned up.'

'Then why apply for the post?'

'So that he would have written evidence to show to his employers that the position he was after did exist. They believed that he went for that interview,' said Leeming, 'and secured the appointment. It meant that his departure aroused no suspicion.'

'Where is Daniel Slender now?'

'Here in London, sir.'

'How do you know that?'

'Because he had always had an ambition to work here. According to the manager at the Chubb factory, he talked of little else. But he was tied to the Midlands by the need to look after his sick mother.'

'If the woman had stayed alive,' moaned Tallis, 'her son would never have got drawn into this conspiracy.' He waved the letter in front of Leeming. 'Look at the fellow's work record. It is admirable.'

'Those who bribed him must have caught him at a weak moment.'

'We need to get to him while he is still alive.'

'Inspector Colbeck feels that we should put out a wanted poster. He came back from Wolverhampton with a good description of Daniel Slender. We should circulate it at once.'

'Yes,' agreed Tallis. 'Have the poster drawn up, Sergeant Leeming. And – quickly! The last thing we need is for this man to finish up on a slab next to William Ings.'

The dog made the discovery. Scampering along the river-bank with his master, he went sniffing at a heap that lay up against a wall. It was covered with sacking and most people had walked past without even noticing it. The little terrier made sure that nobody would ignore it now. With the sacking gripped in his teeth, he pulled hard and exposed a pair of legs, then a body, then a head that was split grotesquely open and crowned with dried blood.

When she saw the corpse, a female passer-by screamed and clutched at her chest, the dog's owner ran to put the animal on his lead and another man went off in search of help. By the time that he returned, with two policemen in tow, he saw that a small crowd was standing around the body with ghoulish curiosity. The policemen ordered everyone to stand back while they checked for vital signs and, finding none, felt in the dead man's pockets for clues as to his identity.

The pockets of his immaculate suit were empty but that did not matter. Sewn into the silk lining of the jacket was the owner's name.

'Daniel Slender,' noted one of the policemen. 'Poor man!'

Inspector Robert Colbeck responded swiftly. The moment he heard about the second murder, he visited the scene of the crime, examined the body and gave permission for it to be moved. Half an hour later, Daniel Slender had been deprived of his new suit, as well as the remainder of his apparel, washed and laid out, beneath a shroud, on a cold slab at the morgue. Victor Leeming joined his colleague to look down at the corpse.

'Those wanted posters will not be needed now,' he said.

'No, Victor.'

'They closed his mouth for good.'

'Mr Slender will never enjoy wearing that new suit of his.'

Leeming was thoroughly perplexed. 'How did they know where to find him, Inspector?' he asked. 'That's what I fail to see. And how did they know where to get hold of William Ings, for that matter?'

'By using an insurance policy.'

'Insurance policy?'

'Yes,' said Colbeck. 'The person behind the robbery realised from the start that both these men would have to be killed. They knew too much and, in the event of arrest, lacked the guile to conceal their secrets. My guess is that he paid them some of the money for services rendered, and promised to give them the balance when the crime was successfully committed.

To do that,' he pointed out, 'Mr Ings and Mr Slender would have had to disclose their whereabouts.'

'What if there's a third accomplice?'

'Then he, too, is likely to be silenced.'

'My feeling is that he works for the Royal Mint.'

'Yet there's no breath of suspicion against anyone there.'

'Someone told the robbers when gold coin was being moved by train. The only person outside the Mint who knew the relevant date was Mr Shipperley at the Post Office and, as we found out when we spoke to him, he is certainly not involved.' Leeming gave a mirthless laugh. 'He'd sooner sell his grandmother to a brothel-keeper.'

'You have a point, Victor.'

'The information must have originated from the Royal Mint.'

'Perhaps you should pay a second visit there.'

'Yes, Inspector.'

'I, meanwhile, will visit Bond Street to speak to Daniel Slender's tailor. He will be able to tell me precisely when the suit was ordered and give me some idea of what manner of man his customer was.'

'A foolish one.'

'Mr Slender was offered a large amount of money to create a new life for himself,' said Colbeck, tolerantly. 'That would be a temptation for anyone in his position. It was too much for William Ings to resist as well.'

'Did you speak to his wife, sir?'

'First thing this morning.'

'How did she receive the news that she was now a widow?'

'Very bravely,' replied Colbeck. 'Mark you, Mrs Ings does have something to console her in her bereavement.'

'And what's that?'

'The best part of two hundred pounds, Victor. The money was put through her letterbox last night by an anonymous hand.'

'Two hundred pounds?' said Leeming in astonishment. 'That's a substantial amount. Who is her benefactor?'

'William Ings.'

'Her husband?'

'Indirectly,' said Colbeck. 'My feeling is that the money paid to him for providing information was given to his wife after his death. The man who authorised payment clearly knew that Maud Ings would be left destitute by her husband's demise. He sought to help her.'

'Murdering her husband is hardly a way to help.'

'Perhaps he is trying to make amends. Do you see what we have here, Victor? A ruthless killer with a conscience. That's a weakness.'

'What about the money paid to Daniel Slender?'

'That has doubtless been repossessed,' said Colbeck, 'because he had no family to whom it could be left. Mr Ings did. However, when I told her where her gift came from, his wife was not at all sure that she should keep it.'

'Why not?'

'She thought that it was tainted money.'

'It could not have come from the proceeds of the robbery.'

'That's what I said to her. In the end, I persuaded her that she had every right to keep the money. Incidentally,' he went on, lowering his voice, 'this is not something that needs to come to the ears of Mr Tallis. He would be certain to misunderstand and might even argue that the money should be taken from the widow.'

'That would be unfair.'

'Then say nothing, Victor. I speak to you in confidence.'

'It would have been very helpful had you done that before,' said Leeming, as he recalled his bruising encounter with the

Superintendent. 'You should have told me that you were thinking of employing Mulryne.'

'You would only have tried to talk me out of it.'

'I would, Inspector. No question about that.'

'Brendan has his uses.'

'With respect, sir, that's beside the point. You kept me ignorant.'

'Only as a means of defending you from Mr Tallis.'

'You did the opposite,' protested Leeming. 'You exposed me to his anger. He demanded to know if you'd discussed your intentions with me and I was forced to lie in order to cover for you.'

'Thank you, Victor. I appreciate that.'

'I can't say that I appreciated being put in that position, sir.'

'You have my profound apologies,' said Colbeck. 'I may have expected too much of Brendan Mulryne. I accept the blame for that. But,' he continued, glancing down at the body once more, 'let us put that mistake behind us. So far, we have a train robbery and two murders to investigate. What we must try to do is to anticipate their next move.'

'To kill their source at the Royal Mint?'

'If there is such a person.'

'There is, Inspector. I feel it in my bones.'

'What I believe is that they will not just sit back and enjoy the fruits of their crime. They want more than the money they stole.'

Leeming pointed a finger. 'Those mail bags.'

'Exactly,' said Colbeck. 'Why go to the trouble of stealing them if there was no profit to be made from their contents? Yes, Victor. I think that it's only a matter of time before we hear about some of the mail that went astray.'

After luncheon at his club, Lord Holcroft decided to take a walk in Hyde Park for the benefit of his constitution.

Accompanied by a friend, he set out at a brisk pace and gave his views on the political affairs of the day. His friend concurred with all that he said. Lord Holcroft was an imposing figure in his dark frock coat, light trousers and silk hat. Now almost sixty, he had the energy of a much younger man and a zest for debate that was indefatigable. He was expressing his reservations about the impending Great Exhibition when someone stepped out from behind a tree to accost him.

'Lord Holcroft?' he inquired.

'Who might you be, sir?' said the other, glaring at the newcomer.

'I'd like a quiet word with you about a certain person.'

'Stand aside, fellow. I never talk to strangers.'

'Even when he has news about Miss Grayle?' whispered the other so that Holcroft's companion did not hear the name. 'Two minutes of your valuable time is all that I ask.'

Lord Holcroft studied the man. Tall, well-dressed and wearing a full beard, the stranger was in his thirties. He had a look in his eye that was politely menacing. Excusing himself from his friend, Holcroft stepped aside to speak to the newcomer. He tried to browbeat him.

'How dare you interrupt my walk like this!' he growled. 'Who are you and what's your business?'

'I came to save you from embarrassment,' said the man, calmly. 'A letter has fallen into our hands that casts an unflattering light on your character. It is written by you to a Miss Anna Grayle, who lives close to Birmingham, and it expresses sentiments that are quite improper for a married man such as yourself.'

'The letter is a forgery,' snapped Holcroft.

'We will let your wife be the judge of that, if you wish.

Lady Holcroft knows your hand well enough to be able to tell us if you wrote the *billet-doux*.'

Holcroft reddened. 'My wife must *never* see that letter.'

'Even though it is a forgery?' teased the other.

'Miss Grayle's good name must be protected.'

'That will not happen if we release the letter to a scandal sheet. Her good name – and your own – would be in jeopardy. I should perhaps tell you, Lord Holcroft,' he lied, 'that we have already been offered a sizeable sum for the missive. We did not, of course, divulge your identity but we explained that you were a person of some importance.'

Lord Holcroft was squirming. His temples began to pound.

'How can I be sure that you have the letter?' he demanded.

'Because I brought a copy with me,' replied the other, taking a sheet of paper from his pocket to give to him. 'You have a colourful turn of phrase, Lord Holcroft. If what you say in the letter is correct, I also have to admire your stamina.'

After reading the copy, Holcroft swore under his breath and scrunched the paper in his hand. He was cornered. Were his wife to see the letter, his marriage would come to an abrupt end. If his disgrace reached a wider audience, he would never recover from the scandal. There was no point in trying to reason with the stranger. Lord Holcroft was forced into a sour capitulation.

'How much do you want?' he asked.

CHAPTER EIGHT

Having worked as a tailor in Bond Street for over thirty years, Ebenezer Trew was inclined to judge everyone by his own high sartorial standards. When he first set eyes on Robert Colbeck, therefore, he took note of the cut and colour of his apparel and saw that he was a man of discernment. Colbeck's height and well-proportioned frame were a gift to any tailor, and his attire served to enhance his air of distinction. Trew was somewhat nonplussed, therefore, to learn that the visitor to his shop that afternoon was a Detective Inspector, and dismayed that he had lost what he hoped would be a potential customer.

Further disappointment followed. Colbeck opened a bag to produce a jacket that the tailor recognised at once. When he saw the bloodstains on the material, Ebenezer Trew winced. He was a short, neat, fastidious man with the hunched shoulders of someone who spent most of his time bent over a work table.

'You know the jacket, I see,' observed Colbeck.

'I could pick out my handiwork anywhere, Inspector.'

'Do you remember the customer for whom you made the suit?'

'Very well. His name was Mr Slender.' He reached out

to take the jacket and looked more closely at the stains on the shoulders. 'This will be almost impossible to remove,' he warned. 'Mr Slender was so proud of his suit. How did it come to be marked like this?'

'Daniel Slender was attacked on the embankment, Mr Trew.'

'Dear me! Was the assault a serious one?'

'Extremely serious,' said Colbeck, 'I fear that your customer was bludgeoned to death.' Trew turned pale. 'If you had not providentially sewn his name into the lining, we might not have identified him.'

'Mr Slender insisted on that. He told me that he had always wanted his name in a suit made by a Bond Street tailor.' He wrinkled his nose. 'The clothing he wore when he first came in here was of poor quality. Not to put too fine a point on it,' he said, 'it was very provincial – quite the wrong colour for him and made with such inferior material. Frankly, Inspector, I'd not have been seen dead in a suit like that.' He chewed his lip as he heard what he had just said. 'Oh, I do apologise,' he added, quickly. 'That was a rather tasteless remark.'

Colbeck studiously ignored it. 'What else can you tell me about Daniel Slender?' he asked.

'That he had obviously never been to a place like this before.'

'Was he shy and awkward?'

'On the contrary,' said Trew, 'he was full of confidence. I've never met anyone who enjoyed the experience of buying a suit from us so much. He gave me the impression that he had come into an appreciable amount of money that allowed him to indulge himself in a way that he had never been able to do before.'

'That fits in with what I know of the man,' said Colbeck.

'Until he came here, Daniel Slender worked as a locksmith in Wolverhampton.'

Trew wrinkled his nose again. 'Those dreadful Midlands vowels travelled with him to London,' he said with mild disgust. 'I could make him *look* like a gentleman, but he would never sound like one.'

'I trust that you concealed your prejudice from him, Mr Trew,' said Colbeck, irritated by the man's snobbery. 'None of us can choose the place where we are born or the accent that we inherit.'

'Quite so, quite so.'

'You, I suspect, hail from the West Country.'

'Yes, I do,' admitted the tailor, hurt that his attempts to remove the telltale burr from his voice had not been quite as successful as he thought. 'But I have lived in London since the age of ten.'

'How many times did you meet Mr Slender?'

'Three, Inspector. He came in to place the order and returned for a fitting. The third time was to collect the suit.'

'And to pay for it.'

'He did that with something of a flourish.'

'Did he ever tell you why he had moved to London?'

'Oh, yes,' said Trew, handing the jacket back to Colbeck. 'It was an ambition that he had nursed for years but domestic concerns kept him in the Midlands. At long last, he told me, he had a means of escape.'

'What else did he say?'

'That he was going to enjoy his retirement.'

'Not for very long, alas,' said Colbeck, sadly. He looked around at the various items of clothing on display. 'Being measured for a suit is usually an occasion for light conversation with one's tailor. Did you find Daniel Slender a talkative man?'

'To the point of garrulity, Inspector.'

'In what way?'

Ebenezer Trew needed no more encouragement. Feeling that he had aroused Colbeck's disapproval, he tried to atone by recalling snatches of the various conversations he had had with his customer. Most of it was irrelevant, but enough was of interest to the detective for him to let Trew ramble on. When the tailor's reminiscences came to an end, Colbeck seized on one remark made by Slender.

'He told you that he intended to move in society?'

'That is what I took him to mean, Inspector,' said Trew. 'I think that his exact words were that he would be "rubbing shoulders with a different class of person." It was one reason why he wanted a new suit.' He gave an ingratiating smile. 'Have I been of any assistance?'

'A little, Mr Trew.'

'Good. I aim to please.'

'Did your customer furnish you with an address?'

'Of course,' said Trew, seriously. 'I insisted on that. Had we not known where he lived, we would not have undertaken the work. We are very punctilious about such matters.' He opened a ledger and leafed through the pages. 'Here we are,' he said, stopping at a page and pointing a finger. 'Mr Slender had lodgings at 74, Delamere Street.' He offered the ledger to Colbeck. 'You may see for yourself, Inspector.'

'There is no need for that, Mr Trew,' said Colbeck, who knew the street well. 'It seems that you were not as punctilious as you imagined. The last time that I was in Delamere Street, it comprised no more than two dozen houses. In other words, Daniel Slender was residing at an address that does not exist.'

Trew was shocked. 'He *lied* to me?' he said with disbelief. 'But he seemed to be so honest and straightforward.'

'Never judge by appearances,' advised Colbeck, putting the jacket back into his bag. 'They can be very misleading.'

'So I see.'

'Goodbye, Mr Trew.'

'One moment, Inspector,' said the tailor. 'I am still trying to come to terms with the notion that one of my customers was murdered. Do you have any idea *why* Mr Slender was killed?'

'Of course.'

'May one know what it is?'

'Not at this stage,' said Colbeck, unwilling to discuss the details of the crime with a man he found increasingly annoying. 'Of something, however, I can assure you.'

'And what is that?'

'He was not killed for his new suit, Mr Trew,' said the detective, crisply. 'Or, for that matter, because he had an unfortunate accent.'

Leaving him thoroughly chastened, Colbeck went out of the shop.

On his second visit, Victor Leeming found the Royal Mint a much less welcoming place. Hoping that the detective had brought good news, Charles Omber was disturbed to hear that no significant progress had been made in the investigation and that suspicions were still harboured about his colleagues. He had defended them staunchly and said that he would take a Bible oath that there had been no breach of security at the Mint. An argument had developed. Omber was determined to win it. Leeming finally withdrew in some disarray.

When he got to Euston Station, he found that Colbeck was already in the waiting room. It was thronged with passengers. The Inspector had suggested they meet there for two reasons. It would not only keep them out of range of the simmering fury of Superintendent Tallis, it would, more importantly, take them back to the place from which the mail train had set out on its doomed journey.

Colbeck saw the jaded expression on the Sergeant's ugly face.

'I take it that you found nothing,' he said.

'Only that Mr Omber has a very nasty temper when his word is challenged. He refuses to accept that the Mint could be at fault.'

'Do you believe him, Victor?'

'No, sir,' said Leeming. 'I have this doubt at the back of my mind.'

'Was Mr Omber deceiving you, then?'

'Not at all. His sincerity is not in question. In fact, he spoke so passionately on behalf of his colleagues that I felt a bit embarrassed for even suggesting that one of them may have leaked information about the movement of gold coin.'

'Yet your instinct tells you otherwise.'

'Yes, Inspector.'

'Then rely on it, Victor. It rarely lets you down.'

'Thank you,' said Leeming. 'How did you get on in Bond Street?'

'I met a tailor whom I would never dare to employ.'

'Why not?'

'Which of the ten reasons would you care to hear first?'

Colbeck told him about his meeting with Ebenezer Trew and why he had disliked the man so much. He explained what the tailor had said about his erstwhile customer. On one point, Leeming wanted elucidation.

'Daniel Slender had *retired*?' he said.

'Apparently.'

'Could he afford to do so, Inspector?'

'He sold the house in Willenhall, remember, and he would have had a certain amount of savings. Then, of course, there is the money that he would have received from the train robbers.'

'More or less than William Ings?'

'More, I should imagine,' said Colbeck.

'Mr Ings got the best part of two hundred pounds.'

'Yet all he did was to tell them that money was being carried by train to Birmingham on a specific day. Mr Slender's contribution was far more critical,' he noted. 'Without those keys and that combination number, they could never have opened the safe so easily. That would have left them with two options – trying to blow it open with a charge of gunpowder or taking the whole safe with them.'

'That would have entailed the use of a crane,' said Leeming.

'And taken far too long. Speed was the essence of the operation and Daniel Slender's help was decisive. I think that he was paid handsomely in advance with a promise of more to come.'

'Much more, probably.'

'Yes,' said Colbeck. 'When you do not intend to part with another penny, you can afford to offer any amount by way of temptation. It may well be that Mr Slender was lured to the embankment last night in the hope of receiving the rest of his pay.'

'Instead of which, his head was smashed in.'

'They do not take prisoners, Victor.'

'Mr Slender must have wished that he had stayed in Willenhall.'

'The attack on him was so ferocious that he had no time to wish for anything. It was a gruesome but quick death. Come with me for a moment,' he said, putting a hand on Leeming's shoulder, 'I want to show you something.'

They walked out of the waiting room and picked their way

through the milling crowd. Colbeck stopped when he reached the first platform. A train had just arrived and passengers were streaming off it. Friends were waiting to greet them. On the other platform, a train was about to depart, and dozens of people had come to wave off their friends or family members. Porters were everywhere, moving luggage on their trolleys, and several other railway employees were in evidence. The noise of a locomotive letting off steam rose above the tumult.

Colbeck nudged his colleague. 'What do you see, Victor?'

'Bedlam, sir.'

'No, you see a thriving industry. You are looking at visible proof of the way that the railways have transformed our lives. Euston Station is as busy as this every day of the week – and so is Paddington. Everybody has somewhere to get to,' said Colbeck, indicating the scene, 'and they choose to travel by rail in order to get there. Why is that?'

'Because they think it is quicker.'

'Demonstrably so.'

'If they travel second or third class, it is certainly cheaper as well.'

'You've missed out the real attraction of the railway.'

'Have I?' said Leeming.

'It is safe. At times, I grant you, it can also be noisy, smelly and a trifle uncomfortable but it is, as a rule, safe. It gets passengers to their appointed destinations in one piece. Railway companies met with great fear and opposition at first,' Colbeck reminded him, 'but the public has now come to trust them. This is the Railway Age.'

'I still prefer to travel by horse.'

'Then you are behind the times, Victor.'

'I am not ashamed of that, Inspector.'

'Nor should you be,' said Colbeck. 'But the point I am trying to make is this. The train robbery is a dangerous precedent. It imperils the safety record of the railway companies. If we do not catch and convict those responsible, then they will surely be emboldened to strike again.'

'And others might be inspired by their example.'

'Exactly. We must solve these crimes soon, Victor.'

'How can we when we have so little to go on?' asked Leeming with a gesture of despair. 'We still know nothing whatsoever about the man who organised the train robbery.'

'But we do,' said Colbeck. 'We know three crucial things.'

'Do we?'

'First, he is a gentleman.'

'Gentleman!' exclaimed Leeming. 'How can you describe someone who is behind such callous murders as a gentleman?'

'Think what else he did, Victor. He may have seen fit to have William Ings killed but he made sure that the widow inherited her husband's money. That was the act of a gentleman.'

'Not in my opinion.'

'Have you forgotten what the tailor told me about Daniel Slender?' asked Colbeck. 'Here was a man from a modest background in the Midlands, suddenly finding himself in London with money in his pockets. And what pleased him most was that he was about to rub shoulders with what he called a better class of person. In short, with gentlemen.'

'What's the second thing we know about this fellow?'

'He was in the army.'

Leeming was surprised. 'You sound very certain of that, sir.'

'I'd put money on it,' said Colbeck, 'and, as you know, I am not a betting man. The train robbery was no random attack. It was a military operation that was planned and, I daresay, rehearsed very carefully. Only someone who is used to commanding a body of men like that could have brought it off. So,' he went on, 'what do we have so far?'

'An officer and a gentleman.'

'Add the most telling thing about him, Victor.'

'He's a cold-blooded killer.'

'Cast your mind back to the robbery itself.'

'It's as you say,' conceded the other. 'He knew when and how to strike and, as a result, got away with the money and the mail bags.'

'What other part of his plan was put into action?'

Leeming needed a moment for consideration. 'The locomotive was deliberately run off the track,' he remembered.

'Yes,' said Colbeck, snapping his fingers. 'Severe damage was inflicted and Caleb Andrews's beloved engine was put out of action for a long time. What sort of person would do that, Victor?'

'Someone who hates trains.'

Sir Humphrey Gilzean sat in an open carriage on the Berkshire Downs and watched his racehorses being put through their paces. Bunched together, they thundered past and left a flurry of dust in their wake. Gilzean's eyes were on the black colt at the front of the group. As they galloped on, its rider used his whip to coax extra speed out of his mount and the colt surged ahead of the others to establish a lead of several lengths. Gilzean slapped his thigh in delight. He turned to his trainer, a big, sturdy man, who sat astride a chestnut mare beside him.

'*That's* what I want from him,' he declared.

'Starlight is a fine horse, Sir Humphrey,' said the trainer.

'Good enough to win the Derby?'

'If he loses, it will not be for want of trying. Starlight has a turn of foot to leave most colts and fillies behind. The secret is to bring him to a peak at just the right time.'

'I rely on you to do that, Welsby.'

'Yes, Sir Humphrey.'

'Starlight was certainly expensive enough to win the Derby,' said Gilzean, as the horses ended their race and trotted back in his direction. 'I expect a return on my investment.'

'Naturally.'

'Make sure that I get it.'

He was about to give some more instructions to his trainer when the distant sound of a train whistle distracted him. Gilzean's eyes flashed and his jaw tightened. He dispatched the trainer with a dismissive flick of his hand then spoke to the driver of the carriage.

'Take me home.'

'Yes, Sir Humphrey.'

'By way of the church.'

The coachman cracked his whip and the two horses pulled the carriage in a semicircle before setting off across the Downs at a steady trot. It was a large estate, parts of which were farmed by tenants. Some of the land was arable but most was given over to herds of dairy cattle and flocks of sheep. Gilzean found the sight of so many animals grazing in the fields strangely reassuring. There was a timelessness about the scene that appealed to him, an unspoilt, unhurried, natural quality that he had known and loved since he was a small child. It was the English countryside at its best.

Sitting erect in the carriage, Sir Humphrey Gilzean was a striking figure in his late thirties, tall, slim, swarthy of complexion and with finely chiselled features. Dressed in the most fashionable attire, he had the unmistakable air of an aristocrat, allied to the physique and disposition of a soldier. Even at his most relaxed, he exuded a sense of authority. As he was driven past the labourers in the fields, he collected an endless sequence of servile nods or obsequious salutes.

The Norman church stood at the edge of the village. Built of local stone, it was a small but solid structure that had withstood the unruly elements for centuries. Its square tower was surmounted by a little steeple with a weathervane at its apex. The churchyard was enclosed by a low and irregular stone wall, pierced by a wooden lychgate. Members of the Gilzean family had been buried there for generations, and it was their money that had kept the church in a state of good repair. When the carriage drew up outside the lychgate, Gilzean got out and tossed a curt command over his shoulder.

'Wait here,' he said to the coachman. 'I may be some time.'

During an investigation, leisure did not exist for Robert Colbeck. Having worked until late, he was back at his desk early the following morning so that he could collate all the evidence that had so far been gathered and address his mind to it when there was little chance of interruption. He had been at Scotland Yard for almost two hours before he was disturbed by the arrival of a clerk.

'Excuse me, Inspector,' said the man, putting his head around the door. 'There's a young lady to see you.'

'Miss Andrews?' asked Colbeck, hoping that it might be her.

'No, sir. She gave her name as Miss Woodhead.'

'Then you had better shown her in.'

When his visitor came into the room, Colbeck got to his feet for the introductions. Nobody could have been less like Madeleine Andrews than the shy, hesitant creature who stood before him in a state of such obvious distress. Bella Woodhead was a short, plump and decidedly plain young woman in nondescript clothing and a faded straw hat. Offered a chair, she sat on the very edge of it. Colbeck could see that her hands were trembling.

'You wished to see me, Miss Woodhead?' he inquired.

'Yes, Inspector. I have something to tell you.'

'May I know what it concerns?'

She swallowed hard. 'Mr Ings,' she murmured.

'William Ings?'

'We read the newspaper this morning and saw the report of his death.' She gave a shudder. 'We could not believe it at first. When we saw that William – Mr Ings, that is – might actually be connected with this train robbery, we were shocked. It was like a blow in the face.'

'How did you come to know Mr Ings?' asked Colbeck.

'I work at the Post Office.'

'I see.'

'Only in a minor capacity, of course,' she said with a self-effacing smile. 'I am merely a clerk there. He was far more senior. Mr Ings was well-respected. The Post Office held him in high regard.'

Colbeck could tell from the way that she said the man's name that she had enjoyed a closer relationship with Ings than any of his other colleagues. Bella Woodhead was too honest and unschooled to disguise her feelings. Stunned by the news of his murder, she had come to make a confession that was clearly causing her intense pain. Colbeck tried to make it easier for her by anticipating what she was going to say.

'I believe that you were very fond of Mr Ings,' he suggested.

'Oh, I was, I was.'

'And he, in turn, was drawn to you.'

'That's what he told me,' she said, proudly, 'and it changed my life. No man had taken the slightest interest in me before. For a time, it was like living in a dream.' Her face crumpled.

'Now I see that he did not mean a word of it.' She looked up at Colbeck. 'Is it true that he was found dead in the Devil's Acre?'

'Yes, Miss Woodhead.'

'In the company of a woman?'

Colbeck nodded and she promptly burst into tears. He came across to put a consoling arm around her shoulders but it was minutes before she was able to speak again.

'Mr Ings betrayed me,' she said, finally controlling her sobs and dabbing at her eyes with a handkerchief. 'He swore that he loved me. He told me that he would leave his wife and that we would be together. Yet all the time . . .'

She put both hands to her mouth to stifle another fit of crying. Colbeck could well understand how the relationship with William Ings had developed. His position at the Post Office would have impressed Bella Woodhead and made her vulnerable to any favour that was shown to her. Patently, Ings had exploited her but the detective could not understand why. Since the man's taste ran to women like Polly Roach and Kate Piercey, why had he turned to someone as virginal and inexperienced as Bella Woodhead?

'Did he offer to marry you?' he wondered, softly.

'Of course,' she replied with a touch of indignation. 'Do you think that I would have become involved with him on any other basis? Mr Ings was a decent man – or so I thought at the time. He told me that he would arrange a divorce somehow. All that happened between us, Inspector, was an exchange of vows. I must ask you to believe that.'

'I accept your word without reservation, Miss Woodhead.'

'Mr Ings wanted everything to be done properly.'

'Properly?'

'He wanted to make me his wife so that we could, in time,

live together openly. That was why he insisted on meeting my parents.'

'Oh?'

'He knew how protective they were of me – especially my father. At first he was very unhappy about my friendship, but Mr Ings persuaded him in the end. Father and he got on well. In fact,' she said, 'when he came to the house, he spent more time talking to my father than he did to me.' She blew her nose into the handkerchief. 'Now I know why.'

'Do you?'

'Yes. Mr Ings only wanted to hear about Father's job.'

'Why?' asked Colbeck. 'Where does your father work?'

'At the Royal Mint.'

It was a warm day but there was nevertheless a fire in the grate. Sir Humphrey Gilzean tossed another bundle of envelopes on to it and, putting one hand on the marble mantelpiece to steady himself, stirred the blaze with a poker. Wisps of black paper went up the chimney.

'That's the last of them, Thomas,' he observed.

'Good,' said the other. 'Such a dreary business, reading through other people's correspondence.'

'Dreary but rewarding. How much did Lord Holcroft give us?'

'Five hundred pounds.'

'This mistress of his must be a remarkable lady if she is deemed to be worth five hundred pounds. Lord Holcroft would rather lose the money than surrender the charms of Miss Anna Grayle.'

'All that money for two pieces of stationery.'

'And not a blow given or a risk taken,' noted Gilzean. 'Blackmail is a much easier way to make a living than by robbing trains. Secrecy is a valuable commodity, Thomas. I wish that we had more of it to sell.'

'So do I, Humphrey.'

They were in the library at Gilzean's house, an extensive property that overlooked a formal garden of almost three acres. Thomas Sholto was the bearded individual who had accosted Lord Holcroft in Hyde Park with a copy of the compromising letter. Like his friend, he was a man of impressive demeanour and military bearing. Sholto was pleased at their record of success.

'Mr Blower was a more difficult target,' he recalled.

'Remind me who he was.'

'The financier who was fishing in murky waters.'

'Ah, yes,' said Gilzean. 'Mr Jeremiah Blower. His letter disclosed confidential information about a forthcoming merger. Had his company known how treacherous he was being, they would have dismissed him on the spot. What value did we set on his ill-judged letter?'

'Three hundred pounds.'

'Yet he refused to pay up.'

'Initially,' said Sholto. 'He made all kinds of wild threats and was even foolish enough to strike out at me. He soon regretted that. I knocked him flat. And because he had the gall to haggle with me, I put up the price. He ended up paying twice as much as we asked.'

'What with Lord Holcroft and the others, we've made a tidy profit out of this little venture. I told you that we should steal the mail bags as well. Admittedly,' said Gilzean, watching the flames die down, 'we had to pick our way through a deal of worthless trivia, but the result more than justified the effort involved. And we learnt a valuable lesson in the process.'

'Be careful what you commit to paper.'

'Precisely, Thomas.'

Sholto rubbed his hands together. 'When do we strike again?'

'Soon,' said Gilzean. 'The important thing was to ensure that there were no loose ends hanging. Thanks to you, the only two people who could have led this Inspector Colbeck to us are now in no position to speak to anyone.'

'Daniel Slender's head cracked open at one blow,' recalled Sholto with a grin. 'It was all over in less than thirty seconds. Mr Ings had a much harder skull.'

'Of more use to us was the fact that both of them had soft brains. They foolishly believed that we'd let them live when they knew too much about us. How could they be so naïve?'

'It served our purpose, Humphrey.'

'Supremely well.'

'Killing the pair of them was child's play,' boasted Sholto.

'It should be for a trained soldier like you, Thomas. The beauty of the two murders is,' said Gilzean, smugly, 'that they help to confuse this gifted detective who is supposed to be on our trail. Inspector Robert Colbeck will never be able to connect the victims with us. We are free to make our next move.'

Superintendent Edward Tallis was in an even more irascible mood than usual. Apart from the criticism he was receiving in the press, he was troubled by toothache and smarting from the reproaches of the Police Commissioners. Two cigars did nothing to dispel his feeling that he was the victim of unjust persecution. Summoned to his office, Colbeck decided to take Victor Leeming with him, not because he thought there would be safety in numbers, but because he wanted his colleague to be given some credit for his intuition.

When Tallis had stopped fulminating, Colbeck said his piece.

'Valuable information has come into our hands, sir,' he explained. 'We have learnt that William Ings befriended a female colleague at the Post Office in order to win the confidence of her father, Albert Woodhead. It transpires that Mr Woodhead is employed at the Royal Mint.'

'So?'

'We now know where the other breach of security occurred. An unguarded remark by Mr Woodhead about the transfer of money was seized on by Mr Ings and passed on to the robbers. Victor's instinct told him that a leak had occurred at the Mint,' continued Colbeck, turning to his colleague. 'I believe that he deserves some praise.'

'Yes,' said Tallis, grudgingly. 'I suppose that he does.'

Leeming took his cue. 'I've just returned from my third visit to the Mint, sir,' he said, 'where I spoke to the manager, Charles Omber. He confirmed that Albert Woodhead had owned up to his folly. Even though it was not deliberate, he has been suspended from his job.'

'And is full of contrition,' said Colbeck. 'After his daughter came to see me this morning, I called on Mr Woodhead and found him in a sorry state. It is not only his humiliating suspension that is upsetting him. The murder of William Ings has brought to the light the cruel way in which he used Miss Woodhead. Her father feels that, to some extent, he may have condoned it.'

'This is all very interesting, Inspector,' said Tallis, brooding behind his desk, 'but where does it get us?'

'It explains exactly where the necessary information came from and it absolves the railway company of any blame.'

'Yes,' added Leeming. 'It also tells us why Mr Ings was paid such a large amount of money. He had vital intelligence to sell.'

'Who bought it from him?' asked Tallis.

'We have yet to determine that, sir.'

'And how much longer do I have to wait before you do?'

'That depends on what he does next,' said Colbeck.

'Next?' repeated Tallis. 'Are you telling me that we may expect another train robbery or additional murders?'

'No, Superintendent. I am simply saying that the man who is behind these crimes will act in character – and that we now have a clear idea of what that character is.'

'So do I. He is cunning, merciless and able to outwit us with ease.'

'He has stayed one step ahead of us so far,' agreed Colbeck, 'but that will soon change. The aspect of his character that I would point to is his rooted dislike of railways. It amounts to abhorrence. I would not at all be surprised to learn that he is a landowner whose property has been encroached upon by a railway company. Robbing that train and wrecking that locomotive was his way of striking back.'

'And?'

'There will be more to come, sir.'

'Why do you think that?'

'This man wants blood.'

Since its mail train was ambushed, the London and Birmingham Railway Company had tightened its security. Two policemen now guarded each end of the various tunnels that punctuated the 112 miles of track between the two cities. No risks were taken. Running to almost a mile and a half, the Kilsby Tunnel in Northamptonshire was the longest on the line and by far the costliest to build, taking all of two years to complete. It was the work of Robert Stephenson and a model of its kind. Most people marvelled at its construction but the three men who crept towards it that evening did not share in the general admiration of an outstanding feat of engineering.

The seized their moment. One of the railway policemen on duty was relieving himself behind a bush and the other was stuffing tobacco into his pipe. Both men were overpowered and tied up without offering any real resistance. The newcomers could carry on with their business. After checking their watches to see how much time they had before the next train, they went into the mouth of the tunnel at the Northamptonshire end. A small barrel of gunpowder was rolled against the brickwork. Loose stones were packed around it to keep it firmly in place.

Having lit the long fuse, the three men scampered to a place of safety and thought about the rich reward that they would earn. It was only a matter of time before the explosion occurred.

Returning to his office, Colbeck was both astonished and delighted to see Madeleine Andrews waiting for him there. She gave him a tentative smile.

'I hope that I am not intruding, Inspector,' she said.

'Of course not.'

'I know how busy you must be.'

'That's a hazard of my profession, Miss Andrews,' he said, indicating the huge pile of papers on his desk. 'Crimes are committed in London every hour of the day. Being a detective means that one is kept constantly on one's toes.'

'Then I'll not hold you up for long.'

'At least, take a seat while you are here.'

'Thank you,' she said, lowering herself on to a chair and spreading her skirt out. 'I really called to see if any progress had been made.'

'A little, Miss Andrews. A little.'

'The report in today's newspaper was not very encouraging.'

'Do not pay too much attention to what you read,' he counselled. 'Newspapers do not always have the full facts at their fingertips and some of them appear to take pleasure in baiting us. I can assure you that we have made more headway than they would lead you to believe.'

'We were horrified to learn that there had been two murders. Is it true that they may possibly be related to the train robbery?'

'Undeniably so.'

'Why were they killed?'

'The murder victims were accomplices who had to be silenced.'

'How terrible!'

'Except for the young woman, that is. She was an innocent person who happened to be in the wrong company at the wrong time.'

'Yet they still cut her throat?'

'We are dealing with ruthless men, Miss Andrews.'

'Father discovered that.'

'How is he, by the way?'

'He gets better each day,' she said, brightening. 'Unfortunately, he also gets angrier and louder. I have difficulty in calming him down.'

'I refuse to believe that. You know exactly how to handle him.'

His fond smile was tinged with disappointment. Madeleine met his gaze and held it for some time, trying to read the message in his eyes while sending a covert signal in her own. Colbeck was strongly aware of the mutual interest between them but he did not feel able to explore it. His visitor eventually broke the long silence.

'I had a more personal reason for coming, Inspector,' she said.

'Indeed?'

'Yes, I feel that I owe you an apology.'

'Whatever for?'

'My behaviour when you called at our house.'

'I saw nothing that could warrant an apology, Miss Andrews.'

'My father spoke out of turn.'

'He does seem to have an impulsive streak.'

'It led him to say something that he had no right to say,' explained Madeleine, 'and I did not wish you to be misled by it. The person that he mentioned – Gideon Little, a fireman – is a family friend, but, as far as I am concerned, he can never be more than that. Father thinks otherwise.'

'Your private life is no business of mine,' he said, trying to ease her obvious discomfort. 'Please do not feel that you have to offer either an apology or an explanation.'

'I just wanted you to understand.'

'Then I am grateful that you came.'

'Really?'

'Really,' he confirmed.

Madeleine smiled with relief. 'Then so am I, Inspector Colbeck.' She got to her feet. 'But I must let you get on with your work. What am I to tell my father?'

'That he has a very beautiful daughter,' said Colbeck, letting his admiration show, 'though I daresay that he already knows that. As for the train robbery,' he went on, 'I can give him no hope of an early arrest. Indeed, I think you should warn him to brace himself.'

'Why?'

'Because the man behind the robbery will be back. In my

view, he is conducting a feud against the railway system and he will not rest until he has inflicted more serious damage upon it.'

'What do you mean?' roared Sir Humphrey Gilzean, striking the side of his boot with his riding crop. 'The attempt *failed*?'

'It was only a partial success,' said Thomas Sholto.

'How partial? Was there no explosion?'

'Yes, Humphrey.'

'Then what went wrong?'

'The gunpowder, it seems, was not in the ideal position. All that it did was to dislodge the brickwork on one side of the tunnel.'

'It was intended to block the entrance completely.'

'That did not happen, alas.'

'Why ever not, Thomas? I gave orders.'

'They were disobeyed,' said Sholto. 'The men decided that they could achieve the same results with a smaller amount of gunpowder than you had decreed. They were proved wrong.'

'Damnation!'

'They've been upbraided, believe me.'

'I'll do more than upbraid them,' snarled Gilzean, slapping the back of a leather armchair with his crop. 'I gave them precise instructions. Had they followed them to the letter, the train that was coming from the opposite direction would have crashed into the debris and put the Kilsby Tunnel out of action for a considerable time.'

'That did not happen, Humphrey. Damage was limited.'

'I *knew* that we should have done the job ourselves.'

'Jukes and the others have never let us down before.'

'They'll not get the chance to do so again,' vowed Gilzean, prowling vengefully around the hall of his house. 'I know that. Instead of disrupting the railway, we simply gave them a salutary warning. The Kilsby Tunnel will be guarded by an army of policemen from now on.' He flung his crop onto the armchair. 'We lost our chance through sheer incompetence.'

'They did not realise how solid that brickwork was.'

'Almost as solid as their heads, by the sound of it. I don't like it, Thomas. This is a bad omen. Until now, everything has gone so smoothly.'

'Our luck had to change at some time.'

'Luck does not come into it, man,' retorted the other. 'It is merely a question of good preparation and perfect timing. That is what served us so well with the train robbery – discipline. Were I still in the regiment,' he said, waving a fist, 'I'd have the three of them flogged until they had no skin left on their backs. Just wait until I see them. Disobey orders, will they?' he cried. 'By God, the next time I try to blow up a tunnel, I'll make sure that each one of those blithering idiots is inside it!'

Madeleine Andrews made no objection this time when he suggested that she might return home in a cab. Shadows were lengthening and Camden began to seem a long way away. As they stood in Whitehall, however, she made no effort to hail a cab and neither did Colbeck. She wished to stay and he wanted her to linger. Their brief conversation in his office had redeemed his whole day. When a cab went past, they both ignored it.

'I read what the newspaper said about you, Inspector.'

'Did you?'

'Yes,' replied Madeleine. 'It listed some of the other cases in which you've been involved. You've had a very successful career.'

'I am only one of a team, Miss Andrews,' he said, modestly. 'Any success that I've enjoyed as a detective is due to the fact that I have people like Sergeant Leeming around me.'

'That face of his would frighten me.'

'Victor has many compensating virtues.'

'I'm sure that he has.' She looked up quizzically at him. 'How did you come to know so much about locomotives?'

'They interest me.'

'Father could not believe that you could tell the difference between a Bury and a Crampton locomotive. That pleased him so much.'

'Good,' said Colbeck, studying her dimples. 'Driving a train has always seemed to be to be an exciting occupation.'

'Not to those who actually do it, Inspector. Father has to work long hours in all weathers. Standing on the footplate in heavy rain or driving snow is an ordeal. And think of the dirt. His clothing gets so filthy that I have to wash it in several waters to get it clean.'

'Has he ever wanted to change his job?'

'No,' she admitted. 'He loves it too much.'

'In spite of what happened to him this week?'

'In spite of it.'

Colbeck grinned. 'I rest my case.'

'Being in a railway family is hard for any woman,' she said. 'Talk to Rose Pike. Her husband was the fireman. Rose will tell you how often Frank has come home with burns on his hand from the firebox or a mark on his face where some flying cinders have hit him. When she heard about the train robbery, she was terrified.'

'Be fair, Miss Andrews. It was a unique event.'

'That made no difference to Rose.'

Colbeck began to fish. 'Coming back to what you were saying about a railway family,' he said, casually. 'Is it because you were brought up in one that you have no desire to marry a railwayman?'

'I've no desire to marry anyone at present,' she replied.

'Yet you have a suitor.'

'An unwanted suitor.'

'Because he works on the railway?'

'No, Inspector,' she said with a shrug. 'Because he is not the right husband for me. Gideon Little is a pleasant enough young man and I have always liked him, but that is the extent of my interest in him.'

'You do not have to account to me for your feelings.'

'I wanted you to appreciate the true position, Inspector.'

'Thank you.'

'Just as I now appreciate your situation.'

'Is it so transparent, Miss Andrews?'

'I think so,' she said, looking him full in the eye. 'You are married to your work, Inspector. It occupies you completely, does it not? Nothing else in your life matters.'

'You may be wrong about that,' said Colbeck with a slow smile. 'Though I suspect that it may take time to convince you of it.' The clatter of hooves made him look up. 'Ah, here's a cab at last!' he noted. 'Shall I stop it or do you reserve the right to hail it yourself?'

'I accept your kind offer, Inspector. Thank you.'

Colbeck raised an arm and the cab drew up alongside them. He had the momentary pleasure of holding her hand to help her into the cab. There was an exchange of farewells. Madeleine gave an address to the driver and he flicked his reins. The horse trotted off up Whitehall. Colbeck had a sudden desire to sit beside her in the cab and continue their conversation indefinitely but other priorities called. Forcing himself to forget Madeleine Andrews, he went swiftly back to his office.

The dark-eyed young man in the ill-fitting brown suit emerged from the doorway where he had been lurking. Gideon Little set off with long strides in pursuit of the cab.

CHAPTER NINE

Darkness had fallen by the time that news of the explosion in the Kilsby Tunnel finally reached Scotland Yard. Superintendent Tallis was not entirely convinced that it was the work of the same people who had robbed the mail train, but Inspector Colbeck had no doubts whatsoever on the subject. He decided to visit the scene of the crime in daylight. Accordingly, early next morning, he and Victor Leeming caught a train that would take them there with a minimum number of stops on the way. Knowing that his companion was a reluctant rail traveller, Colbeck tried to divert him with some facts about their destination.

'What do you know about the tunnel, Victor?' he asked.

'Nothing – beyond the fact that it goes under ground.'

'It's a work of art. On my visit to the Midlands, I went through it twice and was struck by the sheer size of it. The Kilsby Tunnel is cavernous. It's like being in a subterranean kingdom.'

'I'll take your word for it, Inspector.'

'When he undertook the project, Mr Stephenson thought it would be relatively straightforward because they would be cutting their way through a mixture of clay and sand.

Unhappily,' said Colbeck, 'much of it turned out to be quicksand so the whole area had first to be drained. It was slow and laborious work.'

'Like being a detective,' noted the other, lugubriously.

Colbeck laughed. 'Only in the sense that we, too, come up against unforeseen hazards,' he said. 'But our job is far less dangerous than that of the miners who sunk those enormous ventilation shafts or the navvies who dug out all that soil. How many bricks would you say were needed to line the tunnel?'

'Hundreds of thousands, probably,' guessed Leeming, unable to share the Inspector's enthusiasm for the topic. 'I hope that you are not asking me to count them when we get there.'

'It would take you a lifetime, Victor.'

'Why, sir?'

'Because millions of bricks were used,' said Colbeck. 'A steam clay mill and kilns were built on site by Mr Stephenson so that he had a constant supply of 30,000 bricks per day. Imagine that, if you will.' Leeming stifled a yawn. 'The original estimate – would you believe – was for a total of 20 million bricks, some of them made from the clay that was excavated from the tunnel itself.'

'How do you know all this, Inspector?'

'I took the trouble to do some research on the subject.'

'In that library of yours, you mean?'

'Yes, Victor.'

'I wouldn't know where to look.'

'Start with a history of the London and Birmingham Railway,' said Colbeck. 'That was the name of the company that operated this line when the tunnel was built. It was only amalgamated into the London and North Western Railway Company five years ago.'

'Now that's something I *did* know,' said Leeming. 'Every person I spoke to at the company made a point of telling me.' He gave Colbeck a meaningful glance. 'But not one of them mentioned how many bricks there were in the Kilsby Tunnel.'

'Point taken,' said Colbeck, smiling. 'You are not in the mood for a lecture about the railway. Given the choice, I suspect, you would rather be making this journey on horseback.'

'Or in the comfort of a stage coach, sir.'

'Either way, you would have been much slower.'

'Would I?'

'By the time you got to Northamptonshire, I would have been back at my desk in London. Railways are helping to defeat time.'

When the train passed through Leighton Buzzard Station, they were pleased to see that the wrecked locomotive near the Linslade Tunnel had been removed, leaving deep indentations in the grass where it had come to rest. Though the robbery had been a serious crime with murderous consequences, Colbeck was very conscious of the fact that it had introduced him to Madeleine Andrews. He regarded that as an incidental bonus. His mind was filled with pleasant thoughts of her as they crossed the county border.

Stations flashed pass them at regular intervals then – to Leeming's obvious relief – the train began to slow down. The detectives alighted at Crick to be greeted by a familiar sight. The hulking figure of Inspector Rory McTurk came along the station platform to give them a blunt reception.

'What are *you* doing here, Inspector Colbeck?' he asked.

'We wanted the pleasure of renewing your acquaintance,' replied Colbeck, touching the brim of his hat with courtesy. 'I'm sure that you remember Sergeant Leeming.'

'I do,' grunted the Scotsman.

'Good morning, Inspector,' said Leeming.

'Neither of you is needed here. This is railway business.'

'Not when it's related to the train robbery,' asserted Colbeck.

'What makes you think that?'

'I'll tell you when we have examined the scene.' The locomotive was starting up again. 'I see that the line has been reopened.'

'In both directions,' said McTurk. 'A team of men worked through the night to clear the obstruction. Everything is as it should be now.'

'Were there no policemen on duty at the tunnel?'

'Two of them, Inspector. They were both overpowered.'

'What game of cards were they playing *this* time?' asked Leeming.

McTurk scowled. 'Follow me,' he said.

When the train had departed, they went down onto the track and strolled in the direction of the Kilsby Tunnel. McTurk walked with a proprietary strut. Since he was landed with him, Colbeck tried to make use of the combative Scotsman.

'The news reached us by telegraph,' he said. 'Details were scarce.'

'Then how can you link this outrage with the train robbery?'

'I was expecting it.'

'You expected it?' said McTurk. 'Why did you not forewarn us?'

'Because I had no idea *where* they would strike, Inspector, only that an attack of some sort was imminent. From what I gather,' Colbeck went on, 'you had something of a lucky escape.'

McTurk frowned. 'Two railway policemen injured and

an explosion in the longest tunnel on the line – I fail to see how you can talk about luck. It could have been worse,' he admitted, 'much worse, but it is still bad enough.'

He grumbled all the way to the mouth of the tunnel itself. Colbeck and Leeming said nothing to interrupt him. The first thing they noticed was the large pile of rubble to the side of the track that carried up trains to London. Working from ladders and trestles, bricklayers were already trying to repair the damage. Leeming saw an opportunity to air his limited knowledge of tunnel construction.

'Tell me, Inspector McTurk,' he said. 'Do you happen to know how many bricks were used in the Kilsby Tunnel?'

'Too bloody many!' came the tart reply.

Leeming chose not to pursue the conversation.

Colbeck went into the tunnel to examine the full extent of the damage. He tried to work out where the gunpowder must have been when it exploded. McTurk came to stand at his shoulder.

'By the end of the day,' he said, 'it will be as good as new.'

'What about the two men who were attacked?' asked Colbeck. 'Are they as good as new, Inspector?'

'They're still a bit shaken, but they'll be back at work soon.'

'Were they able to give a description of their assailants?'

'No,' said McTurk. 'They were grabbed from behind, knocked unconscious and tied up. They didn't even hear the explosion go off. There's no point in talking to them.'

'Perhaps not.' He felt inside a hole where the brickwork had been blasted away. 'What was the intention behind it all?'

McTurk was contemptuous. 'I'm surprised that a man of your experience has to ask that, Inspector Colbeck,' he said. 'The intention is plain. They tried to close the tunnel in order to disrupt the railway.'

'I think that there is more to it than that.'

'What do you mean?'

'These people do nothing at random, believe me. The explosion would have gone off at a specific time and for a specific purpose. When was the next up train due to enter the tunnel at the other end?'

'Not long before the explosion. Fortunately, it was late.'

'There's your answer, Inspector McTurk.'

'Is it?'

'The tunnel was supposed to collapse just before the train reached it. The driver would have been going too fast to stop. The locomotive would have ploughed into the rubble and the whole train would have been derailed. *That* was their intention,' declared Colbeck. 'To block the tunnel, destroy a train and kill passengers in the process.'

'But there were no passengers on board the train.'

'Then what was it carrying?'

'Goods.'

'Any particular kinds of goods?'

'Why do you ask?'

'Because it may be significant.'

'I don't see how,' said McTurk, irritably. 'My information is that the wagons were simply carrying huge pieces of glass from the Chance Brothers' Factory.'

'Of course!' cried Colbeck. 'That explains it.'

McTurk looked blank. 'Does it?'

'I'm as mystified as Inspector McTurk,' confessed Leeming as he joined them. 'How can some sheets of glass provide the explanation?'

'Think of where they would be going, Victor,' advised Colbeck.

'To the customer who bought them, I suppose.'

'What's so remarkable about that?' said McTurk.

'The customer in question happens to be Joseph Paxton,' replied Colbeck, 'the man who designed the Crystal Palace. And who had the contract for supplying all that glass? Chance Brothers.'

McTurk lifted his hat to scratch his head. 'I'm still lost.'

'So am I,' said Leeming.

'Then you have obviously not been reading all the advertisements for the Great Exhibition. What is it,' said Colbeck, 'but a celebration of British industry? One of the main elements in that is the primacy of our railway system. A number of locomotives will be on display – but only if the structure is finished, and that depends on the supply of the glass panels that were commissioned from Chance Brothers.'

Leeming blinked. 'They were trying to *stop* the Great Exhibition?'

'At the very least, they were doing their best to hamper the completion of the Crystal Palace,' argued Colbeck. 'The explosion was contrived by someone who not only wanted to put the tunnel out of action, he also hoped to delay an exhibition in which the steam locomotive will have pride of place.'

'All I see is wanton damage,' said McTurk, looking around.

'Look for the deeper meaning, Inspector.'

'I've tried. But I'm damned if I can spot it.'

'What happened to the train carrying the glass?' said Leeming.

'I told you, Sergeant. It was late. The driver was a mile or so short of the tunnel when the explosion went off. Must have sounded like an earthquake to him.'

'The noise would have echoed along the whole tunnel.'

'And well beyond,' said McTurk. 'When the driver heard it, he slowed the train immediately. The signalmen at the other end of the tunnel were, in any case, flagging him down.'

'So the sheets of glass were undamaged?'

'They were taken on to London as soon as the line was cleared.'

'Thank you, Inspector McTurk,' said Colbeck, shaking his hand. 'You have been a great help. Forgive us if we rush off. We need to catch the next train back to Euston.'

'Do we?' asked Leeming. 'But we have not seen everything yet.'

'We've seen all that we need to, Victor. The man we are after has just given himself away. I know what he will do next.'

Leaving a bewildered Inspector McTurk in his wake, Colbeck led his companion back towards Crick Station. There was a spring in the Inspector's step. For the first time since the investigation had begun, he felt that he might have the advantage.

It was Gideon Little who told them about the incident. His ostensible reason for calling at the house was to see how Caleb Andrews was faring and to pass on details of the attack on the Kilsby Tunnel. A train on which Little had been the fireman that morning had been as far as Northampton and back. He had picked up all the news. In telling it to Andrews, he was also able to get close to Madeleine once more. She was as alarmed as her father by what she heard.

'Was anyone hurt, Gideon?'

'Only the railway policemen on duty,' said Little, enjoying her proximity. 'They were ambushed and knocked on the head.'

Andrews was rueful. 'I know how *that* feels!'

'Why would anyone damage the tunnel?' asked Madeleine.

'I wish I knew,' said Little. 'It's very worrying. If a train had been coming through at that time, there would have been a terrible crash.'

'Thank heaven that never happened!'

'Railways still have lots of enemies,' said Andrews. 'I'm old enough to remember a time when landowners would do anything to stop us if we tried to go across their property. Boulders on the line, track pulled up, warning fires lit – I saw it all. And it was not just landowners.'

'No,' added Little, mournfully. 'People who ran stage coaches feared that railways might put them out of business. So did canal owners. Then there are those who say we destroy the countryside.'

'We are not destroying it, Gideon. Railways make it possible for people to *see* our beautiful countryside. The many who are stuck in ugly towns all week can take an excursion train on a Sunday and share in the pleasures that the few enjoy. We offer a public service,' Andrews went on with conviction. 'We open up this great country of ours.'

They were in the main bedroom and the driver was resting against some pillows. His arm was still in a sling and his broken leg held fast in a splint. An occasional wince showed that he was still in pain. Pressed for details, Little told him everything that he could about the explosion but his eyes kept straying to Madeleine, hoping to see a sign of affection that never materialised. When it was time for him to go, she showed the visitor to the door but did not linger.

'Goodbye, Madeleine,' said Little.

'Thank you for coming to see Father.'

'It was you that I came to see.'

She forced a smile. 'Goodbye.'

Madeleine closed the door after him then went back upstairs.

'Is there anything I can get you, Father?' she said.

'A pair of crutches.'

'The doctor told you to stay in bed.'

'I'll die of boredom if I'm trapped in here much longer.'

'You've had plenty of visitors,' Madeleine reminded him. 'Frank Pike came yesterday, so did Rose. Today, it was Gideon's turn.'

'He'd be here every day if he had some encouragement.'

She inhaled deeply. 'You know how I feel on that score.'

'Give the lad a chance, Maddy. He dotes on you.'

'Yes,' she said, sadly, 'but I do not dote on Gideon.'

'Your mother didn't exactly dote on me at first,' he confided with a nostalgic sigh, 'but she took me on and – God bless her – she learnt to love me in time. I think I made her happy.'

'You did, Father. She always said that.'

'I miss her terribly but I'm glad that she's not here to see me like this. I feel so *helpless*.' He peered up at her. 'Gideon will be a driver one day, Maddy – just like me. You could do a lot worse.'

'I know that.'

'So why do you give the poor man a cold shoulder?'

'I try to be polite to him.'

'He wants more than politeness.'

'Then he wants more than I am able to offer,' she said.

His voice hardened. 'Gideon is not good enough for you, is that it?'

'No, Father.'

'You think that you are above marrying a railwayman.'

'That's not true at all.'

'I brought you up to respect the railway,' he said with a glint in his eye. 'It served me well enough all these years, Maddy. Your mother was proud of what I did for a living.'

'So am I.'

'Then why are you giving yourself these airs and graces?'

'Father,' she said, trying to remain calm, 'the situation is simple. I do not – and never could – love Gideon Little.'

'You've set your sights higher, have you?'

'Of course not.'

'I'm not blind, Maddy,' he told her. 'Something has happened to you over the past few days and we both know what it is. Run with your own kind, girl,' he urged. 'That's where your future lies. Why look at a man who will always be out of your reach?'

'Please!' she said. 'I don't wish to discuss this any more.'

'I only want to stop you from getting hurt, Maddy.'

'You need rest. I'll leave you alone.'

'Stick to Gideon. He's one of our own. Be honest with yourself,' he said. 'No man in a silk top hat is going to look at you.'

Madeleine could take no more. Her feelings had been hurt and her mind was racing. Holding back tears, she opened the door and went out.

Superintendent Tallis did not even bother to knock. He burst into Colbeck's office in time to find the Inspector poring intently over a copy of the *Illustrated London News*. Colbeck looked up with a dutiful smile.

'Good afternoon, sir,' he said.

'Where have you been, Inspector?'

'To the Kilsby Tunnel and back.'

'I know that,' said Tallis, leaning over the desk at him. 'Why did you not report to me the moment that you got back?'

'I did, Superintendent. You were not in your office.'

'I was in a meeting with the Commissioners.'

'That's why I came back here to do some work.'

'Since when has reading a newspaper been construed as work?'

'Actually,' said Colbeck, turning the paper round so that Tallis could see it, 'I was studying this illustration on the front page. I suggest that you do the same, sir.'

'I do not have time to look at illustrations, Inspector,' rasped the other, ignoring the paper, 'and neither do you. Now what did you learn of value in Northamptonshire?'

'That it really is a charming county. Even Victor was impressed.'

'Did you establish how the tunnel was damaged?'

'I did much more than that.'

'Indeed?'

'I discovered why they chose that particular target. More to the point,' Colbeck announced, 'I believe that I know where they will direct their malign energies next.'

'And where is that, Inspector?'

'At this.' Colbeck tapped the illustration that lay before him. '*The Lord of the Isles*. It's a steam locomotive, sir.'

'I can see that, man.'

'The pride of the Great Western Railway. What more dramatic way to make his point than by destroying this symbol of excellence?'

'Who are you talking about?'

'The man who organised the train robbery and who instigated the attack on the Kilsby Tunnel. If you take a seat, Superintendent,' he said, indicating a chair, 'I will be happy to explain.'

'I wish that somebody would.'

As soon as Tallis sat down, Colbeck told him about the visit to the scene of the latest crime and how he had become convinced of where the next attack would be. Tallis had grave doubts.

'It's a wild guess, Inspector,' he said.

'No, sir. It's a considered judgement, based on what I know of the man and his methods. He is conducting a vendetta against railways.'

'Then why not blow up another tunnel or destroy a bridge?'

'Because he can secure infinitely more publicity at the Crystal Palace. Every newspaper in Britain and several from aboard would report the event. After all, the Exhibition has an international flavour,' said Colbeck. 'The whole civilised world will be looking at it. That is what this man craves most of all, Superintendent – an audience.'

'Why should he pick on the *Lord of the Isles*?'

'Because that will set the standard of locomotive construction for years to come, sir. It repeats the design of Daniel Gooch's *Iron Duke*, built for the Great Western Railway at Swindon. Other locomotives will be on display,' he continued, 'including the famous *Puffing Billy* and the *Liverpool*, designed by Thomas Crampton. Our man may choose one of them instead or create an explosion big enough to destroy all the railway exhibits. Inside a structure like the Crystal Palace, of course, any explosion will have a devastating effect.'

'Only if it were allowed to happen.'

'That is why we must take preventative measures.'

'They are already in hand,' Tallis informed him. 'I attended a first meeting with the Commissioners about security at the Exhibition in November of last year. We recommended that an extra 1,000 police officers were needed.'

'Yes, but only to control the massive crowds that are expected.'

'A moment ago, you mentioned the *Iron Duke*. It may interest you to know that the real Iron Duke, the Duke of

Wellington, advocated a force of 15,000 men. I put forward the notion of swearing in sappers as special constables but it was felt – wrongly, in my opinion – that they would be seen as too militaristic.' He stroked his moustache. 'As an army man, I believe in the power of the uniform.'

'The problem is,' said Colbeck, 'that a uniform gives the game away. It sends out a warning. Besides, Superintendent, you are talking about security arrangements *during* the Exhibition. I think that the attack will be made before it.'

'How have you arrived at that conclusion?'

'By putting myself in the mind of the man we are after.'

'But you do not even know his name.'

'I know his type, sir,' said Colbeck. 'Like you, he was a military man. He understands that he must use surprise to maximum effect and strike at the weakest point. Look at the train robbery,' he suggested. 'The weak points were William Ings and Daniel Slender. Once their loyalty had been breached, the ambush could be laid.'

Superintendent Tallis ruminated. Crossing to the desk, he picked up the paper and looked at the illustration of the *Lord of the Isles*. After a moment, he tossed it down again.

'No,' he decided. 'Simply because there was an explosion in the Kilsby Tunnel, I do not foresee an outrage at the Crystal Palace.'

'What if you are mistaken, sir?'

'That is highly unlikely.'

'But not impossible,' reasoned Colbeck. 'If there *is* some sort of attack on those locomotives, you will be blamed for not taking special precautions when you had been advised to do so. All that I am asking for is a small number of men.'

'To do what?'

'Mount a guard throughout the night. Nobody would be

reckless enough to attempt anything in daylight – there would be far too many people about, helping to set up the exhibits.'

'Are you volunteering to lead this guard detail?'

'Provided that I have a free hand to choose my team.'

'It could be a complete waste of time, Inspector.'

'Then I will be the first to admit that I was wrong,' said Colbeck, firmly. 'If, on the other hand, we do foil an attempt to damage the locomotives, you will be given the credit for anticipating it.'

Tallis needed a few minutes to think it over. Inclined to dismiss the idea as fanciful, he feared the consequences if the Inspector were proved right. Robert Colbeck had a habit of coming up with strange proposals that somehow, against all the odds, bore fruit. A man who was ready to endure sleepless nights at the Crystal Palace had to be driven by a deep inner conviction. After meditation, Tallis elected to trust in it.

'Very well, Inspector,' he said. 'Take the necessary steps.'

Thomas Sholto had known him for several years. Educated at the same school, they had been commissioned in the same regiment and served together in India. For all that, he could still be amazed at the dedication that Sir Humphrey Gilzean brought to any project. It was in evidence again when they met that morning to discuss their latest scheme. A large round mahogany table stood in the library at Gilzean's house. Sholto was astounded to see what was lying on it. As well as a detailed floor plan of the Crystal Palace, there was a copy of the *Official Catalogue* for the Great Exhibition.

'How on earth did you get hold of these?' asked Sholto.

'By a combination of money and persuasion,' replied Gilzean, picking up the catalogue. 'This is the first of five parts but the printers only have this one ready for the opening ceremony on May Day. Did you know that there are over 100,000 separate items on show, sent in from all over the world by individual and corporate exhibitors?'

'Prince Albert wants it to be a truly unforgettable event.'

'We will make sure that it is, Thomas.' He put the catalogue down and scrutinised the plan. 'Everything on show is divided into four different classes – Raw Materials, Machinery, Manufactures and Fine Arts.'

'Any mention of the British Army? That's what made the Empire.'

'Only a display of Military Engineering and Ordnance.'

'No bands, no parades, no demonstrations of military skills?'

'No, Thomas. The emphasis is on industry in all its forms.' He drew back his lips in a sneer. 'Including the railways.'

'Where are the locomotives housed, Humphrey?'

'Here,' said Gilzean, indicating a section of the ground floor plan. 'What we are after is in an area devoted to Machinery for Direct Use.'

'On the north side,' observed Sholto. 'It should not be difficult to gain access there. I took the trouble to have a preliminary look at the Crystal Palace when I accosted Lord Holcroft in Hyde Park. It is a vast cathedral of glass that looks like nothing so much as a giant conservatory. But, then, what else should one expect of a man like Joseph Paxton who is a landscape gardener?'

'As far as I am concerned, Thomas, his notoriety lies elsewhere.'

'Yes, Humphrey. He is a director of the Midland Railway.'

'Had he not been,' said Gilzean scornfully, 'he might never have been employed to design that monstrous edifice. I am told, on good authority, that Joseph Paxton came down to the House of Commons last year for a meeting with Mr John

Ellis, Member of Parliament and chairman of the Midland Railway, a ghastly individual with whom I've crossed swords more than once in the Chamber.'

'Yes, Humphrey. I recall how you opposed his Railway Bill.'

'It was a matter of honour. To return to Paxton,' he said. 'When our landscape gardener discovered how poor the acoustics were in the House of Commons, he decried the architect, Mr Barry. He then went on to say that those designing the hall for the Great Exhibition would also botch the job – even though he had not seen their plans.'

'Mr Paxton is an arrogant man, by the sound of it.'

'Arrogant?' said Gilzean, scornfully. 'The fellow has a conceit to rival Narcissus. At a meeting of the board of his railway company, he had the gall to sketch his idea for the building on a piece of blotting paper. That, Thomas, is how this Crystal Palace came into being.'

'On a piece of blotting paper?'

'The design was shown to Ellis, who passed it on to someone in authority and, the next thing you know, Paxton is invited to submit a plan and an estimate of its cost. To cap it all,' said Gilzean through gritted teeth, 'he is given an audience with Prince Albert himself. His Royal Highness was not the only one to approve of the design. Paxton managed to win the support of no less a personage than Robert Stephenson.' He arched an imperious eyebrow. 'The two of them met – appropriately enough – during a train journey to London.'

'The railway has a lot to answer for, Humphrey.'

'More than you know,' returned the other. 'In the early days, when we were doing our best to oppose the scheme, it looked as if the Great Exhibition might not even take place.

It was dogged by all sorts of financial problems. Then in steps Mr Peto, the railway contractor, and offers to act as guarantor for the building by putting down £50,000. Once he had led the way,' said Gilzean, 'others quickly followed. Mr Peto also put his weight behind the choice of Paxton as the architect.'

'At every stage,' noted Sholto, 'crucial decisions have been made by those connected with the railways. You can see how they stand to reap the benefit. When the Exhibition opens, excursion trains will run from all over the country. Railway companies will make immense profits.'

'Not if I can help it, Thomas.'

'The men are in readiness.'

'They had better not repeat their failure at the Kilsby Tunnel.'

'After what you said to them, Humphrey, they would not dare. They are still shaking. You put the fear of God into them.'

'They deserved it.'

'I agree,' said Sholto. 'Have you chosen the day yet?'

'Thursday next.'

'I'll give them their orders.'

'No, Thomas,' said Gilzean, folding up the floor plan, 'I'll do that myself. I intend to be at my town house in London this week. I want to hear those locomotives being blown apart.'

'They'll take a large part of the Crystal Palace with them. That glass is very fragile. It will shatter into millions of shards.' Sholto laughed harshly. 'A pity that it will happen in darkness – it should be a wondrous sight. Farewell to the Great Exhibition!'

'Farewell to the *Lord of the Isles* and all those other

locomotives,' said Gilzean, bitterly. I'll never forgive the railways for what they did to me. My ambition is to act as a scourge to the whole damnable industry.'

The meeting was not accidental. As she came out of the shop, Madeleine Andrews was confronted by Gideon Little, who pretended that he was about to go in. Since he lived half a mile away, and had several shops in the vicinity of his house, there was no need for him to be in Camden at all. After greeting Madeleine, he invented an excuse.

'I thought of calling on your father again,' he said, diffidently.

'He is asleep, Gideon. It is not a good time to visit.'

'Then I'll come another time.'

'Father is always pleased to see you.'

'What about you, Madeleine?'

'I, too, am pleased,' she said, briskly. 'I believe that any friend of Father's is welcome at our house, especially if he is a railwayman.'

'I am not talking about Caleb,' he said, quietly.

'I know.'

'Then why do you not answer my question?'

There was a long and uncomfortable pause. When she walked to the end of the street to buy some provisions, Madeleine had not expected to be cornered by a man whose devotion to her had reached almost embarrassing proportions. She had tried, in the past, to discourage him as gently as she could, but Gideon Little had a keen ally in her father and a quiet tenacity that drove him on past all her of rebuffs. Madeleine had the uneasy feeling that he had been lurking outside the house in case she came out.

'Why are you not at work?' she asked.

'I was on the early shift today.'

'Then you must be very tired.'

'Not when I have a chance to see you, Madeleine.' He offered a hand. 'Let me carry your bag for you.'

'No, thank you. I can manage.'

He was hurt. 'Will you not even let me do that?'

'I have to go, Gideon.'

'No,' he said, stepping sideways to block her path, 'you have walked away from me once too often, Madeleine, and it has to stop. I think it's time you gave me an answer.'

'You *know* the answer,' she said, seeing the mingled hope and determination in his eyes. 'Do I really have to put it in words?'

'Yes.'

'Gideon—'

'At the very least, I deserve that. It's been two years now,' he told her. 'Two years of waiting, wanting, making plans for the two of us.'

'They were *your* plans – not ours.'

'Will you not even listen to what they are?'

'No,' she said with polite firmness. 'There would be no point.'

'Why are you so unkind to me? Do you hate me that much?'

'Of course not, Gideon. I like you. I always have. But the plain truth is – and you must surely realise this by now – that I can never see you as anything more than a friend.'

'*Never*?' he pleaded.

'Never, Gideon.'

Madeleine did not want to be so blunt with him but she had been left with no choice. Her father's condition gave Gideon Little an opportunity to call at the house on a regular basis, and he would try to urge his suit each time. The prospect dismayed

Madeleine. It was better to risk offending him now than to let him harry her and build up his expectations. Wounded by her rejection, Little stared at her in disbelief, as if she had just thrust a dagger into him. His pain slowly gave way to a deep resentment.

'You were not always so cruel to me, Madeleine,' he said.

'You asked for the truth.'

'We were real friends once.'

'We still are, Gideon.'

'No,' he said, glaring at her. 'Since Caleb was injured, something has changed. You no longer have any interest in me. A fireman on the railway is beneath you now.'

'Let me go past, please.'

'Not until we settle this. You've met someone else, Madeleine.'

'I have to get back.'

'Someone you think is better than me. Don't lie,' he said, holding up a hand before she could issue a denial. 'Your father has noticed it and so have I. When you went to see Inspector Colbeck for the second time, I followed you. I saw the way you looked at him.'

Madeleine was furious. 'You *followed* me?'

'I knew that you wanted to see him again.'

'You had no right to do that.'

'Caleb told me how you behaved when the Inspector came to the house. He said that you put your best dress on for him. You never did that for me, Madeleine.'

'This has gone far enough, Gideon,' she asserted. 'Following me? That's dreadful. How could you do such a thing?'

'I wanted to see where you were going.'

'What I do and where I go is my business. The only reason I spoke to Inspector Colbeck again is that he is investigating the train robbery in which Father was injured.'

'Yet you never even mentioned it to Caleb,' said Gideon, hands on his hips. 'When I asked him if you had been back to Whitehall, he shook his head. Why did you mislead him, Madeleine?'

'Never you mind,' she said, flustered.

'But I do mind. This means a lot to me.'

Madeleine tried to move. 'Father will be expecting me.'

'You told me that he was asleep.'

'I want to be there when he wakes up.'

'Why?' he challenged, obstructing her path. 'Are you going to admit that you went out of your way to see Inspector Colbeck again because you like him so much?'

'No,' she retorted. 'I am going to tell him that I do not want you in the house again. I'm ashamed of you for what you did, Gideon.' She brushed past him. 'I will not be spied on by anyone.'

'Madeleine!' he cried, suddenly penitent.

'Leave me be.'

'I did not mean to upset you like that.'

But she was deaf to his entreaties. Hurrying along the pavement, she reached her house, let herself in and closed the door firmly behind her. Gideon Little had no doubt what she felt about him now.

On the third night, Victor Leeming's faith in the Inspector began to weaken slightly. It was well past midnight at the Crystal Palace and there had been neither sight nor sound of any intruders. Leeming feared that they were about to have another long and uneventful vigil.

'Are you sure that they will come, sir?' he whispered.

'Sooner or later,' replied Colbeck.

'Let someone else take over from us.'

'Do you want to miss all the excitement, Victor?'

'There's been precious little of that so far, Inspector. We've had two nights of tedium and, since the place is in darkness, we cannot even divert ourselves by looking at the exhibits. Also,' he complained, shifting his position, 'it is so uncomfortable here.'

Colbeck grinned. 'I did not have time to instal four-poster beds.'

The detectives were in one of the massive exhibition halls, concealed behind *Liverpool*, a standard gauge locomotive designed for the London and North Western Railway by Thomas Crampton. Built for high speed, it had eight foot driving wheels and an unprecedentedly large heating surface. Having learnt its specifications, Colbeck had passed them to Leeming in the course of the first night, trying in vain to interest his Sergeant in the facts that the boiler pressure was 120 per square inch and that the cylinders were 18 by 24 inches. All that Leeming wanted was to be at home in bed with his wife, whose total ignorance of locomotives he now saw as a marital blessing.

'I think that *Liverpool* has a chance of winning a gold medal,' said Colbeck, giving the engine a friendly pat. 'That would really annoy Daniel Gooch at the Great Western.'

'I think that *we* deserve a gold medal for keeping watch like this,' said Leeming, yawning involuntarily. 'Mr Tallis had a feeling that we'd be chasing shadows.'

'Try to get some sleep, Victor.'

'On a floor as hard as this?'

'In any surveillance operation, you have to make the best of the conditions that you are given. We are, after all, indoors,' said Colbeck. 'Would you rather be outside in all that drizzle?'

'No, Inspector.'

'Then cheer up a little. We could be on the brink of an arrest.'

'Then again,' said Leeming under his breath, 'we could not.'

'Go on, Victor. Put your head down.'

'There's no point.'

'Yes, there is. You need some sleep.'

'What about you, Inspector?'

'I prefer to stay on duty. If anything happens, I'll wake you.'

'And if nothing happens?'

'In that case,' said Colbeck, beaming, 'you'll be able to tell your grandchildren that you once slept beneath one of the finest locomotives of its day. Good night, Victor. Remember not to snore.'

There were three of them. Having studied the plan that had been obtained for them by Sir Humphrey Gilzean, they were familiar with the layout of the Great Exhibition. Their leader, Arthur Jukes, a big bulky man in his thirties with ginger whiskers, had taken the precaution of visiting the site on the previous night to reconnoitre the area and to look for potential hazards. They were few in number. Security was light and the guards who patrolled the exterior of the Crystal Palace could be easily evaded. As he and his companions crouched in their hiding place, Jukes had no qualms about the success of the operation.

'We should've done it last night,' said Harry Seymour, the youngest of the three. 'When it wasn't so bleeding wet.'

'This drizzle will help us, Harry. It will put the guards off. They'll want to stay in the dry with a pipe of baccy.'

'So would I, Arthur.'

'You ready to tell that to Sir Humphrey?'

Seymour trembled. 'Not me!'

'Nor me,' said his brother, Vernon, the third of the men. 'It was bad enough facing Tom Sholto after that mishap at the Kilsby Tunnel. But Sir Humphrey was far worse,' he recalled with a grimace. 'I thought he was going to horsewhip us.'

'He'll do more than that if we fail,' said Harry Seymour.

Jukes was confident. 'No chance of that,' he boasted, looking to see of the coast was clear. 'Are you ready, lads?'

'Ready,' said the brothers in unison.

'Then let's go.'

Keeping low and moving swiftly, Jukes headed for the entrance to the north transept. Harry and Vernon Seymour followed him, carrying a barrel of gunpowder between them in a large canvas bag with rope handles. The three of them reached the door without being seen. Jukes had brought a lamp with him and he used it to illumine the lock so that he could work away at it with his tools. In less than a minute, it clicked open and he eased the door back on its hinges. The three of them went quickly inside. Jukes immediately closed the metal cover on the lamp so that the flame would not be reflected in the vast acreage of glass that surrounded them. Having memorised the floor plan, he knew exactly where to go.

Shutting the door behind them, they paused to take their bearings. In the gloom of the transept, everything was seen in ghostly outline. High above them, under a film of drizzle, was the magnificent arched roof of the transept, so tall that it allowed trees to continue growing beneath it, thereby providing an outdoor element in an essentially indoor space. Ahead of them, they knew, was the refreshment court, and beyond that, heard but not seen, was the first of the fountains that had been built. Harry Seymour remembered something else he had seen on the plan.

'We go past the exhibits from India,' he noted.

'So what?' said his brother.

'We could look at that stuffed elephant they got.'

'I saw enough real ones when we was over there, Harry.'

'So did I,' added Jukes, 'and we're not here to admire the place. We got orders. Let's obey them and be quick about it.'

Followed by the two brothers, he swung to the right and took a pathway that led between statues, exhibits and the forest of iron pillars that supported the structure. They did not even pause beside the stuffed elephant with its opulent howdah. Their interest was in the section devoted to Railways and Steam. It was in between an area set aside for Machinery in Motion and one shared by Printing and French Machinery, and Models and Naval Architecture. By the time that the shape of the first locomotive emerged from the darkness, all three of them were feeling a rush of exhilaration. They were about to earn a lot of money.

After peering at the various exhibits, Jukes stood beside one of the biggest on display and ran a hand over it. He was satisfied.

'This is the one,' he declared.

'How do you know?' asked Harry Seymour.

'Because I can feel the name with my fingers. This is the *Lord of the Isles*. Put that gunpowder underneath her, lads, then we'll blow her to smithereens.'

'Let *me* light the fuse this time, Arthur.'

'Nobody is lighting any fuse,' shouted Colbeck.

'Not when I'm in here, at any rate,' said Brendan Mulryne, popping up in the tender and vaulting to the ground. 'Now which one of you bastards was ready to send me to my Maker?'

Colbeck marched towards them. 'All three of you are under arrest,' he said with Victor Leeming at his side. 'Handcuff them, Sergeant.'

'Yes, Inspector.'

But the three men were not going to surrender easily. Swinging the barrel between them, the Seymour Brothers hurled it at Mulryne but he caught it as if it were as light as a feather. He was thrilled that the men were ready to fight. With a roar of delight, he put the barrel down, jumped forward, grabbed them both by their throats and flung them hard against the side of the locomotive. When they tried to strike back, Mulryne hit them in turn with heavy punches that sent them to their knees. Leeming stepped in quickly to handcuff the two captives.

Jukes, meanwhile, had opted to run for it, blundering his way into an area where visitors to the exhibition would be able to see machines in action as they spun flax and silk or made lace. Colbeck went after him. Although he was armed with a pistol, he did not wish to risk firing it inside the glass structure in case it caused damage. Jukes was fast but he was in unknown territory. Colbeck, on the other hand, had visited the Crystal Palace in daylight and had some idea of where the exhibits were placed. While one man collided with heavy items, the other was able to avoid them.

He overhauled Jukes by the rope-making machine, tackling him around the legs to bring him crashing to the ground. Swearing volubly, Jukes kicked him away and tried to get to his feet, but Colbeck tripped him up again before flinging himself on top of the man. They grappled fiercely for a couple of minutes, each inflicting injuries on the other. With an upsurge of energy, Colbeck was eventually able to get in some telling punches to subdue his man. Bloodied and dazed, Jukes put up both hands to protect his face from further punishment.

Colbeck snapped a pair of handcuffs on his wrists before getting up. Mulryne came lumbering out of the darkness to join them. When he saw Jukes on the floor, he was disappointed.

'Why didn't you leave a piece of him for *me*, Inspector?' he said.

CHAPTER TEN

Within the ranks of the Metropolitan Police Force, Richard Mayne had acquired an almost legendary status. A surprise appointment as Joint Commissioner when the force was founded in 1829, he had worked tirelessly to develop effective policing of the capital, and with his colleague, Colonel Charles Rowan, had tried to make London a safer place for its citizens. Since the retirement of Colonel Rowan in the previous year, Mayne had become Senior Commissioner and, as such, made all the important executive decisions.

In the normal course of events, Robert Colbeck had little direct contact with him but, in the wake of the Inspector's success at the Crystal Palace, Mayne insisted on congratulating him in person. First thing that morning, therefore, Colbeck was summoned to his office along with Superintendent Edward Tallis who, in spite of a tinge of envy, emphasised that the idea of setting a trap at the Great Exhibition had come originally from Colbeck.

'Well done, Inspector,' said Mayne, shaking Colbeck's hand.

'Thank you, sir.'

'Both you and your men performed a splendid service.'

'We could not have done so without the active support of the Superintendent,' said Colbeck, indicating Tallis. 'He should have some share of the glory.'

'Indeed, he should.'

He gave Tallis a nod of gratitude and the latter responded with a half-smile. Turning back to Colbeck, the Commissioner appraised the elegant Inspector.

'I trust that you did not dress like that last night,' he said.

'No, sir,' replied Colbeck. 'I would never risk creasing my frock coat or scuffing my trousers in a situation of that kind. More practical clothing was needed. I had a feeling that some violence might occur.'

'Yet only three of you were on duty.'

'I reasoned that we would only have to deal with a few men. That is all it would have taken to set up the explosion. Besides, the less of us, the easier it was to conceal ourselves.'

'I have read your report of the incident,' said Mayne, 'and found it admirably thorough, if unduly modest. Why not tell us what *really* happened, Inspector?'

Clearing his throat, Colbeck gave him a full account of how the arrests were made, praising the work of his two assistants while saying little about his own involvement. The bruising on his face and the bandaging around the knuckles of one hand told a different story. Mayne was enthralled. Irish by extraction, he was a handsome man in his mid-fifties with long wavy hair, all but encircling his face, and searching eyes. As the person in charge of the special police division, raised to take care of security at the Crystal Palace, he had a particular interest in the events of the previous night. Thanks to Colbeck and his men, the reputation of the Metropolitan Police Force had been saved.

'Had they succeeded,' observed Mayne, drily, 'the results

would have been quite horrific. You saved the Great Exhibition from utter destruction, Inspector Colbeck. The very least that you may expect is a letter from Prince Albert.'

'With respect, sir,' said Colbeck, 'I would rather His Royal Highness stayed his hand until this investigation is over. All that we have in custody are three members of a much larger gang. Its leader remains at large and, until he is caught, we must stay on the alert.'

'Have these villains not disclosed his identity?'

'No, sir. They are very loyal to him.'

'Army men, all three of them,' said Tallis, eyebrows twitching in disapproval. 'It shocked me that anyone who had borne arms for this country should lower himself to such an unpatriotic action as this.'

'It is disturbing,' agreed Mayne.

'The Exhibition has the stamp of royalty upon it. To threaten it in this way is, in my book, tantamount to an act of treason. Left to me, they would be prosecuted accordingly.'

'The court will decide their fate, Superintendent.'

'The gravity of this crime must not be underestimated.'

'It will not be, I can assure you of that.'

'If you want my opinion—'

'Another time,' said Mayne, interrupting him with a raised hand. 'Would you mind leaving us alone for a few moments, please?' he asked. 'I'd value a few words in private with Inspector Colbeck.'

'Oh, I see,' said Tallis, discomfited by the request.

'Thank you, Superintendent.'

Tallis paused at the door. 'I'll want to see you in my office later on, Inspector,' he warned.

'Yes, sir,' said Colbeck.

Tallis went out and closed the door behind him. Mayne sat

down behind his desk and waved Colbeck to a chair opposite him. Now that the two men were alone, the mood became less formal.

'The Superintendent is a typical army man,' observed Mayne, 'and I say that in no spirit of criticism. Colonel Rowan was another fine example of the breed. He had a wonderful capacity for organisation.'

'So does the Superintendent, sir,' said Colbeck, giving credit where it was due. 'And unlike Colonel Rowan, he does not insist on retaining his army rank. He chooses to be plain Mister instead of Major Tallis.'

Mayne smiled. 'He will always be Major Tallis to me,' he said, wryly. 'But enough of him, Inspector – tell me a little about yourself.'

'You have my police record in front of you, sir.'

'I am more interested in your life before you joined us. Like me, I believe, you trained as a lawyer. Were you called to the bar?'

'Yes, sir.'

'Why did you not pursue that career? I should imagine that you cut quite a figure in a courtroom.'

'Personal circumstances had a bearing on my decision to turn my talents elsewhere,' explained Colbeck, not wishing to provide any details. 'In any case, I found the life of a barrister far less fulfilling than I imagined it would be.'

'I had the same experience, Inspector. Unless one is successful, it can be an impecunious profession.'

'Money was not that issue in my case, sir. I was disillusioned because I was always dealing with crime after the event, and it seemed to me that, with sensible policing, so much of it could have been prevented from happening in the first place.'

'Prevention is ever our watchword.'

'It's the main reason that I joined the Metropolitan Police Force.'

'You were far more educated than our average recruit.'

'Educated in criminal law, perhaps,' said Colbeck, 'but I had a lot to learn about the criminal mind. One can only do that by pitting oneself against it on a daily basis.'

'Judging by your record, you were an apt pupil.'

'I was fortunate enough to secure an early promotion.'

'It is we who are fortunate to have you,' said Mayne, glancing down at the open file on his desk. 'Though your service record has not been without its minor setbacks.'

'I prefer to see them as my idiosyncrasies, sir.'

'That's not what Superintendent Tallis calls them. He has had to reprimand you more than once. This time, of course,' he went on, closing the file, 'he will have nothing but praise for you.'

'I am not sure about that.'

'You are the hero of the hour, Inspector Colbeck.'

'There were three of us involved in that surveillance, sir.'

'I am well aware of that.'

'What you may not be aware of is the means by which Brendan Mulryne came to be on the scene. Sergeant Leeming had a perfect right to be there,' said Colbeck, 'but there is a slight problem where Mulryne is concerned. To that end, I wonder if I might ask you a favour?'

'Please do,' said Mayne, expansively. 'After your achievements last night, you are in a position to ask anything.'

'Thank you, sir. The truth is that I need your help.'

After making discreet inquiries, Thomas Sholto repaired immediately to Sir Humphrey Gilzean's house. He steeled himself to break the bad news. Ashen with cold fury, Gilzean had already anticipated it.

'They failed,' he said.

'Yes, Humphrey.'

'They let me down again.'

'Not for want of trying.'

'With all that gunpowder, they could not even contrive a small explosion. I lay awake in bed, listening – and nothing happened.'

'That's not quite true.'

Gilzean stamped a foot. 'They'll wish they'd never been born!'

'You would never get close enough to chastise them,' said Sholto. 'The tidings are worse than you feared. Jukes and the Seymour brothers walked into an ambush at the Crystal Palace.'

'An ambush?'

'All three are taken, Humphrey.'

'What!' exclaimed Gilzean.

'They are in police custody. From what I can gather, this Inspector Colbeck laid a trap for them and they walked into it.'

'But how could he possibly know that they would be there?'

'I think that he is much cleverer than we imagined.'

Gilzean's fury changed to concern. Dropping into a high-backed leather armchair, he became pensive. The house was in Upper Brook Street, close enough to Hyde Park for him to hear any explosion that occurred in the Crystal Palace. Long before dawn had broken, he realised that the mission had been unsuccessful but it had never crossed his mind that his men had been arrested.

'We have one comfort,' said Sholto. 'They will not betray us.'

'They have already done so, Thomas.'

'How?'

'By getting themselves caught,' said Gilzean. 'If this Inspector is clever enough to apprehend them, it will not take him long to find out that all three served in our regiment. That will set him on a trail that leads directly to us.'

'Perhaps we should quit London and go into hiding.'

'No, Thomas. There is no danger yet.'

'But there soon will be.'

'Only if we let things take their natural course.'

'What else can we do, Humphrey?'

'Divert them,' said Gilzean, getting to his feet. 'At every stage, we have relied on the slowness and inefficiency of the police. We have out-manoeuvred them with comparative ease. Until now, that is. It seems that we underestimated them, Thomas. They have one man within their ranks who has a keen intelligence.'

'Inspector Robert Colbeck.'

'What do we know about him?'

'Only what we have read in the newspaper.'

'Find out more,' said Gilzean. 'We need to identify his weakness. Is he married? Does he have children? Who are the loved ones in his life? If we have that information in our hands, we can distract him from his investigation and buy ourselves some valuable time.'

'Supposing that he is a bachelor with no family ties?'

'Every man has someone he cares about,' insisted Gilzean, dark eyes gleaming. 'All you have to do is to find out who it is.'

Madeleine Andrews was pleased when the visitor arrived. Still in his working clothes, Frank Pike had called on his way home from Euston Station and he had brought plenty of gossip to share with his friend. After all this time, the fireman was still blaming himself for the injury to Caleb Andrews and he began with another battery of apologies. Madeleine hoped to leave the two men alone in the bedroom, but her father decided to use Pike as a court of appeal.

'What do *you* think, Frank?' he asked.

'About what?'

'Gideon Little.'

'I think he'll be a driver before I am,' said Pike, honestly. 'Gideon may be younger than me but he learns faster. I think that he's one of the best fireman in the company.'

'There you are, Maddy,' said Andrews, pointedly.

'I never doubted his abilities,' she replied.

'Gideon has a bright future ahead of him. All that he needs is a loving wife to support and cherish him.'

Pike grinned. 'Is there an engagement in the wind?' he asked.

'No,' said Madeleine.

'Not yet, anyway,' said Andrews.

'Father!'

'You may come to your senses in the end, Maddy.'

'It would make Gideon the happiest man on the railway,' said Pike, 'I know that. He never stops talking about you, Madeleine. Some of the others tease him about it.'

She was roused. 'So my name is taken in vain, is it?'

'No, no.'

'You and the others are having a laugh at my expense.'

'I'd never do that, Madeleine,' said Pike, overcome with remorse, 'and I'm sorry if I gave you that idea. No,' he went on, 'I promise you that nobody would dare to mock you.'

'They'd have me to answer to, if they did,' said Andrews.

'Gideon is the only one they tease.'

'Yes,' she said. 'About me.'

'About . . . being the way that he is.'

'Besotted with my daughter,' observed Andrews. 'You cannot stay single for ever, Maddy. Choose the right person and marriage is the most wonderful institution ever invented. Am I right, Frank?'

'Yes, Caleb.'

'Do you wish that you were still a bachelor?'

'Not for a moment,' said Pike, chuckling merrily. 'Rose has made me very happy and she seems to be content with me.'

Andrews cackled. 'Heaven knows why!'

'Getting married changed my life for the better.'

'You hear that, Maddy?'

'I can recommend it,' said Pike.

'So can I,' said Andrews. 'How much longer do we have to wait?'

Madeleine did not trust herself to reply. She was fond of Frank Pike and did not wish to have a quarrel with her father in front of him. More to the point, she did not want to deal with an issue that, as far as she was concerned, had finally been settled. Hounded for a decision, Madeleine had told Gideon Little the painful truth. What she had not admitted was that her affections had been placed elsewhere. For a woman like her, Robert Colbeck might be unobtainable but that only served to increase his attraction.

'I'll make some tea,' she said, and went out abruptly.

Since a window had been opened to admit fresh air, the office was free from the stink of cigar smoke for once yet the atmosphere remained unpleasant. Superintendent Edward Tallis was spoiling for a fight. He stood inches away from Inspector Colbeck.

'Whatever did you think you were *doing*?' he yelled.

'Taking the necessary steps to achieve an objective, sir.'

'Brendan Mulryne was supposed to be in custody.'

'Arrangements were made,' said Colbeck.

'What sort of arrangements?'

'I looked more closely at the charges against him, Superintendent. There are several witnesses at The Black Dog in the Devil's Acre, who will swear that Mulryne did not start the affray. He was not even there when it flared up. Mulryne is paid to quell such outbursts. Those he knocked out during the brawl certainly have no complaint against him. They made the mistake of taking on a stronger man. As for the damage he caused to a window,' he revealed, 'nobody is prepared to bring a charge against him on that account.'

'That Irish gorilla assaulted four policemen,' said Tallis.

'Only because they provoked him, sir,' replied Colbeck, 'and they now admit that. I spoke to the custody sergeant. Since he's been behind bars, Mulryne has been a model prisoner. He's even made his peace with the four men who tried to arrest him.'

'Turning on that blarney of his no doubt!'

'Mulryne was one of them, remember. In his heart, I suspect, he would still like to be.'

'Not as long as I have anything to say about it!'

'I raised the matter with Mr Mayne earlier on.'

Tallis was horrified. 'You tried to get Mulryne reinstated?'

'No,' said Colbeck, 'that would have been asking too much, and in any case, it's too late for that. No, Superintendent, I wanted to discuss a point of law with him.'

'When it comes to law, you only need to know one thing with regard to Brendan Mulryne. He's on the wrong side of it.'

'Technically, he's not.'

'He resisted arrest.'

'The four officers involved see it rather differently now.'

'They cannot change their minds about a thing like that.'

'According to Mr Mayne,' said Colbeck, levelly, 'they can. If, on mature reflection, they feel that their report of the incident was slightly inaccurate, they can amend it when they give their statements in court. Like me, Mr Mayne agreed that Mulryne should get off with a small fine.'

'A small fine!' roared Tallis.

'I will be happy to pay it on his behalf.'

'Inspector, he attacked four policemen.'

'I prefer to remember the two villains whom he took on last night, sir. Both were armed but Mulryne squared up to them nevertheless. All that Sergeant Leeming had to do was to snap on the handcuffs.'

'Mulryne had no right to be there in the first place.'

'You said that I had a free hand to choose my men.'

'I assumed they would be from inside the police force.'

'Nobody else could have done what Mulryne did last night.'

'That does not exonerate him, Inspector,' said Tallis, sourly. 'Or you, for that matter.'

Colbeck met his glare. 'Mr Mayne felt that it did, sir,' he pointed out, calmly. 'Since you feel so strongly about it, perhaps you should take it up with him.'

Tallis was halted in his tracks. Whatever else he did, he could not countermand the orders of his superior. Colbeck not only had the Police Commissioner on his side, he had, by effecting the three arrests at the Crystal Palace, earned the admiration of the whole department. A vital breakthrough had at last been made in the investigation. To harry him after such a triumph would be seen as sheer vindictiveness. Tallis retreated to the safety of his desk and took out a cigar from its case. Inhaling deeply as he ignited it, he watched Colbeck through the smoke.

'I will remember this, Inspector,' he said, sternly.

'It is all a matter of record, Superintendent.'

'What do you intend to do now?'

'Question the three men in custody,' said Colbeck. 'They may not give us the name that we want but we can still squeeze some information out of them. Arthur Jukes is their leader. I'll start with him. To be frank, I hoped that you might join me, sir.'

'Me?'

'You know how to speak to an army man.'

'That's true,' said Tallis, slightly mollified, 'though all three of them are a disgrace to their regiment. If they were still in uniform, they'd be court-martialled.'

'Make that point to them,' advised Colbeck. 'If I introduce you as Major Tallis, it will increase your authority. Do you agree, sir?'

Tallis straightened his back. 'Yes, Inspector. I think that I do.'

'And we will need the services of an artist.'

'An artist?'

'To draw sketches of the three men,' explained Colbeck. 'I want to see if Caleb Andrews recognises any of them. Since he is unable to come here to identify the prisoners, we will have to take a likeness of them to him. He might pick out the man who assaulted him.'

'The fireman can do that – what was his name?'

'Frank Pike.'

'Arrange for him to call here.'

'I will, sir,' said Colbeck, smoothly, 'but I think that Mr Andrews is entitled to have a first look at these three men. After all, he was the real victim.'

'True enough.'

'He also deserves to know that we have taken such an important step forward in the investigation. When we finish questioning the prisoners, I'll go across to Camden to apprise him of the situation. I have more than one reason for wishing to see him,' he added, thinking of Madeleine. 'Please put an artist to work as soon as you can.'

Thomas Sholto moved swiftly. In the space of a few hours, he had gathered sufficient information about Robert Colbeck to take back to the house in Upper Brook Street. Sir Humphrey Gilzean was waiting for him. When his manservant showed the visitor into the drawing room, Gilzean got to his feet with urgency.

'Well?' he said.

'I arrived just in time, Humphrey.'

'In what way?'

'When I got to Scotland Yard, there was a crowd of reporters waiting to hear details of the arrests. I mingled with them.'

'Did you get inside?'

'Yes,' said Sholto, 'I pretended that I worked for a provincial newspaper. Nobody paid any attention to me, tucked away at the back.'

'Who gave the statement? Inspector Colbeck?'

'No, it was Superintendent Tallis. A military man, by the look of him. He introduced us to the Inspector but would not let him answer any questions. Tallis has taken some severe criticism in the press,' explained Sholto. 'He wanted to make sure that he was seen in a better light this time. That's why he stole all the attention.'

'So what exactly *did* take place at the Crystal Palace last night?'

'Three men lay in wait near the locomotives. When Jukes and the others gained entry, they were promptly arrested.'

'Three against three? Why did they not fight their way out?'

'They tried, Humphrey, but they were soon overpowered.'

'Inspector Colbeck is a brave man,' said Gilzean, 'but he took a foolish risk when he fought on equal terms. He is obviously no soldier or he would have had a dozen policemen at his back.'

'Nevertheless, he got the better of Jukes and the Seymours.'

'How on earth did he come to be there in the first place? Was it a complete coincidence or a case of inspired guesswork?'

'Neither,' replied Sholto. 'According to the Superintendent, they realised that the shipment of glass for the Great Exhibition was the intended target of the Kilsby Tunnel explosion. That led them on – at least, it led Inspector Colbeck on – to the conviction that the locomotives on display at the Crystal Palace were in potential danger. Last night was the third during which he kept vigil.'

'A patient man, clearly.'

'And a powerful one. It seems that he tackled Arthur Jukes on his own and beat him into submission – even though he had to take a few blows himself.'

'Jukes is a tough character. He would have fought like a tiger.'

'The tiger has now been caged.'

Gilzean nodded soulfully. It had given him pleasure to organise the train robbery, to inflict damage on a railway company and to outwit the detectives who were put in charge of the case. The murders of William Ings and Daniel Slender had been necessities rather than sources of enjoyment, though they had also been carried out in order to muddy the waters of the investigation. Someone, it now transpired, was able to see clearly through muddy waters and it was troubling.

'What manner of man is this Robert Colbeck?' he asked.

'A positive dandy.'

'Yet able to acquit himself well in a fight.'

'I'd not like to take him on, Humphrey.'

Sholto went on to give of description of Colbeck's appearance and behaviour. Since the Inspector was clearly known to the other reporters, Sholto had taken the trouble to talk to as many of them as possible, picking up all kinds of anecdotes about Colbeck. He retailed them to Gilzean, who assimilated all the facts he had been given.

'Tall, handsome, single,' he noted. 'He must be a ladies' man.'

'Apparently not.'

Gilzean was curious. 'Are you telling me that he seeks exclusively *male* company?'

'No,' said Sholto. 'I would never accuse him of that.'

'Then he must have a social life of some kind.'

'One of the reporters told me that Colbeck is something of a mystery. He trained as a lawyer, went to the bar, then, for some inexplicable reason, chose to become a policeman.'

'There's no such thing as an inexplicable reason, Thomas. A man would only make such a radical change of direction if he were prompted by just cause. It would help us if we knew what it was.'

'There was one rumour.'

'Go on.'

'Someone told me that there had been an incident in his past,' said Sholto, 'involving a broken engagement.'

'Now we are getting somewhere!'

'It was some years ago, apparently.'

'Who was the lady in question?'

'I did not get a name.'

'See if you can discover what it is, Thomas,' said Gilzean. 'We may be able to use it as a lever. Inspector Robert Colbeck must have some human contact, surely. No parents still alive, no brothers or sisters, no close friends – I do not believe it. There has to be *someone*.'

'How can we find out?'

'By having him followed.'

'That will not be easy.'

'He does not spend twenty-four hours a day at Scotland Yard. And when he leaves, I doubt if he always goes home to an empty house. Have him followed, Thomas,' he instructed. 'We'll soon unravel the mystery of Robert Colbeck.'

When she finally had some time to herself, Madeleine Andrews chose to read the newspaper cuttings that she had kept since the train robbery. Her father's injuries were mentioned but the name that she paid most attention to was that of Robert Colbeck, wondering how she could manage to meet him again without seeming forward. Madeleine recalled their last conversation and smiled. She was still annoyed that she had been followed to Scotland Yard by Gideon Little but that did not prevent her feeling a pang of sympathy for him. If he were so obsessed with Madeleine that he would shadow her across London, he had to be pitied. She hoped that he would find someone else to whom he could transfer his stifling affections.

There was a loud knock at the door. Fearing that it might be Gideon Little, she was minded to ignore the caller at first but her father's yell from upstairs made that impossible. It might well be another visitor for him and she was grateful for anyone who could offer him some distraction. Putting the cuttings away in a drawer, therefore, she went to open the front door.

'Oh, my goodness!' she cried.

Her exclamation blended pleasure with sheer fright. While she was overjoyed to see Colbeck standing there, she was shocked at the sight of the bruising on his face.

'Hello, Miss Andrews,' he said, raising his hat.

'What happened to you?' she asked with concern.

'That is what I came to tell you.'

She noticed the bandage. 'And your hand is injured as well.'

'A minor problem. Is it convenient for me to come in?'

'Yes, yes,' said Madeleine, backing away and wishing that she had known that he was about to call. 'Forgive my appearance.'

'I see nothing whatsoever wrong with it.'

'This is my working dress, Inspector.'

'And very charming you look in it, Miss Andrews.'

'Thank you,' she said. 'Do you wish to see Father?'

'Yes, please. I have some good news for both of you.'

She led him up the staircase and he watched her hips swaying entrancingly to and fro in front of him. Stepping into the bedroom, he was greeted by a look of surprise from Caleb Andrews.

'Have you been fighting, Inspector?' he said, staring at his face.

'A light scuffle, Mr Andrews,' replied Colbeck. 'Nothing more. My injuries pale beside yours even though we may possibly have come up against the same man.'

'What do you mean?'

'Three arrests were made last night. The men were all members of the gang involved in the train robbery.'

'At last!' said Madeleine.

'We still have to round up the others, of course, but we feel that we are definitely closing in on them now. Last night was a turning point.'

'Tell us why, Inspector,' urged Andrews. 'We want the details.'

Without even saying that they had been acting on his initiative, Colbeck told them about the successful ambush at the Crystal Palace and gave them the names of the three men in custody. Madeleine clapped her hands together in delight but her father shook his head.

'Those names mean nothing to me,' he said.

'Perhaps their faces will, Mr Andrews.'

'You're going to bring the rogues here for me to see them?'

'I already have,' said Colbeck, taking some sheets of paper from inside his coat and opening them out. 'These are only sketches, mark you, but I think that the artist caught the salient features of each man. Here,' he went on, passing the first sketch to Andrews, 'this is Harry Seymour. Do you recognise him?'

'No,' said Andrews, squinting at the paper. 'No, I don't think so.'

'What about his brother, Vernon?'

'Let me see.' He took the second sketch then shook his head. 'No, this is not the man either. He was bigger and with an uglier face.'

'Perhaps it was Arthur Jukes, then,' said Colbeck, showing him the last drawing. 'Ignore the black eye,' he advised. 'That's what I gave him when he had the temerity to fight back. Those whiskers of his are ginger, by the way.'

'It's him!' asserted Andrews, waving the paper. 'This is him!'

'Are you certain?'

'As certain as I am of anything. This is the devil who hit me.'

'Then that's one more charge for him to answer.'

'Frank Pike was there as well,' recalled Madeleine. 'He probably got a closer look at this man than Father.'

'I intend to call on Mr Pike to show him these sketches,' said Colbeck. 'If he agrees with your father that Jukes is the man, he can come and see him in person, just to make sure.'

'Take me along as well, Inspector,' said Andrews.

'No, Father,' said Madeleine. 'You must stay here.'

'I want to tell that villain what I think of him, Maddy.'

'Mr Pike will surely do that on your behalf,' said Colbeck, taking the sketches back and slipping them into his pocket. 'Well, I'm delighted that we have such a positive identification.'

'How many other men are involved?' wondered Madeleine.

'That has yet to be determined, Miss Andrews, but we intend to hunt down each and every one. Apart from the robbery, there are two murders and an explosion at Kilsby Tunnel to be laid at their door.'

'And an attempted outrage at the Crystal Palace.'

'Blowing up those wonderful locomotives?' said Andrews, still appalled at the idea. 'That's worse than a crime – it's downright evil.'

'They were all saved for the visitors to enjoy them,' said Colbeck. 'And what amazing machines they are! After spending three nights lying beneath *Liverpool*, I got to know her extremely well. Mr Crampton is a brilliant man.'

'A genius, Inspector.'

'I only wish that I could persuade Sergeant Leeming of that. He hates trains, I fear, and being forced to sleep under a locomotive did not endear him to the notion of rail travel.'

'Who is Sergeant Leeming?' said Andrews.

'Your daughter will explain – she's met him. Well,' said Colbeck, 'now that I've passed on the glad tidings, I'll be on my way.' He smiled at the invalid. 'I'm pleased to see that you're looking somewhat better, Mr Andrews.'

'I can't say the same about you, Inspector.'

'That's not very tactful, Father,' said Madeleine.

'It's an honest comment, Maddy.'

'It is,' agreed Colbeck. 'When I saw myself in the shaving mirror this morning, I had quite a shock. It looks far worse than it feels.'

After trading farewells, he went downstairs and made for the front door. Madeleine was at his heels, determined to have a word with him alone. When he let himself out, she stood on the doorstep. Colbeck kept his top hat in his hand while he talked.

'I hope that the news will act as a tonic for your father,' he said.

'It will, Inspector. It has certainly cheered me.'

'I have the feeling that he can be a difficult patient.'

'Quite impossible at times.'

'Fretful and demanding?'

'Only on good days, Inspector.'

They shared a laugh and he watched her cheeks dimple again. She had a way of putting her head slightly to one side that intrigued him. For her part, she noticed the sparkle of interest in his eyes. It implanted a distant hope in her breast.

'Where are you going now?' she asked.

'To call on Frank Pike,' he replied. 'After that, I have to go straight back to Scotland Yard.'

'Do you never rest, Inspector?'

'Not when I am in the middle of an investigation.'

'Your family must miss you terribly.'

'I live alone, Miss Andrews,' he said, glad of the opportunity to reveal his circumstances. 'My parents died some years ago and I have never felt it entirely fair to invite anyone to share the life of a detective.' He pointed to his face. 'What wife wishes to see her husband coming home like this, especially after he has been absent from the marital couch for three nights?'

'Some wives have to put up with a lot more than that, Inspector.'

'By choice?'

'Of course,' she said, earnestly. 'If a woman really loves her husband, then she will happily endure all the disadvantages that his job might bring. I know that that was my mother's attitude. Being the wife of a railwayman has many drawbacks, believe me.'

'Is that why you spurned the opportunity yourself?'

'Not at all.'

'But I understood you to say that you had rejected your suitor.'

'Only because he was not the right man for me,' she explained. 'It was nothing to do with his occupation. If Gideon had been the husband of my choice, it would not have mattered whether he were a railwayman or a road sweeper.'

'I see that you are a romantic, Miss Andrews.'

'I have always thought of myself as a practical woman.'

'Even a practical woman can have romantic inclinations,' he said, holding her gaze for a long time. 'However,' he added, putting his hat on, 'I must not keep you talking out here in the street. You have things to do and I have somewhere to go. Goodbye, Miss Andrews.'

'Goodbye, Inspector.'

She offered her hand in the expectation that he would shake it but Colbeck instead brought it to his lips and planted a gentle kiss on it. Madeleine was thrilled and he was pleased with her reaction. The tender moment between them did not go unobserved. Seated in a cab a little way down the street was a man who had followed Colbeck all the way from Scotland Yard. Watching the two of them in conversation, he felt that he would have something of great interest to report.

Superintendent Tallis could not believe his eyes. As he stepped into the corridor, he saw Brendan Mulryne walking jauntily towards him, a broad smile covering his battered face. The Irishman offered his hand.

'Good day to you, Superintendent,' he said, cordially.

'What, in the name of Christ, are you doing here?' demanded Tallis, declining the handshake. 'You should be locked up.'

'I've been released on bail.'

'On whose authority?'

'Mr Mayne himself,' said the Irishman. 'I've just spoken to him. He wanted to congratulate me on the help that I gave at the Crystal Palace. I'm moving up in the world,' he went on, chuckling. 'I never thought that I'd get to meet a Police Commissioner face to face.'

'You should not have been at the Crystal Palace in the first place.'

'Inspector Colbeck wanted me there.'

'He was exceeding his authority.'

'What does it matter, sir?'

'It matters a great deal, Mulryne,' said Tallis, acidly, 'as you should know. A police force is run on discipline. It was a lesson that you never learnt when you were in uniform.'

'There were too many rules and regulations.'

'You managed to break each and every one of them.'

Mulryne beamed. 'I never was a man for half-measures.'

'You were an embarrassment to all of us.'

'Inspector Colbeck doesn't think so. Neither does Mr

Mayne. By the way, Superintendent, did you know that we had something in common – me and the Police Commissioner, that is?'

'Beyond the fact that you both happen to be Irish,' said Tallis, superciliously, 'I can't see the slightest affinity.'

'That's because you don't know my background, see. It turns out that Mr Mayne's father was one of the judges of the Court of King's Bench in Dublin. In short,' said Mulryne, cheerily, 'he must have been the same Judge Mayne that sent my father to prison for three years for a crime that he didn't commit.'

'I should have guessed that you're the son of a convicted criminal.'

'It was the reason I wanted to be a policeman.'

'Old habits die hard, Mulryne.'

'Yes,' said the other, 'so I notice, Superintendent. You still have a habit of smoking those foul cigars.' He sniffed Tallis's lapel. 'Sure, I can smell the stink of them in your clothes.'

Tallis pushed him away. 'Get off, man – and get out of here!'

'Is there any chance of a word with Inspector Colbeck first?'

'No, the Inspector is busy.'

'I don't mind waiting.'

'I'll not have you on the premises. Besides,' he said, 'Inspector Colbeck may be some time. He is about to question one of the men who was arrested last night.'

'Have they given you the names of their accomplices yet?'

'Unfortunately, they have not.'

'Then you should let me talk to them,' offered Mulryne, pounding a fist into the palm of the other hand. 'Put me in a cell with one of them and I'd have him talking his head off inside two minutes.'

'We do not resort to violence.'

'A crying shame!'

'In any case, even you would not be able to beat a confession out of them. I have been interrogating criminals for several years but I could not break down their resistance.'

'Maybe you asked the wrong questions.'

'Inspector Colbeck is seeing one of the men for the second time,' explained Tallis. 'He feels that he now has a means of opening the man's mouth a little.'

Frank Pike had no hesitation in identifying the man. When he saw Arthur Jukes through the bars of his cell, he picked him out immediately as the person who had clubbed Caleb Andrews to the ground and forced the fireman to drive the locomotive off the track. Pike also recognised the Seymour brothers as having been involved in the robbery. Robert Colbeck's problem was to get the fireman out of there. Confronted with the man who had held a pistol on him, Pike wanted retribution and, denied the opportunity to attack the man, he yelled abuse at Jukes through the bars. Jukes replied in kind and the air was blue with ripe language. Colbeck needed the help of Victor Leeming to hustle the visitor out of the area.

When Pike had left, the detectives questioned Jukes in a room that contained nothing beyond a table and three chairs. Still handcuffed, Jukes was surly and withdrawn.

'You have been formally identified as the man who assaulted the driver of that train,' said Colbeck. 'Do you admit the crime?'

'No,' replied Jukes.

'Mr Andrews himself identified the artist's sketch of you.'

'So?'

'We have two eyewitnesses, Mr Jukes.'

'Had Mr Andrews died from his injuries,' said Leeming, 'you might now be facing a charge of murder. That's a hanging offence.'

'Mr Jukes might still have the opportunity to mount the gallows,' Colbeck reminded him. 'The murders of William Ings and Daniel Slender have yet to be accounted for. Were you responsible for those, Mr Jukes?'

'No,' asserted the other.

'Are you sure?'

'I'm no killer, Inspector Colbeck.'

'Yet the army taught you how to take a man's life.'

'That was different.'

'Did you kill anyone when you were in uniform?'

'Only in combat.'

'You have admitted something at last,' said Colbeck, watching the prisoner's eyes. 'We are starting to make progress.'

'What about the explosion at the Kilsby Tunnel?' asked Leeming. 'I suppose that you were not party to that either.'

'No,' said Jukes. 'This is the first I've heard about it.'

'I think that you are lying.'

'You may think what you wish, Sergeant.'

'Since we caught you with a barrel of gunpowder at the Crystal Palace, it's logical to assume that you caused the earlier explosion. You and your accomplices are obviously experienced in such work.'

Jukes was stony-faced. 'Are we?'

'Let me ask you another question,' said Colbeck, changing his tack. 'Why did you leave the army?'

'Because I only enlisted for a certain number of years.'

'What occupation did you take up?'

'That's my business.'

'Discharged soldiers often find it difficult to get employment.'

'I managed,' said Jukes, uneasily.

'Even though you had no trade to follow?'

'One of the Seymour brothers told us that he worked as a slaughterman in an abattoir,' said Leeming. 'Is that the sort of job you were forced to take, Mr Jukes?'

'Of course not,' snarled the prisoner.

'You must have done something,' argued Colbeck. 'When you were arrested, you were wearing a wedding ring. I remember feeling it when you punched me,' he said, rubbing his chin. 'That means you have a wife to support, Mr Jukes. How did you do it?'

'Leave my wife out of this!'

'Do you have children, by any chance?'

'My family do not go short.'

'But they will suffer now, won't they?' Jukes scowled at him before turning his head away. 'What I am trying to suggest to you,' said Colbeck, gently, 'is that you may have been earning a paltry wage – or, perhaps, were actually out of work – when you received the invitation to take part in a train robbery. You are not, by instinct, a criminal, Mr Jukes. What drove you to break the law was the desire to do better for your family.'

'Is that true?' pressed Leeming.

'Does your wife *know* where all that money came from?'

'Did you tell her what you were going to do at the Crystal Palace?'

Jukes said nothing, but his silence was eloquent. As he stared unseeingly in front of him, there was a deep sadness in his eyes. The detectives noted how tense the prisoner's whole body had become.

'There is only one way to help yourself,' advised Colbeck, 'and that is by cooperating with us. Any assistance you give will be looked upon favourably by the judge.'

'It could well lead to a reduction in your sentence,' said Leeming.

'So tell us, Mr Jukes. Who organised the train robbery?'

'Was it someone you met in the army?'

'Or someone you were introduced to by the Seymour brothers? We will catch the man before long, Mr Jukes,' said Colbeck, 'make no mistake about that. But you are in a position to save us time and trouble. Now, then,' he went on, leaning forward across the table, 'why not think of your own plight and seek to ease it? Give us his name.'

'Never,' retorted Jukes.

'Your loyalty is mistaken.'

'You're the one who's mistaken, Inspector. You may have had the luck to catch us but that's as far as you'll get. Harry and Vernon are like me. We'd sooner hang than tell you the name you want. As for catching him before long,' he added with a mocking laugh, 'you are in for a big surprise. He can run rings around the Metropolitan Police Force. You'll never catch him in a month of Sundays.'

It happened in broad daylight. Madeleine Andrews had just made her father comfortable in bed next morning when she heard a knock at the front door. She glanced through the bedroom window and saw a uniformed policeman below. Thinking that he might have brought more news, she hurried downstairs to open the door. The policeman, a bearded man with a polite manner, touched the brim of his hat.

'Miss Madeleine Andrews?' he inquired.

'Yes.'

'I have come with a request from Inspector Colbeck. He wonders if you could spare an hour to call on him at Scotland Yard.'

Madeleine was taken aback. '*Now*?'

'I have a cab to take you there,' said the other, 'and it will bring you back to your house.'

'Did the Inspector say why he wished to see me?'

'No, Miss Andrews, but it must be a matter of some importance or he would not be summoning you like this.' He made to leave. 'I can see that it is not convenient. I'll tell Inspector Colbeck that he will have to meet you another time.'

'Wait,' she said. 'I can come with you. I just need to tell my father where I am going first. Please excuse me.'

'Of course.'

Madeleine went back upstairs, explained the situation to her father and promised that she would not be long. She went quickly into her own bedroom to look at herself in the mirror and to adjust her clothing and hair. When she reappeared at the door, she was wearing a hat.

'This way, Miss Andrews,' said the policeman.

He escorted her to the waiting cab and helped her up into it. As soon as he sat beside her, however, his manner changed abruptly. One arm around Madeleine to restrain her, he used the other hand to cover her mouth with a handkerchief.

'Do as you're told,' ordered Thomas Sholto, 'or you'll never see your precious Inspector Colbeck again.'

The cab was driven away at speed.

CHAPTER ELEVEN

Arthur Jukes gave nothing away. No matter how much pressure they applied, the detectives could not get the answers that they required. They interrogated the other prisoners separately but with the same negative result. Vernon Seymour was openly defiant and his younger brother, Harry, boasted that they would not stay under lock and key for long. He seemed to have a naïve faith that someone would come to his rescue and confound the forces of law and order. When all three men were back in their cells, Robert Colbeck adjourned to his office with Victor Leeming. The Sergeant was not optimistic.

'It's like trying to get blood out of a stone,' he moaned.

'We need to be patient, Victor.'

'We failed. I thought it was a brilliant idea of yours to let Mr Tallis loose on them but even he, with his military background, could not frighten them into revealing the name of their paymaster. Why are they so loyal to this man?'

'I think it's a combination of loyalty and fear,' said Colbeck. 'They know just how ruthless he can be. Even if they were not directly involved in the murders of William Ings and Daniel Slender, they would surely be aware of them. If they betray their leader, they are afraid that they will be signing their own death warrants.'

'But they are in police custody.'

'I regret to admit it, Victor, but there are ways of getting to people even when they are in the most secure prisons. No,' said Colbeck, 'there's little chance that any of them will volunteer the name that we seek. All that we can do is to remain calm, question them at intervals and hope that one of them makes a slip.'

'Which one?'

'Harry Seymour would be my choice. He's the youngest.'

'He's convinced that he is about to be rescued.'

'That proves my point. Whoever has been employing the three men has persuaded them that he is invincible, and that he has the power to get them out of any situation. In other words, he must be a man of considerable influence.'

'Nobody is above the law,' said Leeming.

'This man obviously believes that he is.'

'Where do we go from here, Inspector?'

Colbeck rested against the edge of his desk and pondered. Having caught the three men in the act of committing a heinous crime, he had hoped that they had taken a giant stride forward in the investigation but they had suddenly come to a halt. Evidently, Arthur Jukes and the Seymour brothers had been taught how to behave in the event of arrest. In taking them out of action, Colbeck and his men had performed a valuable service but the rest of the gang was at liberty and there was no simple way of identifying them. What was certain was that the failure of his plot to blow up the locomotives at the Crystal Palace would enrage the man who had set it in motion. Colbeck feared reprisals.

'First, we must find out which regiment they served in,' he said.

'They refused to tell us.'

'We have their names, Victor. It is only a question of checking the records. I leave that to you.'

'Where do I start?' asked Leeming, over-awed by the task.

'With regiments that have served in India.'

'India?'

'You saw the complexion of those three men,' said Colbeck. 'They have clearly spent time in a hot country. Also, Harry Seymour made his first slip. The custody sergeant told me that he had the gall to ask when tiffin would be brought to his cell.'

'Tiffin?'

'It's an Indian word for a midday meal.'

'The bare-faced cheek of the man!' said Leeming, angrily. 'What does Harry Seymour expect – a dozen oysters and a pint of beer, with apple pie to follow? He'll be asking for a butler next.'

'My guess is that all three of them were in an infantry regiment. The brothers would certainly have served together and they treat Jukes with that mixture of jocularity and respect that soldiers reserve for a corporal or a sergeant. When people have been in the army for any length of time,' observed Colbeck, 'they can never entirely shake off its effects.'

'You only have to look at Mr Tallis to see that.'

Colbeck smiled. '*Major* Tallis, please.'

'Did *he* have any idea which regiment they might have been in?'

'Not his own, anyway – the 6th Dragoon Guards. None of them would have lasted a week in that, according to the Superintendent. He had a very low opinion of them as soldiers.'

'Someone obviously values their abilities.'

'The most likely person,' said Colbeck, 'is an officer from the same regiment, someone whom they would instinctively obey. When you find where they served in India, make a list of any officers who have retired from their regiment in recent years.'

'Yes, Inspector.'

'After that, I have another assignment for you.'

Leeming grimaced. 'I thought that you might.'

'Visit all of the slaughterhouses within the London area,' suggested Colbeck. 'If Vernon Seymour used to work in one of them, they'll remember him and might even provide an address.'

'Regiments and slaughterhouses.'

'That should keep you busy.'

'This job never lacks for variety.'

'The more we can find out about those three men, the better.'

'What about Jukes? He's the only one who has a wife and family.'

'So?'

'Should we not try to track them down, sir?'

'No need of that, Victor. You saw the fellow earlier on. The one moment he looked vulnerable was when we touched on his marriage.'

'Yes,' recalled Leeming. 'He obviously cares for his wife.'

'Then she will doubtless love him in return,' said Colbeck. 'When he's been missing long enough, she'll become alarmed and turn to us for help. All that we have to do is to wait.'

'I'll make a start with those regimental records.'

'The Superintendent will be able to offer guidance. I daresay that he'll reel some of the names straight off.'

'I was banking on that, sir.' He opened the door. 'This may take me some time – well into tomorrow, probably. What about you, sir?'

'Oh, I'll be here for hours yet. It will be another late night for me.'

'At least we do not have to spend it underneath a locomotive.'

Colbeck laughed and Leeming went out. Three nights without sleep were starting to take their toll on both of them but the Inspector drove himself on. There was no time to rest on his laurels. The man he was after was still in a position to make further strikes against railways and Colbeck was determined to get to him before he did so. Sitting behind his desk, he took out his notebook and went through all the details he had gathered during his interviews with the three prisoners. What stood out was the similarity of their denials. It was almost as if they had agreed what they were going to say even though they had deliberately been kept in separate cells. Someone had drilled them well.

An hour later, Colbeck was still bent over his desk, working by the light of the gas lamp that shed a golden circle around one end of the room. When there was a tap on the door, he did not at first hear it. A second and much louder knock made him look up.

'Come in!' he called. A clerk entered. 'Yes?'

'Someone wishes to see you, Inspector.'

Colbeck's hopes rose. 'A young lady, by any chance?'

'No, sir. A man called Gideon Little.'

'Did he say what he wanted?'

'Only that it was a matter of the utmost importance.'

'Show him in.'

The clerk went out and left Colbeck to speculate on the reason for the unexpected visit. He remembered that Little was the suitor whom Madeleine Andrews had chosen to turn down. Colbeck wondered if the man had come to blame him for the fact that he had been rejected, though he could not imagine why. As soon as he saw Gideon Little, however, he realised that his visitor had not come to tax him in any way. The man was hesitant and agitated. Dressed in his work clothes, he stepped into the room and looked nervously around it, patently unused to being in an office. Colbeck introduced himself and offered him a chair but Little refused. Taking a few tentative steps towards the desk, he looked appealingly into Colbeck's eyes.

'Where is she, Inspector?' he bleated.

'Who?'

'Madeleine, of course. She came to see you.'

'When?'

'This morning.'

'You are misinformed, Mr Little,' said Colbeck, pleasantly. 'The last time that I saw Miss Andrews was yesterday when I called at the house. What gave you the idea that she was here?'

'You sent for her, sir.'

'But I had no reason to do so.'

'Then why did the policeman come to the house?'

'He was not there on my account, I can promise you.'

'Caleb swore that he was,' said Little, anxiously. 'Madeleine told him that she had to go out for a while to visit you but that she would not be too long. That was the last her father saw of her.'

Colbeck was disturbed. 'What time would this have been?'

'Shortly after eight.'

'Then she's been gone for the best part of the day.'

'I only discovered that when I finished work, Inspector,' said Little. 'I stopped at the house on my way home and found Caleb in a dreadful state. It's not like Madeleine to leave him alone for so long.'

'You say that a policeman called?' asked Colbeck, on his feet.

'Yes, sir. A tall man with a dark beard.'

'Did you actually *see* him?'

'Only from the corner of the street,' explained Little, suppressing the fact that he had been watching the house for the best part of an hour. 'I was going past on my way to work when I noticed that Madeleine was getting into a cab with a policeman. They went off at quite a gallop as if they were eager to get somewhere, so I was curious.'

'Is that why you went to the house and spoke to her father?'

'Yes, I let myself in. The door was on the latch.'

'And what did Mr Andrews tell you?'

'That you wanted to see her at Scotland Yard and had sent a cab to bring her here.' Gideon Little wiped the sweat off his brow with the back of his hand. 'If he was not a policeman, who could that man be?'

'I wish that I knew,' said Colbeck, sharing his concern.

'Do you think that she could have been kidnapped?'

'I sincerely hope that that is not the case, Mr Little.'

'Why else would she disappear for so long?'

'Could she have visited relatives?'

'I doubt it.'

'Or called on friends, perhaps?'

'Not when her father is stuck in bed all day like that,' said Little. 'Madeleine is very dutiful. She would never desert Caleb.'

'No,' said Colbeck, his brain spinning as he saw the implications of the news. 'The only thing that would keep her away from home is that she is being held against her will.'

'That's our fear, Inspector. Find her for us – please!'

'I'll not rest until I've done so, Mr Little.'

'I know that she'll never be mine,' said the other, quivering with apprehension. 'Madeleine made that obvious. But she'll always be very dear to me. I cannot bear the thought that she is in danger.'

'Neither can I,' admitted Colbeck, worried that he might somehow be responsible for her abduction. 'Thank you for coming, Mr Little. I only wish that you'd been able to raise the alarm sooner.'

'So do I, Inspector. What am I to tell Caleb?'

'That we'll do everything in our power to find his daughter. I will take personal charge of the search.' He thought of the injured driver, stranded in his bedroom. 'Is there anyone to look after him?'

'A servant who comes in three days a week. She's agreed to stay.'

'Good,' said Colbeck. 'You get back to Mr Andrews and give him what support you can. I, meanwhile, will institute a search.' He shook his head in consternation. 'Taken away in a cab – wherever can she be?'

Madeleine Andrews was stricken with quiet terror. Locked in an attic room at the top of a house, she had no idea where she was or why she was being kept there. It had been a frightening ordeal. When the policeman had called for her, she had looked forward to seeing Robert Colbeck again and was so lost in pleasurable thoughts of him that she was caught off guard. Once inside the cab, she realised that she had been tricked. The man who overpowered her had slipped a bag over her head so that she could not even see where they were going. The last thing she recalled about Camden was the sound of a train steaming over the viaduct.

She cursed herself for being taken in so easily. The

policeman's voice had been far too cultured for an ordinary constable, and his manner too courteous. What had misled her was that he had behaved more like Colbeck than a typical policeman. That had appealed to her. His demeanour had changed the moment they were in the cab. He had threatened her with physical violence if she tried to resist or cry out, and Madeleine knew that he was prepared to carry out his threat. All that she could do was to submit and hope that she would somehow get out of her predicament.

The room was small and the ceiling low but the place was well-furnished. Under other circumstances, she might even have found it snug. There were bars across the window to discourage any hope of escape over the roof, and she had been warned that, if she dared to shout for help, she would be bound and gagged. Madeleine spared herself that indignity. A manservant had twice brought her meals in the course of the day and, on the second occasion, had lit the oil lamp for her. Though the food was good, she had little appetite for it.

Fearing for her own safety, she was also distressed on her father's behalf. He would be alarmed by her disappearance and, unable to stir from his bed, would be completely frustrated. Madeleine felt that she was letting him down. The other person about whom she was concerned was Robert Colbeck. During her abduction, she had been ordered to obey if she wished to see the Inspector again. Did that mean *his* life was in danger or merely her own? And how had the counterfeit policeman known that she was fond of Colbeck? It was baffling. As she flung herself down on the couch, she was tormented by one question.

What were they planning to do to her?

Sir Humphrey Gilzean believed in dining in style. When he was staying in London, therefore, he always made sure that his cook travelled with him from Berkshire. Over a delicious repast that evening, washed down with a superior wine, he mused on the ironic coincidence.

'You know how much I detest railways, Thomas,' he said.

'They are an abomination to you.'

'So why do you bring a railwayman's daughter to my house?'

'Madeleine Andrews is the chink in Colbeck's armour.'

'Can this really be so?' asked Gilzean. 'The only way their paths could have crossed is as a result of the train robbery. There has been very little time for an attachment to develop.'

'Nevertheless, Humphrey, I was given to believe that it has. The gallant Inspector was seen to take a fond farewell on her doorstep. And while she may only be a railwayman's daughter,' said Sholto with a well-bred leer, 'she is a fetching young woman. I'd hoped that she'd struggle more so that I could have the pleasure of manhandling her.'

Gilzean was strict. 'She must be treated with respect.'

'Am I not even allowed a little sport?'

'No, Thomas.'

'But she might like some company in the middle of the night.'

'Miss Andrews must be unharmed,' insisted Gilzean, filling his glass from the port decanter. 'I draw the line at molestation.'

'Where women are concerned,' teased Sholto, 'you were always inclined to be too soft.'

'I behave like a gentleman, Thomas. So should you.'

'There are times when courtesy is burdensome.'

'Not to me.'

Sholto laughed. 'You really are the strangest creature, Humphrey,' he said. 'Who else would send me off to murder a man then insist that I leave a substantial amount of money with his widow?'

'Mrs Ings needed it – we do not.'

'I always need money.'

'Even you must be satisfied with what we have accrued.'

'It only makes me want more.'

'Apart from what we gained in the robbery, there were the profits from blackmail. In total, it amounted to almost three thousand pounds. We are in a position to be generous.'

'Giving money to that woman was unnecessary.'

'It salved my conscience and appealed to my sense of fair play.'

'Fair play?' echoed the other with a derisive laugh. 'Having her husband killed hardly constitutes fair play.'

'He betrayed her for that money, remember,' said Gilzean. 'He abandoned his wife and family to live with a whore in the Devil's Acre. I have no sympathy for him – but I did feel that Mrs Ings deserved help.'

Sholto was disdainful. 'I do not believe in charity.'

'Cultivate a little benevolence, Thomas.'

'Oh, I have plenty of that,' said the other, 'but I put it to different uses. You see a grieving widow and tell me to put money through her letterbox. When I see a female in distress – Madeleine Andrews, for example – I have the urge to comfort her in a more intimate way and offer my full benevolence.'

'Miss Andrews is only a means to an end.'

'My belief, entirely.'

'I am serious,' said Gilzean, forcefully. 'When she is under my roof, she is under my protection. Dismiss any thoughts you may have about her, Thomas. Miss Andrews is here for a purpose.'

'How long will we keep her?'

'As long as we need her.'

'What about the elegant Inspector?'

'He will surely be aware of her disappearance by now,' said Gilzean, sniffing his port before tasting it, 'and, if he is as enamoured as you believe, he will be extremely fretful. That was my intention – to give Inspector Colbeck something to occupy his mind.'

Robert Colbeck slept fitfully that night, troubled by dreams of what terrible fate might have befallen Madeleine Andrews. The news that she had been kidnapped aroused all of his protective instincts and he came to see just how fond he was of her. It was no passing interest. His affection was deep and intensified by her plight. The thought that she was in great danger left him in a fever of recrimination. Colbeck felt responsible for what had happened. She had been taken, he believed, as a way of striking at him. Because he had arrested three men, Madeleine had become a hostage.

He woke up to the realisation that his efforts to find her had, so far, been fruitless. In the wake of the visit from Gideon Little, he had sent police officers to Camden to question all the neighbours in her street in case any of them had witnessed the abduction. One had remembered seeing a policeman outside the door of Madeleine's house, another had watched the cab setting off, but neither could add to what Colbeck already knew. He had nothing to help him. Madeleine could be anywhere.

Rain was scouring the streets when he stepped out of his house, making London seem wet and inhospitable. Colbeck had to walk some distance along John Islip Street before he found a cab, and his umbrella was dripping. He was glad to get to Scotland Yard. Although it was still early, Superintendent Tallis had already arrived to start work. Colbeck met him in the corridor outside his office. Having been informed of the crisis, Tallis was eager to hear of developments.

'Any news, Inspector?' he asked.

'None, sir.'

'That's worrying. Miss Andrews has been missing for the best part of twenty-four hours. I would have expected contact by now.'

'From whom?'

'The people who abducted her,' said Tallis. 'In cases of kidnap, there is usually a ransom demand within a short time. Yet we have heard nothing. That bodes ill.'

'Not necessarily, Superintendent.'

'It could mean that the poor woman is no longer alive.'

'I refuse to believe that,' said Colbeck. 'If the object were to kill Miss Andrews, that could have been done more easily. Nobody would go to the trouble of disguising himself as a policeman so that he could lure her into a cab, when he could dispatch her with one thrust of a dagger.'

'That's true, I suppose.'

'Look what happened to William Ings and Daniel Slender, sir. They were both killed with brutal efficiency – so was Kate Piercey.'

'You are still making the assumption that this abduction is the work of the train robbers.'

'Who else would kidnap Miss Andrews?'

'She lives in Camden, Inspector. It's not the most law-abiding area of the city. Any woman who is young and pretty is potentially at risk.'

'Of what?'

Tallis was sombre. 'Use your imagination,' he said. 'When we get reports of abductions, young women – sometimes mere girls – are always the victims. They are dragged off to Seven

Dials or the Devil's Acre and forced into the sort of life that Kate Piercey lived.'

'That is certainly not the case here.'

'It's something that we have to consider.'

'No, Superintendent,' said Colbeck. 'You have obviously not seen the house where Mr Andrews and his daughter live. It's a neat villa in the better part of Camden and the neighbours can be trusted. If that were not so, Miss Andrews would never have gone out and left the door on the latch. And there's something else,' he continued. 'On the two occasions when she visited me here, Miss Andrews walked all the way to Whitehall. If she found Camden a source of peril, she would never have ventured abroad on her own like that.'

'You know the young lady better than I do.'

'Miss Andrews is very practical and level-headed. She knows how to take care of herself. Only a man in police uniform could have won her confidence. That, after all,' Colbeck pointed out, 'was how her father was deceived. One of the robbers who flagged the train down was dressed as a railway policeman.'

'I see what you mean. There is a pattern here.'

'The kidnap was an act of retaliation.'

'Against what?'

'The arrest of Jukes and the Seymour brothers.'

'But why pick on Miss Andrews?' said Tallis, puzzled. 'She is only indirectly connected with this investigation. Why choose her?'

'I wish I knew, Superintendent.'

Colbeck sensed that Madeleine had been abducted in order to get his attention, though he did not mention that to Tallis. It was important to be cool and objective in the Superintendent's presence. To confess that he had feelings for Madeleine

Andrews would be to cloud the issue and to incur the other man's criticism. Tallis did not look kindly on members of his division who became involved with women whom they met in the course of their duties. He viewed it as distracting and unprofessional. While he knew nothing of Colbeck's fondness for Madeleine, however, it appeared that someone else did. That unsettled the Inspector.

'What do you think they will do?' asked Tallis.

'Get in touch with us very soon.'

'To demand ransom money?'

'No, sir,' replied Colbeck. 'Caleb Andrews does not have the sort of income that would interest them. Besides, they are not short of funds after the robbery. No, I suspect that they will wish to trade with us.'

'In what way?'

'They will return Miss Andrews if we release the prisoners.'

'Never!'

'They can always be re-arrested, Inspector.'

'What is the point of that?' snapped Tallis. 'We did not go to all the trouble of catching them in order to set them free. Heavens above, man, have you forgotten what they tried to do?'

'No, sir. I was there at the time.'

'The Great Exhibition is the first of its kind, a world fair that enables British industry to show why it has no rivals. A massive amount of money and energy has gone into the venture. Prince Albert has worked valiantly to contribute to its success. Millions of visitors are expected,' he stressed, 'and what they want to see is the Crystal Palace – not a heap of twisted metal and broken glass.'

'I appreciate the seriousness of their crime, Superintendent.'

'They were also involved in the train robbery.'

'That is not the point,' argued Colbeck. 'A young woman's life may hang in the balance here. If you refuse even to listen to their offer, you may be condemning her to death.'

'I will not sanction the release of guilty men.'

'At least, *discuss* it with them.'

'What good will that do?'

'It will earn us time to continue our search,' said Colbeck, 'but its main advantage is that it may keep Miss Andrews alive. Refuse even to listen and you will only anger them. Employ delaying tactics.'

'I make the decisions, Inspector.'

'Of course. I merely offer my advice.'

'If we let these villains go, we will be made to look like idiots.'

'You are thinking solely of your own reputation, sir,' said Colbeck. 'My concern is for the safety of the victim. Miss Andrews has already suffered the shock of abduction and of being locked away. If the one way to ensure her survival is to release Jukes and the Seymour brothers, I'd unlock the doors of their cells myself.'

The journey was a continuing nightmare. Bound, gagged and blindfolded, Madeleine Andrews sat in the coach as it rolled through the suburbs of London and out into the country. The familiar noises of the capital were soon replaced by an almost eerie silence, broken only by the clatter of hooves, the creaking of the vehicle and the drumming of the rain on the roof. The one consolation was that she was alone, not held in the grip of the bearded man who had called at her house with the false message. She could still feel his hot breath against her cheek as he grabbed her.

Hours seemed to pass. Wherever she was, it was a long

way from London. The rain stopped and so did the pace of the horses. When the animals slowed to a trot, she realised that they were letting another coach catch them up. Both vehicles soon came to a halt and there was a discussion between the coachmen. She strained her ears to pick up what they were saying but she could only make out a few words. The door opened and someone gave a grunt of satisfaction. She presumed that they were checking to see that she was still trussed up safely. The door shut again. A minute later, they set off.

Madeleine no longer feared for her life. If they had wanted to kill her, they would surely have done so by now. Instead, she had been imprisoned in a house that, judging by those she could see opposite from the attic window, was in a very respectable part of London. To her relief, she had been treated reasonably well and was subjected to no violence. What she missed most was conversation. The manservant who had brought her food had been ordered to say nothing to her, and the bearded man who tied her up that morning had confined himself to a few threats before carrying her downstairs over his shoulder.

During a normal day, Madeleine would talk to her father, her friends, her neighbours and to various shopkeepers. Conversations with Gideon Little were more fraught but at least he represented human contact. She longed for that now. For some reason, she had been isolated in a way that only served to heighten her fears. The person she really wanted to speak to was Robert Colbeck, to report her misadventure to him, to seek his reassurance, to enjoy his companionship and to listen to the voice she had come to love for its bewitching cadences. Colbeck was her one hope of rescue. It gave them a bond that drew them closer. Knowing that he would be trying hard to track her down helped Madeleine to find a reserve of courage that she did not know existed.

For her sake, she had to maintain hope; for Colbeck's sake, she was determined to keep her spirits up. The agony could not go on forever. He would come for her in time.

Adversity taught Caleb Andrews just how many friends he had. When he had first been injured, most of his visitors had been other railwaymen, people with whom he had worked for years and who understood how he felt when he heard of the damage to his locomotive. The kidnap of his daughter brought in a wider circle of friends and well-wishers. Once the word had spread, neighbours to whom he had hardly spoken before came to offer their help and to say that they were praying for the safe return of Madeleine. Andrews was touched by the unexpected show of concern.

Frank Pike could hear the emotion in his voice.

'There were six of them in here earlier this morning,' he said. 'I thought that the floor would give way.'

'It shows how popular you are,' said Pike.

'I'd prefer to be the most hated man in Camden if I could have Maddy back home, safe and sound. I didn't sleep a wink last night.'

'What do the police say?'

'That they're doing everything they can to find her. Gideon spoke to Inspector Colbeck yesterday, who told him that he'd lead the search himself.'

'That's good news.'

'Is it?' said Andrews, doubtfully.

'Yes. Inspector Colbeck caught those three men at the Crystal Palace. They included that ugly bastard who knocked you out. If he hadn't been locked up,' vowed Pike, flexing his muscles, 'I'd have beaten him black and blue.'

'He's the least of my worries now, Frank.'

'I know.'

'All that I can think about is Maddy.'

'Did nobody *see* her being taken away?'

'Only Gideon,' said Andrews. 'He claims that he was just passing the end of the street, but I think he was standing out there and watching the house. He's so lovesick, he'll wait for hours for the chance of a word with Maddy. If she comes out of this, she'll have reason to thank him.'

'What did he see, Caleb?'

'A policeman with a dark beard, talking to Maddy on the doorstep then helping her into a cab. The driver cracked his whip and off they went. Gideon had no idea that she was being kidnapped. Luckily, he called in here later on. I sent him off to raise the alarm.'

'Is there anything I can do?'

'You've done it just by being here, Frank.'

'I could send Rose over to fetch and carry for you.'

'No,' said Andrews, 'your wife has enough to do as it is.'

'You only have to ask.'

'Rose would have to wait in the queue. I've got dozens of offers.'

Pike grinned. 'All these women, banging on the door of your bedroom – you always did have a way with the ladies, Caleb.'

'Not when my arm was in a sling and my leg in a splint.'

'They want to mother you.'

Andrews became solemn. 'I tell you this, Frank,' he said. 'If they paraded in here naked and danced in front of me, I'd not even look at them. There's only one woman on my mind right now.'

'Maddy.'

'Why the hell can't they *find* her?'

The letter arrived late that morning. Written in capitals on a sheet of exquisite stationery, it was addressed to Inspector Robert Colbeck. The message was blunt.

RELEASE ALL THREE PRISONERS OR MISS ANDREWS WILL SUFFER. WE WILL BE IN TOUCH TO MAKE ARRANGEMENTS.

A shiver ran through Colbeck. It gave him no satisfaction to see that his guess had been right. Madeleine Andrews was being used as a bargaining tool. Colbeck's problem was that the Superintendent was not prepared to strike a bargain or even to pretend to do so. Releasing anyone from custody was like retreating on the battlefield to him. When Colbeck went to his office to show him the letter, Tallis was defiant. He thrust the missive back at the Inspector.

'Nobody tells me what to do,' he asserted.

'Does that mean you are prepared to let Miss Andrews suffer, sir?'

'Not deliberately.'

'Ignore their demands and that is what will happen.'

'It could be bluff on their part,' said Tallis. 'If they harm her in any way, they lose the one lever that they have at their disposal.'

'I prefer to take them at their word, sir.'

'Yes, Inspector. We know you have a fondness for releasing felons from custody. It was by your connivance that Mulryne walked free.'

'Brendan Mulryne is no felon,' retorted Colbeck.

'He is in my eyes.'

'He acted with outstanding bravery at the Crystal Palace.'

'That does not excuse what he did.'

'Mr Mayne felt that it did, Superintendent. I wonder what his reaction to this demand would be?' he said, holding up the letter.

Tallis was hostile. 'Do not go over my head again, Inspector.'

'Madeleine Andrews's life may be at stake.'

'So is your career.'

Colbeck was unperturbed by the threat. Madeleine's safety meant more to him at that moment than anything else. Baulked by his superior, he would have to find another way to secure her release.

'Excuse me, sir,' he said, politely. 'I must continue the search.'

'You can tear that letter up for a start.'

Ignoring the command, Colbeck went straight back to his office and he was delighted to see that Victor Leeming had finally returned. The Sergeant had the weary look of someone who had pushed himself to the limit. Before he allowed him to deliver his news, Colbeck told him about the kidnap and showed him the letter. Leeming's response chimed in with his own. Even if they did not intend to release the prisoners, they should enter the negotiations so that they could purchase some time.

'One other thing you should know,' explained Colbeck. 'Early yesterday morning, a cab driver reported the theft of his vehicle while he was having breakfast. Later the same day, it was returned.'

'You think that it was involved in the kidnap?'

'Yes, Victor. No self-respecting cab driver would have agreed to take part in a crime like that. And the fact that the cab was returned is significant. These people will destroy a steam locomotive but they will not harm a horse. But how did you get on?' said Colbeck, wrinkling his nose. 'You smell as if you've just come from a slaughterhouse.'

'Several of them, sir. And they all stink like old blue buggery. Do you know how many slaughterhouses there *are* in London?'

'I'm only interested in one of them.'

'Needless to say,' complained Leeming, 'it was the last that I visited. However,' he went on, taking out his notebook and referring to a page, 'they did remember Vernon Seymour and they had an address. He lived alone in a tenement near Seven Dials. The landlord there told me that Seymour had come into some money last week and moved out. I saw the room where he lodged – it still had a whiff of the slaughterhouse about it.' He flicked over a page. 'According to the landlord, Seymour received a visit from a tall, well-dressed man with a beard. Shortly after that, he left the place.'

'What about his brother?'

'Harry came there from time to time, apparently. That's all I can tell you.' Leeming turned over another page. 'But I had more success with the regimental records. Mr Tallis gave me a list of possibilities and told me where to find the records. Arthur Jukes, Vernon Seymour and Harry Seymour all served in India in the 10th Queen's Regiment.'

'Infantry?'

'Yes, Inspector. It's the North Lincoln.'

'Any officers listed as retiring?'

'Quite a few,' said Leeming, running his finger down the page. 'I went back five years and wrote down all the names.' He handed his notebook over. 'It's probably easier if you read them for yourself.'

'Thank you.'

Colbeck ran his eye down the list. While he could never approve of Leeming's scrawl, he had to admire his thoroughness. The names were listed alphabetically with their ranks, length of service and date of retirement noted alongside.

'We can eliminate some of these men immediately,' said Colbeck, reaching for the pen on his desk and dipping it in the inkwell.

'Can we, sir?'

'Yes, I refuse to believe that Colonel Fitzhammond is our man. He's given a lifetime's service to the army and will be steeped in its traditions.'

He scratched through the name then put a line through three more. 'We can count these officers out as well. They'll be too old. All that they will want is a quiet retirement.'

'I know the feeling,' said Leeming.

'Two of these men left the army within the last few months,' said Colbeck, pen poised over their names. 'They would not have had the time to set up such a complicated crime as the train robbery. We can cross them off the list as well.' The pen scratched away. 'That leaves five names. No, it doesn't, Victor,' he added, as he spotted a detail. 'I think that it leaves two whom we should look at more carefully.'

'Why is that, Inspector?'

'Because they retired from the army on the same day.'

'Coincidence?'

'Possibly – or they could be friends who joined at the same time.'

'When did they return to civilian life?'

'Almost five years ago,' said Colbeck. 'Of course, we may be barking up the wrong tree but I have the feeling that we may have found something important here. My belief is that one or both of these men was involved in that train robbery.'

'What are their names?'

'Major Sir Humphrey Gilzean and Captain Thomas Sholto.'

'Mr Tallis will never accept that army officers are responsible for the crimes. In his book, they are above suspicion.'

'Then let's first try these two names on someone else,' decided Colbeck. 'Men who served under them.'

Standing in the hallway of Gilzean's country house, Thomas Sholto stroked his beard and watched two servants bringing another trunk downstairs. He turned to his friend.

'You do not believe in wasting time, Humphrey, do you?'

'Forewarned is forearmed,' said Gilzean.

'What if Inspector Colbeck does not run us to ground?'

'Then we have no need to implement our contingency plans. As you know, I'm a great believer in covering all eventualities. This luggage will be loaded into a carriage in readiness for a swift departure.'

'Will our hostage be travelling with us?' asked Sholto.

'Only if we need to take her, Thomas.'

'Given the opportunity, I'd have taken her already.'

'Keep your hands off Miss Andrews.'

'You should at least have let me share the same coach as her.'

'No,' said Gilzean. 'The woman is frightened enough as it is. I do not wish to add to her distress by having you lusting after her. I prefer to encourage your virtues, not indulge your vices.'

Sholto laughed. 'I didn't know that I had any virtues.'

'One or two.'

'What are you going to do with this resourceful Inspector?'

'Keep him guessing, Thomas.'

'How will you contrive that?'

'By pretending that we really do intend to hand over Madeleine Andrews for the three prisoners. A letter will be delivered by hand to him tomorrow, setting up a time and place for the exchange to be made, two days from hence. Only when they arrive at the designated spot will they realise that they've been hoodwinked. By that time,' said Gilzean, leading his friend into the library, 'I will have emptied my bank accounts and put all my affairs in order.'

'Would you really be prepared to turn your back on this house?'

'Yes. It holds too many unpleasant memories for me now.'

'That was not always the case,' Sholto reminded him.

'No, I agree. When I grew up here, I loved it. After my army days were over, I could think of no finer existence than running the estate and keeping a stable of racehorses.' His face hardened. 'I reckoned without the railway, alas.'

'It does not actually cross your land, Humphrey.'

'Perhaps not but it skirts it for over a mile. It's far too close for comfort. Trains from the Great Western Railway go past all the time. If the wind is in the right direction, I can hear the noise of that damned whistle whenever I am in my garden. Nothing makes my blood boil so much as that sound.'

'I hope that you do not have to sacrifice this place,' said Sholto, gazing fondly around the room. 'It's a splendid house. There are some things that you'll miss a great deal about this estate.' He raised an eyebrow. 'One of them, in particular.'

'All that has been taken into consideration,' said Gilzean, knowing what he meant. 'Whatever happens, I will return somehow from time to time to pay my respects. Nobody will prevent me from doing that. It's a sacred duty. Besides,' he went on, his face brightening, 'I have another good reason to come back.'

'Do you?'

'Yes, Thomas. I simply have to be at Epsom on the first

Wednesday in June. I intend to watch my colt win the Derby.'

'What if he loses?'

'That option does not even arise,' said the other, brimming with confidence. 'Starlight is a Gilzean – we never lose.'

'Sir Humphrey Gilzean?' asked Superintendent Tallis, eyes bulging.

'Yes,' replied Colbeck. 'I'm certain of it, sir.'

'Then I am equally certain that you have the wrong man.'

'Why do you say that?'

'Do you know who Sir Humphrey is – and *what* he is?'

'If my guess is right, he's a man with blood on his hands. He not only organised the train robbery, he sanctioned two murders and ordered the kidnap of Miss Andrews.'

'Do you have any other far-fetched claims to offer, Inspector?' said Tallis, incredulously. 'Are you going to tell me, for instance, that Sir Humphrey is about to assassinate the Queen or steal the Crown Jewels?'

'No, Superintendent.'

'Then do not plague me with your ridiculous notions.'

'Sir Humphrey is our man. Take my word for it.'

'Listen, Inspector. I can accept that men from the ranks, like Jukes and the Seymour brothers, may have gone astray but not someone who was once a senior officer. You have no concept of what it takes to become a major in the British Army. I do. It shapes you for life. Sir Humphrey is no more likely to have committed these crimes than I am.'

Superintendent Tallis was peremptory. Colbeck had come into his office to announce what he felt was a critical breakthrough in the investigation, only to have cold water liberally poured over his suggestion by his superior. Remaining calm in the face of the other's intransigence, he tried to reason with him.

'Will you not at least hear what we found out, sir?'

'No, Inspector. The idea is ludicrous.'

'Sergeant Leeming and I do not think so.'

'Then I have to overrule the pair of you. Look elsewhere.'

'We have,' said Colbeck. 'At a man named Thomas Sholto, who was a Captain in the same regiment. Have you heard of him as well?'

'Not until this moment.'

'Then you will not have prior knowledge of *his* innocence.'

'Do not be impertinent.'

'Well, at least do us the courtesy of taking us seriously.'

'Why should I bother to do that?' said Tallis, sourly. 'It is quite obvious to me that neither you nor Sergeant Leeming are aware of who Sir Humphrey is. Did you know, for example, that he is a distinguished Member of Parliament?'

'No,' admitted Colbeck. 'We did not.'

'He has only been in the House for three or four years yet he has already made his mark. Sir Humphrey is already being talked of as a future minister.'

'That does not prevent him from robbing a train.'

'Why should he *need* to do such a thing, Inspector? He's a rich man with a dazzling political career ahead of him. It would be sheer lunacy to jeopardise that.'

'In his mind,' argued Colbeck, 'there was no jeopardy at all. Sir Humphrey did not expect to get caught. That is why the crimes were planned with such precision.'

'Balderdash!'

'If you will not listen to us, I'm sure that Mr Mayne will.'

'The Commissioner will tell you exactly what I do,' said Tallis, jabbing a finger at him. 'Sir Humphrey Gilzean has a position in society. He has neither the time nor inclination to commit crimes.'

'I am persuaded that he had both,' said Colbeck, unmoved

by the Superintendent's belligerence. 'Like you, we had our doubts at first so we sought the opinion of someone else – someone who knew him in the army and who has been employed by him since then.'

'And who was that?'

'Harry Seymour.'

'You questioned him again?'

'No,' replied Colbeck, 'we simply confronted him with two names and watched his reaction. You saw for yourself how convinced he was that he would somehow be set free. So I told him that it could not happen because we had both Sir Humphrey and Thomas Sholto in custody.'

'What did he say to that?'

'Nothing, sir, but his face gave him away. He turned white.'

Tallis shook his head. 'That could simply have been shock at hearing a familiar name from his days in the army.'

'We repeated the process with Vernon Seymour. He was even more dismayed than his brother. Ask Sergeant Leeming,' said Colbeck. 'The look on Vernon Seymour's face was as good as a confession.'

The news forced Tallis to think again. Unwilling to accept that anyone in Gilzean's position would ever be drawn into criminal activity, he tried to refute the claim but could not find the arguments to do so. He had an ingrained respect for Members of Parliament that blinded him to the possibility that they might not always be men of high moral probity. On the other hand, Inspector Colbeck and Sergeant Leeming would not have plucked the name of Sir Humphrey Gilzean out of the air. And it did seem to have upset two of the prisoners in custody. Searching for a means of exonerating Gilzean, he finally remembered one.

'No, no,' he insisted, 'Sir Humphrey would never

contemplate such crimes – especially at a time like this.'

'What do you mean, Superintendent?'

'The man is still in mourning.'

'For whom?'

'His wife. I remember reading of the tragedy in the newspaper.'

'What happened?'

'Shortly before last Christmas, Lady Gilzean was killed in a riding accident. Sir Humphrey is still grieving for her.'

After placing a large basket of flowers in front of the gravestone, Sir Humphrey Gilzean knelt down on the grass to offer up a silent prayer. When he opened his eyes again, he read the epitaph that had been etched into the marble. He spoke in a loving whisper.

'I will repay, Lucinda,' he said. 'I will repay.'

CHAPTER TWELVE

During the ten years of its construction, Robert Colbeck had been past the House of Commons on an almost daily basis, and he had watched it grow from piles of assorted building materials into its full Gothic glory. However, he had never had an opportunity to enter the place before and looked forward to the experience. As he approached from Whitehall, he saw that work was continuing on the massive clock tower, though completion was not anticipated for some years yet. Until then, Members of Parliament would have to rely on their respective pocket watches, opening up the possibility of endless partisan strife over what was the correct time of day.

When he entered the building, he found the atmosphere rather cold and forbidding, as if a church had been stripped of its mystery and given over to purely temporal functions. Unlike those who filed into the Lower Chamber to take their seats, Colbeck was not there for the purposes of debate. All that interested him were the heated exchanges of an earlier year. Repairing to the library, he introduced himself, made his request then sat down at a table with some bound copies of *Hansard* in front of him. As he leafed through the pages of the first volume, he reflected that Luke Hansard, the printer who had started to publish parliamentary debates way back in 1774, must have felt that he was bequeathing a priceless resource to posterity. What he had not anticipated was that he might, one day in the future, help a Detective Inspector to solve a series of heinous crimes.

Colbeck was concentrating on the year 1847 for two principal reasons. It was shortly after Sir Humphrey Gilzean had become a Member of Parliament and he would therefore have tried to make a good impression by taking part early on in the verbal jousting that enlivened the Commons. In addition, it was the year when investment in the railways was at its height, reaching a peak of over £30 million before declining sharply when the bubble later burst with dramatic effect. Colbeck knew that, in 1847, a substantial amount of time had been devoted to the discussion of Railway Bills and that one of the most insistent voices in the debates would be that of George Hudson, M.P. for Sunderland, the now disgraced Railway King.

It did not take him long to find the name of Sir Humphrey Gilzean, Conservative, representing a constituency in his native Berkshire and sitting on the Opposition benches. His maiden speech, unsurprisingly, had been delivered on the vexed question of railways. Opposing a bill for the extension of a line in Oxfordshire, he had spoken with great passion about the urgent necessity of preserving the English countryside from further encroachments by the Great Western Railway. It was not the only occasion when he had raised his voice in anger. Colbeck found several debates during which Gilzean had risen in defiance against those with vested interests in the railway system.

Gilzean's speeches were not confined to the railways. As he flicked through the rhetorical flourishes, Colbeck learnt that the man had firm opinions on almost every subject, deploring the repeal of the Corn Laws by his own party, reviling the Chartists as dangerous revolutionaries who should be suppressed by force, and showing a special interest in foreign affairs. But his heavy artillery was reserved for repeated attacks on the railways. Since it mentioned his favourite poet, Colbeck was particularly interested in a speech that denounced the Great Western Railway.

William Blake, may I remind you – a poet with whom I will not claim any spiritual affinity – once spoke of building Jerusalem in England's green and pleasant land. He was fortunate to die before the industrial infidels made his dream an impossibility. Green pastures are everywhere darkened by the shadow of the railway system. Pleasant land is everywhere dug up, defaced and destroyed in the name of the steam locomotive. When Blake wrote of chariots of fire, he did not envisage them in such hideous profusion, scarring the countryside, frightening the livestock, filling the air with noise and smoke, imposing misery wherever they go. And who benefits from these engines of devastation? The shareholders of the Great Western Railway – vandals to a man!

Colbeck had read enough. With the words still ringing in his ears, he went off in pursuit of someone whose hatred of the railways amounted to nothing short of a mania. Sir Humphrey Gilzean was clearly a fanatic. Convinced that he had identified the man behind the crimes, Colbeck was ready to bring his parliamentary career to an abrupt halt. There was, he acknowledged, one problem. Abducted from her doorstep, Madeleine Andrews was being held by Gilzean and that gave him a decided advantage. The thought made

Colbeck shudder. It also caused him to break into a run when he came out into daylight once more. He had to find her soon.

They kept her in a wine cellar this time. Long, low and with a vaulted ceiling, it seemed to run the full length of the house and contained rack upon rack of expensive wine. Minimal light came in through the small windows that looked out on a trench alongside the wall of the building. Even on such a warm day, the place was cold and damp. It was also infested with spiders and Madeleine Andrews, liberated from her bonds, walked into dozens of invisible webs as she tried to explore her new prison. It was one more source of displeasure for her.

Madeleine was beyond fear now. She felt only disgust and anger at her captors. Though no explanation had been given to her, she had soon worked out that she was a pawn in a game against Scotland Yard as personified by Inspector Robert Colbeck. If they had not been worried by the detective's skills, she believed, they would not have needed to take a hostage. It was firm proof that Colbeck was getting closer all the time. Madeleine just hoped that she would still be unharmed when he finally caught up with her.

Meanwhile, she intended to fight back on her own behalf. Like her father, she had a combative spirit when roused. It was time to issue a challenge, to show her captors that she was no weak and harmless woman. Her first instinct was to smash as many bottles of wine as she could, venting her fury in a bout of destruction. But she saw that a wine bottle was also a formidable weapon. Used in the right way, it might even help her to escape from her dank dungeon. Madeleine picked up a bottle and held it by its neck. She was armed.

It was not long before she had the chance to test her

resolve. Heavy feet were heard descending the steps outside then a key turned in the lock. Keeping the bottle behind her, Madeleine backed against a wall, her heart pounding at her own bravado. When the door swung open, the bearded man who had kidnapped her stepped into the cellar. Thomas Sholto was in a playful mood.

'I wondered how you were getting on,' he said, grinning at her.

'Who *are* you?' she demanded.

'A friend, Madeleine. There's no need to be afraid of me. I'm sorry we have to keep you down here in the cellar, though, in one sense, it may be the appropriate place, for I'm sure that you taste as delicious as any of this wine.' He took a step closer. 'A room is being prepared for you even as we speak,' he told her. 'It is merely a question of making the windows secure so that you will not take it into your pretty little head to try to get away from us. That would be a very silly thing to do, Madeleine.'

'How long are you keeping me here?'

'Until your ardent admirer, Inspector Robert Colbeck, is suitably diverted. I can see why he has been ensnared by your charms.' Sholto came even closer. 'In this light, you might even pass for a beauty.'

'Keep away from me!' she warned, eyes aflame.

'A beauty with real spirit – that's even better.'

'Where are we?'

'In a much nicer part of the country than Camden Town,' he said with a condescending smile. 'You should be grateful to me. Since we first met, I've taken you up in the world. There are not many railwayman's daughters who have stayed in such a fine house as this. At the very least, I think that I deserve a kiss from you.'

'Stand off!'

'But I'm not going to hurt you, Madeleine. Surely you can spare one tiny kiss from those lovely red lips of yours. Come here.'

'No!' she cried.

Ignoring her protest, he reached out for her. Madeleine tried to fend him off with one hand, using the other to swing the bottle out from behind her back. Sholto ducked instinctively but it caught him a glancing blow on the side of the head before continuing on its way to smash into the brickwork. Glass went everywhere and red wine sprayed over the both of them. Having come off far worse than her, Sholto was incensed.

'You little bitch!' he yelled, his forehead cut and his beard glinting with shards of glass. 'I'll make you sorry that you did that.'

Grabbing her by the shoulders, he pushed Madeleine back against the wall and knocked all the breath out of her. Before he could strike her, however, a voice rang out from above.

'Thomas!' shouted Gilzean. 'What are you *doing* down there?'

The cab was driven as fast as the traffic permitted, the driver using both whip and vocal commands whenever a clear space opened up in front of them. Seated inside the cab, Sergeant Leeming asked for details.

'Upper Brook Street?'

'Sir Humphrey Gilzean rents a house there,' explained Colbeck.

'Do you expect him to be at home?'

'That would be too much to ask, Victor.'

'Does the Superintendent know that we're going?'

'Not yet.'

Leeming was worried. 'He'll be angry when he finds out.'

'That depends on what we discover,' said Colbeck. 'For reasons that we both know, Mr Tallis is temperamentally unable to accept that a man like Sir Humprey Gilzean – in mourning for his late wife – would ever stoop to such villainy. Our job is to enlighten him.'

'He does not take kindly to enlightenment.'

'We'll cross that bridge when we come to it.'

'You can go first, sir.'

When the cab arrived at its destination, Colbeck paid the driver and sent him on his way. After sizing the house up, he rang the doorbell and waited. There was no response. He rang the doorbell again and brought the brass knocker into action as well.

'Nobody there,' concluded Leeming.

'We need to get inside somehow.'

'We can't force our way in, sir.'

'That would be quite improper,' agreed Colbeck, slipping a hand into his pocket. 'So we'll try to manage it without resorting to force.'

Making sure that nobody in the street was watching, he inserted a picklock into position and jiggled it about. Leeming was scandalised.

'What on earth are you doing, Inspector?' he asked.

'Making use of a little device that I confiscated from a burglar we arrested earlier this year. He called it a betty and swore that it could open any lock and . . .' he grinned as he heard a decisive click, 'it seems that he was right.'

Opening the door, he went swiftly inside. Leeming followed with grave misgivings. As the door shut behind them, he was very unhappy.

'We are trespassing on private property,' he said.

'No, Victor,' asserted Colbeck. 'We are taking steps to track down a man who is responsible for a series of crimes that include the kidnap of an innocent young woman. While her life is imperilled, we have no time to discuss the legal niceties of home ownership. Action is required.'

Leeming nodded obediently. 'Tell me what to do, Inspector.'

'Search the downstairs rooms. I'll take those upstairs.'

'What are we looking for?'

'Anything that connects Sir Humphrey to those crimes – letters, plans, notes, information about the railways. Be quick about it.'

'Yes, sir.'

While the Sergeant instituted a rapid search of the ground floor, Colbeck went upstairs and checked room after room in succession. Disappointingly, there was nothing that could be used as evidence against Gilzean. Empty drawers and wardrobes showed that he had quit the premises. In doing so, he had taken great pains to leave nothing incriminating behind him. Colbeck went up to the attic. The bedroom at the rear clearly belonged to a manservant because some of his clothing was still there, but it was the room overlooking Upper Brook Street that really interested him.

The moment that Colbeck went into it, he experienced a strange but compelling sensation. Madeleine Andrews had been there. With no visual confirmation of the fact, he was nevertheless certain that she had been held captive in the room, kept in by the stout lock on the door and the bars on the window. Sitting on the edge of the bed, Colbeck ran his fingers gently over the indentation in the pillow. He doubted if she had had much sleep but he was convinced that Madeleine's head had lain there. That discovery alone, in his mind, justified the illegal mode of entry. Colbeck hurried downstairs.

Sergeant Leeming was in the library, sifting through some items he had taken from the mahogany secretaire. He looked up apologetically as the Inspector came into the room.

'I thought that this would be the most likely place,' he said, 'but all I can find is a collection of bills, a few invitations and some notes for a speech at the House of Commons. What about you, sir?'

'She was here, Victor. Miss Andrews was definitely here.'

'How do you know?'

'There was something in the atmosphere of an attic room that spoke to me,' said Colbeck. 'Also, the key was *outside* the door. How many hosts lock their guests in?'

'I searched the other rooms without success, though I can tell you one thing. Judging by what I found in the kitchen bin, Sir Humphrey dined very well last night. He obviously enjoys fine wine. There are dozens of bottles here. As for this desk,' he went on, dropping the bills on to the desk, 'it's been no help at all.'

'Perhaps you've been looking in the wrong place.'

'I've searched every drawer thoroughly.'

'No, Victor,' said Colbeck, 'you searched everything that you could see in front of you. What about the secret compartment?'

'I didn't know that there was one.'

'My father and grandfather were cabinetmakers. I watched both of them build secretaires just like this and they always included a secret compartment where valuable items could be stored.' Bending over the desk, he began to tap various parts of it, listening carefully for a hollow sound. 'All that we have to do is to locate the spring.'

'If there was anything of real value there,' said Leeming, 'then Sir Humphrey would surely have taken it with him.'

'We shall see.'

Along the back of the desk was a row of pigeonholes with matching doors. Leeming had left them open but Colbeck closed them in order to experiment with the carved knobs on each door. After pressing them all in turn, he started to twist them sharply. When that failed to produce a result, he pressed two of the knobs simultaneously. The Sergeant was astonished when he heard a pinging sound and saw a hidden door suddenly flip open. It fitted so beautifully into the side of the desk that Leeming would never have guessed that it was there. Colbeck reached inside to take out the single envelope that lay inside. He looked at the name on the front.

'What is it, sir?'

'A letter addressed to me.'

Leeming's jaw dropped. 'He was *expecting* you to find it?'

'No,' said Colbeck, slitting the envelope open with a paper knife. 'My guess is that it would have been sent to me in due course.'

'How? The house is closed up.'

'I suspect that a manservant has been left behind. His clothing is still upstairs. He would probably have been deputed to deliver this. Yes,' he added, perusing the letter, 'it has tomorrow's date on it. I was not supposed to read it until then. It gives instructions regarding the exchange of the three prisoners for Miss Andrews in a couple of days' time. In other words,' he declared, 'Sir Humphrey never intended that he would trade his hostage for the men in custody.'

'Then why did he send that first demand?'

'To confuse us and to gain himself some leeway. Here,' he said, giving the letter to his companion. 'If this does not persuade the Superintendent that we are on the right trail, then nothing will.'

'I hope that you are right – or we are in trouble.'

'Have faith.'

'It's all that I can cling onto.'

'We have firm evidence here,' said Colbeck, taking the original ransom note from his pocket and holding it beside the letter. 'Do you see what I see, Victor? Same capital letters, same hand, same ink, same stationery. What do you say to that?'

Leeming chuckled. 'Thank God your father was a cabinetmaker!'

Sir Humphrey Gilzean had no sympathy whatsoever for him. As he looked at his friend's wounds and his wine-stained waistcoat, he was filled with disgust for Thomas Sholto.

'All I can say is that it serves you right,' he snarled. 'What madness drove you to go into the wine cellar in the first place? I told you to leave her alone.'

'I was curious,' whined Sholto, examining his face in the drawing room mirror. 'Look what she did to me. Cuts all over my forehead. But for the beard, my face would have been lacerated to bits. And this waistcoat is *ruined*.'

'That's the price of curiosity, Thomas.'

'I was merely going to take her up to her room.'

'You were there for sport,' said Gilzean, coldly, 'so do not even try to deny it. You could not bear the idea of having a pretty young woman at your mercy without taking advantage of the fact.'

'And what is wrong with that?' asked Sholto.

'To begin with, it was against my express orders. I told you that Miss Andrews was not to be molested. Think how terrified she must already be.'

'She was not terrified when she tried to take my head off with that wine bottle. There was real venom in her eyes. The woman attempted to *kill* me, Humphrey.'

'No, Thomas. She tried to escape and I admire her for that.'

Sholto was aghast. 'You admire her for attacking me in that way?' he said, gesticulating wildly. 'She could have split my head open. If you want my opinion, she should be bound and gagged as long as we have her with us.'

'I'll make any decisions regarding Miss Andrews.'

'She's dangerous, Humphrey.'

'Only when provoked,' replied the other. 'Had you not gone to the wine cellar, none of this would have happened. You've always been too hot-blooded, Thomas. Try to curb your desires.'

'Some of us do not share your monastic inclinations,' said Sholto with disdain. Seeing his friend's angry reaction, he was instantly contrite. 'Look, I take that back unreservedly. I did not mean to sneer at you, Humphrey. I appreciate your situation all too well. I know how difficult life has been for you since Lucinda died.'

Gilzean stared at him with a muted rage and indignation. Sholto had touched him on a sensitive spot and he was in pain. It was some while before he allowed himself to speak. Retaining his composure, he gave the other man a simple warning.

'Do not *ever* mention my wife again, Thomas.'

'No, no, of course not.'

'There are limits even to my tolerance of you.'

'I did apologise.'

'That was not enough.'

'Wait a moment,' said Sholto, wilting under his stern gaze and feeling the need to defend himself. 'Do not forget what

I have done on your behalf. Who helped to set up the train robbery? I did. Who committed the two murders? I did. Who ordered Jukes and the Seymour brothers to blow up the Kilsby Tunnel? I did. Who dressed up as a policeman and abducted Miss Andrews from her house? I did. Ask yourself this, Humphrey – where would you be without me?'

'I would not be looking at a man who disobeyed instructions and was nearly brained by a wine bottle as a result.' His voice softened and he tried to make peace. 'Look, I know that you did all those things, Thomas, and I'm eternally grateful, but you've made a handsome profit out of the enterprise.'

'So have you.'

'In my case, there have been losses as well as gains.'

'Only if Inspector Colbeck overhauls us,' said Sholto, 'and what chance is there of that?'

'None whatsoever – for the next few days at least. Meanwhile . . .'

'Yes, yes. I know. Leave Miss Andrews alone.'

'If you don't,' cautioned Gilzean, 'then I'll be the one coming at you with a wine bottle in my hand. And I can assure you that it will not be to offer you a drink.'

Victor Leeming could think of several places that he would rather be at that particular moment. Travelling by train on the Great Western Railway, seated opposite Superintendent Tallis and Inspector Colbeck, he was in considerable discomfort. The improved stability offered by the broad gauge track failed to dispel the queasiness that he always felt in a railway carriage, nor did it still the turmoil in his mind. Since it would be late evening by the time they reached Berkshire, they would be obliged to stay overnight at an inn. It would be the fourth time in a week that he would be separated from his wife and there would be severe reproaches to face when he returned home again.

His uneasiness was not helped by the hostile glances that Tallis was directing at him from time to time. He felt the Superintendent's silent reproof pressing down on him like a heavy weight. Observing his distress, Robert Colbeck tried to divert attention away from his beleaguered Sergeant.

'At least, you must now admit that Sir Humphrey is the culprit,' he said to Tallis. 'That fact is incontrovertible.'

'I was not entirely persuaded by your evidence, Inspector.'

'But that letter was clear proof of his involvement.'

'I am less interested in the letter than in the means by which you acquired it,' said Tallis, meaningfully. 'However, we will let that pass for the time being. No, what finally brought me round to the unpalatable truth that Sir Humphrey Gilzean might, after all, be implicated, was a visit from the wife of Arthur Jukes. While you and Sergeant Leeming were making your unauthorised visit to Upper Brook Street, she called to report the disappearance of her husband.'

'What state was she in?' asked Colbeck.

'A deplorable one. I could not stop the woman crying. When I told her why her husband was missing, she wailed even more. I've never heard such caterwauling. Marriage,' he pronounced with the air of a man who considered the institution to be a species of virulent disease, 'is truly a bed of nails.'

'Only when you're lucky enough to lie on it,' muttered Leeming.

Tallis glared at him. 'Did you speak, Sergeant?'

'No, sir. I was just clearing my throat.'

'Try to do so less irritatingly.'

'What did Mrs Jukes tell you, sir?' said Colbeck.

'Exactly what I expected,' replied Tallis. 'That her husband was the finest man on God's earth and that he would never even think of committing a crime.'

'She should have seen him at the Crystal Palace,' said Leeming. 'Jukes was ready to blow the place up. Fortunately, we were there.'

'Yes, Sergeant – you, Inspector Colbeck and a certain Irishman. That's another thing I'll pass over for the time being,' he said with asperity. 'What I learnt from Mrs Jukes – in between her outbursts of hysteria – was that her husband had been out of work. Then he got a visit from a bearded man whom Jukes later described to her as a captain from his old regiment.'

'Thomas Sholto,' decided Colbeck.

'So it would appear. Soon after that, she told me, her husband came into some money. Enough to pay off his debts and move house.'

Leeming sat up. 'Did Mrs Jukes never ask where his sudden wealth came from?'

'She was his wife, Sergeant. She believed every lie he told her.'

'My wife wouldn't let me get away with anything like that.'

'You are unlikely to rob a mail train.'

'Given the choice, I avoid trains of all kinds, Superintendent.'

'We know this is an ordeal for you, Victor,' said Colbeck with compassion, 'but at least we have a first class carriage to ourselves. You do not have to suffer in front of strangers.'

'That's no consolation, sir.'

'Forget about yourself, man,' chided Tallis. 'Do you hear me telling you about my headache or complaining of my bad tooth? Of course not. In pursuit of villains such as these, personal discomfort is irrelevant. While you and the Inspector were otherwise engaged today, I had a further insight into how many lives have been damaged by these people.'

'Did you, sir?'

'I had a visit from a gentleman whose identity must remain a secret, and who would not confide in me until I had given that solemn undertaking. Do you know what he came to talk about?'

'Blackmail?' guessed Colbeck.

'Yes, Inspector,' continued Tallis. 'Someone had accosted him with a letter he was incautious enough to write to a young man in Birmingham, offering him money if he would care to visit London. I did nor care to pry into the nature of their relationship,' he went on, inhaling deeply through his nose, 'but it clearly put him in an embarrassing position.'

'Is he married, sir?'

'No, but he has reputation to maintain.'

'What price did the blackmailer put on that reputation?'

'Two hundred pounds.'

'Just for writing a letter?' said Leeming.

'A compromising letter, Sergeant,' noted Tallis. 'I advised him not to pay and promised him that the people behind the attempted blackmail would soon be in custody.'

'He had the sense to report it to you,' said Colbeck. 'Others, I fear, did not. Stealing those mail bags must have paid dividends.'

'It did the opposite to the Post Office. They have been swamped with protests from those whose correspondence went astray. There's talk of legal action. Having spoken to this gentleman today, I can see why.'

Victor Leeming sighed. 'Murder, robbery, assault, blackmail, kidnap, destruction of railway property, conspiracy to blow up the Crystal Palace – is there any crime that these devils have *not* committed?'

'Yes,' said Colbeck, thinking about Madeleine Andrews and fearing for her virtue. 'There is one crime, Victor, and the man who dares to commit it will have to answer directly to me.'

Madeleine Andrews was also concerned for her safety. She had been moved to an upstairs room at the rear of the house and, through the wooden bars that had been fixed across the windows that day, she could, until darkness fell, look out on a large, blossoming, well-kept garden that was ablaze with colour. The room had clearly belonged to a maidservant but Madeleine did not object to that. She had not only been rescued from the gloom of the wine cellar, she had access to the meagre wardrobe of the former occupant. Soaked with red wine, her own dress was too uncomfortable to wear so she changed into a maidservant's clothing, relieved that the woman for whom it had been made was roughly the same shape and size as herself.

Unlike Thomas Sholto, she had sustained only the tiniest injuries to her face when the wine bottle shattered. Dipping a cloth into the bowl of water provided, she soon cleaned away the spots of blood on her face. By the light of an oil lamp, she now sat beside the little table on which a tray of untouched food was standing. There was no hope of escape. In daring to fight back, she had given herself away. From now on, they would take extra precautions to guard her.

Her abiding concern was for the bearded man who had cornered her in the cellar. Had they not been interrupted at a critical moment, Madeleine might have been badly beaten. Patently, her attacker had no qualms about striking a woman. Once he had subdued her by force, she feared, he would satisfy the lust she had seen bubbling in his eyes. Another long and sleepless night lay ahead. She looked around for a weapon with which to defend herself but could find nothing that would keep the bearded man at bay. Madeleine felt more exposed than ever.

Her mind turned once more to her father. Like her, he was trapped in a bedroom from which he could not move. She knew that he would be in a torment of anxiety about her and Madeleine blamed herself yet again for putting him in such a position by being so easily gulled. Instead of representing law and order, the policeman who had enticed her away was a dangerous criminal with designs on her. She was glad that her father could not see what she was being forced to endure.

Hunger began to trouble her so she nibbled at some of the food, keeping her ears open for the sound of approaching feet. But nobody came to disturb her. Down in the hall, she heard a clock strike the hours. It was only when the chimes of midnight finally came that she felt able to relax slightly. If the bearded man were going to force himself upon her, he would surely have done so by now. Determined not to sleep, Madeleine nevertheless lay down on the hard bed. How long she stayed awake, she could not tell, but fatigue eventually got the better of her and she dozed off.

She was awake again at dawn, sitting up guiltily as fingers of light poked in through the windows. Madeleine got up to check the door but it was still locked. She drank some milk to bring herself fully awake before washing her face in the bowl. When she looked at the oil lamp, still giving off a faint glow, she realised that she might have a weapon after all. Its heavy base could knock someone unconscious if she were able to deliver a hard enough blow. But the bearded man would be more wary next time. Madeleine would not be able to catch him unawares again.

Tired, frightened, worried about her father, imprisoned in a strange house and wearing someone else's dress, she tried to stave off despair by praying that she would soon be released. Madeleine even included the name of Robert Colbeck in her prayers, more in desperation than in hope. While she knew that he would be searching hard for her, she was afraid that he would never find her in such a remote spot.

Still thinking about him, drawing comfort from the memory of the brief times they had spent together, missing and needing him more than ever, Madeleine drifted across to a window and looked out. The first rays of sunlight were slowly dispelling the darkness and she was able to make out a few ghostly figures moving furtively towards the house through the garden. She blinked in surprise. When she peered out again, she saw that the men seemed to be carrying firearms. Madeleine felt the first surge of optimism since her kidnap.

'Inspector Colbeck!' she exclaimed.

Superintendent Edward Tallis had insisted on taking charge of the operation. Having had the house surrounded by armed policemen, he and Sergeant Leeming approached in an open carriage that had been hired at the nearest railway station. Inspector Colbeck preferred to ride alongside them on a horse. Even in the hazy light, they could admire the size and splendour of the Gilzean ancestral residence. It was a magnificent pile with classical proportions that gave it a stunning symmetry. Hampered by the presence of his superior, Colbeck had to follow a plan of action with which he did not entirely agree. He would certainly not have done what Tallis now did. When the carriage reached the forecourt, the driver reined in the two horses so that the Superintendent could stand up and bellow in a voice that must have been heard by everyone inside the building.

'Sir Humphrey Gilzean and Thomas Sholto!' he boomed. 'My name is Superintendent Tallis of the Metropolitan Police, and I have warrants for your arrest.' Within seconds, two upstairs windows opened. 'I have deployed men all around the house. Give yourselves up now.'

Taking stock of the awkwardness of his situation, Gilzean closed his window immediately but Sholto left his open while he retreated into his bedroom. Moments later, he reappeared with a pistol in his hand and aimed it at Tallis. There was a loud report and the Superintendent's hat was knocked from his head. Leeming pulled him down into the carriage. Colbeck, meanwhile, ordered the driver to take the vehicle out of range, following him as he did so. Sholto had now vanished from the window.

When the carriage came to a stop, Tallis was livid.

'He shot at me!' he cried, indignantly. 'He tried to kill me.'

'No sir,' said Colbeck. 'That was just a warning shot to make you pull back. I told you that it would be unwise to challenge them like that.'

'The house is ringed with policemen. They have no way out.'

'By throwing away our advantage, we may have given them one. Sir Humphrey will surely have planned for contingencies.'

'So did I, Inspector. That's why I brought so many men. Your idea was that you and Sergeant Leeming would make the arrests on your own. What could two of you have achieved?'

'An element of surprise, sir.'

'I am bound to agree,' said Leeming.

Tallis was acerbic. 'Who invited *your* opinion, Sergeant?'

'Nobody, sir.'

'Then keep it to yourself.'

'Of course, sir.'

'All we have to do is to wait here until Sir Humphrey comes to his senses. He will soon see how heavily outnumbered he is and accept that resistance is pointless.'

'I hope so,' said Leeming, picking up the top hat and putting a finger through the bullet hole. 'I believe that was Captain Sholto who fired at you, sir. Obviously, *he* does not think that resistance is pointless.'

Tallis snatched the hat from him and put it beside him on the seat. Colbeck was keeping an eye on the house, waving back any policemen who appeared and indicating that they should take cover. It was not long before the window of Gilzean's bedroom was opened. Fully dressed and with a defiant smile, he surveyed the scene below.

'Congratulations, Superintendent,' he called out. 'I did not expect to see you for days yet – if at all. The credit, I am sure, must go to Inspector Colbeck so I will address my remarks to him.'

'I am in charge here,' asserted Tallis, rising officiously to his feet as he turned to Colbeck. 'And not the Inspector.'

'But you do not have the same personal interest as your colleague. He is a gentleman who will always put the safety of a lady first. Am I right, Inspector Colbeck?'

'What have you done with Miss Andrews?' asked Colbeck.

'She is right here. Quite unharmed – as yet.'

Madeleine was suddenly pulled into view. Colbeck could see that her wrists were bound together and that she was shaking with fear. Gilzean put a pistol to her temple.

'If anyone tries to stop us,' he warned, 'Miss Andrews dies.'

'He would never dare to kill a woman,' said Tallis.

'Call your men off, Inspector Colbeck.'

'I give the orders here.'

'This is no time to argue, Superintendent,' said Colbeck,

his gaze fixed on Madeleine. 'We must obey him or he'll carry out his threat. I'll not trade Miss Andrews's life for anything.' Before Tallis could stop him, he gave a command. 'Stand back, everyone! Let them go!'

'I have not made a decision yet,' protested Tallis.

'Then make it, sir. Do as he says or tell him to blow out her brains. But bear this in mind, Superintendent,' he went on, looking at him with burning conviction, 'if Miss Andrews is killed, or harmed in any way, I will hold you responsible.'

Tallis wrestled with his conscience. Keen to arrest the two men who had sparked the dramatic series of crimes, he did not want a life to be lost in the process, especially that of a defenceless young woman. He was also swayed by Colbeck's intervention. In the end, trying to attest his authority, he barked his own order.

'Stay where you are!' he shouted. 'Lower your weapons and do not try to stop them!' He sat down heavily in his seat. 'I never thought to see the day when I gave in to the threats of a criminal!'

'They will not get far,' Colbeck assured him. 'But next time, I suggest, we should not arrive with such a fanfare. All that we have done is to endanger their hostage.'

Tallis brooded in silence and stared at the house. They were not kept waiting long. The coachman was the first to emerge, running to the stables at the side of the house with a servant in attendance. Against such an emergency, the carriage was already loaded with baggage but the horses had to be harnessed. While that was happening the front door of the house remained shut. When the carriage finally came round the angle of the building, Colbeck dismounted, tethered his horse to a bush and walked briskly up the drive.

'Wherever is he *going*?' demanded Tallis. 'Those men are armed.'

'Inspector Colbeck has taken that into account, sir,' said Leeming.

'I gave him no permission to move.'

'He obviously feels that he does not need it.'

Colbeck strode on until he was no more than twenty yards from the house. When three figures came out, he had a clear view of them. Dressed in a satin cloak with a hood, Madeleine Andrews was being forced along between Gilzean and Sholto. The men stopped when they saw Colbeck standing there, weighing him up with a mixture of cold scorn and grudging admiration.

'Are you bearing up, Miss Andrews?' asked Colbeck.

'Yes, Inspector,' she replied, summoning up a brave smile. 'They have not hurt me.'

'Nor will we if the Inspector has the sense to do as I tell him,' said Gilzean, letting Sholto get into the carriage before pushing Madeleine after him. 'Goodbye, Inspector. I am sorry that our acquaintance has to be so fleeting.'

'Well meet again soon, Sir Humphrey,' said Colbeck.

'I think not, sir.'

Clambering into his seat, Gilzean ordered the coachman to drive off. The policemen could simply watch as the vehicle was allowed to leave the estate unimpeded. Tallis was fuming with impotent rage. When the departing carriage was out of sight, he told his driver to take him to the house. Colbeck was standing at the front door when they arrived.

'Have you taken leave of your senses, Inspector?' said Tallis, getting out of the vehicle to confront him. 'From that distance, they could easily have shot you.'

'I wanted to make sure that Miss Andrews was unhurt.'

'You should not have put your own life in danger, man.'

'I survived,' said Colbeck, removing his top hat and examining it for holes. 'And so did my hat, it seems.'

'This is no time for humour. We have just been compelled to let two of the worst criminals I have ever encountered go free, and all that you can do is to joke about it.'

'Their freedom is only temporary, Superintendent.'

'How can we catch them when we have no idea where they have gone? Their escape was obviously planned.'

'Yes,' agreed Colbeck, 'but they did not expect to put their plan into action for a few days yet. They had to leave in a hurry and that means they will not have had time to cover their tracks. Let us search the house,' he urged. 'Well soon find out where they are heading.'

Madeleine Andrews did not wish to be seated beside Thomas Sholto but it spared her the agony of having to face him during the journey. Instead, as the carriage rumbled along at speed, she was looking at Sir Humphrey Gilzean, a man who paid such meticulous attention to his clothing that she was reminded of Colbeck. She felt a pang of regret that she had got so close to the Inspector only to be dragged away again. For his part, Gilzean was also reminded of someone. It put sadness into his eyes and the faintest tremor into his voice.

'That cloak belonged to my wife,' he said, pursing his lips as a painful memory intruded. 'Nothing but extremity would have made me loan it to another woman, but it is a convenient disguise.'

'Where are you taking me?' she asked.

'Somewhere you would never have dreamt of going.' He saw her glance over her shoulder. 'Do not bother to look for help, Miss Andrews,' he advised. 'They are not following us. I have kept watch on the road since we left the house.'

Sholto was angry. 'How did they get to us so soon?' he growled.

'Do not worry about that now.'

'I do worry, Humphrey. I thought that you had led them astray.'

'So did I,' admitted Gilzean, 'but we have a formidable adversary in this Inspector Colbeck. I'm sure that Miss Andrews will agree. He is a remarkable man.'

'He is,' she affirmed, 'and he will catch you somehow.'

'Not if he values your life,' said Sholto.

'Besides,' added Gilzean, 'the gallant Inspector will have to find us first and there is no chance of that. His writ does not run as far as the place we are going.'

Madeleine was alarmed. 'And where is that?' she said.

'You will see. But when we get there, I'm afraid that I will have to divest you of that cloak. It suited my wife perfectly,' he went on with a mournful smile, 'but it does not become you at all.'

'No,' said Sholto, harshly. 'You belong in the servant's dress.'

'There is no need for bad manners, Thomas,' scolded Gilzean.

'Miss Andrews will get no courtesy from me – not after she tried to crack my head open with a wine bottle.'

'*Noblesse oblige*.'

'To hell with that, Humphrey! Do you know what I hope?' he said, turning to glare at Madeleine. 'In one way, I hope that Inspector Colbeck *does* turn up again.'

'Do you?' she said, quailing inwardly.

'Yes, I do – because it will give me the perfect excuse to put a bullet through your head.'

Madeleine said nothing for the remainder of the journey.

While the servants were being questioned by Superintendent Tallis, the house was searched by Inspector Colbeck and

Sergeant Leeming. The three men met up in the drawing room. Hands behind his back, Tallis was pulling on a cigar and standing in front of the marble fireplace. His expression revealed that he had learnt little from his interrogations.

'It is useless,' he said, exhaling a cloud of smoke. 'The servants were told nothing. Even if they had been, they are so ridiculously loyal to their master that they would not betray him.' He fixed an eye on Leeming. 'What did you find, Sergeant?'

'Only that Sir Humphrey has a lot more money than I do, sir,' replied the other. 'Parts of the house are almost palatial. It made me feel as if I was not supposed to be here.'

'This is where those terrible crimes were hatched.'

'Yes,' said Colbeck, 'and I think that I know why.' He handed Tallis a faded newspaper. 'This was tucked away in a desk drawer in the library. It contains a report of the death of Lady Gilzean.'

'She was thrown from a horse. I told you that.'

'But you did not explain how it happened, Inspector. Read the article and you will see that Sir Humphrey and his wife were out riding when the sound of a train whistle disturbed the animals. Lady Gilzean's horse reared and she was thrown from the saddle.'

'No wonder he detests railways,' commented Leeming.

'Who can blame him?' said Tallis, reading the report. 'It was a real tragedy. Lady Gilzean's neck was broken in the fall. However,' he went on, putting the newspaper on the mantelpiece, 'it is one thing to despise the railway system but quite another to wage war against it.'

'It's time for the steam locomotive to strike back,' said Colbeck.

'What are you talking about, Inspector?'

'This, sir.' Colbeck held up a booklet. 'I found this in the desk. It's a timetable for sailings from the port of Bristol. Sir Humphrey Gilzean and his accomplice are fleeing the country.'

'Going abroad?' gasped Tallis. 'Then we'll never catch them.'

'But we will, sir. They are only travelling by carriage, remember, and they will have to pace the horses carefully. We, on the other hand, will be able to go much faster.' Colbeck smiled at him. 'By train.'

When the carriage reached Bristol, the port was a veritable hive of activity. Though narrow at that point, the estuary was deep enough to accommodate the largest ships and several steamers were moored at their landing stages. Madeleine Andrews viewed it all with utter dismay. Furnished with locks, wharves and quays some 6,000 feet in length, the harbour was a forest of masts through which she could see a vast number of sailors and passengers milling around. Hundreds of seagulls wove patterns in the air and added their cries to the general pandemonium. Madeleine shivered. To someone who had never travelled more than ten miles from London in her entire life, the thought of sailing across the sea induced a positive dread.

Yet she had no option. She had been warned what would happen if she dared to call for help and could not take the risk. With her hood up, she was taken aboard between Sir Humphrey Gilzean and Thomas Sholto, and – to her astonishment – was described as Lady Gilzean, leaving the country on her husband's passport. Before she knew what was happening, Madeleine was taken below to a cabin, where she was tied up and gagged. Sholto stood over her.

'If we have any trouble from you,' he threatened, cupping her chin in his palm, 'I'll throw you overboard.'

'You'll do nothing of the kind,' said Gilzean, easing him

away from her. 'Miss Andrews came to our rescue at the house. Without her, we would now be in custody. Show some appreciation, Thomas.'

'Leave me alone with her – and I will.'

'Come, you need some fresh air.'

'What I need is five minutes with her.'

Gilzean took him by the lapel. 'Did you hear what I said?'

Sholto obeyed with reluctance. After tossing a sullen glance at Madeleine, he left the cabin. Gilzean paused at the open door.

'I am sorry that you got caught up in all this,' he said with a note of genuine apology, 'but there was no help for it. Had your father chosen a different occupation, you would not be here now.' There were yells from above and the sound of movement on the deck. 'We are about to set sail,' he noted with satisfaction. 'Where is Inspector Colbeck now?'

Madeleine could not speak but there was panic in her eyes. Gilzean went out and shut the door behind him, turning a key in the lock. He had been unfailingly polite to her and had shielded her from Sholto, but he was still taking her as a prisoner to a foreign country. As the ship rocked and the wind began to flap its canvas, she knew that they had cast off. Madeleine was out of Inspector Colbeck's reach now. All that she could do was to resort to prayer once more.

A few minutes later, she heard the sound of a key in the lock. Thinking that it would be Thomas Sholto, she closed her eyes and tensed instinctively, fearing that he had slipped back to get his revenge for what had happened in the wine cellar. But the person who stepped into the cabin was Robert Colbeck and the first thing that he did was to remove her gag. When she opened her eyes, Madeleine let out a cry of relief. As Colbeck began to untie the ropes that held her, tears of joy rolled down her cheeks.

'How ever did you find us?' she asked.

'I took the precaution of bringing my *Bradshaw* with me.'

'The railway guide?'

'A steam train will always outrun the best horses, Miss Andrews,' he said, untying her legs and setting her free. 'And I was determined that nobody was going to take you away from me.'

Madeleine flung herself into his arms and he held her tight until her sobbing slowly died down. He then stood back to appraise her.

'Have they harmed you in any way?'

'No, Inspector. But one of them keeps threatening to.'

'His name is Thomas Sholto,' said Colbeck. 'We waited until we saw them come up on deck. There was no point in trying to apprehend them while they had you in their grasp. Stay here, Miss Andrews,' he went on, moving to the door. 'I'll be back in due course.'

'Be careful,' she said. 'They are both armed.'

'They are also off guard. Excuse me.'

Standing at the bulwark, Gilzean and Sholto ignored the people who were waving the ship off from the shore and congratulated themselves on their escape. Gilzean was honest.

'It was a Pyrrhic victory,' he conceded. 'I kept my promise to Lucinda and struck back at the railway, but it means, alas, that I am parted from her for a while. No matter, Thomas. I will be able to slip back from France in time. Meanwhile, we have money enough to live in great comfort and anonymity.'

'What about that little vixen down in the cabin?'

'She will be released as soon as we are safely in France.'

'Released?' said Sholto, mutinously. 'After what she did to me?'

'We have no more need of her, Thomas.'

'You may not have – but I certainly do!'

'No,' decreed Gilzean. 'Miss Andrews has borne enough suffering. As soon as we dock, I'll pay for her return passage and give her money to make her way home from Bristol.'

'But she will be able to tell them where we are.'

'France is a much bigger country than England. Even if they sent someone after us – and that is highly unlikely – he would never find us.'

'According to you, Inspector Colbeck would never find us.'

Gilzean was complacent. 'We have seen the last of him now,' he said. 'Bid farewell to England. We are about to start a new life.'

The detectives crept up until they stood only yards behind the two men. Victor Leeming had a hand on his pistol, but Robert Colbeck favoured a more physical approach. Since it was Thomas Sholto who had spirited Madeleine away, the Inspector tackled him first. Rushing forward, he grabbed Sholto by the legs and tipped him over the side of the ship. There was a despairing cry, followed by a loud splash. Gilzean spared no thought for his friend. He reacted quickly, pulling out a pistol. Before Gilzean could discharge it, Colbeck got a firm hold on his wrist and twisted it so that he turned the barrel of the weapon upwards.

Seeing the pistol, almost everyone else on deck backed away as the two men struggled for mastery. Sergeant Leeming pointed his own gun at Gilzean and ordered him to stop but the command went unheard. And since the combatants were now spinning around so violently, it was impossible for Leeming to get a clear shot at the man. He jumped back as Colbeck tripped his adversary up and fell to the deck on top of him. Gilzean fought with even more ferocity now, trying to wrest his hand free so that he could fire his weapon. Using all his strength, he slowly brought the barrel of the gun around so that it was almost trained on its target. Colbeck refused to be beaten, finding a reserve of energy that enabled him to force the pistol downwards and away from himself.

Gilzean's finger tightened on the trigger and the gun went off. A yell of pain mingled with a gasp of horror that came from the watching crowd. Hearing the sound of the gunshot from below, Madeleine came running up on deck, fearing that Colbeck had been killed. Instead, she found him standing over Gilzean, who, compelled to shoot himself, was clutching a shoulder from which blood was now oozing.

'Why did you not leave him to *me*?' complained Leeming.

'I wanted the privilege myself.'

'But I had a weapon.'

'I am sorry, Victor,' said Colbeck with a weary grin. 'You can arrest Thomas Sholto, but you'll have to haul him out of the water first.' He turned to Madeleine. 'They'll not trouble you again, Miss Andrews,' he promised. 'Horses and ships have their place in the scheme of things but they were not enough to defeat the steam locomotive. That is what brought them down. Sir Humphrey was caught by the railways.'

Richard Mayne, the senior Police Commissioner, looked down at the newspapers spread out on his desk and savoured the headlines. The arrest of the two men behind the train robbery and its associated crimes was universally acclaimed as a triumph for the Detective Department at Scotland Yard. After sustaining so much press criticism, they had now been vindicated. That gave Mayne a sense of profound satisfaction. While he could bask in the general praise, however, he was the first to accept that the plaudits should go elsewhere.

He was glad, therefore, when Superintendent Tallis entered with Inspector Colbeck and Sergeant Leeming. The Commissioner came from behind his desk to shake hands with all three in turn, starting, significantly, with Robert Colbeck, a fact that did not go unnoticed by Tallis. The Superintendent shifted his feet.

'Gentlemen,' said Mayne, spreading his arms, 'you have achieved a small miracle. Thanks to your efforts, we have secured some welcome approbation. The headlines in today's newspapers send a message to every villain in the country.'

'Except that most of them can't read, sir,' noted Tallis.

'I was speaking figuratively, Superintendent.'

'Ah – of course.'

'No matter how clever they may be,' continued Mayne, 'we catch them in the end. In short, with a combination of tenacity, courage and detection skills, we can solve any crime.'

'That is what we are here for, sir,' said Tallis, importantly.

'Our role is largely administrative, Superintendent. It is officers like Inspector Colbeck and Sergeant Leeming on whom we rely and they have been shining examples to their colleagues.'

'Thank you, sir,' said Leeming.

'On your behalf, I have received warm congratulations from the Post Office, the Royal Mint, Spurling's Bank, the Chubb factory, the commissioners for the Great Exhibition and, naturally, from the London and North Western Railway Company. The last named wishes to offer both of you free travel on their trains at any time of your choice.'

'I will certainly avail myself of that opportunity,' said Colbeck.

Leeming frowned. 'And I most certainly will not,' he said.

'On the other hand,' he added with a chuckle, 'if the Royal Mint is issuing any invitations to us, I'll be very happy to accept them.'

'They merely send you their heartfelt gratitude,' said Mayne.

Tallis sniffed. 'Far be it from me to intrude a sour note into this welter of congratulation, sir,' he said, 'but I have to draw to your attention the fact that some of the evidence was not obtained in a way that I could bring myself to approve.'

'Yes, I know, Superintendent. I've read your report.'

'Then perhaps you should temper your fulsome compliments with a degree of reproach.'

'This is hardly the moment to do so,' said Mayne, irritably, 'but, since you force my hand, I will. Frankly, I believe that *you* are the person who should be reprimanded. Had you let your men go to Sir Humphrey's house on their own, they might well have made the arrests there. By making your presence known so boldly, Superintendent Tallis, you gave the game away. That was bad policing.'

'We had the house surrounded, sir.'

'Yet somehow they still managed to escape. In all conscience, you must take the blame for that.'

Trying not to grin, Leeming was enjoying the Superintendent's patent unease, but Colbeck came swiftly to his superior's aid.

'It was a shared responsibility, sir,' he told Mayne, 'and we must all take some of the blame. Against anyone but Sir Humphrey Gilzean, the plan that Mr Tallis had devised might well have worked. And the Superintendent did, after all, prove that he is not chained to his desk.'

'That merits approval,' said Mayne, 'it's true. So let us be done with censure and take pleasure from our success. Or, more properly, from the success that you, Inspector Colbeck –

along with Sergeant Leeming here – achieved in Bristol. Both of you are heroes.'

Leeming pulled a face. 'That's not what my wife called me when I stayed away for another night, sir,' he confided. 'She was very bitter.'

'Spare us these insights into your sordid domestic life,' said Tallis.

'We made up in the end, of course.'

'I should hope so, Sergeant,' said Mayne with amusement. 'Mrs Leeming deserves to know that she is married to a very brave man. You will have a written commendation to show her.'

'Thank you, sir,' said Leeming, happily, 'but I only followed where Inspector Colbeck led me. He is the real hero here.'

'I'm inclined to agree.'

'The only reason that we finally caught up with them was that the Inspector had the forethought to put a copy of *Bradshaw's Guide* in his valise. It told us what train we could catch to Bristol.'

'I regard it as an indispensable volume,' explained Colbeck, 'and I never go by rail without it. Unlike Sergeant Leeming, I have a particular fondness for travelling by train. I am grateful that this case gave me such opportunities to do so.'

'A train robbery certainly gave you the chance to show your mettle, Inspector,' said Mayne, 'and everyone has admired the way that you conducted the investigation. But success brings its own disadvantage.'

'Disadvantage?' repeated Colbeck.

'You have obviously not read this morning's papers.'

'I have not yet had the time, sir.'

'Make time, Inspector,' suggested Mayne. 'Every single reporter has christened you with the same name. You are now Inspector Robert Colbeck – the Railway Detective.'

After considering his new title, Colbeck gave a slow smile.

'I think I like that,' he said.

Madeleine Andrews could not understand it. While she was being held in captivity, all that she wanted to do was to return home, yet, now that she was actually there, she felt somehow disappointed. She was thrilled to be reunited with her father again, trying to forget her ordeal by nursing him with renewed love, but she remained strangely detached and even jaded. Caleb Andrews soon noticed it.

'What ails you, Maddy?' he asked.

'Nothing.'

'Are you in pain?'

'No, Father,' she replied.

'Did those men do something to you that you haven't told me about? Is that why you've been behaving like this?' She shook her head. 'Well, something is wrong, I know that.'

'I'm still very tired, that's all.'

'Then you should let someone else look after me while you catch up on your sleep.' He offered his free hand and she took it. 'If there *was* a problem, you would tell me?'

'Of course.'

'I'll hold you to that,' he said, squeezing her hand. 'It might just be that you are missing all the excitement now you are back here.'

'There is nothing exciting about being kidnapped,' she said, detaching her hand. 'It was terrifying. I wish that it had never happened.'

'So do I, Maddy. But the men who held you hostage will be punished. I only wish that I could be there to pull the lever when the hangman puts the noose around their necks.'

'Father!'

'It's what they deserve,' he argued. 'You saw that report

in the paper. It was Sir Humphrey Gilzean who set the other man on to commit those two murders. That means a death penalty for both of them. Yes,' he went on, 'and they found a list of all his accomplices when they searched that baggage they took off the ship. The whole gang is being rounded up.'

'I was as pleased as you to hear that.'

'So why are you moping around the house?'

'I'll be fine in a day or two.'

There was a knock at the front door and she went to the bedroom window to see who it was. Recognising the visitor, she brightened at once and smoothed down her skirt before leaving the room.

'Ah,' said Andrews, drily. 'It must be Queen Victoria again.'

After checking her appearance in the hall mirror, Madeleine opened the door and gave her visitor a warm smile.

'Inspector Colbeck,' she said. 'Do please come in.'

'Thank you, Miss Andrews.' Colbeck removed his top hat and stepped into the house. 'How is your father?'

'Much better now that he has me back again.'

'You would gladden the heart of any parent.'

'Did you wish to see him?'

'In time, perhaps,' said Colbeck. 'I really called to speak to you. I am sure that you will be relieved to know that everyone who took part in the train robbery has now been arrested.'

'Were they all men from Sir Humphrey's old regiment?'

'Most of them were. They became involved because they needed the money. Sir Humphrey Gilzean had another motive.'

'Yes, I know,' she said. 'He did all those terrible things because he believed that a train had killed his wife.'

'Even before that happened, he had a deep-seated hatred of the railways. The death of Lady Gilzean only intensified it.'

'But to go to such extremes – it's unnatural.'

'It certainly changed him from the man that he was,' said Colbeck, soulfully. 'Though I'd never condone what he did, I have a faint sympathy for the man.'

Madeleine was surprised. 'Sympathy – for a criminal?'

'Only for the loss that he endured. I know what it is to lose a loved one in tragic circumstances,' he confided. 'If I'm honest, Miss Andrews, it's what made me become a policeman.' He sighed quietly. 'Since I could never bring the lady in question back, I tried to protect others from the same fate.' He looked deep into her eyes. 'That was why it gave me so much pleasure to come to your aid.'

'This lady you mentioned,' she said, probing gently. 'Was she a member of your family, Inspector?'

'She would have been,' he replied, 'but she had the misfortune to surprise a burglar in her house one night, and made the mistake of challenging him. He became violent.' He waved a hand to dismiss the subject. 'But enough of my past, Miss Andrews. I try not to dwell on it and prefer to look to the future. That is the difference between Sir Humphrey and myself, you see. In the wake of his loss, he sought only to destroy. I endeavour to rebuild.'

'That's very wise of you.'

'Then perhaps you will help in the process.'

'Me?'

'I know that it is indecently short notice,' he said, watching her dimples, 'but are you, by any chance, free on May Day?'

'I could be,' she said, tingling with anticipation. 'Why?'

'In recognition of what happened at the Crystal Palace,' he explained, 'His Royal Highness, Prince Albert, has sent me two tickets for the opening ceremony. I would deem it an honour if you agreed to come with me.'

Madeleine was overjoyed. 'To the Great Exhibition!'

'Yes,' said Colbeck over her happy laughter, 'there are one or two locomotives that I'd like to show you.'

THE EXCURSION TRAIN

On the appointed day about five hundred passengers filled some twenty or twenty-five open carriages – they were called 'tubs' in those days – and the party rode the enormous distance of eleven miles and back for a shilling, children half-price. We carried music with us and music met us at the Loughborough station. The people crowded the streets, filled windows, covered the house-tops, and cheered us all along the line, with the heartiest welcome. All went off in the best style and in perfect safety we returned to Leicester; and thus was struck the keynote of my excursions, and the social idea grew upon me.

Thomas Cook
Leisure Hour (1860)

CHAPTER ONE

London, 1852

They came in droves, converging on Paddington Station from all parts of the capital. Costermongers, coal-heavers, dustmen, dock labourers, coachmen, cab drivers, grooms, glaziers, lamplighters, weavers, tinkers, carpenters, bricklayers, watermen, and street sellers of everything from rat poison to pickled whelks, joined the human torrent that was surging towards the excursion train. Inevitably, the crowd also had its share of thieves, pickpockets, card-sharps, thimble riggers and prostitutes. A prizefight of such quality was an increasingly rare event. It was too good an opportunity for the low life of London to miss.

There was money to be made.

Extra ticket collectors were on duty to make sure that nobody got past the barrier without paying, and additional railway policemen had been engaged to maintain a degree of order. Two locomotives stood ready to pull the twenty-three carriages that were soon being filled by rowdy spectators. The excitement in the air was almost tangible.

Sam Horlock looked on with a mixture of interest and envy.

'Lucky devils!' he said.

'All I see is danger,' complained Tod Galway, the guard of the train. 'Look how many there are, Sam – all of them as drunk as bleedin' lords. There'll be trouble, mark my words. Big trouble. We should never have laid on an excursion train for this rabble.'

'They seem good-natured enough to me.'

'Things could turn ugly in a flash.'

'No,' said Horlock, tolerantly. 'They'll behave themselves. We'll make sure of that. I just wish that I could join them at the ringside. I've a soft spot for milling. Nothing to compare with the sight of two game fighters, trying to knock the daylights out of each other. It's uplifting.'

Sam Horlock was one of the railway policemen deputed to travel on the train. Like his colleagues, he wore the official uniform of dark, high-necked frock coat, pale trousers and a stovepipe hat. He was a jovial man in his forties, short, solid and clean-shaven. Tod Galway, by contrast, was tall, thin to the point of emaciation, and wearing a long, bushy, grey beard that made him look like a minor prophet. A decade older than his companion, he had none of Horlock's love of the prize ring.

'The Fancy!' he said with disgust, spitting out the words. 'That's what they calls 'em. The bleedin' Fancy! There's nothing fancy about this load of ragamuffins. They stink to 'igh 'eaven. We're carryin' the dregs of London today and no mistake.'

'Be fair, Tod,' said Horlock. 'They're not all riff-raff, crammed into the third-class carriages. We've respectable passengers aboard as well in first and second class. Everyone likes the noble art.'

'What's noble about beatin' a man to a pulp?'

'There's skill involved.'

'Pah!'

'There is. There's tactics and guile and raw courage. It's not just a trial of brute strength.'

'I still don't 'old with it, Sam.'

'But it's manly.'

'It's against the bleedin' law, that's what it is.'

'More's the pity!'

'The magistrates ought to stop it.'

'By rights, they should,' agreed Horlock with a grin, 'but they got too much respect for the sport. My guess is that half the magistrates of Berkshire will be there in disguise to watch the contest.'

'Shame on them!'

'They don't want to miss the fun, Tod. Last time we had a fight like this was six or seven years ago when Caunt lost to Bendigo. Now *that* was milling of the highest order. They went toe to toe for over ninety gruelling rounds, the pair of them, drooping from exhaustion and dripping with blood.'

'Yes – and what did that do to the spectators?'

'It set them on fire, good and proper.'

'That's my worry,' admitted Galway, watching a trio of boisterous navvies strut past. 'These buggers are bad enough *before* the fight. Imagine what they'll be like afterwards when their blood is racing and their passions is stoked up. I fear for my train, Sam.'

'There's no need.'

'Think of the damage they could cause to railway property.'

'Not while we're around.'

'We're carryin' over a thousand passengers. What can an 'andful of policemen do against that lot?'

'Ever seen a sheepdog at work?' asked Horlock, hands on hips. 'If it knows its job, one dog can keep a flock of fifty under control. That's what we are, Tod. Sheepdogs of the Great Western Railway.'

'There's only one problem.'

'What's that?'

'You're dealing with wild animals – not with bleedin' sheep.'

When the excursion train pulled out of Paddington in a riot of hissing steam and clanking wheels, it was packed to capacity with eager boxing fans. There were two first-class carriages and three second-class but the vast majority of passengers were squeezed tightly into the open-topped third-class carriages, seated on hard wooden benches yet as happy as if they were travelling in complete luxury. As soon as the train hit open country, rolling landscape began to appear on both sides but it attracted little attention. All that the hordes could see in their mind's eye was the stirring spectacle that lay ahead of them. Isaac Rosen was to take on Bill Hignett in a championship contest.

In prospect, the fight had everything. It was a match between two undefeated boxers at the height of their powers. Rosen worked in a Bradford slaughterhouse where his ferocity had earned him his nickname. Hignett was a giant Negro who toiled on a Thames barge. It was a case of Mad Isaac versus the Bargeman. North versus South. White versus Black. And – to add some real piquancy – Jew versus Christian. Nobody could remain impartial. The London mob was going to cheer on Bill Hignett and they were baying for blood. As flagons of beer were passed around thirsty mouths, tongues were loosened and predictions became ever more vivid.

'The Bargeman will tap his claret with his first punch.'

'Then knock his teeth down his Jewish throat.'

''E'll 'it Mad Isaac all the way back to Bradford.'

'And slaughter the Yid!'

Such were the universally held opinions of the experts who occupied every carriage. In praising Bill Hignett, they denigrated his opponent, swiftly descending into a virulent anti-semitism that grew nastier with each mile they passed. By the time they reached their destination, they were so certain of the outcome of the fight that they indulged in premature celebrations, punching the air in delight or clasping each other in loving embraces. Anxious to be on their way, they poured out of the excursion train as if their lives depended on it.

There was still some way to go. The field in which the fight was being held was over three miles away from Twyford Station but the fans made no complaint about the long walk. Guides were waiting to conduct them to the site and they fell gratefully in behind them. Some began to sing obscene ditties, others took part in drunken horseplay and one lusty young sailor slipped into the bushes to copulate vigorously with a buxom dolly-mop. There was a prevailing mood of optimism. Expectations were high. The long column of tumult began to wend its way through the Berkshire countryside.

Tod Galway was pleased to have got rid of his troublesome cargo but his relief was tempered by the thought that they would have to take the passengers back to London when they were in a more uncontrollable state. As it was, he found a man who was too inebriated to move from one of the third-class carriages, a second who was urinating on to the floor and a third who was being violently sick over a seat. He plucked at his beard with desperation.

'They've got no respect for company property,' he wailed.

'We're bound to have a few accidents, Tod,' said Sam

Horlock, ambling across to him. 'Take no notice.'

'I got to take notice, Sam. I'm *responsible*.'

'So am I – worse luck. I'd give anything to be able to see the Bargeman kick seven barrels of shit out of Mad Isaac. Do you think anyone would notice if I sneak off?'

'Yes,' said Galway, 'and that means you'd lose your job.'

'Be almost worth it.'

The guard was incredulous. 'You taken leave of your senses?'

'This fight is for the championship, Tod.'

'I don't care if it's for that Koh-i-noor Bleedin' Diamond what was give to Queen Victoria. Think of your family, man. You got mouths to feed. What would your wife and children say if you got sacked for watchin' a prizefight?' Horlock looked chastened. 'I know what my Annie'd say and I know what she'd do. If I threw my job away like that, my life wouldn't be worth livin'.'

'It was only a thought.'

'Forget it. I'll give you three good reasons why you ought to 'ang on to a job with the Great Western Railway. First of all—'

But the guard got no further. Before he could begin to enumerate the advantages of employment by the company, he was interrupted by a shout from the other end of the train. A young railway policeman was beckoning them with frantic semaphore.

Galway was alarmed. 'Somethin' is up.'

'Just another drunk, I expect. We'll throw him out.'

'It's more serious than that, Sam. I can tell.'

'Wait for me,' said Horlock as the guard scurried off. 'What's the hurry?' He fell in beside the older man. 'Anybody would think that one of the engines was on fire.'

The policeman who was gesticulating at them was standing beside a second-class carriage near the front of the train. His mouth was agape and his cheeks were ashen. Sweat was moistening his brow. As the others approached, he began to jabber.

'I thought he was asleep at first,' he said.

'Who?' asked the guard.

'Him – in there.'

'What's up?' asked Horlock, reaching the carriage.

The policeman pointed. 'See for yourself, Sam.'

He stood back so that Horlock and Galway could peer in through the door. Propped up in the far corner was a stout middle-aged man in nondescript clothing with his hat at a rakish angle. His eyes were open and there was an expression of disbelief on his face. A noisome stench confirmed that he had soiled himself. Galway was outraged. Horlock stepped quickly into the carriage and shook the passenger by the shoulder so that his hat fell off.

'Time to get out now, sir,' he said, firmly.

But the man was in no position to go anywhere. His body fell sideward and his head lolled back, exposing a thin crimson ring around his throat. The blood had seeped on to his collar and down the inside of his shirt. When he set out from London, the passenger was looking forward to witnessing a memorable event. Somewhere along the line, he had become a murder victim.

'This is dreadful!' cried Tod Galway, recoiling in horror.

'Yes,' said Horlock, a wealth of sympathy in his voice. 'The poor devil will never know who won that fight now.'

CHAPTER TWO

When the summons came, Inspector Robert Colbeck was at Scotland Yard, studying the report he had just written about his last case. He abandoned it at once and hurried along the corridor. Superintendent Tallis was not a man who liked to be kept waiting. He demanded an instant response from his detectives. Colbeck found him in his office, seated behind his desk, smoking a cigar and poring over a sheet of paper. Tallis spoke to his visitor without even looking up.

'Don't sit down, Inspector. You're not staying long.'

'Oh?'

'You'll be catching a train to Twyford.'

'In Berkshire?'

'I know of no other,' said Tallis, raising his eyes. 'Do you?'

'No, sir.'

'Then do me the courtesy of listening to what I have to say instead of distracting me with questions about geography. This,' he went on, holding up the sheet of paper, 'is an example of the value of the electric telegraph, a priceless tool in the fight against crime. Details of the murder have been sent to us while the body is still warm.'

Colbeck's ears pricked up. 'There's been a murder at Twyford?'

'In a railway carriage, Inspector.'

'Ah.'

'It was an excursion train on the Great Western Railway.'

'Then I suspect I know where it was going, sir,' said Colbeck.

He also knew why the assignment was being handed to him. Ever since his success in solving a train robbery and its associated crimes in the previous year, Robert Colbeck had become known as the Railway Detective. It was a name bestowed upon him by newspapers that had, in the past, mocked the Detective Department of the Metropolitan Police for its apparent slowness in securing convictions. Thanks largely to Colbeck, the reporters at last had reason to praise the activities of Scotland Yard. He had masterminded the capture of a ruthless gang, responsible for armed robbery, blackmail, abduction, criminal damage and murder. Colbeck's reputation had been firmly established by the case. It meant that whenever a serious crime was committed on a railway, the respective company tended to seek his assistance.

Colbeck was, as usual, immaculately dressed in a black frock coat with rounded edges and high neck, a pair of well-cut fawn trousers and an Ascot cravat. His black shoes sparkled. Tall, lean and conventionally handsome, he cut a fine figure and always looked slightly out of place among his more workaday colleagues. None of them could challenge his position as the resident dandy. Edward Tallis would not even have cared to try. As a military man, he believed implicitly in smartness and he was always neatly, if soberly, dressed. But he deplored what he saw as Colbeck's vanity. It was one of the reasons that there was so much latent tension between the two of them. The superintendent was a stocky, red-faced man in his fifties with a shock of grey hair and a small moustache. A chevron of concern was cut deep into his brow.

'You say that you knew where the train was going, Inspector?'

'Yes, sir,' replied Colbeck. 'It was taking interested parties to the scene of a prizefight.'

'Prizefights are illegal. They should be stopped.'

'This one, it seems, was allowed to go ahead.'

'*Allowed*?' repeated Tallis, bristling. 'A flagrant breach of the law was consciously allowed? That's intolerable. The magistracy is there to enforce the statute book not to flout it.' His eyelids narrowed. 'How did you come to hear about this?'

'It's common knowledge, Superintendent.'

'Did you not think to report it?'

'The fight is outside our jurisdiction,' said Colbeck, reasonably, 'so there was no point in bringing it to your attention. All that I picked up was tavern gossip about the contest. But,' he continued, 'that's quite irrelevant now. If a murder investigation is to be launched, I must be on the next train to Twyford.'

'You'll need this,' Tallis told him, rising from his seat and handing him the sheet of paper. 'It contains the few details that I possess.'

'Thank you, sir. I take it that Victor Leeming will come with me?'

'The sergeant will meet you at Paddington Station. I sent him on an errand to C Division so I've dispatched a constable to overtake him with fresh orders.'

'Because of the speed of this message,' said Colbeck, indicating the piece of paper, 'we might even get there before the fight finishes. It can't be much more than thirty miles to Twyford.'

'Report back to me as soon as you can.'

'Of course, sir.'

'And find me the name of the man who sanctioned the running of this excursion train. If he knowingly conveyed people to an illegal prizefight, then he was committing an offence and should be called to account. We must come down hard on malefactors.'

'Railway companies are there to serve the needs of their customers, Superintendent,' Colbeck pointed out. 'They simply carry passengers from one place to another. It's unfair to blame them for any activities that those passengers may get up to at their destination.'

Tallis stuck out his jaw. 'Are you arguing with me, Inspector?'

'Heaven forbid!'

'That makes a change.'

'I would never question your judgement, sir.'

'You do it out of sheer force of habit.'

'That's a gross exaggeration. I was merely trying to represent the position of the Great Western Railway.'

'Then permit me to represent *my* position,' said the other, tapping his chest with a stubby forefinger. 'I want prompt action. A murder has been committed and we have received an urgent call for assistance. Instead of debating the issue, be kind enough to vacate the premises with all due speed and do the job for which you're paid.'

'I'll take a cab to Paddington immediately,' said Colbeck, moving to the door. 'By the way,' he added with a teasing smile, 'do you wish to be informed of the result of the fight?'

'No!' roared Tallis.

'I thought not, sir.'

And he was gone.

* * *

There was a fairground atmosphere at the scene of the prizefight. Descending on it after their trudge across the fields, the high-spirited crowd from London saw that the ring had been set up and that it was encircled by a number of booths and stalls. Pies, sandwiches, fruit and other foodstuffs were on sale and there was a ready supply of beer. A pig was being roasted on a spit. One tent was occupied by a gypsy fortune-teller, who, having first discovered which man each of her clients was supporting, was able to predict the outcome of the contest to his complete satisfaction. A painted sign over another booth – THE GARDEN OF EDEN – left nobody in any doubt what they would find inside, especially as the artist had added a naked lady, with a large red apple and an inviting smile. A group of Negro serenaders was touting for custom under an awning. There was even a Punch and Judy show to entertain the visitors with some make-believe violence before they were offered the real thing.

The Londoners were the last to arrive. Excursion trains from other parts of the country had already brought in a massive audience. Members of the gentry chose to watch the festivities from the comfort of their coaches, carriages and gigs. Farmers had come in carts or on horseback. But the overwhelming number of people would either clamber on to the makeshift stands or search for a good vantage point on the grass. Meanwhile, they could place their bets with bookmakers, play cards, watch the jugglers and tumblers, visit some of the freaks on show or enjoy an improvised dog fight. With beer flowing freely, it all served to whip them up into a frenzy of anticipation.

The inner ring, where the fight would take place, was protected by an outer ring so that spectators could not get close enough to interfere in the contest. The space between the two sets of ropes was patrolled by a number of brawny figures, waddling around like so many bulldogs, ageing pugs with scarred faces, swollen ears and missing teeth, muscular sentries with fists like hams, there to ensure the safety of Mad Isaac and the Bargeman. Veterans of the sport themselves, their advice was eagerly sought by punters who were still unsure on whom to place their money.

By way of introduction, an exhibition bout was staged between two young fighters, still in their teens, talented novices who wore padded gloves to lessen the injuries they could inflict on each other's faces. Later, when they graduated to the bareknuckle breed, they would pickle their hands to harden them and do their utmost to open deep cuts, close an opponent's eye, break his ribs or cover his body with dark bruising. The preliminary contest lacked any real sense of danger but it was lively enough to thrill the onlookers and to give them an opportunity both to jostle for a position around the ring and to test the power of their lungs. After six rounds, the fight came to an end amid ear-splitting cheers. Between the two fighters, honours were even.

With the spectators suitably warmed up, it was time for the main contest of the afternoon. Everyone pushed in closer for a first glimpse of the two men. The Bargeman led the way, a veritable mountain of muscle, striding purposefully towards the ring with a face of doom. His fans were quick to offer their sage counsel.

'Knock 'im from 'ere to kingdom come, Bargeman!'

'Split the lousy Jew in 'alf!'

'Circumcise 'im!'

'Flay the bugger alive!'

The Negro raised both arms in acknowledgement, cheered and booed with equal volume by rival supporters. Isaac Rosen was the next to appear, strolling nonchalantly along as he chewed on an apple and tossed the core to a woman in the throng. He was every bit as tall as Hignett but had nothing like his sheer bulk. Dark-haired and dark-eyed, Rosen grinned happily as if he were on his way to a picnic rather than to an extended ordeal in the ring. It was the turn of the Bradford crowd to offer a few suggestions.

'Come on, Mad Isaac! Teach 'im a lesson.'

'Smash 'im to the ground!'

'Crack 'is 'ead open!'

'Kill the black bastard!'

Both sides were in good voice. As the fighters stripped off their shirts, the cheers and the taunts reached a pitch of hysteria. Wearing cotton drawers and woollen stockings, the boxers confronted each other and exchanged a few ripe insults. Each was in prime condition, having trained for months for this confrontation. Hignett had the clear weight advantage but Rosen had the more eye-catching torso with rippling muscles built up by hard years in the slaughterhouse. A coin was tossed to see who would have choice of corners, a crucial advantage on a day when the sun was blazing down. Fortune favoured the Jew and he elected to have his back to the sun so that it dazzled his opponent's eyes as he came out of his corner.

With two seconds apiece – a bottleman and a kneeman – they took up their positions. The bottleman was there to revive his charge with a wet sponge or a cold drink while the kneeman provided a rickety stool on which the boxer could sit between rounds. All four seconds were retired fighters, seasoned warriors who knew all the tricks of the trade and who could, in the event of trouble, act as additional bodyguards. On a signal from the referee, the Bargeman moved swiftly up to the scratch in the middle of the ring, but Mad Isaac kept him waiting for a moment before he deigned to leave his corner. As they shook hands, there was another barrage of insults between them before the first punches were thrown with vicious intent. Pandemonium broke out among the spectators. They were watching the two finest boxers in the world, both unbeaten, slugging it out until one of them was pounded into oblivion. In an ecstasy of bloodlust, they urged the boxers on with full-throated glee.

'Who discovered the body?' asked Colbeck, coming out of the carriage.

'I did, Inspector,' replied Ernest Radd, stepping forward.

'When was this?'

'Immediately after the passengers had left the train.'

'Could you give me some idea of the time?'

'Not long after noon, Inspector.'

'I knew that it was a mistake to run this train,' said Tod Galway, wringing his hands. 'Something like this was bound to happen.'

'I disagree,' said Colbeck, turning to him. 'This is a very singular occurrence. It's the first murder that I've encountered on a train. One might expect a little over-excitement from the Fancy but not this.'

The detectives had reached the scene of the crime while the fight was still in progress. To clear the line for use by other traffic, the excursion train had been driven into a siding. Inspector Robert Colbeck was accompanied by Sergeant Victor Leeming, a heavyset man in his late thirties with an unprepossessing appearance. One eye squinted at a bulbous nose that had been battered during an arrest and his chin was unduly prominent. Beside his elegant companion, he looked scruffy and faintly villainous. After examining the dead body with Colbeck, the sergeant remained in the doorway of the carriage, blocking the view of the group of railway policemen who had come to stare.

'I knew he was gone as soon as I saw him,' explained Radd, a chubby young man whose cheeks were still whitened by the shock of what he had found. 'But it was Sam here who went into the carriage.'

'That's right,' Horlock chimed in, relishing the opportunity to get some attention at last. 'Horlock's the name, Inspector. Samuel Horlock. Ernie called us to the carriage and, as the more experienced policeman,' he boasted, 'I took over. The man was stuck in the corner. I shook him by the shoulder and he keeled over, losing his hat. That's when we saw them marks around his neck, Inspector. Someone must have used a rope to strangle him.'

'A piece of wire, I think,' said Colbeck. 'Rope would never have bitten into the flesh like that. It would simply have left a red weal where the neck had been chafed. This man was garrotted with something much thinner and sharper.'

'Then we know one thing about the killer,' volunteered Leeming. 'He must have been a strong man. The victim would not have been easy to overpower. Judging by the size of him, there would have been resistance.'

'I found these in his pockets, Inspector,' said Horlock, handing over a wallet and a slip of paper, 'so at least we know his name.'

'You should have left it to us to search him, Mr Horlock.'

'I was only trying to help.'

'In tramping around the carriage, you might unwittingly have destroyed valuable clues.' He looked at the other railway policemen. 'How many of you went in there to gawp at him once the alarm was raised?' Half a dozen of them looked shamefaced and turned away. 'It was not a freak show, gentlemen,' scolded Colbeck.

'We was curious, that's all,' said Horlock, defensively.

'If you'd shown some curiosity during the train journey, the murder might not have occurred. Why did none of you travel in this particular carriage?'

'We never expected trouble in first and second class. Leastways, not on the ride here. It'll be different on the way back,' warned Horlock. 'There's bound to be some drunken idiots with third-class tickets trying to travel back to London in comfort.'

'Nobody can use *this* carriage,' said Galway, anxiously. 'Not with a corpse lyin' there like that. I mean, it's unwelcomin'.'

'The body will travel back in the guard's van,' declared Colbeck.

'I'm not 'avin ' that bleedin' thing in my van, Inspector!' protested the other. 'Gives me the shakes just to look at 'im.'

'Don't worry. Sergeant Leeming and I will be there to protect you.' Colbeck turned to the others. 'Some of you might find a means of carrying the murder victim along the track. There may be a board of some kind at the station or even a wheelbarrow. We need to move him before the passengers return, and to get this carriage cleaned up.'

Four of the railway policemen shuffled off. The rest of them stared resentfully at Colbeck, annoyed that he had taken over the investigation and relegated them to the position of bystanders. Colbeck's refinement, educated voice and sense of authority aroused a muted hostility. They did not like being given orders by this peacock from Scotland Yard. Aware of their antagonism, Colbeck chose to ignore it.

'Sergeant Leeming.'

'Yes, Inspector?' said his colleague.

'Take a full statement from Mr Horlock, if you will,' instructed Colbeck, 'and from Mr Radd. Meanwhile,' he added, pointedly, 'if the rest of you would be good enough to give us some breathing space, I'll make a more thorough examination of the body.'

Blaspheming under their breath, the knot of railway policemen drifted away, leaving only Sam Horlock, Ernest Radd and Tod Galway beside the carriage. Leeming jumped down on to the ground and took out his notebook so that he could question two of the men. Colbeck hauled himself into the carriage and took the opportunity to look at the two items that Horlock had given him. The wallet contained nothing more than a five-pound note and a ticket for the excursion train, but the piece of paper was far more useful. It was a bill for a supply of leather and it contained the name and address of the person to whom it had been sent.

'So,' said Colbeck with compassion, 'you are Mr Jacob Bransby, are you? I'm sorry that your journey had to end this way, sir.'

Putting the wallet and bill into his pocket, he looked more closely at the injury to the man's neck, trying to work out where the killer must have been standing when he struck. Colbeck then studied the broad shoulders and felt the solid biceps. Bransby might have a paunch but he must have been a powerful man. Evidently, he was no stranger to manual work. His hands were rough, his fingernails dirty. A livid scar ran across the knuckles of one hand. His clothing was serviceable rather than smart and Colbeck noticed that his coat had been darned in two places. The hat was shabby.

But it was the face that interested the detective most. Though contorted by an agonising death, it still had much to reveal about the character of the man. There was a stubbornness in the set of his jaw and protective quality about the thick, overhanging brows. Mutton-chop whiskers hid even more of his face and the walrus moustache reached out to meet them. Colbeck sensed that he was looking at a secretive individual, covert, tight-lipped, taciturn, unsure of himself, a lonely creature who travelled without any friends because they would otherwise have been on hand to save his life instead of rushing out of the carriage, leaving him to the mercy of his executioner.

Wishing that the man did not smell so much of excrement, Colbeck searched him thoroughly. Sam Horlock had already been through the pockets so the inspector concentrated on other parts of his clothing. If Bransby had been as furtive by nature as the detective believed, he might have hidden pockets about his person. He soon found the first, a pouch that had been attached to the inside of the waist of his trousers to safeguard coins from the nimble fingers of pickpockets. Horlock had missed the second hiding place as well. Ingeniously sewn into the waistcoat below the left arm, the other pouch contained a large and expensive gold watch.

It was the third find, however, that intrigued Colbeck. As he felt down the right trouser-leg, his hand made contact with a hard, metal object that, on investigation, turned out to be a dagger strapped above the ankle. Colbeck removed it from the leg, unsheathed the weapon and inspected it. He glanced down at the murder victim.

'Well, Mr Bransby,' he said, raising an eyebrow, 'you're full of surprises, aren't you?'

He put the dagger in its sheath and concealed them in his coat. After completing his search, he left the carriage and dropped to the ground, relieved to be able to inhale fresh air again. Colbeck said nothing about what he had found, unwilling to humiliate Horlock in front the others and, in any case, not wishing to share information with railway employees. The four policemen who had walked off to the station came down the track, carrying a large table between them. Colbeck supervised the transfer of the dead body from the carriage to the guard's van. Tod Galway was not happy about the arrangement.

'I don't want 'im in there, Inspector,' he moaned, waving his arms. 'The dirty dog shit 'imself.'

'That was purely involuntary,' said Colbeck. 'If *you* had been killed in that way, I daresay that your own bowels would have betrayed you. Death plays cruel tricks on all of us.'

'But why did this 'ave to 'appen on *my* train?'

'Only the killer can tell us that.'

Leaving him there, Colbeck strolled back towards the front of the train. He was pleased to see that Leeming had finished taking statements from the two men. It allowed him to confide in the sergeant.

Leeming was astonished. 'A gold watch and a dagger?'

'Both cunningly hidden, Victor.'

'Is that why he carried the weapon, sir? To protect the watch?'

'No,' decided Colbeck, 'I fancy that it was there for self-defence and with good cause. Mr Bransby feared an attack of some kind. He did not strike me as a man who slept easily at nights.'

'A guilty conscience, perhaps?'

'He certainly had something to hide. How, for instance, could a man who plied his trade afford such a costly watch? I venture to suggest that you'll find very few cobblers with the requisite income.'

'How do you know that he was a cobbler?'

'Who else would order that amount of leather?' asked Colbeck. 'And there was what could well be cobbler's wax under his fingernails. Not that he was the most dexterous craftsman, mind you. It looked as if a knife slipped at some stage and slit his knuckles open.'

'I see.' Leeming shrugged. 'What do we do now, sir?'

'All that we can do, Victor – wait until the passengers come back. Only a relatively small number travelled here in these second-class carriages. We need to find someone who might remember Jacob Bransby.'

'One of them will remember him extremely well – the killer!'

'Yes, but I doubt if he'll oblige us by turning up so that we can question him. My guess is that he's already slipped away.'

'And miss the chance of seeing a fight like that?' said Leeming in amazement. 'More fool him, I say.' He brightened as an idea struck him. 'I'd love to watch the Bargeman hit lumps out of Mad Isaac. One of the policemen knows where the fight is taking place, sir. Why don't I rush over there to keep an eye on things?'

'Because you'd be too late, Victor.'

'Too late?'

'Look up there.'

Glancing up at the sky, Leeming saw a flock of birds flying in the general direction of London. He sighed as he realised that the fight must be over. The carrier pigeons were carrying word of the result. Several, he knew, would be winging their way to Bradford.

Leeming cupped his hands to shout up at the birds.

'Who *won*?' he yelled. 'Was it the Bargeman?'

* * *

The trouble had begun when the fight was only an hour old. Supporters of Mad Isaac had been inflamed by what they felt were unfair tactics on the part of his opponent. When they grappled in the middle of the ring, the Bargeman used his forehead to crack down on the bridge of the other man's nose and uncorked the blood. As the fighters swung round crazily in an impromptu dance, the men from Bradford thought that they saw the Negro inflict a bite on their man's neck. They shrieked with rage. Rosen was quick to take revenge. Seized by a madness that turned him into a howling wolf, he lifted the Bargeman bodily and flung him to the ground with a force that winded him. What infuriated the London mob was that he seemed to get in a sly kick to the Negro's groin.

Demands for a disqualification rang out on all sides and a few private fights started on the fringes. The Bargeman, however, had great powers of recovery. Helped back to his corner by his seconds, he needed only a swig of water and a brief rest on a wooden stool before he was able to fight again. When the contest restarted, his arms were flailing like black windmills. And so it went on for another forty arduous rounds, advantage swinging first one way, then the other, the audience keeping up such hullabaloo that it was like watching a brawl in Bedlam. When the rowdier element began to take over, brandishing staves and cudgels, the gentry began to withdraw, worried for the safety of their vehicles and their horses in the seething morass of danger.

The end finally came. It was disputed belligerently by almost half of the spectators. Both men had taken severe punishment and were tottering on the edge of complete fatigue. The Bargeman then found the energy to launch one more savage attack, sending his opponent reeling back against the ropes. Moving in for the kill, he tried to get the Jew in a bear hug to crush the last vestiges of resistance but he suddenly backed away with his hands to his eyes. Nobody had seen Mad Isaac use his fingers yet the Bargeman was temporarily blinded. He was then hit with a relay of punches that sent him staggering backwards and, as he was in the act of dropping to one knee to gain quarter, he was caught with a thunderous uppercut that laid him out flat. It was all over.

Cries of 'Foul!' from the Londoners mingled with roars of delight from the Bradford contingent. The noise was deafening. Every one of the Bargeman's fans believed that he had been hit unfairly though, in truth, few had actually witnessed the blow. Most were in no position to see over the ranks of hats in front of them or they were so befuddled with drink that their vision was impaired. Partisans to a man, they nevertheless took up the chant for retribution. The umpires claimed that they had not seen anything underhand and the referee, sensing that a disqualification would put his life at risk, declared Mad Isaac to be the winner. At that precise moment, thousands of pounds were won and lost in bets.

The more sporting members of the Fancy immediately contributed to a purse for the gallant loser, who was carried back to his corner by his seconds. Because the Bargeman had given a good account of himself in the ring, coins were tossed into the hat with generosity. But there were hundreds of people who disputed the decision and sought to advance their argument with fists, whip handles, sticks, stones, clubs and hammers. The two fighters were not the only ones to shed copious blood that afternoon in Berkshire.

At the point when the whole scene was about to descend into utter chaos, someone fired a warning pistol in the air. A magistrate was on his way to stop the event with a detachment of dragoons at his back. It was time to disappear. Brawls were abandoned in mid-punch and everyone took to their heels. Hustled on to separate carts, the Bargeman and Mad Isaac were driven off in opposite directions by their backers, determined that two brave men would not feel the wrath of the law. Hurt, angry and consumed with righteous indignation, the London mob headed towards their excursion train, licking their wounds and cursing their fate. Having invested time, money and high emotion into the contest, they were going home empty-handed. It made them burn with frustration. They had come with high hopes of victory but were slinking away like a beaten army.

'The Bargeman lost,' said Leeming in dismay as the first of them came in sight. 'I can tell from the look of them.'

'Inquire about the fight at a later stage,' ordered Colbeck. 'All that concerns us now are the passengers who were in the same carriage as Jacob Bransby on their way here.'

'Yes, sir.'

'And don't expect me to share your sorrow, Victor. You may as well know that I put a sovereign on Mad Isaac to win.'

Leeming groaned. 'I had two on the Bargeman.'

When the crowd reached the train, all that most of them wanted to do was to tumble into their seats and nurse their grievances. Some were in an aggressive mood and others tried to sneak into first- and second-class carriages without the appropriate tickets. Railway policemen were on hand to prevent them. Those who had been in the same carriage as Jacob Bransby were taken aside for questioning, but only one of them had actually spoken to the man whom Inspector Colbeck described.

'Yes,' said Felix Pritchard. 'I remember him, sir, though he didn't give me his name. Sat next to him, I did – shoulder to shoulder.'

'Did you talk to him?' asked Colbeck.

'I tried to but he didn't have very much to say for himself.'

'What was your impression of the man?'

'Well, now, let me see.'

Felix Pritchard was a tall, rangy young man with a coat that had been torn in the course of the afternoon and a hat that was badly scuffed. A bank clerk by profession, he had pleaded illness so that he could go to the fight but he was now having second thoughts about the wisdom of doing so. Apart from having backed the wrong man and lost money that he could not afford, he had drunk far too much beer and was feeling sick. As a witness, he was less than ideal. Colbeck was patient with him. Pritchard was all that he had.

'Start with his voice,' suggested the inspector. 'Did it tell you where he came from?'

'Oh, yes, he was a true Cockney, just like me, sir.'

'Did he say what he did for a living?'

'That never came up in conversation,' said Pritchard, wishing that his stomach were not so rebellious. 'All we talked about was the fight.'

'And what did Mr Bransby have to say?'

'That, barring accidents, the Bargeman was bound to win.'

'Did he bet money on the result?'

'Of course. We all had.'

'Had he ever seen Bill Hignett fight before?'

'Yes,' said the other. 'He was a real disciple of the sport. Told me that he'd been all over the country to see fights. It was his hobby.'

'What else did he say?'

'Very little beyond the fact that he did a bit of milling in his youth. I think he was handy with his fists at one time but he didn't brag about it. He was one of those quiet types, who keep themselves to themselves.'

'Tell me about the people in the carriage.'

'We were jammed in there like sardines.'

'How many of them did you know?'

'Only one,' replied Pritchard. 'My brother. That's him, sitting in the corner,' he went on, pointing into the carriage at a youth whose face and coat were spattered with blood. 'Cecil chanced his arm against one of those Bradford cullies and came off worst.'

'Did he speak to Jacob Bransby at any point?'

'No, sir. He was sat on the other side of me. Couldn't take his eyes off the woman who was opposite him.'

'A woman?' echoed Colbeck with interest, looking around. 'I've not seen any women getting back into the second-class carriages.'

'She must be making her way back home by other means.'

'What sort of woman was she, Mr Pritchard?'

'*That* sort, sir,' returned the bank clerk.

'Age?'

'Anything from thirty upward,' said Pritchard. 'Too old for my brother, I know that, and too pricey in any case.'

'Why do you say that?'

'She wasn't a common trull you might see walking the streets, sir. I mean, she was almost respectable. Except that a respectable woman wouldn't be going on an excursion train to a fight, would she? She could only have been there for one thing.'

'Did you see her at the contest?'

'In that crowd?' Pritchard gave a derisive laugh. 'Not a chance! Besides, I didn't look. I was too busy cheering on the Bargeman.'

'Apart from Jacob Bransby, your brother and this woman, can you recall anyone else who was in that carriage with you?'

'Not really, sir. They were all strangers to me. To be honest, I've had so much to drink that I wouldn't recognise any of them if they stood in front of me.' He gave a sudden belch. 'Pardon me, Inspector.'

'What happened when the train reached Twyford?'

'We all got out.'

'Did you see Mr Bransby leave his seat?'

'I didn't notice,' admitted Pritchard. 'There was a mad dash for the door because we were so keen to get out.'

'Did the woman leave before you?'

'Oh, no. She had to take her chances with the rest of us. Cecil and me pushed past her in the rush. That was the last we saw of her.'

'So she could have held back deliberately?'

'Who knows, Inspector? If she did, it wasn't because she'd taken a fancy to Mr Bransby. He was an ugly devil,' said Pritchard, 'and he was so miserable. You'd never have thought he was on his way to a championship fight.'

'No?'

'No, sir. He looked as if he was going to a funeral.'

Colbeck made no comment.

CHAPTER THREE

The excursion train reached Paddington that evening without any undue incident. There were some heated arguments in the third-class carriages and a few minor scuffles but the railway policemen soon brought them under control. Most of the passengers were still too numbed by the defeat of their hero, the Bargeman, to cause any mayhem themselves and they were noticeably quieter on their way back. Those in the second-class carriage that had brought Jacob Bransby to Twyford were quite unaware of the fact a murder had taken place there. When he interviewed Felix Pritchard earlier, Inspector Colbeck had been careful to say nothing about the crime, explaining that he was simply making routine inquiries about a missing person. Unbeknown to the excursionists, a corpse travelled back to London in the guard's van with two detectives from the Metropolitan Police and an irate Tod Galway.

'It ain't decent, Inspector,' asserted the guard.

'The body could hardly be left where it was,' said Colbeck.

'You should 'ave sent it back by other means.'

'What other means?'

'Any way but on my train.'

'Mr Bransby had a return ticket in his pocket. That entitles him to be on this particular train and here he will be.'

'Bleedin' liberty, that's what it is!'

'Show some respect for the dead. And to us,' added Colbeck, sternly. 'Do you think we *want* to ride back to London in the company of a murder victim and a grumbling railwayman?'

Galway lapsed into a sullen silence until the train shuddered to a halt in the station. Victor Leeming was given the job of organising the transfer of the dead body to the police morgue, first waiting until the train had been emptied of passengers so that a degree of privacy could be ensured. Colbeck, meanwhile, took a hansom cab back to Scotland Yard and delivered his report to Superintendent Tallis. The latter listened to the recital with mounting irritation.

'Nobody saw a thing?' he asked, shaking his head in wonder. 'A man is throttled aboard a crowded train and not a single pair of eyes witnesses the event?'

'No, sir.'

'I find that hard to believe.'

'Everyone rushed out of the train in order to get to the fight.'

'Then why didn't this Mr Bransby join them?'

'I have a theory about that, Superintendent.'

'Ah,' sighed Tallis, rolling his eyes. 'Another of your famous theories, eh? I prefer to work with hard facts and clear evidence. They are much more reliable guides. Very well,' he conceded, flicking a wrist, 'let's hear this latest wild guess of yours.'

'I believe that the woman was involved.'

'A female assassin? Isn't that stretching supposition too far?'

'She was no assassin,' argued Colbeck. 'The woman was there as an accomplice to distract the victim. While she delayed him, the killer attacked from behind.'

'What put that notion into your head, Inspector?'

'The fact that she was in that carriage at all.'

'There's no mystery in that,' said Tallis, darkly. 'We both know why she was there. Such creatures always follow a crowd. Clearly, she was looking for a better class of customer than she'd find among the ruffians in third-class.'

'I've only Mr Pritchard's word that the woman was, in fact, a prostitute. He could well have been mistaken. He confessed that he'd been drinking before he boarded the train so his judgement may not be altogether sound. What interests me,' Colbeck continued, 'was that the woman did not return to the train at Twyford.'

'Perhaps she went astray.'

'Deliberately.'

'You've no means of knowing that.'

'I have this instinct, sir.'

'We need more than theory and instinct to solve this murder, Inspector. We need definite clues. So far you seem to have drawn a complete blank.' He glowered at Colbeck. 'What's your next move?'

'To visit the home of the deceased. He wore a wedding ring so he must have a wife and family. They deserve to know what has happened to him. I intend to go to Hoxton at once.'

'What about Sergeant Leeming?'

'He's on his way to the morgue with Mr Bransby, sir. I told him to stay there until the doctor had examined the body in case any important new details came to light. Victor and I will confer later on.'

'For an exchange of theories?' said Tallis with gruff sarcasm.

'Useful information can always be picked up from the

doctor even before a full autopsy is carried out. He may, for instance, give us a more accurate idea of what murder weapon was used.'

'Bring me news of any progress that you make.'

'Of course, sir.'

'Soon.'

'We'll do our best.'

'I trust that you will. I've already had the railway company on to me, demanding an early arrest. A murder on one of their trains is a bad advertisement for them. It deters other passengers from travelling. The crime must be solved quickly. But they must bear some responsibility,' said Tallis, wagging a finger. 'If the Great Western Railway hadn't condoned an illegal fight and transported the sweepings of the slums to it, this murder would never have been committed.'

'It would, Superintendent,' said Colbeck, firmly, 'albeit at another time and in another place. Theft was not the motive or the man's wallet would have been taken. No,' he insisted, 'this was not an opportunist crime. It was a calculated homicide. Jacob Bransby was being stalked.'

At the time when the Domesday Book had been compiled, Hoxton was a manor of three hides, held by the Canons of St Paul's. It had been a tranquil place with green pastures and open meadows intersected by the river along which mills were conveniently sited. There was not the tiniest hint of its former rural beauty now. A part of Shoreditch, it belonged to a community of well over 100,000 souls in an unsightly urban sprawl. It was one of the worst parts of London with poverty and overcrowding as the salient features of its dark, narrow, filthy, cluttered streets. As the cab took him to the address on the tradesman's bill, Robert Colbeck reflected that Hoxton was hardly the district in which to find a man who carried a gold watch and a five pound note on his person. The dagger, however, was a more understandable accessory. In many parts of the area, a weapon of some sort was almost obligatory.

Colbeck was well acquainted with Hoxton, having been assigned a beat there during his days in uniform. He was wearily familiar with its brothels, gambling dens, penny gaffs, music halls, seedy public houses and ordinaries. He knew the rat-infested tenements where whole families were crammed into a single room and where disease ran amok in the insanitary conditions. He remembered the distinctive smell of Hoxton with its blend of menace, despair and rotting food. What had always struck him was not how many criminals gravitated to the place to form a thriving underworld but how many decent, hard-working, law-abiding people also lived there and managed to rise above their joyless surroundings.

After picking its way through the busy streets, the cab turned a corner and slowed down before stopping outside a terraced house. It was in one of the better parts of Hoxton but there was still a distinct whiff of decay about it. Children were playing with a ball in the fading light or watching an ancient man struggling to coax music out of his barrel organ. When they saw the cab, some of the younger ones scampered across to pat the horse and to ask the driver for a ride. Colbeck got out, paid his fare and knocked on the door of Jacob Bransby's house. There was a long wait before a curtain was twitched in the window. Moments later, the door opened and the curious face of a middle-aged woman peered around it.

'Can I help you, sir?'

'Mrs Bransby?'

'Yes,' she said after a considered pause.

'My name is Detective Inspector Colbeck,' he explained,

displaying his warrant card. 'I wonder if I might have a word with you?'

Alarm sounded. 'Why? Has something happened to my husband? I expected him back before now.'

'Perhaps I could come in, Mrs Bransby,' he said, softly. 'This is not something that we should be discussing on your doorstep.'

She nodded and moved back to admit him. Removing his top hat, he stepped into a small passageway and waited until she shut the door behind them. Louise Bransby led him into the front room that was better furnished than he had expected. A lighted oil lamp bathed it in a warm glow. Over the mantelpiece was a picture of the Virgin Mary. On the opposite wall was a crucifix. The carpet had a new feel to it.

'Why don't you sit down?' he suggested.

'If you say so, Inspector.'

'Is there anyone else in the house?'

'No,' she said, lowering herself into an armchair. 'Jake and I live here alone. Our son has a home of his own now.'

'Is there a friend or a neighbour you'd like to call in?'

'Why?'

'You might need some company, Mrs Bransby.'

'Not from anyone round here,' she said, sharply. 'We have no friends in Hoxton.' She took a deep breath and steeled herself. 'I'm ready, Inspector. Tell me what brought you here.'

Louise Bransby was a plump woman in a blue dress that had been worn once too often. She had curly brown hair and an oval face that was disfigured by a frown. Colbeck sensed a quiet toughness about her that would make his task slightly easier. Whatever else she did, Louise Bransby seemed unlikely to collapse in hysterics or simply pass out.

'I'm afraid that I have some bad news for you,' he began.

'It's not his heart again, is it?' she asked with concern. 'The doctor warned him against getting too excited but Jake just had to go to that fight. He loved boxing. It gave him so much pleasure. He'd go anywhere to watch it.' She leant forward. 'Has he been taken ill?'

'It's worse than that,' said Colbeck, sitting on the upright chair beside her. 'Your husband is dead.' As she convulsed momentarily, he put a sympathetic hand on her shoulder. 'I'm so sorry, Mrs Bransby. I hate to be the bearer of such sad tidings.'

She bit her lip. 'It was bound to happen sooner or later,' she said, wiping away a tear with her hand. 'I knew that. Jake would drive himself so. And I was afraid that it would all end once we came here. Moving to Hoxton was a bad mistake.'

'How long have you been in the house?'

'A couple of months.'

'Where were you before?'

'Clerkenwell.'

'Why did you come here?'

'That's private, sir,' she said, evasively. 'Not that it matters any more, I suppose. If my husband has died, I can get away from this place.' She clutched her hands to her breast. 'If only Jake had listened to that doctor! He was told to take it easy.' She read the look in Colbeck's eyes and stiffened. 'There's something you haven't told me, isn't there?' she asked, warily. 'It wasn't his heart, after all.'

'No, Mrs Bransby,' he said, gently. 'There's no way to hide the truth, I fear. Your husband was killed this afternoon.'

'Killed?' she gasped. 'There's been an accident?'

'Unfortunately not. At some time around noon today, Mr Bransby was murdered on an excursion train.'

'Holy Mary!' she exclaimed.

She looked up at the picture of the Virgin, crossed herself

then brought both hands up to her face. Louise Bransby was too stunned to say anything. Lost in a world of her own, she needed several minutes to recover her composure. Colbeck waited beside her, ready to offer physical support if need be, relieved that she did not burst into tears or howl with anguish as other women had done in similar circumstances. Imparting news of a tragedy to a wife was a duty that had fallen to him more than once in Hoxton and it had always been an uncomfortable task.

When she eventually lowered her hands, her eyes were moist but there was no overt display of grief. Louise Bransby was a woman who had learnt to keep her emotions under control in difficult situations and Colbeck suspected that she had had a lot of experience in doing so. There was an innate strength about her that he admired, a practical streak, a capacity for dealing with things as they were instead of clinging on pointlessly to how they had been. He offered her a handkerchief but she shook her head.

'Is there anything that I can get you, Mrs Bransby?' he inquired.

'No, Inspector.'

'A glass of water, perhaps?'

'I'll be well in a moment.'

'Are you sure there isn't a friend I could invite in?'

'Yes,' she said with sudden contempt. 'Quite sure. I don't want anyone here knowing my business. I can manage on my own.' She made an effort to pull herself together. 'How did it happen?'

'This may not be the time to go into details,' he said, trying to keep the full horror from her at this stage. 'Suffice it to say that it was a quick death. Your husband would not have lingered in agony.'

'Where was he killed?'

'At Twyford Station. When the train stopped, everyone rushed to get off. Evidently, someone took advantage of the commotion to attack Mr Bransby.' Hands clasped in her lap, she gazed down at them. 'We found a bill for some leather on him. Was your husband a cobbler?'

'Yes, Inspector.'

'Did he work from home?'

'He has a shed in the yard at the back of the house.'

'The bill is your property now,' he said, reaching inside his coat, 'and so is his wallet.' Colbeck extracted them and set them on a small table close to her. 'There were also a few coins in a secret pocket,' he went on, fishing them out to place beside the other items. 'That was not all that we found on your husband, Mrs Bransby.' She glanced up. 'Do you know what I'm talking about?'

'His watch.'

'It's a very expensive one.'

'But paid for, Inspector,' she declared, 'like everything else in this house. Jake *earned* that watch, he did. He worked hard for it. That's why he took such good care of it. I sewed the pouch into his waistcoat for him. That watch was got honestly, I swear it.'

'I'm sure that it was,' said Colbeck, producing the watch from a pocket and giving it to her. 'But it was a rather unexpected thing to find on your husband.' He brought out the dagger. 'And so was this. Do you know why he carried it?'

'This is a dangerous place to live.'

'I know that. I walked the beat in Hoxton as a constable.'

'Jake never felt safe here.'

'Then why did you move to this part of London?'

'We had to go somewhere,' she said with an air of resignation. 'And we'd tried three or four other places.'

'Couldn't you settle anywhere?' he probed.

'My husband was a restless man.'

'But a cobbler depends on building up local trade,' he noted. 'Every time you moved, he must have had to search for new customers.'

'We got by.'

'Obviously.'

'And we never borrowed a penny – unlike some around here.'

'That's very much to your credit, Mrs Bransby.'

'We had too much pride, Inspector. We *cared*. That's why I dislike the neighbours. They have no pride. No self-respect.'

There was an edge of defiance in her voice that puzzled him. Minutes ago, she had learnt of the murder of her husband yet she seemed to have set that aside. Louise Bransby was more concerned with correcting any false impression that he might have formed about a humble cobbler who lived in an unwholesome part of the city. Colbeck did not sense any deep love for the dead man but his wife was showing a loyalty towards him that verged on the combative.

'How long were you married, Mrs Bransby?' he asked.

'Twenty-eight years.'

'And you have a son, you say?'

'Yes. His name is Michael.'

'Any other children?'

'No, Inspector,' she replied, crisply. 'The Lord only saw fit to allow us one son and we would never question His wisdom.' After glancing down wistfully at the gold watch, she turned back to Colbeck. 'Do you have any idea who did this terrible thing to Jake?'

'Not at the moment. I was hoping that *you* might be able to help.'

'Me?'

'You knew your husband better than anybody, Mrs Bransby. Did he have any particular enemies?'

'Jake was a good man, Inspector. He was a true believer.'

'I don't doubt that,' said Colbeck, 'but the fact remains that someone had a reason to kill him. This was no random act of murder. Mr Bransby was carefully singled out. Can you think of anyone who might have had a grudge against him?'

'No, Inspector,' she replied, avoiding his gaze.

'Are you quite certain?' he pressed.

'Yes.'

'Did he have arguments with anyone? Or a feud with a rival cobbler, perhaps? To take a man's life like that requires a very strong motive. Who might have had that motive, Mrs Bransby?'

'How would I know?' she said, rising to her feet as if flustered. 'Excuse me, Inspector, this terrible news changes everything. I've a lot of thinking to do. If you don't mind, I'd like to be left alone now.'

'Of course,' he agreed, getting up immediately, 'but there is one request that I have to make of you, I fear.'

'What's that?'

'The body will need to be formally identified.'

'But you know that it was Jake. You found those things on him.'

'All the same, we do need confirmation from a family member.'

'I want to remember my husband as he was,' she said. 'I'd hate to see him.' Her voice trailed off and there was a long pause. She became more assertive. 'I'm sorry but I can't do it.'

'Then perhaps your son would replace you. He'll have to be told about his father's death. Does he live close by? I'll pay him a visit this evening and apprise him of the situation.'

'No, no, you mustn't do that.'

'Why not?'

'You keep Michael out of this.'

'One of you has to identify the body,' Colbeck told her. 'The doctor is unable to put the correct name on the death certificate until we are absolutely sure who the man is.'

She bit her lip. 'I *know* it's my husband. Take my word for it.'

'We need more than that, Mrs Bransby.'

'Why?'

'There are procedures to follow. I appreciate that you might find it too distressing to visit the morgue yourself so I'll have to ask your son to come in your place. Where can I find him?'

A hunted look came into her eyes. Her lips were pursed and the muscles in her face twitched visibly. Wrestling with her conscience, she turned for help to the Virgin Mary, only to be met with apparent reproof. It made her start. After swallowing hard, she blurted out the truth.

'I didn't mean to lie to you, Inspector,' she confessed. 'I was brought up to believe in honesty but that was not always possible. You must understand the position we were in.'

'I'm not blaming you for anything,' he promised, trying to calm her. 'And I do sympathise with your position. It can't have been easy for either of you to be on the move all the time, pulling up roots, finding new accommodation, living among strangers. You told me that your husband was restless. I believe that he also lived in fear.'

'He did – we both did.'

'Is that why you never stayed long in one place?'

'Yes, Inspector.'

'What kept you on the run?'

'They did,' she said, bitterly. 'That's why we had to hide

behind a lie. But sooner or later, someone always found out and our lives were made a misery. It was so painful. I mean, someone has to do it, Inspector, and Jake felt that he was called. We prayed together for a sign and we believed that it was given to us.'

'A sign?'

'Jake would never have taken the job without guidance.'

'I don't quite follow, Mrs Bransby.'

'Guttridge,' she corrected. 'My name is Mrs Guttridge. Bransby was my maiden name. We only used it as a disguise. As a policeman, you must have heard of my husband – he was Jacob Guttridge.'

Colbeck was taken aback. 'The public executioner?'

'Yes, sir. Jake was not only a cobbler – he was a hangman as well.'

Victor Leeming did not like visiting the police morgue. The place was cold, cheerless and unsettling. He could not understand how some of those who worked there could exchange happy banter and even whistle at their work. He found it worryingly inappropriate. To the detective, it was an ordeal to spend any time in such an oppressive atmosphere. Robust, direct and fearless in most situations, Leeming was oddly sensitive in the presence of the deceased, reminded all too keenly of his own mortality. He hoped that he would not have to stay there long.

The doctor took time to arrive but, once he did, he was briskly professional as he examined a body that had been stripped and cleaned in readiness. After washing his hands, Leonard Keyworth joined the other man in the vestibule. Short, squat and bearded, the doctor was a bustling man in his late forties. Leeming stood by with his notebook.

'Well, Doctor?' he prompted.

'Death by asphyxiation,' said Keyworth, staring at him over the top of his pince-nez, 'but I daresay that you worked that out for yourself. It was a very unpleasant way to die. The garrotte was pulled so tight that it almost severed his windpipe.'

'Inspector Colbeck thought a piece of wire was used.'

'Almost certainly. The kind used to cut cheese, for instance.'

'How long would it have taken?'

'Not as long as you might suppose,' said the doctor. 'I can't be sure until I carry out a post-mortem but my guess is that he was not a healthy man. Cheeks and nose of that colour usually indicate heavy drinking and he was decidedly overweight. There were other telltale symptoms as well. I suspect that he may well have been a man with a heart condition, short of breath at the best of times. That might have hastened his death.'

'A heart attack brought on by the assault?'

'Possibly. I'll stay with my initial diagnosis for the time being. The prime cause of death was asphyxiation.'

'Right,' said Leeming, wishing that he could spell the word.

'This time, it seems, someone finally succeeded.'

'In what way?'

'It was not the first attempt on his life, Sergeant.'

Leeming blinked. 'How do you know?'

'When a man has a wound like that on his back,' said the doctor, removing his pince-nez, 'it was not put there by accident. There's an even larger scar on his stomach. He's been attacked before.'

'No wonder he carried a weapon of his own.'

'A weapon?'

'He had a dagger strapped to his leg,' explained Leeming.

'Then he was obviously unable to reach it. The killer had the advantage of surprise, taking him from behind when he least expected it. Do you have any notion of the victim's identity?'

'According to a bill in his pocket, his name was Jacob Bransby.'

'A manual worker of some kind, I'd say.'

'The inspector is fairly certain that he's a cobbler.'

'Not a very good one, it appears.'

'Why not?'

'Because he has too many discontented customers,' said Keyworth with a mirthless laugh. 'Three of them at least didn't like the way that he mended their shoes.'

Robert Colbeck did not linger in Hoxton. Having learnt the dead man's real name and discovered his other occupation, the inspector decided that revenge was the most likely motive for the murder. However, since Louise Guttridge knew nothing whatsoever of her husband's activities as a public executioner – a deliberate choice on her part – there was no point in tarrying. After warning her that details of the case would have to be released to the press and that her anonymity would soon be broken, he managed to prise the address of her son out of her, wondering why she was so reluctant to give it to him. Colbeck took his leave and walked through the drab streets until he could find a cab. It took him at a steady clatter to Thames Street.

Michael Guttridge lived in a small but spotlessly clean house that was cheek by jowl with the river. He was a fleshy man in his twenties who bore almost no facial resemblance to his father. His wife, Rebecca, was younger, shorter and very much thinner than her husband, her youthful prettiness already starting to fade in the drudgery of domestic life. Surprised by a visit from a detective inspector, they invited Colbeck in and were told about events on the excursion train. Their reaction was not at all what the visitor had anticipated.

'My father is *dead*?' asked Guttridge with an unmistakable note of relief in his voice. 'Is this true, Inspector?'

'Yes, sir. I went to the scene of the crime myself.'

'Then it's no more than he deserved.' He put an arm around his wife. 'It's over, Becky,' he said, excitedly. 'Do you see that? It's all over.'

'Thank God!' she cried.

'We don't have to care about it ever again.'

'That's wonderful!'

'Excuse me,' said Colbeck, letting his displeasure show, 'but I don't think that this is an occasion for celebration. A man has been brutally murdered. At least, have the grace to express some sorrow.'

Guttridge was blunt. 'We can't show what we don't feel.'

'So there's no use in pretending, is there?' said his wife, hands on hips in a challenging pose. 'I had no time for Michael's father.'

'No, and you had no time for me while I lived under the same roof with my parents. I had to make a choice – you or them.' Guttridge smiled fondly. 'I'm glad that I picked the right one.'

'Were you so ashamed of your father?' asked Colbeck.

'Wouldn't *you* be, Inspector? He was a common hangman. He lived by blood money. You can't get any lower than that.'

'I think you're doing him an injustice.'

'Am I?' retorted Guttridge, angrily. 'You didn't have to put up with the sneers and jibes. Once people knew what my father did, they turned on my mother and me as well. You'd have thought it was us who put the nooses around people's necks.'

'If your father had had his way,' his wife reminded him, 'you would have.' Rebecca Guttridge swung round to face Colbeck. 'He tried to turn Michael into his assistant. Going to prisons and killing people with a rope. It was disgusting!' Her eyes flashed back to her husband. 'I could never marry a man who did something like that.'

'I know, Becky. That's why I left home.'

'What trade *do* you follow?' said Colbeck.

'An honest one, Inspector. I'm a carpenter.'

'When were you estranged from your parents?'

'Three years ago.'

'I made him,' said Rebecca Guttridge. 'We've had nothing to do with them since. We've tried to live down the shame.'

'It should not have affected you,' maintained Colbeck.

'It did, Inspector. It was like a disease. Tell him, Michael.'

'Rebecca is right,' said her husband. 'When I lived with my parents in Southwark, I'd served my apprenticeship and was working for a builder. I was getting on well. Then my father applied for a job as a hangman. My life changed immediately. When the word got round, they treated me as if I was a leper. I was sacked outright and the only way I could find work was to use a false name – Michael Eames.'

'It's my maiden name,' volunteered Rebecca. 'I took Michael's name at the altar but we find it easier to live under mine. There's no stain on it.'

'I'm sorry that you see it that way,' said Colbeck. 'I can't expect either of you to admire Mr Guttridge for what he did, but you should have respected his right to do it. According to his wife, he only undertook the job because of religious conviction.'

'Ha!' snorted the carpenter. 'He always used that excuse.'

'What do you mean?'

'When he beat me as a child, he used to claim that it was God's wish. When he locked me in a room for days on end, he said the same thing. My father wouldn't go to the privy unless it was by religious conviction.'

'Michael!' exclaimed his wife.

'I'm sorry, Becky. I don't mean to be crude.'

'He's gone now. Just try to forget him.'

'Oh, I will.'

'We're free of him at last. We can lead proper lives.'

Michael Guttridge gave her an affectionate squeeze and Colbeck looked on with disapproval. During his interview with Louise Guttridge, he had realised that some kind of rift had opened up between the parents and their son but he had no idea of its full extent. Because of their family connection with a public executioner, the carpenter and his wife had endured a twilight existence, bitter, resentful, always on guard, unable to outrun the long shadow of the gallows. They were almost gleeful now, sharing a mutual pleasure that made their faces light up. It seemed to Colbeck to be a strange and reprehensible way to respond to the news of a foul murder.

'What about your mother?' he asked.

'She always took my father's part,' said Guttridge with rancour. 'Mother was even more religious than him. She kept looking for signs from above. We had to be guided, she'd say.'

'Mrs Guttridge had no time for me,' Rebecca put in.

'She tried to turn me away from Becky. Mother told me that she was not right for me. It was not proper. Yes,' he went on, wincing at the memory, 'that was the word she used – proper. It was one of my father's favourite words as well. You can see why we never invited them to the wedding.'

'They wouldn't have come in any case,' observed Rebecca.

'They never thought I was good enough for their son.'

'Becky was brought up as a Methodist,' explained her husband. 'I came from a strict Roman Catholic family.'

'I gathered that,' said Colbeck, recalling his encounter with the widow, 'but, when I asked about your mother, I was not talking about the past. I was referring to the present – and to the future.'

'The future?'

'Your mother has lost everything, Mr Guttridge. She and your father were obviously very close. To lose him in such a cruel way has been a dreadful blow for her. Can't you see that?'

'Mother will get by,' said the other with a shrug. 'Somehow or other. She's as hard as nails.'

'It sounds to me as if you've inherited that trait from her.'

'Don't say that about Michael,' chided Rebecca.

'I speak as I find.'

'My husband is the kindest man in the world.'

'Then perhaps he can show some of that kindness to his mother. Mrs Guttridge is in great distress. She's alone, confused, frightened. She's living in a house she dislikes among people she detests and the most important thing in her life has just been snatched from her.' Colbeck looked from one to the other. 'Don't you have the slightest feeling of pity for her?'

'None at all,' snapped Rebecca.

'Put yourself in her position. How would *you* cope if it had been your husband who had been murdered on a train?'

'I won't even think such a horrid thought!'

'Inspector Colbeck has a point,' admitted Guttridge as family ties exerted their pull. 'It's unfair to blame Mother for what happened. It was my father who took on that rotten job and who made me hate my name. And he's gone now – for good.' He gave a wan smile. 'Maybe it is time to let bygones be bygones.'

'No, Michael,' urged Rebecca. 'I won't let you do that.'

'She's my mother, Becky.'

'A woman who looked down on me and said that I was not fit to be your wife. She insulted me.'

'Only because she didn't know you properly.'

'She didn't *want* to know me.'

'I can't turn my back on her,' he said, earnestly.

'You managed to do it before.'

'That was because of my father.'

There was a long, silent battle between them and Colbeck did not interfere. Michael Guttridge was at last afflicted by a modicum of guilt. His wife remained cold and unforgiving. At length, however, she did consent to take his hand and receive a conciliatory kiss on the cheek. Colbeck chose the moment to speak up again.

'I came to ask you a favour, Mr Guttridge,' he said.

'Eames,' attested his wife. 'Everyone knows us under that name.'

'Listen to what the inspector has to say,' said her husband.

'Someone has to identify the body,' explained Colbeck, 'and your mother is not able to do that. It will only take a few moments but it has to be done for legal reasons. Would you consent to come to the morgue to make that identification?'

Guttridge was uncertain. 'I don't know.'

'Let *her* go,' said Rebecca. 'It's not your place.'

'In the absence of the wife, an only son is the obvious person,' remarked Colbeck. 'It's crucial that we have the right name on the death certificate. A false one will not suffice. We don't want to compel a family member to perform this duty,' he cautioned, 'but it may come to that.'

The young carpenter walked to the window and looked

out into the darkness. His wife stood at his shoulder and whispered something in his ear but he shook his head. Guttridge eventually turned round.

'I'll do it, Inspector.'

'Thank you, sir,' said Colbeck, glad to have wrested the concession from him. 'It can wait until morning, if you prefer.'

'No, I need to get it over with as soon as possible.'

'Wait until tomorrow,' advised Rebecca. 'That will give us time to talk about it. I don't want you to go at all.'

'The decision has been made,' said Colbeck, anxious to separate husband and wife. 'We'll take a cab there immediately.'

Guttridge nodded. 'I'm ready, Inspector.'

'Michael!' protested his wife.

'It has to be done, Becky.'

'Have you forgotten everything that he *did* to us?'

'No, I haven't,' said Guttridge, grimly. 'I'm only doing this to spare Mother the trouble and to give myself some pleasure.'

'Pleasure?' reiterated Colbeck in surprise. 'I can't promise that you'll find much pleasure in the police morgue, sir.'

'Oh, but I will, Inspector.'

'How?'

'I'll enjoy something that I've wanted for over twenty years.' He was triumphant. 'I'll be able to see for certain that my father is dead.'

CHAPTER FOUR

Because of its proximity to Scotland Yard, one of the pubs frequented by members of the Detective Department was the Lamb and Flag, a well-run establishment with a friendly atmosphere, a cheery landlord and excellent beer. While he waited for Colbeck to arrive, Victor Leeming nursed a tankard of bitter, taking only occasional sips so that he could make it last. Seated alone at a table on the far side of the bar, the sergeant consulted his watch. The lateness of the hour worried him. He was still wondering what had kept the inspector when Colbeck came in through the door, exchanged greetings with other police colleagues and made his way across the bar through the swirling cigarette smoke.

'I'm sorry to keep you waiting, Victor,' said Colbeck, joining him. 'Can I get you something else to drink?'

'No, thank you, sir. One is all that I dare touch. If I'm late back, as I will be, I can tell my wife that it's because of my work. Estelle accepts that. Let her think that I've been drinking heavily, however, and all hell will break loose. She'll call me names that I wouldn't care to repeat.'

'I'm glad you brought up the subject of names.'

'Are you, sir?'

'Yes, I've a tale to tell you on that score. Excuse me a moment.'

Colbeck went across to the counter and ordered a whisky and soda for himself. When he returned to the table, he took off his hat and sat opposite Leeming, who was in his customary sombre mood. Colbeck raised his glass to his companion.

'Good health, Victor!'

'I could do with it and all, sir,' admitted Leeming. 'Five minutes in that morgue and I feel as if I'm ready for the slab myself. It fair turns my stomach to go in there. How can anyone *work* in a place like that?'

'It takes special qualities.'

'Well, I don't have them. I know that. It's eerie.'

'I didn't find it so when I was there earlier,' said Colbeck, tasting his drink. 'Nor should you, Victor. By now, you should have got used to the sight of dead bodies. Over the years, we've seen enough of them and the one certain thing about policing this city is that we'll be forced to look at many more before we retire.'

'That's what depresses me, Inspector.'

'Learn to take it in your stride, man.'

'If only I could,' said Leeming, solemnly. 'But did you say that you'd been to the morgue as well?'

'I was accompanying the son of the murder victim. He made a positive identification of the body – all too positive, as it happens.'

'What do you mean?'

'That I've never seen anyone laugh in those circumstances before. And that's what Michael Guttridge did. When he looked at his father, he seemed to think it an occasion for hilarity.'

Leeming was nonplussed. 'Michael Guttridge?' he said.

'How could he be the son? The dead man's name was Bransby.'

'It was and it wasn't, Victor.'

'Well, it can't have been both.'

'As a matter of fact, it can.'

Colbeck told him about the visit to Hoxton and drew a gasp of amazement from the other when he revealed that the man who had been killed on the excursion train was none other than a public hangman. The sergeant was even more surprised to learn of the way that Michael Guttridge and his wife had behaved on receipt of the news of the murder.

'That's disgraceful,' he said. 'It's downright indecent.'

'I made that point very forcefully to the young man.'

'And he actually laughed over the corpse?'

'I took him to task for that as well.'

'What did he say?'

'That he couldn't help himself,' said Colbeck. 'In fairness, once we left the building, he did apologise for his unseemly conduct in the morgue. I suppose that I should be grateful that his wife was not with us. Given her intransigent attitude to her father-in-law, she might have stood over the body and applauded.'

'Has she no feelings at all?'

'Far too many of them, Victor.'

Colbeck explained about her relationship with the Guttridge family and how it had made the iron enter her soul. A father himself, Leeming could not believe what he was hearing.

'My children would never treat me like that,' he said, indignantly.

'You'd never give them cause.'

'They love me as their father and do as they're told – some

of the time, anyway. If I was to die, they'd be heartbroken. So would Estelle.'

'What if you were to become a public executioner?'

'That would never happen!'

'But supposing it did, Victor. Let me put it to you as a hypothetical question. In that event, would your children stand by you?'

'Of course.'

'How can you be so sure?'

'Because we're a real *family*,' said Leeming with passion. 'That's all that counts, sir. Blood is thicker than water, you know. Well, we see it every day in our work, don't we? We've met some of the most evil villains in London and they always have wives and children who dote on them.'

'True.'

'Murderers, rapists, screevers, palmers, patterers, kidnappers, blackmailers – they can do no wrong in the eyes of their nearest and dearest.'

'That's a fair point.'

'Look at that man we arrested last month on a charge of beating a pimp to death with an iron bar. His wife swore that he didn't have a violent bone in his body. She never even asked what he was doing in that brothel in the first place.'

'Guttridge's case is somewhat different.'

'It all comes back to family loyalty,' insisted Leeming. 'Most people have got it. If he had nothing to do with his father for three years, this Michael Guttridge was the odd man out. How could he turn his back on his parents like that? I mean, how could he look at himself in the shaving mirror of a morning?'

'Very easily, Victor. He'd had a miserable childhood.'

'It makes no difference, sir. There are *obligations*.'

'You were clearly a more dutiful son than Michael Guttridge. The pity of it is,' said Colbeck, drinking some more whisky, 'that it robs us of a valuable line of inquiry. Since he shunned his father all that time, Michael was unable to give me the names of any possible suspects. Come to that, nor was the dead man's wife.'

'We're in the dark, then.'

'Not necessarily. One thing is self-evident. If you supplement your income as a cobbler by hanging people, you are not going to make many friends. Jacob Guttridge must have aroused undying hatred among the families of his various victims.'

'Lots of them will have wanted to strike back at him.'

'Exactly,' said Colbeck with a sigh. 'Our problem is that we may well end up with far too many suspects. Still, you've heard *my* story. What did you discover at the morgue?'

'Very little beyond the fact that the place scares me.'

'Whom did you speak to?'

'Doctor Keyworth.'

'Leonard's a good man. He knows his job.'

'What he told me,' said Leeming, flicking open the pages of his pad in search of the relevant place, 'was very interesting.'

He gave a halting account of his talk with the doctor, struggling to read his own writing by the light of the gas lamp. Colbeck was not surprised to learn that there had been two earlier attacks on Guttridge. It accounted for the fact that he was armed when he went out in public.

'Doctor Keyworth will have more to tell us when he's finished cutting him up,' said Leeming, closing his book. He opened it again at once. 'By the way, sir, how do you spell asphyxiation?'

Colbeck chuckled. 'Differently from you, I expect.'

'I wrote in "strangling" just to be on the safe side.'

'An admirable compromise, Victor.'

'So where do we go from here?'

'You must go home to your wife and family while I have the more forbidding task of placating the superintendent. Because it's bound to attract a lot of publicity, Mr Tallis wants a bulletin about this case every five minutes. That's why I suggested that we meet here,' said Colbeck, lifting his glass. 'I felt that I needed a dram before facing him.'

'I'd need a whole bottle of whisky.'

'His bark is far worse than his bite.'

'Both frighten me. Will Mr Tallis still be in his office this late?'

'The rumour is that he never leaves it. Give the man his due – his dedication is exemplary. Mr Tallis is married to his job.'

'I'd prefer to be married to a woman,' confided Leeming with a rare smile. 'When I get back, Estelle will make me a nice cup of tea and tell me what she and the children have been up to all day. Then we'll climb into a warm bed together. Who does all that for the superintendent?'

'He has his own rewards, Victor.' Colbeck became businesslike. 'Tomorrow, we start the hunt for the killer. You can begin by reviewing the executions that involved Jacob Guttridge. Start with the most recent ones and work backward.'

'That could take me ages.'

'Not really. He was only an occasional hangman, taking over the work that others were unable to tackle. If he'd had a regular income from the noose, Guttridge wouldn't have had to keep working as a cobbler – or to live in such a small house.'

'I'll get in touch with the Home Office. They should have details.'

'All they will tell you is who was sentenced to be hanged,

the nature of the crime and the place of execution. You must dig deeper than that. Find out everything you can about the individual cases. I'm convinced that that's where we'll track down our man.'

'And woman, sir.'

'What?'

'You thought he had a female accomplice.'

'It's a strong possibility.' Colbeck drained his glass. 'Get a good night's sleep, Victor. You need to be up at the crack of dawn tomorrow to make a start.'

'What will you be doing, sir?'

'Learning more about the mysterious Jacob Guttridge.'

'And how will you do that?'

'By talking to the man who has been the hangman for London and Middlesex for over twenty years.'

'William Calcraft?'

'He's the only person really qualified to talk about Guttridge in his professional capacity. Hangmen are an exclusive breed. They cling together. Calcraft will tell me all I need to know about the technique of executing a condemned prisoner.' Colbeck's eyes twinkled. 'Unless you'd rather talk to him, that is.'

'No, thank you,' replied Leeming with a shiver.

'It might be an education for you, Victor.'

'That's what I'm afraid of, sir.'

'In a sense, he is a colleague of ours. We provide his customers.'

'I wouldn't want to get within a mile of a man like that. Think how much blood he's got on his hands. He's topped dozens and dozens. No, Inspector, I'll leave Mr Calcraft to you.'

* * *

Word of any disaster travelled with amazing speed among railwaymen. Whenever the boiler of a locomotive burst, or a train came off the track or someone was inadvertently crushed to death between the buffers, news of the event soon reached those who worked in the industry. Caleb Andrews was employed by the London and North Western Railway, one of the fiercest rivals of the GWR, but he had heard about the murder at Twyford by mid-evening. It was the main topic of discussion among the drivers and fireman at Euston. To learn more about what had occurred, he was up even earlier than usual so that he could walk to the newsagent's to collect a morning paper. When he got back home, he found breakfast waiting for him on the table. His daughter, Madeleine, who lived alone with her father and who ran the household, was as anxious for detail as he was.

'What does it say, Father?' she asked.

'I haven't had time to read it yet,' said Andrews, taking a leather case from his inside pocket. 'Let me put my glasses on first.'

'A murder on a train! It's terrifying.'

'First one I've ever come across, Maddy.'

'Do they tell you who the victim was?'

Sitting at the table, Andrews put on his spectacles and squinted through the lenses at the front page of the newspaper. His eyebrows shot up and he released a whistle of surprise through his teeth.

'Well,' pressed Madeleine, looking over his shoulder. 'What was the man's name?'

'Jacob Guttridge,' he replied. '*The* Jacob Guttridge.'

'Am I supposed to have heard of him?'

'Every criminal in London has, Maddy. He's a Jack Ketch.'

'A hangman?'

'Not any more. He's not as famous as Mr Calcraft, of course, but he's put the noose around lots of guilty necks, that much I do know. It says here,' he went on, scanning the opening paragraph, 'that he was on an excursion train taking passengers to a prizefight.'

'I thought they were banned.'

'There are always ways of getting around that particular law. I tell you this, Maddy, I'd have been tempted to watch that fight myself if I'd been given the chance. The Bargeman was up against Mad Isaac.'

Andrews put his face closer to the small print so that he could read it more easily. A diminutive figure in his early fifties, he had a fringe beard that was salted with grey and thinning hair that curled around a face lined by a lifetime on the railway. Renowned among his colleagues for his blistering tongue and forthright opinions, Andrews had a softer side to him as well. The death of a beloved wife had all but broken his spirit. What helped him to go on and regain a sense of purpose was the presence and devotion of his only child, Madeleine, an alert, handsome, spirited young woman, who knew how to cope with his sudden changes of mood and his many idiosyncrasies. She had undoubtedly been her father's salvation.

When he got to the end of a column, Andrews let out a cackle.

'What is it?' she said.

'Nothing, nothing,' he replied, airily.

'You can't fool me. I know you better than that.'

'I came across another name I recognised, that's all, Maddy. It would have no interest for you.' He gave her a wicked smile. 'Or would it, I wonder?'

Her face ignited. 'Robert?'

'Inspector Colbeck's been put in charge of the case.'

'Let me see,' said Madeleine, excitedly, almost snatching the paper from him. Her eye fell on the name she sought. 'It's true. Robert is leading the investigation. The murder will soon be solved.'

'The only crime I want to solve is the theft of my paper,' he complained, extending a hand. 'Give it here, Maddy.'

'When I've finished with it.'

'Who went to the shop to buy it?'

'Eat your breakfast, Father. You don't want to be late.'

'There's plenty of time yet.'

She surrendered the newspaper reluctantly and sat opposite him. Madeleine was delighted to see that the Railway Detective was involved in the case. When the mail train had been robbed the previous year, her father had been the driver and he was badly injured by one of the men who had ambushed him. Robert Colbeck had not only hunted down and arrested the gang responsible for the crime, he had rescued Madeleine when she was abducted and used as a hostage. As a result of it all, the two of them had been drawn together into a friendship that had grown steadily over the intervening months without ever quite blossoming into a romance. Colbeck was always a welcome visitor at the little house in Camden.

Andrews remained buried in the newspaper article.

'We should be seeing the inspector very soon,' he observed.

'I hope so.'

'Whenever he's dealing with a crime on the railway, he drops in for my advice. I know that you like to think he comes to see you,' teased Andrews, 'but I'm the person that he really wants to talk to, Maddy. I've taught him all he knows about trains.'

'That's not true, Father,' she responded, loyally. 'Be fair

to him. Robert has always taken a special interest in trains. When you first met him, you couldn't believe that he knew the difference between a Bury and a Crampton locomotive.'

But she was talking to herself. Andrews was so engrossed in the newspaper account that he did not hear her. It was only when he had read every word about the murder on the excursion train three times that he set the paper aside and picked up his spoon. He attacked his breakfast with relish.

'One thing, anyway,' he said as he ate his porridge.

'What's that?'

'You'll have a chance to wear that new dress of yours, Maddy.'

'Father!' she rebuked.

'Be honest. You always make a special effort for the Inspector.'

'All I want is for this dreadful crime to be solved as soon as possible.' She could not hide her joy. 'But, yes, it will be nice if Robert finds the time to call on us.'

Once he had set his mind on a course of action, Inspector Colbeck was not easily deflected. The search for William Calcraft took him to four separate locations but that did not trouble him. He simply pressed on until he finally ran the man to earth at Newgate. He did not have to ask for Calcraft this time because the hangman was clearly visible on the scaffold outside the prison, testing the apparatus in preparation for an execution that was due to take place the next day. Colbeck understood why extra care was being taken on this occasion. Calcraft had bungled his last execution at Newgate, leaving the prisoner dangling in agony until the hangman had dispatched him by swinging on his feet to break his neck. Reviled by the huge crowd attending the event, Calcraft had also been pilloried in the press.

Colbeck waited until the grisly rehearsal was over then introduced himself and asked for a word with Calcraft. Seeing the opportunity for a free drink, the latter immediately took the detective across the road to the public house that would be turned into a grandstand on the following day, giving those that could afford the high prices a privileged view of the execution. Colbeck bought his companion a glass of brandy but had no alcohol himself. They found a settle in a quiet corner.

'I can guess why you've come, Inspector,' said Calcraft, slyly. 'The murder of Jake Guttridge.'

'You've obviously seen the newspapers.'

'Never read the blessed things. They always print such lies about me. Criminal, what they say. Deserves 'angin ' in my opinion. I'd like to string them reporters up in line, so I would.'

'I'm sure.'

'Then cut out their 'earts and livers for good measure.'

'I can see why you're not popular with the gentlemen of the press.'

William Calcraft was an unappealing individual. One of eleven children, he had been raised in poverty by parents who struggled to get by and who were unable to provide him with any real education. The boy's life had been unremittingly hard. Calcraft was in his late twenties when he secured the post of public executioner for London and Middlesex, and the capital provided him with plenty of practice at first. Notwithstanding this, he showed very little improvement in his chosen craft. Coarse, ugly and bearded, he was now in his fifties, a portly man in black frock coat and black trousers, proud of what he did and quick to defend himself against his critics with the foulest of language. Conscious of the man's reputation, Colbeck did not look forward to the interview with any pleasure.

'How well did you know Jacob Guttridge?' he began.

'Too well!' snarled the other.

'In what way?'

'Jake was my blinkin' shadow, weren't 'e? Always tryin' to copy wor I did. 'Cos I was an 'angman, Jake takes it up. 'Cos I earned a crust as a shoemaker, Jake 'as to be a cobbler. Everythin' I did, Jake manages to do as well.' He smacked the table with the flat of his hand. 'The bugger even moved after me to 'Oxton, though 'e couldn't afford to live in Poole Street where I do. I'd never 'ave stood for that, Inspector.'

'I get the impression that you didn't altogether like the man,' said Colbeck with mild irony. 'You must have worked together at some point.'

'Oh, we did. Jake begged me to let 'im act as my assistant a couple of times. Watched me like an 'awk to see 'ow it was done. Then 'e 'as the gall to say that 'e can do it better. Better!' cried Calcraft. 'You're lookin' at a man who's topped some of the worst rogues that ever crawled on this earth. It was me who 'anged that Swiss villain, Kervoyseay.'

'Courvoisier,' said Colbeck, pronouncing the name correctly. 'He was the butler who murdered his employer, Lord William Russell.'

'Then there was Fred Mannin' and 'is wife, Marie,' boasted the other. 'I strung the pair of 'em up at 'Orsemonger Lane a few years back. They danced a jig at the end of my rope 'cos they killed 'er fancy man, Marie Mannin', that is. Nasty pair, they were.'

Colbeck recalled the event well. He also remembered the letter of protest that was published in *The Times* on the following day, written by no less a person than Charles Dickens. An execution that Calcraft obviously listed among his successes had, in fact, provoked widespread disapproval.

There was a gruesome smugness about the man that Colbeck found very distasteful but his personal feelings had to be put aside. He probed for information.

'Does it worry you to be a figure who inspires hatred?' he asked.

'Not at all,' returned Calcraft with a chuckle. 'I thrives on it. In any case, most of the cullies who come to goggle at an 'angin' looks up to me really. They're always ready to buy me a drink afterwards and listen to my adventures. Yes, and I never 'ave any trouble sellin' the rope wor done the job. I cuts it up into slices, Inspector. You've no idea 'ow much some people will pay for six inches of 'emp when it's been round the neck of a murderer.'

'Let's get back to Jacob Guttridge, shall we?'

'Then there's another way to make extra money,' said Calcraft, warming to his theme. 'You lets people touch the 'and of the dead man, see, 'cos it's supposed to cure wens and that. Don't believe it myself,' he added with a throaty chuckle, 'but I makes a pretty penny out of it.'

'Some of which you give to your mother, I understand.'

As Colbeck had intended it to do, the comment stopped Calcraft in his tracks. Two years earlier, the hangman had been taken to court for refusing to support his elderly mother, who was in a workhouse. Though he earned a regular wage from Newgate, and supplemented it by performing executions elsewhere in the country, he had had the effrontery to plead poverty and was sharply reprimanded by the magistrate. In the end, as Colbeck knew, the man sitting opposite him had been forced to pay a weekly amount to his mother, who, though almost eighty, preferred to remain in a country workhouse. It was a case that reflected very badly on the public executioner.

'I'm a dutiful son,' he attested. 'I done right by my mother.'

'It's reassuring to hear that,' said Colbeck, 'but it's Mr Guttridge that I came to talk about. You claimed just now that you don't mind if people hate you because of what you do. Jacob Guttridge did. He was so nervous about it that he used a false name.'

'That's why 'e'd never be another Bill Calcraft.'

'He obviously tried to be.'

'Jealousy, that's wor it was. Jake knew, in his 'eart, that I was the master. But did 'e take my advice? Nah!' said Calcraft with contempt. 'I told 'im to use a short drop like me but 'e always used too much rope. Know wor 'appened at 'is first go?'

'No,' said Colbeck. 'Tell me.'

'Jake allowed such a long drop that 'e took orff the prisoner's 'ead, clean as a whistle. They never let 'im work at Norwich again.'

'Were there other instances where mistakes were made?'

'Dozens of 'em, Inspector.'

'Recently, perhaps?'

'There was talk of some trouble in Ireland, I think.'

'What kind of trouble?'

'Who knows? I don't follow Jake's career. But I can tell this,' said Calcraft, slipping his thumbs into his waistcoat pockets. 'If I was in the salt-box, waitin' to be took to the gallows, I'd much rather 'ave someone like me to do the necessary than Jake Guttridge.'

'Why do you say that, Mr Calcraft?'

'Because I tries to give 'em a quick, clean, merciful death and put 'em out of their misery right way. It's not 'ow Jake did it.'

'No?'

'That psalm-singin' fool made their sufferin' worse before

they got anywhere near the scaffold. A condemned man needs peace and quiet to fit 'is mind for the awful day. Last thing 'e wants is someone like Jake, givin' 'im religious bloody tracts or readin' poetry and suchlike at 'im. All that a public 'angman is there to do,' announced Calcraft with the air of unassailable authority, 'is to 'ang the poor devil who's in the condemned cell. Not try to save 'is blinkin' soul when the likelihood is that 'e ain't got one to save. Follow me, Inspector?'

Even allowing for natural prejudice, Colbeck could see that the portrait painted of Jacob Guttridge was very unflattering. Driven to take on the job by a combination of need and religious mania, he had proved less than successful as a public executioner. Yet he still had regular commissions from various parts of the country.

'Have you never been afraid, Mr Calcraft?' he asked.

'No, Inspector. Why should I be?'

'A man in your line of work must have had death threats.'

'Dozens of 'em,' confessed the other with a broad grin. 'Took 'em as a compliment. Never stopped me from sleepin' soundly at nights. I been swore at, spat at, punched at, kicked at, and 'ad all kinds of things thrown at me in the 'eat of the moment, but I just got on with my work.'

'Do you carry any weapons?'

'I've no need.'

'Mr Guttridge did. He had a dagger strapped to his leg. You and he are as different as chalk and cheese,' said Colbeck, stroking his chin. 'Both of you did the same office yet it affected you in contrasting ways. You walk abroad without a care in the world while Jake Guttridge sneaked around under a false name. Why did he do that?'

'Cowardice.'

'He was certainly afraid of something – or of someone.'

'Then the idiot should never 'ave taken on the job in the first place. A man should be 'appy in 'is work – like me. Then 'e's got good reason to do it properly, see?' He held up his glass. 'Another brandy wouldn't come amiss, Inspector. Pay up and I'll tell you about 'ow I topped Esther 'Ibner, the murderess, 'ere at Newgate. My first execution.'

'Another time,' said Colbeck, getting up. 'Solving a heinous crime like this takes precedence over everything else. But thank you for your help, Mr Calcraft. Your comments have been illuminating.'

'Will you be 'ere tomorrow, Inspector?'

'Here?'

'For the entertainment,' said Calcraft, merrily. 'I always work best when there's a big audience. Maybe Jake will be lookin' down at me from a front row seat in 'eaven. I'll be able to show 'im wor a proper execution looks like, won't I?'

His raucous laughter filled the bar.

Louise Guttridge had been unfair to her neighbours. Because she shut them out of her life, she never really got to know any of them. She was therefore taken aback by the spontaneous acts of kindness shown by unnamed people in her street. All that most of them knew was that her husband had died. Posies of flowers appeared on her doorstep and condolences were scrawled on pieces of paper. Those who could not write simply slipped a card under her door. Louise Guttridge was deeply moved though she feared that more hostile messages might be delivered when the nature of her husband's work became common knowledge.

As in all periods of crisis, she turned to her religion for succour. With the blinds drawn down, she sat in the front room, playing with her rosary beads and reciting prayers she had learnt by heart, trying to fill her mind with holy thoughts so that she could block out the horror that had devastated her life. She was dressed in black taffeta, her widow's weeds, inherited from her mother, giving off a fearsome smell of mothballs. Her faith was a great comfort to her but it did not still her apprehensions completely. She was now alone. The death of her husband had cut her off from the only regular human contact she had enjoyed. She had now been delivered up to strangers.

Closing her eyes, she offered up a prayer for the soul of the deceased and coupled it with a plea that his killer should soon be caught, convicted and hanged. In her mind, one life had to be paid for with another. Until that happened, she could never rest. While the murderer remained at liberty, she would forever be tortured by thoughts of who and where he might be, and why he had committed the hideous crime.

Hoxton was to blame. She was fervent in that belief. Disliking and distrusting the area, she wished that they had never moved there. The tragedy that, from the very start, she felt was imminent had now taken place. The irony was that it had prompted a display of sympathy and generosity among her neighbours that she had never realised was there. In losing a husband, she had gained unlikely friends.

She was still lost in prayer when she heard a knock on her door. The sudden intrusion alarmed her. It was as if she had been shaken roughly awake and she required a moment to gather herself together. A second knock made her move towards the front door. Then she hesitated. What if it were someone who had discovered she was the wife of Jacob Guttridge and come to confront her? Should she lie low and ignore the summons? Or should she answer the door and simply brazen it out? A third knock – much firmer than the others – helped her to make her decision. She could hide no longer behind her maiden name. It was time to behave like the woman she really was – the widow of a hangman. Gathering up her skirt, she hurried to the door and opened it wide.

Louise Guttridge was so astonished to find her son standing there that she was struck dumb. He, too, was palpably unable to speak, seeing his mother for the first time in three years and unsure how his visit would be received. Michael Guttridge looked nervous rather than penitent, but the very fact that he was there touched her. Louise's feelings were ambivalent. Trying to smile, all that she could contrive was a grimace. He cleared his throat before speaking tentatively.

'Hello, Mother.'

'What do you want?' she asked, suspiciously. 'Have you come here to gloat?'

'Of course not.' He sounded hurt. 'May I come in?'

'I don't know, Michael.'

'But I'm your *son*.'

'You were – once.'

And she scrutinised him as if trying to convince herself of the fact.

'I knew that you'd need my advice,' said Caleb Andrews, nudging his elbow. 'Whenever there's a crime on the railway, bring it to me.'

'Thank you for the kind offer,' said Colbeck, amused.

'How can I help you this time, Inspector?'

'Actually, it was Madeleine I came to see.'

'But *I'm* the railwayman.'

'Stop playing games, Father,' said his daughter. 'You know quite well that Robert would not discuss a case with you.'

'All right, all right,' said Andrews, pretending to be

offended. 'I know when I'm not wanted. I'll get out of your way.'

And with a wink at Madeleine, he went off upstairs to change out of his driver's uniform. Left alone with her, Colbeck was able to greet her properly by taking both hands and squeezing them affectionately. For her part, Madeleine was thrilled to see him again, glad that she had taken the precaution of wearing her new dress that evening. Colbeck stood back to admire it and gave her a smile of approval.

'We saw your name in the newspaper,' she said. 'I can see why the Great Western Railway asked for you.'

'It's a double-edged compliment. It means that the investigation falls into my lap, which is gratifying, but – if I fail – it also means that I take the full blame for letting a killer escape justice.'

'You won't fail, Robert. You never fail.'

'That's not true,' he admitted. 'I've made my share of mistakes since I joined the Metropolitan Police. Fortunately, I've been able to hide them behind my occasional successes. Detection is not a perfectible art, Madeleine – if only it were! All that we can do is to follow certain procedures and rely on instinct.'

'Your instinct solved the train robbery last year.'

'I did have a special incentive with regard to that case.'

'Thank you,' she said, returning his smile. 'But I don't think that I was your only inspiration. I'd never seen anyone so determined to track down the men responsible for a crime. Father was very impressed and it takes a lot to earn a word of praise from him.'

'He's so spry for his age.'

'Yes, he's fully recovered from his injuries now.'

'He's looking better than ever. And so are you,' he added, standing back to admire her. 'That dress is quite charming.'

'Oh, it's an old one that you just haven't seen before,' she lied.

'Everything in your wardrobe becomes you, Madeleine.'

'From someone like you, that's a real tribute.'

'It was intended to be.' They shared another warm smile. 'But I haven't asked how your own career is coming along.'

'It's hardly a career, Robert.'

'It could be, if you persist. You have genuine artistic talent.'

'I'm not so sure about that,' she said, modestly.

'You have, Madeleine. When you showed me those sketches you did, I could see their potential at once. That's why I introduced you to Mr Gostelow and he agreed with me. If you can learn the technique of lithography, then your work could reach a wider audience.'

'Who on earth would want to buy prints of mine?'

'I would for a start,' he promised her. 'What other woman could create such accurate pictures of locomotives? Most female artists content themselves with family portraits or gentle landscapes. None of them seem to have noticed that this is the railway age.'

'From the time when I was a small girl,' she said, 'I've always done drawings of trains. I suppose that it was to please Father.'

'It would please a lot of other people as well, Madeleine. However,' he went on, 'I didn't only come here for the pleasure of seeing you and talking about your future as an artist. I wanted to ask a favour.'

'Oh?'

'It concerns this murder on the excursion train.'

'How can I possibly help?'

'By being exactly what you are.'

'The daughter of an engine driver?'

'A kind and compassionate young woman,' he said. 'It fell to me to break the news of her husband's death to his widow, and I did so as gently as I could. In the circumstances, Mrs Guttridge bore up extremely well, almost as if she'd been preparing for such an appalling event. One can understand why. Her husband had been attacked twice before.'

'Was he injured?'

'Quite seriously.'

'I still don't see where I come in, Robert.'

'Let me tell you,' he said, taking her arm to move her to the sofa and sitting beside her. 'I had the distinct feeling that Mrs Guttridge was holding something back from me, something that could actually help the investigation. I don't think that she was deliberately trying to impede me but I was certain that she did not tell me all that she could.'

'The poor woman must have been in a state of shock.'

'It's the reason that I didn't press her too hard.'

'What do you want me to do?'

'Relate to her in a way that I can't, Madeleine. She sees me as a detective, a figure of authority and, most obvious of all, as a man. Mrs Guttridge could not confide in me. I could sense her resistance.'

'Is she any more likely to confide in someone like me?' asked Madeleine, guessing what he wanted her to do. 'You're trained to cope with these situations, Robert. I am not.'

'It doesn't require any previous experience. Your presence alone would be enough. It would make her feel less uneasy. With luck,' he said, 'it might break down that resistance I mentioned.'

'What exactly do you want me to do?'

'First of all, I want to assure you that you're under no compulsion at all. If you'd rather stay clear of the whole thing . . .'

'Don't be silly,' she interrupted, relishing the opportunity of working alongside him. 'I'll do anything that you ask. Coming from a railway family, I have a particular interest in solving this crime.'

'Thank you.'

'Just give me my instructions.'

'The first thing I must do is to swear you to secrecy,' he warned her. 'What I'm asking is highly irregular and my superintendent would tear me to pieces if he were to find out. I won't even breathe a word of this to Victor Leeming, my sergeant. He'd frown on the whole notion.'

'I won't tell a soul – not even Father.'

'Then welcome to the Detective Department,' he said, shaking her hand. 'You're the first woman at Scotland Yard and I could not imagine a better person to act as a pioneer.'

'You might think differently when you see me in action.'

'I doubt that, Madeleine. I have every confidence in you.'

'It will be an education to watch the Railway Detective at work.'

'That may be,' he said, enjoying her proximity, 'but I fancy that you're the one who'll achieve the breakthrough that we need. In this case, it may be a woman's touch that will be decisive.'

CHAPTER FIVE

No matter how early he arrived at work, Victor Leeming could never get there before Edward Tallis. Having made a special effort to reach Scotland Yard by seven o'clock that morning, Leeming was dismayed to see the superintendent coming out of his office and pounding down the corridor towards him like an army on the march.

'Good morning, sir,' said the sergeant.

'What time do you call this, man? We've been here for hours.'

'*We*, Superintendent?'

'Inspector Colbeck and I,' growled Tallis. 'At least, I have one person who understands the importance of punctuality, even if deficient in other respects. While you sleep, the criminal underworld is about its nefarious business. What kept you?' A note of censure came into his voice. 'Family matters, no doubt.'

'It was my wife who got me out of bed so early, sir.'

'Indeed?'

'Yes,' said Leeming, thrown on the defensive. 'As soon as we'd had breakfast with the children, I made my way here.'

'You know my opinion of marriage. It gets in the way.'

'We can't be on duty all the time, Superintendent.'

'We should be, Sergeant – metaphorically speaking, that is. Admit a distraction into your life and you weaken your effectiveness.'

'Estelle is no distraction – nor are my children.'

'I dispute that.'

'We're human beings, sir,' argued Leeming, stung by the attack on his family, 'not monks. What do you want – a celibate police force?'

'I want men beneath me who put their work first.'

'That's what I've always tried to do. And so has Inspector Colbeck.'

'While awaiting your arrival,' said Tallis, pointedly, 'he and I have been studying the research that you did into Jacob Guttridge's record as a hangman. Though I have to admit that I'm not entirely sure that we're looking in the right place.'

'Why not, sir?'

'The killer may have no connection whatsoever with the man's former occupation. He might not even have known who Guttridge was.'

'Then what was his motive?'

'Villains of that stripe need no motive,' said the superintendent, corrugating his brow until his eyebrows met in the middle. 'They have a destructive urge that is set off by drink or simply by an argument.'

'Inspector Colbeck believes that—'

'I am fully aware of what the Inspector believes,' snapped the other, cutting him off, 'but I prefer to keep an open mind. Make a wrong assumption at the start of an investigation and you find yourself going in circles.'

'We know that, sir. Here, however, we have a significant clue.'

'Do we?'

'The Inspector saw it immediately,' said Leeming. 'The manner of the victim's death is critical. It would have been easier to stab him and much quicker to shoot him or bludgeon him to death. Instead, a piece of wire was used to strangle him.'

'I'm familiar with the details.'

'A man who made his living by the noose died in the same way. The killer carefully chose the means by which he took revenge.'

'Did he?'

'I think so, sir.'

'I wonder.'

'The Inspector's argument is very convincing.'

'Not to me,' said Tallis, inflating his chest, 'because it is unproven. We've had killers before who favour the garrotte. Foreigners, usually. And there are footpads who like to disable their victims that way. This could be the work of someone quite unrelated to Guttridge's activities on the scaffold. A murderous Italian, for instance.'

'The train was full of them, sir,' said Leeming, attempting humour.

Tallis glared at him. 'Are you being facetious, Sergeant?'

'No, no. I meant that there would have been villains on board.'

'Then I'll let it pass.'

'Thank you, Superintendent.'

'Now that you're finally here, let's have some work out of you.'

'I plan to spend the entire day sifting through all the information that I gathered about various executions.'

'You'll find that the Inspector has saved you some of the trouble.'

'How?'

'By getting here at the crack of dawn and applying himself to the task in hand.' He stepped in closer to the sergeant. 'Do you see how efficient a man can be when he's not hampered by a wife and children?'

'Only a family can make life worthwhile, sir,' contended Leeming.

'Tell that to Inspector Colbeck. But you had better be quick about it. He'll be leaving soon to pay a second visit to Mrs Guttridge.'

Robert Colbeck offered his hand to help her up into the hansom cab. When he and Madeleine Andrews were safely ensconced inside, they were taken on a noisy, twisting, jolt-filled journey from Camden to Hoxton. They were driven down crowded streets, past busy markets, through heavy horse-drawn traffic and beneath a railway bridge over which a train decided to pass at that precise moment. The pungent smells of London were all around them. While Madeleine savoured the pleasure of being shoulder to shoulder with him, Colbeck patiently instructed her in what she had to do when they reached their destination.

'The most important thing is to win her confidence,' he told her. 'Don't ask her anything at all at first. Let her volunteer any information that she wishes to give us.'

'Yes, Robert.'

'If she has the feeling that you are there solely to interrogate her, we'll get no response at all. Let her come to you, Madeleine.'

'How will you introduce me?'

'As a friend. Someone travelling with me.'

'Not as a detective?' she teased.

'That would rather give the game away. Besides,' he said,

'you're not there to search for anything. All you have to do is to listen.'

She laughed. 'I'm used to doing that at home.'

'Was your father always so garrulous?'

'Not when my mother was alive,' she replied. 'In fact, the two of them were remarkably quiet. They'd just sit together happily of an evening without exchanging a word while I got on with my sketching. It's only since her death that Father became so talkative.'

'I can understand that, Madeleine.'

The coach eventually deposited them outside the house in Hoxton and they alighted to discover a fine drizzle starting to fall. An inquisitive dog was sniffing the petals of some flowers that had been left on the doorstep by a caring neighbour. At the approach of the visitors, the animal ran away and Colbeck was able to retrieve the posy. His gaze was then drawn to the noose that had been crudely painted on the front door of the house, clear evidence that Jacob Bransby's true identity had been revealed to the people of Hoxton.

'Don't go in there, sir,' cautioned a boy. 'It's an 'angman's 'ouse.'

'Really?' said Colbeck.

'It'll prob'bly be 'aunted.'

'Thank you for the warning.'

The boy ran off to join some friends at the end of the street. Before Colbeck could knock on the door, it opened of its own accord and Louise Guttridge appeared with an elderly Roman Catholic priest, his face a mask of benignity. When she recognised the detective, she introduced Father Cleary and the two of them were introduced in turn to Madeleine. After an exchange of niceties, the clergyman left. The visitors were invited into the house and shown into the front room.

Since the blinds were down, it was very gloomy but the Virgin Mary caught what little light was left and seemed to glow in appreciation.

'These were outside,' said Colbeck, handing the flowers to Louise Guttridge. 'A kind gesture from a neighbour.'

'Did you see what was on the front door?' she asked.

'Yes,' he replied. 'When was that put there?'

'Some time in the night.'

'Has there been anything else? Warning letters? Broken windows? Unpleasant items being pushed through the letterbox?'

'Not so far, Inspector.'

'I'll call in at the police station later on and make sure that the officers on this beat pass much more often than usual.'

'Thank you.'

'Although the sensible option would be for you to move out.'

The woman shrugged helplessly. 'Where can I go?'

'We have a spare room at our house,' offered Madeleine, taking pity on her. 'You could come to us for a while.'

'That's very kind of you, Miss Andrews, but I couldn't. I'll stay here till I can sell the house and get out for good.'

Her pallor was accentuated by the black dress and there were bags under her eyes that showed how little sleep she had had since receiving news of her husband's murder. But she was not in distress and the visit of her parish priest had undoubtedly bolstered her.

'I came to tell you that the body has been identified,' said Colbeck. 'Your son was prevailed upon to come to the morgue with me.'

'Yes, Inspector. He told me.'

Colbeck was startled. 'You've *seen* him?'

'He called here yesterday.'

'What did he say, Mrs Guttridge?'

'Very little,' she replied. 'Michael said all that he needed to say three years ago when he married that spiteful creature against our will. Rebecca Eames turned our son against us.'

'Yet he does appear to have made the effort to come here.'

'Yes.' There was a long pause before she remembered the rules of hospitality. 'But do sit down, please. May I get you something?'

'A cup of tea would be welcome,' said Colbeck. 'Miss Andrews?'

'Yes, please.'

The other woman indicated the chairs. 'Take a seat while I get it.'

'Let me help you,' said Madeleine, following her out to the kitchen.

Left alone, Colbeck was able to study the room more carefully than he had been able to do on his first visit. Whatever her shortcomings as a mother, Louise Guttridge was a fastidious housekeeper. There was not a hint of dust to be seen anywhere. The mirror on one wall had been polished to a high sheen, the tiles around the fireplace gleamed, and the picture rail looked as if it had been painted that morning. She had even run a vigorous duster around the pot holding the aspidistra and over the black-leading on the grate. Trapped in a false identity and confined largely to the house, she had made it as habitable as possible.

Nor had her spiritual cleanliness been neglected. The crucifix and the Virgin Mary looked down on a well-thumbed Bible and a Catholic missal, side by side on the small table. Colbeck could all but smell the incense in the air. The two women seemed to be taking their time in the kitchen but he did not worry about that. The longer they were alone together, the more likely it was that Madeleine could learn something of consequence. He was especially pleased with the way that she had offered the older woman shelter at her own home, a truly sympathetic response to the predicament in which Louise Guttridge found herself.

Colbeck sat down and waited, noting that there was virtually no sign of anything in the room that had been put there by the deceased. A man who was so passionate about prizefighting might be expected to have a few sporting prints on the wall. His twin occupations of cobbler and hangman had also been excluded but that was understandable. It was pre-eminently his wife's domain, leading Colbeck to wonder just how much time the husband had spent in there with her. While Guttridge had also been religious, his regular consumption of alcohol – confirmed by the post-mortem – had pointed to someone with all too human failings. The former hangman might pray with his wife for guidance but, Colbeck was certain, he did not take her to a public house with him, still less to a boxing match.

The others finally came in from the kitchen and it was Madeleine who was carrying the tray. It was a promising sign. The older woman moved the Bible and the missal so that the tray could be set down on the table. Louise Guttridge stood beside it, ready to pour the tea.

'Mrs Guttridge has just told me about her husband's collection,' said Madeleine, sitting opposite Colbeck. 'It's in the spare room.'

'A collection?' he repeated. 'Of what kind?'

'To do with his work,' explained the widow, removing the tea cosy so that she could take hold of the handle. 'Jacob liked to keep souvenirs. A cup of tea, Miss Andrews?'

'Yes, please,' said Madeleine.

'Help yourself to milk and sugar.'

'Thank you, Mrs Guttridge.'

Colbeck bided his time until his own cup had been poured and he had added a splash of milk. The revelation about the spare room filled him with hope. He stirred his tea.

'Why didn't you mention this collection before?' he wondered.

'Because it was nothing to do with me,' said Louise Guttridge, taking a seat with her own cup of tea. 'Jacob never let me in there – not that I would have cared to see such horrible things, mind you. He kept the room locked.'

'Do you have the key?'

'Yes, Inspector. I found it when I was going through my husband's things last night. But I couldn't bring myself to go into the room.'

'Somebody will have to do so,' said Madeleine, casually. 'Would you like Inspector Colbeck to spare you the trouble? I'm sure that he will have no qualms about what he might find.'

'None at all,' he added, grateful for the ease with which she had made the suggestion. 'I'd be only too glad to help.'

'The decision is yours, Mrs Guttridge.'

The other woman hesitated. Tempted to accept the offer, she felt that it would be an invasion of her privacy and that – at such a vulnerable moment for her – was deeply troubling. In her eyes, there was another drawback. The detective might relieve her of a repellent task but, in the process, he might discover things that she did not wish to know about her late husband. Colbeck was quick to point out a more positive result of any search.

'My job is to catch your husband's killer,' he reminded her. 'It may well be that your spare room contains clues that will lead me to him. It's imperative that I be given access to it.'

'It was Jacob's room. Nobody else was allowed in there.'

'I think that I should find out why, don't you?' Louise Guttridge agonised over the decision for a full minute.

'I'll get the key,' she said at length.

When he got to the top of the stairs, Colbeck took the opportunity to peer into the main bedroom at the front of the house. Immaculately clean, it contained a dressing table, an upright chair, a wardrobe with mirrors and a bed over which another crucifix kept guard. The room was small but uncluttered and he saw the hand of the wife at work once again. He went across to the back room and slipped the key into the lock, wondering what he would find on the other side of the varnished timber. Opening the door, he stepped into another world.

The contrast could not have been greater. The tiny, cramped room was the complete antithesis of the other parts of the house. Where they had been spick and span, Jacob Guttridge's den was in total disarray. In place of the odour of sanctity there was a lingering smell of decay. Instead of looking up to heaven, the hangman preferred to stare down into the mouth of hell. The only pieces of furniture in the room were a long table and a single bed, both littered with newspapers, pieces of rope, advertisements for executions and other grim mementos of his craft. Most ghoulish of all were items of clothing that had been worn by condemned men and, more particularly, by women, their names written on scraps of paper that had been pinned to the material.

The walls, too, were covered in drawings, warrants, newspaper articles and curling advertisements, haphazardly arranged but all the more striking as a result. Amid the hideous catalogue of death, Colbeck noticed prints of prizefighters – one of them was the Bargeman – but the overwhelming impression was of a black museum in which Jacob Guttridge had gloried with almost necrophiliac pleasure. Had the law permitted it, the detective mused, the hangman would have parboiled the heads of his victims and had them dangling from the ceiling like so many Chinese lanterns. Guttridge had relished his work.

Below in the front room, Louise Guttridge was being distracted by Madeleine, sublimely unaware of the essential character of the man with whom she had slept for so many years in the shadow of a crucifix. The house that bore her clear imprint was really a façade behind which she could hide as Mrs Bransby. It was the back bedroom that told the truth about the building and its owner. Colbeck resolved that the wife should not be subjected to the discovery that he had just made. Even with the aid of Father Cleary, he was not sure that she would survive the ordeal.

He began a slow, methodical search, first stripping the walls and sorting the various items into piles. Some of the fading newspaper cuttings referred to executions that he had carried out years before. Any periodical in which Guttridge had been mentioned had been saved, even if the comments about him were unfavourable. Under a collection of death warrants on the table, Colbeck found the hangman's invoice book. Each page was neatly printed in italics with spaces left for him to fill in the date, his current address and details of the execution that he was agreeing to undertake. Sent to the High Sheriff of the relevant county, it was signed: 'Your obedient Servant, Jacob Guttridge.'

The hangman had been ubiquitous. Colbeck found a record of his work in places as far apart as Aberdeen, Bodmin, Lancaster, Cambridge, Taunton, Glasgow, Swansea, Bury

St Edmunds and Ireland. A tattered account book listed his various fees, copied out laboriously in a spidery hand. There was also a series of squiggly notes about the technique of hanging, complete with rough sketches that showed comparative lengths of the drop, relative to the weight of the condemned person. But it was the last discovery that excited Colbeck the most and made his search worthwhile. Concealed under a ballad about the execution of a man in Devizes was something that Guttridge had not put on display. It was a note, scribbled on a piece of brown paper in bold capitals.

N IS INERCENT. IF YOU HANGS HIM,
WEEL KILL YOU.

The warning message was unsigned.

What took you so long up there, Robert?' asked Madeleine Andrews.

'There was a lot to see in that room.'

'You seem to have brought most of it with you.'

She indicated the bundle that lay between his feet. The two of them were in a cab, on their way back to Camden via the local police station, and they had taken some cargo on board. With the permission of Louise Guttridge, Colbeck had gathered up everything that he felt would distress her and wrapped it all in a cloak that had once belonged to a certain Eleanor Fawcett, hanged at Ipswich the previous summer for poisoning both her husband and her lover. Colbeck could only guess at the impulse that had made the hangman keep it as a treasured souvenir. He was grateful that the widow would never know just how depraved her husband had been. When the two of them had knelt before their Maker, they were sending their supplications in opposite directions.

'What exactly is in there?' said Madeleine.

'Evidence.'

'Of what sort?'

'That's confidential,' he said, not wishing to upset her with details of what he had found upstairs. 'But I haven't thanked you properly yet, Madeleine,' he continued, touching her arm. 'Because of you, I have some vital new information. I'm deeply grateful.'

'I was only too glad to help.'

'I'm sorry to have placed such a burden on you.'

'That was not how I saw it, Robert.'

'Good. What did you make of Mrs Guttridge?'

'I felt sorry for her,' said Madeleine with a sigh. 'She's in such desperate straits. Yet you would hardly have known it from the way that she was bearing up. When my mother died, I was helpless with grief for weeks and Father was even worse. We walked around in a complete daze. That's not what Mrs Guttridge is doing and her husband didn't die of natural causes, as Mother did. He was murdered only a few days ago.'

'She's a very unusual woman.'

'I've never met anyone like her, Robert. Somehow, she's managing to keep everything bottled up inside her.'

'Mrs Guttridge has been doing that since her husband first took on the job as a public hangman. She convinced herself that she should support his choice of occupation yet it cost her both her identity and her peace of mind. It also meant that she had no real friends.'

'Her life was snatched away from her.'

'Yes, Madeleine,' he noted, sadly. 'In a sense, she was another of his victims. That rope of his effectively destroyed Louise Guttridge by turning her into someone she did not really wish to be.'

'Perhaps that's why she's unable to mourn him properly.'

'It was a strange marriage, that much is apparent.'

'What will happen to her?'

'Who knows? All that I can do is to offer her some protection by making sure that her street is patrolled regularly. The one thing that will be of real benefit for her, of course, is the arrest and conviction of the man who committed this crime.'

'And you say that you found new evidence?'

'Yes, Madeleine.'

'So my visit was not a waste of time.'

'I could not have achieved any progress without you.'

'Does that mean you'll ask your superintendent to take me on?'

Colbeck grinned. 'Even I would not be brave enough to do that,' he confessed. 'No, your sterling assistance must go unreported but by no means unappreciated.' He squeezed her hand. 'Thank you again.'

'Call on me any time, Robert. It was exciting.'

'It's one of the reasons that I became a policeman. There's nothing quite as stimulating as taking a giant step forward in an investigation,' he said, smiling, 'and that's what I feel we did this morning.'

Still smarting from the rebuke he had received on his arrival, Victor Leeming spent the whole morning at Scotland Yard trying to finish the work that Colbeck had started and assimilate the mass of material that had been assembled. As well as a list of executions carried out by Guttridge over the past two years, Leeming had also found descriptions of the man's career in back copies of various London newspapers. One even contained an artist's impression of the execution of a woman in Chelmsford who, too weak to stand, had been strapped into a chair before being hanged. Leeming felt his stomach lurch. He moved quickly on to the next case he had listed.

Brisk footsteps could be heard in the corridor outside and he steeled himself for yet another abrasive encounter with Superintendent Tallis. Instead, it was Inspector Colbeck who came in through the door with a large bundle under his arm. Leeming got to his feet with relief.

'I'm so glad to see you, Inspector,' he said.

'It's always pleasing to receive a cordial welcome.'

'I've been studying Jacob Guttridge's work and it does not make happy reading.' He shuffled some sheets of paper. 'I know that you made a start on all this but I've more or less finished it off.'

'Well done, Victor,' said Colbeck, dropping the bundle on his desk.

'What have you got there, sir?'

'The contents of a private museum. Most of it, anyway. I had to leave the bottles of brandy that were hidden under the bed. The fact that her husband was a secret drinker is one shock that I can't keep from Mrs Guttridge. The items in here, however,' he said, undoing the knot in the cloak so that it fell open to display its contents, 'would have caused her a lot of unnecessary suffering.'

'Why?'

'Judge for yourself, Victor.'

'What *are* all these things?'

'Trophies.'

'Saints preserve us!' exclaimed Leeming as he saw the lengths of rope that had been used in various executions and tagged accordingly. 'There's everything here but the dead bodies themselves.'

'Wait until you come to the religious tracts and the poems.'

'Poems?'

'Written by Jacob Guttridge.'

While the sergeant sifted his way through the relics, Colbeck told him about the visit to Hoxton, omitting only the fact that Madeleine Andrews had been with him. He then showed him the threatening note that he had found at the house.

Leeming studied it. 'Who is N, sir?'

'That's what we have to determine.'

'It could be Noonan,' said the other, snapping his fingers. 'I was looking at the case just before you came in. Sean Noonan was hanged for murder in Dublin a year ago.'

'Then he's unlikely to be our man.'

'N stands for Noonan, doesn't it?'

'Yes,' agreed Colbeck, 'but it's unlikely that a surname would be used. In all probability, that note was sent to Mr Guttridge by a family member or by a close friend of the condemned man, and they would surely refer to him by his Christian name. We should be looking for a Neil, Nigel or Norman.'

'None of those spring to mind, sir.'

'Where's that list?'

'Wait!' said Leeming. 'There was a Nairn McCracken from Perth.'

'Too long ago,' decided Colbeck, picking up the paper from the table and studying it. 'I'm convinced that we want a more recent case. According to this, McCracken was executed in 1849. I don't think that someone would wait three years to wreak revenge on his behalf.'

'Maybe they'd already had two attempts. Doctor Keyworth told us that there were scars on the body of the deceased.'

'Put there in separate incidents, that much is clear. According to the post-mortem, the stomach wound was several years old, inflicted long before Guttridge went anywhere near Perth.' He tapped the list. 'Now this is much more promising.'

'Who is he, sir?'

'Nathan Hawkshaw. Executed less than a month ago.'

'I remember him. It was in Maidstone.'

'What do we know about the case?'

'Precious little. He murdered someone called Joseph Dykes. That's all I can tell you, Inspector. I could find no details.'

'Then I'll have to go in search of them.'

'To Kent?'

'It's not far by train.' He smiled as Leeming pulled a face. 'Yes, I know that you hate rail travel, Victor, so I won't subject you to the ordeal just yet. I've a more attractive assignment for you.'

'I won't find searching through this lot very attractive,' complained Leeming, gazing down at the items in the cloak. 'What sort of man would want to keep things like this?'

'One with a rather macabre outlook on life – and on death, for that matter. Have no fear. We'll lock all this away for the time being.' He tied the cloak into a knot again. 'What I need you to do for me is to find the answer to something that's puzzled me from the start.'

'And what's that, sir?'

'How did the killer know that Jacob Guttridge would be on that excursion train and in that particular carriage?'

'He must have followed him.'

'Granted,' said Colbeck, 'but how did he find him in the first place? You've seen the lengths that Guttridge went to in order to preserve his anonymity. He changed his name, moved house often and never got too friendly with his neighbours.'

'So?'

'Whoever tracked him down went to enormous trouble.'

'Then bided his time until Guttridge caught that excursion train.'

'No, Victor. The killer could not possibly have watched that house in Hoxton day and night. It's dangerous enough for those who live there. A stranger would be taking serious risks if he lurked in those streets.'

'What's the explanation then?'

'I'm not sure,' said Colbeck, removing his hat and running a hand through his dark, wavy hair. 'At least, not entirely sure.'

'But you have a theory, I can tell.'

'Perhaps.'

'Come on, sir. I know that look in your eye.'

'The superintendent calls my theories misbegotten brainstorms.'

'Who cares what he calls them? They usually turn out to be right in the long run. You have a gift for putting yourself into the mind of the criminal and Mr Tallis can't understand that. Neither can I, if truth be told,' he said, cheerfully. 'What's your theory, sir?'

'Most of Jacob Guttridge's time was spent at home, working as a cobbler in his shed. His wife confirms that. Now, what would get him out of the house?'

'An execution.'

'What else?'

'Going to Mass every Sunday. We know that he was devout.'

'In every way,' observed Colbeck with a glance at the bundle on his desk. 'He worshipped at more than one altar. But where else might he have gone, Victor?'

'I don't know.'

'Yes, you do. Think. Where was he killed?'

'On an excursion train.'

'Why was he there?'

'He was on his way to a prizefight.'

'Then *that* may be how he was tracked.'

'Was it, sir?'

'Mr Guttridge was one of the Fancy. He idolised those bareknuckle boxers and couldn't miss an opportunity to see a championship contest.'

'But a fight like that comes around once in a blue moon.'

'A public contest might,' said Colbeck, 'but there are exhibition bouts being staged all the time for real followers of the sport. And I can guess where Mr Guttridge went to watch them.'

'Where?'

'Bethnal Green. His hero was Bill Hignett.'

'The Bargeman? How do you know that, sir?'

'Because there was a signed print of him at the house. If he wanted to see Hignett in action, all that he had to do was to go to the Seven Stars in Bethnal Green and watch him spar. There's a room at the back of the inn where the Bargeman trains and passes on his skills to a lot of younger boxers.'

'And you think that Mr Guttridge went there?'

'Almost certainly. It allowed him to do two things that were very important to him – enjoy some milling and drink his fill.'

'He could get his beer much closer to home than that.'

'Not in Hoxton,' reasoned Colbeck. 'That was on his doorstep and he was careful to keep his neighbours at arm's length in case he let slip his guilty secret. He'd feel safer in Bethnal Green as part of a crowd that cheered on Bill Hignett.'

'How does the killer fit into your theory?'

'Rather hazily at the moment,' admitted Colbeck, thinking it through. 'Somehow, he discovered that Mr Guttridge had a passion for boxing, followed him to Bethnal Green and established that he would be going to the fight near Twyford on that day. All that he had to do then,' he concluded, taking a handkerchief from his pocket by way of demonstration, 'was to wait at Paddington station until his victim arrived, stay on his heels and get into the same second-class carriage. When the excursion train stopped at Twyford and the hordes charged off,' he went on, using the handkerchief like a garrotte, 'he choked the life out of his victim.'

Leeming fingered his throat uneasily. 'Put that away, sir.'

'I was just trying to illustrate a point.'

'So what do you wish me to do?'

'Go to the Seven Stars and mix with the regular patrons. Ask if any of them recall a Jake Bransby – don't use his real name because we can be certain that *he* didn't do so. And be discreet, Victor. Someone may have realised that Bransby was really Jacob Guttridge, the hangman. Choose your words carefully.'

'I will.'

'You may even get a chance to meet the Bargeman, if he's recovered from the fight.'

'What about the killer?'

'If he *did* trail Mr Guttridge there,' said Colbeck, tucking his handkerchief into his pocket, 'it should be possible to find out. Only the true disciples of pugilism would stand for ages around that boxing ring in Bethnal Green. A stranger would be noticed immediately. Make your way there, Victor. See if any outsider drifted into the Seven Stars in recent weeks. If at all possible, get a description of him.'

'Right, sir,' said Leeming, pleased with his instructions. 'If nothing else, this will get me out from under the superintendent's big feet. I'll go immediately. What about you, sir?'

'I'll be on a train to Maidstone,' replied Colbeck, taking a copy of *Bradshaw's Guide* from his desk drawer. 'I want to find out if N really does stand for Nathan Hawkshaw.'

The county town of Kent lay at the heart of what was popularly known as the Garden of England. Rich soil and a temperate climate combined to make it a haven for fruitgrowers and the hops were reckoned to be the finest in the kingdom, spreading satisfaction and drunken stupor far and wide among the nation's beer drinkers. A parliamentary and municipal borough, Maidstone was an assize town with a long and varied history, its earlier ecclesiastical dominance reflected in the ancient, but expertly restored, Pilgrims' Chapel, its ruined priory, its noble palace, formerly belonging to the Archbishop of Canterbury, and its imposing churches.

It was situated at a well-chosen point on the River Medway, a wide and sometimes turbulent waterway, the main artery of the town for centuries. From the wharves that lined the river, large quantities of local stone, corn, fruit, sand and other goods were shipped, and over fifty barges traded there regularly, giving employment to hundreds of people. The Medway was crossed by a stone bridge with five arches, and plundered assiduously by the local anglers. Occasional flooding was deemed to be an acceptable price to pay for the convenience of living beside such an important river.

Robert Colbeck reached the town by courtesy of the South Eastern Railway, the journey a continuous pleasure to someone who enjoyed travelling by train as much as he did. Since there was no direct line from London to Maidstone, he was obliged to change at Paddock Wood and eventually came into the station at the end of Hart Street on the western side of the town. It was market day and, though he did not get there until mid-afternoon, hundreds of customers still haggled beside the stalls, booths and carts that lined High Street, Week Street and King Street. Someone rang a hand bell, the last of the livestock complained noisily in their pens and the din was compounded by the incessant clucking of poultry in their baskets and by the competing cries of the vendors.

Even from the railway station, Colbeck could hear the noise and he was grateful that he did not have to walk directly through the market, where his elegant attire would make him incongruous among the more homespun garments on show. As it was, he attracted a lot of curious glances. Maidstone prison was a forbidding sight. Erected behind the Sessions House, it had four hundred night cells and was encircled by a high perimeter wall that acted as a stern warning to any would-be malefactors. The man on duty at the gate was so unaccustomed to the appearance of a detective inspector from Scotland Yard that he refused to admit Colbeck until word had been sent to the governor.

There was a long delay. Taken aback by news of his unexpected visitor, Henry Ferriday nevertheless agreed to see him, deciding that he would not have come all that way from London unless it were on a matter of some importance. Colbeck was admitted and escorted to the governor's office, a small, untidy, cheerless room that overlooked the exercise yard. Ferriday welcomed him with a warm handshake and an inquisitive frown. He waved the detective to a chair.

'Well,' he said, resuming his own seat behind the desk, 'to what do we owe the pleasure of this visit, Inspector?'

'I'm hoping that you can help me with an investigation.'

'We are always ready to do that.'

'It concerns the murder of Jacob Guttridge.'

'Yes,' said Ferriday, shaking his head, 'we saw mention of

that in the newspapers. He was here only a matter of weeks ago, you know.'

'Was it the first time he'd carried out an execution at Maidstone?'

'No, no, Inspector. It would have been his third visit.'

Henry Ferriday was a lean man of middle years with hollow cheeks and large, mobile eyes. He had compensated for a dramatic loss of hair by trying to grow a beard but the experiment had been only a limited success. In his black frock coat, and with his sharp features, he looked like a giant crow. While he talked, he kept peering nervously over his shoulder as if fearing that someone would smash a way through the barred window behind him. From the way that the governor talked, Colbeck judged him to be a kind, humane man who had come into the prison service out of a sense of vocation and who still retained vestiges of an idealism that had largely melted away in the white-hot furnace of daily experience.

'In the past,' he explained, 'we were happy with Mr Guttridge's services – insofar as any happiness can attend an execution, that is. Personally, I find them rather disgusting events and I hate being forced to witness them. My digestion is never the same for days afterwards.'

'Tell me about the most recent execution, if you will.'

'Nathan Hawkshaw?'

'Yes, Governor. Was he a local man?'

'He was a butcher in Ashford, twenty miles or so from here. And butchery was involved in his crime, alas,' he said, tossing another glance over his shoulder. 'Hawkshaw was hanged for the murder of Joseph Dykes whom he hacked to death with a meat cleaver. It was a brutal assault. And the worst of it was that Hawkshaw refused to show the slightest remorse. He said that he was glad Dykes was dead though he insisted that he was innocent of the crime.'

'Was there any doubt about his guilt?'

'Not as far as the court was concerned, Inspector, and we are guided by the sentences that they hand down. Hawkshaw's was a capital offence so we sent for Mr Guttridge.'

'Do you happen to know the details of the case?' asked Colbeck. 'I'd be grateful for anything that you can tell me. This was the last execution carried out by Mr Guttridge and it may have some bearing on his death.'

'I fail to see how.'

'Humour me, if you please. I came in search of facts.'

'Then the person you should be talking to,' said Ferriday, getting up to cross to the door, 'is our chaplain, the Reverend Jones. He struggled hard with Nathan Hawkshaw but to no avail.' He opened the door. 'Narcissus will furnish you with all the details you need.'

'Narcissus?'

'That's his name, Inspector. Narcissus Jones.' He spoke briefly to someone in the corridor outside then closed the door. 'Our chaplain is Welsh. He's a man of strong opinions.'

'Not always the case with a man of the cloth.'

'Prison plays havoc with a man's spiritual values. Even the most pious Christian will question his faith when he has worked in this godforsaken hell-hole for any length of time. Yet it has not affected the chaplain in that way,' said Ferriday, brushing an imaginary speck of dust from his lapel so that he had an excuse to look behind him. 'If anything, life within these walls has only reinforced his commitment.'

'That's comforting to hear.'

'Narcissus Jones is a species of saint.'

Colbeck was not at all sure that he wanted to discuss

a murder investigation with a Welsh saint but he had no alternative. In any case, after the fulsome praise that the governor had heaped on the man, the detective was interested to meet him. Ferriday seemed to be slightly in awe of the chaplain, almost to the point of deference. Colbeck fished.

'You say that Nathan Hawkshaw protested his innocence?'

'Most prisoners do that, Inspector,' said the other, wearily. 'The worse their crimes, in my experience, the louder they deny their guilt. Hawkshaw was unusual in one respect, though, I have to concede that.'

'Oh?'

'A campaign was launched on his behalf.'

'What sort of campaign?' asked Colbeck. 'A plea for his release?'

'A full-throated demand for it,' replied Ferriday. 'Quite a sizeable number of people were involved. They had leaflets printed, claiming that Hawkshaw was innocent and they even brought banners and placards to the execution. It made the ordeal even more horrible.' There was a tap on the door. 'Ah, that will be the chaplain.' He raised his voice. 'Come in!'

The door opened and the Reverend Narcissus Jones stepped into the room. He was even taller than Colbeck, a solid man in his forties with broad shoulders and huge hands. Dark hair of impressive luxuriance fell back from the high forehead and almost touched the edge of his clerical collar. His features were rugged, his nose bulbous, his eyes small and darting. Colbeck's first impression was that he bore less resemblance to a species of saint than to a species of farm animal. Ferriday was still on his feet. Introduced to the newcomer, Colbeck got up to exchange a handshake with him and to feel the power in his grip. Reverend Narcissus Jones liked to display his strength.

When all three of them were seated again, the governor

explained the purpose of Colbeck's visit. The piggy eyes of the chaplain flashed.

'Oh, I remember Nathan Hawkshaw,' he said in a lilting voice that was deeper and more melodious than anything Colbeck had ever heard coming from a human mouth before. 'Distressing case. Very distressing. One of my rare failures as a chaplain. Is that not so, Governor?'

'You did your best.'

'I wrestled with him for days on end but I could find no way to awaken his conscience. Hawkshaw was adamant. Kept insisting that he was not responsible for the killing, thereby adding the crime of deceit to the charge of murder.'

'The chaplain even had to overpower the man,' recalled Ferriday.

'Yes,' said Jones, piqued by the memory. 'The prisoner was so incensed with anger that he dared to strike at me and – what was far worse in my eyes – he had the audacity to take the Lord's name in vain as he did so. I felled him with a punch – God help me!'

'After that, we had to keep him under restraint.'

'From what the governor has been telling me,' said Colbeck to the muscular priest, 'this Nathan Hawkshaw was not the only person convinced of his innocence. He had a group of supporters, I believe.'

'A disorderly rabble from Ashford,' said Jones with a loud sniff. 'Thirty or more in number. They even tried to rescue Hawkshaw from the prison but the attempt was easily foiled. Instead, they chose to disrupt the execution.'

'Fortunately,' added Ferriday, 'we had advance warning that there might be trouble. Extra constables were on duty to keep the crowd under control and they were certainly needed.'

'That was largely Mr Guttridge's fault. He stirred them up

to the very edge of mutiny. I've never seen such incompetence on a scaffold.'

'What happened?' asked Colbeck.

'The hangman made a few mistakes,' said Ferriday, mildly.

'A few?' boomed Jones. 'Let us be brutally frank, Governor. The fellow made nothing *but* mistakes. To begin with, he tried to take over my job and offer the prisoner spiritual sustenance. That was unforgivable.' He checked himself and spoke with more control. 'I know that one should not speak ill of the dead – especially if they die by violence – but I find it hard to think of Mr Guttridge without feeling a surge of anger. Giving the prisoner a religious tract, indeed! Reading a ridiculous poem at him! And that was not the sum of his imperfections. As soon as he arrived here, we could smell the brandy on his breath.'

'Most executioners need a drink to steady their hand,' remarked Colbeck, tolerantly. 'Mr Calcraft is noted for his fondness for the bottle.'

'I had a drink myself beforehand,' confessed Ferriday.

'That may be, Governor,' said Jones, tossing his hair back, 'but you did not let it interfere with the discharge of your duties. That was not the case with Mr Guttridge. He tripped on the steps as he went up on to the platform.'

'Nervousness. The baying of that huge crowd upset him.'

'It did not upset me and many of them were abusing me by name.'

'You were an example to us all, Narcissus.'

'With the exception of the hangman.'

'What exactly did he do wrong?' inquired Colbeck.

'Everything, Inspector,' the Welshman told him. 'I thought that Hawkshaw was a benighted heathen but, to his credit, at the very last, he showed a glimmering of Christian feeling. When he saw there was no escape from his fate, he finally began to pray. And what does that fool of an executioner do, Inspector?'

'Tell me.'

'He pulled the bolt before the prayers were over.'

'It was most regrettable,' commented Ferriday.

'Mr Guttridge lost his nerve,' accused Jones, 'and fled from the scene without even checking that he had done his job properly.'

'I take it that he hadn't,' said Colbeck.

'No, Inspector. When the trap sprang open, Hawkshaw somehow contrived to get his heels on the edge so that he did not fall through it. You can imagine how that inflamed the crowd. The mood was riotous.'

'What did you do?'

'The only thing that we could do,' said Ferriday, flicking a glance behind him to check for eavesdroppers. 'I had Mr Guttridge brought out again and ordered him to dispatch the prisoner quickly. But, when he tried to push Hawkshaw's feet away from the trap, the man kicked out violently at him and – the sight will stay for me forever – his supporters urged him on with manic cries as they fought to get at us. Truly, I feared for my own life.'

'In the end,' said Jones, taking up the story, 'Mr Guttridge beat his legs away and he dropped through the trap, but the fall did not break his neck. He was jerking wildly around in the air. Everyone could see the rope twisting and turning. That really made passions rage.'

'I sent Guttridge below to pull on his legs,' said Ferriday, swallowing hard, 'but he could not even do that properly. One of the warders had to assist him. Nathan Hawkshaw was left hanging there, in agony, for well over five minutes. It was an abomination.'

'And Mr Guttridge was to blame?' said Colbeck.

'Regrettably, he was.'

'If all this took place in front of his loved ones, it must have fired some of them up to seek revenge against him.'

'Death threats were shouted from all sides.'

'I deplore those threats,' said Jones, 'but I sympathise with the impulse to make them. If I'm honest – and honesty is the essence of my character – *I* could have called for Mr Guttridge's head at that point in time. He was a disgrace to his calling. *Ieusi Mawr*!' he exclaimed with an angry fist in the air. 'Had there been another rope on the scaffold, I'd gladly have hanged that drunken buffoon alongside the prisoner, then swung on his legs to break that worthless neck of his.'

Henry Ferriday turned to Colbeck with a weak smile.

'I did warn you that the chaplain had strong opinions,' he said.

CHAPTER SIX

Before he set out, Victor Leeming took the precaution of changing into a shabby old suit that he kept at the office for just such occasions. Although it was invariably crumpled, the clothing he wore to Scotland Yard every day was too close to that of a gentleman to allow him an easy passage through Bethnal Green, the most miserable and poverty-stricken district in the whole of the city. His aim was to be as nondescript as possible so that he could merge with his surroundings. For that reason, he traded his hat for a battered cap and his shoes for a pair of ancient boots. When he left the building, he looked more like a disreputable costermonger than a detective. Some of the cabs that he tried to hail refused to stop for him, fearing that he would be unable to pay his fare.

It was over a year since he had been in Bethnal Green but he remembered its notorious reek all too well. No sooner did he reach the area than it assaulted his nostrils once more. In a space enclosed between a hoarding on either side of the Eastern Counties Railway was a vast ditch that had been turned into an open sewer, filled with ever-increasing quantities of excrement, dead cats and dogs, rancid food and disgusting refuse of every imaginable kind. Passing within thirty yards of this stagnant lake, Leeming had to put a hand across his nose to block out the stench. Denizens of Bethnal Green had long been habituated to the stink of decomposition.

The Seven Stars lay on the edge of an infamous area known as the Nichol. Named after Nichol Street, one of its main thoroughfares, it was a stronghold for villains of every kind, fifteen acres of sin, crime and sheer deprivation that operated by rules entirely of its own making. Leeming was a brave man, raised in one of the roughest parts of London, but even he would not have tried to walk alone through the Nichol after dusk. Its filthy streets, shadowed lanes and dark passages were a breeding ground for thieves, pickpockets and prostitutes. Its squalid tenements, slum cottages and ramshackle pubs teemed with beggars, orphans, destitute families, ruthless criminals and fugitives from the law. Bethnal Green was a haven for the most desperate characters in the underworld.

Glad that he was visiting the place in broad daylight, Leeming noticed how many animals were roaming the streets. Snarling cats fought over territory with furious commitment while skinny dogs scavenged among the rubbish. The undernourished horses and donkeys that pulled passing carts looked as if they could barely stand. Loud squawks and even louder yells of encouragement disclosed that a cockfight was being held nearby. Unwashed children played desultory games or lounged in gangs on corners. Cries of pain came from behind closed doors as violent men asserted their dominance over wives and mistresses.

Wherever he went, Leeming knew, dozens of pairs of eyes were upon him. He had never endured such hostile surveillance before. It was like a weight pressing down on him. When he entered the Seven Stars, however, the burden was immediately lifted. He collected a few casual looks from the ragged patrons scattered around the bar but they were too busy enjoying their drinks or their gossip to bother overmuch about the newcomer. Leeming sauntered across to the counter and ordered some beer. Filled with chairs and tables, the room was large, low and in a state of obvious neglect but its atmosphere was welcoming enough. The landlord served his customer with a toothless grin.

'There you are, sir,' he said as he put a foaming tankard on the counter. 'Best beer in Bethnal Green.'

'So I heard.' Leeming paid for the drink then sipped it, managing a smile even though it was far too bitter for his taste. 'And he was right. You serve a good brew.'

'Ben, sir. Everyone calls me Ben. I own the place.'

'You run a good house, Ben.'

'Thank you.'

'My first visit won't be my last.'

The landlord appraised him. 'Where are you from, sir?'

'Clerkenwell.'

'Ah, I see.' A burst of cheering and applause came from the back of the establishment and Leeming turned his head questioningly. 'The lads are staging a bout or two. Fond of milling, sir?'

'That's why I came.'

'Then you're in the right place.'

Ben Millgate beamed proudly. He was a short, stubby man in his fifties with a bald pate that was tattooed with scars, and a craggy face. No stranger to a brawl himself, he had other scars on his bare forearms and both ears had been thickened by repeated punishment.

'Did you see the fight at Twyford?' asked Millgate.

'No – worse luck! I'd have given a week's wages to be there.'

'The Bargeman was robbed and so were we.'

'That's what I was told,' said Leeming, nodding seriously. 'They reckon that Mad Isaac fought dirty.'

'That lousy Jew was full of tricks,' said Millgate, wiping his nose with the back of his hand. 'So were his friends. I was there and saw it with my own eyes. When the Bargemen staggered back against the ropes, one of Mad Isaac's men punched him in the kidneys. Another time, he was hit with a cudgel. And, three times in a row, that sneaky Jew kicked him when he was on the ground.'

'He should have been disqualified.'

'The referee and the umpires had been bribed.'

'They must've been,' agreed Leeming. 'Rotten, I call it. I had money on the Bargeman to win. He's a true champion.'

'And fought like one as well. Gave no quarter.'

'So I gather. My friend was there to support him. More or less worships the Bargeman. In fact, it was Jake who told me about your beer. Comes in here a lot to watch the young boxers learning their craft.'

'Jake, you say?'

'Jake Bransby.'

'Oh, yes,' said Millgate, cheerily, 'I know him.'

'He's a bit on the quiet side.'

'That's him, sir, and no question. A shy fellow but he understands milling. He comes in regular, does Jake. Friend of yours, is he?'

'A good friend.'

'When I drew up a list to see how many of us would be going to the fight, Jake was one of the first to call out his name.'

'You went there as a group?'

'The Seven Stars sent over a hundred people to Twyford,'

bragged Millgate. 'Well, you'd expect it. The Bargeman trains here.'

'How is he now, Ben? He must've taken a real beating.'

'Took one and gave one to Mad Isaac. But he's as strong as an ox. Back on his feet within a day or two. As a matter of fact,' he went on, head turning towards the back room as more applause rang out, 'he's watching the novices showing off what they've learnt.'

'Then I'll take the opportunity to shake his hand,' said Leeming with genuine interest. 'I've followed his career from the start. I knew he had the makings of a champion when I saw him fight Amos Greer in a field near Newport Pagnell.'

'I was there as well. The Bargeman fair killed him.'

'He did at that. Greer was out cold.' He glanced around the bar. 'So all your regular customers went on that excursion train, did they?'

'Every last one of them.'

'What about newcomers?'

'Newcomers?'

'Strangers. People who drifted in for the first time.'

'We don't get many of those at the Seven Stars.'

'In that case, they would have stuck out.'

Millgate smirked. 'Like a pig in a pair of silk drawers.'

'Can you recall anyone who popped in here recently?' asked Leeming, pretending only casual interest. 'When you were drawing up that list for the excursion train, I mean?'

Ben Millgate's face went blank and he scratched the scars on the top of his head. A memory eventually seemed to come to the surface.

'Now that you mention it, sir,' he said, 'there *was* someone and he was certainly no Bethnal Green man. I could tell that just to look at the bugger. Odd thing is, he was asking about your friend, Jake Bransby.'

'Really? Could you describe this man?'

'Annie was the one who spoke to him, sir – she's my wife. You'd best ask her about it. Annie'll be in the back room with the others,' said Millgate, moving away. 'I'll take you through so that you can meet her. Bring your drink and you'll see the Bargeman in there as well.'

'Wonderful!' said Leeming.

Millgate lifted a hinged flap in the counter and opened the little door to step through into the bar. He led the visitor to the room at the rear then stepped back so that Leeming could enter it first. His arrival coincided with the loudest cheers yet as one of the young boxers knocked his opponent to the floor with a well-timed uppercut. The sergeant was instantly enthralled. Crowded around the ring were dozens of people, veteran fighters, local men who followed the sport, eager youths hoping to take it up and a few women in gaudy dresses. Leeming also noticed a couple of well-dressed gentlemen, standing near the edge of the ring, members of the Fancy in search of new talent to sponsor, potential champions on whom they could wager extravagant amounts.

The fallen boxer got to his feet and was quickly revived by his bottleman. Scolded, advised and ordered to fight harder, he came out for the next round with greater determination. Both men pounded away at each other. Ordinarily, Leeming would have watched with fascination had his attention not been diverted to the far corner where a legendary prizefighter was standing. It was the first time he had seen his hero so close and he marvelled at the size and bearing of the man. In the course of their fight, Isaac Rosen had left his signature all over Bill Hignett's face. One eye was still closed, both cheeks were badly puffed and there were ugly gashes above his eyebrows. The Bargeman's hands were heavily bandaged and some more bandaging could be seen under the brim of his hat but the various wounds only increased the man's stature in Leeming's eyes. He felt an almost childlike thrill.

Millgate, meanwhile, had been talking to his wife and to a couple of men standing beside her. They looked across at Leeming. Annie Millgate, a stringy woman with a vivacity that took years off her, tripped over to the visitor and took him companionably by the arm.

'I can tell you about that man, sir,' she said, pulling him away, 'but not in here. It's like Bedlam when a fight starts. Come into the yard where we can talk proper.'

'Thank you.'

'My husband says that you know Jake Bransby.'

'Very well,' replied Leeming, still admiring the Bargeman. 'He's told me about the Seven Stars so many times.'

'This way, sir.'

Annie Millgate opened a door and ushered him through it. Leeming found himself in a yard that was filled with empty crates and barrels. A mangy dog yelped. The detective turned to smile at the landlord's wife.

'You must be Annie,' he said.

But there was no time for proper introductions. Before he knew what was happening, Leeming was grabbed from behind by strong hands and spun round. Held by one man in a grip of iron, he was hit hard by someone who had been taught how and where to punch. The tankard fell from Leeming's fingers, hitting the ground and spilling its contents over his boots. His nose was soon gushing with blood and his body felt as if it were being trampled by a herd of stampeding horses. A fearsome blow to the chin sent him to the ground where he was kicked hard. The mangy dog sniffed him then licked his face.

Ben Millgate came out to get in a gratuitous kick of his own.

'Jake Bransby?' he said with a sneer. 'Think we can't read, do you? It was in all the newspapers. That two-faced bastard was a public hangman and he got what he deserved on that train.'

'What shall we do with him, Ben?' asked his wife.

'Like us to finish 'im off?' volunteered one of the men.

'We'd enjoy that,' said the other, baring his jagged teeth.

'No,' decreed Millgate, spitting on the ground. 'Annie will search him for money first then you can toss this nosey devil into a cesspit so that he'll stink of Bethnal Green for weeks to come. That'll teach him to come lying to me about Jake Bransby!'

'My father taught me how to make a Dog's Nose,' he said, stirring the concoction with a spoon. 'You got to get the proportions right, you see, Inspector. Warm porter, gin, sugar and nutmeg. Delicious!'

'I'm sure,' said Colbeck.

'Will you join me?'

'No, thank you, Sergeant. It's too strong for me.'

'My favourite tipple at the end of the day.'

The two men were in the snug little cottage that belonged to Sergeant Obadiah Lugg, a seasoned member of Maidstone's police force. Having learnt that it was Lugg who had arrested Nathan Hawkshaw on a charge of murder, Colbeck tracked him down in his home on the edge of the town. A portly individual in his forties with a big, round, rubicund face, Lugg had an amiable manner and a habit of chuckling at the end of each sentence. He settled into the chair opposite his visitor and sipped his drink with patent relish.

'Perfect!' he cried.

'You deserve it, Sergeant. You do a valuable job in the town.'

'There's only fifteen of us in all, you know – two sergeants and a body of twelve men with Tom Fawcett as our inspector. Fifteen of us to police a town with over 20,000 people in it.'

'It must be hard work,' said Colbeck.

'Hard but rewarding, Inspector. When the force was founded in 1836, I joined it right away. I was a railway policeman before that. We made a difference from the start. The streets of Maidstone used to swarm with bad characters and loose women but not any more,' he said with a chuckle. 'Everyone will tell you how we cleaned the place up. Of course, Tom must take most of the credit.'

'Tom? Is that the Tom Fawcett you mentioned?'

'That's him. A drum major in the army before he took over here and he made us all stand to attention.' Colbeck gave a half-smile as he thought of Superintendent Tallis. 'Trouble is that Tom is near seventy so he can't go on forever. Do you know what he told me?'

'I'd love to hear it, Sergeant,' said Colbeck, steering him away from his reminiscences, 'but I have a train to catch soon. What I'd really like you to tell me about is the arrest of Nathan Hawkshaw.'

'He resisted. I had to use my truncheon.'

'What were the circumstances of the crime?'

'There'd been bad blood between him and Joe Dykes for some time,' recalled Lugg, taking another sip of his drink. 'Hawkshaw had been heard threatening to kill him. Then this fair was held at Lenham and that's when it happened. The two of them had this quarrel. Next thing you know, Dykes is found dead behind some bushes. And I do mean dead,' he added with a chuckle. 'The body had been hacked to pieces like it was a side of beef.'

'Were there any witnesses?'

'Several people saw the argument between them.'

'Were any blows exchanged?'

'No, Inspector, nothing beyond a few prods and pushes. Everyone reckons that Dykes just laughed and went into the pub. An hour later, he'd been slaughtered.'

'So there were no witnesses to the actual killing?'

'None, sir. But it had to be Nathan Hawkshaw.'

'Why?'

'Because he hated Dykes so much. Think of them threats he'd made. And,' declared Lugg, as if producing incontrovertible proof, 'the murder weapon was one of Hawkshaw's meat cleavers. He admitted that.'

'Yet he protested his innocence.'

'I've never met a villain who didn't do that.'

'Nor me,' said Colbeck with a pained smile. 'You can catch them red-handed and they always have a plausible explanation. Tell me about Hawkshaw. Had he been in trouble with the police before?'

'They've only two constables in Ashford so it's hardly a police force. I interviewed both men and they spoke well of Nathan Hawkshaw. Said he was a good butcher and a decent family man. He kept himself out of mischief.'

'What about Dykes?'

'Ah,' replied Lugg, 'he was much more of a problem. Drunk and disorderly, assaulting a constable, petty theft – Joe Dykes had seen the inside of prison more than once. Nasty piece of work, he was. Even the chaplain found him a handful when he was put in Maidstone prison.' He grinned broadly. 'What did you think of Narcissus?'

Colbeck was tactful. 'The Reverend Jones seemed to be dedicated to his work,' he said, quietly. 'It must be a thankless task.'

'I feel sorry sometimes for those shut away in there. Nobody quite like a Welshman for loving the sound of his own voice, is there? Narcissus can talk the hind leg off a donkey. Imagine being locked in a cell with him preaching at you through the bars.' He let out a cackle and slapped his thigh. 'No wonder Hawkshaw tried to hit the chaplain.'

'You heard about that incident?'

'Narcissus Jones told everyone about it, Inspector. That's the kind of man he is – unlike the governor. Henry Ferriday would never tell tales about what happens behind those high walls. He's more secretive.'

'If Hawkshaw struck out at the chaplain,' noted Colbeck, 'he must be inclined to violence. Yet you say he'd no record of unruly behaviour.'

'None at all, Inspector.'

'What caused the animosity between him and Dykes?'

'All sorts of things.'

'Such as?'

'Emily, for a start.'

'Emily?'

'Nathan Hawkshaw's daughter. Dykes tried to rape her.'

When he first came to his senses, Victor Leeming was lying in a cesspit surrounded by jeering children. There was blood down the front of his jacket and every part of his body was aching violently. Through his swollen lips, he could not even muster the strength to shout at those who were enjoying his misfortune. In trying to move, he set off some fresh spasms of pain down his arms and legs. His body seemed to be on fire.

It was the foul smell and the humiliation that finally got him out of there. Braving the agony, he hauled himself upright, relieved to find that he could actually stand on his own feet. While he gathered his wits, the children subjected him to another barrage of abuse. Leeming had to swing a bruised arm to get rid of them.

A frail old woman took pity on him and explained that there was a pump in a nearby street. Dragging himself there, he doused himself with water in order to bring himself fully awake and to get rid of the worst of the malodorous scum in which he was coated. When he slunk away from the pump, Leeming was sodden. Since no cab would dare to stop for him, he had to trudge all the way back to Whitehall in squelching boots, afraid that he might be accosted in the street by a uniformed constable on suspicion of vagrancy. Because of the smell, everyone he passed gave him a wide berth but he eventually got back to Scotland Yard.

Brushing past a couple of amused colleagues, he dived into the washroom, stripped to his underclothing and washed himself again from head to foot. He could not bear to look in a mirror. When he saw the bruises on his body, his first thought was how his wife would react to the hideous blotching. His sole consolation was that nothing appeared to be broken although his pride was in dire need of repair. The discarded suit was still giving off an appalling stink so he bundled it up, gathered the other items of clothing and peeped out of the door. Seeing that the coast was clear, he tried to make a dash for his office but his weary legs would only move at a slow amble. Before the injured detective could reach safety, a bristling Edward Tallis suddenly turned into the corridor and held his nose in horror.

'Damnation!' he exploded. 'Is that *you*, Leeming?'

'Yes, Superintendent.'

'What on earth is that repulsive stench?'

Leeming sniffed the air. 'I can't smell anything, sir.'

'Well, everyone within a mile can smell *you*. What have you been doing, man – crawling through the sewers?' He saw the bruises on the sergeant. 'And how did you get those marks on your body?'

'I was assaulted,' said Leeming.

'By whom?'

'Two men in Bethnal Green. They knocked me unconscious.'

'Dear me!' said Tallis, mellowing instantly. 'You poor fellow.'

Showing a compassion that took Leeming by surprise, he moved forward to hold him by the arm and help him into the office that the sergeant shared with Inspector Colbeck. The superintendent lowered the stricken detective into a chair then took the suit from him so that he could dump it in the wastepaper basket. After opening the window to let in fresh air, he returned to take a closer look at Leeming.

'No serious injuries?' he inquired.

'I don't think so, sir.'

'Let me send for a doctor.'

'No, no,' said Leeming, embarrassed to be sitting there in his underclothing. 'I'll be fine, sir. I was lucky. All I have are aches and pains. They'll go away in time. I just need to put on some clean things.'

'These, meanwhile, can go out,' decided Tallis, grabbing the wastepaper basket and tipping its contents unceremoniously through the open window. 'I'm sorry but I found that stink so offensive.' He replaced the basket beside the desk. 'Why don't I give you a few minutes to get dressed and spruce yourself up?'

'Thank you, Superintendent.'

'Comb your hair before you come to my office.'

'I will, sir. I didn't mean to turn up in this state.'

'Was it an unprovoked assault?'

'Yes and no,' said Leeming, ruefully. 'I think I upset someone when I asked a wrong question.'

'Well, I shall want to ask a few right ones in due course,' growled Tallis, resuming his normal role as the established martinet of the Detective Department. 'The first thing I'll demand to know is what the blazes you were *doing* in Bethnal Green?'

'Making inquiries, sir.'

'About what? No, no,' he said, quickly, stopping him with a raised palm before he could speak, 'I can wait. Make yourself presentable first. And dab some cold water on those lips of yours.'

'Yes, Superintendent.'

'I'll expect you in ten minutes. Bring the inspector with you. I've no doubt that he'll be as interested as I am to hear how you got yourself in that condition.'

'Inspector Colbeck is not here at the moment.'

'Then where the devil is he?'

'In Maidstone.'

'Maidstone!' echoed the other. 'He's supposed to be solving a crime that took place in an excursion train at Twyford. Whatever has taken him to Maidstone?' He shuddered visibly. 'You don't need to tell me that. Inspector Colbeck has developed another theory, hasn't he?'

'Based on sound reasoning, sir.'

'And what about your visit to Bethnal Green?' asked Tallis with undisguised sarcasm. 'Was that based on sound reasoning as well?'

'Yes, sir.'

'You and I have something in common, Sergeant.'

'Do we, Superintendent?'

'Yes, we do. We're both martyrs to the inspector's predilection for wild and often lunatic theories. So,' he said, pulling out his cigar case from an inside pocket, 'he decided to go to Maidstone, did he? I suppose that I should be grateful it was not the Isle of Wight.'

The return journey gave Robert Colbeck valuable thinking time. As the train rattled along, he reflected on what he had learnt from his visit to Kent. Henry Ferriday and the Reverend Narcissus Jones had explained with dramatic clarity how the hangman's performance on the scaffold had embedded a fierce hatred in the family and friends of the condemned man. On his two previous visits to the town, Guttridge must have acquitted himself fairly well in order to be invited back a third time. It was to prove his downfall. Colbeck had no doubt whatsoever that the murder in the excursion train had been committed by someone who was in the crowd outside Maidstone prison on the fateful day.

Obadiah Lugg had also been a useful source of information. He was not only keen to describe how he had arrested Nathan Hawkshaw and taken him into custody, he was able to show his visitor copies of the local newspapers that contained details of the case and lurid accounts of the execution. Like the hangman, Lugg was a man who hoarded souvenirs of his work but, in the case of the chuckling sergeant, they were far less disturbing. Along with the other members of the Maidstone police force, and supported by dozens of special constables, Lugg had been on duty during the execution of Hawkshaw and gave his own testimony to the ineptitude of the hangman and the effect that it had on an already restive crowd.

What interested Colbeck were the contradictory assessments of Hawkshaw's character and he struggled to reconcile them. As a butcher, the man had been liked and respected, leading an apparently blameless existence and causing no problems for the two constables representing law and order in Ashford. During his arrest, however, he had to be overpowered by Obadiah Lugg and the two men whom the sergeant had wisely taken with him in support. At the prison, too, Hawkshaw had resorted to violence at one point though – having met Narcissus Jones – Colbeck could well understand how the chaplain's robust Christianity might prove irksome. Yet the same man who had struck out in frustration at an ordained priest had elected to pray on the scaffold before he was hanged. Was he an innocent man, searching for divine intervention in his hour of need, or had he finally admitted guilt before God and begged forgiveness for his crime?

It was clear that those who knew Hawkshaw best had a genuine belief in his innocence, an important factor in Colbeck's judgement of the man. Yet the evidence against him had been strong enough to support a death sentence and, according to all the reports of the trial that the detective had read in Lugg's collection of newspapers, Hawkshaw had been unable to account for his whereabouts at the time of the murder. It was a point that the prosecution team had exploited to the full and it had cost the prisoner his life.

Robert Colbeck was a former barrister, a man who had abandoned the histrionics of the courtroom to grapple with what he considered to be the more important tasks of preventing crime wherever possible and hunting down those who committed it. He could see from the newspaper accounts that Hawkshaw had not been well defended by his barrister and that all the publicity had gone to the flamboyant man who led the prosecution. Wanting to know much more about the conduct of the trial, Colbeck made a note of his name and resolved to contact him.

Tonbridge flew past the window of his first-class carriage but the Railway Detective was too lost in thought to notice it. He spared only a glance as they steamed through Redhill, his mind still engrossed by the murder of Joseph Dykes at Lenham and its relationship to a calculated killing on an excursion train. One thing was undeniable. Nathan Hawkshaw had motive, means and opportunity to kill a man he loathed. Since his daughter had been the victim of a sexual assault by Dykes, it was only natural that the butcher would confront him. Whether that confrontation led to a murderous attack, however, was an open question.

When he reached London, Colbeck had still not decided whether an innocent or a guilty man had gone to the gallows in Maidstone. The prison governor had insisted that the case was firmly closed now that Hawkshaw had been executed. The inspector disagreed. It was time to resurrect the hanged man. One way or another – however long it might take – Colbeck was determined to find out the truth.

'How are you getting on, Maddy?' asked Caleb Andrews, standing behind her to look at the painting. 'Oh, yes,' he said, patting her on the back in appreciation, 'that's good, that's very good.'

'I'll have to stop soon. It's getting dark.'

'Sit beside the oil lamp.'

'I prefer natural light. I can see the colours properly in that.'

'You have a real gift, you know.'

'That's what Robert said.'

Madeleine stood back to admire her work, glad of her father's approval because he would not judge her work on artistic merit. As an engine driver, his concern was with accuracy and he could find no fault with her picture of a famous locomotive. After adding a touch more blue to the sky against which the *Lord of the Isles* was framed, she dipped her brush in a cup of water to clean it.

'You'll be painting in oils next,' said Andrews.

'No,' she replied. 'I prefer watercolours. Oils are for real artists.'

'You *are* a real artist, Maddy. I think so and I know that Inspector Colbeck does as well. He's an educated man. He knows about these things. I'm proud of you.'

'Thank you, Father.'

'That's the *Lord of the Isles* and no mistake,' he went on, slipping an arm around her shoulders. 'You've painted everything but the noise and the smell of the smoke. Well done!'

'It's not finished yet,' she said, moving away to take her paints and brush into the kitchen. She came back into the living room. 'I just hope that Robert likes it.'

'He'll love it, Maddy – or I'll know the reason why!'

Andrews laughed then watched her take the painting off the easel before standing both against the wall. He had always got on well with his daughter and enjoyed her affectionate bullying, but he knew that a time would come when she would inevitably move out.

'Has the inspector said anything to you?' he wondered, idly.

'About what?'

'Well . . .' He gave a meaningful shrug.

'About *what*?' she repeated, looking him in the eye.

'Something that a handsome man and a pretty young woman usually get round to talking about.'

'Father!'

'Well – has he?'

'Robert and I are just friends.'

'That's all that your mother and me were until she let me kiss her under the mistletoe one Christmas,' he remembered with a fond smile. 'The trouble was that her parents came in and caught us. Her father gave me such a talking to that my ears burnt for a week. People were very strict in those days and I believe it was a good thing.' He shot her a quizzical glance. 'Do you think I'm strict enough with you, Maddy?'

'*You're* the person who needs a firmer hand,' she said, giving him a peck on the cheek, 'not me. And I've no complaints about the way you brought me up. How many other daughters have been allowed to sneak on to the footplate of a locomotive as I once was?'

'I could've lost my job over that.'

'You took the risk because you knew how much it meant to me.'

'And to me, Maddy. It was something we could *share*.' He sat down on the sofa. 'But you didn't answer my question. Have you and the inspector got any kind of understanding?'

'Yes,' she replied with a touch of exasperation, 'we understand that we like each other as friends and that's that. Robert is too involved with his work to spare much time for me and I'm too busy running this house and looking after you.'

'At the moment.'

'Please!'

'Things could change.'

'Father, will you stop going on about it?'

'Well, I'm bound to wonder. He'd make a fine catch, Maddy.'

'Listen to you!' she cried. 'When I first met Robert, you kept telling me not to waste my time on someone who was out of my reach. He was above me, that's what you said. Too good for a girl from Camden.'

'That was before I got to know him proper. He may look fine and dandy but his father was only a cabinetmaker, a man who worked with his hands. I can respect that.'

'Try respecting me for a change.'

'I always do.'

'No, you don't, Father,' she said, vehemently. 'Left to you, I'd have been married off to Gideon Little, a fireman on the railway, somebody who suited you, regardless of what I felt about him. Now you're trying to push me at another man you like. Don't you think that I have the right to choose my own husband?'

'Calm down, calm down,' he said, getting to his feet.

'Then stop badgering me like this.'

'I was curious, that's all.'

'Robert and I are good friends. Nothing more.'

'It always starts out that way.'

'Nothing more,' she insisted. 'You must believe that.'

'Oh, I do, Maddy, but I can't ignore the signs.'

'What signs?'

'Him taking you out in that cab, for a start.'

'It was only for a ride,' she said, careful to say nothing about the visit to Hoxton. 'What was wrong with that?'

'Only that it's strange that a detective in the middle of a murder investigation can find time to take anyone for a ride in a hansom cab. Some of the neighbours saw him pick you up from here. They told me how attentive he was.'

'Robert is a gentleman. He's always attentive.'

'Then there's the other signs,' he pointed out, marshalling his case. 'The ones you can't hide, no matter how much you try.'

'What are you talking about?'

'The way your voice changes when you mention him. The way your face lights up when he calls here. And look at that painting you've been working on,' he added, indicating it. 'When someone spends that amount of time and effort on a present for a man, he begins to look like more than a friend.'

'Robert loves trains, that's all.'

'There – you have a bond between you.'

'Father—'

'I've got eyes, Maddy. I can see.'

'Well, will you please stop *looking*!' she shouted.

Caught on a raw spot, Madeleine was torn between anger and embarrassment. It was no use asking her father to accept the situation because she did not fully comprehend it herself. When her emotions were in a tangle, however, the last thing she needed was to be questioned about her friendship with Robert Colbeck. Unable to contain her fury, she snatched up the painting and fled upstairs. Andrews heard her bedroom door slam shut. Annoyed with himself for upsetting her, he nevertheless felt able to sit down with a wry smile.

'I must remember to get some mistletoe for Christmas,' he said.

Even in the uncertain light from the gas lamp, Colbeck could see the damage inflicted on his face and, when Leeming got up to greet him, the sergeant let out a grunt of pain. It was late evening when the inspector got back to his office in Scotland Yard and he was distressed to find his colleague in such blatant discomfort. There was also a faint but very unpleasant whiff coming from him.

'What happened, Victor?' he asked.

'I saw seven stars at the Seven Stars,' said Leeming, laughing at his own feeble joke. 'I was fool enough to mention the name of Jake Bransby and took a beating for it.'

'How badly were you hurt?'

'I'll live, Inspector – just about. The superintendent was so worried that he wanted to call in a doctor to examine me. Mr Tallis also made me wash three times but I still can't get rid of that stink.'

'How did you acquire it in the first place?'

'The worst possible way.'

Leeming had been waiting for a chance to tell his story to a more sympathetic audience and he left no detail out. What he could not tell Colbeck was who actually assaulted him and how he got from the yard at the rear of the public house to a cesspit some streets away. As he described the attack itself, his injuries started to throb violently and his swollen lips felt as if they had been stung by wasps. Reaching the end of his narrative, he took a long sip from the glass of water on the desk.

'I blame myself for this,' said Colbeck, apologetically.

'Why, sir?'

'I should never have sent you there.'

'I was getting on well until I tried to be too inquisitive.'

'I was hoping that they had not yet made the connection between Jacob Bransby and the public hangman but it was too much to ask. You have to admire his courage.'

'Yes,' agreed Leeming. 'Going in there among the ruffians of Bethnal Green when he must surely have stretched the necks of a few villains from that part of London. Just as well they never knew who he was or they'd have done more than sling him in a cesspit.'

'Your visit was not entirely wasted, Victor.'

'I hoped you'd say that.'

'You found out that almost everyone at the Seven Stars went off to support the Bargeman in that fight. They even drew up a list.'

'With a certain person from Hoxton near the top.'

'When the killer learnt that,' said Colbeck, 'he didn't need to follow his victim in search of the right moment to strike. He knew that Guttridge would be on that excursion train – so he waited.'

'With that woman.'

'With or without that woman, Victor. That's another little mystery for us to solve. Was she involved or was she just another passenger?'

'I've no idea.'

'Perhaps we'll find out when we go to Ashford tomorrow.'

Leeming gaped. 'Ashford?'

'If you feel strong enough to accompany me.'

'Yes, yes. Of course.'

'Are you certain about that?'

'Yes, I am,' said the other, straightening his shoulders. 'It'll take more than a few punches to keep me out of action, sir – though my wife may not see it that way. I'm dreading the moment when I walk through that door tonight. You know how Estelle can carry on.'

'Would you like me to speak to her?'

'Oh, no.'

'But I can tell her what sterling work you were doing for us in Bethnal Green when you were set upon. Praise can be soothing.'

'Estelle will need more than a few kind words from you to calm her down, sir. Leave my wife to me. I know how to handle her. Meanwhile,' he went on, nodding in the direction of the door, 'make sure you have a good story ready for the superintendent. He'll come storming in here any moment to ask why you went to Maidstone.'

'How did he react when you struggled back here earlier?'

'He seemed very sorry for me at first – even helped me in here. And being the superintendent, of course, he wanted retribution. Assaulting a police officer is a serious offence.'

'Except that they didn't know what your occupation was.'

'Thank God! I'd not be alive now, if they had.'

'Nobody involved in law enforcement is very welcome in Bethnal Green,' said Colbeck, 'and we both know why. It's the children I feel sorry for. They have no choice. If they're born there, crime is the only means by which they can survive.'

'Too true, sir.'

'So what did Mr Tallis want to do?'

'Send a bevy of constables to arrest the landlord and his wife,' said Leeming with a grimace, 'but I managed to talk him out of that. It was those two bruisers who set about me and I'd never recognise them again. Even if I did, it would be my word against that of everybody else in the Seven Stars and they'd swear blind that I was lying. I've got no witnesses to speak up for me.'

'That doesn't mean that we let these bullies get away with it, Victor,' said Colbeck, sharply, 'but I'm glad that you dissuaded the superintendent from any precipitate action. It needs a more subtle approach. When time serves, we'll pay another visit to the Seven Stars.'

Leeming was vengeful. 'I'll look forward to that, sir.'

'Look forward to what?' demanded Tallis, bursting in through the door in time to hear the words. 'Ah!' he said, seeing Colbeck, 'you've deigned to return from your unauthorised visit to Maidstone, have you?'

'It was a very productive trip, sir,' replied Colbeck.

'That's beside the point.'

'You must allow me some latitude in a murder inquiry.'

'I asked to be kept abreast of any developments. That means you inform me of your movements *before* the event rather than after it.'

'When I made the decision to go to Maidstone, you were in a meeting with the Commissioners and I could not interrupt that.'

'Then you should have waited until the meeting was over.'

'I'll not make any progress in this investigation by sitting on my hands in here, Superintendent,' said Colbeck, evenly. 'You demanded a speedy result so I moved with urgency.'

'So did I,' Leeming put in.

'Be quiet, Sergeant,' barked Tallis.

'Yes, sir.'

'And have a good bath before you come here tomorrow. You still smell like something that crawled out of a blocked drain.'

'Victor will not be in the office tomorrow,' said Colbeck. 'He and I will be going to Ashford in Kent.'

'How kind of you to tell me, Inspector!' returned the other with mock sweetness. 'It's always comforting to know where my detectives actually are.' His voice hardened. 'I trust that you have an extremely good reason for wanting to hare off to Kent again.'

'Yes, sir. That's where the killer of Jacob Guttridge lives.'

'And what makes you think that?'

'The inspector has this theory, sir,' interjected Leeming, earning himself such a glare of naked hostility from Tallis that he wished he had not spoken. 'I'd better leave it to him to explain.'

'Thank you, Victor,' said Colbeck.

Legs wide apart, Tallis folded his arms. 'I'm waiting, Inspector,' he said, coldly. 'I want to hear about this productive trip to Kent.'

'So do I,' said Leeming, eager to learn what progress had been made. 'You obviously fared a lot better than I did today. Did you get to Maidstone prison, Inspector?' He caught Tallis's eye again and took a hasty step backwards. 'Sorry, sir. I didn't mean to hold him up.'

Colbeck had made copious notes during his visit but he had no need to refer to them. His training as a barrister had sharpened his memory and given him an ability to assemble facts in the most cogent way. His account was long, measured and admirably lucid, making it easy for both men to understand why he had spent so much time in Maidstone. Victor Leeming was intrigued to hear about such colourful characters as Reverend Narcissus Jones and Obadiah Lugg but it was the accumulation of pertinent facts that weighed much more with the superintendent. It was not long before the folded arms dropped to his side and the stern expression faded from his countenance.

When the recitation finally ended, Tallis came close to a smile.

'You've done well, Inspector,' he admitted.

'Thank you, sir.'

'It looks as if you may at last have stumbled on a theory that has a grain of truth in it. Notwithstanding that, we are still a long way from making an arrest and that is what the Great Western Railway wants.'

'It's what we all want.'

'Then when do you expect it to take place?'

'In the fullness of time,' said Colbeck, smoothly.

'I need something more specific to tell the railway company,' said Tallis, 'and to appease the pack of reporters who keep knocking on my door.' He glanced at Leeming. 'I thank heaven that none of them were here when the sergeant returned from Bethnal Green in all his glory. I tremble to think what the newspapers would have made of that.'

'I'd have been a laughing stock,' wailed Leeming.

'It's the bad publicity that concerns me. This Department has more than its share of critics. Whatever we do, we must not give them ammunition they can use against us.' He turned to Colbeck. 'So what do we tell them?'

'The same thing that we tell the railway company,' said Colbeck with a confident smile. 'That we have made significant progress but are unable to disclose details because the killer would be forewarned and might be put to flight. More to the point,' he continued, 'the sergeant and I want to be able to shift our interest to Kent without having any reporters barking at our heels.'

'How long will we be in Ashford, sir?' asked Leeming, worriedly.

'A couple of days at least, Victor. Maybe more.'

'Then we'd have to stay the night there?'

'Your wife will have to forego the pleasures of matrimony for a short while, I fear,' said Colbeck, 'but she will be reassured by the fact that you're engaged in such an important investigation.'

'Only when you've taken that bath, Sergeant,' stipulated Tallis.

'Yes, sir,' said Leeming.

'I expect my men to be smart and well groomed.' He turned

a censorious eye on the elegant inspector. 'Though there is no need to take my instructions in that regard to extremes.'

'We'll take an early train to Ashford,' said Colbeck, ignoring the barbed comment from his superior. 'I suggest that you bring enough clothing for five days, Victor.'

'Five days!' gulped Leeming. 'What about my wife?'

'She is not included in this excursion,' said Tallis, sourly.

'Estelle will miss me.'

'The sooner we bring this investigation to a conclusion,' observed Colbeck, 'the sooner you'll be back with your family. But we must not expect instant results here. The only way to solve the murder of Jacob Guttridge is to find out what really happened to Joseph Dykes.'

'But we know that,' asserted Tallis. 'He was killed by Hawkshaw.'

'That's open to question, Superintendent. Far be it from me, as a barrister, to question the working of the judicial system, but I have a strange feeling – and it is only a feeling, not a theory – that there was a gross miscarriage of justice on the scaffold at Maidstone.'

CHAPTER SEVEN

Nothing revealed the essential difference between the two men as clearly as the train journey to Ashford that morning. Inspector Robert Colbeck was in his element, enjoying his preferred mode of travel and reading his way through the London newspapers as if sitting in a favourite chair at home. Sergeant Victor Leeming, on the other hand, was in severe discomfort. His dislike of going anywhere by train was intensified by the fact that his body was a mass of aching muscles and tender bruises. As their carriage lurched and bumped its clamorous way over the rails, he felt as if he were being pummelled all over again. Leeming tried to close his eyes against the pain but that only made him feel queasy.

'How can you do it, sir?' he asked, enviously.

'Do what, Victor?'

'Read like that when the train is shaking us about so much.'

'One gets used to it,' said Colbeck, looking over the top of his copy of *The Times*. 'I find the constant movement very stimulating.'

'Well, I don't – it's agony for me.'

'A stagecoach would bounce you about just as much.'

'Yes,' conceded Leeming, 'but we wouldn't have this terrible noise and all this smoke. I feel safe with horses, Inspector. I hate trains.'

'Then you won't take to Ashford, I'm afraid.'

'Why not?'

'It's a railway town.'

Lying at the intersection of a number of main roads, Ashford had been a centre of communication for generations and the arrival of its railway station in 1842 had confirmed its status. But it was when the railway works was opened seven years later that its geographical significance was fully ratified. Its population increased markedly and a sleepy agricultural community took on a more urban appearance and edge. The high street was wide enough to accommodate animal pens on market day and farmers still came in from a wide area with their produce but the wives of railwaymen, fitters, engineers and gas workers now rubbed shoulders with the more traditional customers.

The first thing that the detectives saw as they alighted at the station was the church tower of St Mary's, a medieval foundation, rising high above the buildings around it with perpendicular authority, and casting a long spiritual shadow across the town. A pervading stink was the next thing that impressed itself upon them and Leeming immediately feared that his bath the previous night had failed to wash away the noxious smell of the cesspit. To his relief, the stench was coming from the River Stour into which all the town's effluent was drained without treatment, a problem exacerbated by the fact that there were now over six thousand inhabitants in the vicinity.

Carrying their bags, they strolled in the bright sunshine to the Saracen's Head to get a first feel of Ashford. Situated in the high street near the corner with North Street, the inn had been the premier hostelry in the town for centuries and it was able to offer them separate rooms – albeit with low beams and undulating floors – at a reasonable price. Colbeck was acutely aware of the effort that it had cost the sergeant to get up so early when he was still in a battered condition. He advised him to rest while he ventured out to make initial contact with the Hawkshaw family. Within minutes, Leeming was asleep on his bed.

Colbeck, meanwhile, stepped out from under the inn's portico and walked across the road to the nearby Middle Row, a narrow, twisting passage, where Nathan Hawkshaw and Son owned only one of a half a dozen butchers' stalls or shambles. The aroma of fresh meat mingled with the reek from the river to produce an even more distinctive smell. It did not seem to worry the people buying their beef, lamb and pork there that morning. Poultry and rabbits dangled from hooks outside the shop where Nathan Hawkshaw had worked and Colbeck had to remove his top hat and duck beneath them to go inside.

A brawny young man in a bloodstained apron was serving a female customer with some sausages. Colbeck noted his muscular forearms and the dark scowl that gave his ugly face an almost sinister look to it. When the woman left, he introduced himself as Adam Hawkshaw, son of the condemned man, a hulking figure who seemed at home among the carcasses of dead animals. Hawkshaw was resentful.

'What do you want?' he asked, bluntly.

'To establish certain facts about your father's case.'

'We got no time for police. They helped to hang him.'

'I've spoken to Sergeant Lugg in Maidstone,' said Colbeck, 'and he's given me some of the details. What I need to do now is to get the other side of the story – from you and your mother.'

Hawkshaw was aggressive. '*Why*?'

'Because I wish to review the case.'

'My father's dead. Go back to London.'

'I understand the way that you must feel, Mr Hawkshaw, and I've not come to harass you. It may be that I can help.'

'You going to dig him up and bring him back to life?'

'There's no need for sarcasm.'

'Then leave us alone, Inspector,' warned Hawkshaw.

'Inspector?' said a woman, coming into the shop from a door at the rear. 'Who is this gentleman, Adam?'

Colbeck introduced himself to her and discovered that he was talking to Winifred Hawkshaw, a short, compact, handsome woman in her thirties with a black dress that rustled as she moved. She looked too young and too delicate to be the mother of the uncouth butcher. When she heard the inspector's request, she invited him into the room at the back of the property that served as both kitchen and parlour, leaving Adam Hawkshaw to cope with the two customers who had just come in. Colbeck was offered a seat but Winifred remained standing.

'I must apologise for Adam,' she said, hands gripped tightly together. 'He's taken it hard.'

'I can understand that, Mrs Hawkshaw.'

'After what happened, he's got no faith in the law.'

'And what about you?'

'I feel let down as well, Inspector. We were betrayed.'

'You still believe in your husband's innocence then?'

'Of course,' she said, tartly. 'Nathan had his faults but he was no killer. Yet they made him look like one in court. By the time they finished with him, my husband had been turned into a monster.'

'It must have affected your trade.'

'It has. Loyal customers have stayed with us, so have our friends who knew that Nathan could never have done such a thing. But a lot of people just buy meat elsewhere. This is a murderer's shop, they say, and won't have anything to do with us.'

There was resignation rather than bitterness in her voice. Winifred Hawkshaw did not blame local people for the way that they reacted. Colbeck was reminded of Louise Guttridge, another woman with an inner strength that enabled her to cope with the violent death of a husband. While the hangman's widow was sustained by religion, however, what gave Winifred her self-possession was her belief in her husband and her determination to clear his name.

'Are you aware of what happened to Jacob Guttridge?' he asked.

'Yes, Inspector.'

'How did the news of his murder make you feel?'

'It left me cold.'

'No sense of quiet satisfaction?'

'None,' she said. 'It won't bring Nathan back, will it?'

'What about your son?' he wondered. 'I should imagine that he took some pleasure from the fact that the man who hanged his father was himself executed.'

'Adam is not my son, Inspector. He was a child of Nathan's first marriage. But, yes – and I'm not ashamed to admit this – Adam was thrilled to hear the news. He came running round here to tell me.'

'Doesn't he live here with you?'

'Not any more.'

'Why is that, Mrs Hawkshaw?'

'Never you mind.' She eyed him shrewdly. 'Why did you come here, Inspector?'

'Because the case interested me,' he replied. 'Before I joined the Metropolitan Police, I was a lawyer and was called to the bar. Almost every day of my life was spent in a courtroom involved in legal tussles. There wasn't much of a tussle in your husband's case. From the reports that I've seen, the trial was remarkably swift and one-sided.'

'Nathan had no chance to defend himself.'

'His barrister should have done that.'

'He let us down as well.'

'The prosecution case seemed to hinge on the fact that your husband was unable to account for his whereabouts at the time when Joseph Dykes was killed.'

'That's not true,' she said with spirit. 'Nathan began to walk home from Lenham but, when he'd gone a few miles, he decided to go back and tackle Joe Dykes again. By the time he got there, it was all over.'

'Mr Hawkshaw was seen close to the murder scene.'

'He didn't *know* that the body was lying there.'

'Were there witnesses who saw him walking away from Lenham?'

'None that would come forward in court.'

'Where was your stepson during all this time?'

'He was at the fair with his friends.'

'And you?'

'I was visiting my mother in Willesborough. She's very sick.'

'I'm sorry to hear that, Mrs Hawkshaw.'

'It's the least of my worries at the moment. If things go on as they are, we may have to sell the shop – unless we can prove that Nathan was innocent.'

'To do that, you'll need to unmask the real killer.'

'Gregory and I will do it one day,' she vowed.

'Gregory?'

'A friend of the family, Inspector.' A half-smile of gratitude flitted across her face. 'I don't know what we'd have done without Gregory Newman. When others were turning away, he stood by us. It was Gregory who said we should start a campaign to free Nathan.'

'Did that involve trying to rescue him from Maidstone prison?'

'I know nothing of that,' she said, crisply.

'An attempt was made – according to the chaplain.'

Her facial muscles tightened. 'Don't mention that man.'

'Why not?'

'Because he only added to Nathan's suffering. Reverend Jones is evil. He kept on bullying my husband.'

'Is that what he told you?'

'Nathan wasn't allowed to tell me anything like that. They only let me see him in prison once. We had a warder standing over us to listen to what was said. Nathan was in chains,' she said, hurt by a painful memory, 'as if he was a wild animal.'

'So this information about the chaplain must have come from a message that was smuggled out. Am I right?' She nodded in assent. 'Do you still have it, by any chance?'

'No,' she replied.

Colbeck knew that she was lying. A woman who had made such efforts to prove her husband's innocence would cherish everything that reminded her of him, even if it was a note scribbled in a condemned cell. But there was no point in challenging her and asking to see the missive, especially as he already knew that there was an element of truth in its contents. The Reverend Narcissus Jones had made the prisoner's last few hours on earth far more uncomfortable than they need have been.

'Does this Mr Newman live in Ashford?'

'Oh, yes. Gregory used to be a blacksmith. He had a forge in St John's Lane but he sold it.'

'Has he retired?'

'No, Inspector,' she said, 'he's too young for that. Gregory took a job in the railway works. That's where you'll find him.'

'Then that's where I'll go in due course,' decided Colbeck, getting to his feet. 'Thank you, Mrs Hawkshaw. I'm sorry to intrude on you this way but I really do want the full details of this case.'

She challenged him. 'You think it's us, don't you?'

'I beg your pardon?'

'You're not really interested in Nathan, are you?' she said with a note of accusation. 'You came to find out if *we* killed that dreadful hangman. Well, I can tell you now, Inspector, that we're not murderers. Not any of us – and that includes my husband.'

'I'm sorry if I gave you the wrong impression,' he told her, raising both hands in a gesture of appeasement. 'Very few cases are reviewed in this way, I can assure you. I would have thought it would be in your interest for someone to examine the facts anew with a fresh pair of eyes.'

'That's not all that brought you here.'

'Perhaps not, Mrs Hawkshaw. But it's one of the main reasons.'

'What are the others?'

He gave a disarming smile. 'I've taken up enough of your time. Thank you for being so helpful.' He was about to leave when he heard footsteps descending the stairs and a door opened to reveal a fair-haired girl in mourning dress. 'Oh, good morning,' he said, politely.

The girl was short, slender, pale-faced and exceptionally

pretty. She looked as if she had been crying and there was a vulnerability about her that made her somehow more appealing. The sight of a stranger caused her to draw back at once.

'This is my daughter, Emily,' said Winifred, indicating her. 'Emily, this is Inspector Colbeck from London. He's a policeman.'

It was all that the girl needed to hear. Mumbling an excuse, she closed the door and went hurriedly back upstairs. Winifred felt impelled to offer an explanation.

'You'll have to forgive her,' she said. 'Emily still can't believe that it all happened. It's changed her completely. She hasn't been out of here since the day of the execution.'

Victor Leeming was dreaming about his wedding day when he heard a distant knock. The door of the church swung open but, instead of his bride, it was a plump young woman with a wooden tray who came down the aisle towards him.

'Excuse me, sir,' she said, boldly.

'What?'

Leeming came awake and realised that he was lying fully clothed on the bed in his room at the Saracen's Head. The plump young woman was standing inside the doorway, holding a tray and staring at his bruised face with utter fascination.

'Did you hurt yourself, sir?' she asked.

'I had an accident,' he replied, leaping off the bed to stand up.

'What sort of accident?'

'It doesn't matter.'

'It would to me if I had injuries like that.'

'Who are you and what do you want?'

'My name is Mary, sir,' she said with a friendly smile, 'and

I work here at the Saracen's Head. The other gentleman told me to wake you with a cup of tea at eleven o'clock and give you this letter.' She put the tray on the bedside table. 'There you are, sir.'

As she brushed his arm, he stepped back guiltily as if he had just been caught in an act of infidelity. It was a paradox. As a policeman in earlier days, Leeming had been used to patrolling areas of London that were infested with street prostitutes yet he was embarrassed to be alone in a room with a female servant. Mary continued to stare at him.

'Thank you,' he said. 'You can go now.'

'I don't believe it was an accident.'

'Goodbye, Mary.'

'Did it hurt, sir?'

'Goodbye.'

Ushering her out, he closed the door and slipped the bolt into place. Then he stirred some sugar into the tea and took a welcome sip. A clock was chiming nearby and his pocket watch confirmed that it was exactly eleven o'clock, meaning that he had slept for over two hours. Grateful to Colbeck for permitting him a rest, he opened the envelope on the tray and read his instructions, written in the neat hand that he knew so well. Leeming was not pleased by his orders but he seized on one benefit.

'At least, I don't have to go there by train!' he said.

Ashford was the home of the South Eastern Railway Company's main works, a fact that gave the town more kudos while inflicting a perpetual clamour upon it during working hours. The construction of a locomotive was not something that could be done quietly and the clang of industry had now become as familiar, if not as euphonious, as the tolling of a church bell. Robert Colbeck was delighted with an excuse to visit the works and he spent some time talking to the superintendent about the locomotives and rolling stock that were built there. To find the man he was after, Colbeck had to go to the boiler shop, the noisiest part of the factory, a place of unremitting tumult as chains were used to manoeuvre heavy pieces of iron, hammers pounded relentlessly and sparks flew.

Gregory Newman was helping to lift a section of a boiler into position. He was a big man in his forties with a mop of dark hair and a full beard that was flecked with dirt. He used a sinewy forearm to wipe the sweat from his brow. Colbeck waited until he had finished the job in hand before he introduced himself, detached Newman from the others and took him outside. The boilerman was astonished by the arrival of a detective from Scotland Yard, especially one as refined and well dressed as Colbeck. He took a moment to weigh up the newcomer.

'How can you work in that din?' asked Colbeck.

'I was born and brought up in a forge,' said Newman, 'so I've lived with noise all my life. Not like some of the others. Three of the men in the boiler shop have gone stone deaf.'

'I'm not surprised.'

'They should have stuffed something in their ears.'

Newman had a ready grin and an affable manner, the fruit of a lifetime of chatting to customers while they waited for their horses to be shod or for him to perform some other task in his forge. Colbeck warmed to the man at once.

'Why did you stop being a blacksmith?' he said.

'This job pays me better,' replied the other, 'and locomotives don't kick as hard as horses. But that's not the real reason, Inspector. I used to hate trains at first but they've grown on me.'

'They're the face of the future, Mr Newman.'

'That's what I feel.'

'Though there'll always be a call for a good blacksmith.'

'Well, *I* won't hear it – not with all that hullabaloo in the boiler shop. It's a world of its own in there.' His grin slowly faded. 'But you didn't come all the way here from London to hear me tell you that. This is about Nathan, isn't it?'

'Yes, Mr Newman. I've just spoken with his wife.'

'How is Win?'

'Holding up much better than I dared to expect,' said Colbeck. 'Mrs Hawkshaw was very helpful. The same, alas, could not be said of her stepson. He doesn't have much respect for the law.'

'How could he after what happened?'

'Was he always so truculent?'

'Adam is a restless lad,' explained Newman, 'and he likes his own way. When he lived at home, he and Nathan used to argue all the time so I found him a room near the Corn Exchange. There's no real harm in Adam but he won't let anyone push him around.'

'How does he get on with his stepmother?'

'Not too well. Win is a good woman. She's done all she could for him but he was just too much of a handful for her. Then, of course, there was the problem with Emily.'

'Oh?'

'Adam was always teasing her. I'm sure it was only meant in fun,' said Newman, defensively, 'but I think it went too far sometimes. Emily's scared of him. It wasn't good for them to be sleeping under the same roof. They've nothing in common.'

'They share the same father, don't they?'

'No, Inspector. Emily is not Nathan's daughter.'

'I assumed that she was.'

'Win's first husband was killed in a fire,' said Newman, sadly, 'and she was left to bring up a tiny baby on her own. She and Nathan didn't get married until a year later. His wife had died of smallpox so he had a child on his hands as well – Adam.'

'I'm told that you were close to the Hawkshaws.'

'We've been friends for years.'

'Was it a happy marriage?'

'Very happy,' returned the other, as if offended by the query. 'You can see that from the way that Win fought for his release. She was devoted to her husband.'

'But you ran the campaign on his behalf.'

'It was the least I could do, Inspector. Nathan and I grew up together in Ashford. We went to school, fished in the Stour, had our first pipe of tobacco together.' He smiled nostalgically. 'We were only twelve at the time and as sick as dogs.'

'Was Mr Hawkshaw a powerful man?'

'Stronger than me.'

'Strong enough to hack a man to death, then?' asked Colbeck, springing the question on him to gauge his reaction.

'Nathan didn't kill Joe Dykes,' asserted the other.

'Then who did?'

'Go into any pub in the town and you'll find a dozen suspects in each one. Joe Dykes was a menace. Nobody had a good word for him. If he wasn't getting drunk and picking a fight, he was stealing something or pestering a woman.'

'From what I heard, he did more than pester Emily Hawkshaw.'

'Yes,' said Newman, grimly. 'That was what really upset Nathan. The girl is barely sixteen.'

'I met her briefly earlier on.'

'Then you'll have seen how meek and defenceless she is.

Emily is still a child in some ways. She was running an errand for her mother when Joe Dykes cornered her in a lane. The sight of a pretty face was all he needed to rouse him. He grabbed Emily, pinned her against a wall and tore her skirt as he tried to lift it.'

'Didn't she scream for help?' asked Colbeck.

'Emily was too scared to move,' said Newman, 'let alone call out. If someone hadn't come into the lane at that moment, heaven knows what he'd have done to her.'

'Was the incident reported to the police?'

'Nathan wanted to sort it out himself so he went looking for Joe. But, of course, he'd run away by then. We didn't see hide nor hair of Joe Dykes for weeks. Then he turned up at the fair in Lenham.'

'Were you there yourself?'

'Yes, Inspector.'

'Did you go with Nathan Hawkshaw?'

'No,' said Newman, 'I rode over there first thing on my own. I've a cousin who's a blacksmith in Lenham. A fair brings in plenty of trade so I helped him in the forge that morning. It made a nice change from the boiler shop.'

'So you didn't witness the argument that was supposed to have taken place between Hawkshaw and Dykes?'

'I came in at the end. There was such a commotion in the square that I went to see what it was. Nathan and Joe were yelling at each other and the crowd was hoping to see a fight. That's when I stepped in.'

'You?'

'Somebody had to, Inspector,' Newman continued, 'or things could have turned nasty. I didn't want Nathan arrested for disturbing the peace. So, when Joe goes off to the Red Lion, I stopped Nathan from following him and tried to talk some sense into him. If he wanted to settle a score, the square in Lenham was not the place to do it. He should have waited until Joe came out of the pub at the end of the evening when there was hardly anyone about.'

'So there would have been a fight of some sort?'

'A fight is different from cold-blooded murder.'

'But your friend was clearly in a mood for revenge.'

'That's why I had to calm him down,' said Newman, scratching his beard. 'I told him to go away until his temper had cooled. And that's what Nathan did. He set out for Ashford, thought over what I'd said then headed back to Lenham in a much better frame of mind.'

'Did he have a meat cleaver with him?'

'Of course not,' retorted the other.

'One was found beside the body. It had Hawkshaw's initials on it.'

'It was not left there by Nathan.'

'How do you know?'

'To begin with,' said Newman, hotly, 'he wouldn't have been so stupid as to leave a murder weapon behind that could be traced to him.'

'I disagree,' argued Colbeck. 'All the reports suggest that it must have been a frenzied attack. If someone is so consumed with rage that he's ready to kill, he wouldn't stop to think about hiding the murder weapon. Having committed the crime, Hawkshaw could have simply stumbled off.'

'Then where was the blood?'

'Blood?'

'I spoke to the farm lad who discovered the body, Inspector. He said there was blood everywhere. Whoever sliced up Joe Dykes must have been spattered with it – yet there wasn't a speck on Nathan.'

'He was a butcher. He knew how to use a cleaver.'

'That's what they said in court,' recalled Newman, bitterly. 'If he'd been a draper or a grocer, he'd still be alive now. Nathan was condemned because of his occupation.'

'Circumstantial evidence weighed against him.'

'Is that enough to take away a man's life and leave his family in misery? I don't give a damn for what was said about him at the trial. He was innocent of the crime and I want his name cleared.'

Gregory Newman spoke with the earnestness of a true friend. Colbeck decided that, since he had supervised the campaign to secure the prisoner's release, he was almost certainly involved in the doomed attempt to rescue him from Maidstone prison and in the upheaval during the execution. For the sake of a friend, he was ready to defy the law. Colbeck admired his stance even though he disapproved of it.

'You heard what happened to Jake Guttridge, I presume?'

'Yes, Inspector.'

'What did you think when you learnt of the hangman's death?'

'He was no hangman,' said Newman, quietly. 'He was a torturer. He put Nathan through agony. When she saw the way that her husband was twitching at the end of the rope, Win passed out. We had to take her to a doctor.'

'So you didn't shed a tear when you heard that Guttridge had met his own death by violent means?'

'I neither cried nor cheered, Inspector. I'm sorry for any man who's murdered and for those he leaves behind. Guttridge is of no interest to me now. All I want to do is to help Win through this nightmare,' he said, 'and the best way to do that is to prove that Nathan was not guilty.'

'Supposing – just *supposing* – that he was?'

Newman looked at him as if he had just suggested something totally obscene. There was a long silence. Pulling himself to his full height, he looked the detective in the eye.

'Then he was not the person I've known for over forty years.'

Colbeck was impressed with the man's conviction but he was still not entirely persuaded of Hawkshaw's innocence. He did, however, feel that the conversation had put him in possession of vital information. If the butcher had been wrongly hanged, and if Colbeck worked to establish that fact, then Gregory Newman would be a useful ally. Though the boiler maker had little trust in policemen, he had talked openly about the case with the inspector and made his own position clear. There was much more to learn from him but this was not the time.

'Thank you, Mr Newman,' said Colbeck.

'Thank you for taking me away from work for a while.'

'I may need to speak with you again.'

'As you wish, Inspector. Do you want my address?'

'No, I think that I'd rather call on you here at the works.'

Newman grinned. 'Are you that fond of locomotives, Inspector?'

'Yes,' said Colbeck, smiling. 'As a matter of fact, I am.'

Unable to hire a trap, they settled for a cart that had been used that morning to bring a load of fish to Ashford and that still bore strong aromatic traces of its cargo. When it set off towards Lenham and hit every pothole in the road, Victor Leeming could see that he was in for another painful ride. His companion was George Butterkiss, one of the constables in the town, a scrawny individual in his thirties with the face of a startled ferret. Thankful to be driven, Leeming soon began to regret his decision to ask Butterkiss to take him. The fellow was overeager to help, even in a uniform that was much too big for his spare frame, and he was desperately in awe of the Metropolitan Police. He spoke in an irritating nasal whine.

'What are our orders, Sergeant?' he asked, whipping the horse into a trot. 'This is wonderful for me, sir. I've never worked for Scotland Yard before.'

'Or ever again,' said Leeming under his breath.

'What are we supposed to do?'

'*My* instructions,' said Leeming, keen to stress that they had not been directed at Butterkiss, 'are to visit the scene of the crime, examine it carefully then speak to the landlord of the Red Lion.'

'I know the exact spot where Joe Dykes was done in.'

'Good.'

'Sergeant Lugg showed it to me. He and his men came over from Maidstone to arrest Nathan Hawkshaw. There was no point, really. They should have left it to us.'

'Did you know Hawkshaw?'

'My wife bought all her meat from him.'

'What sort of man was he?'

'Decent enough,' said Butterkiss, 'though he wasn't a man to get on the wrong side of, I know that to my cost. Of course, I wasn't a policeman in those days. I was a tailor.'

'Really?' said Leeming, wishing that the man had stayed in his former occupation. 'What made you turn to law enforcement?'

'My shop was burgled and nobody did anything about it.'

'So you thought that you could solve the crime?'

'Oh, no, Sergeant. There was no chance of that. I just realised how horrible you feel when your property has been stolen. It was like being invaded. I wanted to save other people from going through that.'

'A laudable instinct.'

'Then there was the other thing, of course.'

'What other thing?'

'The excitement,' said Butterkiss, nudging him. 'The thrill of the chase. There's none of that when you're measuring someone for a new frock coat. Well, I don't need to tell you, do I? You're another man who loves to hear the sound of a hue and cry.' He gave an ingratiating smirk. 'Would someone like me be able to work at Scotland Yard?'

'Let's talk about the case,' insisted Leeming, wincing as the wheel explored another pothole with jarring resonance. 'Do you think that Hawkshaw was guilty?'

'That's why they hanged him.'

'He wouldn't have been the first innocent man on the gallows.'

'There was no doubt about his guilt in my mind,' attested the driver. 'He and Joe Dykes were sworn enemies. It was only a matter of time before one of them did the other in. Joe broke into the butcher's shop once, you know.'

'Then why didn't you arrest him?'

'We couldn't prove it. Joe used to taunt Nathan about it. Boasted that he could walk in and out of any house in Ashford and nobody could touch him.'

'*I'd* touch him,' said Leeming, 'good and hard.'

'We gave him warning after warning. He ignored us.'

'What was this business about Hawkshaw's daughter?'

'It was his stepdaughter, Emily. Pretty girl.'

'Is it true that Dykes assaulted her?'

'Yes,' said Butterkiss. 'Someone disturbed them just in time.'

'Was the girl hurt?'

'Emily was very upset – who wouldn't be if they were

pounced on by someone like Joe Dykes? It was a big mistake for her to go down that lane. It was one of his places, you see.'

'Places?'

'He used to take women there at night,' said the other, confidingly. 'You can guess the kind of women I mean. Even in a place like Ashford, we have our share of those. Joe would take his pleasure up against a wall and then, as like as not, refuse to pay for it.'

'And that's where this girl was attacked?'

'She thought she'd be safe in daylight.'

'It must have been a terrifying experience.'

'That's what fired Nathan up. He was very protective towards Emily. He went charging around the town in search of Joe but he'd had the sense to make himself scarce. If Nathan had caught him there and then,' said Butterkiss, flicking the reins to get a faster pace out of the horse, 'he'd have torn him apart. I've never seen him so angry.'

'Was he carrying a weapon of any kind?'

'A meat cleaver.'

Travelling with George Butterkiss had its definite compensations. Annoying as his manner might be, he was a fount of information about Ashford and its inhabitants and, since the murder case had been the only major crime in the area during his time as a policeman, he had immersed himself in its details. Victor Leeming overcame his dislike of the man and let him talk at will. Long before they reached Lenham, he had acquired a much clearer understanding of what had brought him and Colbeck to Kent.

'Is this it, Mr Butterkiss?' he asked.

'Yes, Sergeant. The very spot.'

'Where exactly was the body lying when discovered?'

'Here,' said the policeman, dropping obligingly to the

ground and adopting what he believed to be the appropriate position. 'This is where the torso was, anyway,' he added. 'Some of the limbs were scattered about. They never found the other bit.'

'What other bit?'

Butterkiss got to his feet. 'Joe Dykes was castrated.'

It was the first time that Leeming had heard that particular detail and it shook him. They were in a clearing in the woods near Lenham, a quiet, private, shaded place that would have beckoned lovers rather than a killer and his victim. Birds were singing, insects were buzzing, trees and bushes were in full leaf. To commit a murder in such a tranquil place was like an act of desecration.

'Who found the body?'

'A lad from a nearby farm, taking a short-cut home from the fair.'

'I'll need to speak to him.'

'He was the one who spotted Nathan close to here.'

'Let's talk to the landlord of that pub first,' said Leeming. 'That was where Dykes was drinking before he came out to meet his death.'

'Will this go into your report, Sergeant?'

'What?'

'The way I was able to demonstrate where the corpse lay,' said Butterkiss with a willing smile. 'I'd appreciate a mention, sir. It will help me to get on as a policeman. A lot of people in Ashford still treat me as if I was still a tailor. But I'm not – I'm one of *you* now.'

Leeming choked back a comment.

Since there were so few customers that afternoon, Adam Hawkshaw elected to close the butcher's shop early. After bringing in everything that had been on display on the table outside, he took off his apron and hung it up. Then he opened the door at the rear of the shop and went into the room. Winifred Hawkshaw was seated beside Emily with a comforting arm around the girl. Both of them looked up. After a glance from her mother, Emily went off upstairs. Winifred stood up to confront her stepson.

'I told you to knock before you came in.'

'Why?' he asked, insolently. 'It's my house as well.'

'You moved out, Adam.'

'I still own a share of this place now that my father's dead. He always said that he'd leave it to me.'

'He changed his mind.'

'You *made* him change it, you mean.'

'I don't want another row with you,' she said, wearily. 'Not now, please. You'll be able to see the will in due course.' She noticed that he had no apron on. 'Have you shut up shop already?'

Adam was surly. 'No point in staying open,' he said. 'The only customer I had this afternoon was a woman who didn't buy anything. Came to complain about the beef we sold her. And you know why.'

'Yes.' Winifred bit her lip. 'We can't get the best meat any more. Mr Hockaday refused to supply us when your father got arrested.'

'So did Bybrook Farm. We have to pay a higher price now for meat that's only half as good. It's killing our trade.' He heard footsteps over his head and looked up. 'How is she now?'

'Much the same.'

'Has she started to talk again yet?'

'No, Adam,' she replied, sorrowfully. 'Emily has hardly spoken more than a few words to me since this all began. She spends most of her time up there in her room, frightened to come out.'

'She never was one for saying much.'

'Emily needs time to recover – just like the rest of us. We could all do with a period of peace and quiet.'

'How can we get that when some inspector from London turns up to cause trouble?' he snarled. 'You were wrong to talk to him like that.'

'Why?'

'Policemen are all the same, even fancy ones like that. You never know what they really want.'

'I know what Inspector Colbeck is after.'

'What?'

'He wants to find out who killed the public hangman.'

'So do I,' said Adam, eyes glinting, 'because I'd like to shake his hand. Guttridge being murdered was the one good thing to come out of all this. I hope he died in torment.'

'That's a vile thing to say!' she chided.

'He killed my father.'

'I lost a husband that day, Adam,' she told him, 'but I don't want vengeance against those involved. I just want the stain to be wiped away from our name so that we can hold up our heads in this town again.'

'We may not be staying long enough for that.'

'We *have* to, Adam. We can't crawl away in disgrace.'

'The shop is the only thing that keeps us here,' he said, jerking a thumb over his shoulder, 'and most people walk straight past it. I'm not a butcher any more. I'm Nathan Hawkshaw's son – a killer's whelp.'

It was remarkable how much information they had garnered between them in the course of one day. When the two detectives met over a meal at the Saracen's Head that evening, Robert Colbeck and Victor Leeming compared notes and discussed what their next move ought to be. Though no firm conclusions could yet be reached, the inspector felt that the visit to Ashford had already proved worthwhile.

'He's here, Victor,' he announced. 'I feel it.'

'Who is?'

'The killer.'

'Which one, sir?'

'I beg your pardon?'

'The man who murdered Joseph Dykes or the one who finished off Jacob Guttridge in that excursion train?'

'The second of the two. That's what brought us here, after all. Until we've solved that particular crime, Mr Tallis will hound us from morn till night – and he's quite right to do so.'

'That's the only advantage of being here,' said Leeming, rubbing a buttock as he felt another twinge. 'We're out of the superintendent's earshot. We can breathe freely.'

'Not with that smell from the river.'

'Going back to Nathan Hawkshaw for a minute.'

'Yes?'

'Before we came here, you had a few doubts about his guilt.'

'More than a few, Victor.'

'And now?'

'Those doubts remain,' said Colbeck, spearing a piece of sausage with his fork. 'I spent the afternoon talking to people in the town who knew the butcher well – his friends, his doctor, even the priest at St Mary's Church. They all agreed that it was so out of character for Hawkshaw to commit murder that they couldn't believe he was culpable.'

'I've come round to the opposite view, sir.'

'Why?'

'According to George Butterkiss, there was another side to the butcher. He liked an argument for its own sake. When he used to be a tailor – Butterkiss, that is, not Hawkshaw – he made a suit for him and got a mouthful of abuse for his pains. It was as if Hawkshaw was finding fault on purpose so that he could have a good quarrel with the tailor.'

'Did he buy the suit in the end?'

'Only when Butterkiss had made a few slight changes.'

'Maybe there *were* some things wrong with it.'

'I don't think so,' said Leeming, munching his food. 'Butterkiss reckons that he only started the argument so that he could get something off the price. The tailor was browbeaten into taking less for his work. That's criminal.'

'It's business, Victor.'

'Well, it sums up Hawkshaw for me. He was no saint.'

'Nobody claims that he was,' said Colbeck, 'and I know that he could be argumentative. Gregory Newman told me that Hawkshaw and his son were always gnawing at some bone of contention. It's the reason that Adam Hawkshaw moved out of the house. Nothing you've said so far inclines me to believe that Hawkshaw was a killer.'

'You're forgetting the daughter, sir.'

'Emily?'

'When she told her stepfather she'd been assaulted by Dykes, he grabbed a meat cleaver and went out looking for him. That doesn't sound like an innocent man to me.'

'What it sounds like is someone who acted purely on impulse. He may have brandished a weapon but that doesn't mean he would have used it – especially in a public place where there'd be witnesses. In those circumstances,' said Colbeck, 'most fathers would respond with blind rage. You have a daughter of your own, Victor. What would you do if some drunken oaf molested Alice?'

'I'd be after him with a pair of shears!' said Leeming.

'I rest my case.'

'Only because you didn't meet the lad who saw Hawkshaw near the place where the murder occurred. I did, Inspector. He gave evidence in court that, when he walked home through the woods, Hawkshaw was trying to hide behind some bushes. He was furtive,' insisted Leeming, 'like he'd done something wrong.'

'Did the youth speak to him?'

'He tried to but Hawkshaw scurried off into the undergrowth. Why did he do that if he had nothing to hide?'

'I don't know,' admitted Colbeck.

'It was because he'd just hacked Joseph Dykes to death.'

'Maybe, maybe not.'

'I'll stick with maybe, sir. The victim was castrated, remember. Only a father who wanted revenge for an attempted rape of his daughter would do that. It has to be Hawkshaw.'

'Did you talk to the landlord of the Red Lion?'

'Yes,' said Leeming. 'He gave evidence in court as well. He told me that Dykes went in there that day, drank a lot of beer and made a lot of noise, then rolled out as if he didn't have a care in the world.'

'What was he doing in that wood?'

'I can't work that out, sir. You'd only go that way if you wanted to get to the farm beyond. It was where that lad worked, you see. My theory is that Dykes may have made himself a den in there.'

'Take care, Victor!' said Colbeck with a laugh. 'We can't have you succumbing to theories as well. In any case, this one doesn't hold water. If there had been a den there, it would have been found when the police made a thorough search of the area.'

'Dykes slept rough from time to time. We know that for certain.'

'But even he wouldn't bed down in the middle of the afternoon when there was a fair to enjoy and several hours more drinking to get through. What took him there at that specific time?'

'Hawkshaw must have lured him there somehow.'

'I think that highly unlikely.'

'How else could it have happened?'

'I intend to find out, Victor,' said Colbeck. 'But only after we've caught the man who stalked Jake Guttridge on that excursion train.'

'We know so little about him, sir.'

'On the contrary, we know a great deal.'

'Do we?' asked Leeming, drinking his beer to wash down his food. 'The only thing we can be sure of is that he's almost illiterate.'

'Why do you say that?'

'Because of that warning note you found at Guttridge's house.'

'Go on.'

'It was nothing but a scrawl. Half the words weren't even spelt properly. The person we want is obviously uneducated.'

'I wonder,' said Colbeck. 'People who can't write usually get someone to do it for them. The man who sent that message to the hangman may have *wanted* to appear unlettered by way of disguise. But there's another factor to weigh in the balance here.'

'Is there, sir?'

'The man who killed Jake Guttridge may not be the one who sent him that note. He could well be someone else altogether.'

'That makes him even more difficult to track down,' said

Leeming, popping a potato into his mouth. 'We're looking for a needle in a very large haystack, Inspector.'

'A small haystack, perhaps,' said Colbeck, sipping his wine, 'but that should not deter us. We know that we're looking for a local man with some connection to Nathan Hawkshaw. Someone so outraged at what happened to his friend that he'd go in search of the hangman to wreak his revenge. The killer was strong, determined and cunning.'

'Have you met anyone who fits that description, sir?'

'Two people at least.'

'Who are they?'

'The son is the first,' Colbeck told him. 'From the little I saw of him, I'd say he had the strength and determination. Whether he'd have the cunning is another matter.'

'Who's the other suspect?'

'Gregory Newman. He was Hawkshaw's best friend and he led the campaign on his behalf. My guess is that he even tried to rescue him from Maidstone prison and he'd have to be really committed to attempt something as impossible as that.'

'If he was a blacksmith, then he'd certainly be strong enough.'

'Yes,' said Colbeck, 'but he didn't strike me as a potential killer. Newman is something of a gentle giant. Since the execution, all his efforts have been directed at consoling the widow. He's a kind man and a loyal friend. The priest at St Mary's spoke very highly of him. Gregory Newman, it transpires, has a bedridden wife whom he looks after lovingly, even to the point of carrying her to church every Sunday.'

'That *is* devotion,' agreed Leeming.

'A devoted husband is unlikely to be a brutal murderer.'

'So we come back to Adam Hawkshaw.'

'He'd certainly conform to your notion that an uneducated

man sent that note,' explained Colbeck, using a napkin to wipe his lips. 'When I left the shop yesterday, he was lowering the prices on the board outside. He'd chalked up the different items on offer. Considering that he must have sold pheasant many times, he'd made a very poor shot at spelling it correctly.'

Leeming grinned. 'He's lucky he didn't have to spell asphyxiation.'

'He's certainly capable of inflicting it on someone.'

'It's that warning note that worries me, sir.'

'Why?'

'Guttridge had one and he ended up dead.'

'So?'

'According to George Butterkiss,' said Leeming, pushing his empty plate aside, 'someone else had a death threat as well. Sergeant Lugg, that policeman from Maidstone, told him about it. The note that was sent sounds very much like the one that went to the hangman. The difference is that the man who received it just laughed and tore it up.'

'Who was he, Victor?'

'The prison chaplain, sir – the Reverend Narcissus Jones.'

Though his job at Maidstone prison was onerous and wide-ranging, Narcissus Jones nevertheless found time for activities outside its high stone walls. He gave regular lectures at various churches and large audiences usually flocked to hear how he had conceived it as his mission to work among prisoners. He always emphasised that he had converted some of the most hardened criminals to Christianity and sent them out into society as reformed characters. With his Welsh ancestry, he had a real passion for choral singing and he talked lovingly about the prison choir that he conducted. Jones was a good speaker, fluent, dramatic and so steeped in biblical knowledge that he could quote from Old and New Testaments at will.

He had been on good form at Paddock Wood that night, rousing the congregation to such a pitch that they had burst into spontaneous applause at the end of his talk. Everyone wanted to congratulate him afterwards and what touched him was that one of those most effusive in his praise was a former inmate at the prison who said that, in bringing him to God, the chaplain had saved his life. When he headed for the railway station, Jones was still beaming with satisfaction.

He did not have long to wait for the train that would take him back to Maidstone. Selecting an empty carriage, he sat down and tried to read his Bible in the fading light. A young woman then got into the carriage and sat opposite him, gaining a nod of welcome from the chaplain. He decided that she had chosen to join him because the sight of his clerical collar was a guarantee of her safety. She was short, attractive and dark-haired but she was holding a handkerchief to her face as if to dab away tears. At a signal from the stationmaster, the train began to move but, at the very last moment, a man jumped into the carriage and slammed the door behind him.

'Just made it!' he said, sitting down at the opposite end from the others. 'I hope that I didn't disturb you.'

'Not at all,' replied Jones, 'though I'd never care to do anything as dangerous as that. Are you going as far as Maidstone?'

'Yes.'

'And what about you, my dear?' asked the chaplain, turning to the woman. 'Where's your destination?'

But she did not even hear him. Unable to contain her sorrow, she began to sob loudly and press the handkerchief to her eyes. Jones put his Bible aside and rose to his feet so that he could bend solicitously over her. It was a fatal error. As soon as the chaplain's back was turned to him, the other man got up, produced a length of wire from his pocket and slipped it around the neck of Narcissus Jones, pulling it tight with such vicious force that the victim barely had time to pray for deliverance. When the train stopped at the next station, the only occupant of the carriage was a dead prison chaplain.

CHAPTER EIGHT

Robert Colbeck had always been a light sleeper. Hearing the footsteps coming up the oak staircase with some urgency, he opened his eyes and sat up quickly in bed. There was a loud knock on his door.

'Inspector Colbeck?' said a voice. 'This is Constable Butterkiss.'

'One moment.'

'I have a message for you, sir.'

Colbeck got out of bed, slipped on his dressing gown and unbolted the door. He opened it to admit George Butterkiss who had come to the Saracen's Head at such speed that he had not even paused to button up his uniform properly.

'What's the problem, Constable?'

'I'm sorry for the delay,' gabbled Butterkiss, almost out of breath, 'but they didn't realise that you were in Kent. They sent a telegraph message to London and it was passed on to Scotland Yard. When they found out you were in Ashford, they asked us to get in touch with you straight away.'

'Calm down,' said Colbeck, putting a hand on his shoulder. 'Just tell me what this is all about.'

'There's been another murder, sir.'

'Where?'

'In a train on its way to Maidstone.'

'Do you know who the victim was?'

'The prison chaplain – Narcissus Jones.'

Colbeck felt a pang of regret. 'Where's the body?'

'Where it was found, sir,' said Butterkiss, deferentially. 'They thought you'd want to see it before it was moved.'

'Someone deserves congratulations for that. I hope that the same person had the sense to preserve the scene of the crime so that no clues have been lost. Sergeant Leeming needs to hear all this,' he went on, stepping into the passage to bang on the adjoining door. 'Wake up. Victor! We have to leave at once.'

Leeming took time to come out of his slumber and to adjust to the fact that someone was pounding on the door. He eventually appeared, bleary-eyed and wearing a flannel nightshirt. Colbeck invited him into his own room then asked Butterkiss to give a succinct account of what he knew. It was a tall order for the former tailor. Overwhelmed at being in the presence of two Scotland Yard detectives, albeit it in night attire, he started to jabber wildly, embroidering the few facts he knew into a long, confused, meandering narrative.

'That's enough,' said Colbeck, cutting him off before he had finished. 'We'll find out the rest when we get there.'

Butterkiss was eager. 'Will you be needing my assistance, sir?'

'You've already given that.'

'There must be something that I can do, Inspector.'

'There is,' said Colbeck, glad to get rid of him. 'Arrange some transport to get us to the station as fast as possible.'

'Very good, sir.'

'Only not that cart that stinks of fish,' warned Leeming.

'I'll find something,' said Butterkiss and he rushed out.

'Get dressed, Victor. We must be on our way.'

The sergeant was hungry. 'What about breakfast?'

'We'll think about that when we reach Maidstone. Now hurry up, will you? They're all waiting for us.'

'What's the rush, Inspector? The chaplain isn't going anywhere.' Leeming put an apologetic hand to his mouth. 'Oh dear! I shouldn't have said that, should I?'

The baker's shop in North Street was among the earliest to open and Winifred Hawkshaw was its first customer that morning. Clutching a loaf of bread still warm from the oven, she was about to cross the high street when she saw two familiar figures coming towards her on a little cart. Gregory Newman gave her a cheery wave and brought the horse to a halt. Seated beside him and swathed in a rug, in spite of the warm weather, was his wife, Meg, a thin, wasted creature in her forties with a vacant stare and an open mouth.

'Good morning,' said Winifred. 'How is Meg today?'

'Oh, she's very well,' replied Newman, slipping a fond arm around his wife, 'aren't you, Meg?' She looked blankly at him. 'It's Win. You remember Win Hawkshaw, don't you?' His wife nodded and gave Win a crooked smile of acknowledgement. 'She's not at her best this time of the morning,' explained her husband, 'but the doctor said that she must get plenty of fresh air so I take her for a ride whenever I can.' He looked up as a few dark clouds began to form. 'We went before work today because it may rain later.'

'You're wonderful with her, Gregory.'

'You were there when I made my marriage vows before the altar. In sickness and in health means exactly what it says, Win. It's not Meg's fault that she's plagued by illness.'

'No, of course not.'

'But how are you? I've been meaning to call in.'

'I'm fine,' said Winifred. 'Well, as fine as I'll ever be, I suppose.'

'What about Emily?'

'She's still the same, I'm afraid. Emily seems to be lost in a bad dream most of the time. I just can't reach her, Gregory.'

'Things will improve soon.'

'Will they?' she asked with a hint of despair. 'There's been no sign of it so far. Emily can go a whole day without even speaking.'

Newman glanced at his wife to show that he had experienced the same problem many times. Win marvelled at the patience he always showed. She had never known him complain about the fact that he had to care for a woman whose mind was crumbling as fast as her body. His example gave Win the courage to face her own domestic difficulties.

'Did an Inspector Colbeck come to see you, Gregory?'

'Yes,' he said with a grin. 'We had a nice, long chat that kept me out of that madhouse of a boiler room for a while. I took him for a shrewd man though he was far too smartly dressed for a town like Ashford.'

'I talked to him as well. Adam refused.'

'That was silly of him.'

'He hates policemen.'

'I don't admire them either,' confessed Newman, 'but I'm ready to accept their help when it's offered. We know that Nathan didn't commit that murder but we still haven't managed to find out who did. I reckon that this Inspector Colbeck might do the job for us. I'll speak to Adam and tell him to talk to the inspector.'

'I can't promise it will do any good.'

'How is he?'

'Still hurting like the rest of us,' said Winifred, 'but he wants to hurt someone back. It doesn't matter who it is to him. Adam just wants to strike out.'

'Are you still having trouble at the shop?'

'Our custom is slowly drying up. Mr Hockaday won't supply us with meat any more and Bybrook Farm turned us down as well.'

'Bybrook!' he said, angrily. 'That's unforgivable.'

'No, Gregory. It's only natural.'

'Nathan was not guilty of that murder.'

'He was hanged for it – that's enough for them.'

'Let me go to Bybrook Farm and have a word.'

'There's no point.'

'There's every point, Win. You've been buying their meat and poultry for years. It's high time someone told them about loyalty.'

'It's good of you to offer,' she said, reaching up to squeeze his arm, 'but you can't fight all our battles for us. You've done more than enough as it is and we can never repay you.'

'I don't look for repayment. I simply want to see some justice in this world. Think of all the money that Nathan paid to Bybrook Farm over the years – and to Silas Hockaday. They ought to be *ashamed*.'

'You'd better go. I don't want to make you late for work.'

'We must talk more another time.'

'I'd like that, Gregory.'

'And so would I.' He turned to his wife. 'Wouldn't I, Meg?' She continued to stare unseeingly in front of her. 'One of her bad days, I'm afraid. Meg will be better next time we meet.'

'I'm sure.' She raised her voice. 'Goodbye, Meg.'

'Goodbye, Win,' he said, clicking his tongue make the

horse move off again. 'And I won't forget to speak to Adam. He listens to me.'

'Sometimes.'

'He's the man of the house now. He's got responsibilities.'

'Yes,' she murmured, 'that's the trouble.'

After watching the cart rattle on up the high street, she went back to Middle Row in time to find her stepson trying to chalk up some information on the board outside the shop. He wrote in large, laborious capitals.

'Good morning, Adam,' she said. 'You're up early.'

He smirked. 'I didn't sleep at all last night.'

'When was the body actually discovered?' asked Inspector Colbeck.

'First thing this morning,' replied Lugg.

'Why was there such a delay?'

'It was the last train from Paddock Wood and it stayed here all night. When it was due to leave this morning, someone tried to get into this carriage and found the chaplain.'

'Didn't anyone check that the carriages were empty last night?'

'The guard swears that he walked the length of the train and looked through all the windows but, of course, he couldn't see anyone lying on the floor now, could he?'

Colbeck was pleased to encounter Sergeant Obadiah Lugg again but he wished that it could have been in more propitious circumstances. After taking a train from Ashford, the two detectives had changed at Paddock Wood so that they could travel on the Maidstone line. News of the crime had spread quickly through the town and a crowd had gathered at the station to watch developments. Colbeck was relieved to see that Lugg had deployed his men to keep the inquisitive and the purely ghoulish at bay while the inspector went about his work.

The scene that confronted him was very similar to the one he had found at Twyford, except that the wider gauge of the Great Western Railway had allowed for a carriage with more generous proportions. The prison chaplain was lying on his back, his mouth agape, his eyes wide open as if straining to leave their sockets. Rigor mortis had set in, turning the face into a marble carving of pain. Above his clerical collar was a dark red circle of dried blood. When he knelt to examine the wound, Colbeck saw that something very sharp and unyielding had cut deep into the neck of Reverend Narcissus Jones.

There were signs of a struggle – the victim's clothing was in disarray, his hair was unkempt, the padding on one seat had been badly torn – but it was one that the chaplain had clearly lost. Underneath his head was his Bible, acting as a spiritual pillow. On the floor near his hand was a small button that did not belong to the victim. Colbeck picked it up and saw the strands of cotton hanging from it.

'He managed to tear this from his attacker by getting a hand behind him,' said Colbeck. He indicated the gash in the padding. 'That could well have been caused by the heel of his shoe when he was threshing about.'

'The chaplain wouldn't give up without a fight, Inspector.'

'Unfortunately, he was caught off guard.'

'How?' said Lugg. 'If there are only two of you in a carriage, it's hard for one man to surprise the other.'

'Not if a third person distracts the victim.'

'A third person?'

'A woman, for instance,' explained Colbeck. 'When I spoke to the stationmaster at Paddock Wood, he remembers a woman on the platform though he didn't see her board the train.'

'Very few women travel alone at that time of the evening.'

'Exactly. That's why this one interests me.'

'I've talked to our own stationmaster,' said Lugg, keen to show that he had not been idle, 'and he recalls that the train was two-thirds empty when it reached Maidstone. Albert knew most of them by name because he's been here for years. No stranger got off that train, he swears to that. Only regular travellers on the line.'

'The killer and his accomplice – if there was one, that is – would never have stayed on the train until it reached here. My guess is that the murder took place shortly after they left Paddock Wood because the killer could not take the risk that someone might get into the same carriage when they stopped at Yalding.'

'In that case,' concluded Lugg, 'he must have strangled the chaplain to death then made his escape at the station.'

'No, Sergeant.'

'Why not?'

'Because someone might have seen him getting off the train,' said Colbeck. 'And if, as I believe, there was a woman with him, they would surely have been noticed by the railway staff.'

Lugg was baffled. 'Then where and how did they get off, sir?'

'I can't give you a precise location but it's somewhere the other side of Yalding. The train slows down well short of the station and there's a grassy bank that runs along the side of the line.'

'You think that the killer jumped off?'

'That's what I'd have done in his place, wouldn't you?'

'Well, yes,' said Lugg, wrinkling his brow in concentration. 'I suppose that I would, sir. Except that I'm a bit old for anything as daring as leaping out of a moving train.'

'Approaching the station, it only goes at a snail's pace but it would still take some agility to get off. That tells us something about the killer.'

'What about this woman you mentioned?'

'She, too, must be quite athletic.'

'Younger people, then?'

'We'll see, Sergeant, we'll see.'

'Two people, leaping from the train,' said Lugg, rubbing his chin as he meditated. 'Surely, some of the other passengers would have spotted them doing that.'

'Only if they happened to be looking out of the window at the time. This, as you can see, is near the end of the train. There are only two carriages and a guard's van behind it. Naturally,' he went on, 'we'll speak to all the passengers who were on that train last night but, since there were so few of them, I doubt that we'll find a witness.'

'No, Inspector. If someone had seen people hopping off the train, they'd have reported it by now. The killer obviously chose the point to jump off very carefully.'

'Someone who knows this line well.'

Colbeck continued with his meticulous examination of the body and the carriage while Lugg looked on with fascination. After searching the dead man's pockets, Colbeck lifted the head so that he could slip the Bible out from under it. He opened it at the page with the marker in it and read the text.

'Amazing how his head came to rest on that, isn't it?' said Lugg with his characteristic chuckle. 'Almost as if God's hand was at work.'

'It was the killer's hand, Sergeant,' announced Colbeck. 'He put the Bible there deliberately so that he could leave us this message.'

'Message?'

'St Paul's Epistle to the Romans – chapter 12. He's crossed out verse 19 in order to make his point.'

'And what's that?'

'Something that every Christian knows – Vengeance is mine; I will repay, saith the Lord.' He closed the Bible and put it aside. 'It seems as if someone is determined to do the Lord's work for Him.'

Victor Leeming had been efficient. Having taken statements from the guard and the stationmaster, he had located a handful of passengers who had travelled on the train the previous evening and spoken to them as well. When he saw Colbeck coming down the platform towards him with Sergeant Lugg, he went swiftly forward to meet the inspector.

'One of the managers of the South Eastern Railway is here, sir,' he said. 'He wants to know when the service can be resumed – so do all the people you see queuing outside the ticket office.'

'As soon as the body is removed,' said Colbeck, 'the train is all theirs, but I'd recommend that they detach that particular carriage. Nobody will want to travel in it now, anyway. Can you pass that on, Sergeant Lugg?'

'Yes, Inspector,' replied Lugg, 'and I've got men standing by with a stretcher – and with a blanket. The chaplain deserves to be covered when we carry him past that mob. I'm not having them goggling at Mr Jones. It's indecent.'

'Well, Victor,' said Colbeck as the policeman waddled off, 'have you discovered anything of value?'

'Not really, sir.'

'I thought not.'

'It was getting dark by the time that the train reached Maidstone last night so the guard couldn't see much when he glanced in through the windows. To be honest,' he added, 'I doubt if he even looked. He was too anxious to get home to his supper.'

'What about the stationmaster? Albert someone, I gather.'

'Albert Scranton, crusty old soul. He recognised all the people who got off that train and said that everything looked perfectly normal. He wonders if the murder could have happened during the night.'

'While the train was out of commission?'

'Yes, Inspector – after he'd closed the station.'

'And how did the chaplain come to be in the railway carriage of a train that wasn't going anywhere?'

'That's what I asked him,' said Leeming. 'Mr Scranton reckoned that he could have been tricked into meeting someone here.'

'Impossible,' said Colbeck, dismissing the notion at once. 'There was a ticket in the dead man's pocket showing that he was travelling from Paddock Wood to Maidstone. Since he didn't get off here, he must have been killed during the journey.'

'So where did the murderer get off?'

'Somewhere on the other side of Yalding station.'

Leeming blinked. 'While the train was still *moving*?'

'Yes, Victor. It's only three miles or so between Paddock Wood and Yalding. The chaplain must have been dispatched shortly after the train left so that the pair of them had time to make their escape.'

'The pair of them?'

'I'm fairly certain that he had an accomplice.'

'You mean that woman?'

'Let's be off,' said Colbeck, using a hand to ease him into a walk. 'I'll give you all the details on the way there.'

'Where are we going, sir?'

'To prison, Victor.'

Henry Ferriday was more apprehensive than ever. Unable to sit still, he paced nervously up and down his office in the vain hope that movement would ease the tension that he felt. A rap on the door startled him and he called for the visitor to identify himself before he allowed him in. It was one of the men on duty at the prison gate, bringing news that two detectives from Scotland Yard were waiting to see him. Minutes later, Robert Colbeck and Victor Leeming were escorted to the governor's office. When the sergeant was introduced to Ferriday, he was given a clammy handshake. All three men sat down.

'This is an appalling business,' said Ferriday, still reeling from the shock. 'Quite appalling.'

'You have my deepest sympathy,' said Colbeck, softly. 'I know how much you relied on the chaplain.'

'Narcissus was vital to the running of this prison, Inspector. He exerted such influence over the inmates. I don't know how we'll manage without him. He's irreplaceable.'

'Is it true that he had a death threat some weeks ago?'

Ferriday was taken aback. 'How on earth do you know that?'

'That's immaterial. It was in connection with the execution of Nathan Hawkshaw, wasn't it?'

'Yes, it was.'

'Did you happen to see the note?'

'Of course. Narcissus and I had no secrets between us.'

'Can you recall what it said?'

'Very little, Inspector. Something to the effect of "We'll kill you for this, you Welsh bastard"—only the spelling was dreadful. It was clearly written by an ignorant man.'

'Ignorant men can still nurture a passion for revenge.'

'Did you take the threat seriously?' asked Leeming.

'Yes, Sergeant.'

'And what about the chaplain?'

'Narcissus shrugged it off,' said Ferriday, 'and threw the note away. He refused to be frightened by anything. That was his downfall.'

'Did he take no precautions outside the prison?' said Colbeck.

'He didn't need to, Inspector. Well, you've met him. He was a big man, strong enough to look after himself. And having worked with villains for so long, he had a second sense where danger was concerned.'

'Not in this case,' observed Leeming.

'Do we have any idea what actually happened?' said Ferriday, looking from one to the other. 'All I know is that his body was discovered in a railway carriage this morning. How was he murdered?'

Colbeck gave him a brief account of his examination of the murder scene and told him that the body had now been removed from the train. The governor flinched when he heard about the Bible being placed under the head of the dead man and the verse that had been picked out.

'What kind of vile heathen are we dealing with here?' he shouted.

'A very clever one,' admitted Colbeck. 'This is the second murder that he's committed on a train and he's escaped on both occasions.'

'He must be caught, Inspector!'

'He will be.'

'This is one execution in which I'll take some pleasure,' said the governor, bunching his fists. 'He deserves to hang until every last breath is squeezed out of his miserable body.' He collected himself. 'Narcissus Jones was a great man. The whole prison will mourn him. It's not given to many chaplains to possess such extraordinary gifts.'

'He was a striking individual,' agreed Colbeck.

The governor looked over his shoulder. 'This prison is a sewer,' he said, contemptuously. 'We have the scum of the earth in here.'

'There's no need to tell us that,' said Leeming with a dry laugh. 'Our job is to catch the devils and send them on to places like this.'

'Most of them sneer at authority and go straight back to a life of crime as soon as we let them out. At least,' Ferriday went on, 'that's what used to happen until Narcissus Jones was appointed here. He gave the men a sense of hope and self-respect. He *improved* them as human beings. That's what made him so popular among the men.'

Colbeck had doubts on that score. 'I take it that the chaplain had a room at the prison?' he said.

'Yes, Inspector. He more or less lived within these walls.'

'But he did venture out?'

'From time to time.'

'What we need to establish is how the killer knew that he would be travelling on that train from Paddock Wood.'

'I can tell you that,' said Ferriday. 'The chaplain was much in demand as a speaker at churches and Christian gatherings. Most of the invitations he received had, of necessity, to be turned down because of his commitments here, but he did like to give a talk or take a service somewhere once or twice a month.'

'Events that would have been advertised in a parish magazine.'

'And in the local newspapers, Inspector Colbeck. Our

chaplain was a man of some renown. If you go to the church in Paddock Wood where he spoke yesterday, I daresay you'll find that they had a board outside for weeks in advance with details of his talk. It was St Peter's, by the way,' he added. 'They'll be horrified to hear the news.'

'So will everyone else,' said Leeming. 'Killing a man of the cloth is about as low as you can sink. I mean, it's sacrosanct.'

'Sacrilege,' corrected Colbeck, gently.

'I call it diabolical,' said Ferriday.

While they were talking a distant noise had begun inside the prison, slowly building until it became audible enough for them to become aware of it. All three of them looked at the window. The sound got progressively louder, spreading swiftly from wing to wing of the establishment with gathering force. Raised voices could be heard but the dominating note had a metallic quality to it as if a large number of inmates were using implements to beat on the bars of their cells in celebration. In its menacing rhythm, a concerted message was being sent to the governor by the only means at the prisoners' disposal. As the noise rose to a climax, Leeming looked across at the governor.

'What's that?' he asked.

'I'll have it stopped immediately,' declared Ferriday, getting up angrily from his seat and going to the door. 'That's intolerable.'

'Someone has heard the news of his death already,' noted Colbeck as the governor flung open the door to leave. 'Perhaps the chaplain was not as universally popular as you believed.'

The loss of Emily Hawkshaw's appetite was almost as worrying to her mother as the long silence into which the girl had lapsed. She refused more meals than she ate and, of those that were actually consumed, the major portion was always left on the plate. Emily was in no mood to eat anything at all that morning.

'Come on, dear,' coaxed Winifred. 'Try some of this bread.'

'No, thank you.'

'It's lovely and fresh. Eat it with a piece of cheese.'

'I'm not hungry.'

'Some jam, then.'

'No.'

'You must eat *something*, Emily.'

'Leave me be, Mother.'

'Please – for my sake.' The girl shook her head. 'If you go on like this, you'll make yourself ill. I can't remember the last time you had a decent meal. In the past, you always had such a good appetite.'

They were in the room at the rear of the shop, facing each other across the kitchen table. Emily looked paler than ever, her shoulders hunched, her whole body drawn in. She had never been the most lively and outgoing girl but she had seemed very contented in the past. Now she was like a stranger. Winifred no longer knew her daughter. As a last resort, she tried to interest her in local news.

'Mr Lewis, the draper, is going to buy the shop next door to his premises,' she told her. 'He wants to expand his business. Mr Lewis is very ambitious. I don't think it will be long before he's looking for another place to take over as well.' She gave a sigh. 'It's nice to know that someone in Ashford is doing well, because we're not. Things seem to get worse each day. Adam says that hardly anybody came into the shop this morning.' Her voice brightened. 'Oh, I saw Gregory earlier on, did I tell you? He was taking his wife for a drive before he went off to the railway works. I know that *we* have our sorrows,' she continued, 'but we should spare a thought for Gregory. His wife has been like that for years and she'll never get any better. Meg can't walk and she can't speak. She has to be fed and seen to in every way by someone else. Think what a burden that must place on Gregory yet somehow he always stays cheerful.' She bent over the table. 'Can you hear what I'm saying?' she asked. 'We have to go on, Emily. No matter how much we may grieve, we have to go on. I know that you loved your father and miss him dreadfully but so do we all.' Emily's lower lip began to tremble. 'What do you think he'd say if he were here now? He wouldn't want to see you like this, would he? You have to make an *effort*.'

'I'll go to my room,' said Emily, trying to get up.

'No,' said Winifred, extending a hand to take her by the arm. 'Stay here and talk to me. Tell me what you *feel*. I'm your mother – I want to help you through this but I need some help in return. Don't you understand that?'

Emily nodded sadly. Winifred detached her arm. There was a long, bruised silence then it seemed as if the girl was finally about to say something but she changed her mind at the last moment. After a glance at the food on the table, she turned towards the door. Temper fraying slightly, Winifred adopted a sterner tone.

'If you won't eat your meals,' she warned, 'then there's only one thing I can do. I'll have to call the doctor.'

'No!' cried Emily, suddenly afraid. 'No, no, don't do that!'

And she fled the room in a flood of tears.

It was early evening before the two detectives finally got back to Ashford, having made extensive inquiries in both Maidstone and Paddock Wood. Both of their notebooks were filled with details relating to the latest crime. On reaching the station, they were greeted by the three defining elements of the town – the grandeur of its church, the smell of its river and the cacophony of its railway works. A steady drizzle was falling and they had no umbrella. Colbeck was still grappling with the problems thrown up by the new investigation but Victor Leeming's mind was occupied by a more immediate concern. It was the prospect of dinner at the Saracen's Head that exercised his brain and stimulated his senses. The only refreshment they had been offered all day was at the prison and the environment was hardly conducive to any enjoyment of food. When they turned into the high street, he began to lick his lips.

As they approached the inn, they saw that George Butterkiss was standing outside, his uniform now buttoned up properly and his face aglow with the desire to impress. He stood to attention and touched his helmet with a forefinger. Thoroughly damp, he looked as if he had been there some time.

'Did you find any clues, Inspector?' he asked, agog for news.

'Enough for us to act upon,' replied Colbeck.

'You will call upon us in due course, won't you?'

'If necessary, Constable.'

'How was the chaplain killed?'

'Quickly.'

'We can't discuss the details,' said Leeming, irritated by someone who stood between him and his dinner. 'Inspector Colbeck was very careful what information he released to the press.'

'Yes, yes,' said Butterkiss. 'I understand.'

'We know where to find you, Constable,' said Colbeck, walking past him. 'Thank you for your help this morning.'

'We appreciated it,' added Leeming.

'Thank you!' said Butterkiss, beaming like a waiter who has received a huge tip. 'Thank you very much.'

'By the way,' advised Leeming, unable to resist a joke at his expense. 'That uniform is too big for you, Constable. You should see a good tailor.'

He followed Colbeck into the Saracen's Head and made for the stairs. Before they could climb them, however, they were intercepted. Mary, the plump servant, hurried out of the bar. She subjected Leeming's face to close scrutiny.

'Those bruises are still there, Sergeant.'

'Thank you for telling me,' he said.

'Is there nothing you can put on them?'

'We were caught in the rain,' explained Colbeck, 'and we need to get out of these wet clothes. You'll have to excuse us.'

'But I haven't told you my message yet, Inspector.'

'Oh?'

'The gentleman said that I was to catch you as soon as you came back from wherever it is you've been. He was very insistent.'

'What gentleman, Mary?'

'The one who's taken a room for the night.'

'Did he give you a name?'

'Oh, yes,' she said, helpfully.

Leeming was impatient. 'Well,' he said, as his stomach began to rumble, 'what was it, girl?'

'Superintendent Tallis.'

'What!'

'He's going to dine with you here this evening.'

Suddenly, Victor Leeming no longer looked forward to the meal with quite the same relish.

Gregory Newman finished his shift at the railway works and washed his hands in the sink before leaving. Many of the boilermen went straight to the nearest pub to slake their thirst but Newman went home to see to his wife. During working hours, Meg Newman was looked after by a kindly old neighbour, who popped in at intervals to check on her. Since the invalid spent most of her time asleep, she could be left for long periods. When he got back to the house, Newman found that the neighbour, a white-haired woman in her sixties, was just about to leave.

'How is she, Mrs Sheen?' he asked.

'She's been asleep since lunch,' replied the other, 'so I didn't disturb her.'

'Did she eat much?'

'The usual, Mr Newman. And she used the commode.'

'That's good. Thank you, Mrs Sheen.'

'I'll see you tomorrow morning.'

'I'll take Meg for another ride before I go to work.'

He went into the house and opened the door of the front room where his wife lay in bed. She stirred. Newman gave her a token kiss on the forehead to let her know that he was back then he went off to change out of his working clothes. When he returned, his wife woke up long enough to eat some bread and drink some tea but she soon dozed off again. Newman left her alone. As he ate his own meal in the kitchen, he remembered his promise to Winifred Hawkshaw. After washing the plates and cutlery, he looked in on his wife again, saw that she was deeply asleep and slipped out of the house. The drizzle had stopped.

He knew exactly where he would find Adam Hawkshaw at that time of the evening. A brisk walk soon got him to the high street and he turned into the Fountain Inn, one of the most popular hostelries in the town. The place was quite full but nobody was talking to Hawkshaw, seated alone at a table and staring into his tankard with a quiet smile on his face.

Walking jauntily into the bar, Newman clapped Hawkshaw on the shoulder by way of greeting. He then bought some beer for both of them and took the two glasses across to the table.

'I was hoping to catch you, Adam,' he said, sitting down.

'Just in time. I'll have to leave soon.'

'Where are you going?'

'That would be telling.'

Adam Hawkshaw grinned wolfishly then finished the dregs of his own drink before picking up the other tankard. He seemed in good spirits. Raising the tankard to Newman in gratitude, he took a long sip.

'How's business?' asked Newman.

'Bad,' said the other, 'though it did pick up this afternoon. Best day we've had all week. What about you, Gregory?'

'Boiler-making is a good trade. I was never apprenticed to it but those years in the forge stood me in good stead. The foreman is amazed how quickly I've picked things up.'

'Do you miss the forge?'

'I miss chatting to the customers,' said Newman, 'and I loved working with horses but the forge had to go. It was unfair on Meg to make so much noise underneath her bedroom. The new house is much quieter and she can sleep downstairs.'

'How is she?'

'As well as can be expected.' Newman leant over the table. 'But I haven't told you the news yet,' he said with a glint. 'One advantage of working by the railway station is that word travels fast. Our foreman heard it from the guard on a train to Margate. He's dead, Adam.'

'Who is?'

'The prison chaplain.'

'Never!'

'Murdered on a train last night,' said Newman, 'and I'm

not going to pretend I wasn't pleased to hear it. Narcissus Jones made your father suffer in that prison.'

'Yes.'

'And someone called him to account.'

Adam Hawkshaw seemed unsure how to react to the tidings. His face was impassive but his eyes were gleaming. He took a long drink of beer from his tankard then wiped his mouth with a sleeve.

'That's great news, Gregory,' he said. 'Thank you.'

'I thought you'd be delighted.'

'Well, I don't feel sorry for that Welsh bastard, I know that.'

'Win ought to be told. It might cheer her up.' Newman sat back. 'I spoke to her early this morning. She said that you wouldn't talk to Inspector Colbeck.'

'Nor to any other policeman,' said Hawkshaw, sourly.

'But he might help us.' The other snorted. 'He might, Adam. We've all tried to find the man who *did* kill Joe Dykes but we've got nowhere so far. And we have jobs to do, people to support. This detective has the time to conduct a proper search.'

'Keep him away from me.'

'If we can convince him that your father was innocent, we'll get him on our side – don't you see?'

'He thinks we killed that hangman.'

'That doesn't mean we don't *use* him, Adam.'

'Forget it.'

'Win agrees,' said Newman. 'If we cooperate with this inspector, he may do us all a favour and help to clear your father's name. You want the man who really killed Joe Dykes to be caught, don't you?'

Hawkshaw gave him a strange look then took another

long sip from his tankard. Wiping his mouth again, he got to his feet.

'Thanks for the beer, Gregory.'

'Where are you going?'

'I've got to see somebody.'

Without even a farewell, Adam Hawkshaw walked out of the bar.

Robert Colbeck was sporting a red silk waistcoat when he joined his superior for dinner and Edward Tallis glared at it with unconcealed distaste. Victor Leeming's apparel was far more conservative but he was criticised by the superintendent for being too untidy. It did not make for a pleasant meal. Tallis waited until they had ordered from the menu before he pitched into the two detectives.

'What the deuce is going on?' he demanded. 'I send you off to solve one railway murder and a second one is committed.'

'We can hardly be blamed for that, sir,' said Colbeck.

'But it happened right under your noses.'

'Paddock Wood is some distance from here and the chaplain was killed somewhere beyond it. We have a rough idea of the location.'

'How?'

'Because we walked beside the line,' said Leeming, able to get a word in at last. 'The inspector's theory was right.'

'It wasn't a theory, Victor,' said Colbeck, quickly, 'because we know that the superintendent frowns upon such things. It was more of an educated supposition.'

'Don't try to bamboozle me,' warned Tallis.

'It would never cross my mind, sir.'

Leeming took over. 'Inspector Colbeck believed that the killer committed his crime soon after the train left Paddock

Wood, then jumped off it before it reached the first station at Yalding.'

'A preposterous notion!' said Tallis.

'We proved it.'

'Yes,' said Colbeck. 'A shallow embankment runs alongside the line outside Yalding. We found a place where there were distinct footprints, as if someone had landed heavily and skidded down the grass. My supposition was correct.'

'I dispute that,' said Tallis. 'Those marks could have been caused by someone else – children, playing near the line, for instance.'

'A child would not leave a murder weapon behind, sir.'

'What?'

'We found it in some bushes close to the footprints.'

'A piece of wire,' said Leeming, 'covered in blood.'

'Then why didn't you bring it back with you?' asked Tallis. 'That's the kind of evidence we desperately need.'

'It's upstairs in my room, Superintendent,' Colbeck reassured him. 'The stationmaster at Yalding was kind enough to give me a bag in which to carry it. So at least we know where and precisely how the prison chaplain met his death.'

'What we really need is a suspect.'

'Two of them, sir.'

Tallis was sceptical. 'Not this phantom woman again, surely?'

'She was no phantom, sir,' said Leeming. 'There were two clear sets of footprints beside the railway line. The inspector guessed it the moment we heard the news. The woman was there to distract the victim.'

'Both of them will hang when they're caught.'

'Yes,' said Colbeck, 'for the two murders.'

'You're certain we're dealing with the same killer here?'

'Without a shadow of doubt, sir.'

'Convince me,' said Tallis, thrusting out his chin.

Colbeck had rehearsed his report in advance. It was clear and concise, containing a description of what the inspector had found at the scene of the crime and the supporting evidence that had been gathered. Leeming felt impelled to add his own coda.

'We even called at St Peter's Church in Paddock Wood,' he said. 'They still had the board that advertised the talk by the Reverend Jones. A large congregation turned up with lots of strangers among them.'

'Including, I should imagine, the killer,' said Tallis.

'He and this woman must have followed the chaplain to the station and seized their opportunity.'

'Yes,' said Colbeck. 'They realised that there wouldn't be many people on that train so there was a good chance that their victim would get into an empty carriage. The rest we know.'

'It means that I now have *two* railway companies demanding action from me,' complained Tallis. 'If anything, the management of the South Eastern Railway is even more strident. They say that disasters come in threes. Which is the next railway company to harry me?'

The waiter arrived with the first course and the discussion was suspended for a little while. Colbeck nibbled his bread roll and Leeming overcame his discomfort in the presence of the superintendent to tuck into his soup. Only when Tallis had tasted his own first mouthful of soup was he ready to resume.

'This all began with an illegal prizefight,' he noted.

'With respect, sir,' said Colbeck, 'it goes back before that. It really started with the murder of Joseph Dykes.'

'That case is closed.'

'Not to the people who believe Hawkshaw was wrongly hanged.'

'Courts of law do not make errors on that scale.'

'It's conceivable that they did so in this instance,' said Colbeck. 'But, in one sense, it doesn't really matter. It's a question of perception, sir. The people who supported Nathan Hawkshaw saw what they honestly believed was an innocent man going to the gallows. They went to exhaustive lengths on his behalf.'

'So?'

'One of those people is the man we're after, Superintendent, and there are dozens to choose from. What happened at Twyford, and on that train last night to Maidstone, is rooted here in Ashford. The killer is probably less than a couple of hundred yards from where we sit.'

'Then find him, Inspector.'

'We will. Meanwhile, precautions have to be taken.'

'Of what kind?'

'We have to ensure that Jacob Guttridge and Narcissus Jones are not joined by a third victim,' said Colbeck. 'We're dealing with a ruthless man here. He may not be content with killing the hangman and the prison chaplain. Other people may be in danger as well.'

'What other people?'

'For a start,' said Leeming, chewing a bread roll, 'the policeman who came here to arrest Hawkshaw. His name is Sergeant Lugg.'

'Empty your mouth before you speak,' snapped Tallis.

'Sorry, sir.'

'Sergeant Lugg has been warned,' said Colbeck, 'but the person we need to contact is the barrister who led the prosecution team. He tore the case for the defence apart and made the guilty verdict inevitable.'

'What's his name?'

'Patrick Perivale, sir. I'm wondering if he received one of those death threats as well.'

'Where are his chambers?'

'In Canterbury. I'm sending Victor over there tomorrow.'

Leeming was uneasy. 'Not by train, I hope.'

'By any means you choose. Mr Perivale must be alerted.'

'Very sensible,' said Tallis. 'We don't want another murder on our hands. You, I presume, will be remaining here, Inspector?'

'Yes, sir,' replied Colbeck, 'but I require your assistance. The petition for the release of Nathan Hawkshaw was sent to the Home Secretary, who refused to grant a reprieve. I'd be grateful if you could get a copy of the names on that petition from the Home Office.'

'Can't you ask for the names from that fellow who organised the campaign? What did you call him – Gregory Newland?'

'Newman, and the answer is no. He knows why we're in the town and he's not going to betray one of his friends by volunteering his name. We'll have to dig it out for ourselves. The only place we can get the full list is from the Home Office.'

'Use your influence, Superintendent,' said Leeming.

'We'd be eternally grateful, sir.'

Tallis was unconvinced. 'Will that really help to solve the murder of the prison chaplain?'

'And that of Jacob Guttridge,' said Colbeck, firmly. 'Somewhere in that list of names is the man that we want and – in all probability – his female accomplice.'

Winifred Hawkshaw was pleased to see her visitor. After a fruitless attempt to get her daughter to eat anything more than a slice of apple, she gave up and slumped in a chair. Emily retired to her room once more. Winifred could do nothing but brood on a malign fate. A once happy home was now a place of unrelieved misery. The arrival of Gregory Newman lifted her out of her gloom.

'Hello,' she said, accepting a kiss on the cheek. 'Come in.'

'I won't stay long,' he told her, removing his hat and going into the parlour ahead of her. 'I have to get back to Meg soon.'

'Of course. Sit down for a moment, anyway.'

'I will.'

'Can I get you some tea?'

'No, thank you.' Newman took a seat and Winifred sat opposite him. They exchanged a warm smile. 'I had a few words with Adam earlier on. He was in a peculiar mood.'

'He's been strange all day, Gregory. But at least he was civil to us and we must be thankful for that. Since the execution, Adam's been like a bear with a sore head.'

'I had some glad tidings for him.'

'Oh?'

'The prison chaplain was murdered on a train last night.'

'Mr Jones?' She gave a cry of delight but was instantly penitent. 'God forgive me for rejoicing in the death of another!'

'You're entitled to rejoice, Win.'

'No, it's wrong. He was a man of the cloth.'

'Are you forgetting what Nathan said about him?'

'It makes no difference. This is awful news. How did he die?'

'I don't know the details,' said Newman, disappointed by her response. 'Our foreman passed it on to me. All that he picked up was that the chaplain was found dead in a railway carriage at Maidstone.'

'Did you tell this to Adam?'

'Yes, and I thought that he'd be glad as well.'

'Wasn't he?'

'It was difficult to say, Win. There was hardly any reaction at all and that was surprising when you think of the way that he damned the chaplain at the execution. It's odd,' Newman went on, scratching his beard, 'but it was almost as if Adam already knew.'

'How could he?'

'I don't know and he didn't stay long enough for me to find out. He rushed off. Adam said that he had somewhere to go and, judging by the way he left, it must have been somewhere important.'

'He told me that he didn't sleep at all last night.'

Newman was puzzled. 'Then what is the lad up to?' He dismissed the subject and turned his attention to her. 'Let's put him aside for the moment, shall we? The person I'm really worried about is you, Win.'

'Why?'

'You looked so drawn and harassed when I saw you this morning. So desperately tired. To be honest, I thought you were sickening for something.'

'Don't fret about me, Gregory.'

'But I do.'

'I'm worn down, that's all,' she explained. 'This whole business has dragged on for so long. Nathan's arrest was such a shock to me and the trial was unbearable. As for the execution . . .'

'You shouldn't have been there. I did try to stop you.'

'He was my husband. I *had* to be there.'

'It was too much to ask of any wife, Win. It was foolish to put yourself through all that suffering outside Maidstone prison.'

'Nathan wanted me, Gregory. I gave him my word.'

She looked down at her hands as unpleasant memories surged back to make her temples pound. He could see her struggling to compose herself. Newman gave her time to recover. When she eventually glanced up, she manufactured a smile.

'I'm sorry. I try not to think about it or the pain floods back.'

'I know.'

'At least Emily was spared the sight. It would have been cruel to make her go with us. She adored Nathan – he could *talk* to her somehow. Emily always turned to him for help, not me.'

'He was a good father to her.'

'She trusted him.'

He looked upwards. 'She spends all her time in her room?'

'Yes, it's so worrying. She won't eat and she won't speak to me.'

'Would you like *me* to talk to her?'

'You?'

'Yes,' said Newman, persuasively. 'Emily and I always got on very well. She adored horses so she'd spend hours watching me at work in the forge. She talked all the time then. If a horse was well behaved, I'd let her hold the bridle sometimes. Emily liked that.'

'Nathan always talked about buying her a pony of her own.'

'Let me see if *I* can draw her out.'

Win was hesitant. 'I'm not sure that it would do any good.'

'It will certainly do no harm. Bring her down.'

'Well . . .'

'And leave us alone for five minutes,' he suggested.

Winifred considered the request for some time before she agreed to it. At length she went upstairs and Newman could hear a muted discussion with her daughter. Emily's voice then rose in protest but it was instantly silenced by her mother's rebuke. After another minute, tentative footsteps came down the stairs and the girl entered the room.

Newman stood up and gave her a welcoming smile.

'Hello, Emily,' he said.

'Hello.'

'I haven't seen you for a while. Come and sit down so that I can have a proper look at you.' She glanced nervously around the room then perched on the edge of an upright chair near the door. 'That's better,' he said, resuming his own seat. 'I was just talking to your mother about the way that you used to hold the horses for me at the forge.'

'Yes.'

'You enjoyed that, didn't you?' Emily nodded. 'I don't work as a blacksmith any more but I've still got my own horse and cart. If ever you want to come for a ride, you only have to ask. You can take the reins.'

'Thank you.'

'It's important to get out. You mustn't lock yourself away in your room like a hermit. We all miss Nathan terribly,' he went on, lowering his voice to a soothing whisper. 'When I take my wife to church on Sundays, the first prayer I say is for your father. Do you pray for him as well?'

'All the time.'

'But we haven't seen you in church for weeks. You mustn't be afraid of what other people may say,' he told her. 'You've just as much right as anyone to go to St Mary's. There are one or two narrow-minded busybodies who may turn up their noses when they see anyone from this family but you've nothing at all to be embarrassed about, Emily. Your father was innocent.'

'I know,' she said, 'that's what makes it so hard to bear.'

'You loved him dearly, didn't you?' said Newman. 'Nathan was so proud of you. He was always talking about his lovely daughter. That's how he thought of you, Emily – as his own child. And you looked on him as your real father, didn't you?'

'I tried.'

'You were a proper family, all four of you.'

She shifted on her seat. 'Can I go now, Mr Newman?'

'Am I upsetting you in some way?'

'No, no.'

'Because we both want the same thing, Emily, you know that, don't you? I'll strain every bone in my body to prove that your father did not commit that crime. That's why I got that petition together,' he said, 'and you saw how many people signed that.'

'You did so much for us, Mr Newman.'

'Then let me do a little more,' he offered, spreading his arms. 'Let me help you through this period of mourning. *Share* your grief, Emily. Talk to your mother about it. Come to church with us and show the town that you can bear this loss because you know in your heart that your father was not a killer. Stand up and be *seen*.'

'I can't, Mr Newman,' she said, shaking her head.

'Why not?'

'Don't ask me that.'

'But we're entitled to know. Your father was the best friend I ever had, Emily,' he said, soulfully, 'and I stood by him until the end. I'll not give up on him now. Nathan may be dead but he still needs us to speak up for him, to show everyone how hard we'll fight to protect his good name. You care, don't you?'

'Yes,' she said, tearfully. 'I care more than anyone.'

'Then why can't you open your heart to us?'

She stood up. 'Let me go,' she bleated, taking out a handkerchief.

'Wait,' he said, getting up to cross over to her. 'Just tell me one thing, Emily. Why are you pushing away the people who love you? Mourn for your father with the rest of us.'

'No, Mr Newman!'

'It's the right and proper way.'

'I'm sorry but I can't do it.'

'Why ever not?'

'You wouldn't understand.'

'Why not?' he pressed.

She looked him in the eyes. 'Because I feel too *ashamed.*'

CHAPTER NINE

After a hearty breakfast and a discussion as to how the investigation would proceed, Superintendent Edward Tallis was driven in a trap to Ashford Station to catch a train back to London. Both detectives were pleased to see him go but it was Victor Leeming who really savoured his departure. Slapping his thigh, he let out a controlled whoop of delight.

'He's gone at last!' he cried.

'He was only here for about twelve hours,' Colbeck pointed out.

'It seemed much longer somehow. If I have to spend a night away from my wife, I'd rather not do it under the same roof as Mr Tallis. It unsettled me, knowing that His Lordship was only a few doors away. I took ages to get off and I expect that you did as well.'

'No, I slept extremely well.'

'Well, I didn't. It's not the same without Estelle,' said Leeming. 'I missed her, Inspector.'

'And I'm sure that she missed you just as much, Victor. The sooner we solve these crimes, the sooner you can get back to her.'

Having bidden farewell to their superior, they were still under the portico outside the Saracen's Head. It was relatively early but the town was already busy. People were bustling around the streets, shops were getting ready to open and the pandemonium from the railway works showed that the first shift of the day had begun. Across the road from them, an ironmonger was going slowly through his morning routine of displaying his wares outside his shop. He heaved out a long tin bath.

'That's what I could do with,' said Leeming, covetously. 'A bath.'

'Take one back to your wife as a present.'

'I meant that I'd like to soak in warm water for half an hour.'

'I was only teasing you,' said Colbeck, smiling. 'There's no time for either of us to relax, I fear. You need to be on your way to Canterbury.'

'How will I find this Mr Perivale?'

'His chambers are in Watling Street. Get his address from there.'

'What if he doesn't live in the city?'

'Then go out to where he does live,' instructed Colbeck. 'The man could be unaware of the danger that he's in. But that's not the only reason you must speak to him, Victor. He was a key figure in the trial of Nathan Hawkshaw. I've several questions I'd like you to put to him,' he said, extracting a folded sheet of paper from his pocket and handing it over. 'I've written them down for you. Peruse them carefully.'

'Wouldn't it be better if you put them to him in person?'

'Ideally, yes.'

'You were a barrister. You talk the same language as this man.'

'Unfortunately, I can't be in two places at once.'

'Where will you be, sir?'

'Here in Ashford, for the most part,' replied Colbeck. 'I

want to make some inquiries at the station, then I need to have a longer talk with Winifred Hawkshaw and with Gregory Newman. To mount the sort of campaign that they did was a formidable challenge to anyone yet they brought if off somehow.'

'It failed all the same.'

'That's irrelevant. When I paid my first visit to Maidstone, I saw some of the leaflets calling for Hawkshaw's release, and Sergeant Lugg showed me the advertisements placed in the local newspapers. They were all well written and must have cost money to produce. Who penned that literature and how could they afford to have it printed?'

'Are they likely to tell you?'

'It depends how I ask.'

'I'd better go and find Constable Butterkiss,' said Leeming. 'He's promised to drive me to Canterbury in a trap. If he keeps on at me about the Metropolitan Police, it's going to be a very long journey. Oh, I do hope that I can get back home soon!' he went on, earnestly. 'I miss everything about London. And so do you, I daresay, sir.'

'My place is here in Kent at the moment.'

'Even you must have regrets.'

'Regrets?'

'Yes,' said Leeming, broaching a topic he had never touched on before. 'You must be sorry to be apart from Miss Andrews. I know that you like to spend time with her occasionally.'

'I'll certainly look forward to seeing her again,' admitted Colbeck, smiling to himself at the unexpected mention of her name, 'but Madeleine understands that my work always takes precedence.'

'That won't stop the lady missing you, sir.'

* * *

Madeleine Andrews scanned the newspaper report with a combination of interest and horror. Her father was eating his breakfast before going off to work. She indicated the paper.

'Have you seen this?' she asked.

'I read it on the way back from the shop, Maddy. When I saw that Inspector Colbeck was on the front page again, I knew you'd want to see it for yourself.'

'A prison chaplain has been murdered.'

'Yes.'

'What kind of monster could want to kill a priest?'

'Oh, I can think of one or two priests *I'd* like to have met in a dark alley,' said Andrews with a grim chuckle.

'Father!' she said, reproachfully.

'I'm only being honest, Maddy. When I was a boy, there was a Canon Howells at St Saviour's who could make a sermon last a whole afternoon, and he'd give you such a clout if you dozed off in the middle. I should know. I had a clip around my ear from him more than once.'

'This is not something to joke about.'

'It's no joke. I'm serious. Canon Howells was a holy terror and his deacon, Father Morris, was even worse.' He swallowed the last of his porridge. 'But I don't think you have to look very far to find the man who killed that Reverend Jones.'

'What do you mean?'

'It was obviously someone who'd been in Maidstone prison.'

'That's not what Robert thinks,' said Madeleine, pointing to the article on the front page. 'He's certain that the murderer was the same man who killed the public hangman in that excursion train.'

'Yes, a former prisoner with a grudge.'

'Robert is the detective. You keep to driving trains.'

'I'm entitled to my opinion, aren't I?' he asked, combatively.

'You'd give it in any case,' she said, fondly, 'whether you're entitled to or not. You've got an opinion on everything, Father. Nobody can silence Caleb Andrews – even when he's wrong.'

'I'm not wrong, Maddy.'

'You don't know all the facts of the case.'

'I know enough to make a comment.'

'I'd sooner trust Robert's judgement.'

'Well, he does have an eye for picking things out,' he said, wryly, 'I have to admit that. After all, he picked you out, didn't he?'

'Please don't start all that again,' she warned. 'You should be off.'

'Let me finish this cup of tea first.'

'Which train are you driving today?'

'London to Birmingham.'

'You must know that route by heart.'

'I could drive it with my eyes closed,' he boasted, draining his cup and getting up from the table. 'Thanks for the breakfast, Maddy.'

'You need a good meal inside you at the start of the day.'

'You sound like your mother.'

'What time will I expect you?'

'Not too late.'

'Will you be going for a drink first?'

'Probably,' he replied, taking his hat from the peg behind the front door. 'I'll call in for a beer or two and tell them all what I think about this latest murder. They listen to me.'

'Do you give them any choice?'

'I've got this instinct, Maddy. Whenever there's a serious crime, I always have this strange feeling about who committed it. Look at this case of the dead chaplain.'

'It's shocking.'

'The person who done him in just has to be someone who was locked up in that prison and took against the Reverend Jones. It was the same with that hangman,' he went on, putting on his hat and opening the front door. 'All prisoners hate Jack Ketch because he could be coming for them with his noose one day.'

'Yes,' she said, immersed in the paper again.

'That's enough to make anyone want revenge.'

'Maybe.'

'I know that I would if I was put behind bars.'

'Of course.'

'Goodbye, Maddy. I'm off.'

'Goodbye.'

'Don't I get my kiss?' he whined.

But she did not even hear his complaint. Madeleine had just noticed a small item at the bottom of the page. Linked to the main story, it reminded her poignantly of the last time that she had seen Robert Colbeck. An idea suddenly flashed into her mind. Caleb Andrews had to manage without his farewell kiss for once.

As soon as the shop opened, Adam Hawkshaw brought some meat out and started to hack it expertly into pieces before setting them out on the table. Other butchers were also getting ready for customers in Middle Row but all they had in response to their greeting was a curt nod of acknowledgement. The first person to appear in the passage was Inspector Colbeck. He strolled up to Adam Hawkshaw.

'Good morning,' he said, politely.

'I've nothing to say to you.'

'Are you always so rude to your customers?'

'Customers?'

'Yes,' said Colbeck. 'I didn't come to buy meat but I am shopping for information and I'm not leaving until I get it. If you insist on refusing to speak to me, of course, I may have to arrest you.'

'Why?' rejoined the other, testily. 'I done nothing wrong.'

'Obstructing a police officer in the exercise of his duties is a crime, Mr Hawkshaw. In other words, a decision confronts you.'

'Eh?'

'We can either have this conversation here and now or we'll have it when you're in custody. It's your choice.'

'I got to work in this shop.'

'Then we'll sort this out right away, shall we?' said Colbeck, briskly. 'Where were you the night before last?'

'That's my business,' retorted Hawkshaw.

'It also happens to be my business.'

'Why?'

'I need to establish your whereabouts during that evening.'

'I was in my room,' said the other, evasively. 'Satisfied now?'

'Only if we have a witness who can verify that. Do we?' Hawkshaw shook his head. 'I thought not.'

'I was on my own.'

'Gregory Newman told me that you rented a room near the Corn Exchange. There must have been someone else in the house at the time. Your landlord, for instance?'

'I can't remember.'

'I'll ask him if *he* remembers.'

'He wouldn't know,' said Hawkshaw. 'I come and go as I please.'

'I've just been talking to the stationmaster at Ashford station. He recalls a young man of your build and colouring, who took a train to Paddock Wood on the evening in question.'

'It must have been someone else, Inspector.'

'Are you quite certain of that?'

Hawkshaw met his gaze. 'I was alone in my room all evening.'

'Studying the Bible, I daresay.'

'What?'

'No,' said Colbeck on reflection, glancing at the board beside him. 'I don't think you have much time for reading – or for writing either. That's evident. I doubt if you'd even know where to find St Paul's Epistle to the Romans, would you?' Hawkshaw looked mystified. 'There you are,' Colbeck went on, 'that wasn't too difficult was it? I'll have some more questions for you in time but I'll not hold you up any longer. I need to speak to your stepmother now.'

'She's not in,' claimed the butcher.

'Then I wonder whose face I saw in the bedroom window when I crossed the high street just now. Is it possible that Mrs Hawkshaw has a twin sister living over the shop?' Hawkshaw glowered at him. 'Excuse me while I speak to someone who's a little more forthcoming.'

Meat cleaver in his hand, Hawkshaw moved across to block his way but the determination in Colbeck's eye made him change his mind. He stood aside and the detective went into the shop before tapping on the door at the rear. It was not long before he and Winifred Hawkshaw were sitting down together in the parlour. He held his top hat in his lap. She was watchful.

'I finally had a conversation with your stepson,' he said.

'Oh?'

'He seems to be having a problem with his memory.'

'Does he, Inspector?'

'Yes, Mrs Hawkshaw. He tells me that he spent the night before last alone in his room yet a witness places him – or someone very much like him – at the railway station that evening. Have you any idea where he might have been going?'

'Adam was where he said he was.'

'How can you be so sure?'

'Because we brought him up to be honest,' said Winifred, stoutly. 'I know you think he might have had something to do with the murder of the prison chaplain but you're wrong. Adam is like his father – he's been falsely accused.'

'I haven't accused him of anything, Mrs Hawkshaw.'

'You suspect him. Why else are you here?'

'I wanted to eliminate him from my inquiries,' said Colbeck, levelly, 'and I did so by discovering if he had any acquaintance with the New Testament. Patently, he does not. The reason I wanted to see you is to ask a favour.'

She was suspicious. 'What sort of favour?'

'When your husband was arrested, several people rallied around you and supported your campaign.'

'Nathan had lots of friends.'

'Did you keep a record of their names?'

'Why should I do that?'

'Because you knew how to organise things properly.'

'That was Gregory's doing, Inspector.'

'I fancy that you were intimately involved in every aspect of the campaign, Mrs Hawkshaw. You had the biggest stake in it, after all. He was your husband. That's why you fought tooth and nail to save him.'

'Yes,' she said, proudly, 'and I'd do the same again.'

'I respect that.'

'Yet you still think Nathan was guilty.'

'Oddly enough, I don't,' he told her. 'In fact, having learnt more details of the case, I'd question the safety of the conviction.'

'Do you?' Winifred Hawkshaw regarded him with frank distrust. 'Or are you just saying that to trick me?'

'Trick you into what?'

'I'm not sure yet.'

'All I want to know is who helped you in your campaign and how you funded the whole thing? There's no trickery in that, is there?'

'I can't remember all the names,' she said. 'There were far too many of them. Most people paid a little towards our expenses.'

'And what about the rescue attempt at Maidstone prison?'

'I told you before – I know nothing of that.'

'But you must have approved of it.'

'If I thought I could have got my husband out,' she said, 'I'd have climbed over the wall of the prison myself.' She looked at him quizzically. 'Are you married, Inspector?'

'No, I'm not.'

'Then you'll never understand how I felt. Nathan was everything to me. He came along at a very bad time in my life when I had to fend alone for Emily and myself. Nathan saved us.'

'But he wasn't your first husband, was he?'

'No, he wasn't. Martin was killed in an accident years ago.'

'In a fire, I believe. What were the circumstances exactly?'

'Please!' she protested. 'It's painful enough to talk about one husband who was taken away from me before his time. Don't ask me about Martin as well. I've tried to bury those memories.'

'I'm sorry, Mrs Hawkshaw. It was wrong of me to bring it up.'

'Have you finished with me now?'

'One last question,' he said, choosing his words with care. 'Your second husband had good reason to loathe Joseph Dykes. What impelled him to go after the man was the assault on your daughter, Emily. Can you recall what she told you about that incident?'

'Why you should want to know that?'

'It could be important. What precisely did she say to you?'

'Nothing at all at the time,' answered Winifred, 'because I wasn't here. I was visiting my mother. It was Nathan who had to console her. As soon as he'd done that, he left Adam in charge of the shop and charged off to find Joe Dykes.'

'With a meat cleaver in his hand.'

'You sound just like that barrister at the trial.'

'I don't mean to, Mrs Hawkshaw,' he apologised. 'Your daughter had just been through a frightening experience. She must have told your husband enough about it to make him seek retribution. Though I daresay that she reserved the full details for you.'

'No,' she confessed. 'That's the strange thing. She didn't.'

'But you're her mother. Surely, she confided in you?'

'If only she had, Inspector. I tried to get the story out of her but Emily refused to talk about it. She said that she wanted to forget it but there's no way that she could do that. In fact,' she went on as if realising something for the first time, 'that's when it really started.'

'What did?'

'This odd behaviour of hers. Emily pulled away from me. We just couldn't talk to each other properly again. I don't know what Joe Dykes did to her in that lane but I was his victim as well. He took my daughter away from me.'

* * *

Victor Leeming was in luck. When he got to the venerable city of Canterbury, he discovered that Patrick Perivale was at his chambers, interviewing a client. The detective did not mind waiting in the gracious Georgian house that served as a base for the barrister. After a ride through the countryside with Constable George Butterkiss at his most aggravating, Leeming felt that he was due some good fortune. Taking out the piece of paper that Colbeck had given him, he memorised the questions by repeating them over and over again in his head. Eventually, he was shown into a large, well-proportioned, high-ceilinged room with serried ranks of legal tomes along one wall.

Standing in the middle of the room, Patrick Perivale did not even offer him a handshake. A smart, dark-haired, dapper man in his forties with curling side-whiskers, he wore an expression of disdain for lesser mortals and he clearly put his visitor in that category. The bruising on Leeming's face made him even less welcome to someone who resented unforeseen calls on his time.

'What's this all about, Sergeant?' he inquired, fussily.

'The trial of Nathan Hawkshaw.'

'That's history. There's no cause to reopen it.'

'I simply want to discuss it, sir.'

'Now?' said Perivale, producing a watch from his waistcoat pocket and looking at it. 'I have another appointment soon.'

'You'll have to hear me out first,' said Leeming, doggedly.

'Must I?'

'Inspector Colbeck was most insistent that I should warn you.'

'About what?' asked the other, putting his watch away. 'Oh, very well,' he went on, going to the chair behind his desk. 'I suppose that you'd better sit down – and please make this visit a short one, Sergeant.'

'Yes, sir.' Leeming lowered himself into a high-backed

leather armchair that creaked slightly. 'Are you aware that the man who hanged Nathan Hawkshaw was murdered recently?'

'I do read the papers, you know.'

'Then you'll also have picked up the information that the Reverend Jones, the prison chaplain from Maidstone, was killed the night before last in a railway carriage.'

'Is this some kind of test for me on recent news events?'

'Both murder victims received death threats from someone.'

'Not for the first time, I warrant.'

'But it was for the last,' stressed Leeming. 'One of them heeded the warning but was nevertheless killed. The other – the chaplain – took no notice of the threat and lost his life as a result.'

'I was truly sorry to hear that,' said Perivale. 'I met the chaplain once and he struck me as a fellow of sterling virtue – not always the case with Welshmen. As a nation, they tend to veer towards the other side of the law.'

'Did *you* receive a death threat, sir?'

'That's none of your damned business, Sergeant!'

'I think that it is.'

'I refuse to divulge any information about what I receive in relation to my cases. It's a question of professional confidentiality.'

Leeming was blunt. 'I'd say it was a question of staying alive.'

'That's a very offensive remark.'

'There's a pattern here, sir. Two people have had—'

'Yes, yes,' said the barrister, interrupting him. 'I can see that, man. When you deal with criminal law, you inevitably make enemies but that does not mean you let the imprecations of some worthless villain upset the even tenor of your life.'

'So you *did* get a death threat.'

'I didn't say that. What I am telling you – if only you had the grace to listen – is that I am very conscious of the dangers appertaining to my profession and I take all sensible precautions. To be more precise,' he continued, opening a drawer to pull out a gun, 'I always carry this when I go abroad in the streets. It's a Manton pocket pistol.'

'Jacob Guttridge was armed as well but it did him no good.'

'Thank you for telling me, Sergeant.' He put the pistol away then stood up. 'Now that you've delivered your message, you can go.'

'But I haven't asked the questions yet, sir.'

'What questions?'

'The ones given to me by Inspector Colbeck.'

'I don't have time to play guessing games.'

'The inspector used to be a barrister,' said Leeming, irritated by the other man's pomposity. 'Of course, he worked in the London criminal courts where they get the important cases that provincial barristers like you would never be allowed to touch. If you don't help me,' he cautioned, 'then Inspector Colbeck will come looking for you to know the reason why. And he won't be scared off by that toy pistol of yours either.'

Patrick Perivale was checked momentarily by Leeming's forthrightness but he soon recovered his natural arrogance. One hand on a hip, he gave a supercilious smile.

'Why did your inspector leave the bar?'

'Because he wanted to do something more worthwhile.'

'Nothing is more worthwhile than convicting criminals.'

'They have to be caught first, sir,' said Leeming. 'Besides, you don't always see justice being done in court, do you? I've sat through too many trials to know that. I've watched guilty men go free because they had a clever barrister and innocent men convicted because they didn't.'

'I hope that you don't have the effrontery to suggest that Nathan Hawkshaw was innocent.'

'I don't know the facts of the case well enough, sir, but Inspector Colbeck has studied it in detail and he's raised a few queries.'

'He's too late. Sentence has been passed.'

'It was passed on the hangman and the prison chaplain as well.'

'Are you being frivolous, Sergeant?'

'No, sir,' said Leeming, 'I was just pointing out that this case is by no means over for those who feel aggrieved on Hawkshaw's behalf. Two lives have been lost already. We'd like to catch the killer before anyone else joins the list. To do that, we need your help.'

'What can I possibly do?'

'Tell us something about the trial. Newspaper reports can only give us so much. You were *there*.'

'Yes,' said the other with self-importance, 'and I regard it as one of my most successful cases. The reason for that is that I refused to be intimidated. I had to walk through a baying crowd outside the court and defy the howling mob in the public gallery.'

'The judge had them cleared out, didn't he?'

'Not before they'd made their point and weaker vessels would have been influenced by that. I was simply spurred on to get the conviction that Hawkshaw so obviously deserved.'

'And how did you do that?'

'By making him crack under cross-examination.'

'He maintained his innocence until the end.'

'But he'd already given himself away by then,' said Perivale with a note of triumph in his voice. 'He could not give a convincing explanation of where he was at the time of the murder. That was his undoing, Sergeant. He had no alibi and I taunted him with that fact.'

'He claimed that he walked away from Lenham to think things over and then returned in a calmer frame of mind.'

'Calmer frame of mind – balderdash! The fellow was in a state of sustained fury. He had to be to inflict such butchery on his victim. It was an assault of almost demonic proportions.'

'I know. I visited the scene of the crime.'

'Then you'll have seen how secluded it was. Hawkshaw chose it with care so that he'd not be disturbed.'

'But how did he persuade Dykes to join him there?'

'That's beside the point.'

'I don't think so,' said Leeming, remembering one of Colbeck's notes. 'Dykes would hardly agree to meet him in a private place when he knew that the butcher was after him. He'd have stayed drinking in the Red Lion where he was safe. And what proof is there that Hawkshaw was in that part of the woods, anyway?'

'He was seen there by a witness.'

'After the event. Yet there was no blood on him.'

'You're dragging up the same feeble argument as the defence,' said the barrister. 'Because there was no blood on him, they argued, he could not have committed such a violent crime. Yet there was a stream nearby. Hawkshaw could easily have washed himself clean.'

'What about his clothing? He couldn't wash blood off that.'

'Quite right. That's why his coat mysteriously disappeared.'

'His coat?'

'Yes,' continued Perivale, almost crowing over him. 'That's one little detail that you and the inspector missed. When he went to that fair in Lenham, Hawkshaw was wearing a coat.

A number of witnesses testify to that, including his son. Later, however, when he was observed by the youth returning to the farm, he had no coat on and was thoroughly dishevelled, as if he'd been involved in vigorous exercise. In other words,' he said, coming to the end of his peroration, 'he discarded his coat because it was spattered with the blood of his victim.'

'Was the coat never found?'

'No – he must have buried it somewhere.'

'Then why wasn't it discovered? The police searched the area.'

'They were only looking for a certain part of Joseph Dykes's anatomy that had gone astray – a fact that tells you everything about the mentality of the killer. Taken together, the missing coat and the absence of an alibi put Hawkshaw's neck into the hangman's noose. Hundreds of people were at that fair with more arriving every minute. If Hawkshaw really had walked off towards Ashford, somebody *must* have seen him but no witnesses could be found.'

'So where do you think he was?'

'Searching the wood for a place to commit a murder.'

'In the hope that Dykes would happen to pass by later on?'

'He enticed him there somehow.'

'I wouldn't be enticed by an angry butcher with a meat cleaver.'

'You never met Nathan Hawkshaw,' countered the barrister. 'He was an evil man and capable of any ruse. You never saw the murder dancing in those black eyes of his. When I had him in the dock,' he said, raising a finger, 'I showed the jury what he was really like. I put him under such stern cross-examination that this decent, kind, popular, reasonable man that all his friends claimed him to be suddenly turned into a snarling animal. I've never seen such a vivid expression of guilt on the face of any prisoner.'

'You have no reservations about that trial then?'

'None whatsoever.'

'What's happened since has not alarmed you in any way?'

'I'm upset that two men have died unnecessarily and in such a brutal way, but I have no fears at all for my own safety. When I led the prosecution in that trial, I was doing my bounden duty.'

'And you believe that you convicted the right man.'

'Without a scintilla of doubt,' said Perivale, lapsing into his courtroom manner. 'The evidence against Nathan Hawkshaw was quite overwhelming. Any other barrister in my place – including your Inspector Colbeck – would have done exactly the same thing as me and striven hard for a death sentence.'

'I hope that you won't make a habit of this, Inspector,' said Gregory Newman with a laugh. 'If you keep taking me away from my work, the foreman will start to dock my wages.'

'I won't keep you long.'

'We could hardly talk in the boiler shop.'

'That's a pity,' said Colbeck. 'I'd have been interested to see more of what goes on in there.'

'You really like locomotives, don't you?'

'They fascinate me.'

'They fascinate lots of people, Inspector, but only if they're running along railway lines. You're the first person I've ever met who wants to see how they're built.'

'Very noisily, by the sound of it.'

Newman grinned. The two men were standing outside the railway works in Ashford. A train was just leaving the station, adding to the industrial uproar and sending up clouds of smoke into an overcast sky. Colbeck waited until it had rolled past them.

'I like to know the way that things are put together,' said Colbeck. 'I come from a family of cabinetmakers, you see. As a boy, I was always intrigued at the way that my father could take a pile of wood and turn it into the most exquisite desk or wardrobe.'

'There's nothing quite so fancy in making a boiler.'

'It takes skill and that impresses me.'

'You wouldn't say that if you worked here,' said Newman. His grin was inviting. 'What can I tell you this time, Inspector?'

'I'd like to hear how far you've got.'

'In what?'

'Your search for the man who *did* kill Joseph Dykes.'

'Not as far as we'd like,' conceded the other, 'but we won't give up. The trouble is that we have such limited time. That holds us back.'

'Us?'

'Me and the friends helping me.'

'How many of them are there?'

'A handful,' said Newman, 'and you can include Win Hawkshaw as well. Nobody is more eager to track down the culprit than Win.'

'Do you have any suspects?'

'Yes, Inspector. One, in particular.'

'Why didn't you mention him before?'

'Let's be frank about this. You didn't come to Ashford because you thought Nathan was innocent, did you? You only came to find out who killed Jake Guttridge and now you have the murder of the prison chaplain on your plate.'

'All three murders are closely linked.'

'But only two of them have any interest for you,' said Newman.

'That's untrue. If you have any new information relating to the murder of Joseph Dykes, I want to hear it.'

'Why?'

'I told you, Mr Newman. I like to know the way that things are put together, whether they're desks, wardrobes, steam locomotives or crimes. I thrive on detail.'

The other man scratched his beard as he pondered. Like Winifred Hawkshaw, he had a deep distrust of policemen but he seemed to sense that Colbeck might be different from the general run.

'His name is Angel,' he said.

'Your suspect?'

'Yes. We don't know his surname – he may not even have one – but he's been through here a number of times over the years. I once shod a horse for him, only to discover that he'd stolen it from Bybrook Farm.'

'Did you report it to the police?'

'Of course, but Angel was long gone by then. I didn't catch sight of him again for eighteen months. He moves around, Inspector. He's half-gypsy. That type never settle.'

'Why do you think that he was Dykes's killer?'

'He was at that fair in Lenham. I saw him going into the Red Lion with my own eyes. According to the landlord, he and Joe Dykes had a disagreement over something or other. When Joe left, Angel must have sneaked out after him.'

'Do you have any proof of that?'

'None at all. But we know how Angel can harbour grudges.'

'Dykes was killed with a meat cleaver belonging to Nathan Hawkshaw. How could this man possibly have got hold of that?'

'By stealing it, Inspector. The day before the fair, it went missing from the shop along with a number of other items. Nathan told them that at the trial,' said Newman with a hint of anger, 'but they didn't believe him. That weasel of a prosecution barrister said that Nathan could have faked the burglary himself.'

'Was this other man – Angel – mentioned in court?'

'I raised his name but nobody would listen to me.'

'You have no firm evidence, then?'

'Not yet, maybe,' said Newman, 'but I'll beat it out of Angel when he shows that ugly face of his in Ashford again.'

'I should imagine he'll have the sense to keep well clear of here.'

'We'll find him somehow, Inspector.'

'And then?'

Newman grinned. 'He'll be passed on to the police.'

'I hope so,' warned Colbeck. 'We don't want anyone taking the law into their own hands. You said that a small number of you are looking out for this man.'

'That's right.'

'Perhaps you'd give me their names, Mr Newman. And while we're on the subject, I'd appreciate the names of everyone who supported the campaign to free Hawkshaw.'

'I'm afraid that I can't do that, Inspector.'

'Why not?'

'Because there are far too many of them to remember. In any case, some people simply gave some money to our fighting fund. They only did that if they could remain anonymous.'

'I see.'

'As for the handful I mentioned, you've already met one of them.'

'Adam Hawkshaw?'

'Yes. The others wouldn't want their names to be known.'

'Is that a polite way of saying that you won't divulge them?'

'I can see why you became a detective,' said Newman with amusement. He became brusque. 'If you want us on your side, you've got to help us in return. Angel is the man we want. Find him, Inspector.'

'There are other suspects at the top of my list first.'

'An innocent man was hanged. Doesn't that matter to you?'

'It matters a great deal, Mr Newman. Innocent or guilty, his death has already provoked two murders. What other crimes are there to come?' He changed his tack. 'How well do you know Emily Hawkshaw?'

'As well as anyone, I suppose,' said Newman, hunching his shoulders. 'My wife and I were not blessed with children – Meg was struck down when she was still a young woman. Nathan let us share his family. Both of the children used to come and watch me at the forge, especially Emily. She was there every day at one time.'

'Why has she drawn away from her mother?'

'What makes you ask that?'

'I spoke to Mrs Hawkshaw earlier,' explained Colbeck. 'She was upset at the way that she and her daughter seem to have lost touch. She traced it back to the assault made by Joseph Dykes.'

'That put the fear of death into Emily.'

'Then you'd expect her to turn to her mother. Yet she didn't.'

'I know.'

'Have you any idea why that might be?'

'No, Inspector,' said Newman, sadly. 'I don't. As a matter of fact, I had a word with the girl yesterday and asked her why she spurned her mother at a time when they needed to mourn together. At first, Emily wouldn't say anything at all. When I pushed her, she told me that she wanted to be left alone because she felt ashamed at Nathan's death.'

'Ashamed?'

'She feels responsible for it somehow.'

'That's absurd.'

'She's only a young girl, after all. In her eyes, none of this would have happened if she hadn't been attacked in that lane. She ran home in tears to Nathan and he swore that he'd make Joe Dykes pay. Can you see it from Emily's point of view, Inspector?'

'Yes – she gave her stepfather a motive.'

'It helped to put him on that scaffold.'

'Was Emily at the fair that day?'

'Yes, she went with Adam.'

'Did they stay together?'

Newman chuckled. 'I can see that you don't know much about country fairs,' he said. 'It's a big event for us. We don't just go there to buy and sell. There are games, dances, races, competitions and they even put on a little play this year. Emily and Adam would have split up and enjoyed the fair in their own way.'

'Did either of them witness the argument with Dykes?'

'I can't honestly say.'

'You were the one who stopped Hawkshaw from going into the Red Lion after Dykes. You persuaded him to go home, didn't you?'

'That's right, Inspector.'

'Then why didn't either of the children go as well?'

'I've no idea. I was back in my cousin's forge by then.'

'I find it surprising that Emily, in particular, didn't go with him.'

'He was in no real state for company, Inspector. He stalked off.'

'But I'm told he was very protective towards his stepdaughter.'

'He was, believe me.' He caught sight of someone out of the corner of his eye. 'Ah,' said Newman, grimacing, 'the foreman has come out to see why I'm not earning my pay. I'll have to go, Inspector.'

'Of course. Thank you for your help.'

'If you want to talk to me again, come to my house in Turton Street. Number 10. You'll find me sitting with my wife most evenings,' he said, walking away. 'I don't go far from Meg.'

'I'll bear that in mind,' said Colbeck.

There were several moments when Madeleine Andrews regretted the impulse that had taken her to Hoxton again, but she felt obscurely that her visit might be of some help to Robert Colbeck and that made her stay. Never having been in a Roman Catholic church before, she felt like an intruder and, since she was wearing black, the charge of impostor could be levelled at her as well. The morning newspaper had printed the bare details of Jacob Guttridge's funeral. Madeleine was one of a pitifully small congregation. The widow and the other mourners occupied the front row of seats while she remained at the rear of the church.

Even from that distance, she found the service profoundly moving, conducted by Father Cleary in a high-pitched voice that reached every corner of the building without effort. The burial was even more affecting and, though she only watched it from behind one of the statues in the graveyard, Madeleine felt as if she were actually part of the event. Louise Guttridge tossed a handful of earth on to the coffin then turned away. The rest of the mourners took their leave of Father Cleary and dispersed.

To Madeleine's horror, the widow walked slowly in her direction. The interloper had been seen. Madeleine feared the worst, expecting to be castigated for daring to trespass on private grief, for attending the funeral of a man she had never known and could not possibly admire. Pursing her lips, she braced herself for deserved censure. Louise Guttridge stopped a few yards from her and beckoned with a finger.

'Come on out, please,' she said.

'Yes, Mrs Guttridge,' agreed Madeleine, emerging from her refuge.

'I thought it was you, Miss Andrews.'

'I didn't mean to upset you in any way.'

'I'm sure that you didn't. You came out of the goodness of your heart, didn't you?' She looked around. 'That's more than I can say for my son. Michael and his wife could not even bother to turn up today. You, a complete stranger, have more sympathy in you than our only child.'

'It was perhaps as well that he did stay away, Mrs Guttridge.'

'Yes, you may be right.'

'At a time like this, you don't want old wounds to be opened.'

'That's true, Miss Andrews.'

'Your son has his own life now.'

'Rebecca is welcome to him!'

Louise Guttridge's face glowed with anger for a second then she went off into a reverie. It lasted for minutes. All that Madeleine could do was to stand there and wait. She felt highly embarrassed. When she saw that Father Cleary was heading their way, Madeleine squirmed and wished that she had never dared to go to Hoxton that morning. She began to move slowly away.

'Perhaps I should go, Mrs Guttridge,' she said.

'No, no. Wait here.'

'I sense that I'm in the way.'

'Not at all,' said the other woman, taking her by the wrist. 'Stay here while I speak with Father Cleary. I need to talk to you alone afterwards.' She gave a semblance of a smile. 'And don't worry about me, Miss Andrews. Jacob has been laid to rest now and I'm at peace with myself. God has provided.'

Edward Tallis was feared for the strong discipline he enforced but he was also respected for his effectiveness. As soon as he reached London, he drafted a letter to the Home Office in response to Colbeck's request. Sent by hand, it prompted an instant response and he was able to dispatch the document to Ashford. It arrived by courier that afternoon as Robert Colbeck and Victor Leeming sat down to a late luncheon at the Saracen's Head. The inspector took the long sheet of paper out of the envelope with a flourish.

'Here it is, Victor,' he said, unfolding it. 'The petition I wanted.'

'Well done, Mr Tallis!'

'I knew that he wouldn't let us down.'

'I never believed that the Home Secretary would bother to keep this sort of thing,' said Leeming. 'I imagined that he'd tear it into strips and use them to light his cigars.'

'You're being unfair to Mr Walpole. His duty is to consider every appeal made on behalf of a condemned man. In this case, he did not see any grounds for a reprieve.'

'They wanted more than a reprieve, sir.'

'Yes,' said Colbeck as he read the preamble at the top of the petition. 'It's an uncompromising demand for Nathan Hawkshaw's freedom, neatly written and well worded.'

'How many names in all?'

'Dozens. Fifty or sixty, at least.'

Leeming sighed. 'Will we have to speak to them all?'

'No, Victor. My guess is that the man we're after will be somewhere in the first column of names. Those are the ones they collected first, the ones they knew they could count on.'

'Who's at the top, sir – Hawkshaw's wife?'

'Yes,' replied Colbeck, 'followed by his son. At least, I take it to be Adam Hawkshaw's signature. It's very shaky. Then we have Gregory Newman, Timothy Lodge, Horace Fillimore, Peter Stelling and so on. The one name we don't seem to have,' he said, running his eye down the parallel columns, 'is that of Emily Hawkshaw. Now, why wouldn't the girl sign a petition on behalf of her stepfather?'

'You'll have to ask her, Inspector.'

'I will, I promise you.'

'Are there any women on the list – apart from the wife, that is?'

'Quite a few, Victor. By the look of it, most of the names are beside those of their husbands but there are one or two on their own.'

'Perhaps she's one of them.'

'She?'

'The female accomplice you believe is implicated.'

'I think that there's a good chance of that. However,' said Colbeck, setting the petition aside, 'let's order our meal and exchange our news. I long to hear how you got on. Was your visit to Canterbury productive?'

'Far more productive than the journey there and back, sir.'

'Constable Butterkiss?'

'He keeps on treating me as if I'm a recruiting sergeant for the Metropolitan Police,' grumbled Leeming. 'I had to listen to his life story and it was not the most gripping adventure I've heard. Thank heavens I never became a tailor. I'd hate to be so servile.'

'He'll learn, I'm sure. He's raw and inexperienced but I sense that he has the makings of a good policeman. Bear with him, Victor. Apart from anything else, he can help us to identify the people on this list.'

The waiter took their order and went off to the kitchen. Leeming was able to describe his jarring encounter with Patrick Perivale. He quoted some of the barrister's remarks verbatim.

'He was exactly the sort of man you said he'd be, Inspector.'

'The egotistical type that never admit they can make a mistake. I've met too many of those in the courtroom,' said Colbeck. 'Winning is everything to them. It doesn't matter if a human life is at stake. All that concerns them is their standing as an advocate.'

'I could see how Mr Perivale had built his reputation.'

'Why – did he hector you?'

'He tried to,' said Leeming, 'but I put him in his place by telling him that you'd been a barrister in London.'

'No word of thanks for warning him, then?'

'He was insulted that we'd even dared to do so.'

'Outwardly, perhaps,' decided Colbeck, 'but it was all bravado. I can't believe that even he will ignore the fact that two murders have already been committed as a result of that trial.'

'I agree, sir. I reckon that he loaded that pistol of his as soon as I left. At one point,' said Leeming with a laugh, 'I thought he'd fire the thing at me. I got under his skin somehow.'

'You were right to do so, Victor, or you'd have learnt nothing.'

'What worried me was that detail about the missing coat.'

'Yes, that disturbs me as well.'

'Hawkshaw was unable to explain its disappearance.'

'I can see why the prosecution drew blood on that point,' said Colbeck, thoughtfully. 'It further undermined Hawkshaw's defence. Nothing you've told me about him has been very flattering or, for that matter, endearing, but Mr Perivale must be an able man or he'd not have been retained in the first place. Unlike us, he saw all the evidence and made a judgement accordingly. I'm beginning to wonder if my own assumptions have been wrong.'

'You think that Hawkshaw was guilty?'

'It's a possibility that we have to entertain, Victor.'

'Then why are so many people certain of his innocence?' asked Leeming, touching the petition. 'They must have good cause.'

'Yes,' said Colbeck, 'they must. But thank you for making the journey to Canterbury. It's thrown up some valuable information.'

'What about you, sir?'

'Oh, I, too, have made a number of discoveries.'

Colbeck went on to describe what he had gleaned from the various people to whom he had talked that morning. In the middle of his account, the first course arrived and they were able to start their meal while the inspector continued. Leeming seized on one detail.

'Adam Hawkshaw went to Paddock Wood that night?' he said.

'Someone resembling him did.'

'Can't you get the stationmaster to make a positive identification? All we have to do is to take Hawkshaw along to the station.'

'Even if it *was* him on that train from Ashford, it doesn't mean that he was implicated in the murder. Adam Hawkshaw can barely write. How could someone that illiterate be able to pick out a verse in the Bible to serve his purpose?'

'Was he travelling alone?'

'Yes, Victor, and that's another point in his favour. He had no female companion. Given his surly manner,' said Colbeck, 'I doubt if he ever will have one. I'm certain that he lied to me about being at home that evening but I don't think he's a suspect for the chaplain's murder.'

'Who else travelled from Ashford to Paddock Wood on that train?'

'Several people. Some of the men from the railway works live there and use the line regularly. The only reason that Adam Hawkshaw – or the person who looked like him – stayed in the stationmaster's mind was that he was so irascible.'

'I still think that Hawkshaw needs watching.'

'He'll stay under observation, Victor. Have no fear.'

'What about this other character?' asked Leeming, spooning the last of his soup into his mouth. 'This gypsy that they're looking for?'

'His name is Angel, apparently.'

'He could turn out to be an Angel of Death.'

'If he really exists.'

'Is there any doubt about that, Inspector?'

'I don't know,' said Colbeck, sprinkling more salt on his food. 'I'm not entirely sure how I feel about Gregory Newman. He's very plausible but he's obviously keeping certain things from me. This story about someone called Angel being the potential killer of Dykes might just be a way of misleading us.'

'Why would Newman want to do that?'

'We're policemen, Victor. We represent the law that sent his best friend to the gallows. He could be trying to confuse us out of spite.'

'I'm confused enough already,' admitted Leeming.

'We can soon find out if Newman was telling the truth. You simply have to ask your assistant if he's even heard of this man, Angel.'

'My assistant?'

'Constable Butterkiss,' said Colbeck, 'and while you're at it, show him this petition and ask him where we could find the first ten people on that list, excluding Newman and the Hawkshaw family.'

'Why must I always be landed with George Butterkiss?'

'The two of you clearly have an affinity, Victor.'

'Is that what it's called?' Leeming was disconsolate. 'I can think of a very different word for it, sir.' He sat back while the waiter cleared the plates away. 'What will you be doing this afternoon?'

'Trying to speak to Emily Hawkshaw. There's something about her behaviour that troubles me. I want to find out what it is.'

Emily lay on her bed and stared up at the ceiling. She was so preoccupied that she did not hear the tap on the door. When her mother came into the room, the girl sat up guiltily.

'You startled me,' she said.

'I didn't mean to do that, Emily. I just came to warn you.'

'About what?'

'Inspector Colbeck just called again,' said Winifred Hawkshaw. 'He's very anxious to talk to you.'

Emily was alarmed. 'Me?'

'Yes.'

'Why?'

'It's nothing to be afraid of, dear,' said her mother, sitting on the bed beside her. 'He needs to ask you a few questions, that's all.'

'Is he still here?'

'No, I thought you'd need fair warning so I told him that you were asleep. The inspector will be back later.'

'What do I say to him?'

'The truth, Emily. He's trying to help us.'

'None of the other policemen did that.'

'Their minds were already made up. They'd decided that your father was guilty and that was that. Inspector Colbeck is different. You'll have to speak to him, dear. He won't go away.'

'What does he want to know?'

'You'll find out when he comes back.'

'Didn't he say?'

'He did wonder why you didn't sign that petition for your father's release,' said her mother, 'and I told him it was because you were too young, but he still felt your name should have been there. So do I, really.' She touched the girl's arm. 'Why wasn't it?'

'I don't know.'

'Gregory asked you to sign but you refused.'

'I had too many things on my mind,' whimpered the girl. 'I just couldn't bring myself to do it somehow. As soon as I saw that list of names, I lost heart. I *knew* that it would do no good.'

'It showed everyone what we felt, Emily.'

'I felt the same.'

'Then you should have been part of it.'

Emily stifled a cry then began to convulse wildly. Putting her arms around the girl, her mother tried to control the spasms but to no avail. Emily seemed to be in the grip of a seizure.

'What's wrong with you?' asked Winifred, tightening her hold on her daughter. 'Emily, what's wrong?'

Robert Colbeck had been in the town for over twenty-four hours without really exploring it properly. While he waited to speak to Emily Hawkshaw, therefore, he decided to stroll around Ashford and take the measure of the place. It also gave him an opportunity to reflect on what he had learnt earlier and to sift through the evidence that Leeming had obtained from his visit to Canterbury. The solution to the two murders aboard trains, he felt, still lay buried in the case of Nathan Hawkshaw. Until he could unearth the truth about the first killing, he was convinced that he would never catch those responsible for the other crimes. Deep in thought, he ambled gently along.

Industry was encroaching fast but Ashford was still largely a pleasant market town with a paved high street at its heart and an ancient grammar school that, for well over two hundred years, had educated privileged pupils and turned them into useful citizens. Shops dominated the centre of the town. It was in the sidestreets that houses, tenements and artisans' villas abounded. Having stopped to admire the soaring church tower of St Mary's, Colbeck read some of the inscriptions on the gravestones surrounding it, sobered by the thought that Nathan Hawkshaw had been deprived of his right to a last resting place there.

Continuing his walk, he went in a loop around the town so that he could see every aspect of it, his striking appearance causing much interest among the townspeople and more than a few comments. When he finally returned to the high street, he elected to call once more on Emily Hawkshaw but, before he could turn into Middle Row, he saw what at first he took to be some kind of mirage. Walking towards him with purposeful strides was an attractive young woman in a dress that he had seen once before. Colbeck rubbed his eyes to make sure that they were not deceiving him. At that moment, the woman saw him and quickened her step at once. Colbeck was astonished and excited to see her.

It was Madeleine Andrews.

CHAPTER TEN

Robert Colbeck escorted her into the Saracen's Head and indicated some chairs. When they sat opposite each other near the window, he beamed at her, still unable to believe that she had come all the way from London to see him. For her part, Madeleine Andrews was delighted to have found him so quickly and to have been made so welcome. She was amused by the look of complete surprise on his face.

'What's the matter, Robert?'

'Did you really take the train by yourself?' he asked.

'My father's an engine driver,' she reminded him. 'I'm well used to the railway, you know.'

'Young ladies like you don't often travel alone. Except, of course,' he added, gallantly, 'that there's nobody quite like you, Madeleine.' She smiled at the compliment. 'You create your own rules.'

'Do you disapprove?'

'Not in the least. But how did you know where to find me?'

'Your name was on the front page of the newspaper. The report said that you were conducting an investigation in Ashford.'

'Ah, well,' he said with a sigh, 'I suppose it was too much

to ask to keep my whereabouts secret for long. We'll have a batch of reporters down here in due course, assailing me with questions I refuse to answer and generally getting in my way. I'd hoped to avoid that.' He feasted his eyes on her. 'I'm so pleased to see you, Madeleine.'

'Thank you.'

'Where were you going when I saw you in the high street?'

'To the Saracen's Head.'

'You *knew* that I was staying here?'

'No,' she replied, 'but I guessed that you'd choose the best place in the town. When I asked at the station where that would be, they directed me here.'

He laughed. 'You're a detective in your own right.'

'That's what brought me to Ashford.'

Mary interrupted them to see if they required anything. Colbeck ordered a pot of tea and some cakes before sending the girl on her way. He switched his attention back to Madeleine again.

'I'm a detective by accident,' she explained. 'I don't know why but, when I saw that Jacob Guttridge's funeral was being held today, I took it into my head to go to it.'

He was stunned. 'You went to Hoxton *alone*?'

'I do most things on my own, Robert, and I felt perfectly safe inside a church. Unfortunately, there was hardly anyone there for the service. It was very sad.'

'What about Michael Guttridge?'

'No sign of him – or of his wife. That upset his mother.'

'You spoke to her?'

'Yes,' said Madeleine. 'I didn't mean to. I kept out of the way during the ceremony and didn't think that she even knew I was there. But Mrs Guttridge did notice me somehow. She said how grateful she was to see me then invited me back to the house.'

'What sort of state was she in?'

'Very calm, in view of the fact that she'd just buried her husband. Mrs Guttridge must have a lot of willpower. After my mother's funeral, I was unable to speak, let alone hold a conversation like that.'

'I put it down to her religion.'

'She told me that her priest, Father Cleary, had been a rock.'

'Why did she invite you back to the house?'

'Because she wanted to talk to someone and she said that it was easier for her to speak to a stranger like me.'

'So you were a mother-confessor.'

'Mrs Guttridge seemed to trust me,' said Madeleine. 'She didn't admit this but I had the feeling that she was using me to get information back to you. She's not an educated woman, Robert, but she's quite shrewd in her own way. She knew that you only took me to the house because she was more likely to confide in a woman.'

'I'm glad that I did take you, Madeleine,' he said with an admiring glance. 'Extremely glad.'

'So am I.'

'Much as I like Victor, you're far more appealing to the eye.'

'Oh, I see,' she said with mock annoyance, 'I was only there as decoration, was I?'

'Of course not,' he replied. 'I took you along for the pleasure of your company and because I thought that Mrs Guttridge would find you less threatening than a detective inspector from Scotland Yard.'

'She did, Robert.'

'What did you learn this time?'

'Quite a lot,' said Madeleine. 'After we left the house that day, she prayed for the courage to go into the room that her husband had always kept locked. It was a revelation to her.'

'I took away the most distressing items in his bizarre collection but I had to leave some of his souvenirs behind – and his bottles of brandy.'

'It was the alcohol that really upset her. She only agreed to marry Jacob Guttridge because he promised to stop drinking. She firmly believed that he had. But what disturbed her about that room,' she went on, 'was how dirty and untidy it was. She called it an animal's lair. You saw how house-proud she was. She was disgusted that her husband spent so much time, behind a locked door, in that squalor.'

'Gloating over his mementos and drinking brandy.'

'It helped Mrs Guttridge to accept his death more easily. She said that God had punished him for going astray. When she saw what was in that room, she realised that her husband's life away from her was much more important to him than their marriage. I tried to comfort her,' said Madeleine. 'I told her that very few men could meet the high moral standards that she set.'

'Jacob Guttridge went to the other extreme. He executed people on the gallows then gloried in their deaths.' Colbeck chose not to mention the hangman's passion for retaining the clothing of his female victims. 'It gave him a weird satisfaction of some sort. But I'm holding you up,' he said, penitently. 'Do please go on.'

'It was what she told me next that made me come here, Robert. On the day when he hanged Nathan Hawkshaw, his wife expected him home that night. But he never turned up.'

'He was probably too afraid to leave the prison in case the mob got their hands on him. What explanation did he give her?'

'That he was delayed on business.'

'Had that sort of thing happened before?'

'Once or twice,' she said. 'Mrs Guttridge was vexed that, as soon as he got home on the following day, he went straight out again to see some friends in Bethnal Green.'

'He must have been going to the Seven Stars.'

'What's that?'

'A public house where fighters train. As an avid follower of the sport, Guttridge knew it well – though he called himself Jake Bransby whenever he was there. Over a hundred people from the Seven Stars went to that championship contest on the excursion train.'

'How did you find that out?'

'Victor Leeming visited the place for me,' said Colbeck, 'though he was not exactly made welcome.' He flicked a hand. 'However, I'm spoiling your story. I'm sorry.'

'It was what happened afterwards that puzzled Mrs Guttridge,' she said, 'though she thought nothing of it at the time.'

'Of what?'

'That evening – when he got back from Bethnal Green – her husband seemed to have been running and that was most unusual for him. He was out of breath and sweating. For the next few weeks, he never stirred out of the house after dark. He used to go off to these "friends" regularly, it seems, but he suddenly stopped altogether.'

'Did she know why?'

'Not until a few days after her husband had been murdered. One of her neighbours – an old Irish woman – was leaving some flowers on her step when Mrs Guttridge opened the door and saw her there. They'd never talked properly before,' said Madeleine, 'but they'd waved to each other in the street. The old woman lived almost opposite.'

'And?'

'She remembered something.'

'Was it about Guttridge?'

'Yes, Robert. She remembered looking out of her bedroom window the night that he came hurrying back home. A man was following him. He stood outside the house for some time.'

'And Guttridge said nothing to his wife about this man?'

'Not a word. I thought it might be important so I made a point of calling on the old lady – Mrs O'Rourke, by name – when I left.'

'That was very enterprising.'

'She told me the same story.'

'Was she able to describe this man?'

'Not very well,' said Madeleine, 'because it was getting dark and her eyesight is not good. All she could tell me was he was short and fat. Oh, and he walked in this strange way.'

'With a limp?'

'No, he waddled from side to side.'

'Age?'

'Mrs O'Rourke couldn't be sure but the man wasn't young.' She smiled hopefully. 'Was I right to pass on this information to you?'

'Yes,' he said, 'and I'm very grateful. It could just be someone he fell out with at the Seven Stars but, then, a man spoiling for a fight wouldn't have gone all the way back to Hoxton to confront him. He would have tackled Guttridge outside the pub,' he went on, recalling what had happened to Leeming. 'It sounds to me as if this man was more interested in simply finding out where Guttridge lived.'

'Do you think that he might be the killer?'

'It's possible, Madeleine, but unlikely.'

'Why?'

'A short, fat man with a strange walk doesn't strike me as someone who could overpower Jacob Guttridge, not to mention Narcissus Jones. I shook hands with the prison chaplain. He was a powerful man.'

'Then who do you think this person was, Robert?'

'An intermediary,' he decided. 'Someone who found out where the hangman lived and who established that he'd be on that excursion train. He could be the link that I've been searching for,' said Colbeck, 'and you've been kind enough to find him for me.'

'Ever since you took me to Hoxton, I feel involved in the case.'

'You are – very much so.'

Mary arrived with a tray and set out the tea things on the table. She stayed long enough to pour them a cup each then gave a little curtsey before going out again. Colbeck picked up the cake stand and offered it to Madeleine.

'Thank you,' she said, choosing a cake daintily, 'I'm hungry. I was so anxious to get here that I didn't have time for lunch.'

'Then you must let me buy you dinner in recompense.'

'Oh, I can't stay. I have to get back to cook for Father. He likes his meal on the table when he comes home of an evening.' She nibbled her cake and swallowed before speaking again. 'I made a note of the train times. One leaves for London on the hour.'

'I'll come to the station with you,' he promised, 'and I insist that you take the rest of those cakes. You've earned them, Madeleine.'

'I might have one more,' she said, eyeing the selection, 'but that's all. What a day! I attend a funeral, go back to Hoxton with the widow, talk to an Irishwoman, catch a train to

Ashford and have tea with you at the Saracen's Head. I think that I could enjoy being a detective.'

'It's not all as simple as this, I'm afraid. You only have to ask Sergeant Leeming. When he went to the Seven Stars in Bethnal Green, he was beaten senseless because he was asking too many questions.'

'Gracious! Is he all right?'

'Victor has great powers of recovery,' Colbeck told her. 'And he's very tenacious. That's imperative in our line of work.'

'Is he here with you in Ashford?'

'Of course. At the moment, he's questioning one of the local constables and he'll stick at it until he's found out everything that he needs to know.'

'Let's start with the names at the top of the list,' said Victor Leeming, showing him the petition. 'Do you know who these people are?'

'Yes, Sergeant.'

'Begin with Timothy Lodge.' He wrote the name in his notebook. 'Does he live in Ashford?'

'He's the town barber. His shop is in Bank Street.'

'What manner of man is he?'

'Very knowledgeable,' said George Butterkiss. 'He can talk to you on any subject under the sun while he's cutting your hair or trimming your beard. What you must never do is to get him on to religion.'

'Why not?'

'Timothy is the organist at the Baptist church in St John's Lane. He's always trying to convert people to his faith.'

'We can forget him, I think,' said Leeming, crossing the name off in his notebook. 'Who's the next person on the list?'

'Horace Fillimore. A butcher.'

'That sounds more promising.'

'Not really, Sergeant,' contradicted Butterkiss. 'Horace must be nearly eighty now. Nathan Hawkshaw used to work for him. He took the shop over when Horace retired.'

Another name was eliminated from the notebook as soon as Leeming had finished writing it. The two men were in an upstairs room above the tailor's shop where Butterkiss had once toiled. Having sold the shop, he had kept the living accommodation. Even in his own home, the constable wore his uniform as if to distance himself from his former existence. Pleased to be involved in the murder investigation again, he described each of the people on the list whose signatures he could decipher. One name jumped up out him.

'Amos Lockyer!' he exclaimed.

'Who?'

'Right here, do you see?'

'All I can see is a squiggle,' said Leeming, glancing at the petition. 'How on earth can you tell who wrote that?'

'Because I used to work alongside Amos. I'd know that scrawl of his anywhere. He taught me all I know about policing. He left under a cloud but I still say that this town owed a lot to Amos Lockyer.'

'Why was that?'

'He was like a bloodhound. He knew how to sniff out villains.'

'Yet he's no longer a policeman?'

'No,' said Butterkiss with patent regret. 'It's a great shame. Amos was dismissed for being drunk on duty and being in possession of a loaded pistol. There were also rumours that he took bribes but I don't believe that for a second.'

'Why were you surprised to see his name on the list?'

'Because he doesn't live here any more. Amos moved away a couple of years ago. The last I heard of him, he was working on a farm the other side of Charing. But the main reason that I didn't expect to see his name here,' said Butterkiss in bewilderment, 'is that I'd expect him to side with the law. How could he call for Nathan Hawkshaw's release when the man's guilt was so obvious?'

'Obvious to you, Constable,' said Leeming, 'but not to this friend of yours, evidently. Or to everyone else on that list.'

'How many more names do you want to hear about?'

'I think I have enough for the time being. You've been very helpful, especially as you've been able to give me so many addresses as well.' He closed his notebook. 'Inspector Colbeck wanted to know if you'd ever heard of a man called Angel.'

'Angel?' Butterkiss gave a hollow laugh. 'Everyone in Kent has heard of that rogue.'

'There is such a person then?'

'Oh, yes. As arrant a villain as ever walked. Nothing was safe when Angel was around. He'd steal for the sake of it. He made Joe Dykes look like a plaster saint.'

'We were told that he may have been at the Lenham fair.'

'I'm sure that he was because that's where the richest pickings are. Angel loved crowds. He was a cunning pickpocket. At a fair in Headcorn, he once stole a pair of shire horses.'

'Someone had *those* in their pocket?'

'No, no,' said Butterkiss, unaware that he was being teased. 'They were between the shafts of a wagon. When the farmer got back to the wagon, the horses had vanished. Angel had gypsy blood and gypsies always have a way with animals.'

'Did you ever meet him?'

'I tried to arrest him once for spending the night in the Saracen's Head without paying. The nerve of the man!'

'What happened?'

'It was raining hard and he needed shelter. So he climbed in, as bold as brass, found an empty room and made himself at home. Before he left, he stole some food from the kitchen for breakfast.'

'The fellow needs locking up for good.'

'You have to catch him first and that was more than I managed to do. Angel is as slippery as an eel. The person who can really tell you about him is Amos Lockyer.'

'Why?'

'Because he had a lot of tussles with him,' said Butterkiss. 'Amos managed to find him once and put him behind bars. Next morning, when he went to the cell, the door was wide open and Angel had fled. The next we heard of him, he was running riot in the Sevenoaks area.'

'How would he have got on with Joseph Dykes?'

'Not very well. Joe was just a good-for-nothing, who stole to get money for his beer. Angel was a real criminal, a man who turned thieving into an art. He boasted about it.'

'Was he violent?'

'Not as a rule.'

'What if someone was to upset Angel?'

'Nobody would be stupid enough to do that or they'd regret it. He was a strong man – wiry and quick on his feet.'

'Capable of killing someone?' said Leeming.

'Angel is capable of *anything*, Sergeant.'

Winifred Hawkshaw was so concerned about her daughter that she went to call the doctor. Occupied with other patients, he promised to call later on to see the girl. The anxious mother went straight back to Middle Row and up to Emily's bedroom. To her dismay, it was empty. After searching the other rooms, she rushed downstairs where Adam Hawkshaw was starting to close up the shop for the day.

'Where's Emily?' she asked.

'I've no idea.'

'She's not in her room – or anywhere else.'

'I didn't see her go out.'

'Have you been here all the time?'

'Yes,' he said. 'Except when I went to buy some tobacco.'

'Emily's run away,' decided her mother.

'That's silly – where could she go?'

'I don't know, Adam, but she's not here, is she? Emily hasn't been out of the house for weeks but, as soon as my back is turned, she's off. Lock up quickly,' she ordered. 'We've got to go after her.'

'She'll come back in her own good time,' he argued.

'Not when she's in that state. I've never known her have a fit like that. There's something very wrong with Emily. Now, hurry up,' she urged. 'We must find her!'

Surrounded by a graveyard in which leafy trees threw long shadows across the headstones, St Mary's Church had stood for four centuries. It was at once imposing and accessible, a fine piece of architecture that never forgot its main function of serving the parish. Emily Hawkshaw attended the church every Sunday with her family and they had always sat in the same pew halfway down the nave. This time, she ignored her usual seat and walked down the aisle to the altar rail before kneeling in front of it. Hands clasped together, she closed her eyes tight and prayed for forgiveness, her mind in turmoil, her body shaking and perspiration breaking out on her brow. She was in a positive fever of contrition.

Madeleine Andrews had travelled from London to Ashford in a second-class compartment but Colbeck was so happy to see her, and so grateful for the information she brought, that he insisted on buying her a first-class ticket for the return journey. He removed his hat to give her a kiss on the hand then waved her off, standing wistfully on the platform until the train had rounded a bend and disappeared from sight. Deeply moved by her visit, Colbeck felt that it had been more than a pleasant interlude. What she had learnt in Hoxton might well serve to confirm his theory about how a man who courted anonymity had been traced to his home. Madeleine's attendance at a funeral had been opportune.

Deciding to call on Emily Hawkshaw again, Colbeck left the station and made for Church Street. He had already resolved to say nothing to his sergeant about the unheralded visitor. Victor Leeming was too old-fashioned and conventional to believe that a woman could be directly involved in the investigative process. It was better to keep him – and, more importantly, Superintendent Tallis – ignorant of Madeleine's part in the case. The Metropolitan Police was an exclusively male preserve. Robert Colbeck was one of the very few men who even dallied with the notion of employing female assistants.

As he approached St Mary's Church, his mind was still playing with fond memories of taking tea with Madeleine at the Saracen's Head. A loud scream jerked him out of his reverie. Ahead of him, pointing upwards with horror, was a middle-aged woman. The handful of people walking past the church immediately stopped and followed the direction of her finger. Colbeck saw the slim figure at once. Holding one of the pinnacles on top of the tower was a young woman in a black dress, trying to haul herself on to the parapet. It was Emily Hawkshaw.

Recognising her at once, Colbeck broke into a run and

dashed into the church, shedding his hat and frock coat as he did so and diving through the door to the tower. He went up the steps as fast as he could, going up past the huge iron bells and feeling a first rush of air as he neared the open door at the top. When he emerged into daylight, he saw that Emily was poised between life and death, clinging to the pinnacle while standing precariously on the parapet. Intent on flinging herself off, the girl seemed to be having second thoughts.

Colbeck inched slowly towards her so that he would be in her field of vision. In order not to alarm her, he kept his voice calm and low.

'Stay there, Emily,' he said, 'I'll help you down.'

'No!' she cried. 'Stay back.'

'I know that you must hate yourself even to think of doing this but you must remember those who love you. Do you really want to *hurt* your family and your friends?'

'I don't deserve to be loved.'

'Come down from there and tell me why,' he suggested, moving closer. 'Killing yourself will solve nothing.'

'Keep away from me – or I'll jump.'

'No, Emily. If you really meant to do it, you'd have gone by now. But you knew that there would be consequences, didn't you? Others would suffer terribly, especially your mother. Don't you think she's been through enough already?'

'I've been through it as well,' sobbed the girl.

'Then share your suffering with her. *Help* each other, Emily.'

'I can't.'

'You must,' he said, gently. 'It's the only way.'

'God will never forgive me.'

'You won't find forgiveness by jumping off here. To take your own life is anathema. To do it on consecrated ground makes it even worse. This is a church, Emily. You understand what that means, don't you?'

She began to tremble. 'I just can't go on.'

'Yes, you can. It won't always be like this. Time heals even the deepest wounds. You have a long life ahead of you. Why destroy it in a moment of despair? You're loved, Emily,' he said, taking a small step towards her. 'You're loved and *needed*.'

The girl fell silent as she considered what he had said and Colbeck took it as a good sign. But she was still balanced perilously on the edge of the parapet. One false move on his part and she might jump. From down below, he could hear sounds of a crowd gathering to watch. Emily Hawkshaw had an audience.

'You know that this is wrong,' he told her, moving slightly closer. 'You were christened in this church and brought up in a God-fearing household. You know that it mustn't end this way. It will leave a stain on the whole family.'

'I don't care about that.'

'What *do* you care about? Tell me. I'm here to listen.'

'You wouldn't understand,' she said, trembling even more.

'Then come down and talk to someone who would understand.' He ventured another step. 'Please, Emily. For everyone's sake – come down.'

The girl began to weep and cling more desperately to the pinnacle. It was as if she finally realised the implications of what she had intended to do. Suddenly, she lost her nerve and began to panic. Emily tried to turn back but her foot slipped and she lost her hold on the pinnacle. There was a gasp of horror from below as she teetered on the very brink of the parapet, then Colbeck darted forward to grab her and snatched her back to safety.

Emily Hawkshaw fainted in his arms.

* * *

After another tiring day in the boiler shop, Gregory Newman was eager to get home to Turton Street. As he came out of the railway works, however, he found Adam Hawkshaw waiting to speak to him.

'Good evening, Adam,' he said, cheerily.

'Can you come to the shop?' asked the other. 'Mother wants to talk to you as soon as possible.'

'Why – what's happened?'

'Emily tried to commit suicide.'

'Dear God!'

'She was going to throw herself off the church tower.'

'What on earth made her do that?'

'We don't know, Gregory.'

'Where is Emily now?'

'She's in bed. The doctor gave her something to make her sleep.'

'Did she change her mind at the last moment?'

'No,' said Hawkshaw with a tinge of resentment. 'That Inspector Colbeck went up the tower and brought her down again. We saw him catch her as she was about to fall. It's a miracle she's alive.'

'This is terrible news!' exclaimed Newman.

'Then you'll come?'

'Of course. Let me go home first to take care of my wife then I'll come straight away. How has Win taken it?'

'She's very upset.'

'Emily – of all people! You'd never have thought she'd do anything as desperate as this. Whatever could have provoked her?'

'She took fright when Inspector Colbeck wanted to question her.'

'And did he?'

'No, Emily ran away before he came back. She sneaked out when we weren't looking. We were searching for her when we heard this noise from the churchyard. We got there in time to see it all.'

Newman started walking. 'Tell Win I'll be there directly.'

'Thanks,' said Hawkshaw, falling in beside him.

'Did Emily really mean to go through with it?'

'She didn't say. When she was brought down from the tower, she was in a dead faint. She came out of it later but she refused to tell us anything. Emily just lay on the bed and cried.'

'The doctor was right to give her a sedative.'

'I'm worried, Gregory,' said Hawkshaw, showing a rare touch of sympathy for his stepsister.

'So am I.'

'What if Emily tries to do that again?'

The suicide attempt was also being discussed over a drink at the Saracen's Head. Victor Leeming was astonished by what he heard.

'Why did she do it, Inspector?' he asked.

'I'm hoping that that will emerge in time.'

'A young girl, throwing her life away like that – it's unthinkable.'

'Emily had come to the end of her tether.'

'She must have been in despair even to consider suicide. I mean, it's the last resort. You're only driven to that when there seems to be absolutely no future for you.' He gave a shrug. 'Was she so attached to her stepfather that she couldn't live without him?'

'I don't know,' said Colbeck. 'What is clear, however, is that Emily Hawkshaw is consumed with guilt over something.

She's nursing a secret that she's not even able to divulge to her mother.'

'Is there any chance she'll confide in you, sir?'

'I doubt it.'

'But you saved her life.'

'She may resent me for that. I brought her back to the very things she was running away from. We'll have to wait and see, Victor. However,' he went on, as Leeming drank some beer, 'tell me what you discovered. Did you find Constable Butterkiss at all helpful?'

'Very helpful.'

Putting his glass aside and referring to his notebook, Leeming described the people on the petition whom he considered to be potential suspects. Of the ten names that he had written down, six had acquired a tick from the sergeant. All of the men lived in or near Ashford and had a close connection with Nathan Hawkshaw.

'Did you ask him about Angel?' said Colbeck.

'I did, Inspector, and there certainly is such a man.'

'Would he have been at that fair in Lenham?'

'Definitely.'

Leeming passed on the details given to him by George Butterkiss and argued that Angel had to be looked at as a potential suspect for the murder of Joseph Dykes. The man whose name had first been voiced by Gregory Newman had a long record of criminality. He had been in the right place at the right time to attack Dykes.

'But we come back to the old problem,' said Leeming. 'How could Angel have persuaded Dykes to go to such a quiet part of the wood?'

'He couldn't, Victor – and neither could Nathan Hawkshaw.'

'So how did the victim get there?'

'I can think of only one possible way.'

'What's that, Inspector?'

'Dykes had been drinking heavily,' said Colbeck, 'and probably looked to spend most of the day at the Red Lion. What was the one thing that could get him out of that pub?'

'A knife in his ribs.'

'There was a much easier way. A woman could have done it. When you returned from the scene of the crime, you told me that it was a place where young couples might have gone. I think that someone may have deliberately aroused Dykes's lust.'

'From what I hear, that wouldn't have taken much doing.'

'Once she had lured him to the wood, the killer could strike.'

'Yes,' said Leeming, warming to the notion. 'The woman was there to distract the victim. If that's what happened, it's just like those two murders on the train.'

'It's uncannily like them,' agreed Colbeck, 'and it raises a possibility that has never even crossed our minds before. Supposing that all three murders were committed by the same man?'

'Angel?'

'Hardly.'

'Why not?'

'I can accept that he's a legitimate suspect for the murder of Dykes but he had no motive to kill the hangman or the prison chaplain. No, it must be someone else.'

'Well, it absolves Hawkshaw of the crime,' observed Leeming. 'If the same man is responsible for all three murders, Hawkshaw must have been innocent. He couldn't have killed two people after he was dead.'

'There's another fact we have to face,' said Colbeck, taking a sip of his drink as he meditated. 'This is pure speculation, of course, and we may well be wrong about this. But, assuming we're not, then the man who butchered Joseph Dykes in that wood allowed someone else to go to the gallows on his behalf.'

'Then why did he go on to commit those revenge murders?'

'Guilt, perhaps.'

'Remorse over the way that he let an innocent man be hanged?'

'Perhaps. He may be trying to make amends in some perverse way by killing the people whom he feels made Nathan Hawkshaw's last hour on earth more agonising than it need have been.'

'It doesn't add up, sir.'

'Not at the moment, Victor, but it opens up a whole new line of inquiry.' He glanced down at the petition. 'And it suggests that someone on this list needs to be caught very quickly indeed.'

'Yes, he could have killed *three* victims.'

'Four,' said Colbeck. 'You're forgetting Nathan Hawkshaw.'

'Of course. He had the most lingering death of all. He was made to take the blame for someone else's crime.'

'That's what it begins to look like.' He picked up the petition. 'We must make our first calls this evening. And if we have no success with this part of the list, we must work our way through the rest of it – and that includes the women.'

'Wait a moment, sir.'

'Yes?'

'Would someone who let Hawkshaw go on trial for a murder that he didn't commit then sign a petition for his release?'

'What better way to disguise his own guilt?'

'That's true. Who do we start with, sir?'

'Peter Stelling. He's an ironmonger. We can rely on him to have a ready supply of wire. We'll have to see if his stock contains anything resembling the murder weapon we found near Paddock Wood.'

'Does that mean we cross Angel off the list?'

'For the moment. From what you've told me about him, we'd have the devil's own job tracking him down.'

'We'd need Amos Lockyer to do that, Inspector.'

'Who?'

'He was a policeman here for years,' said Leeming, 'and he helped Constable Butterkiss a great deal. Lockyer was dismissed for being drunk on duty and carrying a loaded firearm. According to Constable Butterkiss, he was a real bloodhound. He was the only person who ever managed to find Angel and arrest him.'

'Where is this man now?'

'Working on a farm near Charing, apparently. At least, that's what Butterkiss told me. He reveres the man though he was amazed to see his name on that petition.'

'I don't recall an Amos Lockyer there,' said Colbeck, studying the document closely. 'Where is he?'

'Right there,' said Leeming, pointing to the illegible squiggle in the first column. 'I couldn't read it either but that's definitely him. Lockyer's father used to be a watchman in the town. That's what got him interested in being a policeman.'

'You never mentioned him earlier.'

'That was because I'd crossed him off my list.'

'Simply because he was once a local constable?'

'No, sir. I'd need a better reason than that. We both know that there are bad apples in police uniform as everywhere else. I only crossed off Amos Lockyer when Butterkiss told me a little more about him.'

'Go on.'

'To start with,' said Leeming, 'he's no spring chicken. And he has a bad leg. A poacher he tried to arrest shot him in the thigh. I can't see him leaping out of a moving train, can you?'

'Yet you say he had great skill in finding people?'

'That's right. Lockyer was famed for it.'

Colbeck thought hard about what Madeleine Andrews had learnt in Hoxton. Jacob Guttridge had been followed by an older man with an unusual rolling gait. It was too much of a coincidence.

'I'll speak to the ironmonger on my own,' he decided.

'What about me?'

'Go back to Constable Butterkiss and tell him that your need his services again.' Leeming pulled a face. 'Yes, I know that he's not your idea of a boon companion, Victor, but this is important.'

'Can't it wait until tomorrow?'

'No. Ask him to drive you to Charing at once.'

'Not another long journey with George Butterkiss!'

'You need him to find the farm where this Amos Lockyer works. And when you do,' said Colbeck, 'I want you to bring the man back to Ashford immediately.'

'How is she now, Win?' asked Gregory Newman, his face pitted with concern. 'I was shocked when Adam told me what she tried to do.'

'We all were,' said Winifred Hawkshaw. 'It was terrifying to see her up on that church tower. Thank heaven she was saved! The doctor gave her some pills to make her sleep. Emily won't wake up until the morning.'

'Make sure that she doesn't slip out again.'

'I'll lock the door of her room. It's dreadful to treat my

own daughter like a prisoner but it may be the only way to keep her alive.'

They were sitting in the room at the rear of the butcher's shop. Though he had been home to see to his wife, Newman had not bothered to change out of his work clothes or to have a meal. The crisis required a swift response and he had run all the way to Middle Row. Winifred Hawkshaw was deeply grateful.

'Thank you, Gregory,' she said, reaching out to touch him. 'I knew that I could count on you.' She gave a pained smile. 'You must be so sick of this family.'

'Why?'

'We've brought you nothing but trouble.'

'Nonsense!'

'Think of all those arguments we had with Adam when he was younger. You were the one who stepped in and found him somewhere else to live. Then came Nathan's arrest and all the horror that followed it. And now we have Emily trying to kill herself.'

'Is that what she really did, Win?'

'What do you mean?'

'I'm wondering if she was just trying to frighten you.'

'Well, she certainly did that,' admitted Winifred. 'I was scared stiff when I saw her up there. And I do believe she meant to jump. Why else would she have climbed up on that ledge? It was so dangerous.'

'Do you have any idea what made her do it?'

'Only that she's been very unhappy for weeks – but, then, so have we all. Emily is no different to the rest of us.'

'Adam said that Inspector Colbeck wanted to question her.'

'That's right. He called here earlier for the second time today. I sent him away. I pretended that she was asleep so that

I could warn her that she'd have to talk to a policeman from London.'

'What did she say to that?'

'Well, she wasn't very pleased,' replied Winifred. 'Emily seemed to be afraid of talking to anyone. Then I mentioned the petition again. When I asked her why she didn't sign it, she had this sudden fit. It was like the kind of seizure that my mother sometimes has.'

'Emily needs to be looked at properly by the doctor.'

'I know, Gregory. After I'd calmed her down, I told Emily that I couldn't let her go on like this any longer. But she begged me not to call in the doctor again.'

'Why not?'

'She wouldn't say. Emily just cried and cried.'

'It's been weeks since the execution now,' said Newman, running a hand through his beard. 'I'd have expected her to be over the worst. It's not as if she was actually there, after all.'

'No, I made her stay away.'

'How did she sneak out today?'

'Eventually,' she said, 'I went out to call the doctor and Adam was busy elsewhere. Emily must have picked her moment and gone. As soon as I realised she wasn't here, we went off in search of her. Then we heard all the noise coming from the churchyard.'

'It must have been dreadful for you,' he said, getting up to put an arm around her. 'To lose a child is bad enough for any parent, Win, but to lose one in that way would have been unbearable.'

'Yes,' she whispered, nestling against his body.

'I just can't believe it. Emily was always so trustworthy.'

'Not any more, Gregory.' She pulled back to look up at him. 'I'll be afraid to take my eyes off her from now on. I dread to think what might have happened if Inspector Colbeck hadn't gone up that tower after her.'

'What did he do exactly?' he said, standing away from her.

'He talked to her very quietly and made her change her mind. When she tried to get down again, she slipped and almost fell. Honestly, Gregory, my heart was in my mouth at that moment.'

'But the inspector grabbed her just in time?' She nodded. 'We all owe him thanks for that. I could see that even Adam was upset and he's never got on well with his stepsister.' He resumed his seat. 'You said that Inspector Colbeck called earlier today.'

'Yes, he wanted to question Adam.'

'What about?'

'That murder the other night.'

'It had nothing to do with Adam,' he said, staunchly.

'I know but the stationmaster remembers someone who looked like him, taking a train to Paddock Wood that same night.'

'Lots of people look like Adam. There are two or three young men at the railway works who could be taken for his twin. Did the inspector have anything else to say?'

'A great deal. He came in here to see me.'

'Why?'

'It was rather upsetting, Gregory,' she said, wrapping her arms around her body as if she were cold. 'Out of the blue, he asked me what happened to my first husband. He wanted to know how Martin died.'

'That was an odd thing to ask.'

'He did apologise when I told him I didn't want to talk about that. So he turned to Emily instead. The inspector was interested to know what she said to me after she was attacked by Joe Dykes.'

'But you weren't here at the time, were you?'

'No, I was over in Willesborough. She spoke to Nathan.'

'And – like any father – he went charging off after Joe. I remember him telling me about it afterwards,' said Newman. 'He said that this fierce anger built up inside him and he couldn't control himself. It was just as well that he didn't catch up with Joe that day.'

'But it helped to hang him all the same,' she said, grimly. 'Going off in a temper like that. There were half a dozen witnesses who couldn't wait to stand up in court and talk about the way they'd seen him running down the street with a cleaver.'

'I'd have done no different if Emily had been my daughter.'

'I suppose not.'

'Joe Dykes was a menace to any woman.' He sat back in his chair. 'So what did you tell Inspector Colbeck?'

'The truth – that Emily wouldn't talk to me about it.'

'She confided in Nathan.'

'Yes, and he told me what she said but it was not the same. I wanted to hear it from my daughter's own lips. And there was another thing that worried me at the time, Gregory.'

'What was that?'

'Well,' she said, 'Nathan and I had always been very honest with each other. Yet when I tried to talk to him about Emily, and what she'd said when she came running back here that day, I had the feeling that he was holding something back. I only ever got part of the story.'

It took Colbeck less than two minutes to establish that Peter Stelling was not the killer. Since he had a business to run, and a wife and four children to look after, the ironmonger would not have had the necessary freedom of movement. In addition,

Stelling was such a mild-mannered man that it was difficult to imagine him working himself up into the fury symbolised in the slaughter of Joseph Dykes. The second name on Colbeck's list did not keep him long either. As soon as he learnt that Moses Haddon, a bricklayer, had been in bed for a week after falling from a ladder, he was able to remove his name from the list. In the case of both men, however, he took the trouble to ask if they could describe Amos Lockyer for him. Each man spoke well of the former policeman and said that he was short, stout and well into his fifties. They confirmed that the wound in his leg had left him with a rather comical waddle.

He owed a debt of gratitude to Madeleine Andrews for providing a possible link between Lockyer and Jacob Guttridge, and it gave him his first surge of optimism since they had arrived in Ashford. Relishing the memory of Madeleine's surprise visit to the town, he went on to question the next person, wearing a broad smile on his face.

She was in the kitchen when she heard the front door open and shut.

'Where have you *been*?' she asked, chastising her father with her tone of voice. 'Your dinner is getting cold.'

'I was held up, Maddy,' said Caleb Andrews, coming into the kitchen to give her a conciliatory kiss. 'We got talking about the murder of that prison chaplain and time just flew by.'

'Helped along by a couple of pints of beer no doubt.'

'A man is entitled to a few pleasures in life.'

Madeleine served the meal on to two plates and set them on the table. She sat opposite her father and passed him the salt. He shook a liberal quantity over his food.

'They all agreed with me, you know,' he said.

'You mean that they didn't dare to disagree.'

'The killer was someone who served time in Maidstone prison.'

'I'm not so sure, Father.'

'Well, I am,' he asserted, stabbing the air with his knife. 'For two pins, I'd give you the money to take a train to Ashford so that you can tell Inspector Colbeck what I said. He'd know where to look then.'

'Oh, I fancy that he can manage without your help.'

'I have this feeling in my bones, Maddy.'

'Save it for your workmates,' she advised. 'Robert is a trained detective. He knows how to lead an investigation and it's not by relying on suggestions from every Tom, Dick and Harry.'

'I'm not Tom, Dick or Harry,' he protested. 'I'm your father and, as such, I've got connections with this case. I told them all that Inspector Colbeck had come calling here.'

'Father!'

'Well, it's true, isn't it?'

'I don't want you and your friends gossiping about me.'

'What am I supposed to tell them – that you've taken the veil?'

'Don't be silly.'

'Then stop pretending that you and the inspector are not close. You're like a locomotive and tender.' He swallowed a piece of meat. 'Well, maybe not *that* close.' He winked at her. 'Yet, anyway.'

Her gaze was steely. 'You're doing it again, aren't you?'

'It's only in fun, Maddy.'

'How would you like it if I stopped cooking your meals for you and told you it was only in fun?'

'That would be cruel!'

'At least, you'd know how I feel.'

'Maddy!' She picked at her own food and he watched her for a moment. 'Look, I'm sorry. I let my tongue run away with me sometimes. I won't say another word about him. I promise you.' He sliced up his beans. 'What have you been doing with yourself all day?'

'Oh, I had a very quiet time,' she said, determined to conceal from him where she had been. 'I cleaned the house then read for a while.'

'Did you work on the painting?'

'A little.'

'When are you going to give it to him?'

'When it's ready, Father. And,' she told him, pointedly, 'when you're not here to embarrass me.'

'I wouldn't embarrass you for the world.'

'You've done it already since you walked through that door.'

'Have I? What did I say?'

'I'd rather not repeat it. Let's talk about something else.'

'As you wish.' He racked his brain for a new subject. 'Oh, I know what I mean to tell you. When you read the paper this morning, did you see that Jake Guttridge was being buried today?'

'Really?'

'I bet he was there as well.'

'Who?'

'The killer. The man who strangled him on that excursion train. I'd bet anything that he turned up at the funeral just so that he could get in a good kick at the coffin. It's exactly the sort of thing that he'd do.'

Madeleine ate her dinner, not daring to say a word.

Because they had been asked to bring someone back with them, Victor Leeming and George Butterkiss travelled in the cart that had taken them to Lenham on their first journey together. This time it smelt in equal proportions of fish, animal dung and musty hay. The potholes made an even more concerted assault on the sergeant's buttocks and he was glad when they finally reached Charing, a charming village on the road to Maidstone. His aches and pains increased in intensity when he learnt that they had gone there in vain. The farmer for whom Amos Lockyer had worked told them that he had sacked the man months earlier for being drunk and unreliable.

Hearing a rumour that Lockyer had taken a menial job on the staff at Leeds Castle, they rode on there, only to be met with another rebuff. After only a short time in service at the castle, Lockyer had failed to turn up for work and vanished from his lodging. Nobody had any idea where he could be. George Butterkiss drove his unhappy passenger back towards Ashford. The road seemed bumpier than ever.

'Why is the inspector so keen to speak to Amos?' asked Butterkiss.

'I don't know,' said Leeming.

'Does he want him to help in the investigation?'

'Possibly.'

Butterkiss beamed. 'It will be wonderful to work alongside him once again,' he said. 'Amos Lockyer, me and two detectives from the Metropolitan Police. A quartet like that is a match for any villain.'

Conscious that he would have to listen to his zealous companion all the way back, Leeming gritted his teeth. When rain began to fall, he swore under his breath. It was the last straw.

'We'll be soaked to the skin,' he complained.

'I know what Amos would have done at a time like this,' said Butterkiss, remaining resolutely cheerful. 'Never let things get on top of you – that was his motto. If Amos was sitting where you are, Sergeant, do you know what he'd suggest?'

'What?'

'That we sing a song to keep up our spirits.'

'Don't you dare!' warned Leeming, turning on him. 'I don't want my spirits kept up after this wild goose chase. If you sing so much as a single note, Constable Butterkiss, you'll be walking all the way home.'

Adam Hawkshaw waited until it was quite dark before he opened the door of his lodging and peeped out. The rain was easing but it was still persistent enough to keep most people off the streets that evening. When he saw that nobody was about, he pulled down his hat, stepped on to the pavement and pulled the door shut behind him. Hands in his pockets, he walked swiftly off into the gloom.

Robert Colbeck was beginning to get worried. He had expected Leeming and Butterkiss to be back hours earlier with the man they had sought. Charing was no great distance from the town, miles closer than Lenham. Even if they had had to go to an outlying farm, they should have returned by now. The combination of rain and darkness would slow them down but not to that extent. Colbeck wondered if they had encountered trouble of some sort. He sat near the window of his bedroom for what seemed like an age before he finally heard the rattle of a cart below.

Hoping that they had at last come back, he went downstairs and hurried to the door, ignoring the rain and stepping out from under the portico. By the light of the street lamps, to his relief, he saw a wet and disgruntled Victor Leeming, seated on the cart beside an equally sodden George Butterkiss. There was no third person with them. Before he could even greet them, however, Colbeck was aware of a sudden movement in the shadows on the opposite side of the street. A pistol was fired with a loud bang. The noise frightened the horse and it bolted down the high street with the driver trying desperately to control it. Taken by surprise, Leeming was almost flung from the cart.

Robert Colbeck, meanwhile, had fallen to the ground with a stifled cry and rolled over on to his back. Satisfied with his work, the man who had fired the shot fled the scene.

CHAPTER ELEVEN

It was ironic. Robert Colbeck, the assassin's intended target, suffered nothing more than a painful flesh wound in his upper arm whereas Victor Leeming, who just happened to be nearby at the time, collected a whole battery of cuts and bruises when he was hurled from the cart as it overturned. The sergeant was justifiably upset.

'It's not fair,' he protested. 'All that I expected to do was to ride to Charing to pick someone up. Instead of that, I'm drenched by rain, bored stiff by Constable Butterkiss, beaten black and blue by that vicious cart of his, then flung to the ground like a sack of potatoes.'

'You have my sympathy, Victor.'

'And on top of all that, we came back empty-handed.'

'That was unfortunate,' said Colbeck.

They were in his room at the Saracen's Head, free at last from the inquisitive crowd that had rushed out into the street to see what had caused the commotion. Colbeck's injured arm had now been bandaged and the doctor had then treated Leeming's wounds. Back in dry clothing again, the sergeant was puzzled.

'Why are you taking it so calmly, sir?' he asked.

'How should I be taking it?'

'If someone had fired at me, I'd be livid.'

'Well, I was annoyed at the damage he did to my frock coat,' said Colbeck, seriously. 'I doubt if it can be repaired. And the blood will have ruined my shirt beyond reclaim. No,' he continued, 'I prefer to look at the consolations involved.'

'I didn't know that there were any.'

'Three, at least.'

'What are they?'

'First of all, I'm alive with only a scratch on me. Luckily, the shot was off target. The man is clearly not as adept with a pistol as he is with a piece of wire.'

'You think that it was the killer?'

'Who else, Victor? He's frightened because we are closing in on him. That's the second consolation. We've made more progress than we imagined. The man is right here in Ashford. He's given himself away.'

'What's the third consolation, sir?'

'He thinks that he killed me,' said Colbeck. 'That's why I fell to the ground and stayed there. Also, of course, I didn't want to give him the chance to aim at me again. Believing I was dead, he ran away. There was no point in trying to chase him because I had this searing pain in my arm. I'd never have been able to overpower him. Much better to give him the impression that his attempt on my life had been successful.'

'He's in for a nasty surprise.'

'Yes, but it does behove us to show additional caution in future.'

'I will,' said Leeming. 'I'll never ride on that blessed cart again!'

'I was talking about the killer. He's armed and ready to shoot.'

'You mentioned a pistol just now.'

'That's what it sounded like,' said Colbeck, 'though I couldn't be sure. It all happened in a split second. One of the first things we need to do is to find the bullet. That will tell us what firearm was used.'

'We'll have to wait until daylight to do that.'

'Yes, Victor. In the meantime, we need to talk to Butterkiss.'

'Keep him away, Inspector! He almost did for me.'

'He tried his best to control that runaway horse.'

'But he still managed to overturn the cart,' said Leeming, ruefully. 'And while I hit the ground and took the impact, Constable Butterkiss simply landed on top of me. He wasn't really hurt at all.'

'Nevertheless, I'd like you to fetch him.'

'*Now*, sir?'

'If you feel well enough to go. His local knowledge is crucial to us. Give him my compliments and ask if he can spare us some time.'

'I don't need to ask that. If we're not very careful, he'd spare us twenty-four hours a day. The man is so blooming eager.'

'Eagerness is a good quality in a policeman.'

'Not if you have to ride beside him on a cart!' Leeming went to the door. 'Will you come down to meet him, sir?'

'No,' said Colbeck, glancing round, 'this room is more private. And nobody will be able to take a shot at me in here. Be careful how you go.'

'Yes, Inspector.'

'And you might ask him to bring needle and thread.'

'Why?'

'He was a tailor, wasn't he? Perhaps he can repair my coat.'

* * *

When the visitor called, George Butterkiss was regaling his wife with the story of how he had fought to control the galloping horse in the high street. He broke off to answer the door and was delighted to hear the summons delivered by Victor Leeming.

'I'll get my coat at once, Sergeant,' he said.

'Talking of coats,' said the other, detaining him with a hand, 'the inspector has a problem. That bullet grazed his arm and left a hole in his sleeve. He's very particular about his clothing.'

'Inspector Colbeck would be a gift to any tailor.'

'Can you help him?'

'I'll need to see the damage first. A simple tear can be easily mended but, if the material has been shot away, it may be a question of sewing a new sleeve on to the coat.'

Butterkiss ran swiftly up the stairs. When he reappeared soon afterwards, he was back in police uniform even though he only had to walk thirty yards or so to the Saracen's Head. His enthusiasm was quite undiminished as they strolled along the pavement together. The sergeant found it lowering.

'I haven't told you the good news,' said Butterkiss.

'Is there such a thing?'

'Yes, Sergeant. When I took the horse back and explained what had happened, the owner examined the animal carefully. It had no injuries at all. Isn't that a relief?'

'I'd have had it put down for what it did to me.'

'You can't blame the horse for bolting like that.'

'Well, I'm in no mood to congratulate it, I can tell you.'

'How do you feel now?'

'Vengeful.'

'I thought that we had a lucky escape.'

'What's lucky about being thrown head first from a moving cart?'

Butterkiss laughed. 'You will have your little joke, Sergeant.'

They turned into the Saracen's Head and went up the stairs. When they were let into Colbeck's room, they were each offered a chair. The inspector perched on the edge of the bed.

'Thank you for coming so promptly, Constable,' he said.

'Feel free to call on me at any hour of the day,' urged Butterkiss.

'We need your guidance.'

'It's yours for the asking, Inspector.'

'Then I'd like you to take another look at these names,' said Colbeck, handing him the petition. 'Are you ready, Victor?'

'Yes, sir,' said Leeming, taking his notebook dutifully from his pocket. 'I'll write down all the relevant details.'

'We drew a blank with the first batch of names. Can you take us slowly through the next dozen or so, please?'

'If I can read their handwriting,' said Butterkiss, poring over the document. 'There are one or two signatures that defy even me.'

'Do your best, Constable.'

'You can always count on me to do that.'

Taking a deep breath, he identified the first name and described the man in detail. As soon as he learnt the age of the person, Colbeck interrupted and told him to move on to the next one. Leeming's pencil was busy, writing down names then crossing them out again. Of the fifteen people that Butterkiss recognised, only seven were deemed to be worth closer inspection.

'Thank you,' said Colbeck. 'Now turn to the women, please.'

Butterkiss lifted an eyebrow. 'The women, sir?'

'As opposed to the men,' explained Leeming.

'But a woman couldn't possibly have committed those

murders on the trains nor could one have fired that shot at you, Inspector.'

'You are mistaken about that,' said Colbeck. 'Earlier this year, the sergeant and I arrested a woman in Deptford who had shot her husband with his army revolver. The bullet went straight through his body and wounded the young lady who was in bed with him at the time.'

'Dear me!' exclaimed Butterkiss.

'Never underestimate the power of the weaker sex, Constable.'

'No, sir.'

He addressed himself to the petition once more and picked out the female names that he recognised. Most were found to be very unlikely suspects but three names joined the sergeant's list.

'Did you make a note of their details, Victor?' asked Colbeck.

'Yes, Inspector.'

'Good. You can talk to those three ladies tomorrow.'

'What about me?' said Butterkiss.

'I have two important tasks for you, Constable.'

'Just tell me what they are.'

'I want you to find Amos Lockyer for me.'

'I'll do it somehow,' vowed Butterkiss. 'What's the other task?'

Colbeck reached for his frock coat. 'I wonder if you could look at this sleeve for me?' he said. 'Tell me if it's beyond repair.'

Winifred Hawkshaw was on tenterhooks. Whenever she heard a sound from the adjoining bedroom, she feared that her daughter had woken up and was either trying to open the door or to escape through the window. After a sleepless night, she used her key to let herself into Emily's room and found her fast asleep. Putting a chair beside the bed, Winifred sat down and kept vigil. It was an hour before the girl's eyelids fluttered. Her mother took hold of her hand.

'Good morning,' she said, sweetly.

Emily was confused. 'Where am I?'

'In your own bed, dear.'

'Is that you, Mother?'

'Yes.' Winifred rubbed her hand. 'It's me, Emily.'

'I feel strange. What happened?'

'The doctor gave you something to make you sleep.'

'The doctor?' The news brought Emily fully awake. 'You let a doctor touch me?'

'You'd passed out, Emily. When the inspector brought you down from that tower, you were in a dead faint.'

The girl needed a moment to assimilate the information. When she remembered what she had tried to do, she brought a hand up to her mouth. Her eyes darted nervously around the room. She felt trapped.

'We need to talk,' said Winifred, softly.

'I've nothing to say.'

'Emily!'

'I haven't, Mother. I meant to jump off that tower.'

'No, I can't believe that,' insisted her mother. 'Is your life so bad that you could even *think* of such a thing? It's sinful, Emily. It's so cruel and selfish and you're neither of those things. Don't hurt us any more.'

'I wasn't doing it to hurt you.'

'Then what made you go up there in the first place?'

'I was afraid.'

'Of what?'

'Everything.'

Emily began to sob quietly and her mother bent over to hug her. The embrace lasted a long time and it seemed to help the girl because it stemmed her tears. She became so quiet that Winifred wondered if she had fallen asleep again. When she drew back, however, she saw that Emily's eyes were wide open, staring up at the ceiling.

'Promise me that you won't do anything like this again,' said Winifred, solemnly. 'Give me your sacred word of honour.' A bleak silence ensued. 'Did you hear what I said, Emily?'

'Yes.'

'Then give me that promise.'

'I promise,' murmured the girl.

'Say it as if you mean it,' scolded Winifred. 'As it is, the whole town will know what happened yesterday and I'll have to face the shame of that. Don't make it any worse for me, Emily. We *love* you. Doesn't that mean anything to you?'

'Yes.'

'Then behave as if it does.'

'I will.'

Emily sat up in bed and reached out for her mother. Both of them were crying now, locked together, sharing their pain, trying to find a bond that had somehow been lost. At length, it was the daughter who pulled away. She wiped her eyes with the back of her hand and made an effort to control herself.

'You need more time,' said Winifred, watching her closely. 'You need more time to think about what you did and why you did it.'

'I do.'

'But I'll want the truth, Emily.'

'Yes, Mother.'

'I have a right to know. When something as wicked and

terrible as this happens, I have a right to know why. And I'm not the only one, Emily,' she warned. 'The vicar will want to speak to you as well.'

'The vicar?'

'Taking your own life is an offence against God – and you made it worse by trying to do it from a church tower. The vicar says that it would have been an act of blasphemy. Is that what you meant to do?'

'No, no,' cried Emily.

'Suicide is evil.'

'I know.'

'We couldn't have buried you on consecrated ground.'

'I didn't think about that.'

'Well, you should have,' said Winifred, bitterly. 'I don't want two members of the family denied a Christian burial in the churchyard at St Mary's. You could have ended up like your father, Emily. That would have broken my heart.'

Emily began to tremble violently and her mother feared that she was about to have another fit but the girl soon recovered. The experience she had been through was too frightful for her to contemplate yet. Her mind turned to more mundane concerns.

'I'm hungry,' she announced.

'Are you?' said her mother, laughing in relief at this sign of normality. 'I'll make you some breakfast at once. You need to be up and dressed before he calls.'

'Who?'

'Inspector Colbeck. He was the person who saved your life.'

A long sleep had revived Robert Colbeck and got him up early to face the new day. The stinging sensation in his wound had been replaced by a distant ache though his left arm was still rather stiff when he moved it. Before breakfast, he was outside the Saracen's Head, standing in the position that he had occupied the previous evening and trying to work out where the bullet might have gone. Deciding that it must have ricocheted off the wall, he searched the pavement and the road over a wide area. He eventually found it against the kerb on the opposite side of the high street. Colbeck showed the bullet to Victor Leeming when the latter joined him for breakfast.

'It's from a revolver,' said the inspector.

'How can you tell, sir? The end is bent out of shape.'

'That happened on impact with the wall. I'm going by the size of the bullet. My guess is that it came from a revolver designed by Robert Adams. I saw the weapon on display at the Great Exhibition last year.'

'Oh, yes,' said Leeming, enviously. 'Because we saved Crystal Palace from being destroyed, you were given two tickets by Prince Albert for the opening ceremony. You took Miss Andrews to the Exhibition.'

'I did, Victor, though it wasn't to see revolvers. Madeleine was much more interested in the locomotives on show, especially the *Lord of the Isles*. No,' he went on, 'it was on a second visit that I took the trouble to study the firearms because they were the weapons that we would be up against one day – and that day came sooner than I expected.'

'Who is this Robert Adams?'

'The only serious British rival to Samuel Colt. He did not want the American to steal all the glory so he developed his solid-frame revolver in which the butt frame and barrel were forged as a single piece of metal.'

'And this was what they fired?' said Leeming, handing

the bullet back to him. 'You thought that it came from a pistol.'

'A single-cocking pistol, Victor. Adams used a different firing mechanism from the Colt. I'm sufficiently patriotic to be grateful that it was a British weapon,' said Colbeck, pocketing the bullet. 'I'd hate to have been shot dead by an American revolver last night.'

'Who would own such a thing in Ashford?'

'A good point.'

'You were right to stay on the ground when you were hit, sir. If it was a revolver, it could have been fired again and again.'

'Adams designed it so that it would fire rapidly. What probably saved me was that the self-cocking lock needed a heavy pull on the trigger and that tends to upset your aim.'

'Unless you get close enough to the target.'

'We'll have to make sure that he doesn't do that, Victor.'

Having finished his breakfast, Colbeck sat back and wiped his lips with his napkin. Leeming ate the last of his meal then sipped his tea. He pulled a slip of paper from his pocket.

'You want me to talk to these three women, then?'

'Ask them why they signed that petition.'

'One of them lives in a farm near Wye.'

'Then I suggest that you don't go there by cart. Take a train from Ashford station. Wye is only one short stop down the line.'

'What will you be doing, sir?'

'Going back to source.'

'Source?'

'I'm going to have a long-overdue talk with Emily Hawkshaw,' said Colbeck. 'This whole business began when she had that encounter with Joseph Dykes. It's high time that the girl confided in me. After what happened on the top of that church tower yesterday, I feel that Emily owes me something.'

Caleb Andrews had been driving trains for so long that he knew exactly how long it took him to walk to Euston Station from Camden. He also knew how important punctuality was to a railway company. After a glance at the clock, he got up from the table and reached for his hat.

'I'm off, Maddy.'

'Goodbye,' she said, coming out of the kitchen to give him a kiss.

'What are you going to do today?'

'I hope to finish the painting.'

'One of these fine days,' he said, 'you must come down to Euston and do a painting of me on the footplate. I'd like that. We could hang it over the mantelpiece.'

'I've done dozens of drawings of you, Father.'

'I want to be in colour – like the *Lord of the Isles*.'

'You *are* the Lord of the Isles,' she said, fondly. 'At least, you think you are when you've had a few glasses of beer.'

Andrews laughed. 'You know your father too well.'

'Try not to be late this evening.'

'I will. By the way,' he said, 'you needn't bother to read the newspaper this morning. There's no mention at all of Inspector Colbeck. Without my help, he's obviously making no progress.'

'I think that he is. Robert prefers to hide certain things from the press. When he's working on a case, he hates having any reporters around him. They always expect quick results.'

'The inspector had an extremely quick result. As soon as he got to Ashford, someone else was murdered on a train.'

'Father!'

'You can't be any quicker than that.'

'Go off to work,' she said, opening the door for him, 'and forget about Robert. He'll solve these murders very soon, I'm sure.'

'So am I, Maddy. He's got a good reason to get a move on,' said Andrews with a cackle. 'The inspector wants to get back here and have his painting of the *Lord of the Isles*.'

Robert Colbeck was pleased with the way that the sleeve of his frock coat had been replaced. George Butterkiss had done such an excellent job sewing on a new sleeve that Colbeck was able to wear the coat again. Looking as spruce as ever, he turned into Middle Row and raised his top hat to a woman who went past. Adam Hawkshaw was displaying joints of meat on the table outside the shop. The inspector strolled up to him.

'Good morning,' he said, breezily.

'Oh.' The butcher looked up at him, visibly shocked.

'You seem surprised to see me, Mr Hawkshaw.'

'I heard that you'd been shot last night.'

'Who told you that?'

'Everyone was talking about it when I got here this morning.'

'As you can see,' said Colbeck, careful to give the impression that he was completely uninjured, 'reports of the incident were false.'

'Yes.'

'Might I ask where you were yesterday evening?'

'I was at my lodging,' said Hawkshaw. 'On my own.'

'So there's nobody who could confirm the fact?'

'Nobody at all.'

'How convenient!'

The butcher squared up to him. 'Are you accusing me?'

'I'm not accusing anybody, Mr Hawkshaw. I really came to see how Emily was after that unfortunate business at the church.'

'Emily is well.'

'Have you seen her this morning?'

'Not yet.'

'Then how do you know she is well?'

'Emily doesn't want you upsetting her, Inspector.'

'Your stepsister was upset long before I came here,' said Colbeck, firmly, 'and I intend to find out why.'

Before Hawkshaw could reply, the detective went past him into the shop and knocked on the door at the rear. It was opened immediately by Winifred Hawkshaw. She invited him in.

'I was expecting you to call,' she said.

'Really? You can't have heard the rumour then.'

'What rumour?'

'The one that your stepson managed to pick up somehow.'

'I haven't spoken to Adam yet. I've stayed close to Emily.'

'That's understandable,' said Colbeck. 'Yesterday evening, when I was standing outside the Saracen's Head, someone tried to shoot me.'

'Good gracious!'

'Being so close, you must surely have heard the bang.'

'Now that you mention it,' said Winifred, pushing back a wisp of stray hair, 'I did hear something. And there was the sound of a horse and cart, racing down the high street. I was in Emily's room at the time, too afraid to leave her in case she woke up and tried to . . . well, you know. I stayed there until I was exhausted then went to my own bed.'

'How is Emily?'

'She's still very delicate.'

'She would be after that experience.'

'Emily doesn't remember too much of what happened.'

'Then I won't remind her of the details,' said Colbeck. 'Some of them are best forgotten. Has the doctor been yet?'

'He promised to call later on – and so did the vicar. Emily is unwilling to see either of them, especially the doctor. She begged me to send him away.'

'What about me?'

'I can't pretend that she was keen to speak to you, Inspector, but I told her that she must. Emily needs to thank you.'

'I'm just grateful that I came along at the right time.'

'So are we,' said Winifred, still deeply perturbed by the incident. 'But what's this about a shot being fired at you, Inspector? Is it true?'

'I'm afraid so.'

'Someone tried to *kill* you? That's terrible.'

'I survived.'

'Do you have any idea who the man was?'

'Yes, Mrs Hawkshaw,' he replied, 'but let's not worry about me at the moment. Emily is the person who deserves all the attention. Do you think that you could bring her down, please?'

'Of course.'

'Has she given you any idea why she went up that tower?'

'Emily said that she was afraid – of everything.'

Winifred went off upstairs and Colbeck anticipated a long wait as the mother tried to cajole her daughter into speaking to him. In fact, the girl made no protest at all. She came downstairs at once. When she entered the room, she looked sheepish. Winifred followed her and they sat beside each other. Colbeck took the chair opposite them. He gave the girl a kind smile.

'Hello, Emily,' he said.

'Hello.'

'How are you this morning?'

'Mother says I'm to thank you for what you did yesterday.'

'And what about you?' he asked, gently. 'Do you think I earned your thanks?'

'I don't know.'

'Emily!' reproved her mother.

'I'd rather she tell the truth, Mrs Hawkshaw,' said Colbeck. 'She's probably still bewildered by it all and that's only natural.' He looked at the girl. 'Do you feel hazy in your own mind, Emily?'

'Yes.'

'But you do recall what took you to the church?'

Emily glanced at her mother. 'Yes.'

'It was because you were so unhappy, wasn't it?'

'Yes, it was.'

'And because you miss your stepfather so very much.' The girl lowered her head. 'I'm not going to ask you any more about yesterday, Emily. I know you went up that tower to do something desperate but I think that you changed your mind when you actually got there. However,' he went on, 'what interests me more is what happened all those weeks earlier. You were attacked by a man named Joseph Dykes, weren't you?'

Emily looked anxiously at her mother but Winifred did not bail her out. She gave her daughter a look to indicate that she should answer the question. Emily licked her lips.

'Yes,' she said, 'but I don't want to talk about it.'

'Then tell me what happened afterwards,' invited Colbeck.

'Afterwards?'

'When you came running back here. Who was in the shop?'

'Father.'

'What about your stepbrother?'

'Adam had gone to Bybrook Farm to collect some meat.'

'So you only told your stepfather what happened?'

'Nathan was her father,' corrected Winifred. 'In every way that mattered, he was the only real father that Emily knew.'

'I accept that, Mrs Hawkshaw,' said Colbeck, 'and I can see why Emily should turn to him.' His eyes flicked back to the girl. 'What did your father say when you told him?'

'He was very angry,' she said.

'Did he run off immediately?'

'No, he stayed with me for a while.'

'Nathan said she was terrified,' explained the mother. 'He had to calm her down before he could go after Joe Dykes. By that time, of course, Joe had vanished.'

'Let me come back to your daughter,' said Colbeck, patiently. 'You were not to blame in any way, Emily. The chain of events that followed was not your doing. You were simply a victim and not a cause – do you understand what I'm saying?'

'I think so,' said the girl.

'You don't need to take any responsibility on to your shoulders.'

'That's what I told her,' said Winifred.

'But Emily didn't believe you – did you, Emily?'

'No,' muttered the girl.

'Why not?'

'I can't tell you.'

'Then answer me this,' said Colbeck, probing carefully. 'What happened afterwards?'

'Afterwards?'

'Yes, Emily. When your father got back to the shop after he'd failed to find the man who assaulted you. What happened then?'

A look came into her eyes that Colbeck had seen before. It was a look of sudden fear and helplessness that she had given when she felt that she was going to fall to her death from the church tower. The interview was over because Emily was unable to go on but Colbeck was content. He had learnt much more than he had expected.

Notwithstanding his dislike of rail travel, Victor Leeming had to admit that it was quicker and safer than riding beside George Butterkiss on a rickety cart that gave off such pungent odours. The journey to Wye was so short that he barely had time to admire the landscape through the window of his carriage. It was his third call that morning. Having spoken to two of the women and satisfied himself that they could not have been implicated in the crimes, Leeming was on his way to meet the last person on his list.

Wye was a quaint village with a small railway station at its edge. It took him only ten minutes to walk to the address that Butterkiss had given him. Kathleen Brennan lived in a tied cottage on one of the farms. When he knocked on the door, all that the sergeant knew about her was that she worked there and brought produce in to Ashford on market days. Butterkiss had not warned him how attractive she was.

When she opened the door to him, he discovered that Kathleen Brennan was a woman in her twenties with a raw beauty that was set off by her long red hair and a pair of startling green eyes. Even in her working dress, she looked shapely. She put her hands on her hips.

'Yes?' she asked with a soft Irish lilt.

'Miss Kathleen Brennan?'

'*Mrs* Brennan.'

'I beg your pardon. My name is Detective Sergeant

Leeming,' he told her, showing her his warrant card, 'and I'd like to ask you a few questions, if I may.'

'Why?'

'It's in connection with the murder of Joseph Dykes. May I come in for a moment, please?'

'We can talk here,' she said, folding her arms.

'As you wish, Mrs Brennan. You signed a petition, I believe.'

'That's right.'

'Do you mind telling me why?'

'Because I knew that Nathan Hawkshaw was innocent.'

'How?'

'I just did,' she said as if insulted by the question. 'I met him a lot in Ashford. He was a nice man. Nathan was no killer.'

'Were you at that fair in Lenham, by any chance?'

'Yes, I was.'

'And did you witness the argument between the two men?'

'We all did,' she replied. 'It took place in the middle of the square. They might have come to blows if Gregory hadn't stopped them.'

'Gregory Newman?'

'He was Nathan's best friend. He pulled him away and tried to talk sense into him. Gregory told him to go home.'

'But he came back, didn't he?'

'So they say.'

'And he was seen very close to where the murder took place.'

'I know nothing of that, Sergeant,' she said, brusquely. 'But I still believe that they hanged the wrong man.'

'Have you any idea who the killer might be?'

'None at all.'

'But you were shocked when Hawkshaw was found guilty?'

'Yes, I was.'

'Did you go to the execution?'

'Why are you asking me that?' she challenged. 'And why did you come here in the first place? That case is over and done with.'

'If only it were, Mrs Brennan,' said Leeming, 'but it's had so many tragic consequences. That's why Inspector Colbeck and I are looking into it again. Your name came to our attention.'

'I can't help you,' she said, curtly.

'I get the feeling that you don't *want* to help me.'

Leeming met her gaze. Kathleen Brennan's manner verged on the hostile and he could not understand what provocation he had given her. Without quite knowing why, he was unsettled by her. There was something about the woman that made him feel, if not threatened, then a trifle disturbed. Leeming was glad that they were conversing in the open air and not in the privacy of her cottage.

'You haven't told me if you attended the execution.'

'And I'm not going to.'

'Are you ashamed that you went?'

'I didn't say that I did.'

'But you felt sorry for Nathan Hawkshaw?'

'We all did – that's why Gregory got the petition together.'

'Was he the person who asked you to sign?'

'No,' she said, 'it was Nathan's wife.'

'Did you simply put your name on that list out of friendship?'

Anger showed in her face. 'No, I didn't! You've got no call to ask me that, Sergeant. I did what I believed was right and so did the others. We wanted to save Nathan.'

'Yet you had no actual proof that he was innocent.'

Kathleen Brennan's eyes glinted and she breathed hard through her nose. Leeming could see that his questions had inflamed her. She stepped forward and pulled the door shut behind her.

'I've got to go to work,' she said.

'Then I won't stop you, Mrs Brennan. Thank you for your help.'

'Nathan Hawkshaw was a good man, Sergeant.'

'That's what everyone says.'

'Try listening to them.'

She walked abruptly past him and headed across the field towards the farmhouse on the ridge. Leeming was nonplussed, unsure whether his visit had been pointless or whether he had stumbled on something of interest and significance. As he trudged back to the station, he wondered why Kathleen Brennan had made him so uneasy. It was only when, after a lengthy wait, he caught the return train to Ashford that he realised exactly what it was.

There was an additional surprise for him. As the train chugged merrily along the line, he looked absent-mindedly through the window and saw something that made him sit up and stare. A young woman was riding a horse along the road at a steady canter, her red hair blowing in the wind. The person who had told him that she had to go to work was now riding with some urgency towards Ashford.

Inspector Colbeck was so intrigued by what he had learnt from his meeting with Emily Hawkshaw that he took himself to a wooden bench near St Mary's Church and sat down to think. The square tower soared above him and he looked up at it with misgiving, certain that, if the girl really had committed suicide, then the full truth about the murder of Jospeh Dykes would never be known. Emily was young, immature and in a fragile state but he could not excuse her on those grounds. In the light of what he had discovered, he simply had to talk to her again.

Winifred Hawkshaw was unhappy with the idea. When he returned to the shop after long cogitation, she became very protective.

'Emily needs to be left alone,' she claimed. 'It's the only way that she'll ever get over this.'

'I disagree, Mrs Hawkshaw,' said Colbeck. 'As long as she feels such a sense of guilt, there's always the possibility that she'll attempt to take her own life again – and I may not be on hand next time.'

'My daughter has nothing to feel guilty about, Inspector.'

'Is that what she's told you?'

'No,' admitted Winifred. 'She's told me precious little.'

'That in itself is an indication of guilt. If she's unable to confide in the person closest to her, what kind of secret is she hiding? Whatever it is, it won't let her rest. I simply must see her again,' insisted Colbeck, 'and this time, you must leave us alone together.'

'I couldn't do that.'

'I won't get the truth out of her with her mother there.'

'Why not?'

'Because I believe that it concerns you.'

Winifred Hawkshaw was discomfited. It took time to persuade her to summon her daughter but she eventually acceded to his request. There was an even longer delay as she argued with Emily then more or less forced her daughter to come downstairs. The girl was sullen and withdrawn when she came into the room. She refused to sit down.

'Very well,' said Colbeck, settling into a chair, 'you can stand up. I think that you know why I've come back again, don't you?'

'No.'

'I want the full story, Emily. And let me assure you of one thing. Whatever you tell me is in strictest confidence. I'm not going to pass it on to anyone – not even to your mother. She's the one person who must never know, isn't she? At least, that's what you think now.'

'I don't know what you're talking about.'

'I think you do, Emily. Did your father commit that murder?'

'No!' she retorted.

'Would you swear to that?'

'On the Bible.'

'But would you confess *why* you're so certain about it?' asked Colbeck, lowering his voice. 'No, you wouldn't, would you? Because you had a chance to do just that at the trial.' Emily's cheeks were drained of what little colour they possessed. 'The reason you know that he could not possibly have killed Joseph Dykes is that you were with your father at the time.'

'That's not true!' she cried.

'Except that you never saw him as your real father, did you? He was kind to you. He protected you from Adam. He was your friend.' The girl let out a gasp of horror at being found out. 'You loved him as a friend, didn't you, Emily? There's no question that he loved you. Nathan Hawkshaw went to the gallows rather than betray you.'

'Stop!' she implored.

'It has to come out, Emily,' he told her, getting up to stand beside the girl. 'The truth is a poison that must be sucked out of you before it kills you. I'm not here to judge you or to tell you that what you did was wrong. All I want to do is to find the man who did kill Joseph Dykes then went on to murder two other people. Did your mother tell you what happened yesterday evening?'

'No.'

'This man that we're after tried to shoot me, Emily.' She looked at him with dismay. 'Unless we catch him, there'll be other victims. You're in a position to help us. Do you want more people to be killed as a result of what happened that day at Lenham fair?' She shook her head. 'Then tell me the truth. You'll be helping yourself as much as me.'

Emily stared up at him with a fear that was tempered with a wild hope. Colbeck could see that she was wrestling hard with her demons. The guilt that had been oppressing her for weeks was now bearing down like a ton weight.

'You won't tell Mother?' she whispered.

'That's something that only you should do, Emily.'

'I feel so ashamed.'

'I think that your father – your friend, I should say – deserved to bear the greater shame. You were too young to understand what was happening. He was much older – he knew.'

'I loved him.'

'And he loved you, Emily, but not in a way that a stepfather should. It cost him his life.' She shuddered. 'I'm sure that he repented at the last. He took the sin upon himself. You don't have to go through life with it hanging over you forever.'

'Yes, I do.'

'Why?'

Emily was not able to tell him yet. She was still shocked and frightened by the way that he seemed to have looked into her mind and discerned her secret. It was unnerving.

'How did you know?' she asked.

'There were clues,' he explained. 'When you were attacked by Dykes, you didn't turn to your mother for help. In fact, you pulled away from her. And, at the very time when you should have been drawn closer as you mourned together, you shut her out.'

'I had to, Inspector.'

'You lost the person you really loved and you felt that you couldn't live without him.'

'I caused him to die.'

'No, Emily.'

'If he hadn't been with me that day, he'd be alive now.'

'And what sort of life would it have been?' asked Colbeck. 'The two of you were lying to your mother and lying to each other. It could never have gone on like that, Emily. It was only a matter of time before you were found out. Think what would have happened then.'

'I hated all the lies and deceit,' she admitted.

'You went along with them out of love but it was never a love that you could show to the world. You asked me how I knew,' he went on, 'and it wasn't only because of the way you treated your mother. There was your fear of the doctor as well.' His inquiry was gentle. 'Are you with child, Emily?'

'I don't know – I may be.'

'If that's the case, then you tried to kill *two* people when you went up that church tower. That makes it even worse. You must have been in despair to do that.'

'I was. I still am.'

'No, Emily. We're drawing that poison out of you. It's going to hurt but you'll feel better for it in the end. You have to face up to what you did instead of trying to run away from it. Most important of all,' he stressed, 'you mustn't take all the blame on your own shoulders.'

'I can't help it, Inspector.'

'You were led astray by your stepfather.'

'That isn't how it was.'

'He admitted his guilt by giving his life to save yours.'

'It was not like that,' she told him, her eyes filling with tears. 'Joe Dykes did touch me in that lane but that was all he did. I only pretended that he did much more than that. Before I ran back here, I even tore my dress. I wanted Nathan to comfort me. That's how it all started,' she said with a sob in her voice. 'I just *wanted* him.'

By the time he got back to the inn, Victor Leeming had decided that his visit to Wye had not been in vain at all. He had something to report. To his disappointment, however, he did not find Colbeck at the Saracen's Head. In the inspector's place were George Butterkiss and a complete stranger. The constable leapt up at once from his chair and came across to Leeming.

'I found him, Sergeant,' he declared, as if expecting a reward.

'Who?'

'Amos Lockyer. Come and meet him.'

He took Leeming across to the table and introduced him to his friend. The two of them sat down opposite Lockyer, a short, fleshy man in his late fifties with an ugly face that was redeemed by a benign smile. His hand was curled around a pint of beer and, from the way he slurred his words, it was clearly not his first drink of the day.

'How did you track him down, Constable?' asked Leeming.

'I remembered the Romney Marshes.'

'Why?'

'Because I once told George that I'd like to retire there,' said Lockyer, taking up the story. 'I had an uncle who was on his last legs and he promised to leave his cottage to me. I got word of his death when I was working at Leeds Castle. *That* was no job for me,' he told them with disgust. 'I wasn't born to fetch and carry for my betters because I don't believe that they were any better than me.' He gave a throaty chuckle. 'So, after I'd buried Uncle Sidney, I decided to retire.'

'That's where I found him,' said Butterkiss. 'At his new home.'

'You did well,' conceded Leeming.

'Thank you, Sergeant. But how have you got on?'

'The first two ladies on that list could be discounted at once, but I'm not so sure about the third. What can you tell me about Kathleen Brennan from Wye?'

'Nothing beyond what I told you before.'

'There was something very odd about Mrs Brennan.'

'You should have asked *me* about her,' said Lockyer, helpfully. 'What's odd about Mrs Brennan is that she's the only woman I know who wears a wedding ring without having been anywhere near a husband.' He grinned amiably. 'A husband of her own, that is.'

'She's not married?'

'No, Sergeant, and never has been.'

'How do you know her?'

'From the time when she used to serve beer at the Fountain,' recalled the older man. 'This was before your time, George, so you won't remember Kathy Brennan. She was very popular with the customers.'

'That was the feeling I had about her,' said Leeming. 'She was too knowing. As if she was no better than she ought to be.'

'Oh, I don't condemn a woman for making the most of

her charms and Kathy certainly had those. They were good enough to start charging money for, which was how she and I crossed swords.'

'You mean that she was a prostitute?' asked Butterkiss.

'Of sorts,' said Lockyer, indulgently. 'And only for a short time until she saw the dangers of it. I liked the woman. She always struck me as someone who wanted a man to love her enough to stay by her but she couldn't find one in Ashford. What made her change her ways was that business with Joe Dykes.'

'I don't remember that,' said Butterkiss.

'What happened?' prompted Leeming.

'Joe was in the Fountain one night,' said Lockyer, 'and he took a fancy to Kathy. So off they go to that lane behind the Corn Exchange. Only she's heard about his reputation for having his fun then running off without paying, so she asked for some cash beforehand.'

'Did he give it?'

'Yes, Sergeant. But as soon as Joe had had his money's worth up against a wall, he attacked the poor woman and took his money back from her. Kathy came crying to me but, as usual, Joe had made himself scarce. He was cruel.'

'In other words,' said Leeming, realising that he had just been given a valuable piece of information, 'Kathleen Brennan had a good reason to hate Dykes.'

'Hate him? She'd have scratched his eyes out.'

It was at that point that Robert Colbeck returned to the inn. Seeing the three of them, he came across to their table. As soon as he had been introduced to Lockyer, he took over the questioning.

'Did you follow Jacob Guttridge to his home?'

'Yes,' replied Lockyer, uncomfortably.

'Then you are an accessory to his murder.'

'No, Inspector!'

'Amos didn't even know that he was dead,' said Butterkiss, trying to defend his former colleague. 'The first he heard about the murder – and that of the prison chaplain – was when I told him about them.'

'It's true,' added Lockyer, earnestly. 'I was stuck on a farm, miles from anywhere. You don't get to read a newspaper when you're digging up turnips all day. When George told me what's been going on, I was shaken to the core.'

'Yet you admit that you followed Guttridge,' noted Colbeck.

'That's what I'm good at – finding where people live.' He took a long sip of his beer. 'I knew he'd lie low in Maidstone prison after the execution so I stayed the night there and waited at the station early next morning. Mr Guttridge caught the first train to Paddock Wood then took the train to London from there. Unknown to him, I was right behind him all the way.'

'Like a shadow,' said Butterkiss, admiringly.

'Not exactly, George, because he walked much faster than me. This old injury slows me right down,' he said, slapping his thigh. 'He almost gave me the slip in Hoxton. I saw the street he went down but I didn't know which house was his. So I waited on the corner until he came out again and I followed him all the way to Bethnal Green.'

'To the Seven Stars,' said Colbeck.

'That's right, Inspector. How did you know?'

Leeming was bitter. 'We know all about the Seven Stars,' he said. 'If you went there, you must have discovered that Guttridge was going to be on that excursion train to watch the big fight.'

'It was the only thing that people were talking about,'

explained Lockyer. 'The landlord was making a list of all those who were going to support the Bargeman. Jake Guttridge was one of the first to put himself forward, though he gave a different name. I don't blame him. The Seven Stars wasn't the place to own up to being a hangman.'

'What happened afterwards?'

'I trailed him back to Hoxton. The trouble was that he spotted me and broke into a run. I had a job to keep up with him but at least I got the number of his house this time. I earned my money.'

'From whom?'

'The person who paid me to find his address.'

'And who was that?'

'Inspector,' pleaded Lockyer, 'I had no idea that he intended to kill Guttridge. I swear it. He said that he just wanted to scare him. If I'd known what I know now, I'd never have taken on the job.'

'Give me his name, Mr Lockyer.'

'I was a policeman. I'd never willingly break the law.'

'His *name*,' demanded Colbeck.

'Adam Hawkshaw.'

Inspector Colbeck took no chances. Aware that Hawkshaw was a strong young man in a shop that was filled with weaponry, he stationed Leeming and Butterkiss at either end of Middle Row to prevent any attempt at escape. When he confronted the butcher in the empty shop, Colbeck was given a sneer of contempt.

'What have you come for *this* time?' said Hawkshaw.

'You.'

'Eh?'

'I'm placing you under arrest for the murders of Jacob

Guttridge and Narcissus Jones,' said Colbeck, producing a pair of handcuffs from beneath his coat, 'and for the attempted murder of a police officer.'

'I never murdered anybody!' protested the other.

'Then why did you pay Amos Lockyer to find the hangman's address for you?' Hawkshaw's mouth fell open. 'I don't think it was to send him your greetings, was it? What you sent him was a death threat.'

'No,' said Hawkshaw, defiantly.

'You'll have to come with me.'

'But I'm innocent, Inspector.'

'Then how do you explain your interest in Jacob Guttridge's whereabouts?' asked Colbeck, snapping the handcuffs on his wrists. 'How do you account for the fact that you were seen taking a train to Paddock Wood on the night of the chaplain's murder?'

'I can't tell you that.'

'No, and you probably can't tell me where you were yesterday evening, can you? Because I don't believe that you were in your lodging. You were cowering in a doorway opposite the Saracen's Head, waiting for me to come out so that you could shoot me.'

'That's not true,' said Hawkshaw, struggling to get out of the handcuffs. 'Take these things off me!'

'Not until you're safely behind bars.'

'I had nothing to do with the murders!'

'Prove it.'

The butcher looked shamefaced. Biting his lip, he grappled with his conscience for a long time. Eventually, he blurted out his confession.

'On the night of the chaplain's murder, I did take a train to Paddock Wood,' he said, the words coming out slowly and with obvious embarrassment, 'but it was not to go after him. I went to see someone and I took the train over there again last night.'

'Can this person vouch for you?'

'Yes, Inspector, but I'd rather you didn't ask her.'

'A lady, then – a young lady, I expect. What was her name?'

'I can't tell you that.'

'Is that because you just invented her?' pressed Colbeck.

'No,' rejoined the other, 'Jenny is real.'

'I'll believe that when I see her, Mr Hawkshaw. Meanwhile, I'm going to make your mother aware of your arrest then take you back to London.'

'Wait!' said Hawkshaw in desperation. 'There's no need for this.' He swallowed hard. 'Her name is Jenny Skillen.'

'Why couldn't you tell me that before?'

'She's married.'

'Ah.'

'Her husband is coming back today.'

Colbeck knew that he was telling the truth. If he had a witness who could absolve him of the murder of Narcissus Jones then he could not be responsible for the other killings.

'Why did you pay Amos Lockyer to find that address?' he asked.

'I wanted revenge,' admitted Hawkshaw. 'When I saw the way that he made my father suffer on the scaffold, I just wanted to tear out his heart. I didn't say that to Amos. I told him that I just wanted to give the man a fright. He agreed to find his address for me, that was all. When he came back, he told me that Guttridge would be at a prizefight in a few weeks' time.'

'So you decided to go on the same excursion train?'

'No, Inspector – I give you my word. If I'm honest, I

thought about it. I even planned what I'd do when I caught up with him. But I don't think I could have gone through with it.'

'Did you discuss this with anyone else?'

'Yes,' said Hawkshaw, 'and he talked me out of it. He told me that I couldn't bring back my father by killing the man who hanged him. He made me see how wrong it would have been and got me to promise that I'd forget all about it. He stopped me.'

'Who did?'

'Gregory – Gregory Newman.'

There were tears in his eyes as he stood beside the bed and looked down at his wife. Meg Newman had not woken all day. She lay in a sleep so deep that it was almost a coma. On the rare occasions when she did open her eyes for any length of time, she inhabited a twilight world of her own in which she could neither speak, move nor do anything for herself. Her husband gazed down at her with a mixture of love and resignation. Then he bent down to give her a farewell kiss that she never even felt.

'You once begged me to do this,' he said, 'and I didn't have the courage to put you out of your pain and misery. I have to do it now, Meg. Please forgive me.'

Gregory Newman put the pillow over her face and pressed down hard. It was not long before his wife stopped breathing.

Having released his prisoner, Colbeck went marching off to the railway works with Leeming and Butterkiss. As a precaution, he deployed them at the two exits from the boiler shop before he went in. When he found the foreman, he had to shout above the incessant din.

'I've come to see Gregory Newman again,' he yelled.

'You're too late, Inspector.'

'What do you mean?'

'He left half an hour ago,' replied the foreman. 'Someone brought word that his wife had taken a turn for the worse. I let him go home.'

'Who brought the message?'

'A young woman.'

Colbeck thanked him then hurried outside to collect the others. When he heard what had happened, Leeming was able to identify the bearer of the message.

'Kathleen Brennan,' he said. 'I think she came to warn him.'

'Let's go to his house,' ordered Colbeck.

They hurried to Turton Street and found the door of the house wide open. The blind had been drawn on the downstairs front window. Colbeck went quickly inside and looked into the front room. Weeping quietly, Mrs Sheen was pulling the sheet over the face of Meg Newman. She looked up in surprise at Colbeck.

'Forgive this intrusion,' he said, removing his hat. 'We're looking for Mr Newman. Is he here?'

'Not any more, sir. He told me Meg had passed on and he left.'

'Where did he go?'

'I don't know,' said Mrs Sheen, 'but he had a bag with him.'

'Thank you. Please excuse me.'

Colbeck came back out into the street again. Butterkiss was keen.

'What can I do, Inspector?' he volunteered.

'Nothing at all. He's made a run for it.'

'I just can't believe that Gregory is involved in all this. He's such a kind and considerate man. Look at the way he cared for his sick wife.'

'He won't care for her anymore.'

'I think I know where he may have gone,' said Leeming.

'Where's that, Victor?'

'To the place where his female accomplice lives.'

'Who is she?'

'Kathleen Brennan. We need to get to Wye straight away.'

'How do you know that this woman is his accomplice?'

'Because I saw her riding towards Ashford earlier on,' said Leeming, 'and now I realise why. I never expected to hear myself say this, Inspector, but I think that we should take a train.'

Kathleen Brennan bustled around the tiny bedroom and gathered up her belongings. She put them in a large wicker basket, threw her clothes over her arm then went down the bare wooden stairs. Gregory Newman was sitting in a chair, brooding on what he had done. Putting everything down on the table, Kathleen went over to comfort him.

'It had to be done,' she said, 'and it was what your wife wanted.'

'I know, Kathy, but it still hurt me.' He gave a mirthless laugh. 'Strange, isn't it? I killed three people I hated and all I felt was pleasure and satisfaction. It's only when I smother someone I loved that I feel like a murderer.'

'It was no life for her, Gregory. It was a blessed release.'

'For Meg, maybe – but not for me.'

'Why do you say that?'

'Because I feel so *guilty*.'

He put his head in his hands. Kneeling beside him, Kathleen coiled an arm around his shoulders and kissed him on the temple. After a while, he looked up and tried to shake off his feelings of remorse. He pulled her on to his lap and embraced her warmly.

'Thank you, Kathy,' he said.

'This is what we both wanted, isn't it?'

'Yes.'

'You always said that we'd be together one day and now we are.'

'I didn't expect it to happen like this,' he said. 'I thought that Meg would have died long ago but she clung on and on. It would have been so much easier if she could have passed away by now.'

'I had to warn you,' she insisted. 'Sergeant Leeming frightened me with his questions. How on earth did he know that I was involved?'

'He didn't but he found his way out here somehow. That was a danger signal, Kathy. You were right to come to me.'

'He mentioned an Inspector Colbeck.'

'Damn the man!' said Newman. 'He's behind all this. He dug away until he unearthed things that I never thought he'd find. Because he was getting closer all the time, I shot him last night. I hoped I'd killed him.'

'It didn't sound like it.'

'Then we must get far away from here, Kathy. It's only a matter of time before they work out that I murdered Joe Dykes and the others.'

'Joe got his deserts for what he did to me,' she said, harshly. 'If you'd given me that cleaver, I'd have killed him myself.' She grinned. 'You should have seen the look in his eye when I brought him out of the Red Lion. By the time we got to the wood, he was panting for me.'

'Making him undress like that made such a difference,' he recalled. 'All that I had to do was to carve him up.' He kissed her full on the lips. 'I couldn't have done it without you, Kathy.'

'Or without Nathan.'

'He was just where we needed him.'

'When I saw what he was doing, I had no qualms about letting him take the blame. I looked on her as my own daughter and Nathan was—'

'Yes, yes,' she interrupted. 'You paid him back.'

'I paid them all back,' he said, proudly.

'And now we can be together at last.'

As they hugged each other again, Robert Colbeck opened the door. He doffed his hat and he stepped into the room. They sprang apart.

'You shouldn't leave the windows open,' warned Colbeck. 'It only encourages eavesdropping.'

'What are *you* doing here?' gasped Newman, getting to his feet.

'I've come to arrest the pair of you.'

'I thought that I shot you.'

'You tried to, Mr Newman, but your aim was poor. You'll pardon me if I don't turn my back and let you have a second attempt with a piece of wire. I know that's your preferred method.' He looked at Kathleen. 'My name is Inspector Colbeck. I believe that you met my sergeant earlier.'

'Kathy is nothing to do with this,' insisted Newman.

'Then why did she ride to Ashford to warn you?' asked Colbeck. 'Sergeant Leeming saw her from the train. Your foreman told me that a young woman with red hair came for you in the boiler shop.' He saw Newman eyeing the open door. 'And before you decide to bolt again, I should warn you that the sergeant is outside with Constable Butterkiss.'

Kathleen was dazed. 'How did you get here so quickly?'

'By train.'

'And you heard us through the window?'

'I'd worked out some of it beforehand,' said Colbeck. 'Once I knew that Nathan Hawkshaw could not possibly have committed that crime, it narrowed the search down. The one thing I would like clarified is what happened to Hawkshaw's coat.'

'Gregory stole it,' said Kathleen.

'Be quiet!' he snapped.

'I think I can guess the circumstances in which it was taken,' said Colbeck, seizing on the detail. 'It was lying there with the rest of his clothing, wasn't it – and with the meat cleaver that he'd brought?'

'How did you know about that?' asked Kathleen, open-mouthed.

'I think you'll be surprised what we know, Miss Brennan.' He produced the handcuffs again. 'We'll spare you the indignity of these,' he said, 'but Mr Newman is another matter. Shall we, sir?'

Gregory Newman heaved a massive sigh and held out his wrists. As soon as Colbeck tried to put the handcuffs on him, however, he pushed the inspector away, grabbed Kathleen by the hand and ran through the door. Constable Butterkiss tried to stop him but was buffeted aside by a powerful arm. Newman ran to his cart and lifted Kathleen up into the seat, intending to whip the horse into a gallop and get free. But he became aware of an insurmountable problem.

'We took the liberty of taking your horse out of the shafts,' said Colbeck, pointing to where the animal was grazing happily, 'in case you tried to escape.' Newman leant over to grab his bag from the back of the cart and thrust his hand into it. 'I also took the precaution of removing this,' said Colbeck, taking out the revolver from beneath his coat. 'Unlike you, I know how to fire it properly.' Newman slumped forward in his seat. 'Are you ready for these handcuffs now, sir?'

They had never seen Superintendent Tallis in such a euphoric mood. He normally smoked cigars in times of stress but this time he reached for one by way of celebration. Colbeck and Leeming stood in his office at Scotland Yard and basked in his approval for once. Cigar smoke curled around their heads like a pair of haloes.

'It was a triumph, gentlemen,' he said. 'You not only solved two murders that occurred on trains, you exonerated Nathan Hawkshaw from a crime that he didn't commit.'

'Too late in the day,' said Leeming. 'He'd already been hanged.'

'That fact has caused considerable embarrassment to the parties involved and I applaud that. Where a miscarriage of justice has taken place, it deserves to be exposed. It will be a different matter for that monster, Gregory Newman.'

'Yes, sir. He's as guilty as sin.'

'So is that she-devil who helped him,' said Tallis, thrusting the cigar back between his teeth. 'They may have disposed of one hangman but there'll be another to make them dance at the end of a rope. When I was a boy,' he went on, nostalgically, 'over two hundred offences bore the death penalty and it frightened people into a more law-abiding attitude. Only traitors and killers can be executed now. I maintain that the shadow of the noose should hang over more crimes.'

'I disagree, Superintendent,' said Colbeck. 'To hang someone for stealing a loaf of bread because his family is starving is barbaric in my view. It breeds hatred of the law instead of respect. Newman and his accomplice deserve to hang. Common thieves do not.'

Tallis was almost jovial. 'I'll not argue with you, Inspector,' he said, 'especially on a day like this. I know that you'll win any debate like the silver-tongued barrister you once were. But I hold to my point. To impose order and discipline, we must be ruthless.'

'I prefer a combination of firmness and discretion, sir.'

'That's the way we solved the railway murders,' said Leeming.

'Yes,' said Colbeck with amusement. 'Victor was firm and I was discreet. We made an effective team.'

Colbeck's discretion had been shown in abundance. He tried to protect those who would be hurt by certain revelations. Though he told the sergeant about his long interview with Emily Hawkshaw, he had suppressed the facts that he knew would scandalise him. Edward Tallis had been told nothing about the relationship between the girl and her late stepfather. Colbeck had not deemed it necessary. The evidence to convict Gregory Newman and Kathleen Brennan was irresistible. There was no need to release intimate details that would be seized on by the press and turn an already unhappy home into an unendurable one.

'How did the widow receive the news?' asked Tallis.

'Mrs Hawkshaw was in a state of confusion, sir,' said Colbeck. 'She was delighted that her husband's name had been cleared but she was shocked that Gregory Newman was unmasked as the killer and the man who sent those death threats. She had trusted him so completely.'

'He must have hated her to let her husband die in his place.'

'I think that he loved her, sir, and felt that Hawkshaw was unworthy of her. In his own twisted way, he thought that he could please her by killing two of the people who had inflicted needless pain on her husband. Yes,' he said, anticipating an interruption, 'I know that there's a contradiction there. How can a man allow someone to go to the gallows in his stead and then avenge him? But it was not a contradiction that troubled Gregory Newman.'

'His life was full of contradictions,' said Leeming. 'He pretends to care for his wife and yet he goes off to see Kathleen Brennan whenever he can. What kind of marriage is that?'

'One that imposed immense strain on him, Victor.'

'You're surely not excusing him, are you?' asked Tallis. 'I'm no proponent of marriage, as you know, but I do place great emphasis on sexual propriety. In my opinion, Newman's relationship with his scarlet women is in itself worthy of hanging.'

'Then there'd be daily executions held in every town,' said Colbeck, bluntly, 'for there must be thousands of men who enjoy such liaisons. If you make adultery a capital offence, sir, you'd reduce the population of London quite markedly.' Tallis bridled. 'No, the problem with Gregory Newman was that he had too much love inside him.'

'Love! Is that what you call it, Inspector?'

'Yes. He was a man of deep passion. When his young wife was taken so tragically ill, that passion was stifled until it began to turn sour. We saw it again in his strange devotion to Win Hawkshaw. We did, Superintendent,' he went on as Tallis scowled. 'He cared for her enough to want to rescue her from an undeserving husband even if it meant sending that husband to the scaffold. Love turned sour is like a disease.'

'It infected him and his doxy,' said Tallis. 'If I had my way, she'd be paraded through the streets so that all could see her shame. The woman deserves to be tarred and feathered.'

Colbeck was glad that he had not confided details of the more serious irregularity that he had uncovered. The superintendent would have been outraged, insisting on the arrest of Emily Hawkshaw on a charge of withholding vital evidence at the trial of her stepfather. Colbeck saw no gain in such an action. The girl had already punished herself far more than the law would be able to do. Before he left Ashford, she had confided one piece of reassuring news to Colbeck. She was not pregnant. No child would come forth from her illicit union to make her shame public. Colbeck had left the girl to work out her own salvation. Thoroughly chastened by all that had happened, she seemed ready to take a more positive attitude to past misdemeanours.

'The rest,' declared Tallis, 'we can safely leave to the court.'

'That's what everyone felt at Hawkshaw's trial,' said Leeming.

'Don't be impertinent, Sergeant.'

'No, sir.'

'Our work is done and – thanks to you, gentlemen – it was done extremely well. I congratulate you both and will commend you in my report to the Commissioners. You have cleansed Ashford of its fiends.'

'We did get some assistance from Constable Butterkiss,' remarked Leeming, ready to give the man his due. 'He found Amos Lockyer for us.'

'That reflects well on him.'

'Yes,' said Colbeck, smiling inwardly as he thought of Madeleine Andrews, 'our success is not solely due to our own efforts, sir. We had invaluable help from other sources.'

The last bit of paint was still drying on the paper when she heard the sound of the hansom cab in the street outside.

Madeleine Andrews was flustered. Certain that Robert Colbeck had come to see her, she was upset to be caught in her old clothes and with paint all over her fingers. She grabbed the painting and hid it quickly in the kitchen, swilling her hands in a bucket of water and wiping them in an old cloth. There was a knock on the front door. After adjusting her hair in the mirror, Madeleine opened the door to her visitor. He was holding a posy of flowers.

'Robert!' she said, pretending surprise.

'Hello, Madeleine,' he said, 'I just wanted to thank you for the help that you gave us and to offer this small token of my gratitude.'

'They're beautiful!' she said, taking the posy and sniffing the petals. 'Thank you so much.'

'You deserve a whole garden of flowers for what you did.'

'I'm so glad that I could help. But you are the only true Railway Detective. You are on the front page of the newspaper once again.'

'Yes, Superintendent Tallis was pleased with that. He feels that our success should be given wide publicity to deter other criminals.'

'He's right.'

'I have my doubts, Madeleine. It only serves to warn them to be more careful in future. If we reveal too much about our methods of detection in newspaper articles, we are actually helping the underworld.'

'Be that as it may,' she said, 'won't you come in?'

'Only for a moment.' He stepped into the house and she closed the door behind them. 'I'm on my way to Bethnal Green to honour a promise I made to Victor Leeming.'

'Oh, yes. You told me that he was set upon at the Seven Stars.'

'That's why I'm letting him lead the raid. I'll only be there in a nominal capacity. We're going to close the place down for a time by revoking the landlord's licence.'

'On what grounds?'

'Serving under-age customers, harbouring fugitives, running a disorderly house. We'll think up plenty of reasons to close the doors on the Seven Stars. And however random they may seem,' he went on, 'I can assure you that those reasons will all have a solid foundation. In his brief and bruising visit there, Victor noticed a number of violations of the licensing laws.'

'And that's where Jacob Guttridge used to go?'

'Only when disguised under a false name.'

'Who was the man who followed him that night?'

'Amos Lockyer,' he replied. 'A policeman from Ashford who was dismissed for being drunk on duty and who took on the commission to make some money. In fairness to him, it never crossed his mind that such dire consequences would result from his work.'

'I'm thrilled that I was able to help you.'

'It will encourage me to call on you again, perhaps.'

Madeleine beamed. 'I'm at your service, Inspector,' she said. 'But while you're here, I have a present for you – though it isn't quite dry yet.'

'A present for me?'

'Close your eyes, Robert.'

'You're the one who deserves a present,' he said, closing his eyes and wondering what she was going to give him. 'How long must I wait?'

'Only a moment.' She took the posy into the kitchen and returned with the painting. Madeleine held it up in front of him. 'You can look now, Robert.'

'Good heavens! It's the *Lord of the Isles*.'

'I knew that you'd recognise it.'

'There are two things you can rely on me to recognise, Madeleine. One is a famous locomotive in all its glory.'

'What's the other?'

'Artistic merit,' he said, scrutinising every detail. 'This really is a fine piece of work. Quite the best thing you've ever done.'

'Then you'll accept it?'

'I'll do more than that, Madeleine. I'll have it framed and hung over the desk in my study. Then I'll invite you and your father to come to tea one Sunday and view it in position.'

'That would be wonderful!'

Madeleine had never been to Colbeck's house before and she felt that the invitation marked a step forward in their relationship. He had been careful to include her father but she knew that he was giving her a small but important signal. Her own signal was contained in the painting and he could not have been more appreciative.

'Thank you, thank you,' he said, unable to take his eyes off the gift. 'It's quite inspiring.'

'Father was very critical,' she said.

'He is inclined to be censorious. I find no fault in it at all.'

'It was my choice of locomotive that upset him. Mr Gooch built the *Lord of the Isles* for the Great Western Railway. Since he works for another railway company, Father thinks that I should have done a painting of one of their locomotives.'

'Mr Crampton's *Liverpool*, for instance? A splendid steam engine. That was built for the London and North Western Railway.'

'*Lord of the Isles* has a special place in my heart,' she said.

'As I was painting it, I recalled that magical day we spent together at the Great Exhibition. That's when I first saw it on display.'

'I, too, have the fondest memories of that occasion,' he told her, looking across at her with affection. 'When the painting has been hung, bring your father to take a second look at it.' He gave her a warm smile. 'Perhaps we can persuade him that you did make the right choice.'

It was the clearest signal of all. Madeleine laughed with joy.

THE RAILWAY VIADUCT

CHAPTER ONE

1852

Something was missing. His preliminary sketch of the Sankey Viaduct was both dramatic and satisfyingly precise, but it needed something to anchor it, a human dimension to give a sense of scale. He knew exactly where to place the figures, and he could easily have pencilled them in, but he preferred to rely on chance rather than imagination. Ambrose Hooper had been an artist for over forty years and his continued success could not simply be attributed to his sharp eye and gifted hand. In all that he did, luck played a decisive part. It was uncanny. Whenever he needed to add a crucial element to a painting, he did not have to wait long for inspiration to come. An idea somehow presented itself before him.

Hooper was a short, slim, angular man in his sixties with a full beard and long grey hair that fell like a waterfall from beneath his battered old straw hat. On a hot summer's day, he had taken off his crumpled white jacket so that he could work at his easel in his shirtsleeves. He wore tiny spectacles and narrowed his lids to peer through them. An experienced landscape artist, it was the first time that he had turned his attention to the massive railway system that had changed the face of the English countryside so radically over the previous twenty years. It was a challenge for him.

Viewed from below, the Sankey Viaduct was truly imposing. It had been opened in 1830 as part of the Liverpool and Manchester Railway and was roughly halfway between the two places. Straddling a valley that contained both a canal and a brook, the viaduct was supported by nine identical arches, each with a span of fifty feet. Massive piers rose up with perpendicular certitude from the piles that had been driven deep down into the waterbeds, and the parapet coping reached a height of almost seventy feet, leaving ample room to spare for the tallest vessels that sailed on the canal. It was a predominantly brick structure, finished off with dressings and facings that gave it an added lustre. In the bright sunshine, it was a dazzling piece of architectural masonry.

Hooper's sketch had caught its towering simplicity. His main objective, however, was to show the stark contrast between the valley itself with its verdant meadows and the man-made intrusions of canal and viaduct. A few cattle grazed obligingly on his side of the waterway and Hooper was able to incorporate them in his drawing, timeless symbols of rural life in the shadow of industry. What he required now were human figures and – as ever, his luck held out – they not only appeared magically before him, they stood more or less in the spot where he wanted them to be.

Two women and a small boy had come to look up at the viaduct. From the way that she held the boy's hand, Hooper decided that the younger woman must be his mother and his guess was that the other woman, older and more fastidious, was her spinster sister, less than happy at being there. She was wearing too much clothing for such a hot day and was troubled by insects that flew in under her poke bonnet. While the boy and his mother seemed quietly excited, the other woman lifted the hem of her dress well above the ground so that it would not trail in any of the cowpats. The visit was clearly for the boy's benefit and not for that of his maiden aunt.

As he put them into his sketch with deft flicks of his pencil, Ambrose Hooper gave each of them a name to lend some character. The mother was Hester Lewthwaite, the wife of a provincial banker perhaps; her son, eight or nine years of age at most, was Anthony Lewthwaite; and the disagreeable third person was Petronella Snark, disappointed in love, highly critical of her sister and not at all inclined to indulge a small boy if it entailed trudging across a meadow in the stifling heat. Both women wore steel-ringed crinolines but, while Hester's was fashionable, brightly coloured and had a pretty flounced skirt, Petronella's dress was dark and dowdy.

He knew why they were there. When he took his watch from the pocket of his waistcoat, Hooper saw that a train was due to cross the viaduct at any moment. It was something he had always planned to use in his painting. A railway viaduct would not suffice. Only a locomotive could bring it to life and display its true purpose. Gazing up, the artist had his pencil ready. Out of the corner of his eye, he then caught sight of another element that had perforce to be included. A sailing barge was gliding serenely along the canal towards the viaduct with three men aboard. Before attempting to sketch the vessel, however, Hooper elected to wait until the train had passed. It was usually on time.

Seconds later, he heard it coming. Mother and child looked up with anticipatory delight. The other woman did not. The men on the barge raised their eyes as well but nobody watched with the same intensity as Ambrose Hooper. Just when he wanted it, the locomotive came into sight, an iron monster, belching clouds of steam and filling the whole valley with its thunder. Behind it came an endless string of gleaming carriages, rattling noisily across the viaduct high above the spectators. And then, to their amazement, they all saw something that they could not possibly have expected.

The body of a man hurtled over the edge of the viaduct and fell swiftly through the air until it landed in the canal, hitting the water with such irresistible force that it splashed both banks. The mother put protective arms around her son, the other woman staggered back in horror, the three men in the barge exchanged looks of utter disbelief. It had been an astonishing sight but the cows accorded it no more than a cursory glance before returning to the more important business of chewing the cud. Hooper was exhilarated. Intending to portray the headlong dash of the train, he had been blessed with another stroke of good fortune. He had witnessed something that no artist could ever invent.

As a result, his painting would now celebrate a murder.

CHAPTER TWO

After a couple of tedious hours in court, Detective Inspector Robert Colbeck was glad to return to Scotland Yard so that he could write a full report on the case, and clear up some of the paperwork cluttering his desk. He got no further than his office door. Superintendent Tallis loomed into view at the end of the corridor and beckoned him with an imperious crook of a tobacco-stained finger. When they went into the superintendent's office, Colbeck could smell the pungent smoke still hanging in the air. It was a telltale sign that a serious crime had been committed. His superior's response to any crisis was to reach for his cigar box. Tallis waved a piece of paper at him.

'This message came by electric telegraph,' he said.

'From where?'

'Liverpool. That's where the body was taken.'

'Another murder?' asked Colbeck with interest.

'Another *railway* murder. It's the reason I'm sending you.'

The inspector was not surprised. After his success in capturing the gang responsible for the daring robbery of a mail train, the press had dubbed him unanimously as the Railway Detective and he had lived up to the name subsequently. It gave him a kudos he enjoyed, a popularity that Tallis resented and a burden of expectation that could feel very heavy at times. Robert Colbeck was tall, lean, conventionally handsome and dressed as usual in an immaculate black frock coat, well-cut fawn trousers and an Ascot cravat. Still in his thirties, he had risen swiftly in the Detective Department, acquiring a reputation for intelligence, efficiency and single-mindedness that few could emulate. His promotion had been a source of great pride to his friends and a constant irritation to his detractors, such as the superintendent.

Edward Tallis was a stout, red-faced man in his fifties with a shock of grey hair and a neat moustache that he trimmed on a daily basis. His years in the army had left him with the habit of command, a passion for order and an unshakable belief in the virtues of the British Empire. Though invariably smart, he felt almost shabby beside the acknowledged dandy of Scotland Yard. Tallis derided what he saw as Colbeck's vanity, but he was honest enough to recognise the inspector's rare qualities as a detective. It encouraged him to suppress his instinctive dislike of the man. For his part, Colbeck, too, made allowances. Seniority meant that Tallis had to be obeyed and the inspector's natural antipathy towards him had to be hidden.

Tallis thrust the paper at him. 'Read it for yourself,' he said.

'Thank you, sir.' Colbeck needed only seconds to do so. 'This does not tell us very much, Superintendent.'

'What did you expect – a three-volume novel?'

'It claims that the victim was thrown from a moving train.'

'So?'

'That suggests great strength on the part of the killer. He would have to pitch a grown man through a window and over the parapet of the Sankey Viaduct. Unless, of course,' he added, handing the telegraph back to Tallis, 'he opened the door of the carriage first.'

'This is no time for idle speculation.'

'I agree, Superintendent.'

'Are you in a position to take charge of the case?'

'I believe so.'

'What happened in court this morning?'

'The jury finally brought in a verdict of guilty, sir. Why it should have taken them so infernally long, I can only hazard a guess. The evidence against Major Harrison-Clark was overwhelming.'

'That may be,' said Tallis with gruff regret, 'but I hate to see a military man brought down like that. The major served his country honourably for many years.'

'That does not entitle him to strangle his wife.'

'There was great provocation, I daresay.'

A confirmed bachelor, Tallis had no insight into the mysteries of married life and no taste for the company of women. If a husband killed his spouse, the superintendent tended to assume that she was in some way obscurely responsible for her own demise. Colbeck did not argue with him or even point out that, in fact, Major Rupert Harrison-Clark had a history of violent behaviour. The inspector was too anxious to be on his way.

'What about my report on the case?' he asked.

'It can wait.'

'Am I to take Victor with me, sir?'

'Sergeant Leeming has already been apprised of the details.'

'Such as they are.'

'Such – as you so rightly point out – as they are.' Tallis looked down at the telegraph. 'Have you ever seen this viaduct?'

'Yes, Superintendent. A remarkable piece of engineering.'

'I don't share your admiration of the railway system.'

'I appreciate quality in all walks of life,' said Colbeck, easily, 'and my fondness for railways is by no means uncritical. Engineers and contractors alike have made hideous mistakes in the past, some of which have cost lives as well as money. The Sankey Viaduct, on the other hand, was an undoubted triumph. It is also our first clue.'

Tallis blinked. 'Is it?'

'Of course, sir. It was no accident that the victim was hurled from that particular place. My belief is that the killer chose it with care.' He opened the door then paused to give the other man a farewell smile. 'We shall have to find out why.'

Sidney Heyford was a tall, stringy, ginger-haired individual in his forties who seemed to have grown in height since his promotion to the rank of inspector. When he had first joined the local constabulary, he had been fearless and conscientious, liked by his colleagues and respected by the criminal fraternity. He still worked as hard as ever but his eminence had made him arrogant, unyielding and officious. It had also made him very proprietorial. When he first heard the news, he let out a snort of disgust and flung the telegraph aside.

'Detectives from Scotland Yard!'

'Yes, sir,' said Constable Praine. 'Two of them.'

'I don't care if it's two or twenty. We don't want them here.'

'No, Inspector.'

'We can solve this crime on our own.'

'If you say so.'

'I do say so, Constable. It was committed on our doorstep.'

'That's not strictly true,' said Praine, pedantically. 'The Sankey Viaduct is halfway between here and Manchester.

Some would claim that *they* have a right to take over the case.'

'Manchester?'

'Yes, Inspector.'

'Poppycock! Arrant poppycock!'

'If you say so.'

'I do say so, Constable.'

'The train in question did depart from Manchester.'

'But it was coming here, man – to Liverpool!'

In the eyes of Inspector Sidney Heyford, it was an unanswerable argument and the constable would not, in any case, have dared to quarrel with him. It was not only because of the other man's position that Walter Praine held his tongue. Big, brawny and with a walrus moustache hiding much of his podgy young face, Praine nursed secret ambitions to become Heyford's son-in-law one day, a fact that he had yet to communicate to the inspector's comely daughter. The situation made Praine eager to impress his superior. To that end, he was ready to endure the brusque formality with which he was treated.

'I'm sure that you are right, Inspector,' he said, obsequiously.

'There is no substitute for local knowledge.'

'I agree, sir.'

'We have done all that any detectives from the Metropolitan Police would have done – much more, probably.' Heyford turned an accusatory glare on Praine. 'How did they get to know of the crime in the first place?' he demanded. 'I hope that nobody from here dared to inform them?'

'It was the railway company who sent the telegraph.'

'They should have shown more faith in us.'

The two men were in the central police station in Liverpool. Both wore spotless uniforms. Inspector Heyford had spent most of the day leading the investigation into the murder.

When he finally returned to his office late that afternoon, the waiting telegraph was passed to him. It had immediately aroused his possessive streak.

'This is our murder. I mean to keep it that way.'

'We were the first to receive reports of it.'

'I'll brook no interference.'

'If you say so, sir.'

'And, for heaven's sake, stop repeating that inane phrase,' said Heyford with vehemence. 'You're a police constable, not a parrot.' Praine gave a contrite nod. 'What time should we expect them?'

'Not for another hour or so at least.'

'How did you decide that?'

'I checked the timetables in *Bradshaw*,' said Praine, hoping that his initiative might be rewarded with at least a nod of approval. Instead, it was met with a blank stare. 'They could not have set out much before the time when that telegraph was sent. If they arrive at Lime Street by six-thirty, they will be here not long afterwards.'

'They shouldn't be here at all,' grumbled Heyford, consulting his pocket watch. 'I need to master all the details before they come. Get out of here, Constable, and give me plenty of warning before they actually cross our threshold.'

'Yes, Inspector.'

'Make yourself scarce, then.'

Walter Praine left the room, acutely aware of the fact that he had failed to ingratiate himself with his putative father-in-law. Until he managed to do that, he could not possibly muster the confidence that was needed to make a proposal of marriage. Glad to be rid of him, Heyford began to read carefully through the statements that had been taken from the witnesses. It was only minutes before there was a timid knock on the door.

'Yes?' he barked.

The door opened and Praine put a tentative head around it.

'The gentlemen from Scotland Yard are already here, sir,' he said, sheepishly. 'Shall I show them in?'

Heyford leapt to his feet. 'Here?' he cried. 'How can that be? You told me that we had at least an hour.'

'I was mistaken.'

'Not for the first time, Constable Praine.'

Quelling him with a glare, Sidney Heyford opened the door wide and went into the outer office, manufacturing a smile as he did so. Robert Colbeck and Victor Leeming were studying the Wanted posters on the walls. Both men had bags with them. After a flurry of introductions, the detectives were taken into the little office and invited to sit down. Heyford was not impressed by Colbeck's elegance. With his stocky frame and gnarled face, Leeming did at least look like a policeman. That was not the case with his companion. To the man in uniform, Colbeck's debonair appearance and cultured voice were completely out of place in the rough and tumble world of law enforcement.

'I'm sorry that it's so cramped in here,' Heyford began.

'We've seen worse,' said Leeming, looking around.

'Much worse,' agreed Colbeck.

'Ashford in Kent, for instance. Six thousand people and only two constables to look after them from a tiny police house.'

'Some towns still refuse to take policing seriously enough. They take the Utopian view that crime will somehow solve itself without the intercession of detective work.' He appraised Heyford shrewdly. 'I'm sure that Liverpool displays more common sense.'

'It has to, Inspector,' said Heyford, sententiously, 'though we are woefully short of men to police a population of well over three hundred thousand. This is a thriving port. When the ships dock here, we've foreigners of all kind roaming our streets. If my men did not keep close watch over them, we'd have riot and destruction.'

'I'm sure that you do an excellent job.'

'That's how I earned my promotion.' He looked from one to the other. 'May I ask how you got here so soon?'

'That was the inspector's doing,' said Leeming, indicating his companion. 'He knows everything about train timetables. I prefer to travel by coach but Inspector Colbeck insisted that we came by rail.'

'How else could we have seen the Sankey Viaduct?' asked Colbeck. 'A coach would hardly have taken us across it. And think of the time we saved, Victor. Travel between Manchester and Liverpool by coach and it will take you up to four and a half hours. The train got us here in far less than half that time.' He turned to Heyford. 'I've always been fascinated by the railway system. That's why I know how to get from London to Liverpool at the fastest possible speed.'

'Inspector Colbeck!' said Heyford as realisation dawned. 'I thought I'd heard that name before.'

'He's the Railway Detective,' explained Leeming.

The information did not endear them to Heyford. If anything, it only soured him even more. Newspaper accounts of Colbeck's exploits had reached Liverpool in the past and they were invariably full of praise. Sidney Heyford felt that he deserved the same kind of public veneration. He took a deep breath.

'We are quite able to handle this case ourselves,' he asserted.

'That may be so,' said Colbeck, briskly, 'but your authority has been overridden. The London and North-West Railway

Company has asked specifically that the Detective Department of the Metropolitan Police Force intercede. Last year, Sergeant Leeming and I were fortunate enough to solve an earlier crime for the same company so we were requested by name.'

Leeming nodded. 'They were very grateful.'

'So, instead of haggling over who should be in charge, I suggest that you give us all the information that you have so far gathered. We shall, of course, be glad of your assistance, Inspector Heyford, but we have not come all this way to have our credentials questioned.'

Colbeck had spoken with such firm politeness that Heyford was slightly stunned. He retreated into a muted surliness. Snatching up the papers from his desk, he told them about the progress of the investigation, reciting the details as if he had learnt them by heart.

'At 10.15 a.m.,' he said, flatly, 'a train passed over the Sankey Viaduct on its way to Liverpool. The body of a man was thrown over the parapet and landed in the canal. When some people on a barge hauled it out of the water – their names were Enoch and Samuel Triggs, a father and son – it was found that the victim had been killed before he was flung from the train. He had been stabbed in the back though there was no sign of any weapon.'

'What state was the body in?' asked Colbeck.

'A bad one, Inspector. When he hit the water, the man's head collided with a piece of driftwood. It smashed his face in. His own mother wouldn't recognise him now.'

'Was there anything on his body to identify him?'

'Nothing. His wallet and watch were missing. So was his jacket.'

'Where is the body now?'

'In the mortuary.'

'I'd like to examine it.'

'It will tell you nothing beyond the fact that he was a young man and a very healthy one, by the look of it.'

'Nevertheless, I want to see the body this evening.'

'Very well.'

'If you don't mind, sir,' said Leeming, squeamishly, 'it's a treat that I'll forego. I hate morgues. They unsettle my stomach.'

Colbeck smiled. 'Then I'll spare you the ordeal, Victor.' He looked at Heyford again. 'There were two men on the barge, you say?'

'Actually,' replied the other, 'there were three, the third being Micah Triggs. He owns the barge but is very old. His son and grandson do most of the work.'

'But he was another witness.'

'Yes, Inspector. He confirmed what the others told me. When they had pulled the man out of the canal, they moored the barge. Samuel Triggs clambered all the way up to the station and caught the next train here to report the crime.' He puffed out his chest. 'He knew that Liverpool had a better police force than Manchester.'

Leeming was puzzled. 'Why didn't the train from which the body was thrown stop at the viaduct? We did. Inspector Colbeck wanted to take a look at the scene of the crime.'

'This morning's train was an express that does not stop at all the intermediate stations.'

'The killer would have chosen it for that reason,' said Colbeck.

'Once he had jettisoned his victim, he wanted to get away from there as swiftly as possible.' He pondered. 'So far, it would appear, we have three witnesses, all of whom were in a similar position. Was anyone else there at the time?'

'According to Enoch Triggs, there were two ladies and a boy on the bank but they fled in fear. We have no idea who they were. Oh, yes,' he went on, studying one of the statements, 'and there seems to have been a man there as well but he, too, vanished. The truth is that Enoch Triggs and his son were too busy trying to rescue the body from the water to notice much else.'

'That takes care of those at the scene of the crime. I presume that you have details of where this barge can be reached?'

'Yes, Inspector.'

'Good. What about the other witnesses?'

'There *were* none,' asserted Heyford.

'A train full of passengers and nobody sees a man being tossed over the side of a viaduct? That's not an everyday event. It's something that people would remember.'

'I'd remember it,' agreed Leeming.

'Well?' said Colbeck. 'Did you make any effort to contact the passengers on that train, Inspector Heyford?'

'How could I?' asked the other, defensively. 'By the time we were made aware of the crime, the passengers had all dispersed throughout the city.'

'Many of them may have intended to return to Manchester. It may well be that some people live there and work here. Did it never occur to you to have someone at the railway station this afternoon to question anyone leaving Liverpool who might have travelled on that train this morning?'

'No, sir.'

'Then we'll need to meet the same train tomorrow. With luck, we should find at least a few people who make the journey daily.'

'Wait,' said Heyford, leafing through the papers. 'There was something else. Oddly enough, it was the old man who told me this.'

'Micah Triggs?'

'He thought the man was thrown from the last carriage.'

'So?'

'That might explain why nobody saw it happen.'

'What about the guard?' said Leeming. 'His van would be behind the last carriage. Why did he see nothing?'

'Because he could have been looking the other way,' said Colbeck, thinking it through, 'or been distracted by something else. It would only have taken seconds to dispose of that body and the last carriage would be the ideal place.' His eyes flicked back to Heyford. 'I take it that you've spoken to the guard, Inspector.'

'No,' said the other. 'When I got to the station, that train had long since left for Manchester with the guard aboard.'

'He would have been back at Lime Street in due course. Guards work long hours. I know their shift patterns. All you had to do was to look at a copy of *Bradshaw's Guide* and you could have worked out when that particular train would return here. We need every pair of eyes we can call on, Inspector. The guard must be questioned.'

'If he'd had anything to report, he'd have come forward.'

'He *does* have something to report,' said Colbeck. 'He may not have witnessed the crime being committed but he would have seen the passengers boarding the train, perhaps even noticed who got into the carriage next to his van. His evidence could be vital. I find it strange that you did not realise that.'

'I had other things to do, Inspector Colbeck,' bleated the other, caught on the raw. 'I had to take statements from the witnesses then arrange for the transfer of the body. Do not worry,' he said, huffily, 'I'll meet that very train tomorrow and interview the guard in person.'

'Sergeant Leeming will already have done so.'

'Will I?' gulped Leeming.

'Yes, Victor. You'll catch an early train to Manchester so that you can speak to the staff at the station in case any of them remember who got into that last carriage. Then you must talk to the guard who was on that train today.'

'What then?'

'Travel back here on the same train, of course,' said Colbeck, 'making sure that you sit in the last carriage. You'll get some idea of how fast you go over the Sankey Viaduct and how difficult it would have been to hurl a dead body into the canal.'

Leeming goggled. 'I hope you're not expecting me to throw someone out of the carriage, sir.'

'Simply use your imagination.'

'What about me?' asked Heyford. 'Is there anything I can do?'

'Several things.'

'Such as?'

'First of all, you can recommend a hotel nearby so that Sergeant Leeming can book some rooms there. Second, you can conduct me to the mortuary and, after that, you can point me in the direction of the local newspapers.'

'Newspapers?'

'Yes,' said Colbeck, tiring of his pedestrian slowness. 'Papers that contain news. People have a habit of reading them. We need to reach as many of them as we can with a description of the victim.'

Heyford was scornful. 'How can you describe a faceless man?'

'By concentrating on his other features – age, height, build, hair colour and so on. His clothing will give us some idea of his social class. In short, we can provide enough details for anyone who knows him to be able to identify the man. Don't you agree?'

'Yes, Inspector.' There was a grudging respect. 'I suppose I do.'

'Have you reached any conclusion yourself?' asked Leeming.

'Only the obvious one, Sergeant – it was murder for gain. The victim was killed so that he could be robbed.'

'Oh, I suspect that there was much more to it than that,' said Colbeck. 'A lot of calculation went into this murder. Nobody would take so much trouble simply to get his hands on the contents of another man's wallet. Always reject the obvious, Inspector Heyford. It has a nasty tendency to mislead.'

'Yes, sir,' grunted the other.

Colbeck stood up. 'Let's get started, shall we? Suggest a hotel then lead me to the mortuary. The sooner we get that description in the newspapers, the better. With luck, he may read it.'

'Who?'

'The other witness. I discount the two ladies and the boy. They'll have been too shocked to give a coherent account. But there was a man on that bank as well. He's the person who interests me.'

Ambrose Hooper put the finishing touches to his work then stood back to admire it. He was in his studio, a place of amiable chaos that contained several paintings that had been started then abandoned, and dozens of pencil drawings that had never progressed beyond the stage of a rough sketch. Artist's materials lay everywhere. Light was fading so it was impossible for him to work on but he did not, in any case, need to do so. What he had achieved already had a sense of completeness to it. The sketch he had made of the Sankey Viaduct was now a vivid watercolour that would serve as model for the much bigger work he intended to paint.

It was all there – viaduct, canal, train, sailing barge, lush green fields, cows and, in the foreground, two women and a small boy. What brought the whole scene together, giving it life and definition, was the central figure of the man who was tumbling helplessly through the air towards the water, a bizarre link between viaduct and canal. Hooper was thrilled. Instead of producing yet another landscape, he had created a unique historical document. It would be his masterpiece.

CHAPTER THREE

Victor Leeming was a walking paradox. The more things he found to dislike about his job, the more attached he became to it. He hated working late hours, looking at mutilated corpses, appearing in court to give evidence, facing the wrath of Superintendent Tallis, having to arrest women, being forced to write endless reports and travelling, whenever he ventured outside London, by rail instead of road. Most of all, he hated being separated for a night from his wife, Estelle, and their children. Notwithstanding all that, he loved being a detective and having the privilege of working alongside the famous Robert Colbeck. Slightly older than the inspector, he had none of the latter's acuity or grasp of detail. What Leeming could offer were tenacity, commitment and an unflinching readiness to face danger.

He slept fitfully that night. The bed was soft and the sheets were clean but he was never happy when Estelle was not beside him. Her love could sustain him through anything. It blinded her to the patent ugliness of her husband. His broken nose and jagged features would have tempted few women. His squint would have repelled most wives. Estelle adored him for his character rather than his appearance, and, as he had discovered long ago, the most hideous man could look handsome in the dark. Night was the time for confidences, for catching up on domestic events, for making plans, for reaching decisions and for sharing those marital intimacies that never seemed to dull with the passage of time. Leeming missed her painfully. Instead of waking up in his wife's arms, he had to go on another train journey. It was unjust.

Over an early breakfast at the hotel the next morning, he had difficulty in staying fully awake. Leeming's yawns punctuated the conversation. Colbeck was sympathetic.

'How much sleep did you get last night, Victor?' he said.

'Not enough.'

'I gathered that.' Colbeck ate the last of his toast. 'Make sure that you don't doze off on the train. I need you to remain alert. When you get to Lime Street, buy yourself a newspaper.'

'Why?'

'Because it will contain a description of the man we need to identify. Memorise it so that you can pass it on to the various people you question in Manchester.'

'Wouldn't it be easier simply to show them the newspaper?'

'No. You must master all the facts. I'm not having you thrusting a newspaper article under their noses. It's important to look everyone in the eye when you talk to them.'

'If I can keep mine open,' said Leeming, wearily. He drained his teacup in a gulp. 'Is it true that the man's shoes were missing?'

'His shoes and his jacket.'

'I can imagine someone stealing the jacket. It would have his wallet and other things of value in it. Why take his shoes as well?'

'They were probably of high quality. The rest of his clothing certainly was, Victor. It is no working man we seek. The murder victim dressed well and had a comfortable income.'

'How much is comfortable, Inspector?'

'More than we get paid.'

Leeming gave a hollow laugh. He finished his breakfast then checked the time. He had to be on his way. Colbeck accompanied him out of the hotel dining room and into a lobby that was decorated with unsightly potted plants. When someone opened the front door, the noise of heavy traffic burst in. Liverpool was palpably alive and busy. Leeming had no enthusiasm for stepping out into the swirling maelstrom but he steeled himself to do so. After an exchange of farewells with Colbeck, he strode off in the direction of Lime Street.

The first thing he noticed when he reached the railway station was the visible presence of uniformed policemen. Inspector Heyford had obviously taken Colbeck's strictures to heart. Leeming bought a return ticket to Manchester then picked up a copy of the *Liverpool Times* from a vendor with a stentorian voice. The murder attracted a banner headline on the front page. Colbeck's appeal for information was also given prominence. There was no mention of Inspector Sidney Heyford. The Liverpool constabulary had been eclipsed by the arrival of two detectives from Scotland Yard. Leeming was glad that nobody in the bustling station knew that he was one of the men dispatched from London. In his present somnambulistic state, he was hardly a good advertisement for the Metropolitan Police.

The platform was crowded, the noise of trains was deafening and the billowing steam was an impenetrable fog that seemed to thicken insidiously with every minute and invade his nostrils. In the previous year, Lime Street Station had been considerably enlarged, its majestic iron structure being the first of its kind. Leeming was unable to see this marvel of industrial architecture. His mind was on the harrowing journey ahead. When the train pulled in and shed its passengers, he braced himself and climbed aboard. The newspaper kept him awake long enough for him to read the front page. Then the locomotive exploded into action and the train jerked forward like an angry mastiff pulling on a leash.

Within seconds, Victor Leeming was fast asleep.

Inspector Robert Colbeck also spent time at Lime Street that morning, but he made sure that he saw every inch of it, struck by how much railway stations had improved in the past twenty years. It did not have the classical magnificence of Euston, but it had a reassuring solidity and was supremely functional. Even though it was used by thousands of passengers every week, it still had an air of newness about it. Colbeck was there to meet the train from which the murder victim had been hurled on the previous day, hoping that Sergeant Leeming's visit to Manchester had borne fruit.

Blackboards had been set up along the platform with a question chalked on them in large capitals – DID YOU TRAVEL ON THIS TRAIN YESTERDAY? – and policemen were ready to talk to anyone who came forward. Colbeck watched with approval. Long before the train had even arrived at Lime Street, however, Constable Walter Praine bore down purposefully on the detective.

'Excuse me, Inspector,' he said. 'May I have a word, please?'

'Of course,' replied Colbeck.

'There's someone at the police station who refuses to speak to anyone but you. He saw your name in the newspaper this morning and says that he has important information for the person in charge of the investigation.' Praine rolled his eyes.

'Inspector Heyford was most upset that the fellow would not talk to him.'

'Did this man say nothing at all?'

'Only that you'd got it wrong, sir.'

'Wrong?'

'Your description of the murder victim.'

'Then I look forward to being corrected,' said Colbeck, eagerly. 'Any new facts that can be gleaned are most welcome.'

Praine led the way to a waiting cab and the two of them were soon carried along bumpy streets that were positively swarming with horse-drawn traffic and handcarts. When they reached the police station, the first person they met was an aggrieved Sidney Heyford.

'This is *my* police station in *my* town,' he complained, 'and the wretched man spurns me.'

'Did he give you his name?' asked Colbeck.

'Ambrose Hooper. He's an *artist*.'

Heyford pronounced the word with utter contempt as if it were a heinous crime that had not yet come within the purview of the statute book. In his codex, artists were shameless outcasts, parasites who lived off others and who should, at the very least, be transported to a penal colony to reflect on their sinful existence. Heyford jerked his thumb towards his office.

'He's in there, Inspector.'

'Thank you,' said Colbeck.

Removing his hat, he opened the door and went into the office. A dishevelled Ambrose Hooper rose from his chair to greet him.

'Are you the detective from London?'

'Yes, Mr Hooper. I am Inspector Colbeck.'

'I thought you didn't come from around here,' said Hooper, looking him up and down. 'Liverpool is a philistine place. It has no real appreciation of art and architecture. It idolises conformity. Those of us who cut a dash with our clothing or our way of life could never fit easily into Liverpool. I hate towns of any kind myself. I choose to live in the country and breathe in free air.'

Ambrose Hooper was wearing his crumpled white jacket over a flowery waistcoat and a pair of baggy blue trousers. A fading blue cravat was at his neck. His straw hat lay on the table beside a dog-eared portfolio. Some paint had lodged in his beard. Wisps of grey hair stood up mutinously all over his head. Colbeck could see that he was a man of independent mind.

'I'm told that you believe I am wrong,' said Colbeck.

'I don't believe it, sir – I *know* it.'

'How?'

'I was there, Inspector.'

'At the Sankey Viaduct?'

'Yes, I saw exactly what happened.'

'Then why didn't you give a statement to the police?'

'Because that would have meant waiting an age until they arrived on the scene,' explained Hooper. 'Besides, there was nothing that I could do. The body was hauled aboard that barge. I felt that it was important to record the event while it was still fresh in my mind.'

Colbeck was delighted. 'You mean that you went home and wrote down an account of all that you'd seen?'

'I'm no wordsmith, sir. Language has such severe limitations. Art, on the other hand, does not. It has an immediacy that no author could match.' He picked up the portfolio. 'Do you want to know what I saw at the Sankey Viaduct yesterday?'

'Very much so, Mr Hooper.'

'Then behold, my friend.'

Untying the ribbon, the artist opened the cover of the portfolio with a flourish to reveal his work. Colbeck was flabbergasted. An unexpected bounty had just fallen into his lap. What he was looking at was nothing less than a detailed photograph of what had actually happened. Having read the statements from the three witnesses on the barge, Colbeck had built up a clear picture of the situation in his mind's eye. Hooper's work enlarged and enlivened that mental image.

'A perfect marriage of artistic merit and factual accuracy,' said Hooper, proudly. 'This is merely a rough version, of course, hastily finished so that I could offer it as evidence. I'll use this as the basis for a much larger and more dramatic painting.'

'It could hardly be more dramatic,' opined Colbeck, scrutinising the work. 'You are a man of talent, sir. I congratulate you.'

'Thank you, Inspector.' He pointed to the three small figures in the foreground. 'I moved the ladies slightly but this is more or less the position they were in. Not that they stayed there for long, mark you. When that poor man suddenly dived over the parapet, Aunt Petronella jumped back as if she'd seen a ghost.'

Colbeck was surprised. 'She was your aunt?'

'Not mine – the boy's. At least, that's what I assumed. They were complete strangers to me but I always like to give people names if I include them in a painting. It lends a sense of familiarity.' He indicated each one in turn. 'This is Hester Lewthwaite – this is her son, Anthony – and here is his maiden aunt, Petronella Snark.' He gave a sly chuckle. 'I suppose that if you've preserved your virginity as long as she had, the sight of a man descending on you from a great height would be quite terrifying.'

Colbeck could not believe his good fortune. Ambrose Hooper had provided the best and most comprehensive piece of evidence he had ever received from a member of the public. It answered so many important questions and saved him so much time. He was pleased to note that Micah Triggs had been so observant. The victim did appear to have been thrown from the last carriage. He remembered his own description of the victim.

'Ah,' said Colbeck, jabbing a finger at the man in the centre of the painting. 'This is where I got it wrong. He's wearing a jacket.'

'And a pair of shoes,' added Hooper.

'Are you absolutely sure that was the case?'

'That's the kind of detail an artist doesn't miss. The shoes were gleaming. They caught the sun as he plummeted down. They're only minute in the painting, of course, but, if you look closely, you'll see that the shoes are definitely there.'

'They are indeed.'

'I'm a stickler for precision.'

'This is remarkable, Mr Hooper,' said Colbeck, shaking him warmly by the hand. 'I can't thank you enough.'

'We also serve who only stand and paint.'

'You've made our job so much easier. What a blessing that you happened to be in the right place at the right time!'

'I have a habit of doing that, Inspector. At first, I used to put it down to coincidence but I've come round to the view that I'm an agent of divine purpose. God *wanted* me to bear witness. I daresay it was also true of Aunt Petronella but she was unequal to the challenge.' He looked at the tiny figure of the murder victim. 'What I'd like to know is how he brought off that wonderful conjuring trick.'

'Conjuring trick?'

'Yes,' said Hooper. 'When he left the train, he was wearing

a jacket and a pair of shoes. How did he get rid of them by the time that the police arrived on the scene?'

'There's no mystery there,' said Colbeck with a wry smile.

'No?'

'He clearly had some assistance.'

Victor Leeming talked to every member of staff he could find at the station. By the time he finished, he felt that he had spoken to half the population of Manchester and all to no avail. Ticket clerks, porters, the stationmaster, his assistants, the engine driver, the fireman, even those who sold newspapers at Victoria Station were asked if they had seen anyone suspicious around the same time on the previous day. In effect, they had all given him the same answer – that it was difficult to pick out any one person from the sea of faces that passed in front of them. Least helpful of all had been the guard in charge of the train on which the murder had occurred. His name was Cyril Dear, a short, skinny, animated individual in his fifties who was highly offended even to be approached by the detective. As he talked to him, his hands were gesticulating madly as if he were trying without success to juggle seven invisible balls in the air.

'I saw nobody getting into the last carriage, Sergeant,' he said. 'I've got better things to do than to take note of where every passenger sits. Do you know what being a guard means?'

'Yes,' said Leeming. 'It means that you have responsibilities.'

'Many responsibilities.'

'One of which is to ensure the safety of your passengers.'

'And that's what I do, Sergeant.'

'It must entail being especially vigilant.'

'I *am* especially vigilant,' retorted Dear, hands now juggling five additional balls. 'I defy any man to say that I'm not. I see things that most people would never notice in a hundred years.'

'Yet you are still quite unable to tell me who occupied the last carriage yesterday morning. Think back, sir,' encouraged Leeming, stifling a monstrous yawn. 'When the train was filling up, what did you observe?'

'What I observe every day – paying passengers.'

'Did none of them stand out?'

'Not that I recall.'

'This is very serious,' said Leeming, as people surged past him to walk down the platform. 'A man who travelled on this same train only twenty-four hours ago was murdered in cold blood then flung over the Sankey Viaduct.'

'I know that.'

'We simply must catch his killer.'

'Well, don't look at me, Sergeant,' said Dear, as if he had just been accused of the crime. 'I have an unblemished record of service on this line. I worked on it when it was the Liverpool and Manchester Railway, all of twenty-two years ago. Cyril Dear's name is a byword for loyalty. Speak to anyone. They'll tell you.'

Leeming groaned inwardly 'I have no wish to talk to another human being in Manchester,' he said, ruefully. 'My throat is sore enough already. Very well, Mr Dear. You are obviously unable to help me at the moment. But if you should happen to remember anything of interest about yesterday's journey – anything at all – please let me know when we reach Liverpool.'

'Climb aboard, sir. We leave in two minutes.'

'Good.'

Leeming had turned to get into the last carriage, only to find, to his dismay, that it was already full. Men and women had taken every available seat. With a sinking feeling, he realised why. Manchester newspapers had carried full details of the murder as well. Ghoulish curiosity had dictated where some of the passengers sat. They wanted to be in the very carriage where it was believed the crime had been committed. As it passed over the Sankey Viaduct, they would no doubt all rush to the appropriate window in a body to look out over the parapet. He found it a depressing insight into human nature.

Colbeck had instructed him to travel in the last carriage. Since he could not obey the order, he decided to solve another problem that had vexed them. He swung round to face Cyril Dear again and asserted his authority.

'I'll travel in the guard's van with you,' he declared.

Dear was outraged. 'It's against the rules.'

'Is it?'

'I could never allow it, sir.'

'But you're not allowing it, Mr Dear. I'm forcing myself upon you.' He summoned up his most disarming smile. 'When we reach Liverpool, you'll have the pleasure of reporting me, won't you?'

When he was angry, the freckles on Inspector Heyford's face stood out more than ever. As he stared at the painting, they seemed to glow with a rich intensity. He turned to confront Ambrose Hooper.

'Concealing evidence is a crime,' he warned.

'But I haven't concealed it,' argued the artist. 'I've brought it to you. There it lies, for all to see.'

'A day late.'

'I can see that you are no painter, Inspector Heyford.'

'I prefer to do an honest job sir.'

'Art cannot be rushed. I had to finish the watercolour

before I presented it to the public. I have my reputation to consider.'

'It remains intact,' Colbeck assured him.

'There is still the question of delay,' insisted Heyford. 'You were a witness, Mr Hooper. Yet you sneaked away from the scene of the crime. Action should be taken against you.'

'Then it should also be taken against Mrs Lewthwaite, her son and her unmarried sister, Miss Petronella Snark. They had just as good a view of the whole thing as me.'

Heyford gaped. 'Who on earth *are* these people?'

'I'll explain later, Inspector,' said Colbeck. 'The fact of the matter is that Mr Hooper has shown us crucial evidence that may help us to identify the dead man.'

'How?'

'He had an expensive tailor. I could see that from his trousers. In all likelihood, the name of that tailor will be sewn inside his jacket.'

'But we do not have his jacket, Inspector Colbeck.'

'We will do in due course. As for Mr Hooper, the only action that should be taken is to commend his skill as an artist and to thank him for his assistance.' He closed the portfolio. 'It's been invaluable, sir.'

'It's the least I could do for the victim,' said Hooper, tying up the ribbon. 'His loss was, after all, my gain. Like any true artist, I paint out of a compulsion but there is, alas, a commercial aspect to my work as well. As a result of the publicity surrounding this crime, my painting will fetch a much higher price.'

Heyford was scandalised. 'It should not be allowed.'

'It should,' said Colbeck. 'You deserve every penny, sir.'

Since they were in Heyford's office, Colbeck felt an obligation to let him see the painting even though the inspector did not appreciate either its quality or its significance. When the artist had left, Colbeck tried to mollify Heyford by praising the way that he had deployed his men at the railway station. The freckles slowly lost their glint though they did flare up again when Colbeck told him how Petronella Snark and her companions had come by their names.

'And what's all this about the jacket?' asked Heyford.

'I'll reclaim it from the person who stole it.'

'And who might that be?'

'A member of the Triggs family, of course,' said Colbeck. 'Before you got there, he also relieved the corpse of its shoes. Now that really is a case of withholding evidence.'

There was a tap on the door. In response to Heyford's invitation, it opened to admit Victor Leeming, drooping with fatigue. He removed his hat to wipe perspiration from his brow with the back of his hand.

'What did you find out, Victor?' asked Colbeck.

'That I never wish to travel by train ever again, sir,' replied Leeming, rubbing his back. 'The journey back to Liverpool rattled every bone in my body.'

'Did you discover any witnesses in Manchester?'

'Nobody saw a thing.'

'Not even the guard?'

'No, Inspector. When the train is in motion, he always sits on the other side of the van so he saw the wrong side of the viaduct as the train passed over it yesterday. I made the fatal mistake of sharing the guard's van with him,' he went on, massaging a sore elbow. 'It's no better than a cattle truck.'

'Did he remember *anything* about yesterday's journey?' said Heyford. 'What about the occupants of that last carriage?'

'They could have been a tribe of man-eating pygmies, for all that he cared. The guard's only concern was that the train was on time.' Undoing his coat, he flopped into a chair. 'Do you mind if I sit down for a while? I'm aching all over.'

'I'm sorry, Victor,' said Colbeck. 'I need you to come with me.'

'Where?'

'To retrieve some stolen property. While you were away, we had an interesting development in the case.' He eased the sergeant to his feet. 'Come on – I'll tell you about it on the way.'

Leeming blenched. 'Not another train journey?'

'Two of them, I'm afraid.'

The *Red Rose* was moored in the canal basin. Micah Triggs sat on the bulwark of his barge and puffed contentedly on his pipe. Well into his seventies, he had a weather-beaten face and a shrunken body but he remained unduly spry for his age. Curled up in his lap, basking in the afternoon sunshine, was a mangy black cat. When he saw three figures walking towards him along the towpath, Micah stood up suddenly and catapulted the animal on to the deck. With a squeal of protest, the cat took refuge beneath the sail.

'Mr Triggs?' asked Colbeck as they got near. 'Mr Micah Triggs?'

'The same,' grunted the old man.

Colbeck introduced himself and his companions, Victor Leeming and Walter Praine. He explained that he was leading the investigation into the murder and thanked Micah for the witness statement that he had given.

'If you work on a barge,' said Micah, shifting his pipe to the other side of his mouth, 'you fish all sorts of odd things out of the canal but this is the first time we found the dead body of a man.'

'Your son and grandson were with you, I believe.'

'Yes, Inspector – Enoch and Sam.'

'How tall would your son be?'

'That's a strange question. Why do you ask it?'

'Curiosity, Mr Triggs. Would he be around your height?'

'No,' replied Micah. 'Enoch is a good foot taller than me and twice as broad. Sam is shorter and has more of my build.'

'Then it's your grandson we need to speak to, sir,' said Colbeck, glancing around. 'Where might we find him?'

'What business do you have with Sam?'

'We just want to clarify something in his statement.'

Micah was suspicious. 'It takes *three* of you to do that?'

'I think I know where he might be, Inspector,' said Constable Praine, sensing that they would get little help from the old man. 'Most of the bargees spend their spare time in the Traveller's Rest.' He pointed to the inn further along the towpath. 'My guess is that he and his father will be in there.'

'Shall I roust them out, sir?' volunteered Leeming.

'No, Victor,' replied Colbeck. 'This is a job for Constable Praine, I think. And no rousting out is required. The only person we need is Samuel Triggs. He sounds as if he'd be the right size. Constable.'

'Yes, Inspector?' said Praine.

'Invite him, very politely, to come and talk to me.'

'I will, sir.'

Pleased with his assignment, Praine went off willingly towards the inn. On the journey there, Colbeck had questioned him closely about the Liverpool Constabulary and, in the course of describing activities at the central police station, the constable had let slip the information that he had conceived a romantic interest in Heyford's daughter. Since Praine was too frightened of the inspector to pursue it any further, Colbeck hoped that he could put in a good word for the young lover by praising his conduct as a policeman. It was the reason he had dispatched Walter Praine to the Traveller's Rest.

'What's going on?' said Micah, warily.

'You tell us, sir,' suggested Colbeck.

'We've done nothing wrong. We helped you.'

'That's true, Mr Triggs, and we were grateful. But another witness has come forward and his statement contradicts all three that were made on the *Red Rose*.'

Micah became aggressive. 'Is someone calling me a liar?'

'Not at all.'

'I told those policemen exactly what I saw.'

'I'm sure, sir.'

Colbeck looked around the barge. Sailing along the canal, the *Red Rose* had a certain grace about it. Close to, however, its defects were glaringly obvious. It was old, dirty and neglected. The sail had been repaired in several places and some of the planks in its deck were badly splintered. Also, it stank. Micah could read his mind.

'It's not my fault,' he said, bitterly. 'I can't afford a new barge. There's not the same money in the canal any more. That bleeding railway is to blame. It's took lots of our trade away from us. And what has it given us in return – a bleeding corpse!'

'I'd much prefer to travel by water,' said Leeming.

'It's in our blood.'

'By water, horse or on my own two feet. Anything but a train.'

Leeming was about to explain his dislike of the railway

when he saw two people emerge from the Traveller's Rest. Constable Praine was strolling towards them with Samuel Triggs by his side. Triggs was wearing the same rough clothing as his grandfather and a similar hat, but the sun picked out something that set him apart from the other bargees. On his feet was a pair of expensive, shiny, black leather shoes. He was a slim young man in his twenties with a defiant smile and an arrogant strut. Triggs saw the detectives looking at his shoes.

'Finders, keepers,' he said.

'They belong to someone else,' Colbeck told him.

'Yes, but 'e's got no bleedin' use for 'em, poor devil.'

'That doesn't give you the right to steal from him, Mr Triggs.'

'It was my reward for pullin' 'im out of the canal.'

'Where's the jacket?'

'What jacket?' returned Triggs with a blank expression on his face. 'There *was* no jacket. Grandpa?'

'No,' said Micah, firmly. 'He had no jacket on, Inspector.'

'Father will tell you the same. Ask 'im.'

'Constable Praine,' said Colbeck, smoothly, 'we are confronted here with what amounts to a collective loss of memory. Three people have somehow forgotten that the corpse was wearing a suit when it fell into the canal. How do you deal with this sort of problem when you come across it?'

'Like this, sir.'

Seeing an opportunity to impress, the policeman grabbed Triggs by the collar and lifted him bodily before dangling him over the edge of the canal. Triggs squawked in protest but he could not get free.

'If I hold him under the water long enough, we might eventually get an honest answer out of him.'

'Leave him alone,' yelled Micah, snatching up a wooden pole to brandish at Praine, 'or I'll split your skull open.'

'That wouldn't be very wise, Mr Triggs,' said Leeming as he squared up to the old man. 'We're already in a position to arrest your grandson for the theft of a pair of shoes. Do you want to share the same cell on a charge of assaulting a police officer?' Micah spat into the water with disgust then flung the pole aside. 'That's better, sir.'

'Now, then,' said Praine, dipping Triggs in the water before pulling him out again, 'have I jogged your memory?'

'Yes!' cried Triggs, capitulating. The constable set him down again. 'It's under the tarpaulin. I was goin' to wear it on special days.'

'But it must have a hole in the back,' observed Colbeck.

'It's only a slit – and you can 'ardly notice the bloodstains.'

Samuel Triggs climbed aboard the barge and lifted the tarpaulin so that he could haul out the smart jacket. Like the black shoes, it looked incongruous against the rest of his apparel. Before he surrendered it, he put a hand to his heart.

'I swear to God there was nothin' in the pockets, Inspector.'

'Sam's right,' confirmed Micah. 'If there'd been a wallet or some papers, we'd have given them to the police. We're not criminals. If we had been, we'd have stripped all his clothes off and slung him back in the canal for someone else to find.'

Colbeck could see that they were telling the truth. He put out a hand. With great reluctance, Triggs passed the jacket to him. Colbeck turned it over and held it up. There was a neat slit where the knife had gone through the material and an ugly stain left by the blood. Its unexpected visit to the dark water of the canal made the jacket lose a little of its shape. Colbeck examined the front of it.

'This was not made by an English tailor,' he decided, studying the cut of the lapels. 'You'll not see this fashion in London.'

'Then where *does* it come from?' asked Leeming.

Colbeck checked the label inside the jacket then looked up.

'Paris,' he said. 'The murder victim was a Frenchman.'

CHAPTER FOUR

Superintendent Edward Tallis had dedicated himself to his work with a missionary zeal. Faced with what he saw as a rising tide of crime, he put in far more hours than anyone else in the Detective Department in the hope of stemming its menacing flow. With too few officers covering far too large an area, he knew that policing the capital city was a Herculean task but he was not daunted. He was determined that the forces of law and order would prevail. Tallis was not the only man to leave the army and join the Metropolitan Police, but the others had all retained their rank to give their names a ring of authority. The only rank that he used was the one confirmed upon him in his new profession. It filled him with pride. Being a detective superintendent was, for Tallis, like sitting at the right hand of the Almighty.

Accustomed to arrive first at Scotland Yard, he was surprised to find that one of his men was already there. Bent over his desk, Robert Colbeck was writing something in his educated hand. Spotting him through the half-open door, Tallis barged into the room.

'What the devil are *you* doing here, Inspector?' he said.

'Finishing my report on the Harrison-Clark trial, sir,'

replied the other. He turned to face Tallis. 'If you recall, I had to postpone it.'

'You are supposed to be in Liverpool.'

'We came back to London last night.'

Tallis was astounded. 'Are you telling me that the murder was solved in the space of two days?'

'Alas, no,' said Colbeck, rising to his feet, 'but the investigation has reached the stage where our presence is no longer required in Liverpool. To be honest, I'm heartily relieved. It's an unlovely place and Victor Leeming was missing his wife badly.'

'Wives do not exist in the Detective Department,' said Tallis, acidly. 'Duty always comes before any trifling marital arrangements. Leeming knows that. He should have been ready to stay in Liverpool for a month, if called upon to do so.'

'That necessity did not arise, Superintendent.'

'I expected the pair of you to spend more than one night there.'

'So did I, sir,' said Colbeck, 'but events took an interesting turn. You'll find a full explanation in the report I left on your desk earlier on. I also took the liberty of opening a window in your office. When I got here, the stench of cigar smoke had still not dispersed from the room.'

'It's not a stench, man – it's a pleasing aroma.'

'Only to those who create it.'

Tallis glowered at him before stalking off to his office. Colbeck sat down again to finish the last paragraph then he put his pen aside. After blotting the wet ink, he picked up the pages and put them in the right order. When he took the report into the superintendent's office, Tallis was reading about the murder inquiry. Colbeck waited until his superior had finished. The older man nodded.

'Admirably thorough,' he conceded.

'Thank you, sir.'

'Though I'm not sure that it's altogether wise to accept the testimony of an artist at face value. In my experience, they're rather shifty fellows whose imagination tends to get the better of them.'

'I put my trust in Ambrose Hooper unreservedly. Those three witnesses on the barge confirmed everything that was in the painting.'

'Thieves and an artist.' Tallis sucked his teeth. 'Such men are hardly reliable.'

'It was only one member of the Triggs family who kept hold of property that did not belong to him, and he is not what anyone would describe as a thief. Samuel Triggs simply seized an opportunity.'

'That's what villains do,' said Tallis, crisply. 'This fellow stole a jacket and a pair of shoes, thereby impeding the investigation. I trust that you arrested him on the spot.'

'I left that to Constable Praine.'

'You mentioned him in your report.'

'A good policeman, sir – strong, quick-thinking and obedient. I told Inspector Heyford that I would be happy to see Praine in the ranks of the Metropolitan Police. It made the inspector look at the man through new eyes.'

What he did not tell the superintendent was that he had also been able to oil the wheels of Walter Praine's romance. Faced with the threat of losing him, Sidney Heyford had been at his most proprietary, offering all manner of blandishments for the constable to stay. At long last, Praine had been able to broach the sensitive subject of marriage to the inspector's daughter.

'I see that you resorted to the press again,' noted Tallis.

'Yes,' said Colbeck. 'I put the same advertisement in

Liverpool and Manchester papers even though the victim is not a local man.'

'How do you know that?'

'Someone would have reported him missing by now, sir. There are not all that many young Frenchmen living in that part of the country, even fewer with this man's income and taste in clothes. We must remember that he was travelling in a first class carriage. Most people on that train settled for second or third.'

Tallis wrinkled his nose. 'I could never lower myself to either.'

'My hope is that our man was visiting someone in Liverpool without warning. Though he had no face, the description of him is very detailed. If he has friends there, he'll be recognised.'

'He could just have been on his way to the docks.'

'Why?'

'To sail home to France, of course.'

'From Liverpool?' said Colbeck. 'I doubt that, sir. He'd choose one of the Channel ports. No, he had another reason for visiting the place and we need to discover what it was.'

'Why didn't you stay there until someone came forward in answer to your request in the newspapers?'

'Because it might take days and I had no intention of sitting there and twiddling my thumbs. We did not exactly have the most cordial welcome from the local police. They felt – quite rightly – that we were treading on their toes.'

'Supposing that nobody responds to your plea?'

'Oh, I'm fairly certain that someone will, Superintendent.'

'What makes you so confident?'

'A reward was offered,' said Colbeck. 'The railway company is anxious for the crime to be solved as soon as possible. They want to assure their passengers that this is an isolated incident. That's only possible if we catch the killer.'

'Quite so.'

'As long as the man is at large, people will fear that he's likely to strike again even though that possibility is remote.'

'Is it?'

'I believe so. Look at the facts. This murder is unique. It was committed in a particular way and at a particular point on the line. It was at a particular time of day as well – when the express train was running. All of the others stop at the Sankey Viaduct though, rather confusingly, that station was renamed Warrington Junction in 1831. Victor and I changed trains there to get to the canal basin.'

'What this does not explain,' said Tallis, tapping the report in front of him, 'is how the killer came to be sharing the carriage alone with his intended victim.'

'There are two possible answers to that, sir.'

'I fail to see them.'

'They could have been known to each other and travelled as friends. That would have meant that the victim was caught off guard.'

'And the second possibility?'

'That's the more likely one,' said Colbeck. 'The carriage may have been first class but other passengers might have wished to choose it. Had they done so, of course, the murderer would have been foiled. Once his victim had entered the carriage, he had to ensure nobody else did.'

'How could he do that?'

'By posing as someone in authority and turning people away.'

'You mean that he pretended to be a railway employee?'

'No, sir. He was wearing a uniform that would deter other passengers while at the same time reassuring the victim when he joined him in the carriage at the time of departure.'

Tallis was furious. 'Only one uniform would do that.'

'Exactly,' said Colbeck. 'The killer was dressed as a policeman.'

Much as he loved his daughter, there were times when Caleb Andrews found her profoundly exasperating. For the third time in a row, Madeleine had beaten him at draughts, a game in which he had once considered himself invincible. The previous evening, she had trounced him at dominoes. Andrews was not a man who suffered defeat with good grace. He began to wish that he had never taught her how to play the games. It was humiliating for him to lose to a woman.

'Another game?' she suggested.

'No, no, Maddy. I've had enough.'

'Your luck may change.'

'It's not a question of luck,' he said, gathering up the counters and putting them back in their box. 'Draughts is a game of skill. You have to be able to out-think your opponent.'

'I just play it for the pleasure.'

Andrews grimaced. It was even more annoying to be beaten by someone who did not take the game seriously. For him, it was a real contest; for Madeleine, it was simply fun. Seeing that he was so discomfited, she got up, kissed him on the forehead and went into the kitchen to make a pot of tea. They were in the little house that they shared in Camden. Andrews was a short, wiry man in his fifties with a fringe beard dappled with grey. There was a suppressed energy about him that belied his age. Since the death of his wife six years earlier, his daughter had looked after him with a mixture of kindness, cajolery and uncompromising firmness.

When the tea had been brewed, Madeleine brought the pot into the living room and set it down on the table with a cosy on it. Now in her twenties, she had inherited her mother's good looks and had the same auburn hair, but Madeleine Andrews possessed an assurance that was all her own. As her father had learnt to his cost, she also had a quick brain. To stave off the pangs of defeat, he tried to lose himself in his newspaper. One item of news immediately caught his jaundiced eye.

'He should have consulted me,' he said.

'Who?'

'Inspector Colbeck. I work for that railway company. I know every inch of our track.'

'Yes, Father,' she agreed, 'but you're only an engine driver.'

'So?'

'You're not a detective like Robert.'

'I could have helped. I could have made suggestions.'

'I'm sure that he appreciates that,' said Madeleine, tactfully, 'but he had to act quickly. As soon as word of the crime reached him, Robert went straight off to Liverpool. He had no time to contact you.'

'Is that what he told you?'

'More or less.'

It was a white lie to appease her father. Caleb Andrews had been the driver of the mail train that was robbed in the previous year and he had been badly injured in the process. Since he was leading the investigation, Colbeck had got to know both Andrews and his daughter well. A warm friendship had soon developed between the detective and Madeleine and it had matured into something far more. Andrews liked to pretend that Colbeck called at the house to increase his knowledge of the railway system by discussing it with a man who had spent his working life on it. But he knew that it was his daughter who brought the detective to Camden.

'When are you likely to see him again, Maddy?' he asked.

'Soon, I hope.'

'Make a point of telling him about my offer.'

'Robert will be very grateful to hear of it,' she said, fetching two cups and saucers from the dresser. 'At the moment, I'm afraid, he's extremely busy.'

'Not according to this.' Andrews peered at the newspaper. 'It's been five days since the murder took place and they've got nowhere. Inspector Colbeck is making another appeal for someone to help the police by identifying the victim. He was a Frenchman,' he added with a loud sniff. 'Fifty years ago, we'd have cheered anyone who killed a Froggy. Now, we arrest them – if we can find them, that is.'

'Robert will find him in due course,' she said, loyally.

'Meanwhile, he's just sitting on his hands.'

'He'd never do that, Father. While he's waiting for information to come in, he'll be helping to solve crimes here in London. Robert never rests. He works terribly hard.'

'So do I,' boasted Andrews. 'Hard and long. I've been at it for over forty years, man and boy. I could have told Inspector Colbeck exactly what it's like to take a train over the Sankey Viaduct because I've done it. He should have come to me, Maddy.'

'I'll tell him that,' she soothed, removing the tea cosy and lifting up the pot. 'When Robert has a moment to spare.'

Nobody was allowed to rest at Scotland Yard. Superintendent Tallis made sure of that. He kept a watchful eye on what his detectives were doing and cracked the whip over any he felt were slacking. There was never any cause to upbraid Robert Colbeck. He was intensely busy. While awaiting further developments in the murder case, he was reviewing the evidence on a daily basis, giving instructions by letter to

Inspector Heyford, deploying his men on other cases, attending meetings within the Detective Department and acting as a legal consultant to his colleagues.

Unlike the majority of those at Scotland Yard, he had not worked his way up through the Metropolitan Police. Colbeck had trained as a barrister and been a familiar figure in the London courts. The murder of someone very dear to him had affected him deeply and made him question the efficacy of what he was doing. He felt that he could make a far better contribution to law enforcement by catching criminals than simply by securing their convictions in court. Fellow detectives made great use of his legal knowledge but Tallis merely envied it. Colbeck's career as a barrister was one more reason why there was so much latent hostility between the two men.

That afternoon began badly. The superintendent's patience was wearing out. After a bruising interview with him—'You are supposed to be the Railway Detective – prove it!'—Colbeck returned to his office and began to go painstakingly through all the evidence yet again, hoping that there was some hitherto unnoticed detail that might help to illumine the whole investigation. He was so absorbed in his work that he did not hear Victor Leeming enter the room.

'Excuse me, sir,' said the sergeant. 'You have a visitor.'

'Oh.' Colbeck glanced up. 'Thank you, Victor. Show him in.'

'It's a lady and a very handsome one at that.'

'Did she say what her business was?'

'No, sir. The only person she wishes to see is you.'

Colbeck got to his feet. 'Then you'd better bring her in.'

Moments later, a tall, stately woman in her thirties came into the office and waited until the door had been closed behind her before she yielded up her name.

'Inspector Colbeck?'

'That's correct.'

'My name is Hannah Critchlow,' she said, 'and I've come in response to the request you inserted in the *Liverpool Times*.'

He was curious. 'You've come all the way from Liverpool?'

'This is not something I wished to discuss with the local police. I had other reasons for being in London, so I decided to speak directly to you. I hope that I can rely on your discretion.'

'Completely,' he said. 'Do sit down, Mrs Critchlow.'

'*Miss* Critchlow,' she corrected.

'I beg your pardon.'

Hannah Critchlow lowered herself into a chair and he resumed his seat behind the desk. Colbeck was surprised to hear that she was unmarried. She had a sculptured beauty that was enhanced by her costly attire. She also had a distinct poise about her and would never go through life unnoticed by members of the opposite sex. Without being told, he knew that she had travelled by train to London in a first class carriage. Colbeck felt a quiet excitement. Given the trouble she had taken to see him, he believed that she would have something of value to impart.

'Before we go any further,' she said, 'there is one thing that I must make clear. I am not here in search of any reward.'

'But if you can provide information that will lead to the arrest of the murderer, the railway company will be very grateful to you.'

'I don't want their gratitude.'

'What do you want, Miss Critchlow?'

'The satisfaction of knowing that this villain is caught. From the reports in the newspaper, it seems to have been an appalling crime. The culprit should not be allowed to get away with it.'

'He won't,' said Colbeck, levelly. 'I can assure you of that.'

'Good.'

While he had been appraising her, she had been sizing him up and she seemed pleased with what she saw. It encouraged her to confide in him. After clearing her throat, she leant slightly forward.

'I believe that they call you the Railway Detective,' she said.

'My nickname is immaterial. The only name that interests me at this point in time is that of the murder victim.'

'When I tell you what it is, Inspector, you will see that your nickname is not at all irrelevant. The gentleman who was thrown from the Sankey Bridge was – if I am right – a railway engineer.'

'Does he have a name, Miss Critchlow?'

'Yes.' There was a long pause. 'Gaston Chabal.'

'What makes you think that?'

'I happen to know that he was coming to England around this time to take a closer look at our railway system. He had an especial interest in the London and North-West Railway so that would account for his presence on the train in question.'

'Gaston Chabal.'

'Yes, Inspector – if I am right.'

'I have a feeling that you are,' he said, writing the name down on a piece of paper in front of him. 'Would it be impertinent of me to ask how you come to know this gentlemen?'

'Not at all,' she replied, adjusting her skirt. 'My sister and I visited Paris earlier this year. In a small way, we are art collectors. We attended the opening of an exhibition one afternoon. M. Chabal was one of the guests.'

'Could you describe his appearance?'

'He was very much like you, Inspector.'

'Me?'

'Yes. M. Chabal was not what I had expected a railway engineer to be any more than you are what I envisaged as a detective. I mean that with the greatest of respect,' she went on. 'Most policemen I've encountered have had a more rugged look to them. As for Gaston – for M. Chabal – he seemed to be far too modish and fastidious to be involved in work on the railways.'

'He was French. They pay attention to their appearance.'

'Yes,' she murmured. 'He was very French.'

'Did he live in Paris?'

'I believe so.'

'You have no address for the gentleman?'

'It was only a casual encounter, Inspector,' she said, 'but I do know that he was an admirer of our railway system. It's much more advanced than the one in France. He felt that he could learn useful lessons by studying it.'

'To some extent, that's true,' said Colbeck, 'but our system has many vices as well as virtues. We do not have a standard gauge on our railways, for a start. That causes immense problems.'

'I would blame the Great Western Railway for that. Mr Brunel insists on using the broad gauge instead of coming into line with the others. And we have too many companies competing with each other to serve the same towns and cities.'

'You seem to know a lot about railways, Miss Critchlow.'

'I've spent a lot of time travelling on them.'

'So have I,' said Colbeck. 'To come back to M. Chabal, do you happen to know if was married or not?'

Her reply was prompt. 'He was a bachelor.'

'Nevertheless, he'll have had a family and friends who need to be informed of his death, not to mention his employers.

Have you any idea how we might contact them?'

'No, Inspector.'

'Do you know if he was engaged on any particular project?'

'Yes,' she replied, a finger to her chin. 'He did mention that he would be working with a British contractor in northern France, but I can't remember exactly where.'

'It must be the railway between Mantes and Caen. It's the only large project in that part of the country. Thomas Brassey is in charge of its construction. Yes, that must be it,' decided Colbeck. 'Thank you, Miss Critchlow. At least I know where to start looking now.'

'I hope that I've been able to help your investigation.'

'Without question. You've cleared up one mystery for us. Is there anything else you can tell me about Gaston Chabal?'

'I'm afraid not. I only met him that once.'

'Was he a handsome man? Did he speak good English?'

'Most people would have thought him handsome,' she said, choosing her words with care, 'and his English was faultless. He once gave a lecture here in London on railway engineering.'

'Bold man. That's rather like carrying coals to Newcastle. Do you know when and where he delivered this lecture?'

'No, Inspector.'

'A pity. It might have been another way to track him.'

'If it really is the man I think.' She rose to her feet. 'Well, I won't take up more of your time, Inspector Colbeck. I've told you all I can so there's no point in my staying. Goodbye.'

'I'll see you out,' he insisted, getting up to cross to the door. 'Are you staying in London?'

'Only until tomorrow.'

'Then permit me to call a cab for you, Miss Critchlow. And if you are an art collector, allow me to recommend the name of a British painter – Ambrose Hooper. I think very highly of his work.'

He opened the door to let her go out first then followed her down the corridor. When they left the building, he hovered on the pavement until an empty cab came into sight. Flagging it down, Colbeck assisted her into the vehicle and made sure that he heard the name of the hotel that she gave to the driver. The man flicked his reins and the horse set off at a steady trot in the direction of Trafalgar Square. Colbeck did not return to his office. Hannah Critchlow had given him a crucial piece of information, but he was much more interested in what she was concealing than in what she had actually divulged. When the next empty cab came along Whitehall, therefore, he put out an arm to stop it.

'Where to, guv'nor?' asked the driver.

'Camden.'

Madeleine Andrews had always been fond of drawing but she did not know that she possessed a real talent until Robert Colbeck had come into her life. Not for her a rural landscape, or a jolly scene at a fair or even a flattering portrait of her sitter. Like her father, her passion was for locomotives and she had sketched dozens of them over the years, honing her skills without even realising that she was doing it. With Colbeck's encouragement, she had shown some of her sketches to a dealer and actually managed to sell two of them.

Bolstered by her modest success, Madeleine always tried to find at least some time in a day to work on her latest drawing. When she had cleaned the house, finished the washing-up and been out to do the shopping, she was back at her easel. Sitting near a window in the living room to get the best of the light, she was in the perfect position to see the cab as it drew up outside. When she saw Colbeck alight, she put her work aside and rushed to open the door.

'Robert! How lovely to see you!'

'I need your help,' he said, kissing her on the cheek. 'Is there any chance that you could spare me an hour or two?'

'Of course,' she replied. 'Where are we going?'

'I'll tell you in the cab.'

'Give me a moment.'

Madeleine went back into the house to leave a short note for her father, then she collected her hat and coat. Colbeck was waiting to help her into the cab before climbing up to sit beside her. Their conversation was conducted to the rhythmical clip-clop of the hooves. He told her about his visitor from Liverpool. Madeleine was interested.

'What made you think she was hiding something?'

'When a married woman tells me that she is single, then I know that she is lying to me. Nobody as fetching as Hannah Critchlow could reach that age without having had dozens of proposals.'

'She might have turned them all down,' said Madeleine.

'That was not the impression I got. She not only has a husband,' Colbeck went on, 'but my guess is that he's connected with a railway company in some way – though not the GWR.'

'Why do you say that?'

'Because of a criticism she made to me about the broad gauge. It was not the kind of remark I'd expect a woman to make – unless her name was Madeleine Andrews, that is. But then, you have a genuine fascination with railways.'

'It's only natural. Father is an engine driver.'

'Hannah Critchlow is different,' he said. 'When she talks about railways, she sounds as if she's quoting somebody else

– her husband, most probably. It was another instance of her concealing something from me. And I didn't believe for a second that she had chanced upon this railway engineer at an art exhibition.'

'Why not?'

'Wait until you meet her, Madeleine.'

'What do you mean?'

'She's a very self-possessed woman with typical English reserve. Such people do not make casual conversation with foreigners. I fancy that she and Gaston Chabal became friends elsewhere. You'd be doing me a huge favour if you could find out the truth.'

'What makes you think that she'd confide in me, Robert?'

'You're a woman. You might be able to break through her defences. It took an enormous effort for her to come forward like this. She must have found Scotland Yard – and me, for that matter – rather intimidating.'

'You're not in the least intimidating,' she said, squeezing his arm affectionately. 'You're always extremely charming.'

'Well, my charm did not work on her, Madeleine – yours might.'

He spent the rest of the journey schooling her in what to say and how to say it. Madeleine was an attentive pupil. It was not the first time he had employed her on an unofficial basis and she had proved extremely helpful in the past. Colbeck knew that he could rely on her to be gently persuasive.

'Does the superintendent know about this?' she said.

'Mr Tallis?' He gave a dry laugh. 'Hardly. You know his opinion of women – they should be neither seen nor heard. If he realised what I was doing, he'd probably roast me over a spit.'

'Even if your methods bring results?'

'Even then, Madeleine.'

They eventually reached their destination in the Strand and pulled up outside a fashionable hotel. He gave her another kiss.

'Good luck!' he said.

It had taken Hannah Critchlow almost a week to gather up enough courage to get in touch with Inspector Colbeck. Now that she had done so, she felt both relieved and anxious. But her overriding emotion was sadness and, no sooner did she return to her hotel, than she burst into tears. It took her a long time to compose herself. When there was a tap on her door, she assumed that it would be a member of the hotel staff. Opening the door, she saw instead that she had a visitor.

'Miss Critchlow?'

'Yes,' said the other, guardedly.

'My name is Madeleine Andrews. I wonder if I might have a private word with you? I'm a friend of Inspector Colbeck.'

'Then why are you bothering me? We've nothing to say to each other. I told the inspector all that I know.'

'That's untrue,' said Madeleine, holding her ground.

'Good day to you.'

'As Hannah Critchlow, you gave him a certain amount of information but, as Mrs Marklew, you may be able to provide more. Why give him one name when you are staying here under another?'

Hannah was suspicious. 'Who *are* you?'

'I told you. I'm a friend of the inspector. If I explained how he and I came to meet, you'll understand why I'm here.'

Hannah Marklew hesitated. She was unsettled by the fact that her disguise had been so easily pierced and she knew that she could be severely reproached for misleading a detective.

At the same time, she found Madeleine personable and unthreatening. There was another telling factor. Her visitor had a sympathetic manner. She was on Hannah's side.

'You'd better come in, Miss Andrews. It is "Miss", I presume?'

'Yes, Mrs Marklew.'

Madeleine went into the room and the other woman shut the door behind them. Hannah indicated a chair but she remained standing when Madeleine sat down.

'What did Inspector Colbeck tell you about me?' said Hannah.

'That you had provided the name of the murder victim and thereby moved the investigation on to another stage. He also told me how eager you were to see the killer brought to justice.'

'I am, Miss Andrews.'

'Then he needs all the help he can get in order to do that.'

Hannah was still wary. 'How do you know the inspector?'

'The same way that you do,' replied Madeleine. 'As a result of a crime. Somebody I know was attacked on the railway in the course of a robbery and Inspector Colbeck was put in charge of the case. Luckily, the injured man survived but it took him months to recover and he still carries the scars from that assault. Because of Inspector Colbeck's efforts, the villain responsible was eventually apprehended with his accomplices.'

'And who exactly was the victim?'

'My father. He almost died.'

Madeleine spoke with quiet intensity. She explained that her father had been in a deep coma and was not expected to live. More suffering had followed. In a desperate attempt to impede the police investigation, she had been abducted and held in captivity until rescued by Robert Colbeck.

'You can see why I have such faith in the inspector,' she said.

'Yes, Miss Andrews.'

'It's the reason I'm so willing to help him now.'

'But I have nothing else to add.'

'I believe that you do, Mrs Marklew. You came all the way from Liverpool to see Inspector Colbeck in person. That suggests it was a matter of importance to you. Otherwise,' Madeleine pointed out, 'you could simply have informed the local police, or even made contact with Scotland Yard by anonymous letter. The inspector believes that you have a personal reason to see this crime solved.'

Hannah studied her carefully as if weighing her in the balance. It was certainly easier talking to a woman in the confines of a hotel room than discussing the case with a detective inspector in an office. Madeleine, she sensed, was discreet. Also, there was a bond between them. Both had endured great pain as a result of a crime committed on the London and North-West Railway. Hannah wondered if she could ease her pain by talking about it.

'Inspector Colbeck is very perceptive,' she said. 'I did know Gaston Chabal rather better than I indicated, but I did not wish to admit that. It might have caused complications.'

'With your husband?'

'Yes, Miss Andrews.' Hannah sat down. 'I love him very much and I do not want to hurt him in any way. The simple fact is that Alexander – my husband – is somewhat older than me and is always preoccupied with business affairs.'

'The inspector thought that he had a connection with railways.'

'It's more than a connection. He's one of the directors of the London and North-West Railway. That's what seems so cruel.

Gaston was murdered on a railway in which my husband is so closely involved.' She hunched her shoulders. 'I suppose that some might see that as an example of poetic justice.'

'How did you first meet M. Chabal?' asked Madeleine.

'It was at a reception in Paris. A major rail link was planned between Mantes and Caen. Since he already has some investments in French railways, my husband was interested in buying shares.'

'And you were invited to go with him?'

'All that I saw was an opportunity to visit Paris,' said Hannah. 'To be candid, I expected the reception itself to be very boring – they usually are. When you get a group of men talking business, you can feel very isolated. Fortunately,' she went on, a wan smile touching her lips, 'Gaston was there. We began talking. A few months later, there was a meeting in London for investors in the project. My husband had to be there, so I made sure that I was as well.'

'Did you meet M. Chabal again?'

'Yes. I suppose that it all sounds a trifle sordid to you. I'm a married woman. I had no right to let a friendship of that nature develop. But the simple fact was that he made me feel unbelievably happy. Gaston reminded me that I was a woman.'

'How did you keep in touch?'

'By letter.'

'So you have an address for him?'

'Yes, Miss Andrews – it's in Mantes. His home was in Paris but he took a lodging in Mantes when they began to build the railway. My letters went there.'

'Inspector Colbeck would like that address, Mrs Marklew.'

'Of course.'

'And any details you have of his life in Paris.' Hannah nodded sadly. 'It must have come as a terrible blow to you when you realised that he was the murder victim on that train.'

'It did. I cried for days.'

'And are you absolutely sure that it was Gaston Chabal?'

'There's no possible room for error, Miss Andrews.'

'How can you be so certain?'

'My husband was away from Liverpool on business,' said Hannah frankly. 'I was waiting at Lime Street station that day to meet the train. Gaston was coming to see me.'

CHAPTER FIVE

'France!' exclaimed Superintendent Tallis, reaching for a cigar to absorb the shock of what he had just been told. 'Heavens above! For centuries, they were our mortal enemies until we put paid to them at Waterloo. Why must you go to France?'

'Because that's the only place we'll find out the full truth,' said Robert Colbeck. 'The crime may have taken place on British soil but I believe that its roots lie across the Channel.'

'We have no jurisdiction there, Inspector.'

'I'm sure that the French police would cooperate with us. The murder victim was a Parisian, after all. They have a stake in this.'

'But they would insist on being in charge,' said Tallis, irritably. 'Before we know it, we'd have their officers crawling about over here.'

'I dispute that, sir.'

'I've had dealings with them before.'

'So have I,' said Colbeck, 'and I found members of the Police de Surêté very helpful. We are kindred spirits.'

'If only that were the case! You seem to have forgotten that the man responsible for founding the Surêté was a known villain who had served time in prison.'

'Vidocq saw the folly of his ways, Superintendent. It was to his credit that he chose to work on the right side of the law. And he achieved some remarkable results.'

'Yes,' said Tallis, lighting his cigar and puffing on it until the end glowed. 'But how did Vidocq get those remarkable results? There was a suspicion that many of the crimes he solved were actually committed by his henchmen. I'd not have allowed anybody under me to resort to that kind of skulduggery. Vidocq was a born criminal. Look what happened to him.'

'He became a private detective twenty years ago, sir.'

'And then?'

'The police eventually closed down his agency because he was using dubious methods.'

'I rest my case – as you barristers say.'

'But that does not invalidate all the good work that he did earlier,' affirmed Colbeck. 'Besides, the Surêté is a much improved police force now. It's not full of men like Eugene Vidocq. How could it be? He was inimitable.'

'He was French,' said Tallis, darkly. 'That's enough for me.'

He pulled on his cigar then exhaled a cloud of thick smoke. It was one more problem with which Colbeck had to contend as he stood before the superintendent's desk. He was not merely hampered by the other man's prejudices against the French, he was forced to conceal both the source and extent of the information that he had received. In using Madeleine Andrews as his unauthorised assistant, Colbeck had risked dismissal but he felt that it had been worth it. What she had discovered from Hannah Marklew had been extraordinary. Once the older woman had started talking about her relationship with Gaston Chabal, she had not stopped. When she reported back to him, Madeleine was able to tell Colbeck a great deal about the character and career of the Frenchman.

'In the first instance, sir,' said Colbeck, 'we do not have to deal with the French police at all. It would be a preliminary inquiry.'

'To what end?'

'Establishing if there were any clear motives why someone would seek the life of the victim.'

'How could you hope to do that in a country full of foreigners?'

'I have a fair command of the language, Superintendent, so I would not be at a disadvantage. In any case, most of the people to whom I intend to speak are English.'

'Really?' said Tallis in surprise.

'You are obviously not familiar with French railways.'

'I regard that as a virtue, Inspector.'

'Their system is far less developed than ours,' said Colbeck, 'so it was natural that they looked to us for expertise. Many of the locomotives they use over there were designed by Thomas Crampton and three-quarters of the mileage of all French railways so far constructed was the work of Thomas Brassey and his partners.'

'What relevance does this have to the case in hand?'

'Gaston Chabal worked for Mr Brassey.'

'Then you do not have to go haring off to France,' said Tallis, flicking cigar ash into a metal tray. 'If this contractor is English, you can call on him at his office.'

'He is not in this country at the moment.'

'How do you know?'

'Because he always supervises major projects in person. This line will run for well over a hundred miles, sir, so it will take a long time to build. Until it's finished, Mr Brassey has moved to France.'

'What about his family?'

'They've gone with him, sir. His wife, Maria, I believe, speaks tolerable French and acts as his interpreter. It's a language that her husband cannot bring himself to learn.'

'Then he's a man after my own heart. Dreadful lingo!'

'Perhaps you can understand now why I need to go there,' said Colbeck. 'Mr Brassey will be wondering what's happened to one of his senior engineers and Chabal's family need to be informed of his death so that they can reclaim the body.'

Edward Tallis thrust the cigar between his teeth. He was loath to send Colbeck abroad on what he believed might be an expensive and unproductive visit. At the same time, he could appreciate the logic of the inspector's argument. Unless the crime was solved, the railway company would keep hounding him. Worse, in his view, was the intensive scrutiny of the press. Newspapers were very willing to trumpet any success the Detective Department achieved but they were equally ready to condemn any failures. Having christened Colbeck as the Railway Detective, they would have no qualms about finding a more derisive nickname for him.

'How long would you be away?' growled Tallis.

'Impossible to say, sir, but we'd be as quick as possible.'

'Would you take Sergeant Leeming with you?'

'With your permission.'

'It's his wife's permission you need to seek, by the sound of it.'

'Victor will do what he's told,' said Colbeck. 'While I'm talking to Mr Brassey, he can question some of the men who work for him.'

Tallis was astounded. 'Are you telling me that the sergeant speaks French?'

'No, sir, and nor will he need to. For a number of reasons, Mr Brassey prefers to employ men from this country.

When he built the Paris to Rouen railway, he took five thousand navvies, miners, carpenters, smiths, brick-makers, bricklayers and other tradesmen with him. He had his own private army.'

'That's what you need over there – for protection.'

'Hostilities with France ceased many years ago, sir.'

'Some of us have long memories.' Tallis chewed on his cigar and regarded Colbeck from under bushy eyebrows. 'How do you come to know so much about Thomas Brassey?'

'I read a number of railway periodicals, sir.'

'What manner of man is he?'

'A very successful one,' said Colbeck. 'He's a good businessman and a caring employer. That's why his men are so loyal to him. He also has the courage to admit his mistakes.'

'Mistakes?'

'Even the best contractors go astray at times, Superintendent. Six years ago, Mr Brassey built the Barentin Viaduct about twelve miles from Rouen.'

'Don't mention viaducts to me, Inspector.'

'This was a massive construction, much higher and longer than the one over the Sankey Valley. There was only one problem with it.'

'And what was that?'

'After a period of heavy rain, it collapsed in ruins. Some people would have invented all manner of spurious excuses, but not Thomas Brassey. His reputation as a contractor was in serious danger. So he admitted liability and at his own cost – some £30,000 – he had the viaduct rebuilt.'

'Did it stay up this time?'

'Oh, yes,' replied Colbeck. 'I've been over it. I think it's one of the most inspiring sights on the French railways. And because it was rebuilt in a mere six months, it meant that he completed the whole project well ahead of schedule, earning himself a bonus of £10,000.'

'The only viaduct that concerns me at the moment is the one from which that fellow was thrown. Why couldn't he have the decency to get himself killed in his native country?'

'I doubt if he was given any choice, Superintendent.'

'I agree,' said Tallis, becoming serious. 'A murder victim is a murder victim, whatever nationality he holds. We must bring his killer to book and do so with all speed.'

'Does that mean you sanction our visit to France?'

'I'll give it my consideration.'

'You just said that speed was essential, sir.'

'I'm treating it as a matter of urgency.'

'Shall I warn Victor that he may be going abroad?'

'Do not run ahead of yourself, Inspector. There are many things to take into account. Leave me alone while I mull them over.'

'Of course, Superintendent.'

The decision had been made. When Tallis stopped making protests about a course of action, it invariably meant that he would in time approve of it. Colbeck left the room with a feeling of triumph. After a period of inertia, the murder investigation had been given a new lease of life. He and Victor Leeming were going to France.

Thomas Brassey came out of the wooden hut that he used as an office and went off to see the damage for himself. He wore his habitual frock coat, waistcoat and check trousers and, although in his late forties, moved briskly across the ground. When he passed a group of navvies, he was given warm smiles or cheerful greetings, and coarser language was immediately suppressed within his earshot. Brassey was a true gentleman with an innate dignity. He lacked the rough and ready appearance of some self-made men and had none of their arrogance or assertive manner.

'When did you discover it?' he asked.

'This afternoon,' replied Aubrey Filton. 'We'd suspended work on the tunnel until fresh materials arrived, but, in view of what's happened, I thought that I'd carry out an inspection.'

'Very sensible of you.'

'This is what I found, sir.'

Filton led the way down the embankment to the mouth of the tunnel. As it was dark inside, he picked up a lantern that was already burning. Brassey followed him into the long cavern. Halfway along it, the contractor expected to see two sets of parallel rails, laid across timber sleepers and bolted tight, the whole track resting on ballast. Instead, he was looking at a confused mass of wood, iron and rock chippings. Rails and sleepers had been levered out of position. The fishplates and bolts that held one length of rail against the end of another had been either broken or twisted out of shape.

'This was done on purpose, Mr Brassey,' said Filton.

'I can see that. Was nobody guarding the tunnel last night?'

'They claim that they were but my guess is that they either fell asleep or were paid to look the other way. This is the fourth incident in a row. Someone is trying to stop us building this railway.'

'Then they'll have to do a lot better than this,' said Brassey, assessing the cost of the damage. 'It's annoying but it won't hold us up for long. As soon as a fresh supply of rail arrives on site, we'll start work in the tunnel again. Meanwhile, we'll post more guards.'

'Yes, Mr Brassey.'

'*Armed* guards.'

'What are their orders?'

'I'll issue those directly.'

They walked back towards the mouth of the tunnel, stepping over the accumulated debris as they did so. Filton, one of the engineers working on the Mantes-Caen railway, was a tall, thin, nervous man in his thirties with a tendency to fear the worst. Brassey had a much more robust attitude to life. What his companion saw as a disaster, he dismissed as a minor setback. Sensing the other man's anxiety, he put a consoling arm around Filton's shoulders.

'Do not worry about it, Aubrey,' he said. 'If someone is trying to hinder us, we'll catch them sooner or later. The important thing is that these delays do not interfere with our overall schedule.'

'I hate the thought that we have enemies in our midst.'

'For every bad apple, we have a thousand good ones.'

'I wonder that you can shrug it off like this, sir,' said Filton.

'Oh, I'm not shrugging it off, I assure you. I take this very seriously – but I'll not let my anger show. I prefer to carry on as if nothing had occurred to halt our progress. I've signed a contract that has time limits on it. I intend to meet them.'

They walked on until they emerged into broad daylight. All around them, men of various trades were working hard. Brassey stopped to watch them. It was very hot and the navvies were dripping with sweat as they toiled away. Many of them were bare-chested in the baking sun. The ceaseless pandemonium of industry rang out across the French countryside as picks, shovels, axes, sledgehammers and other implements pounded away. Birds flew overhead but their songs went unheard beneath the cacophony.

'Is there any finer sight on earth than men building a

railway?' said Brassey, removing his top hat. 'It lifts my spirit, Aubrey.'

'It would lift mine as well if we were not plagued by problems.'

'Four incidents can hardly be called a plague.'

'I think the number might be five, sir.'

'What do you mean?'

'Well,' said Filton, brow corrugated with disquiet, 'I can't help remembering what happened to Mr Ruddles the other week.'

'That was an accident, man.'

'Was it?'

'Of course,' said Brassey, airily. 'It's a law of averages that a scaffold will collapse from time to time. Bernard Ruddles and I had the misfortune to be standing on it when it gave way.'

'You could have been badly injured, sir.'

'I was lucky. I had a nasty fall and was shaken up but I lived to tell the tale. Bernard, alas, was not so fortunate.'

'He broke his leg in two places.'

'I know,' said Brassey. 'I was right beside him at the time. Had we listened to the advice of the French doctors, he would have lost the leg altogether. They were queuing up to amputate. Bernard had the good sense to wait for an English doctor to give an opinion. As a consequence, the leg can be saved.'

'That's not the point, Mr Brassey.'

'Then what is?'

'The scaffold could have been tampered with.'

'It was badly erected, that's all,' Brassey told him. 'I sacked the men responsible. They were not trying to inflict injury on me or on Bernard Ruddles. How could they know when either of us would stand on that particular scaffold?'

'But suppose it had been you who'd broken a leg, sir?'

'I did suppose it, Aubrey, and it made me offer up a prayer of thanks. I landed on level ground but Bernard, alas, hit some rocks. It could so easily have been the other way around.'

'How could we have managed without you, sir?'

'You wouldn't have had to do so.'

'No?'

'Once the leg had been put into a splint, I'd have used a pair of crutches to get round. Nothing would stop me from keeping an eye on a project like this,' he went on, stoutly. 'If I'd broken both legs and both arms, I'd have men to carry me around on a stretcher.'

'Heaven forbid!'

'Never give in, Aubrey – that's my motto.'

'Yes, sir.'

'And always complete a railway ahead of time.'

Brassey put on his hat. They clambered up the embankment and strolled back towards the office. Filton was not reassured by his employer's brave words. Clearly, they had enemies. That was what alarmed him. He felt certain that it was only a matter of time before those enemies struck again.

'By the way,' said Brassey, 'have you seen Gaston Chabal?'

'No, sir.'

'He was due back here days ago.'

'Well, I've seen no sign of him. Wherever can he be?'

'Find out.'

'I'll try, sir.'

'When I engage a man, I expect him to fulfil his duties or give me an excellent reason why he's unable to do so. Gaston has left us in the dark,' said Brassey. 'We need him back here. Unless he turns up soon, he may well find that he is no longer working for me.'

* * *

Victor Leeming had been horrified to learn that he had to go to France with Robert Colbeck. Apart from the fact that he would miss his wife, Leeming knew that he would be condemned to spend long and uncomfortable hours on trains, a form of transport he had come to loathe. There was an even deeper cause for concern. Leeming was uneasy about the temper of the French nation.

'What if they have another revolution while we're here?' he said.

'Then we'll be privileged spectators,' replied Colbeck.

'It wasn't long ago that the barricades went up in Paris.'

'France was not alone, Victor. In 1848, there were revolutions in other parts of Europe as well. Superintendent Tallis feared that we might have riots in London if the Chartists got out of hand.'

'We've had nothing to match the bloodshed over here,' said Leeming, looking through the window of the carriage at some peasants working in the fields. 'There's something about the French. It's in their nature to revolt. They make me feel uneasy.'

The two men were on their way to Mantes. Having crossed the English Channel by packet boat, they had boarded a train at Le Havre and were steaming south. Colbeck had been pleased to note that the locomotive was of English design and construction, but the news brought no comfort to the sergeant. The name of Thomas Crampton was meaningless to him. If the train had been pulled by a herd of giant reindeer, Leeming would have shown no interest. The only thing about France that would bring a smile to his craggy face was the date of their departure from the country.

'Look upon this as an adventure,' urged Colbeck. 'You are seeing a foreign country for the first time and you'll get some insight into the way that it's policed.'

'It seems such a long way to come, sir.'

'Be grateful that the murder victim was not Italian or Swiss. Had that been the case, we'd have had to go much farther afield.'

'I'd prefer to be in London.'

'Amid all that crime and squalor? There's far less danger out here in the countryside, Victor, and it's so much healthier for us to get away from the city.' A beautiful chateau appeared on the horizon. He pointed it out to his companion. 'Isn't it superb?' he said. 'Now there's something you wouldn't see in Whitechapel.'

Leeming was unimpressed. 'I'd still much rather be there.'

'You're too insular,' said Colbeck with a laugh.

'I like my country, that's all. I'm patriotic.'

'I have no quarrel with that.'

The railway had been built in defiance of geography. There were so many hills, valleys and rivers to cross that there was a long sequence of tunnels, cuttings, bridges and viaducts. As they sped across the Barentin Viaduct with its striking symmetry and its panoramic views, Colbeck thought it better not to mention that it had once collapsed into the valley below. Teeth clenched and hands gripping the seat for safety, Leeming was already troubled enough by having to cross it. The magnificent construction had all the qualities of a death trap to him. Only when they were well clear of the viaduct did he find his voice again.

'Why didn't he choose that instead, Inspector?' he asked. 'Why didn't the killer throw his victim over that viaduct instead of coming all the way to England to do it?'

'You're assuming that the murderer was French.'

'Isn't that why we're here?'

'No, Victor,' said Colbeck. 'We are hunting a motive. I'm

fairly certain that the man who killed Gaston Chabal was English and that only the Sankey Viaduct would suffice.'

'In that case, the lady's husband must be involved.'

'I think not.'

'His wife was unfaithful to him – there's the motive.'

'On the face of it, perhaps,' said Colbeck, 'but there are two very good reasons why we can eliminate Alexander Marklew from our enquiries. To begin with, he was quite unaware of the friendship that existed between his wife and M. Chabal.'

'It was more than a friendship, sir. Let's not beat about the bush. It was adultery, pure and simple – except that it was far from pure. I don't hold with it,' declared Leeming, thinking of his wife. 'Marriage vows should be kept.'

'We are not here to sit in judgement on Mrs Marklew. The fact is that, but for the information that she volunteered, we would still be scratching our heads back in Scotland Yard. But there's an even stronger reason why the husband must be discounted,' he went on. 'Mr Marklew is a director of the London and North-West Railway. He would never do anything to create bad publicity for it. Murder is the worst possible advertisement, Victor.'

Colbeck had given him an abbreviated version of what he had learnt from Hannah Marklew, making no reference to the fact that it was Madeleine Andrews who had obtained most of the salient facts. While he did not share the superintendent's dismissive attitude towards women, Leeming would certainly have questioned the use of one in a murder investigation. That was why Colbeck told him only what the sergeant needed to know. Victor Leeming was an able detective but he was shackled to correct police procedure. When it served his purpose, the inspector was ready to ignore it.

'Are you hungry, Victor?' he asked.

'No, sir,' replied Leeming, feeling his stomach. 'Crossing the Channel took away my appetite completely. Besides, I don't think that I'd take to French food.'

'Why not?'

'They eat horses and frogs and snails.'

'Not on the same plate,' said Colbeck with amusement. 'Wait until you taste their wine. If we stay here long enough, you'll acquire a real taste for it. You may even learn some of the language.'

'There's only one thing I want to hear, sir.'

'What's that?'

'The French for "We're going home". Very soon, please.'

Having removed his coat and hat, Thomas Brassey was at his desk, poring over surveyors' maps as he planned the next stage of the Mantes-Caen railway. Each project threw up its own individual challenges and this one was no exception. There were a number of potential hazards to be negotiated. He was grappling with one of them when there was a firm tap on the door. In response to Brassey's call, it opened to admit Inspector Robert Colbeck and Sergeant Victor Leeming. When introductions had been made, Brassey was amazed to hear that they had come all the way from England in order to see him.

'Have I committed a crime of some kind?' he asked.

'Not at all, sir,' said Colbeck. 'We're here on other business. I believe that you employ an engineer called Gaston Chabal?'

'I did employ him, Inspector, but the fellow seems to have vanished into thin air. He's an extremely competent man. If he keeps me waiting any longer, however, he'll find that he no longer has a job here. Nobody is indispensable.'

'M. Chabal will not be returning here, I fear. He's dead.'

Brassey was shocked. 'Dead – poor Gaston!'

When he was told about the murder, he was aghast and felt guilty for harbouring so many unkind thoughts about the engineer's absence. It was no wonder that Chabal had been unable to return.

'Did you know that he went to England?' said Colbeck.

'No, Inspector. He told me that he was going to be in Paris for a few days to see his parents. I'd no idea that he crossed the Channel. Whatever could have taken him there?'

'We believe he went to see a friend, Mr Brassey, but that's not our major concern. What we are looking for is the reason why he was singled out in this way. That reason can only be found in France.'

'Nothing else would have brought us here,' said Leeming, sourly. 'We hope that the effort will have been worthwhile.'

'You must forgive Victor. Rail travel is a torment to him.'

'That boat was even worse, sir. Fair upset me, it did.'

'He misses London,' explained Colbeck. 'He hates to be away from his wife and children.'

'I always bring my family with me,' said Brassey.

Leeming scowled. 'I could hardly do that in my job, sir.'

'No,' agreed Colbeck. 'It might hamper you somewhat. But let's turn our attention to Chabal. He's the important person here. What sort of man was he, Mr Brassey?'

'An extremely able one,' said the contractor. 'Gaston had the sense to learn from good masters. Most of the engineers I employ are English, but Gaston Chabal could match any of them.'

'Did he have any enemies?'

'None that I know of, Inspector. He was very popular. Some of the men used to tease him because he was French, but it was all in good fun. I can't think of any reason why anyone should conceive such a hatred of him that he wanted him dead.'

'And yet someone clearly did.'

'Yes.'

'Have you had any trouble in your camp, sir?' said Leeming.

'We've had the usual fights and drunkenness, but you expect that from navvies. They're a law unto themselves. If you employ them, you have to allow for a certain amount of boisterous behaviour.' Brassey grew pensive. 'On the other hand . . .'

'Well?' prompted Colbeck.

'No, no. It's probably just a coincidence.'

'Let us be the judge of that, sir.'

'The truth is,' confessed Brassey, running a hand across his broad forehead, 'that we've been having a spot of bother here. I've tried to ignore it but Aubrey takes it very seriously.'

'Aubrey?'

'Aubrey Filton, one of the senior engineers. He worked alongside Gaston and he'll be very distressed to hear what's happened to him. Anyway,' he continued, 'there have been three or four incidents here that look as if they're part of a worrying pattern.'

'What sort of incidents, Mr Brassey?'

'Aubrey would be the best person to tell you that.'

'Is he here at the moment?'

'Yes, Inspector. He has an office in the hut at the end.'

'Then I think you should pay him a visit,' said Colbeck, raising an eyebrow at Leeming. 'Break the sad news to him, Victor, and see what memories he may have of Chabal. And make a list of these incidents. They could be significant.'

Leeming nodded and went straight out. Colbeck was glad to be alone with the contractor. He had long been an admirer of Thomas Brassey and had always felt it rather unjust that those who designed locomotives or ran railway companies enjoyed public acclaim while those who actually built the endless miles of track remained in the shadows. The two men appraised each other.

'Do sit down, Inspector,' said Brassey, resuming his own seat.

'Thank you, sir.' Colbeck lowered himself on to a chair. 'This is a treat for me. I've always wanted to see a new stretch of line being laid. We hired a trap in Mantes to bring us out here so I was able to see what you've done so far.'

'Then you've also seen the problems created by the Seine.'

'We followed it for most of the journey.'

'Rivers are the bane of my life, Inspector Colbeck. Bridges and viaducts slow us down so much. If only we had a flat plain across which to construct a railway – flat and arid.'

'Then there would be no triumphs of civil engineering.'

'No triumphs, maybe, but far less sweat and toil.' He shook his head. 'I still can't accept that Gaston is dead. I always found him such an honest fellow. Why tell me that he was going to Paris when he intended to sail to England?'

'He was being discreet, I expect.'

'In what way?'

'There was a lady involved.'

'Ah, of course. Do you know who she was?'

'No,' said Colbeck, determined to honour his promise to keep Hannah Marklew's name out of it. 'But I'm convinced that Chabal was on his way to visit her when he was killed.'

Aubrey Filton was very upset to hear of his colleague's murder. It made him twitch slightly and glance over his shoulder. His office was in a much smaller hut, but it was perfectly serviceable. Victor Leeming glanced at the array of drawings that had been pinned to the wall.

'What are these, Mr Filton?' he said.

'Part of the original survey.'

'Is this your work, sir?'

'I wish it was, Sergeant,' replied Filton, looking enviously across at the wall, 'but my drawings are not quite as neat and accurate as these. Gaston was very gifted.'

'Do you mean that Chabal did these?'

'Most of them. It's all we have to remember him by.'

Leeming was pleased to have the responsibility of questioning Aubrey Filton. It gave him something to do and took his mind off the queasiness that he still felt. Having heard so many French voices since their arrival, he was relieved to be talking to an Englishman.

'Mr Brassey mentioned some incidents,' he said, taking out a notebook and pencil. 'Could you tell me what they were, sir?'

'The most recent happened only yesterday. When I inspected a tunnel, I discovered that someone had levered the rails off their sleepers and scattered the ballast everywhere. A week earlier, we had a more serious setback.'

'Go on, Mr Filton.'

'A fire had been started in one of our storage huts. We were able to stop it spreading but it destroyed everything inside. It slowed us down, Sergeant Leeming. Time costs money in this business.'

'And were there any other incidents?'

'The first was a case of simple theft – at least that's what we thought at the time. But who would want to steal gunpowder?'

'Someone who needed to blast through rock.'

'The second incident was a week later,' said Filton. 'A stack of our timber was pushed into the river. By the time we became aware of it, the sleepers had floated over a mile away.'

'Stolen gunpowder, missing timber, arson in a storeroom and wreckage in a tunnel. These are all serious crimes, Mr Filton. Have you reported them to the police?'

'Mr Brassey chose not to, Sergeant.'

'Oh.'

'He believes that we should take care of our own security and he does not want too much interference from the French. We have enough of that, as it is. In any case,' he continued, 'there's no police force out here in the wilds. The nearest constable is ten miles away. What can one man on a horse do?'

'Travel in comfort,' said the other with feeling. 'From what you tell me, it's evident that somebody is taking pains to delay the building of this railway. This is not wanton damage. It's deliberate.'

'That's what I feel about the scaffolding.'

Filton told him about the way that Brassey and his companion had fallen when the scaffolding had collapsed under them. Leeming duly noted the information down. It was Filton who discerned a clear connection with the murder.

'It's all part of the same plot,' he decided.

'Is it, sir?'

'In killing Gaston Chabal, they've inflicted yet another blow.'

'A critical one at that, Mr Filton.'

'They'll stop at nothing to wreck this railway.'

'Have you any idea who these people might be?' asked Leeming. 'Do you have any suspects in mind?'

'Several of them.'

'Such as?'

'Business rivals, for a start,' said Filton. 'This contract is worth a large amount of money. Mr Brassey was not the only person to put in a tender. He was up against others.'

'French or English?'

'Oh, French. They resent the fact that a contractor has been brought over from England, in spite of the fact that Mr Brassey has such an outstanding record of work in this country.'

'Anybody other than jealous rivals, sir?'

'Resentful navvies. We brought most of our labour with us because it's more reliable, but we've had to take on some Frenchmen as well. They bear grudges.'

'Why would that be?'

'They get paid less than our own men,' said Filton, 'and it's caused a lot of bad blood. Yes,' he went on, warming to his theme, 'I fancy that's where the trouble is coming from – French labour. It's their way of making a protest.'

'Then it has no connection with M. Chabal's death, sir.'

'I believe that it does.'

'Why would someone track him all the way across the Channel,' asked Leeming, 'when they could have killed him here? More to the point, how could a mere labourer possibly know that Chabal was going to England in the first place? I'm sorry, Mr Filton. I think you are forging links where they may not exist.' He consulted his notebook. 'Let's go back to the first incident, shall we? You say that gunpowder was stolen – for what purpose?'

'I dread to think, Sergeant Leeming.'

They moved swiftly. While one man kept watch, the other scuttled along the track in the darkness until he reached one of the largest of the wagons. He packed the gunpowder firmly beneath it and ran a fuse alongside the iron rail. Both men made sure that they were well clear of the danger area before the fuse was lit. When they saw it burning away purposefully in the direction of the wagon, they ran off quickly to their hiding place. The explosion was deafening. Shattering the silence, it lifted the wagon high off the track and blew it into small pieces that were dispersed everywhere at great velocity. Rolling stock in the immediate vicinity was also destroyed in the blast. A section of rail was plucked from the sleepers and snapped apart. Fires started. Injured men screamed in pain. Falling debris killed a dog.

Another incident could be added to the list.

CHAPTER SIX

Robert Colbeck and Victor Leeming were staying at a cottage almost a mile away, but the noise of the blast woke them up. Though railway companies often used gunpowder to shift awkward obstructions, they would never do so at night. To someone like Thomas Brassey, it would be anathema. He was renowned for the care he took to keep any disruption to an absolute minimum in the locality where his men were working. Instead of putting all his navvies in one camp, and risking the uncontrollable mayhem that usually followed the creation of a private town, he placed as many of them as he could in houses, inns and farms in the area to spread them out. It was also a means of developing ties of friendship with local people and that was important.

A nocturnal explosion meant trouble. The two detectives got up at once, dressed in the dark then walked swiftly in the direction from which the sound had come. There was no danger of their getting lost. They simply followed the track that had already been laid. As each new extension was added, it was used to bring fresh supplies of iron, timber, ballast, bricks and other materials required on site. Movement by rail was so much quicker and more efficient than having to rely on horses and carts or using barges on the river. It also helped to raise morale. When they saw that their track was already in operation, those working on it could measure the progress they had already made. They could take pride.

As they got closer, Colbeck and Leeming could see a mass of torches and lanterns. Raised voices were then carried on the breeze towards them. They quickened their step until figures were slowly conjured out of the gloom. Dozens of people were moving about as they tried to establish the full extent of the damage. Thomas Brassey was supervising the operation. Colbeck and Leeming walked through the scattered wreckage to get to him.

'What happened, Mr Brassey?' asked Colbeck.

'We're still not entirely sure,' replied the contractor, 'but it looks as if someone planted gunpowder beneath one of the wagons and blew it to pieces. We'll have to wait until dawn before we can make a complete inventory of the damage.'

'It must have been the stuff that was stolen earlier,' said Leeming, confidently. 'Mr Filton told me about it.'

'Whoever used it knew what he was doing, Sergeant. One wagon was blown apart and four others were damaged beyond repair. As you can see, the track was ripped up as well.'

'Was anyone hurt?'

'Some of the nightwatchmen were injured by the debris but nobody was killed, as far as we know.' He looked around and sighed. 'This is the worst incident yet. Someone is trying to cripple us.'

'No, sir,' said Colbeck. 'This was simply another warning.'

'Warning?'

The detective recoiled from the clamour all round him.

'Is there somewhere a little quieter where we might talk?'

'Of course, Inspector. Come to my office.'

Carrying a lantern, Brassey picked his way carefully through the gathering crowd and led them to the wooden hut. Once inside, he put the lantern on a ledge and lit some oil lamps, one of which was set on the large safe that stood in a corner. Brassey waved them into chairs before sitting down behind his desk.

'What's this about a warning?' he said.

'Somebody wishes you to think again about building this railway. I know that you have a contract to do so,' said Colbeck before Brassey could protest, 'but contracts can be revoked. The object of the exercise, I believe, is to frighten you off.'

'I'm not a man who's easily frightened, Inspector,' said the other with defiance. 'Whatever happens, I'll press on.'

'I admire your courage, sir, but you must expect worse attacks than the one you suffered last night.'

'What could be worse than this?'

'Lots of things,' said Colbeck. 'Blowing up the locomotive, for instance. That would have been far more costly and inconvenient than destroying some wagons. Breaking in here would be another option,' he went on, pointing to the safe. 'If they stole whatever you keep in there, I should imagine that it could create some serious problems for you.'

'It could,' admitted Brassey. 'That safe holds money. My men like to get their wages on time. If the navvies were not paid when they expect it, there'd be ructions. That's why a nightwatchman always patrols this area in the hours of darkness – to guard the safe.'

'You had plenty of men on duty tonight, sir,' Leeming pointed out, 'but the explosion still took place.'

'It means the people responsible must work for you,'

reasoned Colbeck. 'They know exactly where any guards are deployed and they can find their way around in the dark. In short, they're familiar with everything that happens on site. It enables them to stay one step ahead of you all the time.'

'What do you suggest?' said Brassey. 'Do I call in the police?'

'That's a decision only you can make, sir.'

'Well, I wouldn't make it lightly, Inspector. I've tried until now to contain the various setbacks we've suffered. Once I involve the police, our difficulties become common knowledge and newspapers start to take an interest. I'd hate that to happen,' he confided. 'Not everyone in this country is entirely happy to see an English contractor building a French railway. Adverse comment by the press could make things very awkward for us.'

'Then we tackle the situation another way,' decided Colbeck. 'We have to catch the men who are behind all these incidents.'

'And how do we do that?'

'By having someone working alongside them. At the moment, we're trying to solve the problem from the outside. That's a handicap. What we need is someone inside the labour force who can sniff out these villains by rubbing shoulders with them.'

'Such a man would be courting grave danger,' said Brassey.

'Only if he were found out.'

'Navvies are very close-knit. They resent outsiders.'

'Not if the outsider can win their confidence.'

'Inspector Colbeck is right,' said Leeming, glibly. 'We've used this device before and it's always worked. If the right man is chosen, he could unmask the villains in no time.'

'I'm glad that you agree,' said Colbeck, putting a hand on his shoulder, 'because you are the person I had in mind.'

Leeming gasped. '*Me*, sir?'

'Yes, Victor – you can start work this very morning.'

When light finally came, there was no shortage of volunteers to help in the work of clearing up the mess. The fires caused by the explosion had been swiftly put out but, ironically, another one now had to be lit to burn the remnants of the wagons. Two men had been badly hurt in the blast and half a dozen had sustained minor injuries. The dog was duly buried. When the work was finally done, the men stood in a circle around the railway lines that had been hideously distorted by the blast. Threats of violence were made against the culprits.

'They should be hung by their balls from the tallest tree,' snarled Pierce Shannon, 'then we could all throw rocks at the cruel bastards until they bleed to death.'

'I agree with the principle that they should suffer,' said Father Slattery, gently, 'though I'd express myself with more restraint.'

'That's because you're a priest. I can speak the truth.'

'You'll certainly speak *something*, Pierce, for I've never known a man with such a runaway mouth on him as you, but I'm not always sure that it's the honest truth that passes those lips of yours.'

'Whoever did this deserves to be crucified!'

Slattery bristled. 'And I'll not have you filching from the Holy Bible like that. Our Lord died upon a cross – he was martyred on our behalf. Never forget that. It would be sheer sacrilege to punish these evildoers in the same way.'

'What would you do to them, Father?'

'First of all, I'd ask them why they've been harrying us.'

'I can tell you that,' said Shannon, vengefully. 'They're swinish Frenchmen who can't bear the thought that we build better railways than they do. They want to drive us all away.'

'Well, I'm not going anywhere, Pierce.'

'Neither am I – whatever the dirty buggers do to us.'

Many of the navvies had been found accommodation in the surrounding farms and villages, but hundreds of them lived in the makeshift camp they had erected. Pierce Shannon was one of them, a short, compact, powerful Irishman in his thirties with a fondness for strong drink and a hard fight. Since there were so many people like Shannon on his books, Thomas Brassey had allowed a Roman Catholic priest to join them as a kind of missionary among the large Irish contingent, acting as a soothing presence and trying to turn their minds to higher things than merely satisfying their immediate needs.

Eamonn Slattery was a white-haired man in his sixties with a haggard face and an emaciated body. Respected and reviled alike, he loved the community in which he worked and did his best to master the names of as many men as he could. Instead of preaching at them from an imaginary pulpit, he came down to their level and talked in terms that they could understand. He disapproved of the fact that some of the navvies lived with common-law wives – sharing them openly with other men in some cases – but he did not respond with outright condemnation. Instead, he turned his persuasive tongue on the women, telling them how much deeper and more fulfilling their relationships would be if they were blessed by the Church. Since he had been in the camp, he had already performed two marriages.

'Why do you blame the French?' asked Slattery.

'Because they're behind all this trouble we've been having.'

'I see no evidence of it.'

'That's because you weren't here when we were working on the Rouen to Le Havre Railway,' said Shannon, pronouncing the names in a way that any Frenchman would find incomprehensible. 'Because the ballasting was done before the mortar was properly dry, the viaduct at Barentin fell down with a bang. Jesus! The way they turned against us, you'd have thought we'd raped every nun in the country and set fire to that Notre Damn Cathedral.'

'Moderate your language, please,' rebuked the priest.

'They treated us like criminals, Father. It's as well I can't read French because the newspapers went for us with a cat-o'-bleeding-nine tails. Even when we rebuilt the viaduct,' continued Shannon, 'we got no credit for it. We were British scum, taking jobs off the French.'

'That's not the case here, though, is it? The majority of the work force is British but Mr Brassey has also engaged French navvies.'

'Yes, but he pays them only half what we get – quite right, too.'

'They do have cause for resentment, then.'

Shannon was aggressive. 'Whose bleeding side are *you* on?'

'If you could ask me more politely, I might tell you. As it is, I remain sceptical about your claim that Frenchmen were behind that explosion. I'll reserve my judgement, Pierce,' said the priest, meeting his glare, 'and I advise you to do the same.'

'My mind is already made up and the same goes for a lot of us. We're not going to sit back and let these bastards cause even more damage. When we come off shift this evening,' said

Shannon, bunching both fists, 'we intend to settle a few scores with the French.'

'What are you going to do?'

'Well, we're not going to pray with them, I can tell you that.'

The visit to Mantes was a revelation. When he called at the house where Gaston Chabal had lodged, Robert Colbeck had to explain to the landlady why the engineer would not be returning. She was very upset to hear of the murder and had clearly been exceptionally fond of her lodger. Colbeck was allowed to inspect the man's room. The first things he found were some letters from Hannah Marklew, one of which set a date for their rendezvous in Liverpool. On his way to the assignation, her lover had been killed. It was clear from the missives that Hannah had never been involved in such a situation before. She was naïve and indiscreet. She not only signed her Christian name, she gave her full address as well. Colbeck tore up the letters so that they would not fall into anyone else's hands.

Hers were not the only *billets-doux* he found in the room. A Frenchwoman, signing herself with the letter 'D', wrote with even greater passion from somewhere in Paris. She was more circumspect. No address was given in her letters, only the city from where the mail was dispatched. Colbeck checked the rest of the correspondence. Business letters showed that Chabal had built himself a reputation that brought in several offers of work. One person, from England, invited him to return there in order to give some more lectures on his work as a civil engineer. The fee was tempting.

Even when working on a railway, Chabal kept an extensive wardrobe and Colbeck found a jacket identical to the one that had taken an unfortunate dip in the Sankey Canal. There were many other clues to the character of the deceased and they helped to give the inspector a full portrait of him. When he went downstairs, he found the landlady in tears, stunned by the loss of her charming lodger and horrified at the manner of his death. Colbeck told her that, once Chabal's family and friends were informed of his demise, someone would soon come to claim his effects.

Paris was his next destination. Boarding a train at the station, Colbeck went on the short journey from Mantes, intrigued to see what had been for so many years the capital of Europe. It was a city that celebrated the arts, and composers, musicians, dancers, artists, poets and authors from many countries had flocked there in search of inspiration. Chopin, Liszt, Mendelssohn, Donizetti, Rossini, Verdi, Wagner and Heine had all resided there at one time or another. Two English authors whose novels were on Colbeck's bookshelves back home in London – Dickens and Thackeray – had also lived in the city. It was a place of cosmopolitan talent with superb art galleries, concert halls and opera houses to display it.

Colbeck was not disappointed. Driven in a cab along its broad boulevards, he marvelled at its sumptuous architecture and tried to take in its full wonder. The buildings of Paris reflected an empire that no longer existed but that could still stir the imagination. What he noticed was the abundance of outdoor cafes, where customers were enjoying a leisurely drink in the sunshine while reading a newspaper, playing dominoes or talking with friends. Like any major city, Paris had its share of slums and Colbeck saw something of them when he was taken through a maze of back streets. The grinding poverty in the mean tenements was exacerbated by the prevailing stink of the drains.

Before he reported the death of Gaston Chabal to the police, and left them to track down his family, Colbeck wanted to visit the address that Thomas Brassey had given him for the late engineer. The detective hoped to find out a little more about the man on his own account. Once the French police were involved, he would have to surrender the initiative to them. The address was in the Marais, one of the oldest and most interesting parts of the city, and it took its name from the marshes on which it was built. When the cab pulled up in a busy street, he saw that the dead man had owned a tall, narrow house with a hint of Gothic extravagance in its façade. It was large enough to require servants, so Colbeck could expect someone to be at home.

He alighted from the cab and was immediately reminded how much taller he was than the average Frenchman. Most of those who bustled past him were distinctly shorter and had darker complexions. From the hostile glances he was given, Colbeck could see that the passers-by had guessed his nationality. He pulled the bell rope and heard it ring deep inside the house. The door was soon opened by a pretty young woman with a look of hope and expectation in her eyes. When she saw that a stranger had called, she let out a sigh.

Colbeck thought that she could be no more than sixteen or seventeen. It was clear from her manner and her elegance that she was no servant. Since he had been informed that Chabal was unmarried, he assumed that she might be a relative of his. Breaking the sad news to her would be painful but it had to be done. Lifting his hat in a gesture of courtesy, Colbeck gave a smile.

'*Bonjour, Mademoiselle*,' he said.

'*Madame*,' she corrected.

'*Ah*.' He looked down and saw her wedding ring.

'*Vous êtes un ami de Gaston*?' she asked.

It was an awkward question and Colbeck did not wish to answer it on a doorstep when people were walking past all the time. Since he had bad tidings to impart, he needed to do so in privacy. He reached for a polite euphemism.

'*J'ai fait sa connaissance*.'

'*C'est mon marie*.'

Colbeck was shaken. He was talking to Gaston Chabal's wife.

Victor Leeming had been startled when first given the assignment, but he had adapted to the notion very quickly. He was very pleased to be directly involved in the business of detection again. Strong enough to do the work, he also had the facial characteristics to pass as a navvy. For once, his ugliness was a positive advantage. Wearing moleskin trousers, double-canvas shirt, velveteen square-tailed coat, hobnail boots and a mud-spattered felt hat with the brim turned up, he looked almost indistinguishable from the rest of the men. Like them, he even wore a gaudy handkerchief at his neck to add some colour.

Railway work covered a wide variety of skills, each trade commanding a different wage. Leeming met carpenters, blacksmiths, miners, quarrymen, masons, bricklayers, horse keepers and sawyers. Taken on as a navvy, he was responsible to a ganger, a huge man with the rasping tongue and bulging muscularity needed to keep such an unruly group of workers in order. Digging, loading, cutting and tipping were the navvies' traditional tasks. Unskilled work was left to the labourers. Leeming was a cut above them.

When they were building a railway in England, navvies had an allowance of two pounds of beef and a gallon of beer a day. Since they had been in France, however, they had discovered that brandy was cheaper than beer and more potent. It had become the drink of choice for many of them. The fact that they spent their money so freely in the local inns made them more acceptable to the indigenous population. Given a shovel, Leeming was ordered to load spoil into wagons. It was hard, tiring, repetitive work but he did it without complaint. Those alongside him were largely Irish and they tended to work in silence. A group of Welsh navvies further down the line, however, insisted on singing hymns as they used pick and shovel on the rocky ground.

'Will you listen to those bastards?' said Liam Kilfoyle, during a brief rest. 'They never stop.'

'I'm surprised they've got the breath to sing,' observed Leeming.

'They'll work all day, rut all night and sing their heads off while they're doing both. It's unnatural, that's what it is.'

'They sound happy enough.'

'Little things please little bloody minds.'

Kilfoyle was a tall, stringy individual in his twenties with a pair of small, darting eyes in a face that reminded Leeming of a weasel. The sergeant had gone out of his way to befriend the young Irishman, feeding him the story that Brassey had prepared for his new recruit. The problem was that Leeming could only understand half of what Kilfoyle said because the latter kept using colloquialisms that were peculiar to the Irish. He knew the rhyming slang of the London underworld by heart but this was quite different. When in doubt as to his companion's meaning, he simply nodded. Kilfoyle seemed amiable enough. Putting his shovel aside, he undid his trousers and urinated against the wheel of a wagon, breaking wind loudly in the process. He did up his moleskin trousers again.

'Have you worked for Mr Brassey before?' said Kilfoyle.

'No – what's he like?'

'He's a fair man and you'll not find too many of them in this line of business. Some contractors are bloody tyrants, so they are. Real bloodsuckers. Not our Mr Brassey. His only fault is that he won't allow beer to be sold on site. Shovelling earth is thirsty work.'

'You don't need to tell me that,' said Leeming, face and armpits streaming with sweat. 'My throat's as dry as a bone.'

'Mine, too.' Kilfoyle eyed him up and down. 'So where have you worked, Victor?'

'On the London to Brighton.'

'From what I heard, there were some really good fights there.'

'There were, Liam. We were at it hammer and tongs many a time. I've got friends who are still locked up in Lewes Prison because of a riot we caused. They had to call in the troops.'

'It was the same for us when we were building the Chester and Holyhead. A gang of mad Welsh bricklayers from Bangor attacked us and said that all Irish were thieves and rogues. We'd have murdered them, if the soldiers hadn't stopped our fun. You look as if you could handle yourself in a fight,' he went on, noting the size of Leeming's forearms. 'Am I right?'

'I won't let anyone push me around.'

'Then you're one of us.' After slapping the other on the back, he picked up his shovel. 'What do you think of the French?'

'I don't like them, Liam.'

'Ugly sons of diseased whores!'

'It's that gibberish they speak.'

'They hate us, Victor.'

'I know. They see us as invaders.'

'That's why they're trying to stop us,' said Kilfoyle, angrily. 'That explosion last night was set off by those French frigging navvies, sure it was. Well, some of us are not going to let these greasy, bloody foreigners drive us away. We're going to strike back.'

'Strike back?' repeated Leeming, trying to keep the note of alarm out of his voice. 'And who is we, Liam?'

'The sons of Erin.'

'Oh, I see.'

'We'll attack their camp tonight and kick them all the way from here back to Paris. Are you with us, Victor?'

'I'm not Irish.'

'A strong arm and a stout heart is all we ask.'

'Tonight, you say? When and where?'

'That doesn't matter. Are you with us or are you not?'

Leeming had no choice in the matter. If he refused, he would earn Kilfoyle's derision and be ostracised by the rest of the Irish navvies. If that happened, he would find out nothing. He simply had to appear willing.

'Oh, yes,' he said with conviction. 'I'm with you, Liam.'

'Good man!'

They started working in earnest beside each other again.

'Married?' said Thomas Brassey, rising from his seat in surprise. 'I always thought that Gaston was a roving bachelor.'

'That was the impression that he liked to give,' confirmed Colbeck, 'and it obviously convinced some ladies. I now know of two seduced by him and there may be well be more. He seems to have been liberal with his affections.'

'That raises the possibility that Gaston was the victim of an enraged husband, Inspector.'

'But it is only a possibility, sir.'

Robert Colbeck had returned from Paris late that afternoon and called in at Brassey's office to report his findings. The contractor was fascinated to hear what he had learnt.

'What did you think of Paris?' he asked.

'It's a beautiful city, so cultured, so exciting, so urbane.' He held up a small book. 'Do you know Galignani's work? This is a *Stranger's Guide through the French Metropolis*. I bought it on my first visit there several years ago. It's a veritable goldmine of information. I only wish I'd had time to visit some of the sights he recommends.'

'How did Gaston's wife take the news?'

'She almost fainted. Naturally, I suppressed most of the details. There's no need for her to know any of those. Nor did I tell what her husband was doing in England. That would have been cruel.'

'What had he said to her?'

'That he was going to London to deliver a lecture.'

'And she had no suspicion that another woman was involved?'

'None at all, Mr Brassey,' said Colbeck. 'She's young, innocent and very trusting. His death was a devastating blow to her. Luckily, her mother was staying at the house. She was able to comfort her.'

'That's something, anyway.'

'I didn't wish to trespass on private grief any longer so I left.'

'Did you go to the police?'

'Yes,' said Colbeck, 'I gave them a full report of the murder and told them that we were devoting all our resources to the arrest of the killer. They agreed to help in any way, a fact that Mr Tallis will no doubt treat as a phenomenon.'

'Mr Tallis?'

'My superintendent. He has a very low opinion of the French.'

'Oh, they're a civilised nation at bottom,' said Brassey with a guarded affection. 'They make me feel very parochial at times. The trouble is that they are so easily aroused. I was here four years ago when the revolution broke out.'

'That must have been quite frightening.'

'It was, Inspector Colbeck. I was in no personal danger but my business interests were. Success as a contractor depends on stability and France became very unstable. When Louis Philippe was swept from the throne, there was a deep financial crisis.'

'Yes – many people were ruined.'

'I could have been one of them,' admitted Brassey, flicking back his coat tails as he perched on the edge of his desk. 'Stocks and shares fell heavily, none more so than those of the railways.' He pulled a face. 'It was a testing time for us. How much do you know about the French railway system?'

'I know that it's far less developed than ours,' said Colbeck, 'and that it's never attracted anything like the private investment that we enjoy. For that reason, the French government has had to play more of a role – and that's all very well until you have a violent change of government.'

'It's made this project so much more difficult.'

'Do the government interfere?'

'I'm answerable to the Minister of Public Works and he expects to be kept up to date with our progress. That was why Gaston Chabal was so useful to us – I got him to send regular reports in French. No,' Brassey continued, 'our real difficulty lay on the other side of the Channel.'

'In England?'

'It's where so many of our private investors live, Inspector.'

'I see.'

'Ten years ago, they were happy to put money into a venture of this kind, knowing that they'd get an excellent return on their capital. After the revolution, they were much more reluctant. One of them told me that the trouble with the French was that they were *too* French.'

'Emotional, unreliable and prone to overthrow governments.'

'The gentleman in question put it more bluntly than that. Mark you,' said Brassey, 'not all the British investors turned tail. Some had the foresight to see that this railway could pay handsome dividends in time. One of them had the sense to come here to see for himself.'

'Oh?' said Colbeck. 'Who was that?'

'Alexander Marklew. He understands railways.'

'And he's actually been here?'

'In the very early stages,' replied the other. 'I let Gaston Chabal talk to him about the potential of this railway. He had such a persuasive tongue. He managed to persuade Mr Marklew to invest. He also showed him and his wife around Paris – I think that helped.'

'I'm sure that it did.'

Colbeck said nothing about the liaison with Hannah Marklew but it took on a slightly different aspect now. He suspected that part of the reason Chabal had cultivated the lady was to persuade her to urge her husband to buy shares in the railway. The intimacies of the bedroom were not without a commercial significance.

'Clearly,' said Colbeck, 'you were able to raise the finance.'

'Yes, Inspector, but the government remains our paymaster. They've built a whole series of time penalties into the contract. That's why these setbacks are so annoying,' said Brassey, pursing his lips. 'They slow us down and cost us a lot of money.' He saw someone through the window. 'Ah, here's Aubrey.' He crossed to the door to open it. 'Come on in,' he said. 'This is Inspector Colbeck.'

'How do you do, sir?' said Filton.

'Pleased to meet you,' said Colbeck, shaking his hand. 'I believe that you talked earlier to Sergeant Leeming.'

'Yes. I've just come from him.'

'Oh?'

'Now that he's working in disguise, of course, I did not disclose the fact that I knew him. But, as I walked past, he slipped this into my hand.' He gave a note to Brassey. 'It's for you, sir.'

'Thank you, Aubrey.' Brassey unfolded the note and read it. He then offered it to Colbeck. 'I think you should see this, Inspector.'

'Why?'

'More trouble ahead.'

'Really?' Colbeck took the note from him.

'We're going to have a fight on our hands.'

'Between whom?' asked Filton, worried at the prospect.

'The French and the Irish.'

'When?'

'Tonight, according to this,' said Colbeck, reading the message.

'Some Irish hotheads have decided that the French are to blame for all the attacks on us,' said Brassey. 'They're acting as judge and jury. They want summary justice.'

'Some of them just want a fight, I expect.'

'Yes, Inspector. They enjoy a brawl for its own sake.'

'Think what havoc they can wreak,' said Filton, wringing his hands. 'There'll be dozens on both sides who are unfit for work tomorrow. And it won't end there. If there's bad blood between the Irish and the French, there'll be another clash before long.' He spread his arms in despair. 'What on earth are we going to do?'

'He's a friend, I tell you,' said Liam Kilfoyle. 'I can vouch for him.'

'I don't care,' snapped Pierce Shannon. 'He's not coming.'

'But he looks like a real fighter.'

'He's not Irish.'

'Victor supports our cause.'

'After only one day? No, Liam. I don't trust him.'

'Well, I do. I worked alongside him. The French are not going to take this lying down, Pierce. They'll fight back. We need every man we can get. Victor Leeming is on our side.'

'We'll manage without the English bastard.'

It was late evening and, like everyone else who was gathering there, Shannon and Kilfoyle had been drinking. They had also armed themselves. Shannon was carrying a shillelagh that had drawn blood from many a skull in the past, while Kilfoyle preferred a pick handle. The rest of the men had chosen an assortment of weapons, including sledgehammers, shovels and lengths of thick, tarred rope. Brandy had roused passions to a fever pitch. When he joined the others, Victor Leeming found them in a turbulent mood.

'Good evening, Liam,' he said, picking out Kilfoyle by the light of the lanterns. 'When are we going?'

'You're not going any-bloody-where,' retorted Shannon.

'Why not?'

'Because you can clear off out of here.'

Leeming turned to Kilfoyle. 'What's happened?'

'Pierce is not happy about you,' said the other, shuffling his feet in embarrassment. 'I'm sorry, Victor. You can't come.'

'Why not – what's wrong with me?'

'You're a cock-eyed fool of an Englishman, that's why,' said Shannon, waving his shillelagh. 'This is our fight, not yours.'

'I work on this railway as well as you.'

'Yes – for one frigging day!'

'If it was one pissing hour, I'd still want to take a crack at the French,' said Leeming, boldly. 'There's jobs at stake here – mine as well as yours. If the French have been trying to stop us working on this railway, then they deserve a good hiding.'

'See?' said Kilfoyle. 'He's got balls, Pierce.'

Shannon was contemptuous. 'We don't need this ugly bugger,' he said, raising his weapon again. 'Go on – get out of here!'

It was a decisive moment. A menacing ring of Irishmen surrounded him. If he backed down, Leeming knew that he would be finished as a spy because he would be marked down as an outsider. The others would shun him completely. To win them over, he had to convince them that he shared their beliefs and commitment.

'Stop waving that cudgel at me,' he warned, 'or I'll take it off you and stick it up your arse!'

'You and whose bloody army?' demanded Shannon.

'Calm down,' said Kilfoyle, standing between them. 'We don't want you falling out with each other. Our enemy is the French.'

'And the frigging English, Liam.'

'Does that include Mr Brassey?' challenged Leeming. 'Or do you only curse him behind his back? Is he a frigging Englishman as well? Do you sneer at all of us?'

'Mr Brassey is different,' conceded Shannon.

'So am I. That means I come with you.'

'Over my dead body.'

'What's this idiot's name, Liam?'

'Pierce Shannon,' replied Kilfoyle. 'He's one of our leaders. Whatever Pierce says, goes. That's the way it is, Victor.'

'Yes,' reinforced Shannon. 'That's the way it is, shit-face.'

Leeming pretended to accept the decision. He glanced at the leering Irishmen around him. They began to jostle him. Without warning, he suddenly threw a punch that caught Shannon on the ear and knocked him to the ground. Leeming stamped on the hand that was holding the shillelagh, forcing him to release it. Two men grabbed the detective from behind but Shannon wanted personal revenge.

'Leave go of the bastard!' he yelled, struggling to his feet. 'He's all mine. I'll tear out his heart and liver.'

The crowd moved back to give them room. The two men circled each other warily. Leeming could feel the hostility all around him. His one mode of escape was to earn their respect. Shannon lunged at him with both fists flying but the blows were all taken on the protective forearms that Leeming put up. He responded by hitting Shannon hard in the stomach to take the wind out of him, then followed with a relay of punches to the face and body. Blood spurted from the Irishman's nose. It made him launch another attack but Leeming was much lighter on his feet. As Shannon lurched at him, he dodged out of his way and felled him with a vicious punch to the side of his head.

As their leader went down in a heap, three men clung on to Leeming so tight that he was unable to move. Shannon got up very slowly, wiped the blood from his nose with a sleeve then picked up his shillelagh. Eyes blazing, he confronted Leeming. Then he gave a broad grin of approval and jabbed him in the chest.

'I like him,' he announced. 'He's one of us, lads.'

There was a rousing cheer and Leeming was released. Everyone close patted him on the back. Kilfoyle came forward to pump his hand. Leeming was relieved. He had survived one test but a far worse one might lie ahead. In beating one Irishman in a fight, all that he had done was to earn the right to attack the French as part of a mob. It was frightening. Once battle had been joined, there would be many casualties. No quarter would be given. In the uninhibited violence, Leeming could well be injured. He thought about his wife and children back in England. At that moment, he missed them more than ever. The railway was to blame. He realised that. It had not only brought him to a foreign country he disliked, it was now putting his life at risk. Leeming wished that he were hundreds of miles away.

'Come on, Victor,' said Shannon, putting a companionable arm around his shoulders. 'Let's go and kill a few Frenchies.'

CHAPTER SEVEN

'Navvies are a race apart,' said Thomas Brassey. 'I've never met anyone like them for sheer hard work. I respect them for their virtues but I also condemn them for their vices.'

'They've caused so much trouble in England,' observed Robert Colbeck. 'When they've set up camps there, they've terrorised whole communities.'

'You can see why, Inspector. Ordinary, decent, law-abiding people are horrified when they have huge gangs of hooligans on their doorstep. In their place, I'd be scared stiff.'

'Yet you seem to have less problems with your navvies, sir.'

'That's because I won't employ known troublemakers. If I find someone trying to stir up mischief, I get rid of him at once. I also try to reduce friction by keeping different nationalities apart,' he went on. 'The Irish and the Welsh don't always see eye to eye, so I make sure they are never together. It's the same with the French. I never put them shoulder to shoulder with British navvies.'

'Yet you've now got a potential riot on your hands.'

'Only because we're in an unusual position.'

'Have you never faced this situation before, Mr Brassey?'

'No – thank heaven!'

They were travelling through the French countryside in a trap. The horse was moving at a steady trot across the uneven ground and they were shaken up as the wheels mounted the frequent bumps and explored the deep potholes. It was a clear night with a half-moon looking down dolefully from the sky. Behind them were two other traps and a couple of men on horseback. Most of them carried a firearm of some sort.

'What's the worst that could happen?' asked Colbeck.

'That we get there too late.'

'We'd have heard the noise of battle before now.'

'True,' said the other. 'I suppose that the very worst thing that could happen is that news of any violence would get out, and that would surely happen if the French are involved. Activities on this railway would then be reported in the newspapers.'

'You've had bad publicity before.'

'And plenty of it, Inspector, especially in this country.'

'But I understood that you were on good terms with the French government. Mr Filton told me that you'd had dealings with Louis Napoleon himself.'

'A businessman should always cultivate his employers. That's sound common sense. Not that I ever expected to be accountable to a man called Napoleon,' he added with a rueful smile. 'It's a name that conjures up too many ghosts for any Englishman. But I've had to put all that aside. As it happens, on the few occasions when I've met him, I've found him an amenable gentleman.'

'How amenable would he be if French navvies were badly wounded in a fight with the Irish?'

'I hope that I never find out, Inspector Colbeck. That's why I was grateful for your advice. The plan might just work.'

'I've dealt with angry crowds before.'

'I'm sure.'

'Facing a Chartist march was a sobering experience,' admitted Colbeck. 'There were thousands of them and, if truth be told, I had a lot of sympathy with their cause. But I was there to police them so my personal views were irrelevant. Fortunately, no real violence erupted.'

'I pray that we have the same outcome tonight.'

'So do I, Mr Brassey.'

'It's not just the future of *this* railway that's at stake,' said the contractor, 'the next one would also be imperilled.'

'The next one?'

'Linking Mantes to Caen is only the first half of the project. The next stage is to build a railway from Caen to Cherbourg. We would be bidding for the contract to extend the track for that extra ninety miles or so. If we blot our copybook on this venture,' he said with a frown, 'then our chances of securing that contract will be slim.'

'Caen to Cherbourg?' asked Colbeck.

'Yes, Inspector.'

'That would provide a direct link between Paris and the dockyard at Cherbourg.'

'More than the dockyard – they have an arsenal there.'

'That's exactly what I was thinking.'

'Of course, it will take time to build,' said Brassey. 'At a rough guess, we'd not even be starting for another three years. The engineer I'd most liked to have had on the project was Gaston Chabal.'

'Why?'

'His surveys were brilliant and, being French, he got on well with local people while he was there. Gaston's preparatory work on the current railway helped us to land the contract and – because of its accuracy – saved us a lot of money in the process.' Colbeck seemed to have gone off into a reverie. 'Did you hear what I said, Inspector?'

'Every word, Mr Brassey, every single word. I was also reminded of a remark you made a little earlier.'

'Oh – and what was that?'

'You told me that you never expected to be accountable to a man called Napoleon.'

'Well, we fought for so many years against his namesake.'

'Precisely,' said Colbeck. 'Imagine how much more danger we would have been in if Napoleon Bonaparte had had a rail link between Paris and a huge arsenal on the tip of the Normandy peninsular. In that event,' he went on, stroking his chin reflectively, 'you and I might well have been having this conversation in French.'

Victor Leeming was afraid. He was so accustomed to physical violence that, as a rule, it held no fear for him. Most criminals resisted arrest and it was necessary to overpower them. It was an aspect of his work that he enjoyed. But he was now locked into a very different kind of struggle, one in which he had no place to be. Along with over two hundred wild Irishmen, he was trudging across the fields toward the farm where the French navvies had set up their camp. Leeming had sent warning of the attack to Thomas Brassey but he could not see how the contractor could possibly stop it. Carried along by its own momentum, the drunken mob was bent on what it saw as justified revenge. Leeming felt as if he were trapped on a runaway train that was heading at top speed towards a fatal collision.

'Isn't this wonderful?' said Kilfoyle alongside him.

'Yes, Liam.'

'We'll teach them a lesson they'll not bloody well forget.'

'Whose idea was it?' asked Leeming.

'Eh?'

'Launching this attack on the French. Who first thought of it?'

'What does it matter?'

'I was interested, that's all. Was it Shannon?'

'Pierce is one of the leaders,' said Kilfoyle, 'but I fancy it was someone else who made the decision. Pierce just went along with it like the rest of us.' He let out a cackle. 'Oh, we need this so much, sure we do. We've not had a proper fight for months.'

'What will Mr Brassey do?'

'He can't do anything, Victor.'

'I don't want to lose my job over this,' said Leeming, worriedly. 'I've got a family to feed back in England.'

'Your job is safe – and so is mine. That's the reason we stick together. Mr Brassey knows which bloody side his bread is buttered. He can't sack all of us, or the rest of the Irish would walk out.'

'Safety in numbers, eh?'

'Only for us, Victor – not for the French.'

'How many of them are there?'

'Who cares? One Irishman is worth four of the buggers.'

'What about me?'

'You're the fella who knocked Pierce to the ground,' said Kilfoyle, admiringly, 'and I've never seen anyone do that before. You'll have to be in the front line. Pierce wants his best men at his side. Get yourself a weapon, man.'

'Why?'

'Because the French won't be fighting with bare hands, that's why.' He thrust the pick handle into Leeming's palm. 'Here – have this. I'll use my knife instead and poke out a few eyes with it.'

There was no turning back now. Victor Leeming was part

of a ravening pack of Irish wolves that was closing in on their prey. They could smell blood. Shannon pushed through the crowd.

'Come on, Victor,' he urged. 'We need you for the first charge.'

'I'm here,' said Leeming, holding up his pick handle.

'Let's see who can open the most French skulls.'

'Where's the camp?'

'Just over the brow of the hill. In a few more minutes, we'll be haring down on them to massacre the bastards.' He punched Leeming on the shoulder. 'Are you ready for a fight?'

'Ready and willing, Pierce.'

Leeming spoke with more confidence than he felt. He was not merely facing the prospect of injury, he was taking part in a criminal act. If the superintendent ever discovered that he had been party to an affray, he would chew Leeming's ears off. The sergeant was glad that he was well out of Edward Tallis's jurisdiction.

Shannon took him by the arm and dragged him to the front of the marchers. As they went up the hill, Leeming began to have more and more misgivings. He rarely criticised Colbeck's methods but this time, he believed, the inspector had been mistaken. In making his sergeant work as a navvy, he had exposed him to dire hazards. Yet Leeming could not break ranks now. The brow of the hill was only thirty yards away. Once they were over it, there would be carnage.

Then, out of the dark, three figures appeared on the top of the hill. Silhouetted against the sky, they were an imposing trio. Even in the half-dark, Leeming recognised Colbeck, standing in the middle, with Thomas Brassey beside him. He could not identify the third man. Colbeck took out a pistol and fired it into the air. The Irishmen stopped in their tracks.

'That's as far as you go tonight, gentlemen,' said Brassey.

'Why?' demanded Shannon.

'Because I say so – and so does Father Slattery.'

'Yes,' said the priest, stepping forward and raising his voice so that all could hear. 'It's a pity that some of you don't come to a church service with the same kind of enthusiasm. When you want a fight, there's no holding you. When I tell you to join me in fighting the Devil, then it's only the bravest who show their faces.'

'Out of our way, Father!' shouted Kilfoyle.

'I stand here as a representative of Roman Catholicism.'

'I don't care if you're the bleeding Pope!' cried someone.

'The French are Catholics as well,' returned Slattery. 'Would you attack your own kind?'

'Go back to your camp,' ordered Brassey. 'There'll be no brawl tonight. The French are not even here,' he lied. 'They were forewarned to pull out of their tents and shacks.'

'Who by?' called Shannon.

'Me. And I didn't do it to save your skins. Some of you deserve to take a beating – it's the only way you'll see sense. I did it so that you could keep your jobs. This gentleman here,' he went on, pointing at Colbeck, 'is M. Robert, assistant to the Minister of Public Works.' Colbeck raised his hat to the mob and produced a barrage of jeers. 'Before you taunt M. Robert, let me tell you that he's empowered to revoke our contract if he decides that we are not able to fulfil it peaceably. I don't think anyone could construe an invasion of the French camp as a peaceful act.'

'Had you firebrands insisted on a fight,' said Slattery, taking over, 'you'd not only have been sacrificing your jobs and those of all the other navvies from across the Channel. In your wisdom, you'd also have been handing over the work to a French contractor who would refuse to employ a single one of you.'

'Think on that,' said Brassey. 'You'd have been letting me, yourselves and your families down. You'd have had to sneak home in disgrace without any money in your pockets and no work awaiting you in England. Is that what you really want?'

'No, sir,' bleated Kilfoyle.

'What about the rest of you?'

In response came a lot of shamefaced muttering. The fight had suddenly been taken out of the navvies. Several began to slink away at once. Alone in the crowd, Leeming was delighted. A calamity had just been averted by the intervention of Thomas Brassey and Father Eamonn Slattery. But it was the presence of M. Robert that had tipped the balance. Fear of losing their jobs, combined with the certainty that Brassey would never hire any of them again, brought them to heel. More of them turned round and left. The danger was over.

The contractor and the priest had prevented a bloodbath, but Leeming knew that they did not deserve all the credit. The ruse had worked well because Robert Colbeck had devised it. Not for the first time, Leeming had been rescued by the inspector's guile.

As soon as they got back to his office, Thomas Brassey lit a few oil lamps then he unlocked a cupboard and took out a bottle of whisky and three glasses. He poured a generous amount into the glasses then gave one each to Robert Colbeck and Aubrey Filton. The contractor raised his own glass with a smile.

'I think we're entitled to toast a job well done,' he said.

'I never thought that you'd pull it off, sir,' confessed Filton after taking his first sip. 'I thought someone might call your bluff.'

'That's why I suggested that we involve Father Slattery,' said Colbeck, impressed by the quality of the whisky. 'I felt that he would give credence to the whole exercise. I'm still troubled by guilt at having had to deceive an ordained priest like that.'

'He really thought that you were M. Robert.'

'In a sense, of course, that's what I am.' He adopted a French accent. 'M. Robert Colbeck.'

'You spoke the language so well, Father Slattery was taken in.'

'The main thing is that the mob was as well,' said Brassey. 'I shudder to think what chaos would have followed if they'd reached the French camp. They hadn't withdrawn at all.'

'I had a very good reason to make sure that the two parties didn't meet,' Colbeck explained. 'Victor Leeming was in that crowd somewhere. I need him to remain in one piece.'

'He deserves my congratulations for what he did, Inspector.'

'Save them until he delivers the real culprits up to us.'

'Are you sure they're part of the Irish contingent?'

'Yes, Mr Brassey. Their camp is almost adjacent to the railway, so it would be easy for someone to slip out at night to cause damage. The French are nearly a mile away and none of them would be aware of how you deployed your nightwatchmen. The same goes for the Welsh and the rest of your navvies,' said Colbeck. 'They're too far away. No, I believe that the men we're after might well have been in that mob tonight.'

'Would they?' said Filton.

'What better way to take suspicion off themselves than by accusing someone else of the crimes? It's an old trick, Mr Filton.'

'Cunning devils!'

'We played a trick on them tonight,' recalled Brassey. 'It was all your doing, Inspector. You'll have to meet my wife. Her French is almost as fluent as yours. Have dinner with us some time.'

Colbeck smiled. 'That's very kind of you, Mr Brassey.'

'Sergeant Leeming can join us as well.'

'Only when he's finished the task he was set.'

'He was very brave to take it on.'

'Victor has already proved his worth. I just hope that he's not the victim of his own success.'

'In what way?' said Filton.

'Those men we turned back earlier on will know that they were betrayed by someone,' said Colbeck. 'They'll want his name.'

'Then I hope they never discover it.'

'No,' said Brassey with a shiver. 'I wouldn't like to be caught out in the middle of all those Irishmen. They have hot tempers and they don't take prisoners.'

'Sergeant Leeming will have to be careful.'

'Extremely careful, Aubrey.'

'He's done this kind of work before,' said Colbeck, 'though he's never dealt with navvies. As you told me earlier, Mr Brassey, they're a race apart. My hope is that Victor doesn't stick out too much. After tonight, some of those men will be desperate for revenge.'

'It must have been you, Father Slattery,' he said, glowing with rage.

'It was not, Pierce – on my word of honour.'

'You betrayed your own countrymen.'

'That's something I'd never do,' vowed the priest, 'and I'm insulted that you should even suggest it.'

'They knew we were coming.'

'And I'm eternally grateful that they did. Otherwise, you and your drunken ruffians would have committed the most unholy crime.'

'We were fighting on Mr Brassey's behalf.'

'Try telling him that.'

'We were,' said Shannon, vehemently. 'The Frenchies are trying to wreck this railway so that we lose the contract. That way, they can take over. The bastards want us all out of their country.'

'If you conduct yourselves as you did tonight, I'm not surprised. When drink is taken,' said Slattery, 'you turn into wild beasts. You don't belong in civilised company. Truly, I was ashamed of you all.'

They were in the Irish camp, talking by the light of a lantern outside one of the shacks. Most of those who had marched with Pierce Shannon had either gone off to bed or started drinking again. Shannon himself had waited until Father Slattery had reappeared. It was all he could do to keep his hands off the priest.

'I still say that it was you, Father,' he accused.

'Then you'd best bring a Holy Bible so that I can swear on it. That won't mean much to you, godforsaken heathen that you are, but it means all the world to me.' He put his face close to that of the other. 'I did not tell a soul about your plan.'

'But you did know about it.'

'Of course – thanks to you. To get support, you told everybody you could. That's how it must have leaked out. The person to blame is you and that jabbering mouth of yours. It never stops. Someone overheard you and reported it straight away.'

'Is that what Mr Brassey told you?'

'Yes,' replied Slattery. 'He called me to his office and said that he'd received information that there was to be an attack on the French camp. He asked me if I knew who was behind it.'

Shannon was disturbed. 'Did you tell him?'

'Of course not.'

'How do I know that?'

'Because I give you my word. If I'd named you and the other ringleaders, you'd all have been on the first boat back home. If nothing else does, that should prove my loyalty to my nation.'

There was an extended pause while Shannon pondered.

'Thank you, Father,' he mumbled at length.

'I named no names,' said Slattery. 'Tell that to the others.'

'I will.'

'And don't invent any more hare-brained schemes like this.'

'It wasn't me that thought of it.' Shannon lowered his voice. 'What else did Mr Brassey say?'

'Only that you were mad to turn on the French. It could've meant him losing the contract altogether. As it is, the delays have cost him a lot of money. Did you know that there are time penalties of five thousand pounds a month if work is behind schedule?'

'No, I didn't.'

'Well, there are. Mr Brassey showed me the contract.'

'Did he give you the name of the traitor?'

'No, but I still think he was called Pierce Shannon. You opened your mouth once too often.'

'Everybody knew that something was afoot tonight,' said Shannon, 'but only those who were coming knew the time and place. Somehow, Mr Brassey got hold of those details.'

'God works in mysterious ways.'

'This was nothing to do with God. We've got a spy in our ranks.'

'Then you should thank him – he saved your jobs.'

'And what if these bloody raids go on, Father? What if we get another explosion or some more damage in the tunnel? What if someone starts a real fire next time? What would happen to our frigging jobs then? Answer me that.' Shannon was breathing heavily. 'And while you're at it,' he continued, angrily, 'you can answer another bloody question as well.'

'If you could phrase it more sweetly, maybe I will.'

'Since *you* didn't betray us, who, in the bowels of Christ, did?'

Victor Leeming had never spent such an uncomfortable night before. He was, by turns, appalled by what he saw, nauseated by what he smelt and disgusted that human beings could live in such a way. The Irish camp consisted of ragged tents, rickety wooden huts and ramshackle cottages built out of stone, timber, thatch and clods of earth. In such dwellings, there was no trace of mortar to hold things together. Gaps in the roof and walls would, in due course, let in wind, rain and snow. Vermin could enter freely. It was grim and cheerless. Leeming had seen farmyard animals with better accommodation.

When he had been invited to go to the flimsy shack where Liam Kilfoyle slept, he did not realise that he would be sleeping on flagstones and sharing a room with five other people. Two of them were women, and Leeming was shocked when the men beside them each mounted their so-called wives and took their pleasure to the accompaniment of raucous female laughter. It was worlds away from the kind of tender union that Leeming and Estelle enjoyed. Simply being in the same room as the noisy, public, unrestrained rutting made him feel tainted. Kilfoyle, by contrast, was amused by it all. As he lay beside Leeming, he whispered a secret.

'The fat one is called Bridget,' he said, grinning inanely. 'I have her sometimes when Fergal goes to sleep. You can have her as well, if you want to.'

Leeming was sickened by the thought. 'No, thank you.'

'It's quite safe. Fergal never wakes up.'

'I'm too tired, Liam.'

'Please yourself. I'll have Bridget later on.'

Leeming wondered how many more nights he would have to endure such horror. During his days in uniform, he had raided brothels in some of the most insalubrious areas of London but he had seen nothing to equal this. He could not understand how anyone could bear to live in such conditions. What he did admire about the navvies was their brute strength. After one day, his hands were badly blistered and he was aching all over, yet the others made light of the exhausting work. Navvies had incredible stamina. Leeming could not match it for long. To take his mind off his immediate discomfort, he tried to probe for information.

'Liam?'

'Yes?'

'What if we were wrong?'

'Wrong about what?'

'The French,' said Leeming, quietly. 'Suppose that it wasn't them who set off that explosion?'

'It had to be them, Victor.'

'Yes, but suppose – only suppose, mind you – that it wasn't? If it was someone from this camp, for instance, who'd be the most likely person to have done it?'

'What a stupid question!'

'Think it through,' advised Leeming.

'What do you mean?'

'Well, it has to be someone who knows how to handle gunpowder, for a start. It's very easy to blow yourself up with that stuff. Is there anyone here who's had any experience of blasting rock before? I heard that the gunpowder was stolen from near here.'

'It was.'

'Who could have taken it?'

'Some bleeding Frenchie.'

'It's a long way to come from their camp.'

'Yes,' said Kilfoyle slowly, as if the idea had never occurred to him. 'You're right, Victor.'

'So who, in this camp, knows how to handle gunpowder?'

'Not me, I can tell you that.'

'Somebody must have had experience.'

'So?'

'I just wondered who it might be, that's all.'

'He needs catching, whoever the bastard is.'

'Have you any idea at all who it could be?'

'No.'

'Think hard, Liam.'

'Don't ask me.' He fell silent and cupped a hand to his ear so that he could hear more clearly. A loud snore came from the other side of the room. 'That's Fergal,' he said with snigger. 'Fast asleep. I'm off to shag his wife.' He sat up. 'Shall I tell Bridget you'll be over to take your turn after me?'

Leeming's blushes went unseen in the dark.

Caleb Andrews was late getting home that night. When he came off duty at Euston, he went for a drink in a public house frequented by railwaymen and tried to bolster his confidence by beating his fireman at several games of draughts. His winnings were all spent on beer. As he rolled home to Camden, therefore, he was in a cheerful mood. His supremacy on the draughts board had been restored and several pints of beer had given him a sense of well-being. He let himself into his house and found his daughter working by the light of an oil lamp.

'Still up, Maddy?' he asked.

'Yes, Father,' she replied. 'I just wanted to finish this.'

He looked over her shoulder. 'What is it – a portrait of me?'

'No, it's the Sankey Viaduct.'

'Is it? Bless my soul!'

Since his vision was impaired after so much alcohol, he needed to put his face very close to the paper in order to see the drawing. Even then he had difficulty picking out some of the pencil lines.

'It's good, Maddy.'

'You've been drinking,' she said. 'I can smell it on your breath.'

'I was celebrating.'

'Celebrating what?'

'I won ten games of draughts in a row.'

'Are you ready for another game with me?'

'No, no,' he said, backing away. 'I'll not let you take advantage of your poor father when he can't even see straight. But why are you drawing the Sankey Viaduct? You've never even seen it.'

'Robert described it to me.'

'I could have done that. I've been over it.'

'Yes, Father, but you were driving an engine at the time. You've never seen the viaduct from below as Robert has. According to him, it was a painting rather like this that will help to solve the murder.'

'I don't see how.'

Madeleine put her pencil aside and got up from her chair. She explained how Ambrose Hooper had witnessed the body being hurled over the viaduct, and how he had duly recorded the moment in his watercolour of the scene. She felt privileged that Colbeck had confided the information to her. What both she and the inspector knew was that the murder victim had been on his way to an assignation, but it was something she would not confide to her father. Caleb Andrews would have been alarmed to hear that she had been involved in a police investigation. More worrying from Madeleine's point of view was that fact that he was likely to pass on the information over a drink with his railway colleagues. Discretion was unknown to him.

'Why do *you* want to draw the Sankey Viaduct?' he wondered.

'I was just passing an idle hour.'

'You're never idle, Maddy. You take after me.'

'Robert told me so much about it that I wanted to put it down on paper. It's not something I'd ever expect to sell. I was just trying to do what Mr Hooper did and reconstruct the crime.'

'The real crime was committed by the guard on that train,' said Andrews with passion. 'He should have kept his eyes open. If he'd seen that body being thrown from the train, he could have jumped on to the platform at the next stop and caught the killer before he could sneak away.'

'But the guard didn't see a thing, Father.'

'That's my point.' Swaying uneasily, he put a hand on the back of a chair to steady himself. 'I'm for bed, Maddy. What about you?'

'I'll be up soon.'

'Next time you speak to Inspector Colbeck, tell him to consult me. I've got a theory about this crime – lots of them, in fact.'

'I know,' she said, fondly. 'I've heard them all.'

Madeleine kissed her father on the cheek then helped him to the staircase. Holding the banister, he went slowly up the steps. She returned immediately to a drawing that she had embarked on in the first instance because it kept Robert Colbeck in her mind. It was not meant to be an accurate picture of the viaduct. Madeleine had departed quite radically from the description that she had been given. She now added some features that were purely imaginary.

Using her pencil with a light touch, she removed the brook and canal that ran beneath the viaduct by drowning them completely in the foaming waves of the English Channel. On one side of the viaduct, she drew a sketch of a railway station and wrote the name Dover above it. On the other, she pencilled in a tall, elegant man in a frock coat and top hat. England and France had been connected in art. The drawing was no longer her version of what had happened to Gaston Chabal. It was a viaduct between her and Robert Colbeck, built with affection and arching its way across the sea to carry her love to him. As she put more definition and character into the tiny portrait of the detective, she wondered how he was faring in France and hoped that they would soon be together again.

Thomas Brassey did not only expect his employees to work long hours, he imposed the same strict regimen on himself. Accordingly, he arrived on site early that morning to discover that Robert Colbeck was there before him. The inspector was carrying a newspaper.

'You've read the report, I daresay,' noted Brassey.

'Yes, sir.'

'I got my wife to translate it for me. I'm glad that they described Gaston as an outstanding civil engineer because that's exactly what he was. My only concern is that the report of his murder will bring droves of people out here to bother me.'

'I doubt it,' said Colbeck. 'Since the crime was committed in England, reporters would have no reason to visit you. The police, on the other hand, may want to learn more about the deceased so I am sure that they will pay you a call at some time.'

'I hope that you're on hand when they come, Inspector.'

'Why?'

'I need an interpreter.'

'What about your wife?'

'Maria doesn't like to come to the site. And who can blame her?' he said, looking around at the clamorous activity. 'It is always so noisy, smelly and dirty here.'

'Building a railway means making a mess, Mr Brassey.'

The contractor laughed. 'I've made more mess than anybody.'

'All in a good cause.'

'I like to think so.'

Brassey unlocked the door of his office and the two of them went in. Various people began to call to get their orders for the day from the contractor. It was some time before Colbeck was alone again with him. Meanwhile, he had been studying the map of northern France that was on the wall.

'Compared to us,' he remarked, 'they have so few railways.'

'That will change in time, Inspector. Mind you, they've been spared the mad rush that we had. Everyone wanted to build a railway in England because they thought they would make a fortune.'

'Some of them did, Mr Brassey.'

'Only the lucky ones,' said the other. 'The crash was bound to come. When it did, thousands of investors were ruined, credit dried up and everything ground to a standstill. The Railway Mania was over.'

'You survived somehow.'

'We still had plenty of work on our books, in France as well as England. Many of our rivals went to the wall. It was the one good thing to come out of the disaster – we got rid of a lot of crooked promoters, incompetent engineers and contractors who gave us all a bad name. It stopped the rot, Inspector.'

'Is that why you prefer to work in France?'

'My partners and I will go wherever railways need to be built,' said Brassey. 'We've contracts in Canada, Italy and Denmark at this point in time.'

'But this one is your major concern.'

'At the moment.'

'I can understand why,' said Colbeck, glancing at the map. 'If you can secure the contract for the extension of this line from Caen to Cherbourg, you'll have work in France for years to come.'

'That's why nothing must jeopardise the project.'

'We headed off one big threat last night.'

'When will the next one come?'

'I hope that it won't Mr Brassey.'

'But you can offer no guarantee.'

'No, sir. I fear not. What I can tell you is this. Gaston Chabal was murdered in England for reasons that are connected to this railway. As you pointed out to me,' Colbeck went on, 'he was much more than an engineer. He obviously had a pivotal role to play here.'

'He did, Inspector. He was a sort of talisman.'

'In more ways than one, it seems.'

'I knew nothing of Gaston's private life when I took him on,' said Brassey. 'Even if I had been aware of his adulteries, I'd still have employed him. I'm a contractor, not a moral guardian.'

'That's clear from the vast number of navvies you employ.'

'Quite so, Inspector Colbeck. All sorts of irregularities go on in their camps but it's none of my business. As long as a man can do the job he's paid for, he can have three wives and a dozen mistresses.'

'I don't think that Chabal went to that extreme.' Colbeck moved away from the map to look through the window. 'I fear that it will all have come as a great shock to Victor.'

'What?'

'The moral laxity in the camp. He's a married man who tries to lead a Christian life. Some of the antics here will shake him to the core. He won't have seen anything like this before.'

'It's one of the reasons I encouraged Father Slattery to join us.'

'He's a courageous man, taking on such a task.'

'And so is Sergeant Leeming,' said Brassey, a chevron of concern between his eyebrows. 'As a priest, Father Slattery is not in any physical danger. Your sergeant certainly is.'

'Police work entails continuous danger, sir.'

'I just wonder if you have him in the right place.'

'The right place?'

'Well, I agree that the people we are after may be somewhere among the Irish but we've hundreds and hundreds of those. The villains could be bricklayers or quarrymen or blacksmiths. Why do you think they are navvies?'

'Instinct,' replied Colbeck. 'Instinct built up over the years. I feel that it was endorsed last night when that mob went in search of a fight. That was another attempt to disrupt this railway and to put you out of business. The villains used the same device as on the previous night, Mr Brassey.'

'In what way?'

'On the first occasion they used gunpowder. On the second, they used an equally deadly device – human gunpowder. Those Irish navvies were set to explode by the time they reached the French camp. No,' he decided, 'Victor is definitely where he needs to be. He won't thank me for putting him there, but he's in exactly the right place.'

Working so hard left him little time for detection. Victor Leeming had to take on a convincing camouflage and that forced him to toil away for long hours with a shovel in his hands. There were breaks for food and times when he had to satisfy the call of nature. Otherwise, he was kept busy loading spoil into the wagons for hour after fatiguing hour. He talked to Liam Kilfoyle and to some of the others labouring alongside him but they told him nothing of any real use. It was only when the shift finally ended, and the men trooped off to the nearest tavern, that Leeming was able to continue his search. Since he had joined in the march on the French camp, he was accepted. It made it easier for him to talk to the navvies. With a drink in their hands, they were off guard.

Yet it was all to no avail. Most of them refused to believe that an Irishmen could be responsible for the outrages, and none of them could give the name of someone with expertise in using gunpowder. At the end of a long evening, he abandoned his questioning and started to walk back towards the camp with a group of navvies. He braced himself to spend another night in the shack with Kilfoyle and the others, hoping that he would soon be released from that particular torture. The notion of coupling with Bridget, a big, buxom, shameless woman in her thirties, made his stomach heave.

So preoccupied was he in fearful thoughts of what lay ahead that he did not notice he was being followed. When they reached the railway, the men struck. Grabbing him by the shoulders, they pushed Leeming behind a wagon then one of them hit him on the back of the head with something hard and unforgiving. He had no chance to put up any resistance. He fell to the ground like a stone. Sinking into oblivion, he did not even feel the repeated kicks that thudded into his body. In a matter of seconds, it was all over.

CHAPTER EIGHT

Superintendent Edward Tallis was almost hidden by a swirling fug of cigar smoke. He did not like what he saw and he was unhappy about what he heard. While the cigar helped him to relieve his tension, it had another important function. It largely obscured Victor Leeming from his gaze. Seated in front of the desk, Leeming was a sorry sight. His head was heavily bandaged, his face covered in ugly bruises and lacerations, his lower lip twice it normal size. One eye was almost closed, the other looked to the superintendent for a sympathy that was not forthcoming. When he shifted slightly in his chair, Leeming let out an involuntary groan and put a hand to his cracked ribs.

Robert Colbeck was sitting beside the sergeant.

'I think that Victor should be commended for his daring, sir,' he suggested. 'By working alongside the navvies, he was able to foil an attack on the French camp.'

'Yes,' said Tallis, rancorously. 'He was also in a position to get himself all but kicked to death. That's not daring, Inspector, that's tantamount to suicide.'

'I'd do the same again, Superintendent,' said Leeming, bravely, wincing at the pain of speaking.

'You'll do nothing at all until you've recovered, man.

I'm giving you extended leave until you start to resemble a human being again.' He leant forward to peer through the smoke. 'Has your wife seen the state you're in?'

'No, sir,' said Colbeck, trying to spare the sergeant the effort of talking. 'We felt that we should report to you first so that you understood the situation. For obvious reasons, we travelled back to England slowly. Victor could not be hurried in his condition. I thought it best if I speak to Estelle – to Mrs Leeming – before she actually sees her husband.'

'That's up to you, Inspector.'

'I'll tell her how courageous he was.'

'Tell her the truth – he could have been killed.'

'No, Superintendent,' rejoined Colbeck. 'The men who set on him drew back from murder. That would have brought the French police swarming to the site and they did not want that. The beating was by way of a warning.'

'It was my own fault,' admitted Leeming, his swollen lip distorting the words. 'I asked too many questions.'

'I accept my share of the blame, Victor.'

'No, sir. It was the correct decision.'

'I beg to differ,' said Tallis, mordantly. 'Correct decisions do not result in a vicious attack on one of my men that will put him out of action for weeks.'

'You approved of our visit to France,' Colbeck reminded him.

'I've regretted it ever since.'

After giving him a day and night to make a partial recovery from the assault, Colbeck had brought Leeming back to England by means of rail and boat, two forms of transport that only served to intensify the sergeant's discomfort. Scotland Yard had been their first destination. Colbeck wanted the superintendent to see the injuries that Leeming had picked up in the course of doing of his duty. Neither compassion nor congratulation had come from across the desk.

'And what was all that about a Catholic priest?' said Tallis.

'It was Father Slattery who found Victor,' Colbeck told him. 'In fact, he seems to have disturbed the attackers before they could inflict even more damage.'

'Even *more*? What else could they do to him?'

'I didn't have the opportunity to ask them, sir,' said Leeming, rashly attempting a smile that made his whole face twitch in pain.

'Father Slattery is a good man,' said Colbeck. 'He acts as a calming influence on the Irish.'

Tallis indicated Leeming. 'If this is what they do when they're calm,' he said with scorn, 'then I'd hate to see them when they're fully aroused. Navvies are navvies. All over the country, police and local magistrates have trouble with them.'

'Mr Brassey's men are relatively well-behaved, sir.'

'Comment would be superfluous, Inspector.'

Tallis glowered at him before expelling another cloud of cigar smoke. He was trying to rein in his anger. In allowing the two men to go to France, he had had to raid his dwindling budget and account to the commissioner for the expenditure. All that he had got in return, it seemed, was the loss of a fine officer and a succession of tales about the problems encountered by a railway contractor in France.

'None of this has any bearing on the murder,' he announced.

'But it does, sir,' insisted Colbeck. 'If you look at the events carefully, you'll see how the death of Gaston Chabal fits into the overall picture. There's a logical development.'

'Then why I am not able to perceive it?'

'Perhaps you have the smoke of prejudice in your eyes.'

Tallis stubbed out his cigar then waved an arm to dispel

some of the smoke that enveloped him. Before he could take Colbeck to task for his comment, the inspector went on.

'Everything we learnt in France confirmed my initial feeling.'

'And what was that?'

'The answer to this riddle lies across the Channel.'

'It's true,' said Leeming. 'We could feel it.'

'Feeling it is not enough, Sergeant,' said Tallis, coldly. 'I want firm evidence and you have signally failed to provide it. Mr Brassey may be experiencing difficulties on his railway – in spite of the calming influence of this Catholic priest – but it's no concern whatsoever of ours. The Froggies must solve any crimes that take place on French soil. Mr Brassey should call in the local police.'

'I've explained why he's reluctant to do that,' said Colbeck.

'Not to my satisfaction.'

'There's an international dimension to this murder.'

'It took place in this country. That's all that matters to me.'

'We'll only apprehend the killer if we help to solve the crimes that are bedevilling the new railway in France. I must go back.'

Tallis was peremptory. 'Out of the question.'

'Then the murderer of Gaston Chabal will go unpunished.'

'No, Inspector, he must be caught.'

'In that case, sir,' said Colbeck with gentle sarcasm, 'I'll be interested to hear your advice on how we are supposed to catch him. You are clearly in possession of important details that have so far eluded Victor and me.'

'What I am in possession of are these,' said Tallis, lifting a pile of correspondence from his desk. 'They are letters from the railway company, demanding action, and they come on a daily basis. This morning, one of their directors was here in person to ambush me. Mr Marklew did not mince his words.'

'Would that be Mr Alexander Marklew?'

'Yes. Do you know him?'

'Not personally,' said Colbeck, 'but I gather that he's also invested in the Mantes to Caen line. When he hears about the setbacks in France, he may realise that this is a much wider investigation that he imagined.'

'Marklew is only one of my problems,' moaned Tallis. 'I've had the commissioner on my tail as well and an Inspector Sidney Heyford keeps writing from Liverpool, asking me why the great Robert Colbeck has failed to make any discernible progress. That's a theme taken up elsewhere,' he went on, bending down to retrieve a newspaper from his wastepaper basket. 'There's biting criticism of the way that we've handled this investigation and you are now referred to as the Railway Defective.' He thrust the newspaper at Colbeck. 'Take it.'

'I'm not interested in what newspaper reporters think,' said the other. 'They don't understand the complexity of the case. If you'll excuse me, sir, I'll take Victor back home then make arrangements to return to France.'

'No,' said Tallis, pounding the desk. 'You stay in London.'

'I must insist, Superintendent.'

'You are overruled. Nothing on earth would induce me to send you gallivanting off on another pointless French adventure. You belong to the Metropolitan Police not to the Surêté.'

'It looks as if I belong to neither, sir,' said Colbeck, rising to his feet with dignity. 'Since you refuse me permission to go as a member of the Detective Department, then I'll do so as a private individual.'

'Don't talk nonsense, man!'

'I'm quite serious, Superintendent. I feel very strongly

that this case can only be solved in France and I mean to go back there on my own account, if necessary. Give me a few minutes,' he said, as he walked to the door, 'and you shall have my resignation in writing.'

'You can have mine, too,' added Leeming, getting out of his chair with difficulty. 'Inspector Colbeck is right. If you do not have faith in our judgement, then I'll leave the Department at once.'

'Wait!' yelled Tallis.

He could see the futility of blustering. The two of them were in earnest. The loss of Victor Leeming would be a blow but he could be replaced by promoting someone from below. Robert Colbeck, however, was quite irreplaceable. He not only had an unrivalled record of success as a detective, he had a comprehensive knowledge of railways that was founded on a deep love of steam transport. Whenever serious crimes occurred on a railway, the company involved always asked for Colbeck to investigate. If he were to leave Scotland Yard, a huge vacuum would be created. Superintendent Tallis would have to explain to the commissioner why he had forced his best officer to resign, and he could imagine the withering reprimand that he would get in return. It was time to give ground.

'How long would you need in France?' he growled.

'As long as it takes,' replied Colbeck, going back to the desk to pick up the cigar box. 'Perhaps I can offer you one of these, sir?' he said, holding it out. 'It might stimulate your thought processes while I compose my letter of resignation.'

Madeleine Andrews was preparing a meal in the kitchen and musing on the changes that had come into her life since she had met Robert Colbeck. He had not merely urged her to develop her artistic talent to the point where she had actually managed to earn money from it, he had enlarged her world in every way. Until she had met him, Madeleine was happy enough looking after her father and educating herself by means of books, magazines and lectures. It had never crossed her mind that she would one day assist a detective inspector in a murder investigation and become – albeit unofficially – the first woman to have a role at Scotland Yard. Colbeck had brought love, interest and excitement into the house in Camden. Entertaining fond thoughts of him made the most menial chores seem pleasant. When she worked on, there was a smile on her face.

Madeleine had just finished peeling the potatoes when she heard the rasp of wheels pulling up outside the house. Only one person would call on her in a hansom cab. Tearing off her apron, she wiped her hands dry in it then cast it aside. As she rushed to the front door, she adjusted her hair. She flung the door open. When she let Colbeck in, she was enfolded in a warm embrace.

'I was just thinking about you, Robert,' she confessed.

'Good.'

'I had no idea that you were back in England.'

'Only briefly,' he told her. 'I'll be sailing across the Channel again this evening.'

'Why? What's happened? Do you know who the killer is?'

'Stop firing questions at me and I'll tell you what we've managed to find out so far.' He kissed her then led her to the sofa. 'Sit down.'

Holding her hand, he gave her a concise account of the visit to France and made her gasp when he revealed that Gaston Chabal was married. Madeleine recalled her interview at the hotel.

'Mrs Marklew was certain that he was single,' she said.

'I suspect that that's what she wanted to believe.'

'He deceived her cruelly.'

'In two ways,' said Colbeck, sadly. 'He not only enjoyed her favours by posing as a bachelor. Chabal seems to have entered into the liaison for the prime purpose of getting her to persuade her husband to invest in the railway. The French government provided much of the capital required, but private investors were desperately needed. Given the volatile political situation in France, very few people from this country were prepared to risk their money.'

'How callous of him!'

'He'd probably have seen it as a piece of clever engineering.'

Colbeck finished by telling her about the savage beating sustained by Victor Leeming when posing as a navvy. The information made her sit up in alarm.

'Do be careful, Robert!' she exclaimed.

'I always am.'

'I feel so sorry for Sergeant Leeming.'

'His time as a navvy was not wasted, Madeleine. He unearthed a lot of useful intelligence. It's a pity that it had to end this way.'

'I hope that you are not thinking of taking his place.'

'If only I could,' said Colbeck, wryly, 'but it's impossible. With a face like mine, I could never pass as a navvy. Victor could. He looked the part – though he could never have lived that sort of life.'

'Was the work too hard?'

'I think it was the sleeping arrangements that upset him.'

'His wife must have been shocked by what happened.'

'That's why I went into the house first,' said Colbeck. 'I felt that it would be considerate to prepare Estelle beforehand. In fact, she took it very well. She went straight to the cab and helped Victor out. She's been a policeman's wife for years now. It's toughened her.'

'Will the sergeant be replaced?' asked Madeleine

'Not from the Detective Department.'

'Who else would you take to France?'

'Someone who will fit more easily into the scene than Victor,' he told her. 'The last I heard of him, he was working as a dock labourer so I fancy that a trip to France might appeal to him.'

'Who is he, Robert?'

'The genuine article.'

Nature seemed to have destined Aubrey Filton to be the bearer of bad news. He had a face that could transform itself instantly into a mask of horror and a voice that rose by two octaves when he was really disturbed. His arms semaphored wildly.

'It's happened again, Mr Brassey!' he cried.

'Calm down, Aubrey.'

'We must have lost thousands of bricks.'

'How?'

'Somebody carried them to one of the ventilation shafts and dropped them down into the tunnel,' said Filton. 'The bricks were smashed beyond repair and the line has been blocked.'

'When did this happen?' asked Thomas Brassey.

'In the night, sir. They chose a shaft that was furthest away from the camp so that nobody heard the noise. When they'd unloaded the wagon that carried the bricks, they smashed it to pieces. There's no sign of the horse that pulled it.'

Brassey did his best to remain calm, but exasperation showed in his eyes. He was in his office with Filton. On its walls were the maps and charts drawn as a result of various surveys. Had work proceeded at the stipulated pace, they would have been ahead of schedule and Brassey could have marked their progress on one of the charts. Instead, they were hamstrung by the sequence of interruptions. The latest of them was particularly irksome.

'We needed those bricks for today,' said Brassey.

'I've sent word to the brickyard to increase production.'

'It's security that we need to increase, Aubrey. How was anybody able to steal so many bricks without being seen?'

'I wish I knew, sir,' answered Filton, trembling all over. 'How were they able to light that fire, or damage the track in the tunnel, or steal that gunpowder or blow up the wagons? We're dealing with phantoms here, Mr Brassey.'

'No,' affirmed the other. 'Inspector Colbeck correctly identified our enemy. We're dealing with navvies. Nobody else would have had the strength to drop all those bricks down a ventilation shaft. It would take me all night to do such a thing.'

'It would take me a week.'

'What they probably did was to unload a fair number by hand then undo the harness on the horse so that they could tip the whole cart over.'

'I suppose that the horrible truth is that we'll never know.'

'Not until the inspector returns, anyway.'

'Do you really think that he can catch these men?' said Filton, sceptically. 'He hasn't managed to do so thus far and we both saw what happened to Sergeant Leeming.'

'That incident will only make Inspector Colbeck redouble his efforts. Introducing a man into the Irish camp did have advantages. He was able to warn us about that planned attack on the French.'

'What if there's another?'

'That's very unlikely,' said Brassey. 'I think we scared the

Irish by telling them that they'd lose their jobs. Work is scarce back in England. They all know that.'

'It didn't stop some of them from stealing those bricks last night and there'll be more outrages to come. I feel it in my bones.'

'Don't be so pessimistic, Aubrey.'

'There's a curse on this railway.'

'Balderdash!'

'There is, Mr Brassey. I begin to think that it's doomed.'

'Then you must change that attitude immediately,' scolded the other. 'We must show no hint of weakness. The villains are bound to slip up sooner or later. We need another spy in their camp.'

'We already have one, sir.'

'Do we?'

'Of course,' said Filton. 'Father Slattery. He knows everything that goes on in the Irish community. It's his duty to assist us.'

'His main duty is a pastoral one and nothing must interfere with that. If we asked Father Slattery to act as an informer, he'd lose all credibility. What use would he be then? Besides,' he continued, 'he obviously has no idea who the miscreants are or he'd tackle them himself. A priest would never condone what's been going on.'

'So what do we do?'

'Wait until the inspector gets back with this new man.'

'New man?'

'Yes, Aubrey. I'm assured that he will be ideal for the job.'

'Ah,' said Brendan Mulryne, swallowing his brandy in a gulp as if it was his last drink on earth, 'this is the life, Inspector. And to think I might be heaving cargo at the docks all day long.'

'You were working in the Devil's Acre last time we met.'

'I had to leave The Black Dog.'

'Why?' asked Colbeck.

'Because I had a disagreement with the landlord. He had the gall to hit me when I wasn't looking and I take violence from no man. Apart from anything else, he did it at the most inconvenient time.'

'What do you mean?'

'I was teaching his darling wife a few tricks in bed.'

Brendan Mulryne roared with laughter. He was an affable giant with a massive frame and a face that seemed to have been hewn out of solid teak by a blind man with a blunt axe. Though he was roughly the same age as Colbeck, he looked years older. There was an irrepressible twinkle in his eye and he had a ready grin that revealed a number of missing teeth. Mulryne had once been a constable in the Metropolitan Police Force but his over-enthusiasm during arrests led to his expulsion. Having caught a criminal, he had somehow seen it as a duty to pound him into unconsciousness before hauling him off to the police station. He had always been grateful to Colbeck for trying to save him from being discharged.

Since his dismissal, Mulryne had drifted into a succession of jobs, some of them firmly on the wrong side of the law but none that offended the Irishman's strange code of ethics. He would only steal from a thief or commit other crimes against known villains. It was Mulryne's way of restoring what he called the balance of society. In his heart, he was still a kind of policeman and that was why the present situation had so much appeal for him.

Having crossed the Channel the previous evening, they had spent the night in Le Havre before taking the train to Mantes.

Mulryne was a much livelier companion than Victor Leeming. It was his first visit to France and he was thrilled by everything he saw. When the train rattled over the Barentin Viaduct, he gazed down with awe.

'Be-Jesus!' he exclaimed. 'Will you look at that? It's almost as if we was flying, Inspector.'

'Thomas Brassey built the viaduct.'

'Then I'll be happy to shake his hand.'

'Not too hard,' advised Colbeck. 'You've got the biggest hands I've ever seen on a human being. You can crack walnuts with a gentle squeeze. Go easy on Mr Brassey.'

'I will.' His face crumpled with sympathy. 'But I'm sorry to hear about Sergeant Leeming.'

'Victor was unlucky.'

'He taught me a lot when we were both in uniform.'

'You're a detective now, Brendan, in the Plain Clothes Division.'

'Well,' said Mulryne, emitting a peal of laughter, 'clothes don't come any plainer than these.'

He was wearing the same moleskin trousers, canvas shirt and tattered coat that had served him in the docks, and his hobnail boots were also suitable for work on the railway. A shapeless hat completed the outfit but he had removed it when they boarded the train. Mulryne was tickled by the fact that he was dressed like a typical navvy while travelling in a first class carriage.

'I'll be carrying on the family tradition,' he said, proudly.

'Will you?'

'Yes, sir. My father was a navvy in the old days when the word had its true meaning. Father – God bless him – was a navigator who helped to cut canals. I was born in a navvies' camp somewhere along the line.'

'I never knew that, Brendan.'

'I'm a man with hidden secrets.'

'You'll certainly have to hide a few when we get to Mantes.'

'I'll soon charm my way in.'

'That's what Victor thought but they found him out.'

'It takes an Irishman to beguile the Irish, so it does.'

'It's the reason I chose you. Most of them are decent, honest, hard-working men and they couldn't have a better priest than Father Slattery.' He saw Mulryne's glum expression. 'What's wrong?'

'I didn't know I'd have a priest to worry about.'

'Father Slattery is a dedicated man.'

'Yes – dedicated to stopping the rest of us having a bit of fun. It's the reason I couldn't stay in Ireland. It's so priest-ridden. You only had to fart and they'd make you say a novena and three Hail Mary's. The place for a man of the cloth,' he declared, soulfully, 'is in a church and not on a railway.'

'He does valuable work,' said Colbeck. 'More to the point, he knows everyone. That's why you ought to meet him, Brendan. He can introduce you to the others. Father Slattery is a way in.'

'And will I be seeing you at the service on Sunday, Liam Kilfoyle?'

'Yes, Father.'

'You said that last week and the week before.'

'It slipped my mind,' said Kilfoyle, evasively.

'St Peter has been known to let certain things slip *his* mind as well,' cautioned the priest. 'How will you feel when you reach the Pearly Gates to find that he's forgotten all your good deeds?'

'I'll remind him of them.'

'The best way to do that is to attend Mass.'

'I worship in my own way, Father Slattery.'

'That's wonderful! When you come on Sunday, you can give us all a demonstration of how you do it. We can always learn new ways to pray, Liam.' He beamed at Kilfoyle. 'I'll see you there.'

'I hope so.'

'Are you going to let the Lord down yet again?'

Kilfoyle swallowed hard. 'I'll try not to, Father.'

'Spoken like a true Catholic!'

The old man chuckled and went off to speak to a group of men nearby. It was the end of the day's shift and Slattery was trying to increase the size of the congregation in his makeshift, outdoor church. Kilfoyle was glad to see him go. A wayward Christian, he always felt guilty when he talked to the priest. Memories of sinful nights between the thighs of another man's wife somehow thrust themselves into his mind. It was almost as if Father Slattery knew about his moments of nocturnal lechery with Bridget.

'What did that old bastard want?' said Pierce Shannon, coming over to him. 'Did he want you to train for the priesthood?'

'Nothing like that.'

'Be careful, Liam. You'd have to be celibate.'

'Then the job'd not suit me. I've got too much fire in my loins for the church. Father Slattery will have to look elsewhere.'

'Well, it had better not be in my direction.'

'Why not, Pierce? You might end up as a cardinal.'

'If I'm a cardinal, you're the Angel bleeding Gabriel.'

They traded a laugh. Shannon stepped in closer.

'By the way,' he said, casually, 'it's a shame about that

friend of yours, Victor Leeming. He could have been useful to us.'

'Not any more.'

'I suppose the truth is that he just didn't fit in here. Pity – he was a good worker.'

'Victor won't be doing any work for a while.'

'I liked the man. He had a good punch.'

'He was certainly a match for you, Pierce.'

'Only because he caught me unawares that one time,' said Shannon, thrusting out his chest. 'In a proper fight, I reckon that I could kick the daylights out of him.'

'Don't try to do that to Brendan,' warned Kilfoyle.

'Who?'

'Brendan Mulryne. He was helping us to shovel spoil into the wagons today. He's got muscles bigger than bloody pumpkins. He made me feel puny beside him. Brendan could fill two wagons in the time it took me to fill one.'

'What sort of man is he?'

'The best kind – joking all day long.'

'I prefer a man who keeps his friggin gob shut while he works.'

'Then stay clear of Brendan. He can't keep quiet. We got on well together. He feels the same about priests as me. He'd rather roast in Hell than be forced to listen to a sermon.'

'Where's he from?'

'Dublin.'

'And he's a real navvy?'

'With hands like that, he couldn't be anything else.' Kilfoyle saw the giant figure ambling towards him. 'You can meet him for yourself, Pierce. Here he comes.'

Shannon turned a critical eye on Brendan Mulryne, who was smiling amiably at everyone he passed and making cheerful comments as he did so. When he spotted Kilfoyle, he strolled across to him. Mulryne was introduced to Shannon. As they shook hands, the latter felt the power in the other's grip.

'I'm looking for somewhere to sleep tonight,' said Mulryne. 'The ganger told me there'd be room at Pat O'Rourke's. Do you know him?'

'Yes,' replied Kilfoyle, pointing. 'He owns that stone house at the end of the row. Pat will look after you. Built the house himself.'

'How much does he charge?'

'Almost nothing.'

'That's good because I haven't got two bleeding pennies to rub together.' He became conspiratorial. 'Hey, I don't suppose that either of you know how I can pick up a little extra money, do you?'

'In what way?' asked Shannon.

'Any way at all, friend.'

'Such as?'

'On my last job, I made a tidy sum at cockfighting.'

'Nobody will want to fight a cock as big as yours,' said Kilfoyle with a giggle. 'And, if you're talking about the kind with feathers and sharp claws, then Mr Brassey won't allow that kind of thing on any of his sites.'

'What the eye doesn't see, the heart doesn't grieve.'

'I couldn't have put it better,' said Shannon, warming to him at once. 'How else have you made money in the past, Brendan?'

'All sorts of ways. Best of all was prize-fighting.'

'Really?'

'Yes, I'd take on all-comers with one hand strapped behind my back. They not only paid for the chance to take a swing at me,' said Mulryne, 'I got my share of the bets that were laid as well.'

'Very crafty.'

'I've got a devil of a thirst, Pierce. That takes money.'

'Not here,' said Kilfoyle. 'The brandy's dirt cheap.'

'I know. I tried some on the way here. Anyway,' Mulryne went on, 'I'd best find O'Rourke so that I've got somewhere to lay my head tonight. Then it's off to the nearest inn with me.'

'We'll take you there,' volunteered Shannon.

'Thank you, friend. I might hold you to that.' He caught sight of Father Slattery among the crowd and recoiled. 'Is that the bleeding priest they told me about?'

'That's him, large as life.'

'Then keep him away from me.'

'Father Slattery is harmless enough,' said Kilfoyle.

'Not to me, Liam. There's a time and place for priests and this is not it. When I've worked my balls off all day,' asserted Mulryne, 'the last thing I want is a dose of religion. A good drink and a warm woman is all I need and Father Slattery looks as if he's never tasted either.'

Maria Brassey was an excellent hostess. She gave the guests a cordial welcome and served a delicious meal. When he spoke French by demand, Robert Colbeck discovered that she had an excellent grasp of the language. She was delightful company and presided over the table with her husband. After dinner, however, she knew exactly when to withdraw so that the men could talk in private.

'Have you had any success while I was away?' said Colbeck.

'A little,' replied Brassey. 'The nightwatchmen caught two men pilfering but they had nothing to do with all the damage we've suffered. I paid them what I owed and ordered them off the site.'

'That, of course, is another avenue we might explore.'

'What do you mean, Inspector?'

'Discontented former employees. Men with a grudge.'

'You'll not find many of those,' said Aubrey Filton, the other guest. 'Mr Brassey is renowned for his fairness. If the men step out of line, they know they'll be sacked. They accept that.'

'Most of them, perhaps,' said Colbeck. 'But I can see how it would rankle if someone was dismissed from a job that would guarantee two years' work for them.'

'We keep a record of every man we employ.'

'Then I'd like to take a close look at it, Mr Filton.'

The three men were comfortably ensconced in chairs in the living room of the country house that Brassey had rented. It was close enough to the site for him to get there with ease, yet far enough away to be out of reach of the incessant noise that was created. Having grown up on a farm, the contractor always preferred a house that was surrounded by green fields. It made him feel as if he were back in his native Cheshire. He sipped his glass of port.

'How is Sergeant Leeming?' he said.

'Very glad to be back home,' returned Colbeck. 'Victor took a beating but no permanent damage seems to have been done. He simply needs plenty of time to recover.'

'That sort of thing would put me off police work forever,' said Filton. 'It's far too dangerous.'

'Victor is not so easily deterred.'

'And what about this new fellow?'

'Oh,' said Colbeck with a smile, 'you can rely on him. If you set off an explosion under Brendan Mulryne, you'd not scare him away. He has nerves of steel.'

'Then why didn't you bring him here in the first place?' said Brassey. 'Was he assigned to another case?'

'Yes, sir.'

'He doesn't look like a detective at all.'

'He isn't one,' said Colbeck.

'I see. He's an ordinary constable.'

'There's nothing ordinary about Brendan, I promise you. He was trained as a policeman and I had the good fortune to work with him when I was in uniform. When you have to break up a tavern brawl, there's no better man to have beside you than him.'

'I can imagine.'

Colbeck did not reveal that the man he had entrusted with such an important task was, in fact, a dock labourer of dubious reputation who led the kind of chaotic existence that two conventional middle class gentlemen could not begin to understand. The less they knew about Brendan Mulryne, the better. At all events, Colbeck resolved, his name must not get back to Edward Tallis. If the superintendent became aware of the Irishman's presence on site, Colbeck would not have to write a letter of resignation. He would probably be ejected from Scotland Yard with Tallis's condemnation ringing in his ears.

'What interests me is the next stretch of line,' said Colbeck, draining his glass. 'The one that runs from Caen to Cherbourg.'

Brassey held up a palm. 'Give us a chance, Inspector,' he said, jocularly. 'We haven't finished this one yet.'

'And may never do so,' said Filton, gloomily.

'Of course we will, Aubrey.'

'I wonder, sir.'

'Will any French companies put in a tender for the other line?' asked Colbeck. 'Are any contractors here big enough to do so?'

'Yes,' replied Brassey. 'The French were slow starters when it came to railways but they are catching up quickly, and contractors have seen the opportunities that are there. When the time comes, I'm sure that we'll have a number of competitors.'

'What about labour? Are there enough navvies in France?'

'No, Inspector Colbeck, not really. Comparatively few railways have been built here so far. As a result, there's no pool of experienced men on which to draw. We found that out when we built the Paris to Rouen railway some years ago.'

'Yes, I believe that you imported 5,000 from England.'

'It was not nearly enough,' said Brassey. 'I had to cast the net much wider in order to double that number. They were mainly French but they also included Germans, Belgians, Italians, Dutchmen and Spaniards. Do you remember it, Aubrey?'

'Very well,' said Filton. 'You could hear eleven different languages in all. It was quite bewildering at times.'

'As for the line from Caen to Cherbourg, that remains in the future. We've not really had time to think about it.'

'Somebody else might have done so,' said Colbeck.

'I'm sure that other contractors are planning surveys already.'

'Only because they want to build the line.'

'It could be a very profitable venture.'

'Assuming that we do not have another revolution,' said Filton with a tentative laugh. 'You never know with these people.'

'Oh, I think that Louis Napoleon is here to stay.'

'For a time, Mr Brassey.'

'He's a man of great ambition, Aubrey.'

'That's the impression I've had of him,' said Colbeck.

'From all that I've read about Louis Napoleon, he seems to be a man of decisive action. He knows precisely what he wants and how best to achieve it. Well, you've met him, Mr Brassey,' he continued. 'Is that an unfair estimate of him?'

'Not at all. He's determined and single-minded.'

'Just like his namesake.'

'He patterns himself on Bonaparte.'

'That could worry some people. When I said a moment ago that somebody else might have thought about the extension to Cherbourg, I was not referring to your rival contractors. They simply want to build the railway,' said Colbeck. 'What about those who want to stop it from ever being built?'

'Why should anyone want to stop it, Inspector Colbeck?'

'We'll have to ask them when they're finally caught.'

Brendan Mulryne might have been working on the railway for a month rather than simply a day. He related so easily to the people around him that he gained an immediate popularity. Part of a crowd of navvies who descended on one of the inns in a nearby village, he proved to his new friends that he could drink hard, talk their language and tell hilarious anecdotes about some of the escapades in which he had been involved. Since there were others there who hailed from Dublin, he was also able to indulge in some maudlin reminiscences of the city. The night wore on.

To earn some easy money, he issued a challenge. He said that he would pay a franc to anyone who could make him double up with a single punch to his stomach. Those who failed would pay Mulryne the same amount. Liam Kilfoyle was the first to try. Slapping a franc down on the bar counter, he took off his coat and bunched his right hand. Everyone watched to cheer him on and to see how he fared. Mulryne grinned broadly and tightened his stomach muscles. When he delivered his punch, Kilfoyle felt as if he had just hit solid rock. His knuckles were sore for the rest of the night.

Several people tried to wipe the grin from Mulryne's face but none could even make him gasp for breath. In no time at all, he had earned the equivalent of a week's wage and he showed his benevolence by treating everyone to a drink. By the time they rolled out of the inn, Mulryne was more popular than ever. He led the others in a discordant rendition of some Irish ballads. When they neared the camp, the men dispersed to their respective dwellings. Mulryne was left alone with Kilfoyle and Pierce Shannon.

'When you won all that money,' said Shannon, 'why did you throw it all away on a round of drinks?'

Mulryne shrugged. 'I was among friends.'

'I'd have held on to it myself.'

'Then you don't have my outlook on life, Pierce.'

'And what's that?'

'Easy come, easy go.'

'Does it work the same for women?' asked Kilfoyle.

'Yes,' said Mulryne, chortling happily. 'Take 'em and leave 'em, that's what I believe, Liam. Love a woman hard but always remember the queue of other lucky ladies that are waiting for you with their tongues hanging out.'

'What about French women?'

'What about them?'

'Do you like them?'

'I like anything pretty that wears a skirt.'

'They can't compare with an Irish colleen.'

'Women are women to me.'

They walked on until they came to the two parallel tracks that had already been laid. Empty wagons stood ready to be filled on the following day. Kilfoyle saw a chance to win a wager.

'How strong are you, Brendan?' he said.

'Why – do you want to take another swing at me?'

'No, I was wondering if you could lift that.' He pointed to one of the wagons. 'Only a few inches off the rails. Could you?'

'Depends on what you're offering,' said Mulryne.

'A day's wages.'

'They'll be mine to keep, if I win. There'll be no buying you a free drink this time, Liam.'

'If you can shift that wagon, you'll have earned the money.'

'I'll match the bet,' said Shannon, 'if you take it on.'

Mulryne removed his coat. 'I never refuse a challenge.'

It was the last wagon in the line. He walked around it to size it up then uncoupled it from its neighbour. Taking a firm grip of it at the other end, he gritted his teeth and pretended to put all his energy into a lift. The wagon did not budge. Kilfoyle rubbed his hands with glee.

'We've got him this time, Pierce,' he said.

'I just need a moment to get my strength up.' Mulryne took a few deep breaths then tried again in vain. 'This bleeding thing is heavier than I thought. What's inside it – a ton of lead?'

'Do you give up, Brendan?'

'Not me – I'll have one last go.'

'You owe each of us a day's wages.'

'I'll make it two days, if you like,' said Mulryne.

'Done! What about you, Pierce?'

Shannon was more wary. 'My bet stands at one day.'

'Then get ready to hand it over,' said Mulryne, spreading arms further apart as he gripped the wagon once more. 'Here we go.'

Bracing himself with his legs, he heaved with all his might and lifted the end of the wagon at least six inches from the rail. Then he dropped it down again with a resounding clang.

Kilfoyle was amazed. 'You did it!'

'I usually only use one hand,' boasted Mulryne.

'You could have lifted it off the rails altogether.'

'Easily.'

'Here's my money,' said Shannon, paying up immediately. 'I'll have more sense than to bet against you next time.'

'Don't tell the others, Pierce.' Mulryne slapped the wagon. 'I think that this little trick might bring in even more profit. Let's have what you owe me, Liam.'

'Right,' said Kilfoyle, handing over the coins.

'And don't be stupid enough to challenge me again.'

'I won't, Brendan.'

'To tell you the truth,' admitted Mulryne, 'I never thought I could do it. But the chance of winning the bet put new strength into my arms. I'm like an old whore,' he added with a loud guffaw. 'I'll do absolutely anything for money.'

CHAPTER NINE

Robert Colbeck was interested in every aspect of the railways. While he enjoyed travelling on them, he was also very curious about those who brought them into being with the brilliance of their invention or the sweat of their brow. Bridges, aqueducts, tunnels, cuttings, and drainage systems did not burst spontaneously into life. Each and every one had to be designed and built to specification. Colossal earthworks had to be constructed. Timber had to be felled and cut to size. Marshes had to be drained. Stone had to be quarried. Untold millions of bricks had to be made on site before being used to line tunnels, create ventilation shafts, solidify bridges and aqueducts, or stabilise steep embankments. A railway was a declaration of war against a contour map of the area where it was being built. Continuous and unremitting attack was needed.

When he inspected the site with Aubrey Filton that morning, Colbeck was impressed by the amount of work that had been done since the day he had first arrived there with Victor Leeming. Nobody was slacking. Everywhere he looked, men were putting their hearts and souls into their job. Brendan Mulryne, he noticed, was now helping to dig a new cutting, shovelling methodically and building up a vast mound of earth to be taken away to the wagons. Colbeck could hear his distinctive voice above the din.

'You're making headway, Mr Filton,' he observed.

'Not enough of it, Inspector.'

'Where did you expect to be at this stage?'

'At least a quarter of a mile farther on,' said the engineer. 'The French government are slave-drivers. We have targets to meet at the end of every month.'

'Everything seems to be going well now. And we've not had any incidents for the last couple of days.'

'It's the calm before the storm.'

'I don't think so,' said Colbeck. 'I believe it may have something to do with the fact that Mr Brassey took my advice about security. In addition to nightwatchmen, he now has a handful of guard dogs.'

'Yes, they're vicious-looking brutes.'

'That's the intention.'

'I'm glad that they're kept on a leash.'

'They won't be if there's any trouble, Mr Filton. The dogs will be released. The simple fact that you've got them will make any villains think twice before committing a crime. They might be able to outrun a nightwatchman,' said Colbeck, 'but not if he has four legs.'

They strolled on until they reached the forward end of the strenuous activity. Ground rose steadily ahead of them and would need to be levelled before the track could be laid. There would be more digging for Mulryne and the others. Colbeck thought about all the maps and charts he had seen in Brassey's office.

'How good an engineer was Gaston Chabal?' he asked.

'He was outstanding.'

'I'm sure that you are as well, Mr Filton, or you'd not

be employed on such a major project. Was Chabal taken on because he was French or because he had remarkable skills?'

'For both reasons, Inspector.'

'But you can manage without him?'

'We have to,' said Filton. 'Fortunately, we have all the drawings and calculations he did for us, but it's not the same as having the man himself here. Gaston was a delightful fellow.'

'Everyone seems agreed on that.'

'Except his killer.'

'Yes,' said Colbeck, thoughtfully, 'I've been trying to put myself in his position – the killer, that is, not Chabal. Why did he choose the Frenchman as his target? If you wanted to halt the construction of this railway, whom would you murder?'

Filton was offended. 'I have no homicidal urges, I assure you.'

'The obvious person would be Mr Brassey.'

'Yes, that would be a calamity.'

'Who would come next?'

'One of his partners, I suppose.'

'And then it would be the leading engineer, Gaston Chabal.'

'Actually,' said Filton with a rare flash of pride, 'I was slightly senior to Gaston. I've been with Mr Brassey much longer and he always rewards loyalty.'

'In other words, Chabal's death was not a fatal blow to the building of this railway.'

'No, Inspector. It was a bitter blow but not a fatal one.'

'Then he must have been killed for symbolic reasons.'

'Symbolic?'

'He was French,' said Colbeck. 'That was the conclusive factor. A Frenchman thrown from the Sankey Viaduct – I believe that act has a weird symbolism to it.'

'What exactly is it?'

'I've yet to establish that, Mr Filton.'

'Do you still think his killer was an Englishman?'

'I'm as certain as I can be.'

'I wish I had your confidence.'

'Everything points that way, sir.'

'Not to my eyes. What possible connection is there between a crime near the Sankey Viaduct and the ones that have afflicted us here? The two railways involved have nothing whatsoever to do with each other.'

'Yes, they do.'

'What?'

'Mr Alexander Marklew, for a start. He's a director of the London and North-West Railway and a major investor in this one. And there are lots of other hidden links between the two, I feel, if only we could dig them out.'

'All that troubles me is what happens on this project, Inspector. We've had setback after setback. Unless they are checked, they could in time bring us to a dead halt.'

'That's his intention.'

'Who?'

'The man I'm after,' explained Colbeck. 'The one responsible for all the crimes that have occurred. He's very elusive. All I know about him so far is that he's conceived a hatred of this particular railway and a passion for symbols. Oh, yes,' he added. 'One more thing.'

'What's that?'

'The fellow is utterly ruthless.'

Sir Marcus Hetherington left the shareholders' meeting and called a cab with a snap of his fingers. He was a tall, slim, dignified man in his seventies with white hair curling from under his top hat and a red rose in the lapel of his frock coat.

His short, white moustache was neatly trimmed. After telling the cab driver to take him to the Pall Mall, he clambered into the vehicle and settled back. Alone at last, he was able to let his mask of imperturbability drop. His face was contorted with fury and he released a few silent expletives.

It had been a disappointing meeting. Unlike many landowners, he had not seen the advent of railways as a gross intrusion of his privacy or a precursor of the destruction of the England he knew and loved. He was keenly aware of their practical value. Since he was paid a great deal of money by way of compensation, he was happy for a line to be built across his estates. The proximity of the railway station enabled him to reach London much more quickly from Essex than by travelling in a coach. That was a bonus.

Sir Marcus had always considered himself a forward-thinking man. Railways were set to revolutionise the whole country and he wanted to be part of that revolution. As a result, he took some of the capital he had received in compensation from one railway company and invested it in a couple of others. When the market was buoyant, dividends were high and he congratulated himself on his acumen. Once the bubble had burst so spectacularly, however, he had been one of the many victims. At the meeting he had just left, the chairman had informed the assembled throng that no dividends at all would be payable to shareholders for the foreseeable future. It was infuriating.

When he reached the Reform Club, the first thing he did was to order a stiff whisky. Reclining in his high-backed leather chair, he sipped it gratefully and bestowed a patrician smile on all who passed. In the sedate surroundings of the club, he could not let his seething rage show. He had to simmer inwardly. One of the uniformed stewards came across to him and inclined his head with deference.

'There's a gentleman asking for you, Sir Marcus,' he said.

'Did he give a name?'

'He sent his card.'

The steward handed it over and the old man glanced at it.

'Send him in, Jellings,' he said, crisply, 'and bring him a glass of whisky. Put it on my account, there's a good chap.'

Minutes later, Sir Marcus was sitting beside Luke Rogan, a thickset man in his forties with long, wavy black hair tinged with grey and a flat, but not unpleasant, face. Though well-dressed, Rogan looked decidedly out of place in a palatial club that was a home for Whig politicians and their like. There was a flashy quality about the newcomer that made him look rather incongruous beside such a distinguished figure as Sir Marcus Hetherington. When set against the educated drawl of the grandee, his voice sounded rough and plebeian.

'You've more work for me, Sir Marcus?' he inquired.

'I think so, Rogan.'

'Tell me what it is. I've never let you down yet.'

'I wouldn't employ you if you had,' said Sir Marcus, 'and you would certainly not be sitting here now. Tell me, do you read the newspapers on a regular basis?'

'Of course,' replied the other with a complacent grin. 'In my line of business, I have to, Sir Marcus. Newspapers is how I gets most of my work. Well, it's how you and me got together, ain't it? You saw my advertisement and got in touch.'

'What have you noticed in the course of your reading?'

'That the police still have no idea how a certain person was thrown out of a moving railway carriage – and they never will.'

'Their failure is gratifying,' said Sir Marcus, 'I grant you that. But we must never underestimate this fellow, Colbeck. He seems to have an uncanny knack of picking up a trail where none exists.'

'Not this time. Inspector Colbeck is like the rest of them over at Scotland Yard – he's floundering, Sir Marcus.'

'I begin to wonder.'

'What do you mean?'

'I've just come from a shareholders' meeting of a railway company,' replied the other. 'The one thing of interest that the chairman told me was that Colbeck helped to prevent a serious crime from taking place on one of their trains earlier this year. The chairman could not speak too highly of him.'

'Colbeck had some luck, that's all.'

'His success can't be dismissed as lightly as that, Rogan. When I pointed out that the Railway Detective was faltering badly with his latest case, the chairman said that he'd heard a rumour to the effect that the inspector had gone to France.'

Rogan was jolted. 'To France?'

'It was not the kind of information I wanted to hear.'

'Nor me, Sir Marcus.'

'What I want to read about is the damage done to a particular railway line on the other side of the Channel, yet the newspapers have been uniformly silent on the subject.'

'You can't expect them to carry foreign items.'

'That's exactly what I do expect, man. Any periodical worthy of the name should have its own foreign correspondents. *The Times* will always report matters of interest from abroad.'

'This would hardly catch their attention, Sir Marcus.'

'Yes, it would. An Englishman is involved – Thomas Brassey.'

'I'm sure that everything is going to plan.'

'Then why is there no whisper of it in the press? Why is there no report from France about the damage caused to a railway in which they have invested both money and national pride?'

'I can't tell you,' admitted Rogan.

'Then find out.'

'Eh?'

'Go to France, man. Discover the truth.'

'But I'm handling other cases at the moment, Sir Marcus. I can't just drop them to go sailing off across the Channel. Anyway, I've no reason to suspect that the men I engaged will let me down.'

'How much did you pay them?'

'Half the money in advance,' said Rogan, 'just like you told me, the rest to be handed over when the job was done.'

'And *has* the job been done?' pressed Sir Marcus.

'Not yet.'

'Not at all, I suspect. What was to stop these rogues from pocketing the money you gave them and taking to their heels? If that's the case, Rogan – and I hope, for your sake, that it's not – then I am out of pocket as a consequence of your bad judgement of character.'

'Sir Marcus—'

'Don't interrupt me,' snapped the other, subduing him with a frosty glare. 'There's unfinished business here, sir. If you accept a commission, you should see it through as a matter of honour. What you did for me in this country, I applaud. You obeyed your orders to the letter and were handsomely rewarded. But I begin to fear that you have let me down woefully in France itself.'

'That's not true, Sir Marcus.'

'Prove it.'

'I will, if you'll bear with me for a while.'

'My patience is exhausted.' Taking something from his pocket, he slapped it down on the little table that stood between them. 'Take that and study it carefully.'

'What is it?'

'A list of sailings to France. Choose a boat and be on it today.'

'Today?' spluttered Rogan. 'That's impossible.'

'Not if you put your mind to it, man. Now stop arguing with me and be on your way. And whatever else you do,' he added, spitting the words out like so many bullets, 'don't you dare return from that confounded country with bad news for me. Is that understood?'

Rogan gulped down his whisky then grabbed the piece of paper from the table. After pulling out his watch to check the time, he got to his feet and wiped his mouth with the back of his hand.

'Yes, Sir Marcus,' he said, obsequiously. 'It's understood.'

'I don't think we've met before, have we?' said Father Slattery, offering his hand. 'Welcome to France, my friend.'

'The name is Mulryne,' said the other, extending his vast palm for the handshake. 'Brendan Mulryne.'

'I thought it might be. I've heard the stories.'

'Don't believe a word of them, Father. You know what terrible liars the Irish are. I'm just an ordinary lad who likes to keep his head down and get on with his work.'

'Is that why you weren't at church on Sunday?'

Mulryne feigned ignorance. 'I didn't know there *was* a church.'

'Then it's blind you must be, Brendan Mulryne, for everyone in the camp knows where we hold our services. We've no building as such and the altar is an old table with a piece of white cloth over it, but we can still worship the Almighty with the respect He deserves.'

'I'm glad to hear it.'

'I would have thought that sheer curiosity would have brought you along. You must have heard us singing the hymns.'

'No,' said Mulryne. 'I was too far away. The truth is, Father, that I was attending a service in the village church.'

They both knew that it was a lie but Slattery did not challenge him. He had stopped to speak to Mulryne during a break when the navvy was wolfing down some bread and cheese and glistening with sweat. He was not pleased to be cornered by the priest.

'You're a Dublin man, I hear,' said Slattery.

'So I am.'

'And your father was a navvy before you.'

'Are you planning to write my life story?' asked Mulryne. 'You know more about me than I do myself.'

'Would you call yourself a Christian?'

'That I would.'

'And are you a loyal Catholic?'

'Since the day I was born, Father.'

'Then we'll look forward to the time when you join us for worship on a Sunday. They tell me that you've a good voice, Brendan.'

'I can carry a tune,' said Mulryne through a mouthful of bread and cheese. 'I've always been musical.'

'Then maybe you can favour us with a solo some time.'

'Oh, I don't think that the songs I know would be altogether suitable for a church service, Father Slattery. They're Irish ditties to amuse my friends. Nothing more.'

'We'll see, we'll see.'

Slattery gave him a valedictory pat on the arm before moving off. Liam Kilfoyle scrambled down the embankment to speak to Mulryne. He looked after the priest.

'What did he want, Brendan?'

'The chance to preach at me next Sunday.'

'Did you tell him you're not a church-going man?'

'But I am, Liam,' said Mulryne, taking another bite of his lunch. 'I'm a devout churchgoer. As soon as I see a church, I go – as fast as I bleeding can.' They laughed. 'It's not God I have the argument with, you see. I believe in Him and try to live my life by His rules. No, it's that army of creeping priests who get between us. They're in the way. I prefer to talk to God directly. Man to man, as you might say. What about you?'

'I'm too afraid of what God would say to me, Brendan.'

'Confess your sins and cleanse your soul.'

Kilfoyle was uneasy. 'I'll think about it,' he said. 'One day.'

'Make it one day soon.'

'You're starting to sound like a bastard priest now!'

'Sorry, Liam,' said Mulryne, jovially. 'What can I do for you?'

'It's the other way round. I may be able to do you a turn.'

'How?'

'Are you still looking to earn some extra money?'

'I'm desperate.'

'And you don't mind what you have to do to get it?'

'I draw the line at nothing,' Mulryne told him. 'As long as I get paid, I'll do whatever I'm asked. And there's another thing you ought to know about me.'

'What's that?'

'When it's needed, I can keep my big mouth shut.'

'Good,' said Kilfoyle. 'I'll pass the word on.'

* * *

The letter came as a complete surprise. Written in an elegant hand, it was addressed to Colbeck and had been sent to Thomas Brassey's office. It was passed on to the inspector as a matter of urgency. He did not at first recognise the name of Hortense Rivet. As soon as he read the letter, however, he realised that he had met the woman when he called at Gaston Chabal's house in Paris. Madame Rivet had been the engineer's mother-in-law. Since she requested a visit from Colbeck, he did not hesitate. He caught the next available train from Mantes and arrived in Paris with his curiosity whetted. As she was so anxious to see him again, Colbeck hoped that Madame Rivet might have valuable information to pass on to him.

A cab took him to the Marais and he rang the bell once again. On his previous visit to the house, Chabal's wife had opened the door with a glow of anticipatory pleasure on her face. This time, he was admitted by an old, black-clad servant with sorrow etched deeply into her face. She conducted him into the drawing room. Madame Chabal was still prostrate with grief in her bedchamber, but her mother came at once when she heard that Colbeck was there. Hortense Rivet was genuinely touched that he had responded so swiftly to her letter. As she spoke little English, they conversed in French.

'I was not sure that you were still here,' she began.

'I still have many enquiries to make in France, Madame.'

'Do you know the name of the man who killed Gaston?'

'Not yet,' he confessed, 'but we will. I'll not rest until he's caught and punished.'

She looked into his eyes for a full minute as if searching for something. Then she indicated a chair and sat opposite him. Hortense Rivet had impressed him at their first meeting. When he had told Chabal's young wife that her husband had been murdered, she had been quite inconsolable but her mother had shown remarkable self-control, knowing that she had to find the strength to help them both through the harrowing experience. Madame Rivet's beauty had been somehow enhanced by sadness. Wearing mourning dress, she was a slim and shapely woman in her early forties. The resemblance to her daughter was evident. Colbeck could see exactly what the young widow would look like in twenty years' time. It made him wonder yet again how Gaston Chabal could have betrayed such a lovely wife.

'How is your daughter, Madame?' he asked, solicitously.

'Catherine is suffering badly. The doctor has given her a potion to help her sleep. When she is awake, she simply weeps. Since we heard the news, Catherine has hardly eaten.'

'I'm sorry to hear that.'

'I wanted to thank you for the way that you broke the tidings to us, Inspector. It was difficult for you, I know, and I was not able to express my gratitude to you at the time. I do so now.'

'That's very kind of you.'

There was a long pause. She studied his face before speaking.

'You strike me as an honest man, Inspector Colbeck.'

'Thank you.'

'So I will expect an honest answer from you. I would like you to tell me how Gaston was murdered.'

'I've already told you, Madame,' he reminded her. 'He was stabbed to death in a railway carriage.'

'Yes,' she said, 'but you did not tell us where the train was going at the time and what my son-in-law was doing on it in the first place. You spared us details that would only have caused us even more pain. I would like to know some of those details now.'

'The French police were given a full account of the murder.'

'There are reasons why I do not choose to turn to them, Inspector. The main one is that the crime did not occur in France. They only know what they have been told. You, on the other hand,' she went on, 'have been in charge of the investigation from the start. You are aware of every detail. Is that not true?'

'There are still some things we *don't* know,' he warned her.

'Tell me the things that you do.' She saw his reluctance. 'Do not be afraid that you will hurt my feelings, Inspector. I am not as frail as I may look. I have already buried my husband and seen my only son go to an early grave. They both died of smallpox. I have survived all that and found a new life for myself. What I must do now is to help Catherine through this tragedy.'

'I'm not sure that you'd be helping her by disclosing the full details of her husband's death,' said Colbeck, gently. 'They are rather gruesome, Madame.'

'What I am interested in are the circumstances.'

'Circumstances?'

'I think you know what I mean, Inspector.' She got up to close the door then resumed her seat. 'And whatever you tell me, it will not be passed on to Catherine. That would be too cruel.'

'Madame Rivet,' he said, 'we are still in the middle of this investigation and I can only speculate on what we will discover next. As for what you call the circumstances, I fear that you might find them very distressing. Some things are best left unsaid.'

'I disagree, Inspector Colbeck. I do not believe you can tell me anything that would surprise me.' She took a deep breath before going on. 'When he was working on this new railway, my son-in-law rented a room in Mantes.'

'I know. I visited the house.'

'Did it not seem odd to you that he did not live at home and travel to Mantes every day by train? It is not very far. Why did he have to be so close to the railway?'

'He worked long hours.'

'That was one of his excuses. There were several others.'

'I hear a rather cynical note in your voice, Madame.'

'It's one that I take care to hide from Catherine,' she said, grimly. 'You may as well know that I did not wish my daughter to marry Gaston Chabal. He was a handsome man with a good future ahead of him, but I did not feel that I could ever trust him. Catherine, of course, would hear none of my warnings. She was young, innocent and very much in love. For the last two years, she thought that she had been happily married.' She pulled a piece of paper from the sleeve of her dress. 'This is something you may have seen before, Inspector.'

'What is it?'

'One of the letters that were found at the house where Gaston was staying in Mantes. The police returned his effects to us earlier this week. Fortunately,' she said, unfolding the letter, 'I was able to see them first. I've destroyed the others and will make sure that my daughter does not see this one either.'

Colbeck remembered the *billets-doux* he had seen at the lodging. Out of consideration to her, he had taken it upon himself to tear up the letters from Hannah Marklew but it had never crossed his mind that he should also get rid of the anonymous correspondence from the young Parisian woman. He felt a stab of guilt as he realised the anguish he had inadvertently caused and he was grateful that Chabal's wife had not been allowed to read the letters from one of her husband's mistresses. He knew how explicit they had been.

'Did you see any letters, Inspector?'

'Yes.'

'Then you must have read them.'

'I glanced at one or two.'

'Then you appreciate the sort of person who wrote them.'

'I think so.'

'Do you know who Arnaud Poulain is, Inspector?' she asked.

'No, Madame.'

'He is a banker here in Paris, a wealthy and successful man. Gaston convinced him to invest in the railway between Mantes and Caen. My son-in-law was not simply an engineer,' she went on. 'If he could persuade anyone to put money into the project, he earned a large commission. Arnaud Poulain was one of the men he talked into it. As a consequence, others followed Monsieur Poulain's example.'

'Why are you telling me this?' wondered Colbeck, guessing the answer even as he spoke. 'Monsieur Poulain has a daughter.'

'A very beautiful daughter.'

'What's her name?'

'Danielle.'

Colbeck thought of the 'D' at the end of the letters. It seemed as if Chabal had used his guile to ensnare another woman in order to secure some investment for the railway on which he was engaged.

'We may be wrong,' cautioned Madame Rivet. 'I have no proof that Danielle wrote these letters and I will certainly not confront her with them. The girl will have suffered enough as it is. I doubt very much if Gaston mentioned to her that he was married. In a liaison of that kind, a wife must always be invisible.'

'The young lady must have read about his death.'

'The discovery that he was married would have come as a terrible shock to Danielle and, I suspect, to her father. Monsieur Poulain would no doubt have welcomed Gaston into his home. The daughter was used callously as a means of reaching the father. Now, Inspector,' she continued, 'even if Danielle is not the woman who wrote this letter, the fact remains that somebody did and that does not show my son-in-law in a very flattering light.'

'I should have destroyed those letters when I had the chance.'

'You had no right to do so.'

'It would have saved you unnecessary pain.'

'The letters confirmed what I already knew,' she said, tearing the paper into tiny pieces before tossing them into a wastepaper basket. 'So, please, do not hold anything back. What were the exact circumstances of the murder?'

'M. Chabal was on his way to visit a woman in Liverpool,' he said. 'I'm not at liberty to give you her name, but I can tell you that someone close to her was persuaded to invest money in the railway.'

'At least we know what they talked about in bed.' She raised both hands in apology, 'I am sorry, Inspector. That was a very crude remark and I withdraw it. I have been under a lot of strain recently, as you can understand. But,' she added, sitting up and folding her hands in her lap, 'I would still like to hear more about what actually happened that day.'

'Then you shall, Madame Rivet.'

Colbeck was succinct. He gave her a straightforward account of the murder and told her about the clues that had led him to come to France in the first place. What he concealed from her was the series of incidents that had occurred on the new railway that was being built. Hortense Rivet listened with an amalgam of sadness and fortitude.

'Thank you,' she said when he had finished.

'That is all I can tell you.'

'It was more than I expected to hear.'

'Then my visit was not wasted.'

'Catherine is heartbroken now but she will recover in time. She will always nurture fond thoughts of Gaston and I will say nothing to her of the other life that he led. It is over now. He died before his wife could learn the ugly truth about him.' She let out a long sigh. 'Who knows? Perhaps it is better that way.'

Colbeck got up. 'I ought to be going.'

'It was good of you to come, Inspector.'

'Your request could not be ignored, Madame.'

'You will understand now why I wrote to you.'

'I do indeed.'

'Have you learnt anything from this conversation?'

'Oh, yes. I feel as if I know your son-in-law a little better now.'

'Does that help?'

'In some ways.'

'Then there is one last thing you should know about him,' she said, rising from her chair. 'The last time I saw Gaston was in this very room. He had come home for the weekend. He did something that he had never done before.'

'And what was that?'

'My son-in-law was a very confident man, Inspector. He had the kind of natural charm and assurance that always appeals to women.' She gave a faint smile. 'You have the same qualities yourself but I do not think you exploit them as he did. But that's beside the point,' she continued, hurriedly. 'When he got back that day, Gaston was upset. He managed to hide it from Catherine but he did not deceive me.' She pointed to the window. 'It was the way that he stood over there and kept looking into the street.'

'What did you deduce from that, Madame?'

'He was frightened,' she said. 'Someone had followed him.'

Luke Rogan felt sick. He had endured a rough crossing from England and was now being jiggled about by the movement of the train. Any moment, he feared, he would be spilling the contents of his stomach over the floor of the carriage. He tried to concentrate on what lay ahead. When he had visited France before, he felt that he had left everything in order. A deal had been struck and money had changed hands. He had no reason to suppose that he had been double-crossed. The discussion with Sir Marcus Hetherington, however, had robbed him of his certainty. He was no longer quite so confident that his instructions had been carried out.

If the men had betrayed Rogan, it would cost him a lot of money and he would forfeit Sir Marcus' trust in him. He did not wish to upset his most generous client especially as there was a prospect of further work from that source. Everything had gone smoothly for him in England. Rogan had to ensure the same kind of success in France. Failure was not acceptable. If the people he employed had let him down, he would have to find others to do the work in their stead and pay them out of his own pocket. The very notion was galling.

He had come prepared. Excuses would not be tolerated. Had the men in his pay not taken any action as yet, Rogan would not give them a second chance. In his bag, he carried a pistol and a dagger that had already claimed one victim. Punishment would be meted out swiftly. He had not made such a gruelling journey to be fobbed off.

Thomas Brassey was pleased to see Colbeck return to the site. Inviting him into his office, he poured both of them a glass of wine.

'One of the advantages of working in France,' he said, sampling the drink. 'England has much to recommend it, but the one thing that it does not have is a supply of excellent vineyards.'

Colbeck tasted his wine. 'Very agreeable.'

'Did you enjoy your visit to Paris?'

'One would have to be blind not to do that, Mr Brassey. It's a positive feast for the eye – though some areas of the city do tend to assault the nasal passages with undue violence.'

'We have that problem in London.'

'I'm all too aware of it,' said Colbeck. 'Madame Rivet wanted to know how the investigation was progressing. She seemed to have much more faith in us than in the French police. I suppose that I should blame you for that, Mr Brassey.'

'Me?'

'Yes, sir. You set a bad example.'

'Did I, Inspector?'

'Because a British contractor builds railways for the French, they will soon expect British detectives to solve their murders for them as well. But I'm being facetious,' he said. 'The visit to Paris was very profitable. It allowed me to see that glorious architecture again and I learnt a great deal about Gaston Chabal's domestic life.'

'Did you meet his widow?'

'No, only his mother-in-law. What she told me was that

he had a role beyond his duties as an engineer. Apparently, he helped to find investors for this project.'

'Gaston had great powers of persuasion.'

'For which he was rewarded, I gather.'

'A labourer is worthy of his hire, Inspector.'

'He was rather more than a labourer.'

'Nobody could dispute that.'

Colbeck went on to describe, in broad outline, his conversation with Hortense Rivet, exercising great discretion as he did so. There was no need for Brassey to know that some of the shares in his railway had been bought as a result of a relationship between his French engineer and the daughter of a Parisian banker.

'How are things here, sir?' asked Colbeck.

'Mysteriously quiet.'

'The noise was as loud as ever when I arrived.'

'I was referring to the problems that have been dogging us of late,' said Brassey. 'We've had almost five days in a row now without any more nasty surprises.'

'That's good to hear.'

'How long it will last, though, is another matter.'

'Yes, it would be foolish to imagine that it was over.'

'I'd never do that, Inspector. What's made the difference is those guard dogs you suggested we might get. There are only four of them but they seem to have had the desired effect.'

'Don't forget the other form of restraint we imposed.'

'What was that?'

'Brendan Mulryne.'

'He's settled in well, from what I hear.'

'They're still not sure of him,' explained Colbeck. 'That's why they've been so well-behaved of late. They're biding their time as they try to work out if Brendan is friend or foe.'

'He's a very different animal from Sergeant Leeming.'

'But he remains suspect, Mr Brassey. Victor joins the camp as a stranger and, within a day, he starts to show too much interest in what's going on.'

'He paid dearly for that.'

'He tried to rush things, sir.'

'What about Mulryne?'

'I told him to be more circumspect. He'll not rush anything. And you must remember that he's still a new man in the camp, so they're bound to have some reservations about him.'

'You mean that they've stayed their hand because of Mulryne?'

'For the time being.'

'When do you think they will strike again?'

'Soon,' said Colbeck. 'Very soon.'

Brendan Mulryne caroused as usual at the village inn that night and indulged in lively badinage with the others. In a crowd of big, powerful, boisterous, hard-drinking Irishmen, he still managed to stick out. His wild antics and devil-may-care attitude made even the rowdiest of them seem tame by comparison. They had seen him get drunk, watched him fight and heard him sing the most deliciously obscene songs. They had also stood by as he turned his battered charm on the pretty barmaids at the inn. Brendan Mulryne was a vibrant character and they were pleased to have him there.

'Are you coming back to the camp, Brendan?' said someone.

'Hold your hour and have another brandy,' he replied.

'I've no money left.'

'Nor me,' said another man. 'We're off, Brendan.'

Mulryne waved a hand. 'I'll not be far behind you, lads.'

In fact, he was deliberately lagging behind. Liam Kilfoyle

had told him to do so because there might be an opportunity for him to make some money. Mulryne jumped at the invitation. When the place finally emptied, he left with Kilfoyle and began the walk back to the camp. It was not long before someone stepped out of the bushes to join them. Pierce Shannon put an arm on Mulryne's shoulder.

'I'm told you're with us, Brendan,' he said.

'I'm with anyone who pays me.'

'And what are you prepared to do for the money?'

'Anything at all,' said Mulryne, expansively, 'as long as it doesn't involve going to church or getting involved in any way with the bleeding priesthood.'

'That goes for me, too,' said Kilfoyle.

'So you don't mind breaking the law, then?' said Shannon.

Mulryne grinned. 'I'll break as many as you like.'

'We'll be in trouble if we're caught.'

'So what, Pierce? Life's far too short to worry about things like that. Just pay me the money and tell me what I have to do.'

'I'll show you.'

They strode on across the fields until the lights of the camp came into view. Lanterns twinkled and a few of the fires that had been lit to cook food were still burning away. When they got closer to the huddle of shacks and houses, Shannon stopped and waited until the last of the navvies had vanished into their temporary homes.

'This way,' he said.

He struck off to the left with Mulryne and Kilfoyle behind him. They reached the railway line and began to walk along the track. When they came to a line of wagons, Shannon called them to a halt. Mulryne gave a knowing chuckle.

'So that's it,' he said. 'It's another bet.'

'Not this time,' Shannon told him.

'I smell a trick when I see one. You're going to challenge me to lift one of those wagons because you know it's filled to the brim with ballast. I'm not *that* strong,' he said, cheerily, 'and I'm not that stupid either.'

'We don't want you to lift it, Brendan.'

'Then what do you want?'

'You'll see.'

Shannon went off to scrabble around in the dark, then he returned with a long, thick, wooden pole and a length of rope that he had hidden there earlier. Mulryne stared at the pole.

'What's that?' he asked.

'A lever,' replied Shannon.

'Yes, but what's it for?'

'Making money.'

Aubrey Filton had to hold back tears when he escorted the two of them to the scene. Eight wagons had been uncoupled and tipped off the line, spilling their respective cargoes as they did so. The rolling stock had been badly damaged and the mess would take precious time to clear away. Thomas Brassey gave a philosophical shrug, but Robert Colbeck walked around the wagons to look at them from every angle. He bent down to pull out the long wooden pole. Beside it was a length of rope. He held both of them up.

'This is how it was done, I fancy,' he said. 'Someone levered the wagon over while someone else pulled it from the other side with a rope. Those wagons are heavy enough when they're empty. Loaded, they must weigh several tons.'

'It must have taken at least a dozen men.'

Colbeck thought of Mulryne. 'Not necessarily, Mr Filton.'

'Look at the mess they've made!'

'What puzzles me,' said Brassey, staring balefully at the broken wagons, 'is how they contrived to get past the nightwatchmen – not to mention the dogs.'

'That's the other thing I have to report, sir,' said Filton.

'What?'

'It's those guard dogs. Someone fed them poisoned meat.'

Brassey was stunned. 'You mean that they're dead?'

'Dead as a doornail, sir. All four of them.'

CHAPTER TEN

Victor Leeming was a hopeless patient. It was not in his nature to sit quietly at home while he recovered from the beating he had taken. It was wonderful to spend so much time with his wife, Estelle, and to be able to play with the children, but the enforced idleness soon began to vex him. The visitors did not help. A number of police colleagues had called at the house out of genuine concern for Leeming and it was reassuring to know that he had so many friends. What irked him was that they invariably talked about the cases on which they were working, emphasising the fact that, while they were still doing their duty, he was missing all the excitement of being employed by the Metropolitan Police Force. Leeming burnt with envy. He was desperate to go back.

While his facial injuries were starting to fade, however, his ribs remained sore and he could only sleep in certain positions. Returning to work was still out of the question, but that did not mean he had to be shackled all day to the house. He was anxious to know how Inspector Colbeck was getting on in France. He was interested to hear if there had been any developments in the case on this side of the Channel. He was eager to experience the surge of raw pleasure that he always got when he crossed the threshold of Scotland Yard. Victor Leeming wanted to feel like a detective again.

Superintendent Edward Tallis did not give him a warm welcome.

'Is that you, Leeming?' he said with blunt disapproval.

'Yes, sir.'

'You should be in bed, man.'

'I feel much better now,' insisted Leeming.

'Well, you don't look it. Appearance is everything in our profession,' said Tallis, adjusting his frock coat. 'It conveys a sense of confidence and is a mark of self-respect. It's one of the first things that one learns in the army.'

'But we're not in the army, Superintendent.'

'Of course, we are. We're part of an elite battalion that is fighting a war against crime. Uniforms must be kept spotless at all times. Hair must not be unkempt. Slovenliness is a deadly sin.'

'I don't believe that I am slovenly, sir.'

'No, you're far worse than that. Look at you, man – you're patently disabled. The public should be impressed and reassured by the sight of a policeman. If they see you in that state, they are more likely to take pity.'

They had met in the corridor outside the superintendent's office. Leeming had long ago discovered the futility of reminding his superior that his men were no longer in police uniform. In the considered judgement of Edward Tallis, members of the Detective Department wore a form of uniform and those who departed from it – Colbeck was the most notable offender – had to be cowed back into line. Tallis himself looked particularly spruce. It was almost as if he were on parade. In one hand, he carried his top hat. In the other, was a large, shiny, leather bag that was packed to capacity. He ran his eye over the wounded man and spoke without a trace of sympathy.

'Are you still in pain?' he said.

'Now and again, sir.'

'Then why did you drag your aching body here?'

'I wanted to know what was going on.'

'The same thing that goes on every day, Leeming. We are doing our best to police the capital and apprehend any malefactors.'

'I was thinking about Inspector Colbeck,' said Leeming.

'That makes two of us.'

'Have you heard from him, Superintendent?'

'No,' replied Tallis. 'There's a popular misconception that silence is golden. When it comes to police work, more often than not, it betokens inactivity.'

Leeming was roused. 'That's something you could never accuse the inspector of, sir,' he said, defensively. 'Nobody in this department is more active than him.'

'I agree. My complaint is that his activity is not always fruitful.'

'That's unfair.'

'I need evidence. I require signs of life. I want progress.'

'Inspector Colbeck will solve this crime in the end, sir,' said Leeming, putting a hand to his ribs as he felt a twinge of agony. 'He's very thorough. Nothing escapes him.'

'Something did,' observed Tallis. 'He obviously didn't notice that trying to pass you off as a navvy was the same as opening the door of a lion cage and inviting you to go in.'

'It was not like that at all, Superintendent.'

'Then why are you hobbling around like that with a face that would frighten the horses and give small children bad dreams?'

'What happened to me was all my own fault,' asserted Leeming.

'The duty of a senior officer is to safeguard his men.'

'I was given the chance to refuse to do what I did, sir, but I knew how important the task was. That's why I undertook it. I was warned of the dangers beforehand. I accepted the risk.'

'That's in your favour,' conceded Tallis, magnanimously, 'and so is the fact that you have not voiced any grievances since you returned from France.'

'My only grievance is that I'm not able to return to work.'

'That, too, is creditable.'

'I feel that I should be at Inspector Colbeck's side. We work so well together even if I do have to go everywhere by train. Railways upset me. Though, if you want to know the honest truth, sir,' he went on, lugubriously, 'the boat was far worse. I never want to cross the Channel again.'

'It's an experience that I am about to undergo.'

'You, sir?' Leeming was astonished.

'Yes,' said Tallis, clapping his hat on. 'I'm tired of sitting behind my desk and waiting for something to happen. And I'm fed up with being hounded from all sides by people demanding arrests. As I've had no word from Inspector Colbeck since he left, I've decided to go to France to see for myself what – if anything – he is actually doing there.' He marched past Leeming and tossed a tart remark over his shoulder. 'It had better be something worthwhile, that's all I can say!'

'Why did you give up being a barrister?' asked Aubrey Filton.

'I discovered that it was not what I wanted to do.'

'But you seem to have all the attributes, Inspector. You've a quick brain, a fine voice and a commanding presence. I could imagine that you would excel in court.'

'To some degree, I did,' said Colbeck, modestly, 'but there was an artificiality about the whole process that worried me. I felt that I were acting in a play at times and I was not always happy with the lines that were assigned to me.'

'All the same, joining the police was a huge step to take. You were giving up what must have been a very comfortable life for a profession that, by its very nature, is full of danger.'

'Comforts of the body do not bring comforts of the mind.'

'I do not follow,' said Filton.

'Something happened that showed me the limitations of working in a court,' explained Colbeck, calling up a painful memory. 'It involved a young lady who was very close to me and who, alas, died a violent death. I was unable to save her. What that misfortune taught me was that prevention is always better than the cure. Stopping a crime from being committed is infinitely preferable to convicting the culprit once the damage is done. A barrister can win plaudits by sending a killer to the gallows but he's not able to raise a murder victim from the dead.'

'That's true.'

'As a detective,' said Colbeck, 'I've been fortunate enough to prevent murders from taking place. It's given me far more satisfaction than I ever had in court. It's also given me a peace of mind that I never enjoyed before.'

Filton was perplexed. 'Peace of mind from a job that pits you against murderous thugs?' he said. 'That's a paradox, surely.'

'You may well be right, Mr Filton.'

It was the first time that Colbeck had spent any length of time alone with the engineer and he was learning a great deal about the man. Away from the site, Filton managed to lose the harassed look in his eyes and the faint note of hysteria in his voice. He emerged as a polite, well-educated, assiduous man with an unshakable belief in the potential of railways to change the world for the better. The two men had taken a trap and driven to a tavern in the nearest village. Over a meal, they were able to talk at leisure.

'This place is quiet in the middle of the day,' said Filton. 'I'd hate to be here at night when the navvies come pouring in. It must be like Bedlam.'

'They don't seem to have done too much damage,' noted Colbeck, glancing around. 'And I daresay the landlord's profits have shot up since the railway came. He'll be sorry to see you all go when you move on further down the line.'

'If and when that ever happens.'

'It will, Mr Filton. I give you my word.'

'I'd prefer a little of that peace of mind you were talking about.'

'Mr Brassey seems to have his share of that.'

'Yes,' said Filton. 'I admire him for it. Whatever the problems, he never gets unduly alarmed. He's so phlegmatic. I wish that I could be like that. My wife says that I used to be until I started working in France.'

'I didn't know that you were married.'

'I've a wife and three children back in Southampton.'

'That might explain why you lack Mr Brassey's *sang-froid*,' said Colbeck. 'You miss your family. Mr Brassey brings his with him but yours is still in England.'

'I write to my wife as often as I can.'

'It's not the same, Mr Filton.'

'Are you married, Inspector?'

'Not yet, sir.'

'I can recommend the institution.'

'I'll bear that in mind.'

Colbeck drank some more of his wine. For a fleeting moment, he thought about Madeleine Andrews and recalled that it was she who had obtained crucial information from the woman who had called herself Hannah Critchlow. He was delighted that she had been able to help him in that way. As an engineer, Aubrey Filton could expect no assistance at all from his wife. His work separated them. Colbeck's profession actually brought him closer to Madeleine. It was something he considered to be a blessing.

'This is good food,' said Colbeck, 'and the wine is more than passable. Working in France obviously has its compensations.'

'In my opinion,' said Filton, 'they are outweighed by the many disadvantages. Whenever I'm in this country, I'm always afraid that the ground will suddenly shift from beneath our feet.'

'You only had to survive one revolution.'

'It was followed by a *coup d' état* last year, Inspector. After the revolution, Louis Napoleon came to power by democratic means. It was not enough for him. He wanted to be Master of France. So he dissolved the Chamber and seized complete control.'

'I remember it well, Mr Filton. The wonder is not that he did it but that he achieved it with so little resistance.'

'The name of Napoleon has immense resonance here,' said Filton, wryly. 'It stands for discipline, power and international renown. That speaks to every Frenchman.'

'One can see why.'

'Yes, but it has not made our work here any easier. When there are upheavals in Paris, the effects spill over on to us.'

'Your immediate problems are not French in origin,'

Colbeck reminded him. 'They are essentially British. Or, if I may be pedantic, they are Anglo-Irish.'

'And how long do you think they will continue?'

'Not very long, Mr Filton. We are nearing the end.'

'How do you know?'

'Because I planted Brendan Mulryne in their midst.'

'You did the same with Sergeant Leeming.'

'That was different,' argued Colbeck. 'Victor was only there to watch and listen. He would never be taken fully into anyone's confidence. Also, he's far too law-abiding at heart.'

'Law-abiding?'

'He would never commit a crime, Mr Filton.'

'What relevance does that have?'

'Every relevance,' explained Colbeck. 'Brendan is not held back by the same scruples. To become one of them, he'll do what they do without batting an eyelid. We've already seen evidence of that.'

'Have we?'

'Think of those wagons that were overturned. Unless I'm mistaken, Brendan was involved there.'

Filton was outraged. 'Do you mean that he *helped* the villains?'

'Yes, sir.'

'That's disgraceful, Inspector. Policemen are supposed to uphold the law not flout it like that.'

'Brendan is a rather unusual policeman,' said Colbeck with an appeasing smile, 'as you'll soon see. Before they would trust him, they put him to the test. Judging from the way that those wagons were toppled, I think that he passed that test.'

'So he'll be in a position to destroy even more of our property,' protested Filton. 'I thought he was supposed to be on our side. All that you've done is to import another troublemaker. How many more delays is he going to inflict on us?'

'None, I suspect. Brendan is one of them now.'

'Bracing himself for another attack, I daresay.'

'No, Mr Filton,' said Colbeck, nonchalantly. 'Waiting for the moment when he can hand the villains over to us on a plate.'

Luke Rogan festered with impatience. Having reached Mantes and spent the night there, he had to wait a whole day before he could speak to the man he had come to see. Until the navvies came off work that evening, Rogan had to cool his heels in a country he despised. Back in England, he could be earning money by working for other clients. Instead, he was compelled to waste valuable time abroad. Sir Marcus Hetherington, however, could not be disobeyed.

Sending a message had been his first priority. After riding to the site on a hired horse, he tethered the animal to a tree and used a telescope to scan the scene. Hundreds of navvies were at work in the blistering sun and it took him a long time to locate the man he was after. Pierce Shannon was part of the team that was raising a high embankment. A boy was taking a bucket of water from man to man so that they could slake their thirst. Rogan kept a close eye on the boy. When he saw the lad run off to draw more water, he realised that there had to be a spring nearby. It did not take him long to skirt the railway and find the spring.

When the boy came back once more, Rogan was waiting for him to make an offer. In return for the promise of money, the boy was very willing to deliver the message. After filling his bucket, he scampered off. Rogan had no worries that his note would be read by anyone else because most of the navvies were illiterate. In any case, the terse message would have been incomprehensible to anyone but its intended recipient. He lurked near the spring until the boy eventually came for some more water.

'I gave it to him, sir,' he said.

'What was his reply?'

'He'll be there.'

'Good lad.'

After handing over the money, Rogan made his way back to his horse and rode away. When evening came, he was punctual. It seemed an age before Shannon actually turned up at the appointed place. Rogan had been waiting near the derelict farmhouse for an hour.

'Sorry to keep you, sir,' said Shannon, tipping his hat.

'Where've you been?'

'I needed a drink or two first.'

'I told you to come just as soon as you could,' said the other, reproachfully. 'Have you forgotten who's paying you?'

'No, sir.'

'Do you want to stay working in this hell-hole forever?'

'That I don't,' said Shannon. 'When you give us the rest of the money, I'll be able to turn my back on this kind of work for good. I'm minded to have a little farm back home in Ireland, you see.' He looked around at the crumbling walls. 'A house about this size would suit me down to the ground.'

'You won't get another penny until the job is done.'

'Oh, it will be, sir. I swear it.'

'Then why has there been no news of any disruption?'

'News?'

'It should have reached the English newspapers by now,'

said Rogan, tetchily. 'Yet there hasn't been a single word about it.'

'You can't blame us for that, sir.'

'I can if you're trying to pull the wool over my eyes. Be warned, Shannon. Cross me and you'll be in deep trouble.'

The Irishman stiffened. 'Don't threaten me, sir.'

'Then do as you were told.'

'We have done,' said Shannon with wild-eyed indignation. 'We've done every damn thing you suggested and much more. Just because it wasn't in your bleeding newspapers, it doesn't mean that it never happened. The person to blame is Tom Brassey.'

'Why?'

'Because he won't report anything to the French police.'

'Maybe that's because there's nothing to report.'

'Are you calling me a liar?' demanded Shannon, raising a fist.

'Give me a reason not to,' said Rogan, pulling out his gun and pointing it at him. 'Otherwise, the only farmhouse you'll ever spend time in is this one and you'll be doing it on your back.'

'Hey, now wait a minute,' said the other, backing away and holding up both hands in a gesture of conciliation. 'Be careful with that thing, sir. You've no call to point it at me. Pierce Shannon is an honourable man. I've not let you down.'

'Then tell me what you've done.'

'I will.'

Shannon used his fingers to count off the series of incidents that he had contrived, giving sufficient detail of each one to convince Rogan that he was telling the truth. When he heard about the explosion, he lowered his weapon. Shannon and his accomplices had not been idle. There was a whole catalogue of destruction to report back to Sir Marcus Hetherington.

'*Now* will you believe me?' said the Irishman.

'Yes,' replied Rogan, putting the gun away. 'I was wrong to accuse you. And I can see now why Mr Brassey wants to hide his problems from the French police and newspapers. He'd rather try to sort out the trouble for himself.'

'He even put a spy in the camp. We beat him to a pulp.'

'But you still haven't brought the railway to a standstill.'

'We will, sir. I know exactly how to do it.'

'How?'

'That would be telling,' said Shannon with a grin. 'Stay in France for a day or two and you'll find out what we did. They won't be able to keep our next crime out of the newspapers. It's one thing that even Mr Brassey won't be able to hide.'

'I'll need certain proof of what you've done.'

'Then use your own eyes.'

'I'll not stay in this accursed country a moment longer,' said Rogan. 'I've got what I came for and there's too much work awaiting me in England for me to linger here. When it's all over, you know how to get in touch with me.'

'I do at that, sir – though I still don't know your name.'

'You don't need to know it.'

'Why not? You can trust Pierce Shannon.'

'Finish the task and earn your money,' said Rogan, firmly. 'Once I pay you, I never want to set eyes on you again. Go back to Ireland and take up farming. It's a far healthier life than building a railway in France.'

'I'll have no choice,' said Shannon with a laugh. 'Very soon, there'll be no bleeding railway here to build.'

* * *

Robert Colbeck had fulfilled a dream that he had harboured for many years. Dressed as an engine driver, he was standing on the footplate of the locomotive that had recently arrived with twenty wagons filled with ballast from the quarry. His only disappointment was that he was not able to drive the engine. He had only donned the clothing so that he would attract no undue attention. The footplate was the venue for a meeting that he had arranged with Brendan Mulryne. Making sure that he was not seen, the Irishman climbed up beside him.

'Drive me all the way home to Dublin, Inspector,' he said.

'I wish that I could, Brendan, but the line doesn't go that far.'

'It won't go any farther than this, if the buggers have their way.'

'Do you know what their next step will be?' asked Colbeck.

'Yes, sir.'

'Well?'

'They want to bring the whole thing to a stop.'

'And how do they intend to do that?'

Mulryne told him what he had heard. While he knew the place where the attack would be launched, he did not know the precise time. That was a detail that was deliberately kept from him. What was certain was that he would definitely be involved.

'You obviously passed the test they set you,' said Colbeck.

'Tipping over a few wagons? It was child's play.'

'Not to the people who had to clear up after you.'

'Sure, I'd have been happy to do the job myself but that would have given the game away. If they weren't such hard-hearted villains,' said Mulryne, 'I'd have no quarrel with them. They're fellow Irishmen and that means they're the salt of the earth.'

'Do they have no suspicion of you at all?'

'None, sir, but they might start wondering if I don't join them for a drink very soon. I've made quite a bit of money from them, one way and another.' His face clouded. 'I suppose that'd be called the proceeds of crime. I won't have to hand it back, will I?'

'No, Brendan. It's yours to keep.'

'I never keep money, sir. It burns a hole in my pocket.'

'Then enjoy a drink with it,' said Colbeck. 'And, as soon as you know when they're going to strike, find a way to let me know.'

'That I will, Inspector.'

'Do you know who's paying them?'

'I don't know and I've never once tried to find out. I remembered what happened to Sergeant Leeming when he asked too many questions.' Mulryne pointed to his head. 'They think of me as a big man with a tiny brain. I'm stupid old Brendan who'll do anything for money and not worry where it comes from.'

'How many of them are there?'

'Difficult to say, sir. I've only met two.'

'There must be more than that, Brendan.'

'That's why you have to catch them in the act. The whole gang is going to be there next time. At least, that's what Liam told me.'

'Liam?'

'I'll introduce him to you when we meet,' said Mulryne. 'You'll be pleased to make his acquaintance.'

'Will I?'

'He's one of the men who ambushed the sergeant.'

'Ah, I see.'

'Liam boasted to me about it. I had a job to hold myself

back from knocking his head off there and then. Sergeant Leeming is a friend of mine. When the fighting really starts, Liam is all mine.'

'Victor will be pleased to hear about it,' said Colbeck. 'Now, off you go, Brendan. Join the others before they start to miss you. And thank you again. You've done well.'

'I ought to be thanking you, sir.'

'Why?'

'Work with Irishmen all day and drink with them all night – this is heaven for me,' said Mulryne, happily. 'Yes, and there's a barmaid at the inn who's sweet on me. What more can a man ask?'

Colbeck waved him off then allowed himself a few minutes to inspect the locomotive more closely and to run a possessive hand over its levers and valves. He had recognised the design at once. It was the work of Thomas Crampton, the Englishmen whose locomotives were so popular in France. As he indulged his fancy, he wished that Caleb Andrews had been there to teach him how to drive it.

Descending at last from the footplate, he walked across the tracks and headed towards Brassey's office. Instead of his habitual long stride and upright posture, he used a slow amble and kept his shoulders hunched. Engine drivers did not look or move like elegant detectives. When success was so close, he did not wish to make a false move and attract suspicion. His talk with Mulryne had been very heartening and he was delighted that he had brought the Irishman with him. It was only a question of time before the problems at the site would be brought to an abrupt end. Colbeck wanted to pass on the good news to Brassey as soon as possible.

Reaching the office, he knocked on the door and opened it in response to the contractor's invitation. He had expected

Brassey to be alone but someone else was there and it was the last person Colbeck had wanted to see. Superintendent Tallis gaped at him in wonder.

'Is that *you*, Colbeck?' he cried, staring in consternation. 'What are you doing, man? I sent you here to solve a crime, not to play with an engine.'

Madeleine Andrews had had a profitable time. It was one of the days when a servant came to clean the house and do various chores, thus releasing Madeleine to work on her latest drawing. She was not trying to sketch the Sankey Viaduct now. She was working on another sketch of the *Lord of the Isles*, the locomotive that Colbeck had taken her to see at the Great Exhibition the previous year. It had a special significance for her. When evening came, she kept glancing up at the clock, hoping that her father would not be too late.

When he went to work, Andrews always bought a morning newspaper at Euston Station. His daughter never got to read it until he came back home, and she was desperate for more news about Colbeck. If he had made any progress in the murder investigation, it would be duly reported. Madeleine was at the window when she saw her father sauntering along the street. He had made a good recovery from the injuries that had almost cost him his life, and he had his old jauntiness back. She opened the door for him and was disappointed that he was not carrying a newspaper.

'Did you have a good day, Father?' she asked.

'Yes,' he replied. 'I've been to Birmingham and back twice. I've driven along that line so often, I could do it blindfolded.'

'Well, I hope you don't even try.'

'No, Maddy.' He took off his coat and hung it on a hook.

'The place looks clean and tidy,' he said. 'Mrs Busby obviously came.'

'Yes. I was able to get on with my own work.'

'How is she?'

'Still worried about her husband. He has a bad back.'

'At his age?' he said, disdainfully. 'Jim Busby must be ten or fifteen years younger than me. Bad backs are for old men.' He sniffed the air. 'I can smell food.'

'I'll get it in a moment, Father. I just wondered what happened to your newspaper today.'

'What? Oh, I must have forgotten to buy one.'

'You never forget,' she said. 'Reading a paper is an article of faith and you know how much I look forward to seeing it afterwards.'

'Then I suppose I mislaid it today. Sorry, Maddy.'

'Tell me the truth.'

'That is the truth. I left it somewhere by mistake.'

'I think that you did it on purpose.'

'Don't you believe your old father?' he asked with a look of injured innocence. 'I've been very busy today, girl. You can't expect me to remember everything.'

She folded her arms. 'What did it say?'

'Nothing of importance.'

'I know you too well. You're hiding something from me.'

'Why should I do that?'

'Because you're trying to spare my feelings,' she said. 'It's very kind of you but I don't need to be protected. They've said something nasty about Robert, haven't they?'

'I can't remember,' he replied, trying to move past her.

She held his arm. 'You're lying to me.'

'There was hardly a mention of him, Maddy.'

'But what did that mention say?'

She was determined to learn the worst. Caleb Andrews knew how much she loved Colbeck and he wanted to shield her from any adverse criticism of the detective. Having been the victim of a crime himself, he was aware how long it could take to bring the perpetrators to justice. Newspaper reporters had no patience. They needed dramatic headlines to attract their readers. Robert Colbeck had so far failed to provide them. He had paid the penalty.

'There was an article about him,' he admitted.

'Go on.'

'It was cruel. That's all you need to know.'

'What did it say about Robert? Tell me. I'll not be baulked.'

'I think that Inspector Colbeck has an enemy in Scotland Yard,' said Andrews. 'Someone who envies him so much that he's gone behind his back to feed a story to the newspapers.'

'What story?' she demanded.

'A spiteful one, Maddy. According to the article, the inspector has made such a mess of this case that Superintendent Tallis has gone to France to drag him back home in disgrace.'

Tallis spat out the name as if it were a type of venomous poison.

'Brendan Mulryne!' he exclaimed.

'Yes, sir,' confessed Colbeck.

'You dared to engage the services of Brendan Mulryne?'

'He was the ideal person for the task. When I lost Victor, I had to find someone who could blend more easily into the scene.'

'Oh, yes,' said Tallis, maliciously. 'Mulryne would blend in. He's the same as the rest of them – a wild, drunken, unruly Irishman who doesn't give two hoots for authority.'

'That's unduly harsh, Superintendent,' said Thomas

Brassey. 'Most of my Irish navvies are a godsend to me. They do the sort of soul-destroying job that would kill the average man, yet they still manage to keep up their spirits. When I build a railway, they're always my first choice.'

Tallis was spiky. 'Well, I can assure you that Brendan Mulryne would never be *my* first choice. When we kicked him out of the police force, we should have put him in a menagerie where he belonged.'

The three men were still in Brassey's office. The confrontation with Edward Tallis was proving to be even more abrasive than usual. At the very moment Robert Colbeck's carefully laid plan was coming to fruition, his superior had turned up to throw it into jeopardy. What increased the inspector's discomfort was that his reprimand was delivered in front of Brassey. It made the contractor realise that he had been misled.

'I thought that Mulryne was a policeman,' he said.

'He was – at one time,' replied Colbeck.

'And he was a menace to us while he was there,' said Tallis. 'I'll spare you the full inventory of his peccadilloes, Mr Brassey, or we'd be here all night. Suffice it to say that the Metropolitan Police Force is run, like the army, on strict discipline. Brendan Mulryne does not know the meaning of the word.'

'He made several important arrests, sir.'

'Yes, Inspector. But he could not resist hitting his prisoners.'

'When he was in uniform,' Colbeck said, 'there was far less crime in the area he patrolled. Villains were too afraid of him.'

'I'm not surprised. He'd assault them first and ask questions afterwards. That's in blatant defiance of police procedure.'

'Why didn't you tell me all this, Inspector?' asked Brassey.

'Because I didn't feel that it was necessary for you to know, sir,' said Colbeck, awkwardly. 'For the last couple of weeks, this railway had been under siege. If these men were allowed to continue, they would bring this whole project crashing down. I believed that the one person who could save you was Brendan Mulryne and, after my conversation with him just now, I'm even more certain of it.'

'But he appears to be no more than a criminal himself.'

'He is,' agreed Tallis. 'I don't think he means to help us at all. Now that he's here, he's made common cause with the villains. He's an active part of the conspiracy against you. All that Inspector Colbeck has done is to add to your troubles.'

'That's unjust, sir!' Colbeck retaliated.

'Didn't you tell us that he'd wormed his way into their ranks?'

'Only to be able to betray them.'

'We are the ones who've been betrayed. You admitted that he's helped them to cause serious damage to railway property.'

'That was an essential part of his initiation.'

'Ruining those wagons is not what I'd call initiation, Inspector,' said Brassey, critically. 'It's straightforward vandalism.'

'He had to convince them that he could be trusted, Mr Brassey.'

'Well, I can't trust him – not any more.'

'Nor me,' said Tallis. 'I've learnt from bitter experience that the only thing you can rely on Mulryne do to is to create mischief. You had no authority whatsoever to use the rogue, Inspector.'

'Desperate diseases call for desperate remedies,' said Colbeck.

'Mulryne is nothing short of an epidemic!'

'Give credit where it's due, Superintendent Tallis. The man

you traduce so readily helped us to catch those responsible for the mail train robbery last year.'

'Yes,' said Tallis, sourly. 'That was another occasion when your methods were highly questionable. You had no right to involve that reprobate in police business.'

'The end justified the means.'

'Not in my estimation.'

'The commissioner disagreed,' said Colbeck, pointedly. 'He wanted to congratulate Mulryne in person. Are you telling me that the head of the Metropolitan Police Force was at fault?'

Tallis's face twitched. 'What I'm telling you is that this charade has got to stop,' he snapped. 'Mulryne must be arrested immediately with his accomplices.'

'But we don't know who they are, sir.'

'They'll be getting drunk with him right now.'

'In your position,' advised Brassey, 'I'd think again. Only a bold man would try to apprehend an Irish navvy when he's celebrating with his friends. I agree that he should be punished, Superintendent, but you have to choose the right moment.'

'Arresting him would be madness,' argued Colbeck. 'Besides, you have no jurisdiction in this country. When we catch the villains, we'll have to hand them over to the French police.'

'Mulryne will be one of them.'

'But he's our only hope of salvation.'

'That unholy barbarian?'

'I'm bound to share the superintendent's unease,' said Brassey.

'It's not unease,' declared Tallis. 'It's sheer horror.'

'All that he needs is a little time,' said Colbeck. 'What harm is there in giving him that? I'd stake every penny I have that Brendan Mulryne will do what's he paid to do – and by the way, sir,' he added, looking at Tallis, 'all his expenses have come out of my own pocket. That should show you how much faith I have in the man.'

'I admire your loyalty but deplore your judgement.'

Brassey shook his head. 'I have an open mind on all this.'

'Do you want this railway to be built?' Colbeck asked him.

'Of course.'

'Then trust a man who's risking his life to make sure that it is not crushed out of existence. Victor Leeming was out of his depth here and he got a beating for his pains. They couldn't punish Mulryne in the same way,' Colbeck told them. 'He's too big and strong. If they knew that he was about to betray them, they'd kill him outright.'

Brendan Mulryne was in his element. Having arrived late, he made up for lost time by ordering two drinks at a time. He was soon involved in the vigorous banter. Alive to any opportunities to make money, he performed a few feats of strength to win bets from some of the others then bought them a brandy apiece by way of consolation. The rowdy atmosphere was like a second home to him but he was not only there to revel with his friends. Every so often, he darted a glance at one of the barmaids, a buxom young woman with dark hair and a dimple in each cheek. Whenever she caught his eye, she smiled at him.

Towards the end of the evening, Liam Kilfoyle came over to him.

'Stay behind for a while, Brendan,' he said.

Mulryne chuckled. 'Oh, I intend to, Liam, I promise you.'

'Pierce would like a word.'

'As long as it's a short one.'

'He was pleased with the way you tipped over those wagons.'

'Ah, I could have done that on my own without you two pulling on that rope as if you were in a tug-o'-war contest. I like a challenge.'

'You've got one of those coming up, Brendan.'

'When?'

'Pierce will tell you – but not in here.'

Shannon was talking to some friends in a corner, but he had kept an eye on Mulryne throughout the evening as if weighing him in the balance. He wished that he had known the newcomer much longer so that he could be absolutely certain about him but there was no time to spare. The surprise visit of his paymaster had acted as a stimulus. The final attack was at hand. He had other men to help him but none with Mulryne's extraordinary strength. Shannon knew a way to put that strength to good use.

When the bar started to clear, the giant Irishman made sure that he had a brief exchange with the barmaid. He spoke no French and she knew very little English but they understood each other well. Mulryne gave her a wink to seal their bargain. Her dimples were deeper and more expressive than ever. He was by no means the only man to take an interest in her but none of the others could compete. She had made her choice. At length, only the stragglers remained and the landlord began to close up the bar. Mulryne was among the last to leave and he walked away very slowly.

When Shannon and Kilfoyle fell in beside him, he put a friendly arm around each of them and gave a playful squeeze.

'Steady on, Brendan,' said Kilfoyle. 'You'll break my shoulder.'

'I was as gentle as a lamb,' claimed Mulryne.

'You don't know how to be gentle.'

'Oh, yes, I do.'

'Keep yourself more sober tomorrow,' ordered Shannon.

'I *am* sober.'

'I saw how much you drank tonight, Brendan.'

'Then you should have noticed something else,' said Mulryne. 'The more I had, the less drunk I became. It's weak men who fall into a stupor. I've learnt to hold my drink.'

'You'll need a clear head.'

'My head *is* clear, Pierce.'

'I'm giving you an order,' said the other. 'If you don't want to obey it, we'll find someone else.'

'No, no,' said Mulryne, quickly. 'I'm your man. If there's money to be made – real money this time – I won't touch more than a drop tomorrow. I swear it. Is that when it's going to be?'

'Yes.'

'At what time?'

'As soon as it gets dark,' said Shannon.

'I'll be ready.'

'So will I,' said Kilfoyle. 'I've been waiting to escape from this shit hole for weeks. Now, I'll finally get my chance.'

'We all will, Liam,' said Shannon.

'This time tomorrow, I'll be rich.'

'Only if you do as you're told.'

'Thank the Lord that it is tomorrow,' said Mulryne, coming to a sharp halt. The others stopped beside. 'Had it been tonight, I'm afraid, I'd not have been able to oblige you.'

'Why not?' asked Shannon.

'You're with us now,' added Kilfoyle.

'Not tonight.'

'Why have we stopped?'

'Because I have other plans. I thought I might take a stroll in the moonlight. It looks like a perfect night for it.' He beamed at them. 'Good night, lads.'

Brendan Mulryne turned around and began to walk back towards the inn. As he did so, the barmaid came out of the front door and ran on the tip of her toes until his huge arms enveloped her. After a first kiss, the two of them then faded quietly into the shadows. Mulryne was determined to make the most of his visit to France.

CHAPTER ELEVEN

Robert Colbeck never enjoyed having to spend a night under the same roof as Edward Tallis; he did not find it an uplifting experience. He slept fitfully, tormented by the thought that the whole investigation could be endangered by the precipitate action of his superior. The arrival of the superintendent could not have come at a worse time. It had taken Colbeck by surprise and undermined his position completely. It had also exposed the ambiguous involvement of Brendan Mulryne in the exercise, thereby alarming Thomas Brassey and driving Tallis into a rage that three consecutive cigars had failed to soften. It was doubtful if a night's sleep would improve the superintendent's temper.

When he came down for breakfast in the cottage where they were both staying, Colbeck did not even know if he was still employed in the Detective Department at Scotland Yard. Tallis had made all sorts of veiled threats without actually dismissing him. Colbeck's career was definitely in the balance. As they sat opposite each other at the table, there was a distinct tension in the air. It was Tallis who eventually broke it.

'I think that we should cut our losses and withdraw,' he said.

'That would be a ruinous course of action, sir,' protested

Colbeck. 'Having come so far, why pull out now?'

'Because the investigation has not been run properly.'

'We are on the point of capturing the villains.'

'One of whom is Brendan Mulryne.'

'No, Superintendent. He is working for us.'

'He's not working for me,' said Tallis, angrily, 'and he never will. Setting a thief to catch a thief has never seemed to me to be wise advice. A criminal will always have more affinity with criminals than with those trying to catch them. We have a perfect example of that here. Instead of working as an informer, Mulryne has sided with his natural allies because the rewards are greater.'

'You malign him, sir.'

'I know him of old.'

'And so do I,' said Colbeck. 'That's why I picked him.'

'A singularly unfortunate choice.'

'You would not think that if you'd spoken to him yesterday.'

Tallis scowled. 'Nothing on God's earth would persuade me to dress up as an engine driver in order to converse with a man who was drummed out of the police force for using excessive violence. And that was only one of his glaring defects. You've had successes in the past, Colbeck,' he went on, chewing his food noisily, 'but this time, you have bungled everything.'

'I resent that, sir.'

'And I resent your attempt to deceive me with regard to the use of that incorrigible Irishman, Mulryne.'

'This railway line is being built by incorrigible Irishmen. Only someone like Mulryne could mix easily with them. He's done everything I asked of him.'

'You mean that you *incited* him to commit a crime?'

'No, sir.'

'Then how much licence did you grant him?'

'I told him to do whatever was necessary.'

'Even if that entailed wrecking a number of wagons?'

'It worked, sir,' insisted Colbeck. 'Don't you realise that? He's now part of their gang. Brendan Mulryne is in a unique position.'

'Yes, he can inflict even more damage on the railway.'

'He can bring the vandalism to an end.'

'He's much more likely to increase it. The kindest thing we can do for Mr Brassey is to haul Mulryne out of France altogether and take him back to whatever squalid hovel he lives in.'

'We must allow him to finish his work.'

'It is finished – as from today.'

'Even Mr Brassey thought that we should wait.'

'He's a contractor,' said Tallis, finishing his cup of coffee, 'not a policeman. He doesn't understand the way that a criminal mind works. I do. Brassey still finds it difficult to believe that he could be employing callous villains on this project.'

'That's because he has a paternal attitude towards his men, sir. Because he treats them so well, he cannot accept that they would betray him. Thomas Brassey is famed for the care he shows to anyone he employs,' said Colbeck, 'and you must bear in mind that, at any one time, he could have as many as 80,000 men on his books. If any one of them finds a particular job too onerous, Mr Brassey will not simply dismiss him. He's more likely to assign him to an easier task. That's how considerate and benevolent he is. It's the reason his men think so highly of him.'

'The law of averages comes into play here. In every thousand good men, you are bound to have a tiny minority of blackguards. Some of them are employed here,' Tallis continued, 'and they think so highly of the benevolent Brassey that they're prepared to do anything to stop this railway from being built. I'm sorry, Inspector. You may admire the way that he operates,' he said, dismissively, 'but I think that Brassey is too naïve.'

'He's a shrewd and hard-headed businessman, sir. You do not achieve his extraordinary level of success by being naïve.'

'If he has problems here, it is up to him to sort them out.'

'But there is a direct link with the murder of Gaston Chabal.'

'So you keep telling me,' said Tallis, 'but we will not find it by unleashing Mulryne on this railway. All that he will do is to muddy the waters even more.'

'Give him time,' implored Colbeck.

'We are returning to England today.'

'But that would leave Mr Brassey in the lurch.'

'He can call in the French police.'

'Then we'll never find the man who killed Chabal.'

'Yes, we will,' said Tallis. 'If we hunt for him in the country where he resides – England.'

Further argument was curtailed. Tallis got up from the table and stalked off to his room to collect his bag. Colbeck thanked the farmer's wife who had given them such a tasty breakfast and paid her for accommodating them. It was not long before he and Tallis were on their way to the site to take their leave of Thomas Brassey. During the drive, Colbeck made repeated attempts to persuade Tallis to change his mind but the superintendent was adamant. Activities in France had to be brought to an immediate halt. As a courtesy to the contractor, Tallis undertook to explain to him why.

Colbeck was faced with a dilemma. If he wanted to remain as a detective, he had to obey orders and return to London.

If, however, he wanted to pick up a trail that led eventually to the killer, he had to remain in France until the information came to light. He was still wrestling with the dilemma when they arrived. Alighting from the trap, they walked towards Brassey's office. Before they could knock on the door, however, it was opened for them. The contractor had seen them through the window.

'I'm glad that you came, Inspector,' he said. 'She'll speak to nobody but you.'

'She?' said Colbeck.

'A young Frenchwoman. She seems quite agitated.'

'Then I'll talk to her at once.'

Colbeck went into the office and closed the door behind him. Tallis was annoyed at being left outside but he took the opportunity to explain to Brassey why they would be leaving the country that very day. Colbeck, meanwhile, was introducing himself to the barmaid from the village inn, who had befriended Mulryne and spent some of the previous night with him. Because they had got on so well, she had been entrusted with an important message but she would not pass it on until she was convinced that she was speaking to Inspector Robert Colbeck. Only when he had shown her identification, and explained that he was a good friend of Brendan Mulryne, did she trust him.

'*Cette nuit*,' she said.

'*Vous êtes certaine, mademoiselle*?'

'*Oui*.'

'*Merci. Merci beaucoup*.'

Colbeck was so delighted that he wanted to kiss her.

Luke Rogan knew where to find him that late in the day. Sir Marcus Hetherington was at his club, whiling away the evening by conversing with friends about the merits of certain racehorses on which they intended to place a wager. When the steward brought him Rogan's card, Sir Marcus detached himself from the group and retired to a quiet corner to receive his visitor. After crossing the Channel again when the waves were choppy, Rogan was looking distinctly unwell. He refused the offer of a whisky, vowing to touch neither food nor drink until his stomach had settled down. He lowered himself gingerly into a chair beside Sir Marcus.

'Well?' said the old man.

'It was as I told you, Sir Marcus – no need to fear.'

'You saw the men?'

'I spoke to their leader.'

'What did he tell you?'

When Rogan repeated the list of incidents that had occurred on the railway line, Sir Marcus gave a smile of satisfaction. His money had not, after all, been squandered. He now understood why none of the destruction that had been wrought had been reported in the French newspapers.

'This is all very gratifying,' he said.

'To you, Sir Marcus, but not to me.'

'What are you talking about?'

'Taking that boat when the waves were so high,' said Rogan, holding his stomach. 'It fair upset me, Sir Marcus. I feel ill. I went all that way to find out something that I knew already. You should have trusted me.'

'I trust you – but not your friends.'

'Oh, they're not friends of mine.'

'Then what are they?'

'I'd call them the scum of the earth,' said Rogan with a sneer, 'and the only reason I employ them is that I can rely on them to do what they're told. Pay them well and they do your bidding. But you'd never want to call any of them a friend, Sir Marcus. They're ruffians.'

'Even ruffians have their uses at times.'

'Once this is over, I wash my hands of them.'

'That brings us to the crux of the matter,' said Sir Marcus. 'When will this finally be over? What they have accomplished so far is a series of delays and I willingly applaud them for that. Delays, however, are mere irritations to a man like Brassey. He's indomitable. He'll shrug off temporary setbacks and press on regardless. When are your friends – your hired ruffians, I should say – going to make it impossible for him to carry on?'

'Soon.'

'How soon?'

'Within a day or two, Sir Marcus,' said Rogan, confidently. 'That's what I was told. They're going to make one last strike before getting away from the site for good.'

'One last strike?'

'It will be much more than a simple delay.'

'Why?'

'They're going to burn down Mr Brassey's office and destroy all the surveys that people like Gaston Chabal prepared for him. Without anything to guide them, they simply won't be able to go on with the work. But there's more, Sir Marcus,' said Rogan, grinning wolfishly, 'and it will give them the biggest headache of all.'

'Go on.'

'They're going to steal the big safe from the office. It not only contains valuable documents that cannot be replaced, it holds all the money to pay the navvies.'

'So they'll get no wages,' said Sir Marcus, slapping his knees in appreciation. 'By George, this is capital!'

'No money and thousands of angry men to face.'

'Come pay day and Brassey will have a veritable riot on his hands. I take back all I said, Rogan,' the old man added with a condescending smile. 'I should never have doubted your ability to pick the right men for the job. Ruffians or not, these fellows deserve a medal. They'll have brought the whole enterprise to a juddering halt.'

There were five of them in all. One of them, Gerald Murphy, was employed as a nightwatchman so he was able to tell them exactly where his colleagues were placed and how best to avoid them. Another man, Tim Dowd, drove one of the carts that took supplies to various parts of the site. Pierce Shannon, Liam Kilfoyle and Brendan Mulryne completed the gang. When they slipped out of the inn after dark, their leader noted that someone was missing.

'Where's Brendan?' he said.

'Saying farewell to his lady love,' replied Kilfoyle with a snigger. 'He's probably telling her that he'll see her later when, in fact, he'll be on the run with the rest of us.'

'Go and fetch him, Liam.'

'Never come between a man and his colleen.'

'Then I'll get the bastard.'

Shannon turned on his heel but he did not have to go back into the building. Mulryne was already walking towards him, still savouring the long, succulent kiss that he had just been given in the privacy of the cellar. He beamed at the others.

'Ah, isn't love a wonderful thing?' he announced.

'Not if it holds us up,' said Shannon, brusquely. 'Forget about her, Brendan. After tonight, you'll have enough money to buy yourself any pair of tits you take a fancy to.'

'I'm sorry, Pierce. What must I do?'

'Shut up and listen.'

Keeping his voice low, Shannon gave them their orders. Murphy was to act as their lookout and he rehearsed a whistle he would give them by way of a warning. Dowd was to bring his horse and cart to the rear of Brassey's office. Kilfoyle was charged with the task of creating a diversion by burning down Aubrey Filton's office. When all the attention was fixed on that, Shannon himself would start a fire in the contractor's office.

Mulryne was baffled. 'What do *I* do, Pierce?' he asked.

'The most difficult job of all,' said Shannon.

'And what's that?'

'Lifting the safe on to the wheelbarrow that Tim will bring.'

'Oh, that's easily done.'

'It won't be,' warned Kilfoyle. 'I've seen it. That safe will be a ton weight, Brendan.'

'I'll manage it,' boasted Mulryne. 'If it's full of money, I'll make sure that I do. Though it'd be a lot bleeding quicker if we blow open the safe there and then. We can just grab the money and run.'

'That's too dangerous,' said Shannon. 'You can't control an explosion. Besides, we've no more gunpowder left. It's far better to steal the safe and take it away on the cart. By the time they discover it's gone, we'll be miles away.'

'Counting out our share of the money,' said Kilfoyle.

'I'll do that, Liam. You only get what I give you.'

'That's fair,' agreed Mulryne. 'Pierce has done all the hard work, planning everything. It's only right that he should get a little more than the rest of us.'

Shannon looked around them. 'Are we all ready, lads?'

'Yes,' they replied in unison.

'Then let's kill this railway line once and for all!'

* * *

Robert Colbeck had been rescued at the last moment. The information passed on by the French barmaid had persuaded Superintendent Tallis to stay for one more day. He accepted that it might, after all, be possible to catch the men who had caused so much disruption on the railway and, in doing so, discover who their English paymaster was. Along with Thomas Brassey and a group of his most trusted men, Tallis was in hiding not far from the contractor's office. All but Brassey were armed with cudgels or guns. Nobody expected that the Irishmen would give up without a fight.

Determined to be at the heart of the action, Colbeck had put on an old coat and hat so that he could replace the nightwatchman who normally patrolled the area. He carried a lantern in one hand and a stout wooden club in the other. He followed the identical routine as his predecessor so that it would look as if the same man were on duty. When the raid came, he knew, it would take place when he was at the farthest point from the designated target. The first hint of trouble came when he heard a horse and cart approaching. At that time of night, all the drivers should have been fast asleep while their horses were resting in their makeshift stables. Pretending to hear nothing, Colbeck turned away from Brassey's office and began a long, slow, methodical walk to the edge of the camp.

The attack was imminent. He sensed it. As soon as he reached the outer limit of his patrol, therefore, he did not amble back at the same pace. Blowing out his lantern, he ran back towards the office in the dark. Colbeck did not want to miss out on the action.

Everything seemed to have gone to plan. Murphy's whistle told them that the nightwatchman was some distance away from the office. Dowd's horse and cart were in position and he had trundled the wheelbarrow up to the others. Shannon gave the signal, smacking Kilfoyle on the back so that the latter went off to stand by Filton's office, then leading Mulryne and Dowd towards their target. The door of the office had two padlocks on it but Shannon soon disposed of them with his jemmy, levering them off within seconds before prising the door open. Holding a lantern, he went across to the safe. Mulryne followed and Dowd came in with the wheelbarrow.

'Jesus!' said Dowd when he saw the size of the safe. 'I'll never be able to wheel that bloody thing away.'

'Leave it to Brendan,' said Shannon. 'That's why he's here.'

Mulryne bent down and got a firm grip on the safe. When he felt its weight, he lifted it an inch off the floor before putting it down again. He spat on both hands then rubbed them together.

'This is not really heavy,' he boasted. 'Hold up that lantern, will you, Pierce? I need all the light I can get.'

Shannon responded, lifting the lantern up until his whole face was illumined. Mulryne seized his moment. Pulling back his arm, he threw a fearsome punch that connected with Shannon's chin and sent him reeling back. He was unconscious before he hit the floor. Coming into the office, Colbeck had to step over the body. It took Dowd only a moment to realise that they had been duped. Escape was essential. Running at Colbeck, he tried to buffet him aside but the detective was ready for him. He dodged the blow and used his club to jab the man in the stomach. As he doubled up, Colbeck hit him in the face and made him stagger backwards into Mulryne's bear hug.

'Timothy Dowd,' said Mulryne, lapsing back into his days as a constable, 'I'm arresting you on a charge of attempted burglary.'

'You double-crossing bastard!' howled Dowd.

But it was the last thing he was able to say because Mulryne tightened his hold and squeezed all the breath out of him. Kilfoyle came running to see what had caused all the commotion. When he burst in, he almost tripped over Shannon's body.

'What happened to Pierce?' he demanded, bending over his friend. 'Who hit him?'

'I did,' replied Mulryne, triumphantly. 'He'll be out for ages, Liam. I caught him a beauty.'

Kilfoyle let out a roar of anger and pulled out a knife. Before he could move towards Mulryne, however, Colbeck stepped out to block his way. Kilfoyle waved his knife threateningly.

'Who the hell are you?'

'The man who's here to disarm you,' said Colbeck, hitting him on the wrist with his club and making him drop his weapon. 'You must be Liam Kilfoyle.'

'What of it it?'

'I'm a friend of Victor Leeming.'

'That dirty, treacherous, lying turd!'

'He asked me to pass on a message,' said Colbeck, tossing the club aside so that he could use his fists. 'Attacking people from behind is unfair. This is how you should do it.'

He pummelled away at Kilfoyle's face and body, forcing him back by the sheer power of his attack. The Irishman tried to fight back at first but he was soon using both hands to protect himself. When Colbeck caught him on the nose, Kilfoyle stumbled back into the arms of Superintendent Tallis as the latter came into the office.

'Have we got them all?' asked Tallis, holding his man tight.

'Hello there, sir,' said Mulryne, effusively, as if encountering a favourite long-lost relative. 'How wonderful it is to see you again, Superintendent, even if it is on foreign soil. Forgive me if I don't shake hands but Timothy here needs holding.'

'How many of you were there, Brendan?' said Colbeck.

'Five, including me.'

'We've three of them here – that leaves one.'

'He was caught as well,' said Tallis. 'We've got the whole gang.'

'And you saved me the trouble of trying to pick up this bleeding safe,' said Mulryne, giving it a kick. 'It weighs three ton at least.'

'It shouldn't.' Colbeck picked up the fallen lantern and walked across to the safe. He opened the door to show that it was completely empty. 'Thanks to your warning, Brendan, we took the precaution of removing everything of value out of it.'

The interrogation took place in Thomas Brassey's office. It was obvious that Kilfoyle, Dowd and Murphy had no idea who had sponsored their work from England. They were mere underlings who obeyed orders from Pierce Shannon. Accordingly, the three of them were taken away and held in custody. On the following morning, they would be handed over to the French police. Shannon sat in a circle of light provided by a number of oil lamps. Colbeck and Mulryne were present but it was Edward Tallis who insisted on interrogating their prisoner. Hands behind his back, he stood over Shannon.

'Who paid you?' he asked.

'Nobody,' replied the other, rubbing his aching jaw.

'Don't lie to me. Somebody suborned you. Somebody told you to bring this railway to a halt. Who was it?'

'Nobody.'

'So you did everything of your own volition, did you?'

'What's that mean?'

'That it was all your own idea, Pierce,' explained Mulryne.

'Yes, that's right.'

'So why did you do it?' said Tallis.

Shannon gave a defiant grin. 'Fun.'

'Fun? Is it your notion of fun to cause extensive damage to the property of the man who is employing you? Is it your notion of fun to put the thousands of men on this site out of work?'

'Yes.'

'He's a bleeding liar, sir,' said Mulryne.

'Keep out of this,' ordered Tallis.

'But I know the truth. Liam told me. That's Liam Kilfoyle. He's the scrawny one that fell into your arms like an amorous woman when you came in here. Liam reckons this man met up with Pierce and offered him money to wreck this railway – a lot of money. Enough to let them all retire.'

'And who was this man?'

'Liam didn't know.' He pointed at Shannon. 'But he does.'

'Shut your gob!' snarled Shannon.

Mulryne laughed. 'Compliments pass when the quality meet.'

'If I'd known you were a dirty traitor, I'd have killed you.'

'You're in no position to kill anyone,' Tallis reminded him. 'Now stop playing games and answer my questions. Who paid you and why did he want this railway to be abandoned? He's the man who dragged you into all this? Do you want him to get off scot-free?'

'Yes,' said Shannon.

'Who *paid* you, man?'

'Nobody.'

'Tell me, damn you!'

'I just did.'

'Give me a name.'

'Pierce Shannon. Would you like another? Queen Victoria.'

'I'd like you to tell me the truth.'

'I have.'

'Who is behind all this?'

'Nobody.'

Shannon was beginning to enjoy the situation. Resentful at being caught, and infuriated by Mulryne's part in his capture, he was at least getting some pleasure out of frustrating Tallis. No matter how hard the superintendent pressed him, he would volunteer nothing that could be remotely helpful. Tallis kept firing questions at him with growing vexation. Eventually, Colbeck stepped in.

'Perhaps I could take over, sir,' he suggested.

'It's like trying to get blood from a stone,' said Tallis.

'Then let me relieve you.'

'If you wish.'

Tallis withdrew reluctantly to a corner of the room and watched.

Colbeck brought a chair and placed it directly in front of Shannon. He sat down so that he was very close to him.

'When I first came to France,' he told Shannon, 'I brought my assistant with me – Sergeant Victor Leeming.'

'I knew he was a bleeding copper,' said the other with derision. 'I could smell him. I enjoyed beating him up.'

'I'm glad you mention beating someone up because that's the subject I was just about to raise with you. Would you describe your friends – Kilfoyle, Dowd and Murphy – as violent men?'

'They're Irish – they like a decent brawl.'

'The same goes for me,' said Mulryne, happily.

'I'm only interested in Mr Shannon's friends,' said Colbeck.

'At least, they're his friends at the moment. That, of course, may not last.'

Shannon was guarded. 'What are you on about?'

'The contents of your pockets.'

'Eh?'

'When we searched you earlier, you were carrying a large amount of money. A very large amount, as it happens. Where did it come from, Mr Shannon?'

'That's my business.'

'No,' said Colbeck, 'it's our business as well. And it's certainly the business of your three friends. We searched them as well, you see, and they had substantially less money on them. Even allowing for the fact that they had spent some of it on drink, they were clearly paid far less than you for any work that they did.' He turned to Mulryne. 'How much were you paid for tipping over those wagons?'

'A week's wages,' replied Mulryne.

'Mr Shannon had over two years' wages in his pocket, Brendan. Unless, that is, Mr Brassey has been particularly philanthropic. What this all indicates to me is that one person held on to most of the money he'd been paid while the other three were deprived of their fair share. That's robbery. What do you think the others would do to Mr Shannon if they knew the truth?'

'Break every bleeding bone in his body, Inspector.'

'That's the least they'd do, I should imagine.'

'I earned that money,' insisted Shannon. 'I had the brains to plan things. The others are all boneheads.'

'I'll pass on that charming description of their mental powers when I talk to them,' said Colbeck, smoothly, 'and I must thank you for admitting that you were, after all, paid by someone else.' He flicked a glance at Tallis. 'Our first trickle of blood from the stone.'

Shannon sat up. 'I'm not saying another word.'

'Then you're throwing away any hope of defending yourself. When we hand you over to the French police, you'll be charged under their law and in their language. When you get into court,' Colbeck went on, 'you won't understand a single word of what's going on so you'll be unable to offer anything by way of mitigation.'

'What's that?'

'It's a way of shortening the sentence you're likely to get. If you claim – as you did earlier – that everything that happened was your idea, then you'll face several years in prison. If, on the other hand, you were simply obeying someone else's orders – and if you tell us who that someone is – your sentence might be less severe. In fact, I'd make a point of telling the French police how helpful you've been.'

'And he'd tell them in French,' said Mulryne, proudly. 'He speaks the lingo. Doesn't he, Superintendent?'

'Yes,' said Tallis.

'What about you, sir? Do you speak French?'

'I'd never let it soil my lips.'

'To sum up,' said Colbeck, bestowing a bland smile on Shannon, 'it's a pity that you've elected to hold your tongue. You might need it to plead for mercy when we lock you up with your friends and tell them about the monetary arrangements you decided upon. When you get to court, however,' he went on, 'you can talk all you like to no effect because they won't bother to hire interpreters for someone who was caught red-handed committing a crime. Expect a long sentence, Mr Shannon – after your friends have finished with you, that is.' He stood up. 'Let's take him over there, Brendan.'

'With pleasure,' said Mulryne.

'Wait!' cried Shannon, as they each laid a hand on him. 'There *was* someone who put us up to this.'

'Now we're getting somewhere,' said Colbeck.

'But I don't know his name.'

'Do you expect us to believe that?'

'It's true, Inspector – I'd swear on the frigging gospel.'

'There's no need for blasphemy!' shouted Tallis. 'Keep a civil tongue in your head.'

'You must have known who this man was,' said Colbeck. 'How did he get in touch with you in the first place?'

'I was in a police cell,' admitted Shannon. 'Only for a week or so. There was an affray at a tavern in Limehouse and I got caught up in it by mistake. Anyway, this man read about it in the paper and saw that I was a navvy. He came to see me and asked me if I'd ever worked for Tom Brassey. That's how it all started.'

'Go on,' invited Colbeck.

'He tested me out then decided I might be his man.'

'What name did he give?'

'None at all,' said Shannon, 'but I did hear one of the coppers calling him "Luke"—you know, as if they were friends. I called him by that name once and he swore blue murder at me.'

'How did he pay you?'

'He waited until I'd got a job with Mr Brassey and settled in here. Then he told me what to do first so that I could prove myself. Once I'd done that,' said Shannon, 'he paid me the first half of the money so that I'd have enough to take on people I could trust.'

'And cheat easily,' said Mulryne.

'It's their own bleeding fault for being so stupid.'

Colbeck's ears pricked up. 'You say that you had the first

half of the money?' Shannon nodded. 'When would you get the other half?'

'When we brought the railway to a standstill.'

'But how would you get in touch with Luke?'

'He gave me an address in London,' said Shannon. 'I was to leave a message there, saying what we'd done. Once he could confirm it, he promised to leave the second half of the money for me to collect it. And – as God's my witness – that's the truth!'

'We'll need that address,' said Colbeck.

'As long as you don't tell the others about the money.'

'We don't bargain with criminals,' said Tallis.

'It's a reasonable request, sir,' Colbeck pointed out, 'and, now that he appreciates the predicament that he's in, Mr Shannon has been admirably cooperative. Some reward is in order, I believe.'

'Thanks,' said Shannon with great relief.

'We'll need that address, mind you.'

'I'll give it to you, Inspector.'

'There you are, Superintendent,' said Mulryne, hands on his hips. 'You should have let the Inspector question him from the start. He's a genius at getting blood from a bleeding stone.'

Luke Rogan was working in his office when he heard the doorbell ring insistently. He looked out of the front window to see Sir Marcus Hetherington standing there while a cab waited for him at the kerb. Rogan was surprised. The only place they ever met was in the privacy of the Reform Club. If he had come to the office, Sir Marcus must have something of prime importance to discuss. Rogan hurried along the passageway and opened the door. Sweeping in without a word, Sir Marcus went into the office and waited for Rogan to join him.

'What's the matter, Sir Marcus?' asked Rogan.

'This,' said the other, thrusting a newspaper at him. 'This is what is the matter, Rogan. Look at the second page.'

'Why?'

'Just do as I say.'

'Very well, Sir Marcus.'

Rogan opened the newspaper and scanned the second page. He soon realised why his visitor had come. What he was looking at was a report of the arrest of four men who were accused of trying to disrupt work on the railway that was being built between Mantes and Caen. Rogan recognised one of the names – that of Pierce Shannon – and assumed that the others were his accomplices. The name that really jumped up at him, however, was not that of the prisoners but of the man who had helped to capture them.

'Inspector Colbeck!' he gasped.

'Read the last paragraph,' instructed Sir Marcus. 'The much-vaunted Railway Detective believes that he now has evidence that will lead him to the person or persons responsible for the murder of Gaston Chabal. In short,' he said, hitting the top of the desk hard with his cane, 'evidence that points to you and me.'

'But that's impossible!'

'So you assured me.'

'Shannon didn't even know my name.'

'He's obviously told them enough to steer them towards you.'

'He couldn't have, Sir Marcus.'

'Then how do you explain this report?'

'Colbeck is bluffing,' said Rogan, trying to convince himself. 'He's done this before. He pretends to be in possession of more information than he really has in the hope of making someone fly into a panic and give themselves away.'

'The newspaper certainly gave me a sense of panic,' confessed Sir Marcus. 'My wife thought I was having a heart attack when I read that – and I almost did.'

'He knows *nothing*, Sir Marcus.'

'Then how did he manage to arrest four men in France?'

'Pure luck.'

'Colbeck never relies on luck. He believes in a combination of tenacity and cold logic. He's been quoted to that effect more than once. I do not want his tenacity and logic to lead him to me.'

'That's out of the question, Sir Marcus.'

'Is it?'

'I'm the only person that knows you were my client.'

'Do you keep records?' asked the other, glancing down at the desk. 'Do you have an account book with my name in it?'

'Of course not. I know how to be discreet.'

'I hope so, Rogan.'

'Colbeck will not get within a mile of us.'

'What can he possibly have found out?'

'Nothing of value.'

'He must have squeezed something out of those Irishmen.'

'Shannon was the only one I had dealings with. The others don't even know that I exist. And all that Shannon can do is to give them a rough description of me.' Rogan showed snaggly teeth in a grin. 'That means he'd be describing thousands of men who look just like me.'

Sir Marcus relaxed slightly. He removed his top hat and sat down on a chair, resting his cane against a wall. Rogan took the unspoken hint and went to a small cupboard. Taking out a bottle of whisky, he poured two glasses and handed one to his visitor.

'Thank you,' said the old man, tasting the whisky. 'I'd hoped to toast our success but our plans have obviously gone awry.'

'We can try again at a later date, Sir Marcus.'

'This was our chance and we missed it.'

'Bide our time, that's all we have to do.'

'Until a certain detective comes knocking on our doors.'

'That will never happen,' said Rogan, airily. 'The one thing that Shannon knows is an address where he was to leave a message. Nobody at that address knows my name or where I live. It was simply a convenient way of paying Shannon the second half of his fee when his work was completed.'

'But it was not. He failed and you failed.'

Rogan was hurt. 'You can't put the blame on me.'

'You selected this idiot.'

'With the greatest of care, Sir Marcus. I asked a friend about him before I even went near him. He told me that Shannon was full of guile and quite fearless. That's the kind of man we wanted.'

'Then why has he let us down so badly?' asked Sir Marcus. 'And why is Inspector Colbeck coming back to England with such apparent confidence to hunt down Chabal's killer?'

'He's trying to frighten us.'

'He frightened me, I can tell you that.'

'You're as safe as can be, Sir Marcus,' Rogan assured him, taking a first sip of his whisky. 'So am I. London is a vast city. He could search for fifty years and still not find us. Colbeck has no idea where to start looking.'

'There's that address you gave to Shannon.'

'A dead end. It will lead him nowhere.'

'Supposing that he does pick up our scent?'

'I've told you. There's no hope of him doing that.'

'But supposing – I speak hypothetically – that he does? Colbeck has already come much farther than I believed he would so we must respect him for that. What if he gets really close?'

'Then he'll regret it,' said Rogan, coolly.

When he got back from work that evening, Caleb Andrews found a meal waiting for him. Since he had good news to impart about the murder investigation, he surrendered his paper to Madeleine and drew her attention to the relevant report. She was thrilled to read of Robert Colbeck's success in France. Her faith in him had never wavered and she had been disturbed by the harsh criticism he had received in the press. Public rebuke had now been replaced by congratulation. He was once again being hailed for his skill as a detective.

When the meal was over, Andrews was in such an ebullient mood that he challenged his daughter to a game of draughts. He soon repented of his folly. Madeleine won the first two games and had him on the defensive in the third one.

'I can't seem to beat you,' he complained.

'You were the one who taught me how to play draughts.'

'I obviously taught you too well.'

'When we first started,' she recalled, 'you won every game.'

'The only thing I seem to do now is to lose.'

He was spared a third defeat by a knock on the front door. Glad of the interruption, he was out of his chair at once. He went to the door and opened it. Robert Colbeck smiled at him.

'Good evening, Mr Andrews,' he said.

'Ah, you're back from France.'

'At long last.'

'We read about you in the paper.'

'Don't keep Robert standing out there,' said Madeleine, coming up behind her father. 'Invite him in.'

Andrews stood back so that Colbeck could enter the house, remove his hat and, under her father's watchful eye, give Madeleine a chaste kiss on the cheek. They went into the living room. The first thing that Colbeck saw was the draughts board.

'Who's winning?' he asked.

'Maddy,' replied Andrews, gloomily.

'This game was a draw, Father,' she said, eyes never leaving Colbeck. 'Oh, it's so lovely to see you again, Robert! What exactly happened in France?'

'And why did you have to solve crimes on *their* railways? Don't they have any police of their own?'

'They do, Mr Andrews,' replied Colbeck, 'but this was, in a sense, a British crime. It was almost like working over here. British contractors have built most of their railways and French locomotives are largely the work of Thomas Crampton.'

'I'm the one person you don't need to tell that to, Inspector,' said Andrews, knowledgeably. 'In fact, there are far more Cramptons in France than here in England. Lord knows why. I've driven three or four of his engines and I like them. Shall I tell you why?'

'Another time, Father,' said Madeleine.

'But the Inspector is interested in engineering, Maddy.'

'This is not the best moment to discuss it.'

'What?' Andrews looked from one to the other. 'Well, perhaps it isn't,' he said, moving away. 'Now where did I leave my tobacco pouch? It must be upstairs.' He paused at the door. 'Don't forget to show him that picture you drew of the Sankey Viaduct, Maddy.'

He went out of the room and Colbeck was able to embrace

Madeleine properly. Over her shoulder, he saw that the tobacco pouch was on the table beside the draughts. He was grateful for her father's tact. He stood back but kept hold of her hands.

'What's this about the Sankey Viaduct?'

'Oh, it was just something I sketched to pass the time,' she said. 'It's probably nothing at all like the real thing.'

'I'd be interested to see it, all the same.'

'Your work is far more important than mine, Robert. Come and sit down. Tell me what's happened since I last saw you.'

'That would take far too long,' he said, as they sat beside each other on the sofa. 'I'll give you a shortened version.'

He told her about his visit to Paris and his long conversation with Gaston Chabal's mother-in-law. Madeleine was startled by the revelation that the engineer appeared to have seduced another woman for the sole purpose of gaining an additional investor in the railway. She was fascinated to hear of Brendan Mulryne's success as a spy and pleased that Superintendent Tallis had been forced to admit that the Irishman had performed a valuable service.

'Mr Tallis couldn't actually bring himself to thank Brendan in person,' said Colbeck. 'That would have been asking too much. What he did concede was that the notion of putting an informer into the ranks of the navvies had, after all, been a sensible one.'

'Coming from the superintendent, that's high praise.'

'I pointed out that Brendan Mulryne would be an asset if he were allowed to rejoin the police force but Mr Tallis would not hear of it. He'd sooner recruit a tribe of cannibals.'

'Why is he so critical of your methods?'

'There's always been a degree of animus between us.'

'Is he envious of you?'

'It's more a case of disapproval, Madeleine.'

'How could he possibly disapprove of a man with your record?'

'Quite easily,' said Colbeck with a grin. 'Mr Tallis doesn't like the way I dress, the approach I take to any case and the readiness I have to use people such as Brendan Mulryne. Also, I'm afraid to say, he looks askance at my private life.'

She gave a laugh of surprise. 'Your private life!'

'He thinks that you're leading me astray.'

'Me?'

'I was only joking, Madeleine,' he said, putting an arm around her. 'The truth is that Superintendent Tallis doesn't believe that his detectives should *have* a private life. He thinks that we should be like him – unattached and therefore able to devote every waking hour to our job with no distractions.'

'Is that what I am – a distraction?'

'Yes – thank heaven!' He kissed her on the lips. 'Now, let's see this drawing of the Sankey Viaduct.'

'You won't like it, Robert.'

'Why not?'

'It's too fanciful.'

'I love anything that you do, Madeleine,' he said, warmly. 'And it must be worth seeing if your father recommends it.'

'He only saw an earlier version.'

'Please fetch it.'

'I'm not sure that I should.'

'Why are you being so bashful? I really want to see it.'

'If you wish,' she said, getting up, 'but you must remember that it's a work of imagination. It has no resemblance to the real viaduct.' She crossed the room to pick up a portfolio that rested in an alcove. Opening it up, she selected a drawing. 'It was simply a way of keeping you in my mind while you were in France.'

'Then I must have a look at it.'

Colbeck rose to his feet and took the sketch from her hand. He was intrigued. The viaduct dominated the page, but what gave him a sudden thrill of recognition was the way that it connected England and France. It was like a bridge across a wide gulf. He let out a cry of joy and hugged her to him. Madeleine was mystified.

'What have I done to deserve that?' she said.

'You've just solved a murder!'

CHAPTER TWELVE

Victor Leeming was thoroughly delighted when Colbeck called on him that morning. Simply seeing the inspector again was a tonic to him. Time had been hanging with undue heaviness on his hands and he desperately missed being involved in the murder investigation. He felt that he was letting the inspector down. They sat down together in the cramped living room of Leeming's house. He listened attentively to the recitation of events that had taken place in France, only interrupting when a certain name was mentioned.

'Brendan Mulryne?'

'Yes, Victor.'

'There was no reference to him in the newspapers.'

'Mr Tallis made sure of that,' said Colbeck. 'He refused to give any public acknowledgement to Brendan because he felt that it would demean us if we admitted any reliance on people like him. As it happens, I would have kept his name secret for another reason.'

'What's that, Inspector?'

'I may want to employ him again. If his name and description are plastered all over the newspapers, it would make that difficult. He needs to be kept anonymous.'

'I'm not sure that I'd have used him at all,' admitted Leeming.

'That's why I didn't discuss the matter with you.'

'I like Mulryne – he's good company – but I'd never trust him with anything important. He's likely to go off the rails.'

Colbeck smiled. 'In this case,' he pointed out, 'he did the exact opposite. Instead of going off the rails, he kept Mr Brassey on them. Largely because of what Brendan did, the railway can still be built.'

'Then I congratulate him.'

'You have a reason to thank him as well, Victor.'

'Do I?'

'One of the men who gave you the beating was Pierce Shannon.'

'I'm not surprised to hear it. He was a sly character.'

'Brendan laid him out cold on your behalf.'

'I wish I'd been there to do it myself,' said Leeming, grimly.

'The other man who attacked you was Liam Kilfoyle.'

'Liam? And I thought he was a friend of mine!'

'Not any more,' said Colbeck. 'I had the pleasure of exchanging a few blows with Mr Kilfoyle. I let him know what I felt about people who assaulted my sergeant.'

'Thank you, sir.'

Colbeck told him about the capture of the villains and how they had been handed over to the French police the next day. Thomas Brassey and Aubrey Filton had been overwhelmed with gratitude. The second visit to France had been eventful. Colbeck felt satisfied.

'So that part of the investigation is now concluded,' he said. 'What comes next?'

'The small matter of tracking down the killer.'

'Do you have any clues, Inspector?'

'Yes, Victor. One of them came from the most unexpected source, but that's often the way with police work. And I'm a great believer in serendipity.'

Leeming was honest. 'So would I be, if I knew what it meant.'

'Picking up a good thing where you find it.'

'Ah, I see. A bit like beachcombing.'

'Not really,' said Colbeck. 'Beachcombing implies that you deliberately go in search of something. Serendipity depends entirely on chance. You might not even be looking for a particular clue until you stumble upon it in the most unlikely place.'

'Serendipity. I'll remember that word. It will impress Estelle.'

'How is your wife?'

'She's been a tower of strength, sir.'

'Happy to have you at home so much, I should imagine.'

'Yes and no,' said Leeming, sucking in air through his teeth. 'Estelle is happy to have me here but not when I'm convalescing. She'd like more of a husband and a bit less of a patient.'

'You seem to be recovering well.'

Leeming's facial scars had almost disappeared now and the heavy bruising on his body had also faded. What remained were the cracked ribs that occasionally reminded him that they were there by causing a spasm of pain. He refused to give in to his injuries.

'I'm as fit as a fiddle, sir,' he said, cheerily. 'But for the doctor, I'd be back at work right now.'

'Doctors usually know best.'

'It's so boring and wasteful, sitting at home here.'

'Do you get out at all?'

'Every day, Inspector. I have a long walk and I sometimes

take the children to the park. I can get about quite easily.'

'That's good news. We look forward to having you back.'

'I can't wait,' said Leeming. 'Much as I love Estelle and the children, I do hate being unemployed. It feels wrong somehow. I'm not a man who can rest, sir. I like action.'

'You had rather too much of it in France.'

'I like to think that I helped.'

'You did, Victor,' said Colbeck. 'You did indeed.'

'Mind you, I couldn't make a living as a navvy. A week of that kind of work would have finished me off. They earn their money.'

'Unfortunately, some of them tried to earn it by other means.'

'Yes,' said the other with feeling. 'Shannon and his friends were too greedy. They wanted more than Mr Brassey could ever pay them. Pierce Shannon always had an ambitious streak. It's a pity you got so little out of him when you questioned him.'

'That's not true.'

'He couldn't even tell you the name of the man who paid him.'

'Oh, I think that he gave us a lot more information than he realised,' said Colbeck. 'To begin with, we now know how he and his paymaster first met.'

'In a police cell.'

'What does that tell you?'

'Nothing that I couldn't have guessed about Shannon, sir. He got involved in a brawl and was arrested for disturbing the peace. Men like that always get into trouble when they've had a few drinks.' He cleared his throat. 'I'm bound to point out that the same thing happened to Brendan Mulryne after he'd left the police force.'

'He might not be the only policeman that we lost.'

'I don't think that Shannon was ever in uniform, sir.'

'What about the man who employed him?'

'We know nothing whatsoever about the fellow.'

'Yes, we do,' said Colbeck. 'We know that he's able to talk to someone in a police cell, which means that he's either a lawyer, a policeman or someone who used to be involved in law enforcement. I'd hazard a guess that he has friends in the police force, or he'd not have been given such easy access to a prisoner. Also, of course, we do have his Christian name.'

'Luke.'

'You can find out the rest when you get there.'

'Where?'

'To the station where Pierce Shannon was detained.'

Leeming was taken aback. 'You want *me* to do that, sir?'

'You enjoy a long walk, don't you?'

'Yes.'

'And you're chafing at the bit while you're sitting here.'

'I am, Inspector – that's the plain truth.'

'Then you can return to light duties immediately.' His grin was conspiratorial. 'Provided that you don't mention the fact to Mr Tallis, that is. He might not understand. He has a preference for making all operational decisions himself.'

'I won't breathe a single word to him.'

'Not even serendipity?'

'I'm saving that one for my wife.'

'Does that mean you're willing to help us, Victor?'

Leeming struggled to his feet. 'I'm on my way, sir.'

They noticed the difference at once. It was as if a threatening black cloud that had been hanging over the site had suddenly dispersed to let bright sunshine through. In fact, it was raining that morning but nothing could dampen their spirits or that of the navvies. Hectic activity was continuing apace. They were now certain to complete the stipulated amount of work on the railway by the end of the month. The sudden and dramatic improvement made Aubrey Filton blossom into an unaccustomed smile.

'This is how it should be, Mr Brassey,' he said. 'Now that we've got rid of the rotten apples from the barrel, we can surge ahead.'

'Word spread quickly. When they heard about the arrests, the men were as relieved as we were. And you can't blame them,' said Brassey, reasonably. 'If work had ground to a halt here, I'd have been in danger of losing the contract. Thousands of them would have been thrown out of work. Their livelihoods have been saved.'

'And your reputation has been vindicated.'

'I care more about them than about me, Aubrey.'

'You treat them like members of a huge family.'

'That's exactly what they are.'

They were at the window, gazing out at sodden navvies who laboured away as if impervious to rain. There was a new spirit about the way everyone was working. It was almost as if the many wanted to atone for the dire shortcomings of the few by demonstrating their commitment to the project. Eamonn Slattery had noticed it. The priest was standing between the two men.

'Look at them,' he said with pride. 'There's not a navvy alive who can match an Irishman when it comes to hard physical work. The Potato Famine nearly crippled our beloved country but it was a blessing to someone like you, Mr Brassey.'

'I agree, Father Slattery,' conceded the other. 'A lot of the men here emigrated from Ireland. I was glad to take them on. What's the feeling among them now?'

'Oh, they reacted with a mixture of thanks and outrage.'

'Inspector Colbeck deserves most of the thanks.'

'So I hear,' said Slattery with a cackle. 'And there was me, thinking that dandy was working for the Minister of Public Works. He took me in completely but, then, so did Brendan Mulryne.'

'He's the real hero here,' opined Filton.

'The others will miss him. He made himself very popular. Well, there's one good thing to come out of all this.'

'And what's that, Father?'

'I can count on a decent congregation on Sunday,' explained the priest with a grin. 'It's strange how adversity turns a man's mind to religion. They know how close they came to losing their jobs. A lot of them will get down on their knees to send up a prayer of thanks. I'll make the most of it and preach a sermon that will sing in their ears for a week. By next Sunday,' he added, philosophically, 'most of them won't come anywhere near the service.'

'Were you surprised to find out who was trying to disrupt the railway?' asked Brassey.

'I'd always suspected that Shannon might have something to do with it. He was the type. Kilfoyle disappointed me. I thought that Liam would have more sense.'

'What about the other two men?'

'Dowd and Murphy? Weak characters. Easily lead.'

'They'll get no mercy in court,' predicted Brassey. 'This railway has the backing of Louis Napoleon and his government. Anyone who tries to bring it to a halt will be hit with the full weight of the law.'

'The whole sad business is finally over,' said Slattery. 'I think that we ought to console ourselves with that thought.'

'But it isn't over yet.'

'No,' said Filton. 'The murder of Gaston Chabal has still

to be solved. What happened here was entangled with that, Father Slattery.'

'How?'

'The only person who knows that is Inspector Colbeck.'

'Does he know the name of the killer?'

'He will do before long.'

'You sound very confident of that, Mr Filton.'

'He's an astonishing man.'

'It was an education to see him at work,' said Brassey. 'In his own way, Inspector Colbeck reminded me of Gaston. Both share the same passion for detail. They are utterly meticulous. That's why I know that he'll apprehend the killer in due course, Father Slattery.'

'More power to his elbow!'

'The inspector is tireless,' said Filton.

'Yes,' confirmed Brassey. 'His energy is remarkable. Even as we speak, the hunt is continuing with a vengeance.'

Robert Colbeck did not like him. The moment he set eyes on Gerald Kane, he felt an instant aversion. Kane was a short, neat, vain, conservatively dressed, fussy man in his forties, with long brown hair and a thick moustache. His deep-set eyes peered at the newcomer through wire-framed spectacles. His manner was officious and unwelcoming. Even after he had introduced himself, Colbeck was viewed with a mingled suspicion and distaste.

'Why are you bothering me, Inspector?' asked Kane, huffily. 'As far as I'm aware, we have broken no laws.'

'None at all, sir.'

'Then I'll ask you to be brief. I'm a busy man.'

'So am I.'

'In that case, we'll both profit from brevity.'

'This cannot be rushed, Mr Kane,' warned Colbeck.

'It will have to be, sir. I have a meeting.'

'Postpone it – for his sake.'

'Whom are you talking about?'

'Gaston Chabal.'

Gerald Kane raised his eyebrows in surprise, but the name did not encourage him to adopt a more friendly tone. He simply treated his visitor to a hostile stare across his desk. They were in his office, a place that was as cold, ordered and impeccably clean as the man himself. Everything on the leather top of the desk was in a tidy pile. All the pictures on the walls had been hung at identical heights. Kane was the secretary of the Society of Civil and Mechanical Engineers and he seemed to look upon his post as a major office of state. He sounded an almost imperious note.

'What about him, Inspector?' he said.

'I believe that you wrote to him, sir.'

'I don't see why that should concern you. Any correspondence in which I am engaged is highly confidential.'

'Not when one of the recipients of your letters is murdered.'

'I'm well aware of what happened to Chabal,' said Kane without the slightest gesture towards sympathy. 'It's caused me no little inconvenience.'

'He did not get himself killed in order to inconvenience you,' said Colbeck, sharply. 'Since you wrote to invite him to lecture here, you might show some interest in helping to solve the crime.'

'That is your job, Inspector. Leave me to do mine.'

'I will, sir – when I have finished.'

Kane looked at his watch. 'And when, pray, will that be?'

'When I tell you, sir.'

'You cannot keep me here against my will.'

'I quite agree,' said Colbeck, moving to the door. 'This is not the best place for an interview. Perhaps you'd be so good as to accompany me to Scotland Yard where we can talk at more leisure.'

'I'm not leaving this building,' protested Kane. 'I have work to do. You obviously don't realise who I am, Inspector.'

'You're a man who is wilfully concealing evidence from the police, sir, and that is a criminal offence. If you will not come with me voluntarily, I will have to arrest you.'

'But I *have* no evidence.'

'That's for me to decide.'

'This is disgraceful. I shall complain to the commissioner.'

Colbeck opened the door. 'I'll make sure that he visits you in your cell, sir,' he said, levelly. 'Shall we go?'

Gerald Kane got to his feet. After frothing impotently for a couple of minutes, he finally capitulated. Dropping back into his chair, he waved a hand in surrender.

'Close that door,' he suggested, 'and take a seat.'

'Thank you, sir,' said Colbeck, doing as he was told. 'I knew that you'd see the wisdom of cooperating with us. The situation is this. When I was in Mantes recently, I went through Chabal's effects and found a letter written by you. Since it invited him to give a second lecture, I take it that you organised his earlier visit.'

'I did. It's one of my many duties.'

'Where did the earlier lecture take place?'

'Right here, Inspector. We have a large room for such meetings. My colleagues are sitting in it at this very moment,' he went on with a meaningful glint, 'awaiting my arrival for an important discussion.'

'Engineers are patient men, sir. Forget them.'

'They will wonder where I am.'

'Then it will give them something to talk about,' said Colbeck, easily. 'Now, sir, can you tell me why you invited Chabal here?'

'He was a coming man.'

'Do we not have enough able engineers in England?'

'Of course,' replied Kane, 'but this fellow was quite exceptional. Thomas Brassey recommended him. That was how he came to my notice. Gaston Chabal had enormous promise.'

'His lecture was obviously well-received.'

'We had several requests for him to come back.'

'Could you tell me the date of his visit to you?'

'It was in spring, Inspector – April 10th, to be exact.'

'You have a good memory.'

'That's essential in my job.'

'Then I'll take advantage of it again, if I may,' said Colbeck. 'Can you recall how many people attended the lecture? Just give me an approximate number.'

'I represent civil and mechanical engineers,' declared the other, loftily. 'Accuracy is all to us. We do not deal in approximates but in exact measurements. When he first spoke here, Gaston Chabal had ninety-four people in the audience – excluding myself, naturally. As the secretary of the Society, I was here as a matter of course.'

'Were the others all exclusively engineers?'

'No, Inspector. The audience contained various parties.'

'Such as?'

'People with a vested interest in railways. We had directors of certain railway companies as well as potential investors in the Mantes to Caen project. Mr Brassey, alas, was not here but Chabal was a fine ambassador for him.'

'Ninety-four people.'

'Ninety-five, if you add me.'

'I would not dream of eliminating you, Mr Kane,' said Colbeck. 'With your permission, I'd like to plunder that famous memory of yours one last time. How many of those who attended do you recall?'

'I could give you every single name.'

Colbeck was impressed. 'You can remember *all* of them?'

'No, Inspector,' said Kane, opening a drawer to take something out. 'I kept a record. If I'd secured Chabal's services again, I intended to write to everyone on this list to advise them of his return.' He held out a sheet of paper. 'Would you care to see it?'

Colbeck decided he might grow to like Gerald Kane, after all.

Victor Leeming was so pleased to be taking part in the investigation again that he forgot the nagging twinge in his ribs as he walked along. It took him some time to reach his destination. He had been sent to the police station that was responsible for Limehouse and adjoining districts. Close to the river, it was a bustling community that was favoured by sailors and fishermen. Limehouse had taken its name centuries earlier from the lime kilns that stood there when plentiful supplies of chalk could be brought in from Kent. It was the docks that now gave the area its characteristic flavour and its central feature.

When his nostrils first picked up the potent smell of fresh fish, Leeming inhaled deeply and thankfully. The bracing aroma helped to mask the compound of unpleasant odours that had been attacking his nose and making him retch. Streets were coated with grime and soiled with animal excrement and other refuse. Soap works and a leather tannery gave off the most revolting stench. Unrelenting noise seemed to come from every direction. Leeming saw signs of hideous poverty. He could almost taste the misery in some places. Limehouse was an assault on his sensibilities. He was grateful when he reached the police station and let himself in.

A burly sergeant sat behind a high desk, polishing the brass buttons on his uniform with a handkerchief. A half-eaten sandwich lay before him. He looked at his visitor with disdain until the latter introduced himself.

'Oh, I'm sorry, sir,' he said, putting the sandwich quickly into the desk and brushing crumbs from his thighs. 'I didn't realise that you were from the Detective Department.'

'Who am I speaking to?' asked Leeming.

'Sergeant Ryall, sir. Sergeant Peter Ryall.'

'How long have you been at this station?'

'Nigh on seven years, sir.'

'Then you should be able to help us.'

'We're always ready to help Scotland Yard.'

Ryall gave him a token smile. His face had been pitted by years of police service and his red cheeks and nose revealed where he had sought solace from the cares of his occupation. But his manner was amiable and his deference unfeigned. Leeming did not criticise him for eating food while on duty. Having worked in a police station himself, he knew how such places induced an almost permanent hunger.

'I want to ask about a man you kept in custody here,' he said.

'What was his name?'

'Pierce Shannon.'

Ryall racked his brains. 'Don't remember him,' he said at length. 'Irish, I take it?'

'Very Irish.'

'Hundreds of them pass through our cells.' He lifted the lid of the desk and took out a thick ledger. 'When was he here?'

'A couple of months ago, at a guess,' said Leeming. 'When he left here, he went to France to help build a railway.' Ryall began to flick through the pages of his ledger. 'The person I'm really hoping to find is a man who visited Shannon in his cell while he was here.'

'A lawyer?'

'No – a friend.'

'We don't keep a record of visitors, Sergeant Leeming.'

'I was hoping that someone here might recall him. If he was a stranger, he'd have no authority to interview the prisoner in his cell. You'd not have let him past you.'

'That, I wouldn't,' said Ryall, stoutly.

'So how was he able to get so close to Shannon?'

'One thing at a time, sir. Let me locate the prisoner first.' He ran his finger down a list of names. 'I've a Mike Shannon here. He was arrested for forgery in June.'

'That's not him. This man was involved in a brawl.'

'Pat Shannon?' offered the other, spotting another name. 'We locked him up for starting a fight in the market. What age would your fellow be?'

'In this thirties.'

'Then it's not Pat Shannon. He was much older.' He continued his search. 'It would help if you could be more exact about the date.'

'June at the earliest, I'd say.'

'Let's try the end of May, to be on the safe side.' Ryall found the relevant page and went down the list. 'It was warm weather last May. That always keeps us busy. When it's hot and sweaty, people drink more. We attended plenty of affrays that month.' His finger jabbed a name. 'Ah, here we are!'

'Have you got him?'

'I've got a Pierce Shannon. Gave his age as thirty-five.'

'That could be him. Was he involved in a brawl?'

'Yes, sir – at the Jolly Sailor. It's a tavern by the river. We have a lot of trouble there. Shannon was one of five men arrested that night but we kept him longer than the others, it seems.'

'Why?'

'He refused to pay the fine, so we hung on to him until he could be transferred to prison. Shannon was released when someone else paid up on his behalf. He was released on June 4th.'

'Do you know who paid his fine?'

'No,' said Ryall. 'None of our business. We are just glad to get rid of them. His benefactor's name would be in the court records.'

Leeming was pleased. 'Thank you,' he said. 'You've been very helpful. While he was under lock and key here, Shannon had a visit from a man whose first name was Luke. Does that ring a bell?'

'Afraid not – but, then, it wouldn't. I wasn't on duty during the time that Pierce Shannon was held here. I spent most of May at home, recovering from injuries received during the arrest of some villains.'

'You have my warmest sympathy.'

'Horace Eames would have been in charge of custody here.'

'Then he's the man I need to speak to,' decided Leeming. 'If he let Luke Whatever-His-Name-Is into one of your cells, he would have been doing so as a favour to a friend. Inspector Colbeck thinks that friend might have been a policeman himself at one time.'

Ryall closed the ledger. 'Possible, sir. I couldn't say.'

'I need to speak to Mr Eames. Is he here, by any chance?'

'No, he left the police force in July. Horace said that he wanted a change of scene. But he's not far away from here.'

'Can you give me the address, please?'

'Gladly,' said Ryall. 'You probably walked past the place to get here. It's a boatyard. Horace was apprenticed to a carpenter before he joined the police force. He was always good with his hands. That's where you'll find him – at Forrestt's boatyard.'

The shop was in a dingy street not far from Paddington Station. It sold dresses to women of limited means and haberdashery to anyone in need of it. In a large room at the back of the premises, four women worked long hours as they made new dresses or repaired old ones. The shop was owned and run by Madame Hennebeau, a descendant of one of the many French Huguenot families that had settled in the area in the previous century. Louise Hennebeau was a tall, full-bodied widow in her fifties, with a handsome face and well-groomed hair from which every trace of grey had been hounded by a ruthless black dye. Though she had been born and brought up in England, she affected a strong French accent to remind people of her heritage.

She was very surprised when Robert Colbeck entered her shop. Men seldom came to her establishment and the few who did never achieved the striking elegance of her visitor. Madame Hennebeau gave him a smile of welcome that broadened when he doffed his top hat and allowed her to see his face. Colbeck then introduced himself and she was nonplussed. She could not understand why a detective inspector should visit her shop.

'Would you prefer to talk in English or French, Madame?'

'English will be fine, sir,' she replied.

'French might be more appropriate,' he said, 'because I am investigating the murder of a gentleman called Gaston Chabal. Indeed, I have spent some time in France itself recently.'

'I still do not see why you have come to me, Inspector.'

'While I was abroad, crimes were committed on a railway line that was being built near Mantes. The men responsible have now been arrested but, had they done what they were supposed to do, they would have been richly rewarded. To get the reward,' Colbeck explained, 'the leader of the gang was told to come here.'

'Why?' she asked, gesticulating. 'This is a dress shop.'

'It's also a place where a message could be left, apparently.'

'Really?'

'For whom was that message intended?'

'I have no idea. I think there's been some mistake.'

'I doubt it. The man I questioned was very specific about this address. He even knew your name, Madam Hennebeau.'

'*How*?'

'That's what I'd like you to tell me.'

Waving her arms excitedly, she went off into a long, breathy defence of herself and her business, assuring him that she had always been very law-abiding and that she had no connection whatsoever with any crimes committed in France. Her righteous indignation was genuine enough but Colbeck still sensed that she was holding something back from him. He stopped her with a raised hand.

'Madame Hennebeau,' he said, politely, 'you obviously did not hear what I said at the start of the conversation. My visit here concerns a murder investigation. Nothing will be allowed to obstruct me in pursuit of the killer. Anyone who harbours information that may be useful to me – and who deliberately conceals it – will find that they are on the wrong side of the law. Retribution will follow.'

'But I have done nothing wrong,' she said, quivering all over.

'You are protecting someone I need to find.'

'No, Inspector.'

'He may even be hiding here at the moment.'

'That's not true,' she cried in alarm. 'There's nobody here except my women and me.'

'I may need to verify that by searching the premises. If you refuse to help me, Madame Hennebeau, I will have to return with some constables to go through every room. It may be necessary to disturb your seamstresses while we do so but that cannot be helped. As I told you,' he stressed, 'I'll let nobody obstruct me.'

'That is not what I'm doing, Inspector Colbeck.'

'I know when I'm being lied to, Madame.'

'I'm an honest woman. I'd never lie.'

'Do you want me to organise that search?'

'If I could help you, I would.'

'Then tell me the truth.'

'I do not know it myself.' She took a tiny handkerchief from the sleeve of her blouse and dabbed at her watering eyes. 'A gentleman came in here some weeks ago. He asked me if I would receive a message for him in return for some money. That's all I had to do,' she said, earnestly. 'Receive a message and hold it here for him. When it came, I was to put something in the window – a display of green ribbons – so that he could see it as he passed.'

'Was that because he lives nearby?'

'I cannot say. When he saw the signal, he was to pick up the message and leave a reply for whoever had been here. It all seemed so harmless to me, Inspector. I did not realise I was breaking the law.'

'You were not, Madame.'

'I feel as if I was now.'

'What was this gentleman's name?'

'He did not tell me – I swear it.'

'Could you describe him?'

'He was shorter than you, Inspector, and he had broader shoulders. He was not good-looking but he had a pleasant face. I liked him. His hair was thick and turning grey.'

'Could you give me some idea of his age?'

'Ten years older than you at least.'

'Why did he pick here?' wondered Colbeck. 'I can see that he could rely on you do what he asked, but why did he single you out in the first place? Was he ever a customer here?'

'No, Inspector,' she said.

'Then how did you meet?'

'It was some time ago,' she said, hiding her embarrassment behind a nervous laugh, 'and we did not really meet in the way that you imply. He used to wave to me through the window as he passed the shop and we became . . .' She licked her lips to get the words out more clearly. '. . . we became acquainted, as you might say. Then, out of the blue, he stepped into the shop one day.'

'When was this?'

'Weeks ago. I did not even recognise him at first.'

'Why not?'

'Because he was not wearing his uniform. When he used to go past regularly, he always looked very smart. That's why I trusted him, Inspector,' she said. 'He was a policeman.'

The Lamb and Flag was a favourite haunt of Victor Leeming's because it had three outstanding features. It was within walking distance of Scotland Yard, it served excellent beer and it was a tavern that Edward Tallis would never deign to enter. Leeming could enjoy a quiet drink there without fear of being caught in the act by his superior. When he got there, a few of his colleagues were already in the bar and they were very pleased to see him again. They chatted happily with him until Robert Colbeck came in through the door. Understanding at once that the two men wanted to be alone, the others greeted the newcomer with a respectful smile then drifted away. Colbeck brought drinks for himself and his sergeant before choosing a table in the far corner. Leeming quaffed his beer gratefully.

'I needed a taste of that,' he said, wiping the froth from his upper lip. 'I've been very busy today, Inspector.'

'I hope that I didn't overtax you, Victor.'

'Not at all. It felt marvellous to be back.'

'Albeit unofficially,' Colbeck observed.

'Quite so, sir.'

'Did you learn anything of value?'

'Eventually,' said Leeming, taking another long sip as he gathered his thoughts. 'I went to the police station and discovered that Pierce Shannon had been locked up there on May 27th.'

'Disturbing the peace?'

'And causing damage to property, most likely, but he wasn't charged with that. Because he couldn't pay his fine, he was kept in his cell, pending a transfer to prison, but the fine was then paid by an anonymous benefactor.'

'The very man who visited him in prison, I daresay.'

'I can confirm that. I spoke to Horace Eames.'

'Who is he?'

'He spends his time making lifeboats now, sir, but he used to be a policeman in Limehouse. It was Eames who let this old friend of his speak to Shannon in his cell. When he gave me his name, I wanted to make sure that we had the right man so I went to the magistrate's court to check their records.'

'Well done, Victor.'

'Sure enough, the very same person had paid the fine.'

'That's conclusive.'

'Do you know what Luke's other name was?'

'Yes – Rogan.'

Leeming's face fell. 'You've already found out,' he complained.

'Let's call it a joint operation, Victor. We've each confirmed what the other managed to ascertain. While you were in a boatyard, I was at a dress shop in Paddington.'

'A dress shop?'

'It was the place where Shannon was told to leave a message for his paymaster. A French lady owns the shop. She and Rogan seemed to have developed something of a friendship.'

'He was a policeman in that district. So was Horace Eames at one time. They worked together.'

'I went to the station and they told me all about Rogan. It seems that he was a ladies' man,' said Colbeck. 'He developed a habit of enjoying favours from some of the women he encountered on his beat. And not the kind that ever charge for such services, I should add. In return, he kept a special eye on their property. He was a good policeman, apparently, but too fond of disobeying orders. In the end, he was dismissed from Paddington and became a private detective.'

'That's what Eames told me.'

'Did he give you an address for him?'

'He has an office somewhere in Camden.'

'What about his home address?'

'Eames couldn't tell me that, sir,' said Leeming. 'When he left the police force, Rogan moved from his house in Paddington.'

'Not all that far,' said Colbeck, taking a sheet of paper from his inside pocket. 'He needed to keep an eye on the window of that dress shop for a signal that was to be put there. It must have been chosen because of its proximity to his home.' He put the paper on the table. 'Take a look at that, Victor.'

'What is it, sir?'

'A list of people attending a lecture given by Gaston Chabal.'

Leeming picked it up. 'Where did you get this from?'

'The man who organised the event,' said Colbeck, taking a sip of his whisky. 'He's very methodical. As you can see, the names are all in alphabetical order. Check those that begin with an "R". Do you recognise someone?'

'Luke Rogan,' said the other, pointing to the name.

'Now, what is a private detective doing at a meeting that had such specialised interest? He knows nothing about civil engineering. I must be the only policeman in London who would have listened to Chabal with any alacrity.'

'So what was Rogan doing there?'

'Following him,' decided Colbeck. 'Unless I'm mistaken, he even followed the man to Paris. Chabal's mother-in-law told me that he felt someone was watching him. I believe that Rogan stayed on his tail until the moment when he had the opportunity to kill him. I'm also fairly certain that he was wearing a police uniform when he committed the murder. If Chabal was afraid that somebody was stalking him,' he added, 'the one person who would not arouse his suspicion was a police constable.'

'A bogus one.'

'Chabal was not to know that.' He had a second sip of his drink. 'Look at that list again, Victor. Can you see another name that you recognise?'

Leeming let his eye run down the neat column of names. 'Yes,' he declared, 'I know this one – Alexander Marklew.' He tapped the piece of paper. 'That's it, Inspector,' he went on with a note of triumph in his voice. 'We've found the link we needed.'

'Have we?'

'Of course. The only way that Rogan would even have known that that lecture was taking place was if someone took him there. That someone must be Mr Marklew. We've come full circle, Inspector,' he said, pausing to pour down some more beer. 'We're back with the most obvious suspect of all.'

'Who's that?'

'A jealous husband.'

'Husbands are not jealous of things they know nothing about.'

'But he *did* know. He used a private detective to find out.'

'No, Victor. I don't accept that. Alexander Marklew is a person I'd expect to be at such a lecture, but not because he realised that his wife had been unfaithful to him. Had that been the case, he'd surely have challenged Mrs Marklew about it. No,' said Colbeck, taking the list back from him, 'we must look elsewhere on this list.'

'What for?'

'The name of the man who *did* employ Luke Rogan.'

'Then all we have to do is to work through them one by one.'

'There's a more direct way than that, Victor.'

'Is there, sir?'

'Yes,' said Colbeck, pocketing the list and reaching for his whisky. 'I can pay a call on a certain private detective. Luke Rogan is the killer. His arrest must be our first priority.'

Sir Marcus Hetherington's estates were in Essex and he spent a fair amount of time at his country seat. When he was in London, however, he stayed at his town house in Pimlico. It was there, helped by his valet, that he was dressing for dinner. He was too busy adjusting his white tie in a mirror to hear the doorbell ring down below. It was only when he began to descend the staircase that he became aware of the fact that he had a visitor. A manservant awaited him in the hall.

'A gentleman has called to see you, Sir Marcus,' he said.

'At this hour? Damnably inconvenient.'

'I showed him into the drawing room.'

'What was his name?'

'Mr Rogan.'

Sir Marcus reddened. 'Luke Rogan?' he asked, irritably.

'Yes, Sir Marcus.'

Without even thanking the man, Sir Marcus brushed rudely past him and went into the drawing room, closing the door with a bang behind him to show his displeasure. Luke Rogan was admiring a painting of the battle of Waterloo that hung over the fireplace. He spun round to face the old man.

'What the devil are you doing here?' demanded Sir Marcus.

'I needed to see you.'

'Not here, man. I've told you before. You should only make contact with me at the Reform Club. If I am not there, you simply leave a note for me.'

'I preferred to call on you at home, Sir Marcus.'

'But I refrained on purpose from giving you this address.'

'I soon found it out,' said Rogan. 'When someone employs

me, I like to know a little more about them than they're prepared to tell me.'

'Impudent scoundrel!'

'We're in this together, after all.'

'What are you blathering about?'

'Inspector Colbeck.'

Sir Marcus became wary. 'Go on,' he said, slowly.

'He *knows*.'

Luke Rogan had a hunted look about him. He spoke with his usual bravado but there was a distant fear in his voice. Sir Marcus took note of it. Crossing to a table, he removed the stopper from a crystal decanter and poured himself a glass of brandy. He did not offer a drink to Rogan. After replacing the stopper, he threw down half of the brandy before rounding on his visitor. His face was expressionless.

'What do you mean?' he asked with rasping authority.

'Inspector Colbeck came to my office,' replied Rogan.

'When?'

'This afternoon. Luckily, I was out.'

'How did you learn of his visit?'

'The other offices are leased to a firm of solicitors, Sir Marcus. One of their clerks spoke to the inspector. He said that I would be out all afternoon and was not expected to return. As it happens,' said Rogan, 'I did call in earlier this evening.'

'What did Colbeck want?'

'To speak to me, that's all.'

'Was he on his own or did he bring men with him?'

'He came alone. I take that as a good sign.'

'A good sign!' repeated the old man with asperity. 'First of all, you assure me that he will never connect you in a hundred years with what happened in France. Then, when he comes knocking on your door only days later, you describe it as a good sign.'

'I was referring to the fact that he was on his own, Sir Marcus.'

'It only takes one man to make an arrest.'

'That may not be the reason he came.'

'Why else?'

'To make enquiries, maybe,' said Rogan, hopefully. 'My name may have floated in front of him and he came to satisfy his curiosity. I felt that I should warn you, Sir Marcus, but it may be unnecessary. I can't see how Colbeck could possibly link me with the murder.'

'I can,' said the other. 'You slipped up somewhere.'

'But I covered my tracks very carefully.'

'So you tell me.'

'I did, Sir Marcus. I know how policemen work. I left no clues as to my name or my whereabouts.'

'Then how do you explain Colbeck's visit to your office?'

Rogan shrugged. 'I can't,' he admitted.

'So you come running here, you imbecile!' shouted Sir Marcus before downing the rest of his brandy. 'Did it never occur to you that Colbeck might have left a man to watch your office in case you returned? When you did, and learnt what had happened, you might have led him all the way to my door.'

'Impossible!'

'How do you know?'

'Because I left the building by the rear exit,' said Rogan, 'and I changed cabs twice on my way here to throw off anyone who might be following. There was no one, Sir Marcus. I walked around the whole square to be sure before I even rang your bell.'

Sir Marcus put his glass on a table. Flipping his coat tails out of the way, he sank into a leather chair and ruminated for several minutes. Rogan remained on his feet, still trying to work out how Colbeck had managed to identify him as one of the culprits. Having taken such pains to hide behind anonymity, he felt distinctly uneasy, as if layers of protective clothing had suddenly and unaccountably been whisked off him. It made him shiver.

'Where will he go next?' said the old man. 'To your home?'

'No, Sir Marcus. He may have got to my office, but he'll never find out where I live. Even my closest friends don't know that. I keep my address secret and change it regularly. When I go back home tonight,' said Rogan, confidently. 'I'll do so without a qualm.'

'That's more than I'll do.'

'You're perfectly safe here.'

'Not as long as Inspector Colbeck is on the case.' His gaze shifted to the painting above the fireplace and hovered there for while. 'How many men of his standing do they have at Scotland Yard?'

'None at all.'

'He must have an assistant.'

'Victor Leeming was the man beaten up in France,' said Rogan. 'He's not even involved in the case anymore. Colbeck will miss him and that's to our advantage. From what I've heard, Leeming is hard-working and resolute.'

'There must be other capable men in the Department.'

'Not one of them can hold a candle to the Railway Detective.'

'So he is irreplaceable?'

'Completely, Sir Marcus.'

The old man stood up and walked across to stand in front

of the fireplace. He looked up at the swirling action in the oil painting on the wall. As rich memories were ignited, he drew himself up to his full height and stood to attention. He could hear the sound of armed conflict and it brought a nostalgic smile to his lips. When he spoke to Rogan, he kept staring up at the battle of Waterloo.

'Did you ever serve in the army?' he asked.

'No, Sir Marcus.'

'A pity – it would have been the making of you. Military life gives a man the best start in life. It shapes his thinking. It imparts courage and teaches him the virtues of patriotism.'

'Nobody is more patriotic than me,' claimed Rogan.

'Winning a battle is quite simple,' said the old man. 'You have to kill your enemy before he can kill you.' He turned round. 'That way, you remove any threat to your life, liberty and prospects of happiness. Do you understand what I'm saying, Rogan?'

'Extremely well, Sir Marcus.'

'We have an enemy. He's trying to hunt the pair of us down.'

'What do wish me to do?'

'Get rid of Inspector Colbeck,' said the other. 'He's the one man with the intelligence to find us and I'll not let that happen. It's time for him to meet his Waterloo, I fancy. You have your orders, Rogan.'

'Yes, Sir Marcus.'

'Kill him.'

CHAPTER THIRTEEN

Superintendent Edward Tallis was in a buoyant mood for once. He had just received a letter from Thomas Brassey, expressing formal thanks for all the help that had been rendered by the Metropolitan Police Force. The commissioner had then complimented him on his wisdom in dispatching Robert Colbeck abroad and, even though Tallis had been strongly opposed to the notion, he was happy to claim some credit for it now that the French expedition had paid such dividends. But the main reason for the superintendent's good humour was that he was at last in possession of a murder suspect.

'Luke Rogan,' he said, rolling the name off his tongue.

'I have men out looking for him at this very moment, sir.'

'But you do not know his home address.'

'Not yet,' replied Colbeck.

'He sounds like a slippery customer.'

'He is, Superintendent.'

'A former policeman, operating on the wrong side of the law. That's very distressing,' said Tallis, clenching his teeth. 'It sets a bad example. He needs to be caught quickly, Inspector.'

'Rogan is not the only person we need,' Colbeck reminded

him. 'He was merely the agent for someone else. The man who employed him is equally culpable.'

'Unfortunately, we do not have his name.'

'You are holding it in your hands, sir.'

They were in the superintendent's office and there was no sign of a cigar. Cool air blew in through a half-open window. When he had delivered his verbal report, Colbeck had also shown his superior the list of those who had attended Gaston Chabal's lecture. Tallis looked at it more closely and noticed something.

'Why have you put crosses against some of the names?'

'Those are the men I've been able to eliminate, sir.'

'How?' asked Tallis.

'Some of them – Alexander Marklew, for instance – invested a sizeable amount of money in the Mantes to Caen Railway. They are hardly likely to connive at the destruction of the project when they have a financial stake in it.'

'I accept that.'

'As for the other names I have set aside,' said Colbeck, 'that was done so on the advice of Mr Kane.'

'He's the secretary of this Society, isn't he?'

'Yes, sir. Once I had persuaded him to cooperate with me, he was extremely helpful. Mr Kane pointed out the civil engineers who were in the audience that day. Men who make their living from the railway,' Colbeck reasoned, 'would not be inclined to inflict damage on one. They would be violating an unwritten code.'

'So how many names are left?'

'Just over thirty.'

'It will take time to work through them all.'

'If we arrest Rogan, we'll not have to do so. He'll supply us with the name we want. It obviously belongs to a man of some wealth. He spent a large amount on this whole venture.'

'Luke Rogan must have been highly paid to commit murder.'

'I suspect that he needed the money,' said Colbeck, 'which is why he was prepared to take on the assignment. Judging by the size of his office, his business activities were not very profitable. It was very small and he could not afford to employ anyone to take care of his secretarial work.'

'Then why was he chosen?' said Tallis, frowning. 'Wouldn't his paymaster have gone to someone who was more successful?'

'No, sir. That would have been too risky for him. Most private detectives would have refused to have anything to do with such blatantly criminal activities. They are far too honourable. They would have reported to us any such approach. What this man required,' Colbeck said, 'was someone who was less scrupulous, a mercenary who could not afford to turn down such a generous offer. He found what he wanted in Luke Rogan.'

'How soon do you expect to apprehend him?'

'I could not say. He's proving rather elusive.'

'Was there nothing in his office to indicate his whereabouts?'

'Nothing whatsoever,' replied the other. 'I searched the place thoroughly this morning. Rogan was canny. He left no correspondence in his office and no details of any clients.'

'He must have had an account book of sorts.'

'Kept at his home, I presume.'

'Wherever that might be.'

'Mr Kane had an address for everyone on that list so that he could inform them about future events that took place. Luke Rogan had supplied what purported to be his home address but, when I got there, the house did not even exist.'

'What about the police in Paddington?'

'They confirmed that Rogan had always been rather secretive.'

'But they must have known where his abode was,' said Tallis, returning the sheet of paper to Colbeck. 'A police constable would have to register a correct address.'

'That's what he did, sir.'

'Did you visit the place?'

'There was no point,' said Colbeck. 'When he was dismissed from the police force, he moved from the house. Nobody seems to know where he went. Luke Rogan is not married so he has only himself to consider. He can move at will.'

'He must live *somewhere*, Inspector.'

'Of course. I believe it will not be too far from Paddington.'

'Then roust him out.'

'We are doing all that we can, sir.'

'How many men are out looking for him?'

'Hundreds of thousands.'

Tallis glared at him. 'Are you trying to be droll?'

'Not at all,' said Colbeck. 'I'm working from the figures in last year's census. London has a population of well over three million.'

'So?'

'We can discount the large number of people that are illiterate and any children can also be taken out of the equation. It still leaves a substantial readership for the daily newspapers.'

'Newspapers?'

'You obviously haven't read your copy of *The Times* this morning,' said Colbeck, indicating the newspaper that was neatly folded on the desk. 'I took the liberty of placing a notice in it and in the others on sale today.'

'I was about to suggest that you did exactly that,' said

Tallis, reaching for his newspaper. 'Where is the notice?'

'Page four, sir. Why restrict the search to a handful of detectives when we can use eyes all over London to assist us? Somebody reading that,' he said, confidently, 'is bound to know where we can find the elusive Luke Rogan.'

When the cab reached the railway station, Sir Marcus Hetherington alighted and paid the driver. He then bought a first class ticket and walked towards the relevant platform. On his way, he passed a booth from which he obtained a copy of *The Times*. Stuffing it under one arm, he marched briskly on with his cane beating out a tattoo on the concourse. A porter was standing on the platform, ready to open the door of an empty first class carriage for him. Sir Marcus gave him a nod them settled down in his seat. The door was closed behind him.

While he enjoyed travelling by rail, he hated the hustle and bustle of a railway station and he always tried to time his arrival so that he did not have to wait there for long in the company of people whom he considered undesirables. Sir Marcus was not so aristocratic as to believe that trains should be reserved exclusively for the peerage but he did consider the introduction of the third class carriage a reprehensible mistake. It encouraged the lower orders to travel and that, in his opinion, gave them a privileged mobility that was wholly undeserved. When he saw a rough-looking individual, rushing past his carriage with a scruffy, middle-aged woman in tow, Sir Marcus grimaced. To share a journey with such people was demeaning.

Moments later, the signal was given and the train sprang into life, coughing loudly before giving a shudder and pulling away from the platform. Another latecomer sprinted past the carriage to jump on to the moving train farther down. Sir Marcus clicked his tongue in disapproval. Now that they were in motion, he was content. He had the carriage all to himself and the train would not stop until it reached his destination. Opening his newspaper, he began to read it. Since he took a keen interest in political affairs, he perused every article on the first two inside pages with care. When he turned to the next page, however, it was a police notice that grabbed his attention.

'What's this?' he gulped.

The notice requested the help of the public to find Luke Rogan, the prime suspect in a murder investigation, who operated as a private detective from an office in Camden. A detailed description of the man was given and, to his chagrin, Sir Marcus could see that it was fairly accurate. Anyone with information about Rogan's whereabouts was urged to come forward.

'Damnation!' cried Sir Marcus.

He flung the newspaper aside and considered the implications of what he had just read. It was disturbing. If everyone in the capital was looking for Luke Rogan, he could not escape arrest indefinitely. The trail would then lead to Sir Marcus. He began to perspire freely. For a fleeting second, the shadow of the Railway Detective seemed to fall across him.

'If you come down to Euston Station with me,' offered Caleb Andrews, 'I'll show you how it was done.'

'I think I already know,' said Colbeck.

'There are some empty carriages in a siding, Inspector. I could demonstrate for you.'

'Robert is far too busy, Father,' said Madeleine.

'I'm only trying to help, Madeleine. What you have to

do, you see, is to prop the door open while the train is in motion. Someone did just that a few months ago on a train I was driving from Birmingham,' he explained. 'Some villains got on with a strongbox they'd stolen. After a couple of miles, they jammed open the door and flung the strongbox out so that they would not be caught with it.'

'I remember the case,' said Colbeck. 'When they came back later to retrieve their booty, the police were waiting for them. A farmer had found the strongbox in his field and raised the alarm.'

'The point I'm trying to make is that the box was heavy – almost as heavy as that Frenchman. Yet it was slung out with ease.'

'How do you know?' asked Madeleine. 'You weren't there.'

'I was driving the train.'

'But you didn't actually see them throw anything out.'

'Stop interrupting me, Maddy.'

'You make a fair point, Mr Andrews,' said Colbeck, trying to bring the conversation to an end, 'and I'm grateful. But we've moved on a long way from the Sankey Viaduct.'

'You should have come to me at the time, Inspector.'

'I'm sure.'

Colbeck had paid a return visit to Luke Rogan's office to see if there had been any sign of the man. The uniformed policeman who had been keeping the place under surveillance assured him that Rogan had not entered the building by the front or rear doors. Since he was in Camden, only a few streets away from her house, Colbeck decided to call in on Madeleine but it was her father's day off so he had to contend with Caleb Andrews. It was several minutes before he was finally left alone with Madeleine.

'Can I make you some tea, Robert?' she asked.

'No, thank you. I only popped in for a moment.'

'I'm sorry that my father badgered you.'

'I never mind anything that he does,' said Colbeck, tolerantly. 'But for him, we'd never have met. I always bear that in mind.'

'So do I.'

'You were the strongbox thrown from that particular train.'

'I'm not a strongbox,' protested Madeleine with a laugh.

'I was speaking metaphorically.'

'You mean, that I'm very heavy and difficult to open.'

'No,' said Colbeck, giving her a conciliatory kiss. 'I mean that you possess great value – to me, that is.'

'Then why didn't you say so?'

'I was dealing in images.'

'Well, I'd prefer you to speak more directly,' she chided him. 'It would help me to understand you properly. I still don't know what you meant about my drawing of the viaduct helping you to solve a murder. All you would tell me was that it was symbolic.'

'Highly symbolic.'

'It was a sketch – nothing more.'

'Show it to me again,' he invited, 'and I'll explain.'

'In simple language?'

'Monosyllables, if you prefer.'

Madeleine fetched her portfolio and extracted the drawing of the Sankey Viaduct. She laid it on the table and they both scrutinised it.

'What you did was to bridge the Channel between England and France,' he pointed out. 'All the way from Dover to Calais.'

'I drew that picture out of love.'

'But it's a symbol of something that certain people hate.'

'And what's that?'

'I'll tell you, Madeleine. The railway that's being built from Mantes to Caen will not end there. In due course, an extension will be added to take it to Cherbourg.'

'I don't see anything wrong in that.'

'There's an arsenal there.'

'Oh.'

'The railway that Thomas Brassey is constructing will in time provide a direct route between Paris and a main source of arms and ammunition. That's bound to alarm some people here,' he continued. 'It's less than forty years since we defeated France and that defeat still rankles with them. Louis Napoleon, who rules the country, is an emperor in all but name. Emperors need imperial conquests.'

Madeleine was worried. 'Do you think that France would try to *invade* us?' she said, turning to look up at him. 'I thought we were completely safe.'

'I'm sure that we are,' said Colbeck, 'and I'm equally certain that Mr Brassey is of the same opinion. If he believed for one moment that he was endangering his native country by building that railway, he would never have taken on the contract.'

'Then why did someone try to wreck the project?'

'Because he is afraid, Madeleine.'

'Of what?'

'Potential aggression from the French.'

'But you just said that we had nothing to fear.'

'Other people see things differently,' he said, 'and it was only when you showed me this drawing that I realised how they could view what was happening in northern France. A railway between Paris and Cherbourg is a source of intense concern to some Englishmen.'

'All that I can see is my crude version of the Sankey Viaduct.'

'Look beyond it,' he advised.

'At what?'

'The railway that will connect the French capital to a port with military significance.' He gave an apologetic smile. 'I'm afraid that I'm going to have to use a word that you don't like.'

'Will it explain what all this is about?'

'I think so, Madeleine.'

'What's the word?'

'Metaphorical.'

She rolled her eyes. 'We're back to that again.'

'Your drawing is to blame,' he said, indicating it. 'You've created what someone clearly dreads – a viaduct between England and France. In his mind – and we have to try to see it from his point of view, warped as it might be – the railway between Paris and Cherbourg will be a metaphorical viaduct between the two countries. It's a potent symbol of French imperial ambition.'

'Is that why a man was killed?' she said, trying to assimilate what she had been told. 'Because of symbols and metaphors?'

'Chabal was an engineer with an important role in the project.'

'According to father, lots of engineers work on a new railway.'

'Quite true. Mr Brassey has a whole team of them.'

'Why was this particular man murdered?'

'He had the wrong nationality – he was French.'

'Did he have to be thrown from the Sankey Viaduct?'

'I think so.'

'You're going to tell me that that was symbolic as well,

aren't you?' she said. 'It's something to do with whatever you called it a few moments ago.'

'A metaphorical viaduct. I'm only guessing,' he went on, 'and I could be wrong. There are just too many coincidences here. Someone is so horrified at the prospect of that railway being built that he will go to any lengths to stop it.'

'What sort of a man is he, Robert?'

'One who has an implacable hatred of the French.'

'Why?'

'He probably fought against them.'

Nobody else was allowed in the room. It was on the first floor of the mansion and it overlooked the rear garden. It was kept locked so that none of the servants could get into it. The first thing that Sir Marcus Hetherington did when he let himself in was to lock the door behind him. He gazed around the room and felt the familiar upsurge of pride and patriotism. What he had created was a shrine to England's military glory. Banners, uniforms and weapons stood everywhere. Memorabilia of a more gruesome kind were contained in a glass case. Its prime exhibit, a human skull, was something that he cherished. It had belonged to a nameless French soldier who had fallen at the battle of Waterloo. Sir Marcus had killed him.

He wandered around the room, examining various items and luxuriating in the memories that they kindled. Then he crossed to the window. It was a fine day and sunlight was dappling the back lawn, but he was not looking at the garden. His gaze went up to the flag that was fluttering in the breeze at the top of its pole. He gave it a salute. Turning back, he surveyed his collection once more, drawing strength from it, finding consolation, recapturing younger days. On the wall above the mantelpiece was a portrait of himself in uniform. It never failed to lift his heart.

Crossing to a rosewood cabinet, he opened the top drawer and took out a wooden case that he set down on the table. When he lifted the lid of the case, Sir Marcus looked down fondly at a pair of percussion duelling pistols with plated turn-off barrels and walnut stocks inlaid with silver. The weapons gleamed. Packed neatly around them was a small supply of ammunition. He removed the pistols from the case and held one in each hand. The sensation of power was thrilling. It coursed through him for minutes. When it finally began to ease, Sir Marcus started to load the pistols.

Now that he was involved in the investigation once more, Victor Leeming was eager to take on more work. He spent the morning on the hoof, tracking down some of the people who had attended the lecture given by Gaston Chabal. It had been a largely fruitless exercise but it made him feel useful again. Instead of meeting the inspector at the Lamb and Flag, he agreed to visit Colbeck's house in John Islip Street so that they could have more privacy. Robert Colbeck's father and grandfather had been cabinetmakers with a string of wealthy clients. When he inherited the house, he also inherited examples of their work. In the drawing room where he and Leeming sat, a large cupboard, two matching cabinets and a beautiful mahogany secretaire bore the Colbeck name.

'How are you feeling today, Victor?' asked the inspector.

'Tired but happy to be so, sir.'

'You must not overdo it.'

'Knocking on a few doors is no effort,' said Leeming. 'I just wish that I had more to report. None of the four people

I called on could possibly have hired Luke Rogan. You can cross them off the list.'

'That saves me the trouble of bothering with them.'

'How many names are left?'

'Less than twenty. We are slowly whittling them down.'

'Why are you so sure that the man we want actually attended that lecture? If he detested the idea of that railway being built in France, wouldn't he avoid a man who was talking about it?'

'On the contrary,' said Colbeck. 'He'd want to find out as much about it as he could. Also, of course, he'd be keen to take a closer look at Gaston Chabal. The man represented everything that he loathed and feared. No, he and Rogan were there together, I'm certain of it. They may not have sat beside each other – they probably took care to stay apart in order to conceal their relationship – but they were both at that lecture.'

'Then we are bound to find him in the end.'

'Oh, yes.'

Colbeck stirred his tea before tasting it. Leeming had already finished one cup and was halfway through the second. He chewed on the slice of cake that he had been offered.

'What did Mr Tallis have to say about it all?'

'He was pleased, Victor. Or, to put it another way, he smoked no cigars, had no tantrums and was almost disarmingly civil. All that he craves is a little success,' said Colbeck. 'It stops him from being pilloried in the newspapers.'

'Talking of the newspapers, sir, I saw that notice you put in this morning's edition. It's sure to get a response.'

'Not all of it entirely reliable, alas.'

'No,' said Leeming, wearily. 'The promise of a reward does things to some people. They invent all sorts of stories to try to get their hands on the money. But they won't all be fraudulent. There may be some wheat among the chaff, sir.'

'I'm counting on it.'

'You gave a good description of Rogan. It tallied with the one I had from Horace Eames.'

'I also relied on what Madame Hennebeau told me. She was clearly very fond of the man but, then, so were a number of women.'

'Luke Rogan will be on the run by now. You'll have flushed him out of his hiding place good and proper.'

'That was the idea behind using the press,' said Colbeck. 'I wanted to scare Rogan and drive a wedge between him and his employer. When he realises that we've identified his hired killer, the man who set everything in motion will want to distance himself from Rogan. My guess is that he'll go to ground immediately.'

'Here in London?'

'Well, it won't be in France, we may be certain of that.'

While his visitor drained his teacup, Colbeck told him about the conversation he had had earlier with Madeleine Andrews regarding her sketch of the Sankey Viaduct. Leeming was almost as confused by his talk of symbols and metaphors as she had been, but he trusted the inspector to know what he was talking about. What interested him was Colbeck's theory that the man who had engaged Rogan had probably served in the army at one time.

'I wish you'd told me that before, Inspector,' he said.

'Why?'

'I could have asked the people I interviewed this morning if they knew anyone who'd been at that lecture with a military background. It's a small world – engineers and such like. They all seem to know each other.'

'That's in our favour.'

'Do you have any more names for me?'

'Haven't you done enough work for one day?'

'No,' said Leeming, ignoring the stab of pain in his ribs. 'I'm only just starting to warm up, sir. Use me as much as you wish.'

'Mr Tallis would admonish me, if he knew.'

'You employed Brendan Mulryne behind his back and got away with it. Unlike him, I do work at the Detective Department.'

'But you're supposed to be on sick leave, Victor.'

'I'm sick of sick leave. Give me some more names.'

'As you wish,' said Colbeck, taking a slip of paper from his pocket and handing it over. 'There are four more people for you to chase down. Be sure to find out if any of them bore arms against the French at one time. That would make them fifty or more at least.'

'I'll remember that.'

'And take a cab. You don't have to go all over London on foot. Keep a record of your cab fares and I'll reimburse you.'

'You can save your money with this chap, sir,' said Leeming as he saw the first address on the list. 'He lives in Pimlico. That's well within walking distance of here.'

'It is indeed. What's the man's name?'

'Hetherington – Sir Marcus Hetherington.'

The publicity in the newspapers had given him a real fright. Before his landlady or his neighbours could report his whereabouts to the police, Luke Rogan gathered up everything of value and stuffed it into a bag. Then he changed out of the slightly garish attire he usually wore and put on a pair of dungarees, a moth-eaten old coat and a floppy hat. It was a disguise he often used in the course of his work as a private detective and it was so nondescript as to render him almost invisible. After checking his appearance in the mirror, he fled from his house in Bayswater without leaving behind the unpaid rent.

He left his belongings at the house in Paddington of a woman he had befriended during his days as a policeman. He gave her a plausible explanation about why he was dressed as a workman but she needed no convincing. She was a lonely widow who was so pleased to see him that she offered him accommodation for as long as he wished. As she never read a newspaper, there was no possibility that she would link her former lover with a series of horrific crimes. In the short term at least, Rogan had somewhere to hide.

Sir Marcus Hetherington had ordered him to kill Colbeck in order that the murder investigation would lose the man who directed it and make it founder. In view of what the inspector had done, Rogan was now fired by revenge as well. He was anxious to strike back at the person who had exposed him in the newspapers as a wanted felon and spread his name across the whole of London. He knew that he could never return to his old life again. Colbeck had robbed him of his occupation. In recompense, he would deprive the detective of his life.

Rogan had been patient. He knew what his intended victim looked like and where to find him. Lurking outside Scotland Yard until the inspector had emerged, he waited until Colbeck had summoned a cab then flagged down one of his own and ordered it to follow the first vehicle. What he learnt was that Colbeck lived in John Islip Street and that, very soon after his arrival, he had a visitor. While the two men were inside the house, Rogan loitered in a doorway on the other side of the street and bided his time. He felt under his coat for the knife that was thrust into his belt. Having already killed Gaston Chabal, it could now be used to dispatch another man.

Inside the house, the detectives came to the end of their conversation.

'I'll be on my way, Inspector,' said Victor Leeming, rising slowly to his feet. 'Thank you for the tea and cake.'

'When this is all over, we'll celebrate with something a little stronger,' promised Colbeck. 'Before that, I'll want to know how you fared this afternoon.'

'Where will I meet you?'

'At the Lamb and Flag.'

'What time?'

'Shall we say six o'clock?'

'I'll be there, sir.'

'Good.' Colbeck got to his feet and led the way into the hall. 'I'll go back to Scotland Yard to see if anyone has come forward as a result of that notice in the newspapers.'

'And I'll ring some more doorbells.'

'Are you glad to be back in harness again, Victor?'

'Yes, sir – even if I can only manage a trot.' They put on their respective hats and left the house together. Leeming looked up and down the street. 'Not long to go now.'

'I hope not.'

'We'll soon catch Luke Rogan.'

'Yes,' said Colbeck. 'We're getting close. I can feel it.'

They exchanged farewells then parted company. Leeming walked at a gentle pace towards Vauxhall Bridge Road while Colbeck went off in the opposite direction, intending to stop the first empty hansom cab. As none was in view, he continued to stroll briskly along the pavement. He reviewed all the evidence they had so far gathered and it left him with a feeling of guarded optimism. His only worry was that Rogan might leave London to avoid arrest and, possibly, flee the country altogether. If necessary, Colbeck was more than ready to pursue him abroad.

It was minutes before he realised that he was being followed. He did not remember seeing anyone when they came out of the house but he sensed a distinct presence now. When an empty cab came towards him, therefore, he let it pass. Colbeck wanted to know who was on his tail. Moving to the kerb, he glanced back down the street then crossed diagonally to the other side. Out of the corner of his eye, he had seen him. The man had pretended to tie up his bootlace so that he could keep his head down but Colbeck knew at once that it was a ruse. He was being shadowed.

As he walked on, he maintained the same pace, giving no indication that he was aware of someone behind him. They were now on the same side of the street. The gap between them slowly closed until Colbeck could hear the tramp of hobnail boots behind him. That was the danger signal. If he was simply being followed, he knew that the man would stay well back to avoid being seen. The fact that he was moving steadily closer meant that he was going to attack.

Colbeck did not know if the man was a thief or someone with a personal grudge against him. Police work had made him many enemies and he had often received threats from convicted criminals as they were hauled out of the dock to begin a prison sentence. It did not matter who the stalker was. The way to deal with him, he believed, was to invite the attack. When he reached a corner, he turned sharply and went down a narrow lane. He heard footsteps quicken behind him. After a few more yards, Colbeck swung round to confront the man. The sun forewarned him. It glinted on the knife that had suddenly appeared in the stalker's hand. The man lunged forward and thrust hard with his weapon but he could not sink it into the back of an unsuspecting victim this time. Colbeck was ready for him.

Jumping quickly back out of the way, he whisked off his top hat and flung it hard into the man's face to confuse him for an split-second. He grabbed the hand that was holding the knife and turned the point away. They grappled fiercely and it was clear that the man was used to a brawl. Strong and wily, he did everything he could to overpower Colbeck, punching, gouging, spitting into his face, biting his hand and trying to stamp on his toes with his boot. Colbeck responded by tightening his grip. When he managed to manoeuvre the man off balance, he swung him hard against the brick wall. Shaken by the impact, his attacker dropped the knife. Colbeck used a foot to kick it away.

As they grappled once more, Colbeck realised that he was not ideally dressed for a fight. His tight-fitting frock coat did not allow him much flexibility. His adversary, by contrast, had much more freedom of movement. He used it to push Colbeck against the wall then hit him with a relay of punches. Before the detective could fight back, he was kicked in the shin then tripped up. As he fell to the ground, Colbeck heard the ominous sound of torn cloth but he had no time to worry about his coat. The man dived on him and went for his throat, getting both thumbs on his windpipe and pressing hard.

It was the first moment when Colbeck had a proper look at his face. Breathing heavily, the man bared his teeth in a grin of triumph and applied more pressure. Colbeck knew that it must be Luke Rogan. The man was intent on murder. Desperation gave him an extra surge of strength and he rolled suddenly to the left, toppling Rogan and weakening his grip. Colbeck punched him hard in the face until he put up both hands to defend himself. The searing pain in Colbeck's throat had gone but he still had to contend with a powerful adversary. What brought the fight to an end was the arrival of several onlookers. Hearing the commotion, a small crowd began to gather around them. They were witnesses. Rogan had to get away.

Smashing a fist into Colbeck's face, he struggled to his feet and pushed his way past the spectators before running off down the lane. Colbeck was still dazed. By the time he was helped to his feet by two men, he saw that Luke Rogan had vanished. One of the bystanders looked at his torn coat and blood-covered face.

'You all right, guv'nor?' he asked.

'Yes, thank you,' said Colbeck, dusting off his coat.

'Like me to call a policeman, sir?'

Colbeck gave a hollow laugh.

The superintendent had never seen him looking dishevelled before. In all the years they had known each other, Robert Colbeck had striven for a stylishness that Edward Tallis felt was out of place in the Detective Department. Smartness was always encouraged but not to the point of ostentation. Colbeck did not look quite so elegant now. His frock coat was torn, his trousers were scuffed and his face was cut and bruised. Looking into the mirror, he was using a handkerchief to wipe away the blood from his cheek when Tallis burst into his office.

'They told me you were back,' he said, staring in amazement at the unkempt figure before him. 'Whatever happened to you, man?'

'I tried to arrest Luke Rogan, sir.'

'You found him?'

'No, sir,' replied Colbeck. 'He found me.'

'How do you know that it was him?'

'Because he attempted to kill me.' He pointed to the knife that lay on his desk. 'In the same way that he murdered Gaston Chabal.'

Colbeck told him what had happened and how he had been face to face with the wanted man described that morning in the newspapers. When he heard that Rogan had escaped, Tallis wanted him apprehended immediately.

'I'll send out men to scour the area,' he said.

'Too late, Superintendent. I've already done that.'

'I'll not have anyone assaulting my men.'

'He'll be long gone by now,' said Colbeck. 'He ran off as if the hounds of hell were on his tail.'

'And so they will be,' vowed Tallis. 'Dear God! What is the world coming to when a detective inspector can be the victim of a murderous attack only a few blocks from his own doorstep?'

'It's not exactly a daily event, sir.'

'Once is enough.'

'I agree.'

'We knew that Rogan was a villain but it never crossed my mind that he'd be capable of this audacity. Why did he strike at you?'

'Because he identifies me as his nemesis,' said Colbeck. 'Rogan thought he'd committed the perfect murder until we began to breathe down his neck. If he read a newspaper this morning, he'd have seen my appeal for information that would lead to his capture. That could make a man feel vengeful.'

'He's not the only one, Inspector. When I look at you in

that state, I feel vengeful as well. Rogan will pay for this.'

'It's a pity I can't send him a bill from my tailor.' Colbeck examined the long tear under his arm. 'This will need to be repaired and the coat will have to be cleaned. I can't wear it like this.'

'This must not be allowed to happen again.'

'It won't, sir.'

'From now on, you'll have a bodyguard.'

'But it's not necessary.'

'Someone is determined to kill you.'

'Luckily, he failed.'

'He's sure to try again.'

'I think that's the last thing he'll do.'

'Why?'

'Because he knows that I'll be on my guard now,' said Colbeck. 'He'd never have a chance to get that close again.'

'We'll look under every stone in London for him.'

'That could be a wasted exercise, Inspector.'

'Why?'

'Because I don't think he'll stay in the city.'

'He must, if he wants to ambush you again,' said Tallis.

'No, sir. It's too dangerous. Luke Rogan won't show his face here again. He's probably on his way out of London right now.'

'Where do you think he will go?'

'There's one obvious place.'

'Is there?'

'Yes, Superintendent,' said Colbeck. 'He'll want a refuge. He'll scurry back to the man who dragged him into this in the first place. They have a common bond, after all. When we catch them, both will face the prospect of a death sentence.'

* * *

Sir Marcus Hetherington was livid when he was told that he had a visitor by the name of Luke Rogan. Storming out of the library, he went to the front door of his mansion and saw the sorry figure waiting in the porch. Rogan was still wearing the old coat and dungarees. Since he was holding his cap in his hands, the bruises on his forehead and the black eye were clearly visible. Sir Marcus spluttered.

'Whatever brought you here?' he asked.

'We need to settle our account, Sir Marcus.'

'This house is sacrosanct. You're not allowed anywhere near it.'

'I think I am,' said Rogan, pugnaciously.

'And how did you get those bruises?'

'Invite me in and I'll tell you.'

'You're not coming in here.'

Fearing that his wife might see the man, Sir Marcus took him past the stable block at the rear of the house. They went into an outbuilding some distance away so that they could talk without being seen. Rogan told him about the failed attempt on Colbeck's life. The old man was incensed.

'Can't you do *anything* you're told?' he yelled.

'I got rid of that Frenchman for you,' retorted the other.

'Yes, but you didn't bring that railway to a halt, did you? Nor did you stop the police from finding out your identity, thus putting both our lives in danger. And now – *this*!'

'Colbeck saw me coming.'

'You swore to me that you'd kill him.'

'I tried, Sir Marcus. How do you think I got these bruises?'

'The worst thing of all is that you come running here, like a snivelling child who's been beaten at school.'

Rogan became truculent. 'I didn't come for sympathy,' he

said. 'I came for what's owed to me. Now that I have to get out of London, I need every penny.'

'I'm not paying you for something you didn't do.'

'You have to, Sir Marcus. You gave me your word.'

'I've paid you enough already,' said the old man, 'and the money was not well spent. You blundered. And to cap it all, you have the temerity to disturb me in my own home. That's unpardonable.'

'We're in this together.'

'Our association is ended forthwith.'

'You don't get off the hook that easily, Sir Marcus,' said Rogan, squaring up to him. 'If you don't pay me what's due, I'll write a note to Inspector Colbeck and tell him whose idea it was to kill Gaston Chabal and toss him off that viaduct.'

'You wouldn't dare!' howled Sir Marcus.

'What do I have to lose?'

'You're the man they're after, not me. There's a description of you in the newspapers this morning. If you were so careful, how did the police track you down to your office?'

'Give me the money!'

'No!'

'If I go down, Sir Marcus, you'll come with me.'

There was a silent battle of wills. Sir Marcus glowered at him but Rogan met his gaze with unflinching steadiness. The old man was enraged by the lack of respect he was being shown. Hitherto, Rogan had always been deferential. He was now scornful of their social differences. He would not be cowed. Sir Marcus reached a decision. When he had first employed him, Rogan had been an asset to him. He had now become a liability.

'Who knows that you came here?' he asked.

'Nobody.'

'Are you sure?'

'Quite sure, Sir Marcus.'

'Someone must have brought you from the railway station.'

'I walked.'

Sir Marcus was duly impressed. It was almost two miles to the house. If Rogan had walked all the way, it showed how eager he was to get there. Since the house was in an isolated position, the chances that anyone had seen him coming there were very slim. The only other person who had set eyes on the visitor was one of the servants. Feigning repentance, Sir Marcus nodded his head.

'I am indebted to you,' he conceded. 'There's no denying that.'

'I need my money,' said Rogan.

'You'll get it – on the understanding that you'll go far away from here and never return. Is that agreed?'

'You'll never see me again, Sir Marcus.'

'Do I have your word on that?'

'I won't even stay in the country.'

'In that case,' said the old man, 'I'll get what I owe you and I'll add something more. Wait here until I get back.'

Victor Leeming arrived at the Lamb and Flag to find a tankard of beer waiting for him. Colbeck was sitting at a table. When he saw the inspector's face, Leeming was shocked.

'You look worse than me, sir!' he said.

'I feel it, Victor.'

'What on earth happened?'

'I had a chance meeting with Luke Rogan.'

Leeming sat down in the other chair and listened to the story. He was annoyed that he had left Colbeck alone after their meeting in John Islip Street. He felt guilty.

'I should have made sure you caught a cab,' he said.

'I can look after myself.'

'But you might have been killed, sir.'

'A little shaken up, that's all,' said Colbeck. 'What really upset me was that I tore my coat and muddied my trousers. Luckily, I keep a change of clothing in my office. I'd never have ventured in here otherwise.' He drank some whisky. 'What did you learn?'

'You can cross three of the names off that list, sir.'

'Excellent – that takes us down to single figures. Some of the other men working on the case have been busy as well. They managed to eliminate another eight suspects between them.'

'You may be able to get rid of even more.'

'Why?'

'Because I think I struck gold at the first address.'

'The one in Pimlico?'

'Yes, Inspector,' said Leeming before taking a long drink of beer. 'It's a town house owned by Sir Marcus Hetherington. He's gone back to his estates in Essex so I wasn't able to speak to the gentleman himself, but I talked to a servant.'

'And?'

'Sir Marcus had a long and distinguished career in the army.'

'How old would he be?'

'Well into his seventies, apparently.'

'Then he could be our man.'

'I'm fairly certain of it,' said Leeming. 'When I mentioned the name of Luke Rogan, the servant claimed that he had never heard of him. But I had a strong suspicion that he was lying. He's obviously very loyal to his master.'

'Did you press him in the matter?'

'No, sir. I went away. When I'd visited the other three

addresses, I took a cab back to Pimlico and spoke to the same man. This time I showed him that description of Luke Rogan in the newspaper and reminded him that it was a crime to hold back evidence from the police. That rattled him, I could see.'

'Did he buckle?'

'Eventually,' said Leeming. 'He remembered something that had slipped his mind. It seems that a man who called himself Rogan had called at the house only yesterday. That settles it for me, sir.'

'And me,' said Colbeck. 'How quickly can you drink that beer?'

'Why, sir?'

'We're going to catch a train to Essex.'

It was some while before Sir Marcus Hetherington returned and Rogan began to worry. When he stepped outside, however, he saw the old man coming towards him with a small bag in his hand. The sight made him relax. Sir Marcus ushered him back inside and closed the door behind them. Then he held out the bag.

'This is all you get, mind,' he warned. 'Your final payment.'

'Thank you,' said Rogan, snatching the bag.

'Count it out to make sure that it's all there.'

'I will, Sir Marcus.'

There was a little table in the corner. Luke Rogan sat beside it and tipped out the bundle of notes and coins. He began to count the money but did not get far. Taking out a pistol from inside his coat, Sir Marcus shot him in the head from close range. Blood spurted everywhere and stained the banknotes on the table. Rogan slumped forward. Sir Marcus was relieved, convinced that he had just rid himself of the one person who could connect the series of crimes to him. Rogan had deserved what he got. The old man had no sympathy.

Putting the gun aside, he took down an empty sack that was hanging from a nail and used it to cover Rogan's head. Then he opened the door, checked that nobody was about and took hold of the body under the armpits. Rogan was a solid man but Sir Marcus was still strong enough to drag him to the disused well nearby. The corpse plummeted down the shaft and disappeared under the water. The money was soon thrown after Rogan. When he had strewn handfuls of straw down the well, Sir Marcus reclaimed his pistol and went off to change for dinner.

An hour later, he and Lady Hetherington were at either end of the long oak table in the dining room, eating their meal and engaging in desultory conversation. Sir Marcus was chastened by the turn of events. In being forced to kill Rogan, he felt that a chapter in his life had just been concluded. He had to accept that his plan to destroy the railway in France had failed. But at least he was safe. He could now resume his accepted routine, going through the social rounds in Essex with his wife and making regular trips to his club in London. Nobody would ever know that he had once been associated with a private detective named Luke Rogan.

When the servant entered the room, and apologised for the interruption, he shattered his master's sense of security.

'There's an Inspector Colbeck to see you, Sir Marcus.'

'Who?' The old man almost choked.

'Inspector Colbeck. He's a detective from Scotland Yard and he has a Sergeant Leeming with him. They request a few moments of your time. What shall I tell them, Sir Marcus?'

'Show them into the library,' said the other, getting to his feet and dabbing at his mouth with a napkin. 'Nothing to be alarmed about, my dear,' he added to his wife. 'It's probably something to do with those poachers who've been bothering us. Do excuse me.'

The servant had already left. Before he followed him, Sir Marcus paused to kiss his wife gently on the cheek and squeeze her shoulder with absent-minded affection. Then he straightened his shoulders and went out. The detectives were waiting for him in the library, a long room that was lined with bookshelves on three walls, the other being covered with paintings of famous battles from the Napoleonic Wars. Many of the volumes there were devoted to military history.

Robert Colbeck introduced himself and his companion. He gave Sir Marcus no opportunity to remark on his facial injuries. His initial question was all the more unsettling for being delivered in a tone of studied politeness.

'Are you acquainted with a man named Luke Rogan?'

'No,' replied Sir Marcus. 'Never heard of him.'

'You've never employed such an individual?'

'Of course not.'

'I notice a copy of *The Times* on the table over there,' said Colbeck with a nod in that direction. 'If you've read it, you'll have encountered Rogan's name there and know why we've taken such an interest in him. I've a particular reason for wanting to apprehend him, Sir Marcus. Earlier today, he did his best to kill me.'

'Did you instruct him to do that, Sir Marcus?' asked Leeming.

'Don't be so preposterous, man!' shouted the other.

'It's a logical assumption.'

'It's a brazen insult, Sergeant.'

'Not if it's true.'

'Sergeant Leeming speaks with authority,' said Colbeck, taking over again. 'He called at your house in Pimlico this afternoon. According to the servant he met, Luke Rogan visited the house yesterday and spent some time in your company. I think that you are a liar, Sir Marcus.' He gave an inquiring smile. 'Do you regard that as an insult as well?'

The old man would not yield an inch. 'You have no right to browbeat me in my own home,' he said. 'I must ask you to leave.'

'And we must respectfully decline that invitation. We've spent far too long on this investigation to pay any heed to your bluster. The facts are these,' Colbeck went on, brusquely. 'You attended a lecture given by Gaston Chabal, who was working as an engineer on the railway between Mantes and Caen. Because that railway would one day connect Paris with a port that also houses an arsenal, you spied a danger of invasion. To avert that danger, you tried to bring the railway to a halt. That being the case, Chabal's murder took on symbolic significance.' His smile was much colder this time. 'Do I need to go on, Sir Marcus?'

'We are well aware of your military record,' said Leeming. 'You fought against the French for years. You can only ever see them as an enemy, can't you?'

'They *are* an enemy!' roared Sir Marcus.

'We're at peace with them now.'

'That's only an illusion, Sergeant. I knew the rogues when they held sway over a great part of Europe and plotted to add us to their empire. Thanks to us, Napoleon was stopped. It would be criminal to allow another Napoleon to succeed in his place.'

'That's why you had Chabal killed, isn't it?' said Colbeck. 'He had the misfortune to be a Frenchman.'

Sir Marcus was scathing. 'He embodied all the qualities of the breed,' he said, letting his revulsion show. 'Chabal was clever, arrogant and irredeemably smug. I'll tell you something about him that you didn't know, Inspector.'

'Oh, I doubt that.'

'Not content with building a railway to facilitate the invasion of England, he showed the instincts of a French soldier. Do you know what they do after a victory?' he demanded, arms flailing. 'They rape and pillage. They defile the womenfolk and steal anything they can lay their hands on. That was what Chabal did. His first victim was an Englishwoman. He not only subjected her to his carnal passions, he had the effrontery to inveigle money from her husband for the project in France. Rape and pillage – no more, no less.'

'Considerably less, I'd say,' argued Colbeck. 'I spoke to the lady in question and she told me a very different story. She became Gaston Chabal's lover of her own free will. She mourned his death.'

'I saved her from complete humiliation.'

'I dispute that, Sir Marcus.'

'I did, Inspector. I had him followed, you see,' said the old man, reliving the sequence of events. 'I had him followed on both sides of the Channel until I knew all about him. None of it was to his credit. When he tried to take advantage of the lady during her husband's absence, I had him killed on the way there.'

'And thrown from the Sankey Viaduct.'

'That was intentional. It was a reminder of our superiority – a French civil engineer hurled from a masterpiece of English design.'

'Chabal was dead at the time,' said Leeming, shrugging his shouders, 'so it would have been meaningless to him.'

Sir Marcus scowled. 'It was not meaningless to me.'

'We need take this interview no further,' decided Colbeck. 'I have a warrant for your arrest, Sir Marcus. Before I enforce it, I must ask you if Luke Rogan is here.' The old man seemed to float off into a reverie. His gaze shifted to the battles depicted on the wall. He was miles away. Colbeck prompted him. 'I put a question to you.'

'Come with me, Inspector. You, too, Sergeant Leeming.'

Walking with great dignity, Sir Marcus Hetherington led them upstairs and along the landing. He unlocked the door of his shrine and conducted them in. Colbeck was astonished to see the range of memorabilia on show. The sight of the skull transfixed Leeming. Sir Marcus turned to the portrait of him in uniform.

'That was painted when I got back from Waterloo,' he said, proudly. 'I lost a lot of friends in that battle and I lost two young sons as well. That broke my heart and destroyed my wife. I'll never forgive the French for what they stole from us that day. They were *animals*.'

'It was a long time ago,' said Colbeck.

'Not when I come in here. It feels like yesterday then.'

'I asked you about Luke Rogan.'

'Then I'll give you an answer,' said the old man, opening a drawer in the cabinet and taking out the wooden case. He lifted the lid and took out one of the pistols before offering it to Colbeck. 'That's the weapon I used to kill Mr Rogan,' he explained. 'You'll find his body at the bottom of the well.'

Leeming was astounded. 'You *shot* him?'

'He'd outlived his usefulness, Sergeant.'

'It's beautiful,' said Colbeck, admiring the pistol and noting its finer points. 'It was made by a real craftsman, Sir Marcus.'

'So was this one, Inspector Colbeck.'

Before they realised what he was going to do, he took out the second gun, put it into his mouth and pulled the trigger. In the confined space, the report was deafening. His head seemed to explode. Blood spattered all over the portrait of Sir Marcus Hetherington.

Madeleine Andrews was dismayed. It was two days since the murder investigation had been concluded and she had seen no sign of Robert Colbeck. The newspapers had lauded him with fulsome praise and she had cut out one article about him. Yet he did not appear in person. She wondered if she should call at his house and, if he were not there, leave a message with his servant. In the end, she decided against such a move. She continued to wait and to feel sorely neglected.

It was late afternoon when a cab finally drew up outside the house. She opened the door in time to watch Colbeck paying the driver. When he turned round, she was horrified to see the bruises that still marked his face. There had been no mention of his injuries in the newspaper. Madeleine was so troubled by his appearance that she took scant notice of the object he was carrying. After giving her a kiss, Colbeck followed her into the house.

'Before you ask,' he explained, 'I had a fight with Luke Rogan. Give me a few more days and I'll look more like the man you know. And before you scold me for not coming sooner,' he went on, 'you should know that I went to Liverpool on your behalf.'

'Liverpool?'

'The local constabulary helped us in the first stages of our enquiries. It was only fair to give them an account of what transpired thereafter. I can't say that Inspector Heyford was overjoyed to see me. He still hasn't recovered from the shock of accepting Constable Praine as his future son-in-law.'

Madeleine was bemused. 'Who are these people?'

'I'll tell you later, Madeleine,' he promised. 'The person I really went to see was Ambrose Hooper.'

'The artist?'

'The very same.' He tapped the painting that he was holding. 'I bought this from him as a present for you.'

'A present?' She was thrilled. 'How marvellous!'

'Aren't you going to see what it is?' Madeleine took the painting from him and began to unwrap it. 'Because I was engaged in solving the crime, Mr Hooper gave me first refusal.'

Pulling off the last of the thick brown paper, she revealed the stunning watercolour of the Sankey Viaduct. It made her blink in awe.

'This is amazing, Robert,' she said, relishing every detail. 'It makes my version look like a childish scribble.'

'But *that* was the one that really helped me,' he said. 'You drew what was in Sir Marcus Hetherington's mind. Two countries joined together by a viaduct – victorious France and defeated England.'

'Is this Gaston Chabal?' she asked, studying the tiny figure.

'Yes, Madeleine.'

'He really does seem to be falling through the air.'

'Mr Hooper has captured the scene perfectly.'

'No wonder you were so grateful to him at the start.'

'He was the perfect witness – in the right place at the right time to record the moment for posterity. That painting is proof of the fact.'

'It's a wonderful piece of work. Father will be so interested to see it. He's driven trains over the viaduct.'

'I didn't buy it for your father, I bought it for you. It was by way of thanks for your assistance. Do you really like the painting?'

'I love it,' she said, putting it aside so that she could fling her arms around his neck. 'Thank you, Robert. You're so kind.' She kissed him. 'It's the nicest thing you've ever given me.'

'Is it?' he asked with a mischievous twinkle in his eye. 'Oh, I think I can do a lot better than that, Madeleine.'

ACKNOWLEDGEMENTS

With many thanks to Janet Cutler, a former President of the Railway and Canal Historical Society, for her expert advice on Victorian locomotives.